'*See You Tomorrow* is an exceptional novel, as incredible as it is realistic, written with an explosive force and a pulsating passion for Balzac. A majestic page-turner!' Karl Ove Knausgård

'Tore Renberg is one of Norway's finest young writers' Jo Nesbø

'*See You Tomorrow* is an intense, riotous, funny, sexy and thrilling book, full of grit and truth. There is not a single boring sentence. This is a full voltage blast of a novel and Tore Renberg is a *great* writer' Matt Haig

'The greatest storyteller of his generation' *Aftenposten*

'A knockout story ... in 600 pages, Renberg unveils a story that drives the reader to surrender' *Fædrelandsvennen*

'*See you Tomorrow* makes most Norwegian contemporary literature taste like watery tea, and Norwegian crime authors' prose about as elegant and smooth as the Norwegian football team playing against Argentina' *Aftenposten*

'Renberg is one of the most significant epic poets of Norwegian contemporary literature. His ability to read the pulse of a social set, the spirit of an age and an absolutely credible cast of characters is first grade' *Tønsberg Blad*

'600 pages of pure energy ... a charming cock-and-bull story filled with love for twisted criminals, hormonal teenagers and the oil city Stavanger ... this is a novel with momentum. It's entertaining, alternately funny and thrilling' *Dagsavisen*

'A strikingly accurate portrayal of Stavanger's underside ... a collective novel where all participants are portrayed equally clearly, equally credibly and with equal care. *See You Tomorrow* is impressive in every aspect – from its composition, language and credibility to its wit, palette, multiple crescendos. The research for this book must have taken a year of his life' *Adresseavisen*

'Rare linguistic energy, powerful progress and a delightful combination of humour and rawness ... a highlight in Renberg's authorship ... a juicy linguistic orgy fit to be consumed in large quantities' *Hamar Arbeiderblad*

'An author with a literary expression, a human colorfulness, a life-giving love for speed and pace and a completely outrageous devotion to the characters described. One surfs incomprehensibly easily and effortlessly from one situation to another. Not least because the language is so unique and rude, with slang in the most surprising combinations. It is a magnificent book' *Kristeligt Dagblad*

See You Tomorrow is an achievement in technical power. In vital, maximalist prose, the characters' perspectives change in a weaving movement, slowly taking us to an amazing crescendo ... new, fresh and heartfelt' *Expressen*

'A criminal power performance. *See You Tomorrow* is 600 pages of maximalism, not to mention a virtualistic tour de force, which at its best is crushing proof of how productively far you can reach beyond grey standard prose' *Aftenposten*

'An action-packed cross between youth novel and thriller ... an arresting novel where Renberg shows off his best side ... suspenseful from the first till last page' *Bergens Tidende*

'Wow, what a novel! ... Renberg's pitch-black novel from Stavanger is filled with momentum, brutality, humour, poetry and musicality. Renberg possesses a formidable talent for storytelling – a novel of remarkable tempo and drive, and a horror-like ending, grotesque to the point where it becomes comic' *Dagbladet*

'A knockout story ... In 600 pages, Renberg unveils a story that drives the reader to surrender' *Fædrelandsvennen*

See You Tomorrow

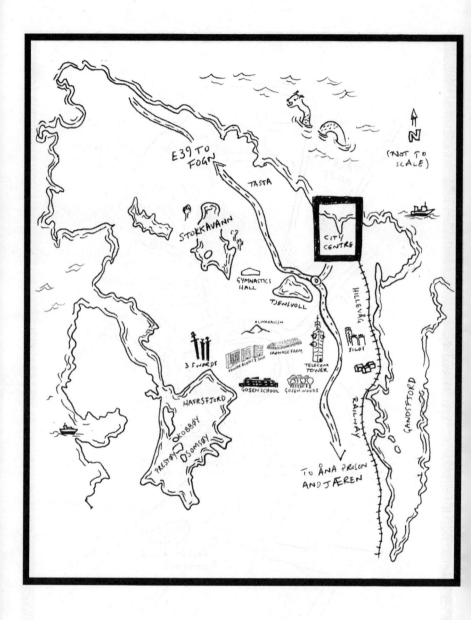

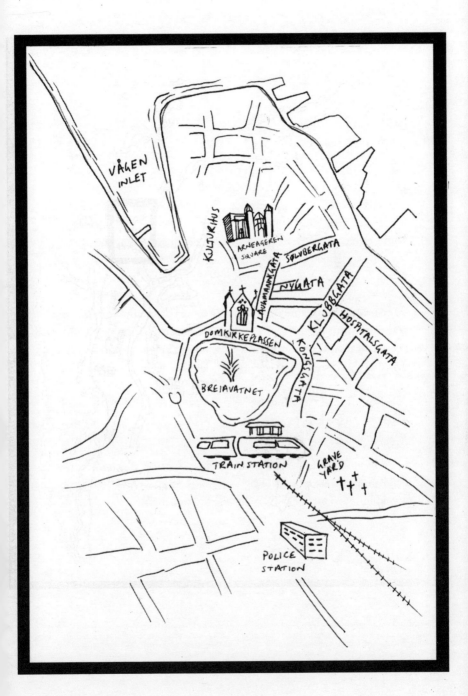

ABOUT THE AUTHOR

Tore Renberg is a multi-award-winning author, who has distinguished himself as a literary critic and TV host for the Norwegian Broadcasting Corporation. A student of philosophy and literature at the University of Bergen, where he met lifelong friend Karl Ove Knausgård, he first achieved major success at the age of 23, with the short-story collection *Sleeping Triangle* and then the novel *The Man Who Loved Yngve,* which was made into a major motion picture. This was followed by four further novels with the same protagonist, which sold over 400,000 copies in Norway. In addition to his work as an essayist and novelist, Tore has played in several bands, and written for the screen and the theatre. His work has been translated into 15 languages.

ABOUT THE TRANSLATOR

Seán Kinsella is from Dublin. He has previously translated works by, amongst others, Kjell Askildsen and Frode Grytten into English. His translation of Stig Sæterbakken's *Through the Night*, was long-listed for the BTBA 2014. He lives in Norway.

See You Tomorrow

Tore Renberg

Translated from the Norwegian by Seán Kinsella

ARCADIA BOOKS

Arcadia Books Ltd
139 Highlever Road
London W10 6PH

www.arcadiabooks.co.uk

First published in the United Kingdom by Arcadia Books 2014
Originally published by Forlaget Oktober, Oslo, as, *Vi ses i morgen* 2013

Copyright © Tore Renberg 2013
English language translation copyright © Seán Kinsella 2014

ISBN 978-1-909807-60-0

Typeset in Garamond by MacGuru Ltd
Printed and bound by CPI Group (UK) Ltd, Croydon CR0 4YY

Arcadia Books gratefully acknowledges the financial support of NORLA.

This book has been selected to receive financial assistance from English PEN's
"PEN Translates!" programme, supported by Arts Council England. English
PEN exists to promote literature and our understanding of it, to uphold
writers' freedoms around the world, to campaign against the persecution and
imprisonment of writers for stating their views, and to promote the friendly
co-operation of writers and the free exchange of ideas. *www.englishpen.org*

Arcadia Books supports English PEN *www.englishpen.org* and
The Book Trade Charity *www.btbs.org*

Arcadia Books distributors are as follows:

in the UK and elsewhere in Europe:
Macmillan Distribution Ltd
Brunel Road
Houndmills
Basingstoke
Hants RG21 6XS

in the USA and Canada:
Dufour Editions
PO Box 7
Chester Springs
PA, 19425

in Australia/New Zealand:
NewSouth Books
University of New South Wales
Sydney NSW 2052

Supported using public funding by
ARTS COUNCIL
ENGLAND

TUESDAY 25 SEPTEMBER

Calling every boy and girl
Calling all around the world
Get ready for love!
Nick Cave

1. **666** (Pål)

His eyes, they feel as if there's sand in them.

As if there's a fine layer of tiny grains on the membrane. It's been like that for weeks now. Nothing helps: not eye drops, not eye ointment, it won't go away. The grains scrape against the membrane. If it keeps up, the particles will perforate the cornea and one day he'll wake up unable to see the world.

Maybe it's just as well.

Getting so sick of this.

It's never going to work out, is it?

Pål wipes the mixer with the cloth, then folds it and hangs it over the tap. He leans on the worktop and fills his lungs with air, as though that would help. He hears the gush of the cistern from the first floor and he exhales, glances at the dog. The border collie is lying on a blanket next to the fireplace.

'Eh, Zitha? Just as well, eh?'

The sound of the cistern subsides and it's peaceful in the house. As peaceful as outside, where not even the lightest leaves on the trees stir beneath the yellow glow of the street lights. Not even the string hanging from the spruce tree moves; the string the girls used to hang milk cartons from, that they had cut holes in and stuck twigs through, so that the great tits could sit there and eat.

Dad? Can we have some raisins? Do birds eat raisins?

The milk carton's gone, his wife's gone, the girls are still here, and so is the string.

Pål squeezes his right eye shut and presses his forefinger against his eyelid in irritation. He turns on the radio. P4. Coldplay. A hit from a few years back. What's it called again? Always so annoying when they don't sing the title. *Now in the morning I sleep alone.* He switches off the radio. Everything is a reference to him, and he's not able to take it in any more. He's not able to watch TV, he's not able to read the papers, he can sit with a book in his hand reading the same page sixteen times over without grasping what's written.

All he can stand is silence, no matter how it might eat away at him.

Autumn came early this year, the first weeks in September were spattered with rain and chased by wind, but the days have suddenly brightened up. It's as though summer wants to bid a final farewell. A glaring white sun sits low in the vast sky. From early morning it casts long shadows along the streets. It's so strong it gives the impression it's going to burn up the sky, and then itself.

Well, Zitha? You think Daddy'll cope?

The dog has one paw curled up under her chest, the other alongside her lupine snout, idle and limp. Zitha takes on a slightly comical expression when she lies down flat on the blanket. Her ears are recumbent on her head, dainty and elegant.

She's a reliable dog, a beautiful dog, and she has no idea about what's going on with her master. Zitha just is. She sleeps. Plays. Runs. Eats. She stands in front of Pål with the same devotion, day in day out, tail wagging, bottom waggling, tongue hanging out.

He looks out of the windows facing the garden. It gets dark earlier now. The street lights are on by half past seven, it's already dusk by then, and within half an hour it's pitch black.

Summer began to ebb a month ago. People were still in T-shirts and shorts then. But soon it was over for the year. The leaves on the birch turned yellow, the rhododendron red, and deciduous trees began to fade. Women had to root out three-quarter length coats, the colours shifted to grey, brown and ochre and there were more and more hats to be seen. People started wearing shawls and scarves, they put away their trainers, and the kids were knocking about in fleece jackets and raingear.

Yeah, birds can eat raisins, they like them.

Is Mum coming back, Dad?

No, I don't think she is.

Good while ago now.

The temperature dropped; the nights got colder. He saw the

neighbour scraping ice off his car windscreen one morning; good thing he's got a garage.

These unnaturally bright days are merely on loan. It's summer's last sigh and not something that will last. His body needs to adjust now, adapt to the new season, to the prolonged gloom that is on its way, to months of cold and darkness. The joints get stiff, the body gets heavy and sleep takes up more room.

Pål rubs his seasonally dry hands together and looks at Zitha. Her breathing is slow and heavy. Who knows if she's dreaming, and who knows what she's dreaming of behind that elegant brow of hers.

Getting incredibly sick of this.

'Zitha!'

He smacks his lips and goes closer to the sleeping dog. She twitches, rises up on her front paws, yawns and stretches. Her tail starts whacking against the floor straight away, her tongue rolls out of her already salivating mouth.

'Yeaah. Come on, Zitha. Yeaah.'

He walks towards the hall, Zitha scampering around his legs. He clears his throat, demonstrably. He says 'Yeah, yeah!' extra loudly as he takes the leash from the top drawer and sees the twinkle in her eyes.

This isn't going to work. Is it?

The girls.

The dog's tail is going like a wind-up toy, she scurries about happily in front of him. Pål rubs his eyes before bending over and feeling the blood tip in his head, as if his skull were a lab flask and everything was following gravity. He rubs Zitha under the chin, looks her in the eyes and meets the same boundless trust she's always prepared to show.

Pål hears a door open upstairs. He puts on his coat, slips his feet into his shoes. He pats his inner pocket to see if the envelope is still there. It is.

They're sharp, collies. Intelligent. When his wife left him and heard he was getting a dog, she said he should get a setter; go hunting like other men. Yeah, you would think that, said Pål. Setters, said Christine, her voice full of admiration, they run themselves into the ground given the chance. Collies, said Pål, they're beautiful and they guard the house, that's the kind of dog I want.

Just to run. To explode, to disappear.

That's what he would like to do. That's what he's felt like doing of late. Run, explode, ready to disappear. In addition to numbness, anxiety, and shame; no one knows what I'm up to.

'Shall I go with you, Dad?'

Footsteps on the carpet above.

The kids are the worst. It feels like Tiril and Malene are all that stand between him and what he is going to do. Malene is the worst. A daddy's girl. She comes down the stairs, he knows her footsteps like he knows his own musty heart.

'Hm? Shall I go with you?'

'No, no.' He can't manage to meet her gaze. 'Get on with your homework.'

'I've finished.'

Pål sends her a puzzled smile. 'I must be mixing you up with someone who doesn't always do their homework. Where's Tiril?'

'At work, I guess.'

'Yeah, of course.'

Malene frowns. She gets that strange grimace around her mouth, the one she has had since she was a baby, the one that makes her look like E.T. He's almost on the verge of tears.

His daughter bends down to Zitha, strokes her snout affectionately, making her eyes narrow and slanted. She puts her face close to the dog's, the dog licks her nose. 'There, there, nice Zitha, nice Zitha, going for a walk with Dad.'

Pål studies her. The strong cheekbones that seem to force her face upwards. Her gymnast's body, strong, supple and erect. Never any nonsense with Malene. Such a pity about that injury. It'll heal soon enough. He smiles, and for a moment he forgets who he is and what it is he has done.

'Can't I come along?'

A daughter standing there asking to go with him. He hopes it will always be like that.

'No,' he says, 'it's late. You've got homework.'

'Dad, I told you, I've finished it.'

'Good,' he says. 'But, it'd be nice if you were here when Tiril gets in.'

'Aww.' She pouts and pulls Zitha close: 'Don't you want to stay here with Malene, eh?'

The dog licks her across the face, the tongue pink, wet, the tail beating the floor.

Next to the hall mirror hangs the old photo of his wife. It has started to fade. The kids wanted it put up after she left. A photo of Mum for the sake of the kids. Funny that. One year you want to tear her eyes out and the next it's like you miss her.

'Someone rang, by the way.'

He's startled out of his musings. 'Hm?'

'On the landline,' says Malene. 'Someone rang. They asked after you.'

'Did they give a name?' He tries to sound as nonchalant as possible.

'No, but they said they'd call back.'

'The rubbish,' he hears Malene say, feeling the fog thicken in his head, wishing he could drop everything and collapse on to the floor. 'Bin collection tomorrow.'

'Oh, yeah, the rubbish,' he says, perplexed. 'What would I do without you?'

Malene stands up, and lets go of the dog. She shrugs. 'That'd be the end of you, Dad.'

'Heh heh. Where's your sister, by the way?'

'I told you, she's at work.'

He rolls his eyes and grins at himself.

'You've become such a scatterbrain.' Malene lets Zitha jump up on her; she takes a paw in each hand and dances with the dog. She sends Pål a playful look: 'Is it your age? Eh? Is my dad an old fogey now?'

'No, no.' He runs his hand over his eyes and laughs awkwardly. 'Just a lot on my mind. Bit too much going on at work. It'll be all right though. Your dad always comes through in the end, you know that.'

Malene peers at him, squinting so intently it makes her cheek-bones even rounder: 'Still sore?'

'Yeah.' He blinks. 'Like there's sand in them.'

'What can it be?'

'Dunno. But I'm sure it'll go away.'

'Have you been to the doctor?'

She's got that grown-up look in her eyes. She looks like Christine when she's like that.

'No, not yet, but I will, of course.' He forces a smile.

'Yeah, well make sure you do, okay?'

Pål suddenly feels his teeth begin to chatter, feels his eyelids close and the oxygen drain from his head. He bends over. Pushes the dog aside, pulls Malene close to him. He swallows a lump in his throat.

He holds her tight, doesn't say a word.

This is never going to work out, he thinks to himself.

'Dad?'

They say you love your kids equally, and you do, but it's different with Malene. He's never quite understood Tiril, never quite connected, like she's off somewhere else, in a whole different direction, moving too fast for him. Is it Thursday she's going to sing?

'Dad? What is it?'

He holds her tight. Swallows, sniffles, blinks. Then he lets go.

'Is it Thursday Tiril is singing?'

'You know it is.'

'Yeah,' he says, shaking his head, 'what are you going to do with me, sentimental fool that I am, eh? Do you know what I was just thinking of? Iron Maiden in *Drammenshallen*, sure it was good, but Maiden in London, Malene, nothing beats that. *Six, six, six, the number of the beast, sacrifice is going on tonight*. Heh heh. Your old rocker dad, eh? Your daft dad has gone all soft. How's your ankle? Soon, Malene, you'll soon be back on the mat. Now, go and do your homework, and I'll take Zitha for a walk.'

She looks at him askance. 'I've done my homework…'

Pål tousles her hair. It feels soothing to the touch. What a girl. He's so proud of having such a great daughter.

Imagine if he told her? Imagine he suddenly told her everything?

'You know what?' He strokes her cheek. 'The two of you should hang up another milk carton for the birds. Autumn's arrived, you know.'

2. **DO YOU WANT ME?** (Sandra)

Am I a storm? Am I electric?

She'll be sixteen in a few months, her forehead is sweaty, under her hairline too. Her mouth is trembling and she knows she needs to hurry up – her knees wobble as she walks. Her heart is wild and emboldened; she feels weak, she feels strong.

One metre sixty-one, two burning eyes, three freckles on her nose, straight blonde fringe and glittering lip gloss.

The white bra, the one she bought without her mother's knowledge, the one her mother would probably think was tawdry, would he like it?

Is she the one he just has to have? Is she irresistible?

Sandra doesn't need any sleep, doesn't need any rest, why sleep the seconds away? She's never going to sleep again, she's going to stay awake twenty-four hours a day, because she doesn't have the time to waste a second of the life she's living.

Terrorism, environmental disasters, financial crises. They might well exist out there, they might well be important, to Mum, to Dad, to the teachers, to grown-ups, but to her they don't exist. The world has vanished. All she's got is heat and dread, haste and apprehension. All she feels is this drizzle within, like a strange rain falling inside her, wonderful and dangerous. Because Sandra is going to meet the one she loves.

He must be there by now?

She clutches the silver cross resting in the hollow of her throat, wipes her damp forehead with her arm. It's embarrassing, she's inherited it from her father. He always has patches of sweat under his arms when he hangs up his jacket after work and says, 'Ah, it's good to be home'.

Maybe she should get herself a headscarf she could tie from the back of her neck round her forehead. Maybe he'd like that. He wouldn't have left yet, would he?

Sandra drags the heavy industrial hoover as quickly as she can across the shop floor. She's not checking the time on her mobile every minute, more like every five seconds and now it's way too late, 20:50.

He's going to be waiting for her by the substation in Gosen Woods. Just by Madlavoll primary school. Close to Gosen kindergarten. She's attended both of them. He'll be waiting for her. And he's not lying now is he, because love, that doesn't lie, does it?

Jesus, imagine if Mum had seen her?

He took her face in those warm hands, his pupils were aglow. She held her breath, felt his thumbs stroke her lips, then he kissed her and said what she wanted to hear: 'I'll be there at nine. See you tomorrow.'

Love doesn't lie.

It's nice outside now. After a few weeks of rain, the September sky is brightening up even though the temperature has dropped and everybody can feel what's coming: there's a nip in the air. Everything living will fade and die.

It's all the same to Sandra. Come rain, come storm, come everything. War could break out, and that would be fine, as long as she gets to be *with him, with him.* The girl can hardly understand what she was doing before she met Daniel. All the days and nights spent with her friends, standing around the schoolyard, hanging about outside the shop, walking arm-in-arm, sniggering, and singing out loud in unison. It seems so insignificant, so stupid, so childish. They can go on about how preoccupied she's become lately. Mira can say it as loud as she likes, *Sandra's let us down, Sandra's losing it.* And Mathilde, poor girl, looks like she lives in squalor, as Mum would say, she can say it too, *Sandra's changed.* Makes no difference what they think, it's air, it's wind, it's really less than nothing. All that matters is running towards the one you love and letting your heart melt into his.

A headscarf.

Yes.

That might be nice.

She doesn't have much left to do now. Vacuum the very back of the shop, then she's finished. Tiril is dragging her feet, she can do what she wants. Once Sandra has finished hoovering, she's out of here. Then she'll hang up her jogging pants and jumper and pull the skinny Met jeans well over her bum, because he's told her he likes them: *I think you're well sexy in those jeans.* She'll put on more lip gloss, because he's told her he likes that too: *I love it when your lips gleam.*

A thousand nervous times she's stood in front of the mirror, trying to find that expression, the one she evidently has, because he said that too: *Oh, you're well cute when you do that.* There's something about her mouth, something about the way her nostrils flare. She's asked him plenty of times, *what do you mean?* She's smacked him on the arm, smiled at him, but all he said was: *I can't explain it, you're just so bloody cute when you do it.*

Am I? You really think so?

Yes, you are, Sandra, You're well cute, fucking hell, you're a flower, you are.

Sandra gets out her mobile again, no messages. 20:52. Hope he hasn't forgotten the time, hope he hasn't grown tired of her, stupid girl, only fifteen.

Ten o'clock, that's what she told Mum and Dad. Her job will take her until ten, because she has to clean the whole shop on her own. There used to be two of them but not any more, and that means it takes a lot longer. But that's a lie, because Tiril is here, and the lie hisses in her head, as if it floods up from her midriff towards her throat: one hour. She had managed to wangle one hour. With him.

Sandra's forehead is sweaty. Yes, Mum, I'll come straight home after work, no, Mum, I won't dawdle, no, Dad, I'm not going to drift around at night. *No one hung out at night midweek when we were young, things were different back then.* Oh, really, so what? If there was one thing she couldn't care less about, it's how things were in the stupid seventies and the idiotic eighties, just like she couldn't care less about the music Dad is always trying to get her to listen to, *real music,* as he calls it. The Police and Sting and all that stuff. People who could play and didn't think real music was made with Pro Tools. Or Mum going on about *Girls Just Want to Have Fun,* Jesus, and all that talk of the cold war and the Berlin Wall – so what? So what? So what?

She's alive *now,* don't they get that?

She's alive now and she's lying through her teeth. It's risky. Mum and Dad could easily find out. They could run into Tiril's dad. They know who he is. They could run into Tiril. The lie is far from watertight. 'Hi Tiril, nice to see you, shame you quit your cleaning job at the shop.'

Dozy Tiril, only fourteen and thinks she is something. She's by the frozen foods with a cleaning spray. Tetchy brat. Sulky and grumpy, always has been. Her sister's not quite as bad, a little quiet maybe, a little serious. The gymnastics talent, Malene, but she's injured her ankle. They're so different, those two. But they're both odd, each in their own way. Everybody knows, knows they're a bit weird. Maybe Mum's right when she raises her eyebrows and says: After all, they haven't grown up with a mum and a dad.

It's so hot.

Sandra sticks out her bottom lip, blows up at her fringe.

It's so unbelievably hot.

The lie is a risk she's willing to take. If they find out they can say what they like, even though they'll probably cut her pocket money and ground her, because what do they know about love? They sit watching box sets on Blu-ray, night after night of *Mad Men* and *The Killing.* Is that love? What do they know about a boy's mouth against hers and his hands on her body, what do they know about the intensity in his eyes when he gazes at her in the darkness of the forest?

Sandra is lying, but it doesn't matter, because she's a child of Heaven. Her willingness to lie attests to the truth of what she's doing. When that's how it is, then it's *right*, then it's the heart that acts. If love wasn't right, what would be right in this world?

Her hand goes to her throat, to her silver cross, the one she got from Aunt Astrid and Uncle Frank for her confirmation, the one with the diamond inset. She squeezes it hard, again.

She's nervous about what's going to happen.

You're precious, Sandra. Remember that.

You won't give yourself to just anybody. Will you, my love?
No, Mum.

She's not just sweaty under her hairline, but on her neck, between her shoulder blades and on her palms. She represses thoughts of her mother and thinks instead about what it says in First Corinthians, about love enduring, believing, hoping for, tolerating all. And she thinks about what the Bible says, that when you were a child, you spoke as a child, thought as a child, and understood as a child, but when you became a man, you put away childish things. That's the way she feels. Everything childish feels so stupid, feels so far away it is inconceivable that it could have been her.

Sandra vacuums as quickly as she can. Tiril glowers at her from under her headphones, with her thick black mascara, listening to Evanescence or My Chemical Romance. Sandra's skin tingles. His hands, his eyes, his voice: *Do you want me? Sexy?*

She hurries, she is close to the bottle return machine and the entrance to the back room, but just before she finishes, she knocks down a display of honey next to the spices. The pyramid collapses, honey jars tumble to the floor and roll in all directions. Sandra's pulse is up under her chin, she curses to herself and quickly falls to her knees to put them back.

'Hey, Tiril? Can you give me a hand?'
She's losing time now. She's losing seconds with him.
Do you want me, Sandra?
'Tiril, give me a hand, will you.'
I'm precious.
I don't give myself to just anyone.
I want you. Take me. Open me. Now. Tonight.

3. **VIVA LA VIDA** (Rudi)

'Hey, Chessi? You there, baby?'

Rudi's coffee-brown eyes move to glance in the rear-view mirror.

'Hey, Chessibaby?'

No reply.

The old Volvo splutters out of the roundabout at Åsen, daylight streaming in the windscreen, and Rudi puts his foot on the pedal. If this is supposed to be a company, and this is a company car, then things are bad. When did they buy it again? Ninety-two. From an old farmer on Finnøy. The Volvo was in a field, under a tarpulin, sheep sniffing around at the edges. It only had 19,000 on the clock. That's how old people are with cars, they treat them as carefully as they would money. Now it had done 270,654 and should have been on its way to Knoksen's knackers yard.

But the Volvo is the same as all the other rubbish you lug around with you year in, year out; you grow so damned attached to it.

'Hey, Chessi?'

Rudi takes another look in the rear-view mirror. She's just sitting there. You'd be hard pressed to find a more pig-headed woman. One little row, Jesus, not even a row, and she won't budge an inch.

His rasping voice reaches a higher pitch: 'Hey, Chessi, are you there, or are you just sitting dreaming about rock ballads and my cock?'

She turns her head and looks out of the window.

That's gratitude for you. A joke, and she looks out the window. Great idea bringing her along to work. It's true what Jani says, that girl was born difficult. She shot out of her mum in December 1972, covered in spikes. She's downright *spiny*. She's always been pale and freckly, rough and sickly and as ugly as an uprooted tree, but she has beautiful big hair, chestnut colour, and hips like shelves, as well as an ass that can make your head spin. Living without her would be utterly impossible.

'Chessi?' Rudi tries to make his voice sound like cotton wool. 'Honeybunch? Only jokin', you know that. Eh? Will we check if there're any concerts coming up? I think Europe are playing at *Folken* soon!'

He allows her time to compose herself. But no. Her cantankerous gaze is fixed on the air in front of her. Those wide-set eyes, which make her resemble some kind of subterranean animal, seem to move even further apart. What about some compassion? *Yourboyfriendoftwentysevenyears, thebaronoflove*, is sitting here and she knows he hasn't slept all night, she knows he has had awful nightmares, but is there an ounce of compassion to be had? Is there the merest hint of a smile? The smallest, kindly word?

Cecilie continues staring out the window while she takes out a pack of cigarettes. Fantastic. Now she's going to punish him. She knows all too well he can't bear anyone smoking in the Volvo. And she knows he's just quit. And she knows how hard it is to kick the habit. Fantastic.

Rudi makes a show of rolling down the window.

They're up and down, these moods of hers. You haven't got a hope in hell of keeping track of them. Yesterday? Yesterday it was super smooth. Movie night in Hillevåg, good old *I Spit on Your Grave* and *Nightmare in a Damaged Brain*. Lo-fi classic night, said Jani, and put out crisps and coke. *Classic Night*. Jani has a way with words. They watched movies, good times and blood and gore it was, even Chessi was in a pretty good mood, lying there in an old pair of jogging bottoms, cuddled up in the crook of his arm. And then, next day? In a rotten mood. Everything's shitty, pissy and crappy. When he's the one, not her, who's had a rough night. He hugged her, but her body was as stiff as a board. He tried to make eye-contact, but her eyes were yellow and fiery. And eventually he lets her know, that she needs to get a fucking grip and be a bit nicer. That was when the storm broke.

But, you got to go to work. No matter how menstrual the weather.

Rudi leans towards the open window, breathes in and out. Chessi sits in the back seat puffing away as if it were the last cigarette she was ever going to have, won't be able to make out her head soon for all the smoke.

He drives through Auglend and takes a left at the southern end of Mosvannet lake, putting the car in a low gear, to get a bit of traction on the uphill climb at Ullandhaugsbakken.

Nicest place on Earth, as Granny used to say. God rest the old bag of bones, as Granddad said when cancer got her. She lay in her sickbed like a crumpled leaf. It was hard seeing her like that. Hi Granny, are you in there? Ah, Rudi, my boy, there's not much left of me, you'll have a slice of cake, won't you? Come to visit your grandmother and get a slice of cake? It was always good to visit Granny. Shoot over to Stokka. He could drive there at any time, pull the Volvo up in front of the house, toot the horn, while it still worked, get inside the house and she would totter into the room wearing that blue dress, radiant as a wrinkly sun. Swiss roll and caffeine-free instant coffee. Yeah, you can laugh, be my bloody guest, but it was one thousand per cent genuine. If there were more people like Granny in the world, you'd hear a lot less about arguments, or the internet or war, that's for sure.

Afeckingworldoffeckinglove.

That's old times for you. They can really take hold.

Sometimes it's a pleasure. Other times it's a pain and they refuse to let you sleep. And you can't do anything but curl up into a ball and wait for it to end, and as for a hug from your girl, well, you can forget about that.

The Volvo hauls itself up the hill in low gear. Rudi feels the hairs on the back of his head crackle as they near the top, as he sees cows grazing in the fields, sees the Ullandhaug Tower stretching up into the sky, and as he gets to the summit: the world opens up to the fjord below. He feels his stomach plummet and his head soar.

Rudi's brown eyes warm up and soften as he drives into his old stomping ground. He feels likes a fag, but if you've quit, then it's all about standing firm. Stay clean, Lemmy. Metal, Motörhead and the old haunts forever.

This landscape, Granny.

You couldn't describe it.

It's true what they say at travel agents, you've got to experience it, you've got to see it with your own two eyes.

Rudi speeds up. He feels his head fizz and shuts his eyes for a few seconds, takes a deep breath, opens them again and goes for it: 'Hey Chessi. You there?' He tries to infuse his voice with as much lightness as possible. 'Eh? You looking? Nicest place on earth, eh?'

'Fucking shithole,' says the voice from the back seat.

Rudi sighs. It's the end of September. You're at work. You're on the road in the Volvo. After weeks of rain, along come a few days of glorious weather, as though a bonus summer had dropped by. You live in the richest country in the world. There's food on the table, and money in the bank, maybe not piles of it, maybe a little less than Jani would like, but enough, and Granny is floating round your head like a crochet angel and life is actually pretty bloody good, and you decide to say something pleasant after a bad morning. *Pleasant*. Not asking much, is it? And that's what you get. It's enough to reduce your whole happy house to rubble.

'Christ, you are a right bitch,' says Rudi, pounding on the steering wheel with his fist.

'Yeah, and when were you planning on treating me any different!'

He sees her shouting, smoke billowing from her mouth.

'Well? What if I want a normal life, and not this bollocks, eh? Fuck's sake, Rudi, you're not a man, you're a dishcloth.'

'A dishcloth?!' Rudi tries to keep his cool so he doesn't explode. 'A dishcloth? Whatthe ... fu ... a ... fu ... dish ... what do you say that for?'

He glances in the rear-view mirror. Now she's crying as well. Brilliant. Dishcloth? The tears run down one pallid cheek, trickle along her narrow nose, taking the make-up with them, it's drama time again. Dramadramadrama. Weird how she only ever cries from one eye. Dishcloth? It's exhausting, that's what it is. They've been together for twenty-seven years now. They *know* one another.

They're like one person! It's like Jani says: she's so dramatic she should start a theatre.

It's not your fault, Rudi. It's congenital. She inherited it from Mum.

'I don't know,' Cecilie says in a low voice. And sniffles. 'I just made it up. Dishcloth.' She looks up, meets his gaze for the first time in a long while. 'I do love you though, Snatchpuss.'

The Volvo trundles by the Iron Age Farm. Cecilie sits pale and freckly with her big hair and shelf hips, and the make-up running down her left cheek spreads out like a river delta from her wet lashes. Her thin, slightly crooked lips, her Easter-yellow teeth and her small mussel ears.

Rudi feels his throat tighten, his stomach swell.

Shit, how he loves that girl.

And shit, how he loves this landscape.

Here's to you, Granny. They were good, those Swiss rolls.

He feels a draught on his neck and rolls up the window. He turns on the radio. Pop music. He's about to switch it off, he knows how anti-pop they are, but he can't. He's heard this song before. Violins. Du-du-du du-du-du du-du-du. Something about a king who used to rule the world. Coldplay? He pretends not to notice the song and hopes Chessi won't notice him listening to it.

Rudi leans forward in the seat, juts out his chin and squints. Now let's see, he thinks, and reduces speed. Down the hill towards the forest. That was what he said. Down towards the shop there. Yeah. Park someplace behind there.

Weird set-up, this. Feels a tiny bit risky.

Keep your wits about you, Jani said. I'm not sure about this.

Rudi turns his head and looks at her.

'Hey, Chessi, come on, we'll knock this on the head. What was it we were arguing about, what was it that stirred up this lousy atmosphere, eh?'

'Don't remember,' says the low voice from the back seat.

'There you have it. It's gone. Vanished! Hey, baby, it's you and me and your ass! You know I'll kill anyone who comes near you. You know you can count on it, count on Rudi whipping out his monster cock and flogging them to death? If anyone other than

Rudi screws you, yeah, so much as fucking looks at you, then I'll break every bone in their body? Oh yeah. Rudi's a real man! Like Granny used to say: I can trust you, Rudi.'

'Oh Jesus...' comes the voice from the back seat. 'Here we go again...'

'Eh?' says Rudi and acts as if he didn't hear what she said.

'Nothing.'

He glances in the mirror. The tears have dried. She sticks the small, pink tip of her tongue out between her thin lips and moistens them.

'Exactly,' he says, fired up at the sight of her, and takes a deep breath: 'Nothing and *kein Problem, Mädchen*. Now we're going to go to work, and there's no telling what we might run into in this forest, but Pål is this guy's name and he's got *ein problem*.' Rudi frowns suddenly, as if he's just thought of something. 'Pål, you don't know anyone called Pål, do you?'

'Pål, eh, no, don't think so.'

'What's going on, Pål shmål,' laughs Rudi, repressing the thought. 'There's only one way out of here: piece by piece! like Slayer say. What's gonna happen, Pålly Bålly? No one knows, baby! Like Foo Fighters say.'

'Queens of the Stone Age.'

'Eh?'

'Queens of the Stone Age. No One Knows.'

'Jesus. Are you gonna nitpick about that now? Who's the dishcloth here?'

Rudi suppresses his irritation and says no more. They draw closer to the woods and the radio is playing Coldplay. It's pop music. And he hates pop music. But those violins and that melody, they get into your brain, and the lyrics, they force their way through your body, and everything reminds you of that troll sitting in the back seat: He's got to have it.

Because he loves it. And he's a man of love.

'Rudi, can you turn off that homo music? It makes me want to puke.'

Rudi pretends not to hear what she said, and raising his voice, making it sound like an engine straining at full pelt, says: 'Yeah,

yeah, dishcloth or not, there's one thing Rudi knows for sure, and that's that tonight, Chessi, tonight I'm going to screw you seven ways to fuckin' Sunday.'

4. THEY'RE SO BLOODY GORGEOUS
(Daniel William)

A little girl, really.

Fifteen years of age. Her mum works at the church, her dad's a lawyer and she oozes naivety. She'll be sixteen in January. If she's telling the truth, that is. She might be adding a few months on to her age. Girls lie all the time, especially about things like that. That's the thing about them. The way they view the truth, it's not the same way we do. The truth is always changing with girls. Runs from their mouths like dribble from old people.

But they're so bloody gorgeous.

So, so bloody gorgeous.

It would be a lot easier living with a man, as his last foster father used to say, before he added: 'Not that I'm a fucking homo.'

Homos. That's just sick. It's one thing to like boys, but not to like girls, that's even worse.

They're so bloody gorgeous.

When there are girls in the room, the rest of the world disappears. It just fucking explodes. There's nothing else in the room other than them. And it's a good feeling, like sniffing glue. Helicopter. Daniel has felt it a thousand times, and he wants to feel it again, because that's the point of this life: if it's good, get more of it.

More, more, more.

If you want to strip this scrap heap of a life down to its essence, then it's girls you're talking about. Daniel can sit behind the drum kit and play, he's a good drummer, a dynamic player, he's as tight as a sphincter, but in his head, while the sticks are hitting the skins, it's girls he's thinking about. They tumble around in his head while he plays. Big ones and small ones; fat ones and thin ones, all kinds of girls. Tits, twats, asses, thighs, lipstick, tights, stockings, blouses, bras, dresses, kerchiefs, make-up, those straps between stockings and panties and everything that goes with a girl. It's been like that ever since he was a little boy. Ever since he was in kindergarten on the other side of the city. There were just as many girls going round in his head when he was playing then as when he was bigger, on the football pitch, practising penalty after penalty, and as there are now when he's banging on the drums.

And what is wrong with that?

Sometimes he gets the feeling people think there's something wrong with it, about life being about girls. But Daniel doesn't care about that. What he wants to do is get his own flat, whenever Child bloody Welfare will let him, work out a couple of times a week, get drunk at the weekends, play in a good band, get some gigs, release some records and get some stuff out on iTunes, YouTube and Spotify, maybe play a few festivals, maybe make a living playing music like Kvelertak, Purified in Blood and Kaizers Orchestra. Dejan's brother – crazy all that stuff Dejan and his family went through in Serbia – Dejan's brother knows a guy who knows one of the guitarists in Purified. Daniel and Dejan saw them at the *Rått og Råde* festival, seriously kickass: *The sky is falling, death is calling, to the grave.* It's not just people in Rogaland who like them, people from Oslo like them too. He just needs to keep at it. If it doesn't work out he'll have to get a job, and he's no wuss, even though his grades aren't great, pass candidate in every subject except PE. He's never shied away from work. If someone tells him to do something, he'll grit his teeth until his jaw aches and do the job, no matter how bloody dirty it is.

Then he'll spend the rest of his time, and money, on girls.

That's what he feels is *meaningful,* as his foster mother and child protection officer say. And if anyone believes that's the wrong way to live your life, then they can just go on believing it. If they feel it's wrong that he thinks girls are so fucking sexy, soft and gorgeous, and he wants to buy them stuff, like houses and make-up and whatever they want, then they can go on feeling it's wrong.

Daniel's rock-hard fuckplan is to find a girl who's not a handful. She has to have her head screwed on and she can't have a face on her in the morning like she's sucking a lemon, and she can't spend three hours deciding what kind of jeans to buy. She has to think the jeans he wants her to wear are the best. He'll be the one looking at her after all. That's the kind of girl he wants for himself. A girl who likes the fact he thinks she's well gorgeous and well sexy, a girl who doesn't look at other boys and isn't running around flirting.

Who knows, maybe he's already found that girl.

Because she is sexy, Sandra.

And she doesn't look at other boys. And she doesn't moan.

The test will be how often she wants to do it with him.

It'll be a shambles if he's together with a woman who only wants to do it a little while he wants to do it a lot. On average once a day, he reckons. So he can't be with someone who only wants it every four days. And there's one other thing that's just as important, and that's that she doesn't poke and pry. He's had enough of that already, from Child Welfare, foster parents, social workers and psychologists, so he doesn't want to be with a girl who pokes and pesters. Respect to Sandra, because she's twigged that. When something comes up in conversation that he can't face talking about, she looks at him with those well gorgeous eyes that make Daniel think of some kind of exotic bird, her lips glisten and it's just like there's light in those three freckles on her nose, and that little mousy mouth of hers drives him nuts, the pursed lips with the slightly protruding teeth, and she gets it, gets that there's certain things you don't want to get into. She's understood what all those childcare losers haven't: if you talk and talk and talk about things, pull them out of the ground like rabbits, then everything goes to shit.

Daniel glances up at the football pitch by the school. He takes his mobile from his leather jacket. 20:52. She's usually on time.

It's shite digging up things best left buried thousands of miles underground.

But the fact that they named him William.

What the fuck were they thinking? Were they at the hospital watching him pop out of his mother and did they think, *ah, we'll have to call him William*. Daniel *William*. What kind of gay name was that?

Daniel spits.

You get the life you're given, it's your job to live it.

It's shite with things that are best left buried thousands of miles underground.

Sometimes he thinks about it. About killing. Just going out and killing somebody. Making a person disappear just because he can. What a release it must be. Clench your fists until they're as hard as wrecking balls, pummel a face until you can't tell it's a face.

Maybe tonight's the night.

Screw.

Screw.

Screw.

5. **AMY LEE** (Tiril)

'Tiril, *please,* can you help me here?'

She sees the honey jars roll across the lino, hears them rattling like the peel of sick bells, sees the sweaty, Christian girl crawling on all fours, and she turns up the volume on the iPhone, wipes the ice cream freezer with the cloth and looks the other way.

Thea is going to sit at the piano and Tiril will stand in front. *I'm so tired of being here, suppressed by all my childish fears.* Thea will be dressed in white: white top, white dress, white tights and white shoes. Whereas she'll be in black: black top, black dress, black tights and black shoes. *And if you have to leave I wish that you would just leave, 'cause your presence still lingers here, and it won't leave me alone.* They're going to blow the roof off the gym hall. *These wounds won't seem to heal, this pain is just too real, there's just too much that time cannot erase.* Tiril feels it on her arms, the hairs standing on end, same as when she heard the song for the first time on YouTube: *When you cried I'd wipe away all of your tears.*

On Thursday. The International Culture Workshop. Kinda daft, but, whatever.

'Tiril! Can you please come and help me here?'

She ignores Christian Girl's desperate pleas and crouches down. Evanescence fills her head as she gives the large surfaces of the freezer a thorough wipe.

Thea's amazing on the piano, she's been playing for years and her parents reckon she could go far. Beethoven and Brahms and all kinds of stuff just flies from her fingers, and she only needs to hear a song and she can play it. It's mad. Her fingers just run across the keys. It's not that easy either, 'My Immortal'. Maybe it's not that hard, like technically, but getting the feeling right, only Thea can do that. And Amy Lee.

And Tiril Fagerland.

They've tried getting hold of a black piano, or a grand, but the school doesn't have anything like that, only an electronic one. But nobody will have a bad word to say about the stage show. They're going to cover the windows in the gym hall with black sheets, drape a black felt cloth over the piano, and Tiril found a five-branched candelabra in Oxfam. The candlesticks in it will shine bright.

You used to captivate me by your resonating light, now I'm bound by the life you left behind.

After the second verse, Tiril's going to let a black, see-through shawl fall down over her face. She'll stand upright, motionless, her gaze fixed on the floor, her body rigid, like a statue, her fingers splayed like a leaf. Then she'll raise her head, slowly, slowly, as she sings the most powerful lines in the song:

I've tried so hard to tell myself that you're gone.
But though you're still with me I've been alone all along.

The plan is for it to be dark when she sings those lines, and then on the final chorus the lights will come up, preferably ones with green and red filters. That's when she needs to give it her all. She needs to sing like Amy Lee, needs to think that *she is Amy Lee*, that she's the one who grew up in Little Rock, Arkansas.

Tiril is going to go there someday. She's going to see the place Evanescence are from. She's going to walk the streets, breathe the air. What would be really amazing would be to see them live in their hometown, like Dad did with Maiden. Dad says he had metal on the brain when he was young, Maiden mainly, and even though he doesn't listen to metal any more he'll never forget that time he saw them in London. He's talked about it loads, about what a fantastic feeling it is, seeing your favourite band in the city they come from. And she'll be the one to do it, not Malene. Tiril will be the one who'll fly to the US, she's the one who'll visit Little Rock, Arkansas.

If there had been eight letters in Evanescence, she would have written it in felt pen on her fingers. But it doesn't fit. Neither does *My Immortal*, or *Little Rock*. Tiril has come up with something else. Something more her style. Eight letters, two hands, two words. The atmosphere in the gym hall is going to be electric, she's going to raise her hands and hold them like a shield in front of her face: LOVE HATE. *These wounds won't seem to heal, this pain is just too real, there's just too much that time cannot erase.*

Burn in hell, Mum.

Tiril gets to her feet. Slinging the washcloth over her shoulder, she presses pause on the iPhone and looks over at Sandra. She's crouched down gathering honey jars, her stupid fingers working away in panic. Tiril takes a few steps towards her.

'Did you say something, by the way?'

Sandra glowers at her while she stacks the last of the jars. She shakes her head.

'I don't get you, Tiril,' she says. 'What exactly have I done to you?'

Tiril stops and leans against the spices.

'It's late,' she says.

'Eh?' Sandra says, blushing.

'You can just go. YOLO.'

'I don't know what you're on about,' says Sandra. She places the last jar on top of the display stand. 'See you later.'

Sandra takes the vacuum cleaner and walks in the direction of the back door. Tiril nods.

Do you think I haven't copped on?

I know where you're off to, shiza.

I know what you're up to, biatch.

I don't like you anyway, not you, your necklace, your BO, your lawyer daddy, your Jesus freak mother or your lies. You think you're so perfect, but you're a Canada Goose minge, a Jimmy Choo ho, a Chanel poontang, a preppy tart, and sorry, but I've news for you: Someday you're going to walk out on the guy you marry, you're going to leave the people around you, you're going to betray your own family, and you're never going to go to Little Rock, Arkansas, because you've no style of your own, slut.

6. **YOU CAN HAVE ME** (Sandra)

Sandra is clammy, her neck feels damp, her back is sweaty and her forehead is moist. She needs to get herself that headscarf, Hennes & Mauritz? She knows that H&M sell stuff that falls apart after the first wash. There are a lot of things her mother's wrong about but she's right about that: *If you want quality, you have to pay for it. Hennes and Mauritz is not the kind of shop that's renowned for its quality, Sandra.*

If she wants to?

He has peered at her with those deep-set eyes of his, they're so far back in his head that sometimes she feels she's going to fall into them. He's put his arms around her and pressed up against her, she's felt how strong and hard he is. When he asks – *Do you want me, Sandra* – he glows. He glows with savage hunger, and right at that moment she thinks that even though she doesn't know if she wants what he's talking about, she wants it just the same. Because he wants to, because he's so hungry.

She knows what she's going to say next time he asks.

Yes, I want you.

Take me, Daniel.

His name is singing in her head from the time she wakes up until she goes to sleep and far into her dreams: Daniel William Moi. He can't bear being named William. It's poncy, he says, as if I'm supposed to be English or something, I can't bloody stand poncy things. But Sandra just wants to take his name in her hands and caress it, cradle it like a bird, stroke its soft feathers with her fingers, put her lips to its head and kiss it. No fucking way I'm letting you use that name, he's told her. Daniel swears quite a lot, she doesn't really like it when people swear, but when he does it she thinks it sounds like a song.

I don't use that name, Sandra, and you're not to use it either, nobody knows I'm called that, just you, and God help you if you tell anyone.

Just her. Just Sandra Vikadal.

I want to know more about you than everybody else.

I want that part of you that nobody else has.

I want to be closer to you than anybody else.

She used to see people in love and think it was gross, she thought boys were annoying, always rowdy and acting stupid, if they weren't called Johnny Depp and weren't hanging on her wall, that is. Now she doesn't recognise the girl she was, because nothing has been as real as this. It's awfully difficult to know if she's doing the right thing. Does she say the things he likes to hear? Does he think it's a turn-off when she sweats like she does? Does he cringe listening to her speak, does he think that tooth of hers is ugly, or her voice sounds stupid? Sometimes when she talks it can sound sort of hollow and lumpy, as though she had a potato in her throat, does he find that disgusting? And what about her age? He says it doesn't matter that she's only fifteen, but sometimes she thinks he's lying, well, not lying of course, people in love don't lie, but still, is he only saying it to cover up how gross he actually thinks it is?

The hardest thing of all is to know if she's good-looking enough.

No matter how many times he tells her she's sexy in those jeans, the pair she lays out flat and takes care not too wash too often, she still doesn't know if it's just something he's saying. If there're a thousand other girls who are just as pretty, whose bums are just as nice. And no matter how often his mouth breaks into that bright smile of his when he sees that expression on her face, the one he thinks is so incredibly cute, she still can't be sure if he's not just putting it on. Even though she trusts him. Of course she does. Because that's love. But still she's nervous, still she takes a long time getting ready.

Her boobs, do they look nice enough?

He stares at them intently, but who knows what he's actually thinking?

She's let him touch them lots of times. It's mad how long he can just stand there, teeth clenched, with that lovely jawline of his, fondling them. Yesterday, she let him kiss them. She took off her bra, in the middle of the woods, her fingers were trembling and she could hardly believe it herself, *the fact she was actually doing it*, as she slipped her hands under her top, unhooked her bra and wriggled it out of her sleeve and stood there, practically naked behind the substation while darkness fell around them. Lord, imagine if someone had come? Imagine someone had seen her standing there, when Daniel opened his bright mouth and said *Oh Jesus, Oh Jesus, they're so fucking beautiful*.

When he said that, she wasn't able to feel anything.

All she was able to do was show herself to him. Because she knew that's what he wanted, it made it her own choice. Show herself and let him touch her breasts, let him kiss them. Then she felt a jolt of happiness through her, but all she could think was: Are they nice enough? Are my boobs as soft and as firm as he wants, are they big enough for him, are they the shape he likes? She doesn't have very small boobs but they're not very big either; compared to the other girls in the class she's probably a little bit bigger than average, but what does that actually mean, and what does Daniel want? Because boys like boobs, she learnt that long ago, and a nice bum, they like that too. But legs? It's not so easy being a girl, not everyone can manage not giving a toss, like Tiril does, not everyone is able to put on a pair of headphones, some goth make-up and rail against the world. It's hard being a girl, because girls are supposed to look so nice all the time, and that doesn't seem fair. Sandra has short legs, her knees are a little knobbly maybe, sometimes she thinks they look like malformed wheels, and Daniel has never mentioned her legs. He's never even looked at them. Her thighs, which are a little thick compared to her body, he's touched those, but not with the same hunger as when he puts his hands on her bum or her breasts. But her legs? Nothing. Doesn't he like them?

My mouth, then? Do you like my mouth, Daniel?

It is small, slightly puckered, my two front teeth do stick out a little and I know they make me look like a rodent. Do you like that? Your little rat-girl?

That's all she wants. To look good enough for Daniel William Moi. *For the rest of her life*, she thinks, glancing at Tiril before taking the vacuum cleaner and going into the backroom. She's unbelievable, that girl. She saw the stack of honey going all over the floor. She heard her asking for help. But she couldn't care less. What's more, she enjoyed it. What is with her? If Sandra told the manager how little work Tiril does, she'd be fired. But Sandra's not a snitch.

20:54

Sandra brings her hand to the crucifix round her neck and squeezes it.

She opens the closet and stows the vacuum cleaner as quickly as she can. Then pulls off her work clothes.

There's never anybody in the woods at night. Round the back of the old school, behind the substation. The only sound they've ever heard is a dog barking. If her friends knew what she was up to they'd shake their heads in disbelief. Jesus, they'd say; going into the woods to meet a seventeen-year-old boy, you do realise what he's after? If they knew *who* she was with, they'd be shocked. They'd be jealous, they'd hardly believe her. *Sandra, you really need to think about this, Daniel Moi, he's not right in the head, everyone knows that.* He's in the sixth form, he rides a moped, he plays in a heavy metal band, he's hot, *but he's not right in the head*, he's from a foster home, people say he's had some seriously screwed-up things happen in his life, he's dangerous, Sandra, you do know that?

If her Mum found out what was happening, she'd freak out. If she heard it was the boy from the foster home, the one who lives with the single mother and her deaf daughter in the flats, she'd break down in tears and start picturing hash, heroin and the end of the world. But no one knows Daniel. They've no clue what that bright mouth of his can say, what those long-fingered hands of his can do or what's stirring in those hungry eyes. They don't realise that he needs her, don't realise that he has an emptiness inside, but Sandra does, and when he says he doesn't want to tell her what happened to him, she understands that. She understands what he's gone through because she can see into his soul, and she's not going to nag him about it, she's promised herself that. She'll never ask what happened, she doesn't listen to rumours, about him having boxed, having beaten up some guy, the thing about his real parents, and that there was something really messed up there. She doesn't listen to gossip, because she is Sandra Vikadal and he is Daniel William Moi.

They can laugh at her, they can trample all over her. They can do what they want.

But they better remember, for all eternity, that they've trampled on love itself.

Because Love, thinks Sandra, love bears all things, love believes all things, love hopes all things, and love, she thinks, taking out her mobile once more, love endures all things.

20:58

You can have me, Daniel William Moi, no matter what it is you're after.

7. LOVE (Rudi)

It's quiet in the car now.

Just the hum of the engine and the sound of the wheels on the tarmac.

Rudi has never liked silence. The feeling of people just waiting to drop a bombshell. Sitting there mulling over some pickle or another they can't face talking about. Speech is silver, Granny said, but silence is golden. Well, Gran, my respect for you is as infinite as the love of the Lord, but that's where we differ.

Rudi has been told loud and clear. On more than one occasion, to put it mildly. That there can be a bit too much gabbing.

Okay!

All right!

But there can be a bit too much bloody silence as well.

Rudi sees the reflection of his face in the rear-view mirror. Behind that, he sees Chessi resting her head against the back seat and closing her eyes. No, love. Who would've believed it that time he called into Jani's house and set eyes on his freckly little sister, lying in her bedroom, getting her brains fucked out beneath posters of horses and dogs? No, those days are long gone, that was Jani's psycho plan. Renting out your sister like she was a movie. You'd have to be right twisted to be at that.

Here you go. Help yourself. This is my sister. Cunt retail.

'Eh? Chessi? You there?'

Good thing she met me, thinks Rudi, replacing the silence with his own thoughts. No telling where she would have wound up if her best customer hadn't caught sight of the person behind the pussy. And, Jesus, the amount of times he's wanted to beat the shit out of those mongrels who got the chance to fuck her before he came on the scene. If he ran into them today he'd skin them alive, bit by bit. It's twenty-seven years since he saw those bulging eyes for the first time. Twenty-seven years since he deserted the Tjensvoll Gang; thanks for the apprenticeship, handy to know you should gaffa-tape a table leg to get a good grip. Handy to know which slim jim to boost a Beamer with. Handy to know how it feels to kick a man in the back of the head! Old memories; salut Tommy Pogo, salut Frax and Stix and Hex, salut Rikke Clit and Baps and J-J-Janne D-D-Dobro, salut Fresi and Christer Imfuckinoff, salut Janka Bat. Rudi needs to be getting on in life. My folks are moving to Hillevåg. Heh heh. Right into the arms of Jani. There's always someone who wants to live outside the law and there's no better leader than Jan Inge Haraldsen, is there now?

Twenty-seven years of love.

'Hmm? Chessi? Baby? Are you there? Ready to do a bit of work?'

No reply.

Give her some time. Ha. Renting out his sister like she was a video. Hard to stomach for a family man like Rudi. But how long are you going to store up old shit? Now everything has calmed down nicely, it's not something they talk about all the time, no more than Rudi can stand anyone bringing up his parents, not to mention that rabid brother of his out in Sandnes, and that psychotic witch he's married to.

They've put it behind them. In the name of love. Chessi and him have stood strong, and what with the unbelievable number of divorces going on all around, society is just about ready to go under: is it any wonder they vote for the Christian Democrats? Listen here, Mr Socialist Homo: walk around in your slippers. Play your protest songs. Listen to The Smiths and The Tits and The Pits. Somebody has to show people what's right and what's wrong in this world, and one thing's for sure, love, that can't be explained, but it's always right, which is pretty much the gist of what it says in The Good Book which Rudi always keeps in the bedside drawer.

She was only thirteen the first time he saw her, and some people may well think that's sick, but Rudi doesn't give a flying fuck what they think. Because the truth is: from the day he saw that chestnut hair, that freckly body and those cracked lips, Rudi knew Cecilie Haraldsen would be his. And that – oh yes – that's just like it was with Granny and Granddad. They stuck together. Weathered all the storms. That's just how it was, *and that's just how it is with Chessi and me,* he thinks and feels a swelling in his chest, the way he always does when something moves him. And the feeling can be just as intense whether you're listening to some good metal or have brought in a nice bit of cash on a warehouse job because you've got a leader who did the groundwork, got hold of a key card and checked times and routines, or like when, for the *fifty thousandth time,* you get an eyeful of what a bloody good woman you *actually* have.

Itsthetwoofusbaby.

Tong's getting out on Friday. Be good that. About time.

Hey Tong, you sick Korean!

Rudi orders himself to give Cecilie more time and meets his own face in the rear-view mirror. No, he thinks, if there's something I bloody well am not, it's good-looking. It's that long line of dishcloths. Dad's side. Dishcloth genes. Looked like pin cushions, the lot of them. A minefield, all over his skin, wrinkled and scarred. And what about a little colour? A little pigment? Oh no, we'll make you pale and anæmic. But we'll make your lips big! Not just a bit big, but biiiiig. And your teeth? Rudi bares his teeth in the mirror. Jesus. They look like nails. They're crooked, all of them, as though they aren't doing anything in his mouth other than fighting. His hair, on the other hand, that's okay. He hasn't started going grey, and as for hair loss, none of that. Colour is a tad dull maybe, this mousy blond tone, hairdo's a bit crap, sort of half long with no style, but it's hair all the same. But good looks, they do not run in the family. Even Granny, that angel, was pig ugly.

A smile spreads across Rudi's face and he can't manage to keep his mouth shut any longer:

'Chessi? You know... fuck, you know... right? That Rudi damn well loves you like crazy? That if you left me I'd kill everyone and everything around me? You know that, right? That you're mine? That I'm yours?'

But no.

'Hmm? Baby? A kind word for a kind man?'
Not a fucking peep.
'Hmm? I yours? You mine?'

8. DEVIL'S TREASURES (Daniel William)

Fifteen. Yeah, so what?

20:54

Daniel pulls out a pack of cigarettes. Takes one out.

In the old days girls had kids when they were fifteen. They were a damn sight more grown up back then. Boys were able to do everything when they were fifteen. No fuss made about how old the girls could be. Now it's all a big to-do. Everything's supposed to be so meaningful the whole time, everything has to be so open and curious and ecological, and he doesn't know what his foster mother and the ones from Child Services are on about. He's been at enough meetings; open get-togethers, my ass – more like they've just made up a load of stuff because they're after getting some ideas in their heads.

For Daniel it's simple.

He pulls his leather jacket tighter around him and lights up the cigarette.

All he wants is to be with girls and get it on with them and for them to get it on with him. Sandra is fifteen and she's fit as fuck. She has a glow around her. He's been with other girls but he's never gone all the way. He's got his hands on tits, licked tits and snogged so much he was almost bored of it – up until he started snogging with Sandra. It was as though his whole mouth became electric, as if something happened, physically, to his tongue, making him just want more.

He's mucked about a lot with tits, he's stuck his fingers into plenty of girls, stuck them in and rubbed. He likes it and all, but sometimes he feels he's lying there rubbing away like you'd scrape at some candle wax stuck to a table. He's kissed a girl between the legs, in a bedroom at a party, but that was a disaster. She was shitfaced, and even though he wasn't that drunk it was no good, she smelt rank, tasted rank too. It'll get better with time. He's going to be a world-beater. Requires practice. A steady relationship. Figure out where to find the right spots, do it the right way.

Daniel balances the cigarette between his lips while he tosses the moped helmet from one hand to the other. Stupid bloody Child Welfare. *What's missing from your life, Daniel?* Wha? Missing? Eh, a moped? *A moped? We can talk about that, Daniel, if you show yourself deserving of the trust placed in you.* Three months later: Ha fucking ha. 20,000 kroner on eBay. Suzuki AC50 from 1978. A sweet second-hand moped at Child Services' expense. Newly overhauled engine, new tyres, wiring, wheel bearings, battery, re-bored barrel and a new piston. The red paintwork was just a little worn, but he fixed that himself.

The ladies like a dude with a bike.

Compared to his mates he's lagging behind when it comes to women. He's the only one in the band who hasn't gone all the way. Dejan has so many women on the go it's nuts, probably because he's a Serb, looks dangerous and has scars across his back and his face. Should see Dejan rolling dice, he looks seriously Mafioso.

Still though, it's strange, because Daniel is popular. He's good-looking, he knows that. But it's just never quite worked out; does he scare the women away?

Daniel takes a drag of the cigarette and leans his head back against the corner of the substation wall while he fiddles with the strap on the helmet. He's getting closer to it with Sandra. Maybe because he's able to behave in a different way with her than with other girls. Maybe he's learnt a little from living with Veronika? It's different when you live with them, you pick up on things, see what girls like and what they don't like. She's okay, Veronika. Bit weird, maybe. All right, so she's deaf, so what? He knows exactly what he'd do to anyone who said a bad word about her, they can just go ahead and try it, if they want their eyes cut out of their heads.

A lot of things have been different with Sandra. He feels he can be more of a man. He can tell her stuff like how sexy she looks in those jeans, and she lights up and beams like a funfair. Same with that facial expression she gets. When her dimples show and the wings of her nose expand and her mouth kind of begins to twitch. Jesus, she's cute when she does that.

Girls.

That's what life's all about.

Bollocks to all that other shit and bollocks to the past, that's for sure.

Play the drums. Work out. Drink beer. But above all, girls.

20:56. She'll be here soon.

It was mental yesterday.

It was as though a glowing light came rolling over the gravel. She came running across the football pitch, her forehead sweaty, small, sexy, shy and sure of herself all at the same time, scared someone might see her. So they went into the woods and got up to a bit of the usual stuff. Hugging and kissing, he put his hand on her ass, both inside and outside her jeans, felt her thighs, placed his hand on her crotch, but only through the jeans, and he pressed himself against her, he always does that, because he gets such a hard-on he doesn't know what to do with it. And then he said the things that make her light up, how sexy she is in those jeans, how cute she looks when she makes that face and that he likes how her lips glitter. And he felt her tits, obviously. You can't be with girls without getting the tit, that'd just be weird. He pulled down her top a little, so he could kiss her nipples. And then.

It was fucking mental.

She stopped and looked at him. When they were tonguing, or maybe when he was trying to work his hand further down her ass. No, it was when he was feeling her tits. They're amazing, he doesn't like big tits, they're too much, big jugs screw up the whole mood, and he doesn't know what to do with really small ones, even though they're sexy in a dirty sort of way. But Sandra's tits, they're amazing. They just sit there looking dead good. So there he was, busying himself with her tits, and then, out of nowhere, she stops and almost pushes him away. She practically had tears in her eyes, they were moist and glistening anyway, and he didn't understand a thing, *shit, is she crying?* But then, all of a sudden, she puts her hands behind her back, while Daniel just stands there thinking *okay, okay, what's going on, keep cool,* and then: Holy fuck.

She starts taking off her bra. In the middle of the woods.

She has her hands round her back and she unhooks the bra, and then, quick as a flash, performs some sleight of hand where she jiggles the strap and pulls the bra out her sleeve, so that her tits are actually just dangling there behind that grey cotton top, and Daniel just breathes, gulps and says *Oh Jesus, Oh Jesus*, and he has no idea what the fuck he's going to do, but he doesn't need to do anything, because this is happening by itself, this well fit girl is standing in front of him taking off her top. Is he in heaven? Are there angels in the air? He's got such a hard-on he thinks he's going to croak, but he just remains standing there, because he needs to take this in, needs to take a photograph and glue it to his brain, if there's one scene from life that he wants to remember every pissy little worthless day, then it's this: Sandra taking off her top in the woods.

Then she stands there.

Just her and her tits.

Some girls. They can look like buttercups. But then. Then they get warmed up. Then something else emerges. Then the floodgates open. They can be some randy little hornbags, so they can.

Oh sweetfuckingjesus, so nice. Almost make you believe in God. It's precisely those kinds of things, like what he experienced there, that happiness is made off. Of course it is.

But a steady relationship?

Daniel's fingers are cold. He feels the urge to scratch them against the rough surface of the substation wall.

Watch yourself, Daniel.

That kind of thing brings about ashes and devil's treasure. Eventually the ground opens up beneath your happiness, and fangs start snapping at you from below.

He puts the chaos out of his mind and flicks the cigarette into the gathering darkness.

20:58.

9. **MY SNATCHPUSS 4 EVER** (Cecilie)

'Hey, baby? You not going to say anything? Eh? Come on, screw napping, darling, youandme? Youandmeandyourbody? Europe, eh?'

The Volvo is approaching Gosen Forest, and the darkness around them is deepening. Rudi's voice fills the car and it's so intense it reeks like a compact stench. Cecilie catches her breath. She rests her neck against the back of the seat, puts her hand in her pocket, takes out a pack of cigarettes and lights up a new one. Europe? She loves Europe, but this isn't about Europe.

His eyes. She sees them in the rear-view mirror. His pupils are zipping round like rubber balls.

Cecilie closes her eyes, inhales the smoke and feels her body relax. I could have had a life, she thinks, I could have had something that was mine, but I don't.

'Eh? Ride on the joycock? Metal up your ass?'

Sometimes she's so tired of that rasping voice, of him going on, that she feels like throwing up just being in the same room. But she loves him as well. In a screwed-up way. It's been like that for as long as she can remember. She loves his blabbermouth, loves his stupid lips that look constantly swollen, and she loves his flapping hands, but she doesn't understand why any more.

Cecilie doesn't have the energy to reply. She misses Dad. That Houston doofus, why did he have to leave? He ruined everything and she's furious with him, but still misses him. You hear me, Dad? You just left, and here I am with Jani and Rudi. What if I want a life as well? Did anybody think of that?

Kids? A house? Some normal stuff?

'Hey? You know, as far as I'm concerned it isn't Rihanna or Michelle Williams that's the hottest chick of 2012! It's you!'

That's what life served her up: sitting at Jani's watching horror movies. Living in the same house for the fortieth year in a row. With a basement smelling of rot, paint peeling off the walls and mouldy old carpets. That's what she's been dished up: being the girlfriend of a guy, two metres tall, with ADHD and bomb-crater skin, who drives around in a stupid Volvo, does break-ins on speed, talks the face off people and has an insane relationship with his family. That's her life: not to have a life of her own.

Cecilie swallows phlegm and exhales.

'Hey, baby, remember the first time? Eh? Twenty-seven years ago, and it's still as good! Eh, why so quiet, Missy Cissy! Heh heh! Do you get it? Cissy?'

Poor Jan Inge. 120 kilos now. That's way too much. Poor, fat boy. He is keeping the house and the business together, but he has little, frightened pinhead eyes, and he is my brother, she thinks. He's never been quite right in the head. People don't know him. They think he's an asthmatic loon with a twisted childhood, and they hear rumours about all the things Videoboy has done, and then they think he's a psycho who just sits there watching horror movies.

But that's not the whole truth.

They don't know what a big heart he has.

It's big enough to beat for the whole world.

'By all means, Chessi. It's up to you! As long as you can suck cock, I won't complain about the lack of words coming out of your mouth. Heh heh, you can say what you want, but we can hold our own, youandmeagainsttheshit! Just take a look around, and I mean right outside the window here, you've got the internet and divorces all day and all night.'

Cecilie looks at Rudi's bobbing head, his hands tapping on the wheel. She knows every inch of that scarred body. Now and then she thinks Rudi is a country and she's a settler there. Sometimes it's a pleasant thought, sometimes it's terrifying.

To think it's possible to loathe a man like I loathe him, and love a man as much as I love him. It doesn't make sense.

Months and years have gone by without anything happening. Days have come, days have gone, and she'll be forty in December.

She can't remember the last time she felt something was happening. But now something is. Something is going on inside of her, and something is going on out there: Tong is getting out on Friday. Cecilie is the one picking him up outside the gates of Åna. Half past eight. Tong. Not the way it was supposed to turn out now, was it?

'Ooh arr, like the farmer said, looks barren 'ere. You'll have to make your own fun.'

She pushes the image of Tong aside and runs her hand under her eye. It feels wet, she sits up, looks at her face in the rear-view mirror to the right of Rudi's head. That vole face of mine. What am I crying for? Look at my make-up. She takes another drag of the cigarette.

Her skin is going to look like ash soon. She is going to be ash soon. She smokes too much. One day she's just going to lie there. *What's that?* A pile of ash. *What was it though, before it turned to ash?* Dunno, no one remembers.

'Baby? Have I ever told you that if the sun went down, and I mean burned out and died, then I wouldn't give a damn, as long as I've got you to light up the house? Eh?'

Cecilie sniffles. He is my snatchpuss, she thinks, no matter how things are. It's Rudi and me. It really is. He is snatchpuss 4 ever.

Coldplay. She saw him. He was sitting there getting into Coldplay.

I hate Coldplay, she thinks.

I want a life, I want a real house, I want a proper man, one who doesn't talk a blue streak and keep spinning like a wheel, I want to hear heavy ballads round the clock, I want my days to feel golden.

Cecilie sighs. 'Rudi boy,' she says, 'we're almost there. You need to get to work.'

I don't know anyone but me who cries from just one eye.

10. HE WALKS INTO THE PITCH DARKNESS
(Pål)

Zitha tugs at the leash once they're outside the house. He can feel how primed the dog is, and he lets her strain forward with her snout to the ground. She needs to be driven by her instincts, needs to live and breathe by them.

The day has been unusually warm, but now night has come and the autumn cold is here again. It's in the air all around him, crackling almost delicately; in a couple of months it will have transformed into winter.

Pål walks over to the rubbish bins. His feet feel heavy, his head feels fried. Is it the green one today? Black? Brown? He looks down the street at the rows of brown bins lined up on either side outside each house, like podgy soldiers. He wheels the bin out in front of the hedge and starts walking down the road with Zitha hurrying ahead of him.

He's been at this so long he's not afraid any more. The most surprising thing is how proficient you become. Living with all the lies isn't difficult. Neither is living with all the covering-up. It's the wide-open world that's difficult to live in.

He comes to Norvald Frafjords Gate and sees the blocks of flats rise up into the sky. The sight of the high-rises has had a hold on him ever since he was little. All the people inhabiting them, all the people living their secret lives, all the people trying to get on. When he was a child and passed them on his way to school – to think it's over thirty years since he did that for the first time – he imagined that everyone living there would one day be pressed out, like meat from a mincer, their eyes, their ears, mouths and hands.

Yeah. That's how it is.

The wide-open world, where nothing is hidden, hard to live in it.

What is with my eyes?

Imagine. These eyes will be forty in a little under a month.

Pål checks his mobile. Soon be nine o'clock. He feels Zitha tug at the leash.

The gap between who he is and what people see has grown so big. It's a strange feeling. Everyone can see him but no one has a clue who they're looking at. They see that guy who's always lived here. Some of the elderly people in the area probably remember him from when he was a kid. They probably recall a normal enough boy, quiet type. The carpenter's son. Yeah, they'd say. Pål Fagerland? He grew up here, nice kid. People his own age might remember the woman living here a few years back. The wife, they'd say, Christine, left him and the kids. Career woman, they'd say. Statoil, made good money, she was a real go-getter. Must have got tired of him. He was a bit humdrum for her, they'd say, strange the pair of them got together in the first place. But what is it they say – opposites attract? She was the one with the money. But imagine leaving the kids, eh? What kind of woman does that? Yeah, times have changed. Mind you, she was generous enough, went to Bergen but let him hang on to the house and that. Poor guy. Works for the local authority, doesn't he? Caseworker or something.

Yeah.

That's probably what they'd say.

Poor guy.

And what is it they see?

A man of average height, dressed in regular clothes. Greying at the temples, round cheeks, childlike skin, hardly any beard and a bashful look in his eyes. His wife was forever saying it, *Pål, can you try looking at people when you're talking to them, it makes them uneasy when your eyes are flitting all over the place.*

Pål isn't the one who pipes up a lot at parents' meetings. He isn't the one who talks loudest in work. He isn't the one who comes out with fresh ideas. He's never been called intense, never been called conspicuous and never been called dangerous. But he has been called kind, been called good and been called reliable. That was what his wife used to say, *I need you, Pål, you bring balance to my life*. Right. Well, suddenly one day you didn't need that any more, did you, Christine?

Pål has always thought that he sees the world as it is.

Seems like that was a bit too boring for her though, doesn't it?

Eh, Christine? Everything you said you needed, everything you said I represented, all that you needed in your life in order for it to make sense. A husband who arrived home at the same time every day, who kept the household in order and took care of all the day-to-day stuff. You started looking in another direction. And then you just left.

Pål, I can't do this any more.

You've been so, so very kind.

You've been so, so very dependable.

But I have to go.

You're just going to leave me here?

You'll manage, Pål.

You're just going to leave the girls?

They'll understand someday, Pål.

Have you lost your bloody mind?

You're strong, Pål, remember that.

Pål scratches Zitha behind the ears. Strong? His eyes are dry, like there's a white light against them. Malene is right: he needs to see the doctor. Strong? He's never felt strong. We've just lived, Pål thinks, from one day to the next, we've tried to do as well as we could. Often, when he hears people discussing their lives, it seems like they're talking about a series of choices they've made. It doesn't feel like that to Pål. It feels, for the most part, as though life were a river and he's been a boat. The girls have gotten bigger. Malene has had her gymnastics. She's practically grown up in that hall – palm guards, chalk, glittering leotards, ice packs and perseverance. Tiril has been a tornado, ferocious intensity, with a restlessness to match. They've travelled backwards and forwards to Bergen a couple of times a month and come home with expensive clothes and make-up: love from Mum. Malene has gone along with being driven to the airport, gone along with being picked up again, and Tiril has hated it from day one. Everything to do with her mother is just fuel to an ever raging fire within her.

He knew Christine could be cynical, but that she could actually go ahead and leave the kids, that was cold. Withdraw from their childhood and stake everything on Statoil and that guy from Bergen. Albeit that was Pål's only consolation: he was left with the kids. The girls had kept things afloat. The drive to gymnastics. The sight of Malene doing backflips, the shouts of the trainer in the hall: Good, Malene! Come on, now straighten up! You need to jump sooner. Wrists straight. Such a shame about that injury; she landed badly on her ankle in the spring, never screamed like that before. She hasn't trained properly since.

Tiril?

Trying to catch her eye, get beyond that wild gaze, never succeeding.

The girls are all he's got. He can't take them over the brink with him. He has to do something, otherwise he may as well put a bullet through his head. Whether or not what he's about to do is a good idea, he doesn't know. But it's the only idea he's got.

Pål halts at the bus stop on Folkeviseveien. He reaches for his inside pocket. 'There, there, Zitha,' he whispers as he takes out the envelope, 'Daddy's just going to get rid of this.' He feels the relief as the envelope lands in the bus shelter bin. Together with all the others. It feels like it's taking all the mould along with it, as if his problems were actually over, and he smacks his lips at Zitha, walks out from under the shelter, back up the hill and doesn't cross over until he's reached the back of the high-rises.

They walk along the footpath, the fields enlarging the landscape around them. Zitha is frisky and happy.

'There, Zitha, there. Go on!'

He walks her every day. Usually up to the fields and forests of Sørmarka, to Hinnaberget, sometimes down to the sea at Møllebukta, but mostly they go to Limahaugen by the Iron Age Farm. Get outdoors, feel like the blood is flowing from Zitha's body over to his. He sees how she tenses up when she picks up the scent of something, sees how her body spurts across the ground. 'Yeah, yeah, Zitha. Go on!' What he likes most is standing on top of Limahaugen, close to the old cairn, and looking down at Hafrsfjord. The three islands, Prestøy, Somsøy and Kobbholmen, lying there like three brothers. He and a mate used to go out there when they were small, to Sømsøy, except they called it Bunny Island on account of all the rabbits running around. Long time ago now.

This is what he likes best. Him, with the dog by his side. If anyone was ever going to paint a portrait of him, then this is what would fill the canvas.

But no one, he thinks, has any idea what I'm up to.

Getting close to nine o'clock.

This isn't going to work out, is it?

Below him lies the forest.

He has the blocks of flats to his right, Limahaugen to his left, and on the horizon the telecom tower at Ullandhaug. Once past the flats, the primary school comes into view. Madlavoll. The one he went to so many years ago. The gym, football pitch, the school building. Brand new in the eighties, seems old now, run-down and out of date. Happens to everything. Everything that was modern, forced to become so faded. Pål looks over at the schoolyard. That's where they played football, where the girls jumped rope, they were there, all of them. Jørgen, Lise, Thomas, Jarle, Bülent, Susanne, Anna and Prince. Prince. What a character. That's all we called him, Prince. He was a damn good breakdancer. Him and Inge. They were the first ones in school to do handstands, had to beat the women off with a stick. Then the girls of course, Hilde, Marianne, ah, she was gorgeous. Funny about the girls you never get. They can haunt you for the rest of your life. And Anne Mette, she became an actor, she did, and then there was Odd ... Odd Jonas, no ... Odd Roger, the guy with the forehead covered in zits, big guy. Yeah, Odd Roger. Something screwed-up there. Wasn't right in the head. Just filled up with hate ... and Pesi ... He died, didn't he? Yeah, junkie. Popped his clogs.

Strange thinking about the old gang.

Feels painful. And it feels good.

And Hasse – imagine, they were so close in secondary school, for a while they were together day and night, and now? They're embarrassed when they meet. Hasse has become a bit of a minor celebrity, works for the Minister of Culture in Oslo. What would he have said if he knew what Pål was doing now? *Jesus, Pål. You're playing with fire. Jesus Christ, Pål, you're heading into the depths of the forest.*

The dog tugs at the leash.

'Yeah, come on, Zitha,' he says, 'Come on.'

He's thought a lot about that school reunion. They arrived one by one, face after face, half-forgotten memories dancing in front of his eyes. Ådne from Class 6B worked for the national health service and had lost his wife to cancer. Bjarne from 6C had MS. Kjartan from 6A had become a multi-millionaire, something to do with selling equipment to the oil business. Tine, Mimi and Anja tottered on high heels, drank gin & tonics and white wine and talked about Thomas Dybdahl, Karl Ove Knausgård and George Clooney, and were on the razz for the first time in ages. A lot of the lads turned up with pear-shaped bodies and potbellies and tried as well as they could to chat about football and the old days. All Pål could think about was how everyone had lost. *Everyone, including me, has lost. We're losing all the time, and we're losing hard, but at the same time our helplessness shines like small, blushing suns.*

Pål passes the kindergarten. Out of the corner of his eye he sees a moped parked over by the old substation. He speeds up, continues down towards Madlamarkveien, crosses over it and enters the wood on the other side. He doesn't take the tarmac path through the wood, he goes into the pitch darkness. He walks carefully through the ferns, the overgrown scrub, the twisted roots, letting Zitha sniff and lead the way.

He stops for a few seconds and turns his face towards the black tops of the trees. A clear, starry sky hangs above them.

There were other people too. Back in his younger days. People who lived in the darkness. People who dared do things he never would. People who crossed lines. People with wild eyes and clenched fists. The Tjensvoll Gang.

Malene mustn't ever find out about this, he thinks. *She must never know what her father was up to.*

He's arranged to meet him at nine o'clock.

11. **O LORD** (Daniel William)

I came down here to fuck these girls
O Lord
I came down here to fuck all of these girls
O Lord
Cause I'm a bad man
Yes I'm a bad man
But I'm a real man

I came down here to kill these girls
O Lord
I came down here to kill all of these girls
O Lord
Cause I'm a bad man
Yes I'm a bad man
But I'm a real man

He's not exactly a songsmith. But then neither are Dejan, Simon or Vegard. So he's been responsible for the lyrics. They're not particularly good, but that's one of the ones he's happy with, one of the ones that feels real.

Daniel remembers one time in third year when they had a writer visit the class, wow, like, *oh, so interesting, Mr Writer Dude, wow, did you really begin writing poetry when you were in second year? You read a thick book by a Russian writer, you say? Oh wow, Mr Writer Dude, I'm so impressed.*

Makes no difference. No one hears what Simon is singing anyway.

But real.

The lyrics of that one song. At least they're real.

Oh Lord.

Daniel checks the time again. 20:59

He often wakes up in the middle of the night, ready to burst he's so aroused. He'll wake up in the dark feeling like he's lying in a cold cave far up in the mountains, where ancient water drips down around his naked feral form, where diseased bats sail above his ringing head, where long curtains of stone hang down through the darkness, where blood boils within those black lungs of his, lungs that look like stone furnaces, where indiscernible spears cut through the foul air now and then, spears glistening with silver and grease, where screams are to be heard, long-drawn-out screams, that begin with a faint, barely audible tinnitus in the distance, before growing and gushing towards him like heavy trains, like jets of pain, banging like bolts against his hearing. Then he knows who's woken, the caveman, the stoneman, the ironman: *He just knows.*

20:59

O Lord

A thousand million kilometres beneath the earth.

Sandra. Now.

12. **THAT WAS KIND OF WEIRD** (Malene)

Adidas Superstar.

It just felt kind of weird.

Malene places her dad's shoes beside one another. The pair he likes best. She knits her brow. They're worn out, those trainers. He ought to get himself a new pair. She's told him. You ought to get a new pair of trainers, Dad. No, no, he said. The more worn in they are, the better.

Dad probably isn't aware she does it. Every night. Places his shoes neatly beside one another. Tiril certainly doesn't spot it. Her head is full of her own stuff. She probably hasn't noticed that he has a pair he wears every day. White with black stripes.

There's no other trainers I feel so comfy in, Dad says.

She gets to her feet.

Felt weird, that hug.

Malene has always been Dad's girl. He has driven her to gymnastics six days a week and she's always felt that he's been hers. She's always crept into his lap and felt it a safe place to be. It's not the kind of thing you think about when you're little, then it's just children's TV, pizza and Saturday treats, but one day you realise that you've always gone to Dad, without really knowing why. She's heard it before: a Daddy's girl. Tiril has said it often enough, that's for sure: go on, run to Daddy.

That hug.

It might not be anything.

But. It *was* weird.

Something about the way he held her. Something about his breathing. He has been acting pretty strangely of late. She never used to think about what he did when they went to bed. It was sort of obvious. He watched TV. He tidied up. He loaded the dishwasher. He hung up clothes to dry. But now? When she says goodnight to him it's like he has an aura of fear about him. How long does he stay up, actually? Maybe he's sad and can't sleep. Maybe he misses having a girlfriend. She has never had a boyfriend herself. She hasn't been quite ready for it. But she's not an idiot, she understands if Dad misses having one. But still. This feels like it's about something else. That hug, for instance. She came out of her room and caught sight of Dad. He was standing in the hall with Zitha. On his way out. And then he just started acting really weird. His bashful eyes grew moist and he suddenly pulled her close, quite roughly, it was totally spooky. Not in a nice way, not in the warm, cosy way he usually does. It was rough.

Malene fixes her eyes on the door, as if it will open merely by her doing so.

Jesus, Tiril's become a real pain in the ass. Fourteen, behaving like an idiot. Fine, they've never been very close, but she is her sister. They've slept in the same room, she's borrowed toys and jewellery, they've taken Zitha out for walks thousands of times and Malene has looked after her since she was small. But now it's as if she's disappeared into some idiotic land of her own, going around scowling at everyone, smearing thick layers of emo make-up on, and thinking Evanescence is the answer to everything in the world. It's fine that she's got her mind on singing next Thursday. It's great that she was picked to perform at the final performance of the International Cultural Workshop, and it's obvious that the director has seen she has talent, it's all good, but it's utterly impossible to get an intelligent word out of her, and she can't be bothered to do her homework, she just lies in bed listening to her iPhone.

Malene puts her forefinger in her mouth, bites right down to the quick.

That hug.

It's just like Sandra at school, she's out of it at the moment. Maybe it's something that happens to everyone, one day you're just out of it? One day you just have to explode? It happened to Mum. Her head was blown open, and she left. Is it going to happen to Malene too? One day, she'll be completely out of it?

She takes a few steps forward. She feels her ankle, it's still sore, how long will it take before she can start training again? She misses it a lot. The smell of the gym hall, the girls in the locker room, that feeling of floating through the air, the kick she gets from it.

She opens the front door, as though to check if he's standing there, right outside. As if she almost believes he is. Dad.

But there's nobody out there. Only the yellow glow of the street lights. Only a row of wheelie bins stretching all the way down to the main road. Only the stars in the night sky. Only this autumnal chill after a bright, warm day.

Dad is forgetting things, and his eyes aren't just dry, they're vacant. As though at times they're far away. He smiles all the time, he smiles when they are eating dinner, he smiles in the mornings, he smiles when he gets in from work, he smiles when he sits with the laptop in the evening and he smiles when they have visitors.

Malene nods.

She hurries to the kitchen, runs her hand across the hob, goes through the living room and checks no candles are burning, tries the handle on the veranda door. Out in the hallway she reaches for her shoes. Slips her feet into them, grabs the green jacket from the peg and puts it on.

She goes out. Because there's something wrong with that smile and she is the daughter of her father, Adidas Superstar.

13. **I'M COMING NOW** (SANDRA)

Love endures all things: There's a tingling on her tongue, as though tiny creatures were dancing across it.

The shop has to be inviting, that's what the manager said when she got the job. When people come through the door in the morning they have to feel welcome. Of course, Mr Spar. They've been happy with her up to now, hard to find fault with Sandra. A good girl, no denying she always has been. Always did her homework, got good marks, kept her room tidy and folded her clothes neatly. Sandra has never been able to live any other way, she gets a guilty conscience from just thinking about not doing things in a neat, proper and orderly fashion. Oh yes, her mother usually says when they have family over, you know Sandra, she was already tidying up toys when she was just a little tot.

She's done her part of the job. The floors are clean. She can go.

'Sandra?'

She gives a start. Suddenly aware of Tiril behind her, standing by the bottle return belt. Her hair is lank, make-up heavy, fingernails black and her gaze harsh. Headphones on. Does she always have to look so angry, is it necessary? Does she have to look like everyone's going to die at any moment?

'Where're you going?' Tiril asks, chewing her gum slowly and pulling off the headphones.

Sandra's can't bring herself to meet those eyes. 'My mum and dad are waiting,' she says, stepping into her shoes. 'You'll lock up, won't you?'

'Yeah, did you think I was going to leave it open or something?'

Tiril responds as if someone has had a go at her. It's weird to think that girl is going to sing in the gym hall on Thursday. She seems like she hates everything and everybody, what is it she's trying to prove? Sandra feels her anger form an aching lump in her chest. She does everything she can to be kind to people, to be open and understanding, everything she can for people to like her. She's used to people being polite. There're a lot of things you could say about Mum and Dad, but she agrees with them that the least you can expect from people is that they're friendly and polite, we only share a short time on this earth together so it's important to meet one another with love and kindness, that's the message of Jesus and the message of love.

Daniel, I'm coming now.

'No, no, I just meant … anyway, look, I've got to run.'

'Okay, so run then.'

Sandra feels a nauseous surge in her stomach. 'Do you know what?' she says firmly, her own boldness making her nervous. 'Do you know what? You can choose, are you aware of that?'

Tiril blinks for a fraction of a second but maintains her composure. 'Choose fucking what?'

'The light or the dark,' Sandra says quickly, startled by herself. She turns and hurries towards the exit.

'How sweet,' says Tiril. She goes back into the shop.

Sandra takes a deep breath, as though she'd done something illegal. She brings her tongue across the dry skin around her mouth and stops in front of the mirror hanging by the back door.

Now Jesus isn't the one I'm going to kiss any more, she thinks. She's never told anyone that she used to kiss Jesus. She'd turn out the light, creep under the duvet, close her eyes, blush, begin to move her lips and then she'd kiss Jesus. Her body would tingle, making her feel warm. But all that has to end, now that she's got her boy.

'Daniel,' she whispers, allowing her lips to part.

'Daniel,' she repeats, while applying a layer of lip gloss.

'Daniel,' her lips mouth, as she adjusts her new bra, trying to get her boobs to sit the way she thinks he'd like.

'Daniel,' she whispers while she fixes her fringe, moves the silver cross into place in the notch of her neck, dries the sweat from her forehead and tries to find that particular facial expression, 'I'm coming now.'

Then she opens the door, feels the air hit her, and she runs.

14. **FOG** (Rudi)

Rudi sees a wizened hand run through her fringe, wiping her teary eye, then a smile play across her mouth.

'Rudi boy,' she says again, and it's so bloody good to hear a friendly word from her that he almost breaks down with joy. 'Yes sir,' she says and sighs, 'you and me, twenty-seven years,' and she has such a beautiful ring to her voice when she talks like that, 'Europe and all kinds of weird and wonderful.'

'Caaarrie, Caaarrie,' sings Rudi, his shoulders swinging.

'Right sexy, that Joey Tempest,' Cecilie says breathily.

Rudi starts slapping his hands on the dashboard, aided by the liberating feeling of drama hour now being over. He overlooks the fact that she just drooled over another man, turns his head and grins at Cecilie.

'You know what,' he says, 'I think you should take a little trip down to ... that ... you know ... that place ... you know. Daddy's treat!'

He sees how flushed she becomes back there, her face shining as though a light's gone on, and Rudi feels he's the one who's flicked the switch.

'Uh-hm,' she says, 'Mariero Beauty.'

'The very place,' Rudi says proudly. 'The name makes no odds to me, could be called Mariero Ass for all I care, but nobody can say Rudi doesn't respect his woman and pay her bills, and if what she needs to feel good is to have sludge and cucumbers and sun-dried tomatoes smeared all over her face, then no one is going to say that Rudi didn't fork out. Eh? Have I ever once refused to pay for something you wanted? Including the times I thought what you wanted to do was bloody idiotic, like lying under a palm tree or—'

'There're no palm trees there, you're—,' she cuts in, but Rudi wants to finish what he's saying:

'Metaphors, baby, they're metaphors – do you know what metaphors are? Pictures. Pictures of things. You say one thing but mean something else and in lots of ways get to say two things at the same time. No, buggered if I know what you're lying under or not lying under as long as it's women tending to you and not men, you can lie down on a bed of oregano as far as I'm concerned—'

'Oreg— heh heh, there's no oregano.'

'No, well, what would I know about what's there or not,' Rudi says, delighted she's happy again, 'but, all the same, as you well know, I have never—'

'No, you have nev—'

'Got in the wa—'

'No, you have n—'

'Or been tight wi—'

'Money, no, you have n—'

'Or let you f—'

'You certainly have not, Rudi boy,' Cecilie says, a wonderful firmness to her voice.

No, he thinks. I treat my woman the way women should be treated. Rudi forms his mouth into a determined pout, moves his hand to his inside pocket, takes out his wallet and pulls out a five hundred note.

'Here,' he says, reaching his right hand back between the front seats. 'Go and make your face shine. Stick it in a bucket of spinach. Yes indeedy. Say hello to Mariero Beauty from Rudi and tell him your face is worth the money. And tell him who's paying.'

'Thank you so much,' he hears from the back seat. 'You're really good to me.'

'Damn right I am,' says Rudi, feeling just how much love is crammed inside the little Volvo.

What a night, he thinks. Cold, clear, so bloody beautiful.

Hey Granny! Should have been around to see this, old hen.

Rudi peers through the windscreen, they're by the forest. 'Okay,' he says, looking at the clock. 20:58. 'Nearly time.'

'Tomorrow,' says Cecilie, kissing the five hundred note with dry lips.

Rudi grins, thinks everything's rosy, wouldn't mind if they played Coldplay on the radio one more time. But what's the song about? Saint Peter, Roman Catholics and bells that ring?

Time to concentrate. That's the thing about love, takes hold of your brain, and if you're not on the ball, it can gobble up the whole world.

Ow! Ow! Stop it!

The phone, Jani's ringtone. He picks it up. 20:59

'Ye yo, brother?'

'Cut that English crap out,' he hears on the other end of the line.

'It's Americano, brother,' he answers, laughing.

'Whatever, it's stupid, you're from Norway, from Rogaland, from Stavanger, from Tjensvoll. Don't put on an act. Now listen, I've just been doing some thinking about this venture of ours,' says Jan Inge.

'Thoughts are free, what were you thinking?'

'Well,' Jan Inge says, wavering. 'There's something foggy about it.'

'Foggy?'

'Yeah, foggy.'

'Okay?'

'I'm dubious. I've got a nose for this kind of thing. We're not exactly in a risk-free line of business.'

'Okay. Will we call it off? Callitaday and pull out? I haven't met him yet—'

'Listen. Working in a risky business means taking risks. You go and meet the guy. But keep your eyes and ears open. Your objective has to be to clarify what's foggy.'

'That was nicely put,' says Rudi.

'That thing you said about remembering the guy, or wondering if you remembered him. What was that?'

'Dunno, just the feeling I got when he called. Or the feeling he got. I don't know. There was something old about it.'

'Old?' Jan Inge's tone is sharp.

'Yeah, old, as in the past.'

'Hm. Old can be good and old can be a mess. Is there anyone who's got something on you?'

'Naah...'

'Stay on your toes. Keep Chessi out of it. She can wait in the Volv—'

Shit!

What was that?

'Hey Chessi, what the fu—'

'Rudi?'

'Yeah, yeah, I'm here, it's just, hold on – *bollocks* – did we hit something? Chessi?'

Cecilie peers out the back window, Rudi slows down and Jani Inge shouts down the end of the line about how he needs to take it easy, he can't be going around attracting attention, Jesus, can't he do anything right, hello, what's happening?

'A cat!' Cecilie cries.

Rudi gulps and breathes easier.

'Just a cat,' he says into the phone.

'Just a cat?!' he hears from the back seat. Rudi glances in the rear-view mirror and sees that she's crying again, and he wonders when this is going to end. Is he going to have to live with this until he's six feet under, is she going to be so difficunt for the rest of her life?

'Sorry, Jani,' he says, 'it was just a cat.'

He can hear Jan Inge breathing heavily.

'You sit yourself down again now,' says Rudi calmly.

'Right, will do,' says Jan Inge. 'Okay, talk to you later, get things sorted out. Keep your eyes open. Ears. Fog and clarity.'

Rudi nods, hears the sound of his best friend putting his inhaler to his mouth, pressing down and sucking in the acrid air. He can picture that fat boy so well it almost hurts.

'Okay, brother, talk soon. You sit down, okay? Pick a classic and open a packet of crisps. *The Hills Have Eyes?*'

Rudi hangs up and indicates a left turn. He swings in by the little shop at the bottom of the hill that's been there as long as he can remember. He pilfered that place empty throughout the entire eighties. Remembers the time he and J-J-Janne D-D-Dobro sauntered out with so many packs of cigarettes in the pockets of their bubble jackets they thought they'd keel over with the weight. Janne Dobro had such black eyes she'd put you in mind of a bird. She's probably selling *Asfalt* magazine now. Liked her heroin, Janne. She was called J-J-Janne D-D-Dobro because of Mini from Haugtussa, he was so small his father took offence every time he clapped eyes on him. Mini was so in love with Janne Dobro he started to stutter every time he saw her.

Used to be called Gosen Grocery Store, now it's part of a chain, Spar. Everything's going to the dogs. The socialists have won. An impersonal society. It's true what Jani says, nobody dares run their own business any more. We're the only ones. The last bastion of independent entreprenuers. But Rudi doesn't park outside the shop, it's too visible. He drives a little further on towards the woods, up a small back road, and brings the car to a halt in a little grove.

'Chessi,' he says, killing the ignition. 'Come on. It was a cat. A cat, okay? We can't do anything about it.'

She's sniffling in the back seat. He recognises the level. It's not disaster sniffling, it's demonstrative sniffling.

'Do you hear me? I'm sorry, but there's nothing we can do about it. Youandme, baby. Mariero Beauty. It's going to be okay. Right? Come on, be a doll now, lie down on the seat, and just keep calm until I get back. And don't smoke, okay? People get all flustered, you know, if they walk past a car filled with smoke and nobody inside. They get suspicious, ring home to the wife, tell her they've come across a car filled with fucking smoke. You can manage without one for a while, right?'

She sniffles again.

'Is this what Jani meant when he said I should go out and get some air?' she says. 'It could have been a kitten, Rudi!'

'No, no, it was a fully-grown cat, didn't you feel the bump? No kitten would have made the car jolt like that. Listen. Chessi. Afterwards,' he says softly, 'afterwards we can drive someplace and sit and look at something. The sea or something. You like looking at the sea. You can teach me that. How to look at the sea.'

Cecilie folds her arms. Doesn't reply.

He recognises the signs. It's all about being smart now. Not making a big deal out of things. He tries to sound as warm as he possibly can: 'Great, baby, so cool of you to take it that way, no one wants to be together with a chick who's high-maintenance. Five minutes, okay, ten tops, then I'm back, who knows, I might come back with a million bucks in my pocket. Then you'll have one million five hundred. Remember, tomorrow, Mariero Beauty!'

No reaction.

Rudi takes a deep breath. Okay, he thinks, all right. He really needs to dig deep here. He looks at her, as directly as he can, he smiles, with as much charm as he can muster, sucks his cheeks in and sings: *Don't want to close my eyes, I don't want to fall asleep, cause I'd miss you babe and I don't want to miss a thing.*

She gulps.

Yesss.

She looks at him.

Laughs a little.

Yesss.

The Aerosmith Trick.

Never fails. Not once since he first did it, standing in front of her, sucking in his cheeks and imitating Steven Tyler, has it failed. The woman just falls apart.

'Baby! Youandme! Daddy has to do a little bit of work now, then I'll be back. Come on, down in the seat with you.'

Rudi gives her a wink. To say she smiles would be an exaggeration, but she wriggles down into the seat in any case.

He opens the door and feels the cold prickle of the September air on the back of his neck. He looks around. The old forest. It's strange being back here. It was Granny's forest in a lot of ways. She spoke about it so much, and all the things she did there when she was little. The flowers she picked and how much better things were before, *in the good old days.* Rudi has never got that out of his head. He often thinks about it, thinks how right Granny was, it was better *in the good old days.* More peace. More style.

Rudi begins to hurry along the path. He glances about him

again, feels the surroundings sucking him in. Then he comes to a halt.

'Hm,' he says, almost loudly.

'Pål,' he says.

'It's as if ... there's something about that name. It ... shit ... it calls something to mind! But what? Hm? Pål, Pål, Pål...'

Rudi walks on. We'll soon see, he thinks, who you are and who you're not, Pål. You called me. You've reached out your hand. And who are you? I'd love a cigarette now. If I'd known it would be this hard to stop then I never would've quit. Women. It's not bloody easy. You've got to be a sly eagle with a good Aerosmith trick in order to be supple enough to get around their corners. Except for Gran. She had her head screwed on. *Skål,* you old jelly roll.

Rudi, without even being aware of it, raises his hand, puts it to his forehead and salutes, while he strides across the forest floor.

Good thing Tong's out on Friday, he thinks. Not the same when the gang isn't together. He brings in good money, Tong. He puts Chessi in better humour, he's always been able to do that. He's a psycho all right. But he's always ready for action.

Pål, Pål, Pål.

Have you taken a beating from me? Is that it?

Are you out for revenge? Is that it?

Are you the devil, Pål?

15. A WOMAN DRESSED IN JEANS AND A LONG-SLEEVED SWEATER WALKS ACROSS A YARD (Jan Inge)

120 kilos now. 120 on the nose. 120 on board.

Jan Inge has been holding the telephone in his hand for almost a minute. He has been standing like a statue on the living-room floor with the phone two feet from his stomach and his eyes turned to the ceiling. Typical me, he thinks, lost in thought. That's what everyone says, that he has great concentration. And no one dares disturb him when he's thinking, there's no one who lacks respect for JANI WHEN HE'S THINKING.

He pictures it like that. In big letters.

Like those neon signs in small American towns beset by gruesome atrocities.

Jan Inge has always been like that, with his head full of big letters.

He puts away the phone. Jan Inge misses the old house telephone. He nods, making the fat on the back of his neck wobble. Grey with red numbers. That telephone worked like a dream, but hi-tech advances meant they had to throw in the towel. So much new technology at the moment that it's becoming a problem. Mobile phones are okay, with top-up cards at any rate, but all this pressure on you to use the internet, it's not good. It's not like it was in the good old days.

There it is again. THE GOOD OLD DAYS. You can't say it without big letters.

Jan Inge glances at the wheelchair at the far end of the hall.

120 on the nose.

It's important Rudi doesn't screw this up. He needs to see through the fog. But if there is one thing Jan Inge has learned, it's that where it seems most foggy, that's where the gold might be, and if you want to get your hands on the gold, you have to venture into the fog. As long as Rudi keeps his wits about him and doesn't start blabbering.

Jan Inge takes the inhaler from the pocket of his jogging pants and sucks. He shuffles across the floor in felt slippers, down the long hallway. He stops in front of the wheelchair.

120 on board.

He has always been fat. Or at least thickset and chubby. So was Mum, may you rest in purgatory, you detestable person. There have always been a few surplus kilos on this body, always a little extra to offer, but 120? He was weighing in at about 100 for a number of years. Nice round number. Easy to relate to. It accorded him a little class, some executive authority. It's only right for a boss to be a few kilos heavier than the others. Rudi, lanky though he is, weighs ninety-five after all. But after a while it started to rise. An occasional check on the scales now and again. Oops. 105. Down to 100. Oops. No, seems to have gone up, this ... 110 ... *Jani 110, since when?*

It rhymes, Tong said, just before he went inside.

They had done a job in Jæren, a clean break-in, got lots of computers, just easy-to-sell stuff that would mean clean cash from Buonanotte. Well planned, well executed. Keys, swipe cards, the whole shebang. There had never been a single mistake on Tong's watch, never been anyone sent down. If there is one man you can count on, it's Tong, because he doesn't count on anyone. Thank Christ he's getting out on Friday. He carried out the job itself perfectly, but then? You'd think he had suddenly become an amateur again. Thirty-five years old, tonnes of experience, and he ends up doing something like that? It's the drugs, Tong. Jan Inge has told him a thousand times. You think your senses are sharpened. But that shit has chomped lumps out of that brilliant brain of yours. We have a policy in this company, we rack up a few lines before we go to work, to get our heads up and running, but we don't degenerate into a gang of junkies. But what do you go and do, Tong? You hit a party in Orre after the job, you stuff your nut full of speed, and God knows what else, and you know how horny that coke makes you, and then you're pulled in for intercourse with a minor.

A month later you're in the dock, faced with two fuming parents and a sobbing girl, all pointing the finger at you, and you claim you had no idea that she was only fourteen.

Jan Inge has said it a million times: listen to me, you horny Korean, the coke has gobbled at your brain, and I know what I'm talking about – my mum drank five bottles of spirits a week and she went as mad as a March hare and as empty as a drum upstairs, and she was a terror and nobody, neither man nor beast, misses that old bitch. Well, all right, Chessi ... poor bag of bones ... maybe she ... no, Chessi remembers shag all. She was only little when Mum died. She can't go around missing someone she practically never set eyes on.

But me, I remember that sicko, and I've nothing good to say about her, no wonder Dad took off when he got that job in Houston.

Jan Inge has spent a good deal of time thinking about it. Thinking about what exactly was wrong with her.

And he has arrived at the conclusion that she lacked something. That she quite simply didn't have it in her to love people.

And that's why Jan Inge has drawn his own conclusions about what is important. To find your own people. To find your own family. To hang on to them. To love them long and love them right. No matter if they make a major blunder that lands them back inside Åna, and no matter if they take 120 kilos on board.

Dad heading to Houston was of little consequence. At least he always sent money, give him his due. Sent money right up until Chessi turned eighteen. And Christmas cards. Or that time in 1985, Jan Inge thought his heart was going to burst out of his chest: a package arrived from Dad in the USA, a package in the post. A SodaStream!

And a huge box with a BETAMAX VCR and a pile of videos. Love from Dad.

He still has the SodaStream. It's down in the basement somewhere. Doesn't work any more. But it worked back then. Every kid in Hillevåg was at the front door slavering after home-made fizzy drinks. They could pick and choose who to let in. Those were the days. Won't ever throw it out, that SodaStream is a trophy.

They were over in Houston a few times, him and Chessi, travelled halfway round the globe on their own; she was so small the first time he had to hold her by the hand for hours. Jan Inge can still remember how clammy their hands got, but forget about trying to let go, then she just wailed as though the plane was going to crash. *No, Janinge.* Those were some trips. Just him and Chessi. Just him and her up in the clouds. *Are we flying now, Janinge?* Yeah. *Are we flying into the sun, Janinge?* It's a great country, the US, free and easy; Dad took them to burger joints, let them do their own thing, watch films and that, while he was at work. As for going back to Norway; that was never going to happen. He was clear about that, they could come and live in the USA, but he was never going back home to Norway.

And he never did come home.

Jan Inge puts the inhaler back into his pocket. He nods to himself. Looks at the wheelchair. It's been sitting there for years. It was Rudi who got hold of it when Chessi broke her foot. Typical Rudi. He'd bend over backwards for her.

People like that, thinks Jan Inge, you hold on to people like that.

Bit foggy, the job they were on at the minute. As long as Chessi manages to keep calm. She has to stay in the car. He can't have her getting under Rudi's feet while he's working. She's too volatile. It's from Mum, thinks Jan Inge, bad genes. She's ill-tempered and difficult, you'd be hard pressed to say otherwise. But she is his sister. And she is Rudi's girlfriend. And that's how it should be.

Jan Inge lowers himself into the wheelchair. It sinks a little beneath his weight, but it supports him well. It's easy to control, a nice little contraption. He smiles. A dark lustre comes over his narrow pinhead eyes and he rolls off down the hall.

He trundles into the living room and over to the table, picks up a remote control, presses minus, and the ceiling lights dim. He continues over to the armchair in front of the flatscreen, remains seated while he shoves the armchair over to the window, and then parks the wheelchair in front of the TV. This is ingenious, he thinks, and then glances out the window and sees how dark it has become outside. Good, working in daylight, that's not for us.

Rudi will manage this. But it's a good thing Tong is getting out on Friday. God bless that little mole of a Korean. He's a demon, but it's been tough without him, been like a football team without a striker, to draw an analogy.

This, thinks Jan Inge, rocking back and forth a little in the wheelchair, this is ingenious.

Then he trundles across the living-room floor. Goes past the hall and manoeuvres himself into the kitchen, where he opens the fridge and takes down a one-and-a-half-litre bottle of coke and a big bowl of chocolates. He opens a kitchen drawer and pulls out a family size bag of paprika crisps, before heaving the goodies on to his lap and wheeling back to the living room.

Jan Inge parks the wheelchair in front of the TV, and takes hold of the remote controls.

No problem having 120 on board with this thing, I'm able to get around like a robot.

God, she was so cute when she was small. Wimpy, awkward and weird. Jan Inge suddenly pictures her as he tears open the crisp bag and arranges the remotes and the goodies in his lap. He's really looking forward to following up *Carnival of Souls* with *Three on a Meathook*. Seeeerious grindhouse. 1973. Maximum low-budget. Dirty as a rubbish heap. Brilliant scene when Billy goes into the house and finds the dead girls, and the harmonica soundtrack really adds to the atmosphere.

He could have written a book on horror by now, after all the films he's seen and studied. It's doubtful there're many people out there with a better collection of horror or more knowledge of the genre than him. It's about time he attended one of the international horror conventions. Show his face. Let them know he exists.

God, Cecilie was so cute back then.

She used to waddle around like a penguin. She'd open that little mouth, her voice all smurfy and nice: Janinge bruuv Cecili sisssa.

Yeah.

I can live with this all right, a cold dark September night in 2012, with coke, treats and a horror movie ready, snuggled up in a wheelchair. It's a starry night outside. After a few harsh autumn weeks, a bright warm day turns up out of the blue. It's a sign, but of what? Joy or the apocalypse? Your best mate is out trying to clarify a slightly foggy job, and it may be twenty-five years since you soared through the clouds with your little sister's hand in yours, but you can still feel the imprint as you sit there in front of the flatscreen, as though she is still clinging to you while you cross the Atlantic.

Yeah.

The fog needs to clear.

Snow flickers on the screen. The old VHS player whines. A woman dressed in jeans and a long-sleeved sweater walks across a yard, over towards a shed. She has shoulder-length hair. Just before she is about to unbolt the door, she turns and looks around. Then she pulls back the bolt, opens it, and goes inside. She screams. Three women hang impaled on meat hooks.

Jan Inge smiles and rocks a little in the wheelchair.

It would be nice to see Dad again.

GOOD MEMORIES.

16. **INDEPENDENT THOUGHTS** (Tiril)

The door slams behind her and Sandra runs off. That daft-looking run of hers. Her right arm under her tits and her tottering legs. Tiril goes into the backroom and grabs a marker from the Spar cup on the break table. She pulls the top off with her teeth and stretches her fingers out in front of her. Which way? Her fingers are thin, her skin is clean and her nails are painted black and bitten down to the quick. They've always been told off for that, both her and Malene; do the two of you have to bite your nails?

Tiril sits down on one of the chairs, sets her jaw, concentrates and begins to write. Letter by letter, going over each twice and making them as decorative as she can.

She clenches her fist, closes her eyes: *This pain is just too real.* Then she hangs up her work clothes and walks into the empty, semi-darkness of the shop. She hears her own footfalls, they resound upon the newly washed lino. Over to one of the tills. Nobody has noticed anything so far. Tiril opens the cabinet with the little key. Not many packs of Prince left. Lots of Marlboro Gold. She fetches out a ten-pack, puts it in her pocket, exhales.

The front doors are locked, she walks into the backroom again, stopping at the bottle deposit belt and tapping the pocket of her jeans to check if she's got the lighter, the little black one. She looks around one last time. Everything is okay. She switches off the ceiling light, turns on the alarm, 8789, and goes out.

Tiril sits down on the loading ramp in front of the deliveries door, half hidden behind the large wheelie bins. Her feet dangling over the ground. Dad is probably out taking a walk, she thinks, while trying to get her blunt nails underneath the plastic wrapping of the cigarette packet. He's probably out with Zitha, she thinks, giving up, bringing the packet to her mouth and tearing the plastic with her teeth.

She sniffles, pulls out a cigarette, puts it between her lips, spins the wheel of the lighter, watches the flame grow and lights it.

There's just so much that time cannot erase.

The worst thing would be if she was standing in front of the whole school, with Thea on the piano, and everything's going well, everything's perfect, and then she forgets the words. Not that she thinks that'll happen, she knows them backwards, but still she worries about it. She just needs to think that she is Amy Lee. That she actually comes from Little Rock, Arakansas, she hasn't grown up here, she doesn't live this pissy life in a little suburb in a stupid oil town in crappy Norway. *Shitty Stavanger doesn't exist.* She has woken up every day of her life and looked out at the Arkansas River, skyscrapers and the big American sky.

'Jesus, Tiril, have you started smoking now as well?' Malene – shit, where did she come from? – is standing in front of Tiril shaking her head. Her arms folded, she rolls her eyes.

Tiril's eyes flash angrily. 'What's it to you?'

Malene assumes a neutral expression and shrugs.

'Yeah, yeah, no surprise there. Jesus, Tiril, you're fourteen. Smoking is lethal.'

Jesus. She's such a bloody old *biddy*.

'Yeah, so? It's lethal to live, in case you didn't know.' Tiril takes a long drag and blows the smoke into her sister's face. 'Are you following me or something?'

Malene sits down beside her on the loading ramp. She shoots a glance at Tiril's hands. 'Jesus. What have you done?'

I knew it, thinks Tiril, I *knew* she'd comment on the tattoo.

'None of your business,' she says, letting the cigarette hang between her lips as she squints her eyes and stretches her hands out towards her sister.

LOVE

HATE

'Lol,' says Malene. 'That's so tweenie. Are you actually going to walk around with that?' Tiril takes a good drag of the cigarette.

Whatever, she couldn't be bothered replying. 'Hey,' she says, 'why has Dad never actually found himself a girlfriend?'

Malene looks at her. 'Well, don't know really ... why do you ask?'

'No reason, am I not allowed to talk now, not allowed to have independent thoughts?'

Malene rolls her eyes. 'Sure, Sure.'

'I mean, Mum got herself a man before she left Dad.'

'You don't know what you're on about,' Malene says sharply.

'Jesus.' Tiril plants her forefinger in her sister's shoulder: 'Listen, you know that Sandra one?'

'In my class?' Malene looks up. 'The one you clean with?'

'Mhm.'

'What about her?'

'Nah, you probably already know. So...'

'Give it a break, what do you mean?'

'Do you know what she's up to?'

'No ... up to? What do you mean?'

Tiril makes a fish-face and blows a perfect smoke ring. 'She's off screwing Daniel William in the woods.'

Malene's lips slowly part. 'What!? *Daniel William?*'

'Mhm.' Tiril nods assuredly. 'Tears out of here after work. Straight over to the woods. Screws.'

'Je-sus.' Malene shakes her head. 'I knew something was up.'

'Yeah, just ask Tiril.'

'*Daniel William.*' Each syllable of his name escapes her mouth slowly. 'That's just ... I mean he's ... Shit. Je-sus.'

The sisters remain sitting beside each other. They smile and shake their heads. Tiril loves the feeling of knowing more about people and what they're up to than Malene, and that she's the one who's clued in, the one who's a tweenie and pissed off all the time.

'Tiril,' says Malene, after a while.

Her tone is stern. She's always talked like that. As if she thinks she's my mother, thinks Tiril. Come on then, out with it, since you're so bloody grown-up, such great mates with Dad and think you can lick your way in everywhere, sitting there smiling saying *yeah, fine*, whenever Mum calls. Come on, out with it, since you think you're such a good judge of who's tweenie in their head and who isn't.

'Tiril,' Malene says again, as though she has a fly in her mouth.

'Yeah? Christ. I'm right here. Are you blind?'

'It's just,' Malene hesitates, 'do you know if there's anything wrong with Dad?'

Tiril turns to face her.

'With Dad? What do you mean?'

'No, I don't know.' That E.T. expression comes across Malene's face. She shrugs. 'No, I don't know. Just seems like something's up.'

'Oh,' says Tiril, taking a last drag of the cigarette before flicking it off the loading ramp and taking a pack of gum from her jeans pocket. 'That's just Dad,' she says, 'he's always been like that.'

'So, you haven't seen him then?'

'Tonight?' Tiril takes a piece of chewing gum and feels the fresh taste spread through her mouth. 'He's never around here anyway. Do you think I'd be sitting here smoking if he was? He's off in the woods. Or in Sørmarka. Or up on top of Limahaugen looking out over the fjord. Him and Zitha.'

'Mhm,' says Malene. 'It's probably nothing.'

She looks at Tiril.

'You should get a haircut,' she says, reaching towards Tiril's hair. 'You're getting split ends.'

'Don't,' Tiril says, pulling away.

Malene's gaze is still fixed on her.

With that look.

Can you please stop, don't give me that look.

'You're so cute,' says Malene, 'it's going to go great on Thursday.'

I'm going to start crying if you look at me like that.

'You don't know anything about it,' says Tiril. 'It might go really badly.'

'No it won't,' Malene says, getting to her feet, 'I'm coming to watch, Dad's coming to watch and everyone's going to be there. Mum would probably be there too if she could. Everyone in the gym hall is going to love you, you're going to be great.'

Tiril looks askance at Malene. The nice gymnastics body.

The supple movements. Malene, you walk like you were royalty, Grandad says. Tiril liked it when she injured her ankle last year. She didn't say it, but she did. Miss Perfect Gymnast had to limp. Poor beautiful bitch.

'Hey. Malene?'

'Mhm?'

'Do you think you can choose, I mean, between light and darkness?'

Tiril sees Malene lift her troubled gaze. Sees it drift over the school, the woods, up towards the telecom tower and the top of the hill, and it almost looks as though she's muttering something.

17. **IT'S A SUN BULLET** (Daniel William)

If you kill someone, you cross the line.

If you never kill anyone, you never cross the line.

If you love someone, you cross the line.

If you never love someone, you never cross the line.

If you cross the line, the earth opens its jaws and swallows you. Love?

Daniel throws the moped helmet back and forth between his hands.

He tilts his head to both sides, stretches his neck and tramps his feet restlessly.

If the fact that he needs to have her is called love, then that's fine. That's what we'll say: I love you. Shit, he's nervous now.

Typical. Just before something's going to happen, it comes, that feeling. The cold and nausea in his stomach, the flashing behind his eyes and that freezing sensation in his temples. He tried to talk to the Child Welfare Officer about it once, told him about how he sometimes got cold and nauseous and felt he was losing control. He said he felt a crackling in his head and a flashing behind his eyes. He said he grew angry, lost the plot. The guy from Child Services was understanding, put his head to one side and asked him how he felt and what he thought and how he wanted to deal with it himself. Just like that psychologist with the stupid glasses, he talked like that too: *And what do you think about it?* Is that all they can do, ask questions and look sympathetic, is that what they learn at university, is that what they get paid for? Do they not bloody well have a solution? Haven't they been studying for forty years in order to give him a *solution*?

Daniel continues throwing the helmet back and forth. If she doesn't come soon then he's going to have to go. It can get too

much. He knows where the danger lies. No matter how caveman
horny he gets, it's like it just tips over, and everything is all fucked-
up and cold. Then he needs to jump on his bike and ride and ride
and ride until his head is like an empty room with all the windows
open.

Do you hear me, Sandra?

Get a bloody move on, I can't take this here.

He swallows and begins knocking his helmet against the brick
wall of the substation. Looks around. What a shithole. Really disgusting, tall weeds and thicket, are they going to lie down and
screw here? It's not on, screwing in all this kak, probably wino piss
and whatnot. It's just not on.

Daniel lets the helmet in his hand come to rest and takes out a
fresh cigarette. He shouldn't smoke so much before she gets here,
his breath will smell bad, but bollocks to that, he needs something
to settle the nerves.

There's lots of oil money round here. Loads of big houses, spe-
cially down by the fjord, not least on the road where Sandra lives,
on Kong Haralds Gate, all filthy rich down there. Daniel always
feels ill at ease when he walks into houses like that, may as well
face it, he doesn't belong in them. But then they hardly belong
there themselves, the money is just an oil fluke. It's not money
they've worked for, it's a windfall, money that rained down upon
them like hell can rain down on other people.

Sandra Vikadal.

Imagine if the two of them end up together. Maybe he'll inherit
heaps of money. He's a lawyer, her dad, rolling in money those
lawyers. Her mother works at the church, plenty of money there
too, in that church system.

Daniel inhales the smoke. He hears a dog bark in the distance.
A car passing on the road behind the woods.

He'll own a car in any case, a car to drive round with his lawyer-
daughter wife, who's always in good humour and who he sleeps
with once a day. That's what his last foster father said. You're not
a man if you don't have your own garden to piss in and a car you
can drive whenever you like. Daniel wants an American car. A
Buick RAM. If he gets rich, he'll buy Veronika a car too. Wonder

what kind of music Veronika would like if she could hear. There's nothing to stop deaf people from driving, is there? She's totally kickass when she sits in front of him smiling in her Buddha position while he's hammering away on the drums. Veronika will get to be around, that's for sure. He'll take bloody good care of her, she can sit in the Buddha position for the rest of her life, listen to him play the drums, break out in that deaf laughter of hers and be as weird as she wants. She can live with him and Sandra, no problem. He just needs to make a shitload of money so they can all live well. Veronika can have a whole Buddha floor to herself. It's just a matter of raking in the money. Good thing he writes songs, that means royalties. Daniel knows he needs to write some new lyrics soon. Dejan is on at him the whole time, come on, songsmith, come on with the poetry shit. Yeah, yeah, he says, I'm working on it. But he isn't. Everything has been blocked lately.

He lifts his head as he hears a sound.

There she comes. Running across the football pitch.

Is it a sun bullet?

Wow, she's slightly knock-kneed. He hadn't noticed. She runs like that and all, knees banging together, one hand under her tits, her head sort of dancing from side to side, her other hand swinging out as though it had a mind of its own, alive, free from the rest of her. Christ she looks gorgeous, looks super sexy running along, God, so fucking foxy, those wobbly legs make her whole body kind of dangle like a doll or something.

Daniel straightens up, he feels a wild electron fire up in his head, he flicks the cigarette out on to the road in front of the kindergarten and runs his hand through his hair, exhales as much as he can and inhales as much fresh air as he's able, feels his face break into a silly smile, feels a rush through his body. He gulps.

Look at that.

Look at her.

Look at her run.

Oh Christ she is so fucking gorgeous.

And just then as he watches her surge towards him, the sentences discharge in his head, like the report of rifle shots, and he knows that soon he'll write some lyrics, true lyrics, real lyrics about the strongest light any person's ever seen: girl light, Sandra light. The eternal light from a muzzle, lyrics nobody needs to bury 1,000 kilometres under the ground.

Yess.

Candyfloss.

18. **HOLY DIVER** (Pål)

A light cleaves its way between the black tree trunks, flashing through the woods. Pål gives a start, he turns his head in the direction of the road and catches a glimpse of a car disappearing down towards the shop.

He tries to regulate his breathing, follow Zitha as nimbly as possible, allow her to traverse the forest floor, not upset her. Zitha isn't a meek dog, but she's never liked cars. *Yeaaah, Zitha, yeaaah, good girl.* Can't have her barking like she did a while ago, mustn't draw any attention to ourselves, that's not on.

Pål draws his coat closer around him. The cold is becoming deep-seated, inching its way into his bones. Must try not to think, just get this done.

Pål hadn't given Rudi a thought in years. But then one day, just as he was opening the post box, retrieving yet another letter bound for the bus shelter bin, an old memory abruptly emerged from the deep. Rudi. Videoboy. An obscure, dim recollection of a day in 1986. Then it slipped away just as suddenly. He began to sift through the memories in his head. He'd heard rumours from time to time. They'd turned out to be as criminal as people thought they would. Could he call them? Surely they wouldn't remember what happened in 1986. That poor girl lying in the room. The sick set-up they had in the house. All the horror movies. Neither he nor Hasse understood it at the time, but now it was easy to see: Jan Inge used the girl as payment for the favours he got people to do. He had people carry out minor thefts for him and he paid them by letting them see uncensored horror films, and giving them all the cola and sweets they wanted. And letting them sleep with the girl. The sister. He rented her out like a whore. She was only thirteen, fourteen maybe. And Pål remembered her well.

He had slipped the envelope into his inside pocket. Then brought out his mobile and sent a text to directory enquiries. His hands were trembling slightly as he punched in the number he'd been given.

'Ye yo, Rudi here, yeah?'

'Hi, eh, it's Pål...'

'*Who?*'

'Pål. Yeah. Fagerland.'

'Okay, Fagerland away.'

'Wha? Eh, listen, you probably don't remember me––'

'Nope, can't say that I do. Who did you say you say you say you say?'

'Pål. Fagerland.'

'No, doesn't ring any bells...'

'Right, I see, well—'

'Out with it, man, out with it, Pål Skål, what brings you round to this haunted house?'

'Well. I ... I was just wondering if you ... if you and your...'

Pål heard a sigh then the person on the other end disappeared.

He walked into the kitchen. Drank some water straight from the tap and tried to understand what had happened. Were they cut off? Did he hang up? He decided to ring again. Put in the number. It rang for a little while.

'Yeah, Rudi.'

'Hi, I think we must've been cut off there. It's Pål again.'

'Yeah.'

'Right, well, I was wondering if you ... or your...'

He disappeared again. The same way. Pål tried to get his head around what had happened. Rudi took the phone. He wasn't disinterested in talking to him. But he hung up. They weren't cut off. Pål nodded to himself. It was obvious he was going about things the wrong way. He punched in the number yet again.

'Hell-o, you've reached Rudi-o, yeah!'

'Hi, Pål again, we seem to be getting cut off, I—'

Silence on the other end of the line.

'Or ... eh ... are we getting cut off?'

Still silence.

'So, anyway, I heard a couple of years back that the two of you, eh, you and that guy Jani, that—'

It happened again. He hung up.

Pål sat down at the kitchen table. Malene and Tiril would be home soon, he couldn't keep at this very much longer. But Rudi was answering the phone. And then Pål said something wrong, and then he hung up. Okay. He put the number in again.

'Yeeeeeep, Rudi here, yeah.'

'Rudi, hi, man! It's Pål here, you know, Pål from the old days, the eighties, eye of the tiger, the final countdown, holy diver...'

'You've been out too long in the midnight sea! Hey, all right, still not ringing any bells, whatsupdude?'

There was a different tone to his voice now.

'Been such a long time. Want to hang? What about meeting up, taking a stroll, say Tuesday night, Gosen Woods, by the big rock, nine o'clock, when I'm out walking the dog?'

'Great plan, Påli, you holy diver. Heh heh! Did you hear Dio died? Shit, that's the way it goes. Talk to you!'

Rudi hung up.

Down, that's what it is, thought Pål and nodded. Down too long in the midnight sea. That clicked. I've just made an appointment. That's how it's done. These people don't accept just anything.

'Yeaaah Zitha, yeaah, good girl,' he whispers, feeling the ground beneath him starting to slope upwards. Zitha keeps moving across the forest floor, sniffing. He stops and looks up at the rock. It doesn't look as big as he remembers. The football pitch is up there, but everything is a lot more open than he remembers.

Pål walks up to the crest and lets his gaze sweep around. It's a long time since he's been here. He chose this spot because he recalled it being overgrown, because in his mind the rock was so big you could stand behind it and hide from the world. But that's completely wrong. That's how memory works. Things are exaggerated, things are diminished and things are moved around.

It's way too exposed. They can't stand here and talk.

Is this a good idea? Seeking out these people?

Pål wipes his right eye with a shaky hand. It has to go away soon. He feels worn out. So worn out by all of it. His eyes, the long nights. Why couldn't he just leave everything the way it was? Why did he have to get into all this? He had everything he needed. The house. The kids. A job. Was it all down to his fingers, his breath, the cold light of night, his empty life, the desire to be sucked into the cold glow of the screen and disappear?

I don't know, he thinks.

I just don't know.

It just happened.

Pål goes over to the rock and leans against it. He inhales and exhales. Wonder how things are with Videoboy's sister now? Maybe she's married with kids, maybe she got herself an education, maybe she lives in another country.

What is it I've been doing, he thinks.

Day after day, evening after evening, night after night.

Footsteps?

Zitha's ears stand on end.

19. **IF IT WAS A KITTEN** (Cecilie)

Cecilie is curled up in the back seat. She isn't very tall. Just one metre fifty-nine. As for curling up, she's good at that. She peers up at the beige upholstery in the roof of the Volvo. There are slashes in it from the time they drove home from a job over in Ålgard. Rudi had taken too much speed and wanted to write 'fuck' with his knife.

She blows out the smoke. It fills the car.

If it was a kitten I'll kill him, she thinks. Maybe I'll just do it anyway. Get rid of his Motörhead T-shirt, get rid of all his shit, get the whole of Rudi out of my head, rewind to the life I had before life began. Kill him. So I can go to his grave, lay down a wreath and whisper: Hi, Rudi, sweetheart, you're dead.

She slides up and rolls the car window down a little to let out some smoke.

Take Cecilie along, she could use a little air. Those lads, what do they think she is? Stupid, that's what. They get up every morning thinking they can make the world how they want it, and they think she's an idiot. And she lets them talk to her as though she is an idiot.

Cecilie slips two pasty fingers out the gap in the window and drops the cigarette, before opening the pack and taking out another. Get some air. How's this getting some air?

She lights the cigarette, inhales deeply and lies back down on the seat.

Bloody Volvo. She's so fucking tired of waiting while the boys are on a job somewhere or other, and she's so fed up of this car. It's uncomfortable to sit in, it stinks, the gearbox is loose, the axle is dodgy and the steering wheel will soon be hanging off. Why can't they get a new car? One like normal people have. But no, no, they're not going to do anything like normal people. A4 people, Jani calls them, and it's obvious he doesn't look up to them.

Cecilie hears a faint noise and raises her head. She ducks down when she sees two young clear-skinned girls come walking up the hill towards Hafrsfjord.

'Friends wouldn't be a good idea,' Rudi says.

'Wouldn't be good for you, Chessi.'

'And not for the company either,' Jani says.

'It's all part and parcel of our profession, we have to keep to our own kind.'

Cecilie brings herself up on to her elbows, looks out and sees the girls are gone.

But imagine she wants some friends? Imagine she does. But she hasn't any. She was banged by every moron who came through the door with a stolen carton of Marlboro, a Walkman or a ghetto blaster; she spread her legs, heard the boys groan, closed her eyes and thought of Dad in Houston. She eats cinnamon buns, takes walks to the sea and has a boyfriend who has problems sleeping and sings Aerosmith songs when he gets nervous. She's allowed go to the skincare clinic once a month.

Cecilie gets up abruptly and opens the door. She puts her feet on the soft earth and looks towards the woods. It's so dark. She doesn't like the darkness, never has, only in movies. She turns and begins walking up the road in the direction they came from. She speeds up. If it was a kitten. She squints ahead of her. It was around here somewhere. What kind of place is this anyway?

Shush shush little baby.

Shush shush little one.

Just be quiet.

Mummy's got five hundred kroner and Mummy's going to the beauty clinic.

You can come along.

Or maybe we'll go to Houston. Say hello to Granddad. You'll like him. He never should have left us. He was such a laugh. It always felt like Christmas Day when he was in the room. His smile was so big it swallowed everything. Doesn't seem like either of his kids have inherited that good humour.

Cecilie halts as she catches sight of something on the road.
She bends over.
It's a hedgehog.
A little bloody hedgehog.

Cecilie lifts it up into her arms. The creature has curled itself
up. It feels like a stinging ball in her hands. It must have scurried
out on to the road on its tiny feet, quickly understood it wasn't a
good place to be, then curled itself up to meet death.

'Mummy is going to look after you,' she whispers to the hedgehog, feeling her anger mount. She turns and stomps back angrily,
a severe sway in her hips. There's a lot you don't know, Rudi, she
thinks, her heels digging into the ground. You think you can just
run over anyone at all and act as if nothing has happened, but
there's a lot you don't have a clue about. Tong would do anything
for me, did you know that? He's getting out on Friday, I'm picking
him up at half eight, and he's one sick Korean and he would do
anything for me, did you know that?

Her speed increases for every step she takes.

Rudi.

We'll kill you, you ugly prick.

20. **IS THIS WHAT YOU WANT?** (Sandra)

Waking up at three in the morning, jolted by a dizzy heart, to stare at the darkness in fear. Being wide awake, feeling how ready her body is, how sharp, anxious and all set it is, as though she were a soldier. *Where are you? What are you doing now? What are you thinking about?* Sandra tilts to one side: *No, you must never leave me, you must never look at anyone but me, nothing must ever change from the way it is now.*

That terrible fear that one day it will end. She refuses to believe it, because Sandra and Daniel are the ones who are going to make it: I will never leave you. I will never look at anyone else. Here are my hands, look, they're touching you, look, they want to caress you, and here's my mouth, look, it wants to kiss you, feel it, it's yours: *Promise me, yes? Do you promise, yes? Sure? Yes? Positive?*

Yes.

Nobody will threaten us.

No.

This will never end.

One day he was just standing there, like a snowdrop when the ground frost releases its hold.

That was only a few weeks ago, and there was a life before this but now it's no more than fading echoes in her body. The girl with three freckles on her nose and the slightly goofy teeth has gone crazy. She can't concentrate on her homework, when her mother and father are speaking it's like they're muttering in the fog. The same with her friends, it's utterly impossible to grasp what they're babbling about.

She knows that relationships fall apart. She knows that people leave one another. But this is different. This is a higher power. This is for the rest of her life.

One day he was just standing there. It was the week Tiril left an hour early to rehearse the Evanescence song. Sandra could feel the sweat making her T-shirt stick to the skin between her shoulder blades while she vacuumed the floor, and in the distance she picked up some sounds from the entrance. Sandra has clear instructions not to open the shop after closing time. They've told her not to talk to anybody if they knock on the glass, because there was an incident a few years ago where a guy managed to break in and threatened one of the cleaners while he stole money and whatnot.

But the sounds wouldn't cease; it was raining cats and dogs out there, and Sandra moved cautiously towards the door, worried about what she was going to see.

There was a boy standing outside with a moped helmet in one hand. He looked so small, so wet, so terribly good-looking and he didn't look dangerous. What did he want? He was trying to form words with his lips; he smiled, pointed at himself to show that he wanted to come in; what was it he was trying to say?

'No,' she said, shaking her head. She pointed at the door while she wagged her finger. She mouthed the words as clearly as she could: 'I can't let you in, I'm not allowed.'

But he just stood there.

He was so good-looking!

His mouth was so ... so bright.

And then she realised who it was. Bewildered, she said: 'Daniel?'

'Yeah.'

She watched him form the words with his lips. It was a super strange moment, she felt it right down to the soles of her feet. It was Daniel William Moi standing there, the boy there were so many rumours about, the foster brother of Veronika from the flats. And the weird thing was that she said his name and smiled at him, stupid Sandra who's only fifteen, and that he actually smiled back, *Daniel William Moi,* the one in sixth form nobody dared talk to, the one all the girls thought was so hot with those deep eyes of his, and dangerous. The fact that she smiled at him and that he smiled back, it was almost unreal.

'Yes,' he repeated, pointing at himself again.

Sandra's eyes began to blink. Was she going to let him in? Now he said that word again, what was it he was saying? He started doing something with his hands too, as if he was drawing in the air, a square, no, a circle, while his lips repeated what he was attempting to say.

He began to laugh, and Sandra couldn't help but laugh as well, it was a really odd situation, two people standing miming and laughing on either side of a glass door. Now he began to write something on the rain-soaked windowpane, what was it?

Sandra went as close as she could. He put the moped helmet down on the ground, his hair was already wet, his face glistening, and when he stood up he traced his forefinger across the glass again. But what he wrote was washed away by the rain.

Now he was standing right against the pane.

Today's paper?

Is that what he said?

He's so gorgeous!

Today's paper?

'What are you saying?' Sandra spoke louder.

He read her lips. He'd probably learnt it from Veronika, the lip-reading, and he repeated, as slowly as he could:

toi

let

pa

per

Sandra burst out laughing, she felt her face crack up. Daniel William Moi was standing there yelling for toilet roll. He was so cute, you could see how white his teeth were when he laughed and he was soaked to the skin. She leaned towards the glass and formed the words as clearly as she could:

'Wait. Wait. Okay? Wait.'

He nodded, and she dashed back through the shop. Sandra knew she was doing something wrong, but it felt right so she did not allow herself time to think, she just ran into the backroom, ran with one arm under her breasts and the other swinging through the air, got the keys to the entrance and whispered to herself: 'I'll do it. I'll just do it.'

'Hi,' he said and laughed as she let him in.

'Quick,' she pulled him further into the shop, away from the windows, 'quick, I'll lose my job if they think I'm letting people in...'

'Right, yeah...' The rainwater was dripping from him and forming small puddles on the floor, he shook his long fingers and sprinkled the droplets around him.

'It's fine,' she said, feeling the perspiration begin in her armpits and under her hairline. 'It's only water.'

'I've been at band practice – I play in a band – and I'd promised Inger, that's my foster mother, to buy toilet paper on the way home, but I forgot the time and got here a bit late, and well...'

He looked at her.

Sandra swallowed.

'Hi,' he said, 'my name's Daniel.'

He extended his hand. She took hold of it and felt small. She released it quickly.

Sandra nodded and swallowed again, 'I know,' she said, something catching in her throat.

He looked at her. For a long time. Sandra tried to look away, because his gaze was so penetrating, but she wasn't able to.

'What's your name?'

His voice was so deep.

'Sandra Vikadal,' she said and curtsied.

She *curtsied!*

'Well, look, you can get toilet roll,' she said hurriedly, to cover what she'd just done. She turned so he wouldn't see how stupid she looked. 'But I'll have to just give it to you,' she said, 'because I can't open the till...'

He laughed as he followed her along the aisle towards the shelves with the toilet paper. 'Theft.'

'Gosh, yeah,' she said.

They stopped in front of the shelves. She grabbed a packet, felt the fear over what she was doing course through her hands, then held it out to him.

He's a lot taller than me, she thought.

And then – it was so unbelievably strange and so unbelievably nice and Sandra has thought about it every day since, as though it were a sign – then he jutted out his chin, giving his face a sort of silly look, and raised his forefinger. He held it in the air in front of her. Then he brought it to her nose, gave it a gentle press and said:

'Now the two of us have a secret, Sandra Vikadal.'

And then?

Then the days, the hours, the minutes and the seconds just came crashing down. They collapsed on top of one another. The following night he was back, she let him in without any questions, the night after that he kissed her in the backroom, and the next night she met him in the woods for the first time, and the next night ... everything merged together, she hardly slept, he took her over, they kissed and kissed and neither mouth could get enough, they touched one another and touched one another and neither pair of hands could get enough, they stared into each other's eyes and Sandra felt she was drowning in them, they entwined hands, and what did they talk about?

The future, countries they would travel to, things they would see, how beautiful the world was right here, right now. They talked about each other, about the storm of emotions that had suddenly arisen one rainy night, they retold and retold their own short history, how he had stood outside the shop with the moped helmet in his hands – *you were so wet!* – how he had tried to make her understand what he was saying – *toilet paper, I said! A thousand times. But you, you thought – I thought it was today's paper!* Over and over again they repeated their own short history, and they thought it was the most important story of all. And every day they came closer. Every day, greater courage in their kisses, every day, greater courage in their hands, every day, greater courage in their words. Every day, a wild joy over recognition – *Oh, you're well sexy in those jeans* – and an equal joy in discovering new things – *Your lips look so beautiful when they gleam like that* – and every day an all-engrossing interest in everything the other person does – *I just have to hear that band, I've never liked metal but I'm sure I'd love them* – and every day a drawn-out farewell, that horrible moment when they had to part:

Oh, do you have to go?

Yeah. I have to.

I hate this.

Me too.

Don't go.

I have to.

I hate this.

See you tomorrow, yeah?

Yeah.

If not I'll die.

Yeah.

You're mine.

I'm yours.

See you tomorrow.

And now?

Now it's serious. Sandra runs across the football pitch and Sandra has decided: she'll lie down, she'll be brave.

She gasps when she catches sight of him by the substation. A pressure lifting from her chest; he hasn't left. She runs faster, as fast as she can and throws herself into his arms.

'Daniel,' she sobs.

'Hey...'

'I've missed you so much! I thought you'd be gone! I didn't think you – I thought—'

'Hey, come on...'

He takes her face in his hands.

'Hey, hey...'

He tilts her chin up with two fingers.

'You...'

He looks her in the eyes.

'Hi,' he says, holding her gaze. 'Do you think Daniel would leave you? Eh? Do you not know Daniel would wait until Friday, until next month, Jesus, until it bloody well started to snow, if it's you he's waiting for?'

She sniffles and feels the tears roll down her cheeks. A 'hhha' escapes her mouth, and Sandra stretches up on her toes, closes her eyes and kisses him, for a long time.

'You taste of salt,' he says, laughing.

'It's the tears,' Sandra says, sniffling. 'Tears of joy.'

'They taste extra nice,' he says.

Then they begin walking into the woods while holding each another. Daniel with his arms around her slender waist, she with her arms up along his back, him backing up, her following his steps. It looks like ballet and that's probably what it is.

Sandra unbuttons her top.

They totter further into the woods. Their breathing is heavy, his hands rove over her backside, she undoes the last button, they kiss one another, whisper 'Here?'

'No, not here, it's too exposed.'

'Further in?'

'Yeah, further in.'

'What about here then?'

'No, across the road, the forest is denser there and no one can see us...'

Then they stop. Sandra is naked from the waist up. He stands there gasping. He places his hands on her breasts and sighs.

'Do you want to do this?' Daniel whispers.

'Yes,' she whispers, closing her eyes, 'yes, it's what I want.'

'Do you want to do this every day for the rest of your life?'

'Yes,' she whispers.

They sink down on to the ground.

'No matter who I am?'

'Yes,' she whispers.

'No matter what has happened to me?'

'Yes, I want to do this every day for the rest of my life.'

'Cool,' says Daniel, 'that's really fucking cool of you.'

21. GET THEE BEHIND ME, SATAN (Rudi)

Rudi strides through the woods. He's a tall man, well over one ninety-five with long arms which don't always know what to do with themselves. His face is pockmarked, his whole body is lop-sided and he looks like a roaming tower moving across the ground.

He stops for a moment to think.

Not many men have as good a woman as he has. Anyone think-ing of laying a hand on her better fucking watch out. You can call it what you want, call it being a psycho, call it jealousy, I call it love and Chessi does too. Do you not think I've looked after her? Do you not think Rudi has given her what she wants? Didn't she get to see Aerosmith at Sweden Rock Festival? Dream until your dreams come true!

Rudi froths saliva between his teeth and continues pounding across the forest floor. Hasn't he taken her to both Rock am Ring and Rock im Park, hasn't he laid the tickets on the table and paid for the whole shebang? Weren't they a fixture at Norway Rock in Kvinesdal until the festival went bust, doesn't she get as many thousands of pints of beer as she wants, didn't she stand and almost weep with joy in front of Motörhead and didn't she almost come when Twisted Sister played 'We're Not Gonna Take It'? Didn't he hold her and rub her back when she puked in the tent in the middle of the night. And hasn't she got an amazing fucking metal tattoo on her back that he paid for? And isn't she allowed to go to that skincare shit, even though he thinks it's disgusting.

Rudi spits into the woods, feeling strong and fair.

She's grumpy and electric, always has been. She's not approacha-ble in the morning, you need to stay weeeell bloody clear of her until she's had her coffee. But those are the kinds of things you just have to cope with when it's love that's at stake, you need to be generous, you need to let her sit in her room and mope – yeah, she can keep that room until she dies, every girl needs to have a room of her own.

Rudi spits again, before halting in his tracks and spinning all the way round.

Here. A wistful feeling sneaks up and strikes Rudi. Gran's cabin could have stood right here. God bless the old bag of bones, they were the good old days. Land, fields, sheep and cows and no mobile bloody phones, no interfuckingnet and nobody ringing up to ask if you're interested in faster broadband; no, mister, I'm interested in your dick on a skewer. Good thing for you, Gran, that you didn't have to live to see this shit.

Focus.

Rudi peers into the forest. He pricks up his ears. A sound? His eyes dart back and forth in the darkness, trying to adjust to the lack of light. He orders his pulse to slow down.

No, no sounds.

Need to get hold of that du-du-du du-du-du du-du-du song. It's impossible to remember the name of it. Coldplay. What is it he's singing? *I used to rule the world.* Chessi is going to put her finger down her throat and puke, heavy ballads all the way there. Rudi can't stand pop either, metal all the way. But that one song there, that takes the roof off the church. He needs to get it on CD, then he won't have to sit wondering if they're going to play it on the radio when he's out in the Volvo, and no way in hell is he getting any SPOTIFUCK or PISSTUNES or YOUSCREW and sitting listening to Mötley on a computer or watching the old videos on a mobile phone, that's an insult to all music.

Tapes. And CDs.

Rudi nods to himself.

He never got into vinyl. Jan Inge likes records. He's got those old country records his dad left behind when he went to the US. Might be hi-fi, but it's just scratches and stress. Rudi has always been of the opinion that if it's good sound you want, just turn up the volume, then you'll hear everything loud and clear. But each to their own, he thinks, I mean, it's not like I sit doing my nails with silver polish and read poetry while the moon glimmers behind a cloud either.

Pity you never had the chance to meet my woman, Gran. Cecilie's her name! Lots of sharp edges but you'd be hard pressed to find better. Granny would've liked her. She's sitting on a silver cloud up there in heaven with flowers in her lap, and one day she's going to say: *Rudi. There you are. Welcome to heaven. Is that right? You became a crook, I see, well, to every man his own life, welcome to heaven!* She had a lot more respect for an individual on God's green earth than the rest of that unspeakable family of his: Get thee behind me, Beast from Sandnes. Is that what a brother is supposed to be like? And is that what a sister-in-law is supposed to be like? Spitting in your own brother's face at Gran's funeral? Telling him you never want to see him again as long as you live?

Rudi breathes in and out deeply.

Who are you, Pål?

The question is: should they move? Away from Jani. Get their own place. A damn hard question. Hard in *every* way. It's by no means certain Jani could handle it. It's by no means certain it'd be good for the company. It could actually ruin *everything*. A damn, damn, damn, damn, damn, damn hard question.

He waves his big hands in front of him in the darkness.

Focus, like Jan Inge says, you need to focus, Rudi. Don't talk too much. Don't get lost in thought.

He takes long strides up towards the rock where he's arranged to meet Pål. He catches sight of him when he's halfway up. Rudi comes to a stop and studies him. There's no immediate recognition. Of course the guy had to have a dog. He needs to start saying it to people. *Dogs prohibited.* Pål looks worn out. His shoulders are slouching, his hands are nervous and his face is sad. He can't say he recognises him.

Rudi continues on and Pål catches sight of him. Rudi gives him a firm nod and assumes his sternest look, Pål raises his hand and gives him a lopsided smile.

'All right?' Rudi halts.

'Yeah, hi, I'm På—'

Rudi glances quickly left and right. 'No,' he says, grabbing Pål by his jacket. 'No, we can't stand here. Come on.'

'Okay...'

They walk down the hill, cross the path and break off into the woods. The dog barks. Rudi hears Pål breathing nervously beside him and lifts his hand up in the air as a signal to remain silent, while continuing to pull Pål after him. He looks intently toward the tree trunks ahead.

'Can you make your dog shut up?' Rudi hisses. 'Or do I have to find a stone to beat his head in with?'

Pål bends down quickly to the dog, whispers in a commanding voice: 'Zitha! Quiet!'

Rudi mutters to himself, annoyed. They cross the road and enter the small forest on the far side, which seems less inviting, less frequented, and after a short time Rudi points toward the substation.

'There,' he says. 'Behind that.'

'Okay?'

'The hum from the substation,' Rudi says. 'Away from prying eyes.'

They tramp through the undergrowth, towards the graffitied brick wall. The substation emits a steady, monotone sound. They stop. Rudi smiles sideways and says:

'Påli dude. I was thinking about you earlier today. You say we've met before? In the old days? Did you massage J-J-Janne D-D-Dobro's melons? Did you live on the same road as Tommy Pogo? Did I steal comics from you? Did I beat you up under the street lights by Tjensvoll Shopping Centre?'

Pål looks down. 'Eh, no, eh, it—'

'No?' Rudi clicks his tongue. 'No?' he laughs. 'Yeah, they were the good old days. That was what made us men, eh?'

'I...' Pål clears his throat. 'I lived here when I was small. Or, I mean. I still live here, and ... yeah, I, or, everyone knew who you were of course, or the Tjensvoll Gang, who all of you were rather, and eh, what all of you, y'know, did—'

'You're struggling a little. Were you afraid of us?'

'Eh...'

'Were you?'

'Everyone was.'

'Heh heh.'

'The whole area was, we—'

'Yeah, yeah,' Rudi interrupts, 'old times. Now our paths cross once again and you've gone grey, my friend, but have I? Heh heh! Can't say I remember you. Okay, Pål, focus. The ball's in your court, we don't have any unfinished business, I haven't beaten you up, you're not out for revenge and I'm guessing you don't want to invite me round for dinner? Heh heh! And if you do, then I've only one thing to say – Rudi ain't no homo! I'd cut my own head off before I'd take a cock up the hole!'

Rudi jabs Pål hard in the chest.

'No,' he says, inhaling what feels like a kilo of air, while thinking that people can say what they like about fresh air being the best thing there is, but when you've quit smoking you know what the real truth is. 'No, you don't get much of a laugh if you're not up for a laugh. So Wally, the dog whisperer, what will we do?'

'Eh .... well—'

Rudi places his hand on Pål's shoulder. 'Nervous? Okay, listen to me. Breathe in. And out. And in. And out. This is what you discover the older you get. All people – *almost all*, there's always an almost – that's the thing. This is what I want to teach my kids, if I have any. *All people – almost all – are okay.* They might look like inside out goatskin, but they're okay. Come on, Kåli, you need to breathe here! In, out, in, out! Yeah. Repeat after me, Tåli: *All people – almost all – are okay.* There's something for you to think about.'

Rudi stops himself. Focus. He takes his hand off Pål and straightens up. Scrutinises him. Just a regular guy. Not much else to say. Could do with a bit more facial hair, maybe. Shy looking.

'So. Pål. Fagerland. What is it this fudgepacker has got on his mind? Have you got a woman, Fåli?'

'Eh ... no...'

'No? Thought as much. You'd know to look at you. Yeah, I can see how things might be tough. If I didn't have—'

Rudi clears his throat. How many times has Jani said it: No names. No stories. Nothing personal. He's said it a billion times.

'Anyway,' Rudi says, 'one day the ladies are going to come knocking on your door too. And that's when you need to start ... yes, so anyhoo ... Pål. Fagerland. What is bothering this guy?'

Pål shifts his feet.

'Spit it out, Gåli. And remember to breathe now.'

Pål gulps. 'The Ace of Spades,' he whispers, glancing up at Rudi. Rudi begins slowly to nod. 'I see,' he says, in recognition. 'Double up or quit?'

Pål looks down at the tall grass. 'Yeah,' he says softly.

'Double stakes or split?' Rudi raises his bushy eyebrows.

'Yeah,' whispers Pål.

His shoulders drooping over. His eyes, so scared looking. Standing there, slouched over. The dog's leash hanging slack from his wrist. His meek, embarrassed voice. Is he crying? Jesus, this guy is in a bad way.

Rudi starts removing his jacket. He pulls the sleeves back the right way round and hands it to Pål. Then Rudy takes off his sweater, which he also hands to Pål. And even though it's beginning to get very cold, he pulls off his T-shirt. Then turns his back to Pål.

'See?'

'Yeah...'

'What do you see?'

'Well...'

'You see that it says Motörhead?'

'Yes,'

'Good.' Rudi turns and takes back his clothes. 'So now you know.'

'I can't get out of it,' he hears Pål say while he puts his clothes back on.

'Staying up at night?'

Pål nods.

'The internet?'

Pål nods again.

'That's what's wrong with the world today,' Rudi says, and spits.

Pål looks at him. 'So I was thinking ... I don't know, maybe it's a stupid idea but I've got into a situation which I can't manage to, y'know, debt collection and...'

'I know, you don't need to explain. Go on...'

'And then I came to think of you and him, what's his name, Jan Inge, and—'

Rudi lifts both hands. 'Whoa! Stop! No names. Erase! Rewind! Dude, no names!'

'Okay, no names, but you two came to mind, from the eighties,' Pål says, his forehead sweaty. 'I have two kids. Two girls. I've done something stupid. I...'

'Yeah?'

'Well, I—'

'Yeah?'

'I need a million.'

'A million?' Rudi laughs.

'Yeah.' Pål nods and looks down at the undergrowth.

'Listen,' says Rudi, slapping Pål on the back, 'sorry I'm laughing here, but ... I mean ... you need a *million*, and—'

Pål's eyes brim with desperation. 'Help me,' he whispers, a lump in his throat. 'Help me, please. I have two daughters—'

'Yeah, don't they have a mother?'

'Yes, but it's ... it's complicated. I'm up to my neck in this...' Pål pauses, swallows, before looking up at Rudi: 'I've no place to go. Please, help me. I'll do anything.'

Rudi nods. He folds his arms.

'Anything,' Pål whispers.

Rudi puts his fingertips against one another, all ten of them, and begins pacing restlessly in front of Pål while he speaks.

'Firstly: It's sad, what's happened to you. You've done something stupid. Secondly: You're not alone, this happens the best of us. Thirdly: You're looking for a solution. That's good. Fourthly: You're a Motörhead man. I appreciate good taste. I like that we're cultural brothers. Do you like Coldplay? No, Rudi's just kidding with you. Heh heh. Sorry. Back to the game, to put it like that. Fifthly: You think we can get our hands on a million?'

'Yeah, I...'

'Do you or don't you?'

'I ... I don't know what I think. I don't know what you ... I just remember ... in the old days, when you were in the Tjensvoll Gang ... people said that...'

'And what makes you think I don't work as a gardener now, or crochet tea cosies?'

'Huh?'

'Go on,' said Rudi. 'Go on.'

'I'm sorry if I ... I just thought ... is there anything I can do to get hold of a million? Then I had the idea of calling you.'

'Ah, Pål. *Is there anything I can do to ...* you've got the right attitude, maestro. You've got in touch with a good company, I'll give you that. You've realised that there's something called expertise. You have what Jani calls intuition. But *is there anything I*—'

They hear a rustling behind them.

'Down!' Rudi puts his hand on top of Pål's head and pushes him down into the bushes. He turns round as quick as a flash, peers back into the woods. 'Down!' he repeats. 'And keep the dog quiet!'

Oh, sweetbabyjesus.

'Rudi, you rotten pimp!'

Cecilie comes storming through the undergrowth. Her eyes are bright red with anger, tears have run down her cheeks, blackening them with smeared make-up, and what is it she's carrying?

'I hate you!'

She comes to a stop just in front of him, with something in her hands – what the hell is that?

'Chessi, what the hell do you think you're doing?!'

She throws it at him, what the fuck is it? He brings his arms up to catch it, a *hedgehog!*

'What are you playing at? Have you lost it completely? I'm at work, twatmuff! At work! You know bloody well that this is unacceptable, what do you think Jani's going to say? I take you out in the Volvo to get a little fresh air, toss five hundred kroner bills your way and you can't manage to sit still for *five little minutes*, you barge in with...' He throws the hedgehog onto the ground. 'You need to fucking get yourself tog—'

Cecilie's lips quiver. She sniffles, goes down on her knees in front of the animal. 'Rudi,' she says, her breathing fitful, 'it's a hedgehog. And you just drove right over it.'

Rudi bends over and hugs her. 'It's okay now. Rudimann is here. I didn't do it on purpose but you can't—'

She frees herself from his arms, gets to her feet and takes a small step backwards. Points towards Pål who appears behind them, his features contorted in a expression of fright.

'Who's that?'

Rudi clasps his hands round the back of his neck and sighs. 'Yeah, this is...' He stops himself. 'This is someone I'm working with.'

'What a lovely dog...'

Cecilie goes down on one knee. She stretches her arms out to the dog. It sniffs its way over, snout to the ground, and enters her embrace. Pål stands nailed to the ground. Not so strange, thinks Rudi, people are usually slightly taken aback when they first meet Chessi.

She gets to her feet. Puts her hand out towards Pål.

'Cecilie,' she says, in a high-pitched voice, shaking the hand of the stranger. 'Cecilie Haraldsen. I'm Rudi's woman. Such a cute dog, what's its name?'

'Zitha,' says Pål, 'she's called Zitha.'

'Zitha, yeaaah,' Cecilie pats the dog across the snout again, gives Pål a pleasant look. 'So, what are the two of you working on then?'

Something seeps into her expression. Her forehead furrows slightly. 'But ... have I ... have I seen you before?'

'No, don't think so,' says Pål. 'No.'

Cecilie nods. 'Just thought I'd seen you before.'

Jan Inge is not going to like this. Cecilie doing as she pleases. Flirting with this Pål guy. Bollocks, thinks Rudi, snapping after his thoughts. Get thee behind me, Satan. She's my whole life. She's the twisted light, she's canary-yellow happiness.

'Okay, Chessi,' he says, 'now you've shown us the hedgehog, are you satisfied? Pål's got troubles, you understand? He's got two daughters, and a mother, their mother that is, but it's complicated, and I think you're just complicating it even further now. Can you head back, so as we can finish off our meeting here?'

22. **DAD'S SHOES** (Malene)

Are you out there, Dad?

Malene is standing on the loading ramp behind the shop. She knows it's at rest but it feels like a boat that's rocking. She's conscious of the stinging in her ankle as she lets her gaze gather what she has in front of her, the houses, the high-rises, the woods, the sky, as though her eyes were somehow magic and could capture everything; the people in the buildings, the forest behind the school, what's happened and what's going to happen.

Dad, what are you up to?

Malene feels a dull thumping from the pulse in her ear. It makes her think of the tension just before a gymnastics competition, her feet on the mat, her body fully concentrated. She feels like she has her dad's shoes in her hands, even though she knows she doesn't. She feels she's standing in the bathroom folding her dad's jeans, even though she knows she isn't. She feels like she's sitting in her dad's lap, even though she's fully aware that she's standing on the ramp.

Tiril lights up another cigarette behind her, the nauseous smell of it drifting her way. She hears her sister shift her feet in irritation.

'Well? Are you just going to stand there staring? Hey? Lol?'

Malene doesn't reply.

Once when she and Tiril were small, Dad fell off the garage roof and broke his arm. Malene had noticed a dead magpie lying up there. A dead bird? Dad would take care of that. But he's clumsy when it comes to that sort of thing. He's not that kind of man. Dad is the type of man who lets the screwdriver slip and gashes his hand, he's the type who stumbles when he goes on top of a garage roof. Malene can remember Mum shaking her head and laughing as they drove to the hospital. She did that a lot, Mum, laughed at people. Always so sure of things, Mum, so sure about everything. Thought people just needed to pull themselves together, thought that everyone had to take care of themselves. That's how she goes on when she rings from Bergen: Everything all right, Malene? And then, before Malene has the time to answer: Good, that's what I thought. Or: How's the ankle? And then, before Malene has a chance to answer: It'll be fine, you'll soon be back on the mat.

Malene was terrified. She can remember the smell in the car as they drove to the hospital. She couldn't take her eyes off Dad's arm, dangling by his side.

'Hey, Maly? That thing I asked you about. Do you think it's true? Y'know, about choosing, between the light and the dark?'

Malene doesn't reply. She knows she's a girl who's one metre sixty-two with high cheekbones and a slender figure, a girl without a best friend, who sometimes feels alone, but never feels lonely. She knows she's a girl who reads books and listens to 'Payphone', 'Hot N Cold', and 'Rolling in the Deep', a girl who likes to feel her body sail through the air. She knows she's a girl who's never had a boyfriend, who's never bunked off school, who's always done her homework and taken things one step at a time. She knows that one day she'll marry a man who won't allow himself be henpecked, who'll carry her as though she were a queen. She knows that one day she's going to leave this town, travel to Bergen or Oslo, and study there. And she knows she'll come home every Christmas. She knows she's cautious, but she knows she's courageous. She feels that if a fire is burning someplace then it's her job to fetch the water.

Malene stretches out her injured foot. It's unstable. Can't rely on it any more. Behind her, Tiril puts out her cigarette.

'Of course you can,' says Malene, without turning to look at Tiril.

Then she whispers into the darkness, low enough for her sister not to hear her: 'It's Malene. Are you out there? Please. Talk to me, Dad. What is it I haven't noticed? Tell me what to do.'

23. LIKE THIS? LIKE THIS? LIKE THIS?
(Daniel William)

Only a matter of moments stand between Daniel and that addictive experience: entering a girl. Up until now it's been a pounding desire, stronger for every day. Envisioned and borne by turbulent currents in his body, raging rapids, which no power can halt, so cold they burn. When he's felt it rise, he's often thought about just going out into the dark, seizing hold of the first girl he sees, dragging her into the forest, throwing her down, peeling her clothes off and drilling a hole in her. He's closed his eyes and clenched his teeth, felt how the power can't be overcome, how it's that which is God. Sparks fly within him, the flash of a million sledgehammers falling on blazing iron, a roaring noise in his head. It's not evil, nor good, but it's real. The earth's crust needs to split, light must be torn, knock-kneed girls need to quiver and glisten, sing and die and be hunted like wounded animals across the great darkness.

What is it that the sight of her breasts does to him? Why do they set off such raving hunger, why must he press his lips against them, why must he cup them in his hands? What is it the sight of her closed eyes gives rise to in him? No, they're *almost closed*, the lids are quivering over her eyeball, like someone at the moment of death, a slightly moist twinkling under the arched lashes. Look at her lips, slightly parted, what is it they do to me? What the fuck is it you do to me?

No one can see them. They're hidden away in an empty wood, now nobody can get in their way. He stares at her. Sandra pulls down the zip on her jeans. She hooks her thumbs into the waistband, lifts her behind, and begins to wiggle free of her jeans while jerking her hips to and fro.

Daniel gasps.

Now she's lying there glistening, now she's lying there glowing. She's only wearing panties. She spreads her legs.

Daniel breathes through his nose, his chest is pounding, the oxygen in his head diminishing, he sets his jaw. Her legs are apart, her knees slightly raised. He kneels down, then bends over her, his palms resting on the soil and weeds.

'Take off your clothes.'

She whispers.

'Daniel, come on, take off your clothes.'

She opens her eyes slightly, liquid gold runs out. Her voice takes hold of him, she could have asked anything at all of him and he'd have done it. Daniel's made up his mind. This is what he was put on this earth for.

'Say it again.'

She smiles.

'Don't smile.'

'Take off your clothes.'

He jerks back up on to his knees, unbuckles his belt, unbuttons his jeans, feeling no nerves, only the hard warmth. He pulls his jeans down to his knees and sees Sandra's eyes fall upon him.

'Oh,' she says.

Your hands. Touch me.

But she doesn't. She just lies there. Her eyes have closed. Your hands, he thinks again. Touch me. But she doesn't. She just lies there. Daniel pulls off his underwear, his erection like a crowbar, then she begins taking off her white panties.

Then she looks up at him:

'Are you sure it's your first time, Daniel?'

He blinks confusedly and fixes his eyes on the strange country she has between her legs, which isn't a flower, isn't an animal, it's impossible to say what it is, he only knows he has to get in there. A dog barks not too far off in the distance, but the sound barely registers in Daniel's consciousness before disappearing again.

'Wha? Yeah – yeah, why are you asking about that now?'

She pulls him close, her hands move down over his body. She touches him, takes hold of him, guides him into her, pushes a whimper of pain aside, and he begins to move, the wild dogs storm across the fields and he can't call them back, it isn't possible to escape this heaven.

'Like this? Daniel? Like this? Like this?'

24. **SAY GOOD NIGHT TO THE GIRLS** (Pål)

Hear about what they did today. Hear about what they're going to do tomorrow. Fix their duvets a little, lean over them, as though they were still two little tots, give them a hug and a kiss on the forehead. Say goodnight to the girls. Go into the kitchen, clean away the day's mess. Bread in the breadbin, load the dishwasher, turn it on, check the calendar to see if you've forgotten anything, a dentist's appointment, a parent-teacher meeting. Let Zitha outside to pee in the garden. Into the sitting room, slide down in the armchair, put your feet on the pouf, three remote controls in your lap, flick through the channels, watch an episode of *Sons of Anarchy* or *Breaking Bad*. Maybe read a few pages of Michael Connelly or Jo Nesbø. Feel the daylight withdraw, see the wind play with the trees outside, see the moon exposed in the sky, hear the night come with corrosive silence. Get up from the chair, walk quietly across the floor, turn out the lights in each room downstairs, open the door to the basement. Tread gingerly on the creaky first step, go down carefully, set your feet on the cold tiles at the bottom. Go in the door to the right of the laundry room, don't turn on any lights, the blinds are drawn, sit down at the computer. Turn it on. Hear the humming of the fan increase, feel your neck tense, an effervescent rush in your temples and your pulse ticking in your throat, as you push aside the sick feeling unfurling in the pit of your stomach. See how the cold light of the monitor blanches the room, your fingers on the keys, sometimes catching sight of your own reflection but not allowing your gaze to fix upon it. Do this, just do this, say that it's soon over, say it's the last time. Betsson. Oddsbet. Betsafe. Centrebet. Username: Maiden. Password: Zitha. Blackjack, live odds, casino, roulette, poker. Bonus. Win. Raise. Win. Lose, lose, lose. Say goodnight to the girls.

Seen from the outside it's obvious that it can't work. It's so obvious he can't understand that he's done it. How long is it since he played his last ever game? A month? No, two weeks? Three days? No. Last night. Last night, he sat in the glow from the screen and played a round of blackjack, adding another few thousand to the debt he's no longer able to deal with. All the letters, the warnings about repossession, collection agencies, all the bills. He doesn't open them. He slips them into his inside pocket, takes them with him on his evening walks with Zitha, and makes sure they all end up in the same rubbish bin at the same bus shelter in Folkeviseveien.

No matter how easy it is to see from the outside, that this could never work out, it's the inside that counts. That's where we live, where we ache and burn, and that's where I've been, Pål thinks, while he stands there trying to conceal his amazement from Rudi and his girlfriend. They're a few metres off, Rudi with his arm around her, bending down, talking to her. There's a hedgehog by their feet.

The inside. That's where I live, he thinks. The nausea, I've become so good at pushing it from me, I've learnt to treat it like a ball I can just wrap my hand around and fling towards the horizon. Turn around, smile at the girls. Hi, Malene. Hi, Tiril.

To think he believed it could work. In retrospect it seems ridiculous, before it seemed easy. *The kids will stay with you, Pål. You get the house, you get the car, you'll get child support and double child allowance. You get everything, Pål. You're going to manage fine.* He pocketed his pride and resentment, accepted her money, as he always had done. Pål worked as a case officer for the local authority and it was written all over him: Never going to earn much money. Like it was written all over her: Going to earn a *lot* of money. And back then, when they started out, nobody could see foresee any trouble.

Why should we think about money troubles? Why should we think about the economic imbalance between us? After all, we share everything, said Christine. Pål made a quarter the amount she did, but he didn't experience any feelings of displeasure about it, just as he didn't feel any displeasure at having an ambitious wife who travelled abroad with Statoil, who constantly worked overtime. He liked that she was on the go, the same way he liked his own ordered life, and instead of thinking that a job with the local authority is an insecure job, because there's no opportunity to earn more money if you should suddenly find your life beginning to go under, he thought that a job with the local authority is a good job, because at least you have one if the world begins to go under.

When she left, things looked okay, Pål didn't need to change his habits, didn't need to start shopping at cheaper supermarket chains or cancel his newspaper subscription. He managed to pay the bills, was able to live like before. The support payments from Bergen were generous. But after a few years things started getting a bit tight. The upkeep on such a big house was expensive. The money from Bergen became more infrequent. And after four or five years Pål had to face the fact that funds were running low. He needed a new lawnmower; he had to get drainage problems outside the house sorted after some damp damage had shown up in the basement. Where was he going to get the money from? He cut down on things here, there and everywhere, food, clothes, holidays, downloaded TV series off the net. But it still wasn't enough. He traded in his car, it didn't help. He borrowed money from his mother, it didn't help. And then one night he began to gamble. Almost out of curiosity. It helped. After a few minutes he was sitting with several hundred thousand in his account. Pål, nervous and grinning, switched off the computer. Never again, he said to himself, and got the area round the house drained and damp-proofed with the money, but a month later he was back in front of the screen, and so began the life he's lived since: win a little, lose a little, win less, lose even more.

It's not just nights he's been playing. Lately he's been in the sitting room with a smile plastered to his face, the laptop on his knees, two windows open, one an online newspaper, the other a gambling site. On Sunday, he'd said, casually, his eyes on the screen: Hey Malene, what's your favourite number? She gave him a strange look and said, eh seven, why do you ask? Oh, was just wondering, he said, betting on seven. What are you doing, Dad?

Hm, ah, just checking the weather forecast in the paper here. Lose. Lose. Lose. Continue. Continue. Continue. Personal loan, maxed-out card, GE Money Bank are throwing loans at people these days, and no one knows who Pål Fagerland is, apart from them: Hi Pål, how's it going? The telephone rings late one night. Listen, we wondered if you wanted to come along to a poker tournament in Riga? Or: Hi Pål, we transferred 500 euros to you today, a little bonus. And when does that call come? Just as he's logged on. After a few day's absence. *They know who you are.* No one else.

The inside.

That's where I live, he thinks. But what is it that's going on inside of me?

He won big one time, felt the money rain down upon him one time, and that one time he's believed it was down to talent, but the laws are such that eventually he'll lose, everything. That's the heart of the game. He knows that. But how does that help? It doesn't, not at all. Pål was terrified of smoking when he was small. It didn't prevent him from starting to smoke. He smoked for seventeen years. The only reason he managed to quit was Malene, when she was ten and lay crying because she was sure her daddy would die. That was something that raked at him on the inside. Pål knows that it's not going to work. But no matter how well he knows it, he still believes in that jackpot every night, the one that can cancel all his debts and make him rich and worry-free.

Zitha rubs her snout against his thigh and Pål feels his jaw loosen, his chin drop, hears himself sigh.

'Yeaah,' he whispers, glancing over at Cecilie and Rudi, 'yeaah, good girl.'

He was amazed when she showed up. She hasn't changed since the time he went into her room. 1986. She's just the same, only more run-down. Just as thin, just as bony, just as discordantly composed. Her skin was soft and pink back then, now it's grainy and grey, but still freckly.

Pål needs to take pains to avoid being recognised. It's not going to go down well if Rudi realises he's been one of her – well – customers. To think she was the first girl Pål was with. Two hundred kroner? Wasn't it two hundred kroner he stole from his mum and dad? They took the bus out to the house in Hillevåg, he and Hasse. Pål handed the money over to Videoboy, was directed towards a room that lay at the end of a long hall. She was lying in there. A little girl under a duvet. Posters on the walls, one of a cat and another of Wham! He undressed. She giggled, he remembers, and lifted the duvet. He got into the bed, put his hands on those tiny tits. He didn't sleep with her, didn't have time, he came as soon as her fingers stroked his dick. Pål felt sick with shame afterwards, ran away from the horror movies and the rented girl and never went back.

And now here she was. She'd become Rudi's girlfriend.

He was always a nutcase, thinks Pål, looking over at the pair of them. Was this a good idea? Help him get hold of a million? Rudi was always twisted but now he seems even more so. Probably the same with criminals as the rest of us, we become ourselves more and more as life goes on, we expand, and it's not only the good sides that grow, the bad ones do too.

The eighties come wafting back to Pål, a time smelling of Sky Channel and late nights, flickering bike lamps, humming dynamos and puddle rock. The Tjensvoll Gang, sick rumours circulated about them. They looked tough, they lived by their own rules, they had the courage not to give a shit, not about school, or teachers, or parents, if they had any. Pål never possessed that kind of courage. Hasse was drawn to it, his curiosity greater than any moral qualms, he had to get to see everything, but Pål grew frightened when he heard about the things they got up to. Even their names scared him, *Rudi, Tommy Pogo, Janka Bat*. People spoke of Rudi's eyes sparkling the time he held a wailing cat in his grip, knocked it on the head with a stone, opened its mouth, placed a firecracker on its still pink tongue, laughed so much he almost retched, closed the cat's mouth, lit the fuse, took a few steps back and said:

'This is the most fun I've ever fucking had, and it hasn't even happened yet.'

People said the cat's head cracked and its eyes exploded like glass. Two weeks later they stole a can of petrol from the garage of a house in Ragnhilds Gate, captured a hedgehog, doused the animal with it and watched the flames rise into the night sky as they discussed what to do next, and did anyone have any drain cleaner at home?

Rudi has placed both hands on Cecilie's shoulders. It looks like he's trying to press her down into the ground. She nods. Then she looks over at Pål while saying something. Pål swallows. Are they talking about him? Has she recognised him?

Rudi looks in his direction.

No, thinks Pål. I need to go. He's going to kill me.

There's a flash in Rudi's eyes. He raises his forefinger.

I need to go. Now.

Rudi begins to walk towards him.

'Nice to meet you, Pål,' says Cecilie, 'I have to be off, so ... see you.'

Pål clears his throat but doesn't manage to get a word out.

She bends over, picks up the hedgehog and begins walking back down through the forest. A bit like a soldier, Pål thinks, and sees Rudi approach. He looks like one of the trees in the forest, like one of the trees has torn its roots up out of the soil and begun ambling across the earth in the darkness.

'Okay, Pål Wall.'

Rudi hawks and spits.

No, no, no. I should never have done this.

Rudi puts his finger on Pål's chest, jabs him hard a few times. 'Listen,' he says. 'Don't worry about it. Woman stuff. You'll know all about it when you get yourself a lady, Påli—'

Woman stuff?

'Sorrysorrysorry, daughters? Two daughters? But no wife? Rudi's not going to stick his nose in. You know all about it. What do I know? Isn't it the very reason someone like you and someone like me are talking? Woman stuff, it's a full-time job, man. You smoke? No?'

They didn't recognise me.

'Quit a few years back,' Pål says, and breathes out.

'Yeah, I quit too. Couple of weeks back. Hell to pay. No. The ladies. Got to have a spine of steel. Love, Snåli. You know about love?'

'Yeah, I've—'

Rudi fixes his eyes on him.

'I'm a man of love, Jåli.'

That look of his, utterly mad. It's like he's going to spontane-
ously combust and lava's going to flow out of his head.

'Never doubt it, not for a fucking minute,' Rudi says, seething.
'You can talk all the shit you like about Rudi but he's a man of
love, never ever doubt that. You hear me, Swalli?'

'Yeah, of co—'

'Good. I can't stand talking to people who don't listen. But. We
can't stand here nattering. Will I tell you what's wrong with the
world today, Wålli? The internet. There you have it. What happened to the human factor? Answer me that, Zålli. The internet.
Don't get me started, brother! The internet, that's what wrong
with the world today. As you well know, my keyboard-clicking
friend. And The Good Book, who reads that nowadays? And the
family, who watches over them nowadays? Okay, Håli, I'll tell you
how we'll do this.'

Say goodnight to the girls, Pål thinks, trying hard to hold back
the tears. I need to get away from here, this is all wrong, I need to
get home and say goodnight to the girls.

25. **A LOW FRIGGING GIRLY THING TO PULL**
   (Tiril)

'Tiril?'

Malene is standing on the loading ramp with her arms folded. Her head moving slowly from side to side, like a leaf in a light breeze.

Tiril bites the top off a fingernail and spits it out on the tarmac. She takes out a fresh cigarette, tucks her chewing gum up between her lip and her front teeth as though it were a pinch of *snus*, produces the lighter, watches the flame light up the darkness before bringing it to the cigarette.

She doesn't reply. Why should she go around answering people all the time? Amazing how someone's always pestering you. Everybody's alone in this world, in case you hadn't noticed, you're born alone and you'll die alone.

'Something's up with Dad.'

Malene turns to her. She speaks in a low voice. She has a forlorn expression on her face. Sometimes Tiril wonders if she practises that look, so people will feel sorry for her. Tiril certainly couldn't be bothered perfecting any bogus expressions of her own, even though she's the one they should feel sorry for, because she's the one who's fourteen, she's the one with a horrible body, the one without any friends, while Malene gets everything handed to her, just sits there in Dad's lap being the understanding, talented little gymnast with good grades.

'I can just feel it,' Malene says, still speaking in a hushed tone. 'There's something up with Dad.'

She can just *feel* it.

Jesus.

'Relax,' says Tiril. 'You're so dramatic. He's out taking Zitha for a walk. That's what he does every night. Zitha is a dog, she needs to be taken for walks. It's not Dad there's something wrong with, it's you.'

Malene crouches down right in front of her. Tiril doesn't like it. She doesn't like it when people get all in her face. It's like when that Norwegian teacher crops up behind her shoulder, smelling of coffee and asks so veeeeeeeery gently *how are you getting on here, Tiril.* Just great, Miss, get lost and sort out your own life, on your period, are you?

She blows smoke straight into her sister's face.

'You need to quit that, it's disgusting.' Malene waves the smoke away with a grimace.

'No. It's great. Cancer of the future, pleasure of the present.'

'Knock it off. Listen to me,' says Malene. 'I can feel it, you understand?'

Tiril shakes her head: 'You can feel it. You know what, I'm so bloody fed up of you thinking you can *feel* how things are with Dad.'

'Tiril, stop—'

'Who do you think you are? Dad's girlfriend? The way you go round tidying his things, as if he didn't have his own life, do you think he likes that? Do you think he likes you putting away his Adidas and folding his trousers, I don't know what you're thinking, I mean, it's sick! You're, like, his daughter! And then you sit on his knee as if you were even younger than me. Jesus, it's disgusting.'

Malene recoils. Her eyes screw up slightly and the corners of her mouth begin to quiver.

Jesus, now she's going to start crying.

That is a frigging low girly thing to pull.

She's never going to be like that, she's never going to cry unless she's in real pain. Harshini and Vera both do it as well, they've been at it since first class, crying about nothing and then the whole class gathers round them and it's all pooooooor you, Harshini, and poooooor you, Vera. Jesus, it's not *poooooor* anyone, or if it was it should be Kia Pogo, she's actually paralysed, she actually *has* a reason to think everything's fucked up. No, it's just a low, frigging, girly thing to do because they're weak and don't have the guts to deal with things themselves. It was cool when Frida Riska tore into them, Vera and Harshini both, went over to them and said: 'Girls, enough of the crocodile tears. You hear me?'

Tiril gets to her feet. She looks away.

Mhm. There's the sniffling.

Time for the waterworks now, maybe? Pooooor me who's always looking after Dad. Pooooor me who does all the housework. Ungrateful you, who just goes round giving out and being pissed off. Isn't that what you're going to say?

Malene stands up, grabs hold of Tiril's arm. She tries to pull herself loose – 'what are you doing? Are you going to hit me now as well?' – but her sister clutches her tight.

'You can say what you want, Tiril.' Malene looks her in the eyes. 'You can say what you want about me, we can talk about that another time, when you've had a chance to think about it. But this here, this is about Dad. Understand?'

Tiril tears herself free from Malene's grip. She stares at her while fixing her clothes.

'Is that so? You think you're the only one who's ever right? You think you're the only one with eyes in their head? Don't you? That you're the only one who can think and understand and actually has a brain?'

'No. I—'

'No! So quit it and … just quit it! What is it you want?'

Malene looks down. 'I'm sick of arguing with you, Tiril,' she says quietly.

Tiril takes a last drag of the cigarette, drops it, puts it out with her foot and dislodges the chewing gum from beneath her lip. She takes a few steps along the loading ramp and looks over towards the school. Some day she's going to get out of here, and she's never going to come back. She'll get away from here, away from Madla, away from Gosen, away from poxy fucking Stavanger.

'I'm not arguing,' Tiril says coolly, 'I'm discussing.'

Behind her, she hears Malene let out a heavy sigh. 'Yeah,' she says. 'Whatever.'

Her hands hang by her sides. Malene stands there with her nice body. And Tiril stands there with her horrible body and a pain in her stomach. Two boys skate by in the car park below. One of them points at the girls and shouts something. It's Bunny's little brother and that guy from Haugtassa, Hassan. Tiril extends her middle finger, holds it up to them and shouts: 'Fucking retard!'

Can't she give it a rest.

Standing there breathing so heavily.

'Yeah, yeah!' sputters Bunny's little brother. 'Emo! Looking forward to you making an asshole of yourself on Thursday! International Cunt Workshop!'

'Wanker!' shouts Tiril, hears them laughing and watches them skate out of sight. Bunny's little shit of a brother, cheeky little prick. Not a day goes by without him making some remark, something wrong with that guy.

'Listen...' she says, without looking at Malene. 'I didn't mean it.'

'Right, right,' her sister says hastily. 'Whatever. I'm heading home. See you when I see you'

Tiril bites her lip. 'Look...' she takes a deep breath: 'That thing about the clothes. I didn't mean it. Dad likes it. I'm sure he does. It's just ... you always have to be so ... it's like, you always have to do the right thing the whole time. When did you get your period, by the way?'

Malene looks like E.T. again, she gives a little start and laughs. Tiril grins.

'Well, I—' Malene stops herself. Looks closely at Tiril. 'But have you—'

'No, no. I'm as clean and pure as a preacher's sheets. Heh heh.'

'Summer last year,' Malene says, 'right after we got home from Copenhagen. It's a real hassle.'

Tiril looks around. It's a hassle, yeah, but it sucks being the last in the class to get it. Not that she'd want to have been the first, not like Amalie, that was so embarrassing, she got it super early, but if it doesn't come soon she's going to start to wonder if there's something wrong with her, no matter how much it hurts.

She doesn't have Malene's nice figure. She doesn't have Malene's eyes. She isn't good, nice and kind like Malene, but she has the eyes of Amy Lee, and she, too, is able to see. Bunny's little brother and his mate skating by the low-rises. The woods. The school. The telecom tower. The hill.

Tiril feels the cold worming its way into her body. All right, she thinks, hopping down off the loading ramp. Fleet of foot, clear in mind. All right.

'Come on,' she says, setting off.

'Huh?'

'Limahaugen.'

'Huh?' Malene scuttles after her.

'Well? Didn't you want to look for Dad?'

'Yeah, but—'

'Well then, come on,' says Tiril, continuing up the hill by the school, 'and I'll prove to you nothing's wrong. Dad is standing up there, I'll bet you a hundred kroner on it. He's standing up there, on top of Limahaugen looking out over the fjord, Zitha by his side, her tail wagging, and when we get there she'll come running and barking, but then you're the one, Malene, who's going to have to explain what we're doing there, okay?'

Tiril stops in front of the flats, turns and breathes on her sister.

'Well, have you got a hundred? I'm not going if you don't.'

Malene nods and takes a banknote from her pocket.

'Do I smell of smoke?'

Malene sniffs.

'It'll go away.' Tiril hurries uphill toward Limahaugen. 'Dad will be disappointed, you know, if he finds out. Think you might need glasses by the way, you're making a lot of weird faces, maybe your eyesight is bad.'

Bunny's little brother, that prick.

Tiril clenches her fists.

Guess who's going to get a taste of Tiril tomorrow.

26. SHE BRUSHES OFF LEAVES, GRASS AND MOULD (Sandra)

'Like that? Daniel? Like that?'

It hurts a little. She has the weight of a boy lying on top of her, his entire bodyweight. Only a few moments ago she thought about just abandoning herself to it, and she managed too, but now she's suddenly thinking there's a boy on top of her, she's never experienced that before and he's thrusting something inside her. Ouch.

It stops abruptly. She feels a trickling sensation ease through her body and it doesn't hurt so much any more.

I love this boy, she thinks. I love this. He's all mine.

Why is he stopping? Why is he pulling out of me? Sandra opens her eyes as she feels Daniel getting up. She props herself up on her elbows, covering her naked breasts. He's on his knees in front of her, features tightly drawn, looking away, looking into himself.

'Daniel? What is it?'

He doesn't answer. His face is contorted, his eyes wide open, as though his pupils are just going to disappear. Sandra draws her legs back, feels a tightening in her chest.

'Daniel? Is there something wrong?'

He holds his hands in front of his crotch, he's quivering all over, sweating, not looking at her. Sandra reaches out despairingly, her hands touching his stomach.

'Don't!' he hisses, getting up and pushing her away.

'What is it?' She sobs. 'Daniel? What have I done wrong? You know I love you, you know I just want ... it was nice, Daniel!'

They hear the sound of a dog barking, not far from them. Daniel pulls up his jeans, giving her a stern look as he crouches down.

'Daniel, I—'

'Shhh!'

He brings a finger to his lips. He shoots her another severe look. Sandra feels her throat go cold and a sweat break out under her hairline. She's never seen him like this before, it's scary.

But she does as he says. Keeps quiet.

Footsteps. They hear footsteps. Moving quickly over the ground, nearby. They both crouch down further. Daniel zips up the flies of his jeans. Sandra pulls her panties on hurriedly, wiggles her hips into her jeans and nervously fastens the buttons on her top one by one. They look around for the source of the footsteps. That dog, the barking of that dog, they've heard that before. Is someone spying on them? My God, it could be someone from the class. It could be Mum, it could be Dad.

Daniel points. Once again he puts a finger to his lips. Sandra feels her stomach throb with fear, she looks around anxiously. Now he gives a firm nod, his teeth clenched, in the direction of the woods. What is it she's supposed to see?

There. A girl.

Or, a woman.

She's walking between the trees. God, she's walking right towards them. A woman, she's carrying something, what is it, a *cat*? It's an animal in any case, and she doesn't look good, this woman, not at all, frail and rough with unruly witchlike hair, shabby clothes and smudged make-up – there's that dog barking again.

'Down!' whispers Daniel and lies down flat on the ground.

Sandra does the same. Her heart pounding in her chest.

The woman walks by. It's a hedgehog she's carrying. It's the weirdest-looking thing, the woman is tiny and as thin as a sheet of paper, around forty or something, with crooked teeth and red eyes, walking along muttering to herself.

She continues on down towards the road.

They get back up when she's out of sight. They try to look at one another but can't manage to. Sandra has tears running down her cheeks and feels like she's ruined everything. She did something wrong but doesn't know what, and now he's furious. Wasn't she good enough at it? Were her hands not skilled, did she use her tongue wrong, was her body not attractive? Has he slept with hundreds of girls before her and just thought she was horrible, stupid, small and tight and no good at anything? Please, Daniel, give me one more chance, I'll be better, I promise, I'll do everything the way you want.

'There's someone here,' he says, in a low voice.

She's about to say something, but he puts his hand over her mouth.

What's he on about? How can he talk like that after what's happened?

There's that dog barking again.

He turns. Whispers: 'Understand?'

Sandra nods, she feels so small and stupid that she obeys everything he says.

Then they hear it, both of them. The sound of someone laughing.

'We have to go,' he says. 'It's not safe here.'

Sandra feels like she's going to shatter into a thousand pieces. There's nothing about Daniel to indicate they've slept together, that they've looked as far into one another's eyes as people can.

'We can't be here,' he says, straightening his jacket. 'We'll just walk calmly across the path, me first and then you half a minute after.'

Daniel stops.

'Fuck. Where's my helmet?'

'Helmet?'

'Fuck,' he says again. 'Never should have—' He shakes his head. 'Okay. Me first. Then you follow half a minute later. I'll take the Suzuki. You walk home.'

Home?

She's not able to get up, not able to breathe, she can only cry.

'Get a grip, Sandra.' He's not looking at her. 'Get up. Don't sit there blubbering. I'm off now, you follow after.'

She gets to her feet unsteadily. I have to do what he says, she thinks, otherwise he'll leave me. He knows about this sort of thing. He's older than me.

'Okay,' she says, mustering her most grown-up smile. 'Half a minute,' she adds, trying to sound upbeat. She leans forward, gives him a peck on the cheek. 'So, did you like it?'

His eyes flit around, avoiding her gaze.

'Hm? Yeah, yeah, it was great, see you tomorrow.'

What's with you, Daniel William Moi?

How can you be so cold?

Are you a dangerous boy, Daniel William Moi?

She wants to hurl herself at him, wants to hit him more than anything, hit him with both hands, but she refrains. She smiles, brushes off leaves, grass and mould, and says: 'Yeah. Sure. See you tomorrow.'

27. **VOLVO** (Jan Inge)

He's pleased with this wheelchair.

Jan Inge rocks slightly forward and back while watching a movie. It handles like a dream, much better than you'd think to look at it. Ingenious idea Rudi had that time. Chessi needs a wheelchair. Where do they have wheelchairs? Wherever sick people are. Where are there sick people? At the hospital. Okay. Rudi drives to the hospital. He just walks straight in the door. He sees a wheelchair: That's mine.

Rudi at his best. Utterly fearless.

Easy to change course too. Jan Inge brakes hard in front of the living-room table and turns the chair smoothly around. Carrying 120 here, after all. About time Rudi called. But that's Rudi's style, if you take him on you have to be willing to take on the best and the worst, like beer and calories, to make a comparison. But loyal? People have come and gone in this company, good people who've accepted Jani's leadership style and realised this isn't some half-ass gang, bad people who haven't understood a single rule, people who've run themselves into the ground on drugs, made for a lousy atmosphere and been disloyal.

A cushion wouldn't go amiss, if you were planning on sitting here for a while. And some kind of headrest. Be surprised if Tong couldn't knock something up. There're few things he can't fix up, it'll be good to have him around again.

Jan Inge grins at the TV as though it were an old friend, and that's what it is, after all. A classic, *Three on a Meathook*. Well made, if you consider the budget and the fact it came out in 1973. Yeah. That scene's so good. The axe isn't even big, just a little hatchet, and it chops the woman's head right off.

There. Darkness. Zoom in on the house.

The father walking around calling out to Billy.

Why didn't you listen?

It's too late now.

That's what's so good about horror movies. They're all about it being too late. If Jan Inge ever writes that book, he can call it something along those lines.

It's Too Late.

A Study of Horror Movies.

By Jan Inge Haraldsen.

That bloody surname. It doesn't command any respect. He'd have to change his name if he was going to be a writer.

Jan Inge Wilson.

Doesn't sound that good.

What are writers called?

Hamsun.

He can't remember that many writers from school. But then again there weren't many days he went to school.

Jan Inge Hamsun

That has a certain ring to it.

JAN INGE HAMSUN

Vibrant. But a bit Nazi.

Knausgård? Jan Inge Knausgård?

Bit boring. Bit German.

Jan Inge Nesbø?

Bit used-up.

Spielberg? Jan Inge Spielberg?

Not enough like a writer.

Jan Inge Cash.

No. He's not really a writer-writer, Johnny Cash.

Nooo ... Jan Inge ... what's his name...

Yess.

JAN INGE KING.

It's Too Late. A Study of Horror Movies.

By Jan Inge King.

Jan Inge pivots a little on the wheelchair, nodding to himself.

It's all about grabbing hold of life while you can.

Some people have that little extra. The company was vulnerable when Tong went inside. Cash flow was better when he was working. He can be a bit iffy upstairs but that's the drugs. And as soon as that's out of the picture, which Tong promises it is, then it's hard to find fault. It'll be good to have him home, then the gang will be all together, then they can avoid having to trust people they half know as well as complete strangers. Melvin. Tødden. God, he's happy to be rid of that sick hippie, and Hansi, what a disgusting individual. He'd start jabbering away when he was drunk. When Rudi drinks he just wants to sing, dance, shout, mess about and screw Chessi, but when Hansi drank he wanted to hit the town, then he'd start blabbering, and then it's not far to the copshop on Lagårdsveien 6, and before too long you've got Tommy Pogo standing at your door. Well, anyway, all that's behind us now. Have to organise a party for Tong on Friday. Show him that we care. That he's bloody well welcome back.

WELCOME HOME, YELLOW SUBMARINE, WE'VE MISSED YOU.

That's what's important, thinks Jan Inge, filling his mouth with crisps. Keeping the gang together. Being a good leader. He saw a programme about business executives on TV, and after listening to them, he can't say he breaks with any of the fundamental principles of sound leadership. Trust. Presence. Ambition. Resolve. Seeing your co-workers. Seeing their good sides. Supporting them. Inspiring them. Being there for them in adversity. No, Jan Inge can't see that he breaks with any of the fundamental principles. On the contrary, they're precisely the same basic principles he adheres to when it comes to leadership:

No drugs (only when we're on a job!).

No to porn (ruins your head!).

Never harm individuals (what have they done to us? Are we animals?).

No to excessive violence and weapons (= copshop on Lagårdsveien 6!).

Small jobs = good jobs (get too big, Lagårdsveien 6!).

Yes to break-ins, no to hold-ups (Lagårdsveien 6!).

Keep calm! (Chaos is our enemy!)

Only talk to your own people (who else can you trust?).

Focusfocusfocus (!!!).

The biggest danger is Rudi and Chessi moving out. That's not a pleasant thought. What he needs to do is make sure things are so good for them in the old house that the issue doesn't arise. A charter holiday? Is that what they want? Jan Inge can surprise them and splash out. He could spring a surprise trip on them. And what about the SodaStream? How about he actually digs it out to see if it can be fixed?

LEADERSHIP.

'No,' Jan Inge says aloud. He rocks a little back and forth. On the TV screen a dead girl lies in a bathtub filled with a mixture of water and blood. 'No,' he says again, even louder. His voice fills the room, as though he were addressing someone. 'No,' he repeats firmly, 'need to get back down to a hundred. Too much of a good thing, this here.'

Why are you doing this! What do you want!

That's Rudi's ringtone. Jan Inge is torn away from his meandering thoughts and reaches out for the telephone. 'Yep, Jan Inge King speaking.'

'King?'

Jan Inge rolls his blueberry eyes.

'Okay, Mr King, noisy at your end, what are you … hang on, hang on, I'm listening, hang on, *Three on a Meathook?* Ha ha. You study day and night, you do.'

Jan Inge grabs the remote control and mutes the sound.

'Always on the hunt for knowledge. So, what gives?'

'The Volvo won't need repairs.'

'No?'

'Nope.'

'But we need to go through it together.'

Jan Inge squeezes the mobile phone between his jaw and shoulder, turns the wheelchair and trundles toward the door to the veranda.

'Oh?'

'A few details we need to take a look at.'

'But no repairs?'

'No.'

'Otherwise everything went okay with the Volvo?'

'What do you mean?'

There's something amiss with Rudi's voice.

'Well, just wondering if everything else was okay with the Volvo?' Jan Inge rocks back and forth in the wheelchair.

'Eh ... yeah? I mean yeah! Yeah. Everything's good with the Volvo.'

'Okay, well, if you say so.'

'*Kein problem*. Back to your studies!'

Jan Inge hangs up. Then he unlocks the door to the veranda, shoves it open and feels the white September night meet him. He feels the chill of a slight prickle on the top of his head. His bald spot's getting bigger, but can't do anything about that, runs in the family, bad hair. He seesaws the wheelchair gracefully over the doorsill, steering with steady hands, rocking a little back and forth before gliding out on to the veranda. Never fails, that whole Volvo thing, he thinks, surveying the run-down garden. Weeds and shit. All that junk and other crap lying about rotting. It attracts attention. They ought to have a clean-up soon. Straighten out company HQ. They can just talk about the Volvo and they understand one another. Don't need any set code, can just talk about the Volvo.

And that, he thinks contentedly, despite the presence of a creeping unease over what may have occurred; that is the innermost secret.

To be so tight with your colleagues that you understand everything. That you need only listen to the sound of their voices to figure out what kind of humour they're in. That you don't need to look in their eyes for more than a moment to know what's going on.

That to me is VOLVO.

28. **TITANIUM** (Malene)

The sisters walk across the fields by The Iron Age Farm.

They've been here before. All the kids in the area have been here. First in kindergarten, a herd of children out in the rain or wind, and then in primary school. Out to look at the ruins of the Iron Age houses situated on the slope between the high-rises and Limahaugen, with a view over Hafrsfjord, where the battle which united Norway into one kingdom took place: 872, Harald Fairhair.

They're surrounded by darkness, ahead of them they can see the red signal lights of the telecom tower at Ullandhaug, they can see the lights from passing cars down on Madlamarkveien, and they don't have the energy to talk.

The first girl is angular and ungainly, with small hips and a boyish stride, she's bent forward and moves with a jerky gait. Her chin juts out, her eyes often narrow and often flash with anger. She's good at football, has a foul mouth and wears heavy make-up. The other girl has grown-up features and beautiful, high cheek-bones. The first one has said she wants to be an environmental activist with Amnesty and write songs of her own. The other has said she is going to concentrate on gymnastics, continue studying in any case, perhaps something within sport or health.

She might well be a little anxious about the future. Anxious it could present further changes.

It was a normal training session. A Thursday afternoon at the end of May. Spring was in bloom, the air full of birch pollen, the summer holidays were right around the corner and Malene had had a good season. After a difficult winter where she had felt stiff and heavy, she was back in form. She'd done well in the regional finals, third place on the beam, a good routine on the parallel bars had given her second place behind Ylva from Sandnes Gymnastics

Club, and she'd executed a lovely vault where she'd finished with her first double somersault in a championship and taken home her first gold medal. In the Norwegian Cup in Trøgstad she'd been on the winners' podium again, third place in the vault and parallel bars.

Malene trained six days a week all season. She could feel her own strength, she could trust both her mind and her body, and people remarked how she had a new gracefulness about her. She'd grown, was elegant and had gone from being a good gymnast to being considered one of the best in the region. Not as ruthless as Mia, her best friend in the club and not as solid or tough as the Russian twins in Stavanger Gymnastics Club, but people viewed her differently than before. The jump was still the weakest part of her routine, she still lacked the necessary explosiveness, but she trained with determination and she knew everything was moving in the right direction. She had been doing gymnastics since she was seven years old and now she was reaping the rewards.

She was standing. The hall was full of girls, young beginners who practised their first round-off backflip, girls of ten in the advanced group doing arm support swings on the parallel bars. They giggled, ran and landed on the crash mat, Sigrid Ueland making comments the whole time: Bravo, Ingrid! Shuttle runs! Don't play with the hoop, Nora! What kind of wrist is that, Tuva? The vaults are all right, Mia, but otherwise you're too careful! You'll get a half-point more for a proper finish! You're going to get a Christmas present from me, Pia! You're running like a bunch of old ladies! Legs together! Legs together!

Without Sigrid, Malene would never be where she is. A powerhouse of a woman with a steely personality, a legend in the city, gymnastics champion and PE teacher, over fifty years of age but still very strong in both mind and body, imperious as well as ambitious on behalf of the girls, with crimson lipstick beneath bright green eyes.

'Malene! The double!'

Sigrid called out to her and Malene hurried from the beam over to the iPhone laying on the little table by the benches and wall bars. The other girls cleared off the mat and made room. Malene turned up the volume, 'Titanium', David Guetta & Sia. She always has to have loud music on when she's going to do her elements, it gives her energy and shuts out the world. Then she took up position in a corner of the hall. She allowed the music to play a little until it rose to a pumping tempo, she tensed her body and could feel Sigrid's eyes boring into her. The younger girls began chanting her name until it resounded throughout the hall – just as she'd done for the bigger girls when she was smaller, cheered them on, given them the noisy support they needed to get their adrenalin going.

'Come on, Malene! Come on, Malene!'

I won't fall, I am titanium. She began her run up. Not too many steps, she ran as hard as she could, did a chassé, perfect, not too short, went into a somersault, over into a backflip – was it a bit too high? A bit too far?

Malene felt a millisecond of nervousness as she sailed through the air performing the double backflip, but it all went so fast she didn't have time to think, and then she landed. Pain screeched through her body. It felt as though her right ankle had been torn right off. She screamed, fell on to the mat and clutched her foot. In the very same second she knew what had happened. Talus fracture. She erupted in a flood of tears. Sigrid came running over as she shouted to one of the others: 'Mia, ice!'

Malene was in more pain than she'd ever known, but all she could think of while Sigrid examined her foot with a seasoned eye, was: 'Now I won't be able to do gymnastics for months. Maybe never again. All the work I've put in to get here has been wiped out.'

'Pia! Turn off the music! Ice and tape!' Sigrid's powerful voice rang out through the hall. The music stopped, Pia ran. The smaller girls stood around Malene with their hands to their mouths and eyes large as saucers.

One small mistake was all it took. Had she not been concentrating? Had she done something wrong in the chassé? No. It was the backflip. It was too high.

'There's only one thing to do now, Malene,' Sigrid said calmly. 'You put this behind you,' she continued as she taped the ice pack tight around Malene's ankle before elevating it and stating that they'd have to go to A&E to get an X-ray. 'You'll be back in this hall next week, even if you come on crutches, you're coming along with us to camp in the summer, do you hear me?'

Malene nodded and writhed in pain.

'You're not going to let this fester, you're not going to let it get to you. Do you understand?'

She nodded again.

'You'll be back on the mat in a few months and this won't affect you.'

Malene began strapping her ankle and icing it regularly, she went to the gymnastics hall to begin training herself back up carefully, but as the weeks went by she felt less and less at ease. Her friends, who'd been so considerate to start with, were occupied with their own things, her injury wasn't exotic anymore. Malene felt stupid, her fear wouldn't release her and she limped her way through the whole of the summer holidays. She avoided meeting Sigrid's eyes because she knew what they were saying: Don't quit, Malene. She began doing exercises, began going to the physiotherapists, but the ankle wouldn't heal. Every day she checked it when she got out of bed in the morning: was it stronger today? Every second of the day went to thinking about the pain and just as Sigrid had feared, the pain won out, over Malene's mind as well. Then summer came round again, with the Olympics in London, a few of the other girls travelled to England with Sigrid, they saw sixteen-year-old Gabby Douglas beat Victoria Komova, but Malene didn't go along. She sat home reading text messages from the UK: 'Mally, you should have been here.'

Everyone says change is a good thing. Malene isn't so sure about that. Tiril loves change. She hated it when Mum left but apart from that she loves everything new. She throws herself into one new thing after the other, never looks back, just keeps on going.

They've always said we're like night and day, Tiril and I. Am I the day, then? Is she the night?

The sisters continue on up the hill towards the top of Limahaugen. It's not windy, there isn't even a hint of a breeze, but still it feels colder as they get higher up, and Malene considers what Dad always says about it being the nicest place in the world and thinks how true that is.

'Look at that,' he likes to say, 'eh? Take a look. The fjord down there. Those three islands out there. Eh?'

You don't get it, Tiril. You're so knotted up in your emo brain that you don't understand. One day you'll suddenly have been cocky one time too many. Suddenly the pain you flirt with will turn serious. Suddenly you'll have lost everything you can't live without. What do you think life is? A game about suffering?

They stop at the top of the hill. Look at one another.

Dad isn't there. Zitha isn't there.

Tiril gives a self-assured shrug. She purses her lips, assumes that cheeky look, the one that makes her look like a fox. 'There you go,' she says and blows a bubble with her chewing gum. It bursts in the wind with a dry snap. 'Now what do you say? Isn't it just like I said?'

Malene grabs hold of her sister. And then she slaps her across the face.

29. **HERE'S TO YOU MR HEDGEHOG** (Cecilie)

A dog. A nice little dog. A black-and-white one, maybe. Would you like that? Baby? A black and white one?

Cecilie carries the hedgehog in her arms, resting against her stomach. It still feels warm to her, as though death hadn't prevailed just yet.

He looked kind, that Pål guy, she felt it in her gut. His eyes looked frightened, but kind all the same, he had shiny skin. He ought not to get mixed up with them. He doesn't belong in our world, thinks Cecilie.

Rudi's actually kind as well, he's just not always able to show it, he's just not always able to show it, just so much crap with him. ADHD. That's what he says. 'It's the ADHD, Chessi, you know how it makes me act. But so what. Never bothered me,' he says. But that's bullshit. She's well aware of that. It's a load of bullshit. When a guy sits there jiggling his foot day in day out for forty years then it does something to him. He's got beetles on his brain.

Cecilie emerges from the darkness of the woods and walks over to the car. Holding the hedgehog with one hand, she opens the boot. There's usually all kinds of odds and ends in there. It's a storeroom so to speak, the Volvo. She picks up a hammer, looks at it, thinks it over, then takes it out and slams the boot. With the hammer in one hand and the hedgehog resting against her stomach she takes a few steps into the woods. She halts when she comes to a little patch of grass.

Yeah.

You can rest here.

Mr Hedgehog.

Here's to you. Sorry.

Cecilie puts the hedgehog down carefully. It sinks down and

spreads out a little, as though it were breathing out heavily. 'Look, baby,' she whispers. 'Do you see the hedgehog? Do you see, its ears are just as small as your Mummy's, see? It's lovely, isn't it?'

She waits, as if for an answer, and nods.

'Yeah,' she whispers. 'It's really lovely. Now we'll bury it. Hallelujah.'

Cecilie takes hold of the hammer and begins making a furrow with the cleft end, the part you pull out nails and things like that with, whatever it's called. Yes, she thinks, you can tell by looking at people if they're kind or not and that guy Pål, he looked kind.

She has a calm feeling in her chest. Digging up the earth does her good. Friends of my own, she thinks, girls. No. She'd just feel stupid if she had a load of friends. They'd know all kinds of stuff while she doesn't know too much at all.

But it would be nice to have some friends all the same.

But if she was to have friends she couldn't have Rudi.

But if she sets Tong on Rudi?

Then there'll be war.

The strongest will win and the weakest will die.

Five hundred kroner to take away my ashes.

Cecilie gets to her feet. She looks at the little grave she's made. 'See,' she whispers and points. 'There we go. Hmm?'

Again she waits, as though for an answer.

'Yeah. You're right. It's deep enough now. Cheers, Mr Hedgehog. You can rest here, can't you?'

She crouches down and picks up the animal. It's cold now. Stiffer as well. She lays it down in the hollow and covers it with earth.

I could always get a job, she thinks. Could find something to do with plants and flowers. I'm good at working with soil. Jesus, I'm so lucky I don't have to work, Jani says. Work? Do you know how much money people would pay not to work? says Rudi.

But I'm good at screwing.

I've been good at that since I was small.

Cecilie puts her foot over the soil and flattens it with the tip of her shoe. Then she stands there for a few moments looking at what is just a plain patch of earth, before grabbing the hammer and heading back towards the car.

She lights up a cigarette.

Jani never misses Mum, he hates her. Cecilie hates her too, but sometimes she misses her as well. In a way. Maybe not in a Mum-the-way-she-was way, but Mum all the same. Mum the way she could be, perhaps. Mum the way she wasn't? Is that possible? To miss Mum the way she wasn't?

But Dad.

He was always so happy. Dad was like a funfair.

If Cecilie was to make a list of her top five heavy rock ballads, then it'd be:

'Dream on' by Aerosmith. Obviously. 'Carrie' by Europe. 'Still Loving You' by Scorpions. 'Dreamer' by Ozzy. 'When the Children Cry' by White Lion. And 'Jump' by Van Halen. But that would make six. No matter. David Lee Roth would have to be on there. Even though 'Jump' isn't a ballad. Puss would say it wasn't a good list if there's no Motörhead. It's not her fault Lemmy's no good at ballads.

'Baby,' she whispers. 'We're going to listen to heavy rock, you and me. We're going to raise our hands in the air and listen to heavy rock, you and me.'

Cecilie snaps out of the thoughts going round her head as she spots a boy emerging from the woods. She lowers her head, puts her hand to her stomach and looks at the ground. A girl follows just after. She shivers a little, looks away, trying to make herself invisible.

Puss.

Sometimes she wants to kill him and sometimes she wants to marry him. It's practically the same thing, Cecilie feels.

Baby, she thinks, watching the boy and girl scurry out of sight. We'll get Uncle Jani to fix up a nice room for you in the basement. And then we'll get a nice dog, you and me. A black-and-white one. Or maybe we can get a place of our own. A house. Maybe.

I smoke too much but I need a cigarette now.

I'm not pretty but Rudi thinks I am.

And so does Tong. Friday. That's when I'm picking him up and then anything could happen.

Cecilie makes her way back over to the hedgehog's grave. Once again she pats the topsoil with the tip of her shoe.

30. THEY'RE TAKING OVER THE WHOLE WORLD (Daniel William)

A thousand kilometres underground.

I want to go down, I want to go down, a thousand kilometres beneath the earth. To the place where dreams are boiled in rusty oil drums, where feet scrape across bleeding stones, where small boys pluck squirrel eyes under the light from hanged girls. You're going down, you hear me? A thousand kilometres under the earth. Don't touch me, you hear, don't fucking touch me. You can just lie there, you bitch, you can just lie on your back, being all sexy, closing your eyes and whimpering with glossy lips but you have no idea, you hear me, no idea.

Daniel darts like a ragged dog across the forest floor. Setting his heels down hard into the ground, gritted teeth, breathing through his nose with his fists clenched. If he could hit someone he would; smash a face to a pulp, kick someone in the guts, break them up and hollow them out until they were dust.

Nobody is ever going to put their hands on me again.

Play the drums while Veronika watches, drink with Dejan and the others, work out until I'm built like a brick shithouse. Full stop.

Bury girls a thousand kilometres underground.

He slid in and out of her, once, twice, then it cascaded through him. It was impossible to control. He shouted at himself, pull back, keep calm, but it didn't help. It was just a wild storm. No matter what he did, no matter what he screamed at himself, it was impossible to hold back. It pumped through him and he just about managed to pull out of her, just about managed to cover himself with his hands before it blasted out of him, wave after wave.

So unbelievably embarrassing. So unmanly.

Daniel keeps a look out for his helmet. Have to just strike that whole girl idea, shit plan anyway, having yourself depend on something as fickle as a girl. What the hell did he do with that bloody helmet. There you have it. Girls, they screw your head up. Just because they're gorgeous. He's been walking around like an idiot the last few weeks, a silly grin on his face, only sleeping two or three hours a night, thinking about roses and all kinds of girly crap, even thinking about a house and kids, no wonder he just tossed his helmet someplace. It's not right, hardly recognise myself, he thinks, as though nothing matters any more, apart from her, apart from her body, apart from getting inside her.

He doesn't like it.

Daniel speeds up.

Losing control.

I don't like that one fucking bit.

Anyhow, it's the last time I'll ride out to these woods and snog a fifteen-year-old who sings in a choir, wears a cross round her neck, has a lawyer daddy and a Jesus freak for a mother and thinks the world is a lollypop.

> *Cotton Candy, sunbullet mine*
> *Explode my body out of time*
> *Bowlegged baby, how you shine*
> *Running over space and time*
>
> *Bring my shovel, bring my axe*
> *Bring my rifle, fill your cracks*
> *First I fuck you, then I kill you*
> *First I fuck you, then I kill you*
>
> *Cause I see you running, whore*
> *I see you running, whore*
> *Bandylegged you set ashore*
> *Away with another man*

Daniel nods to himself as he feels the lyrics tick out in his head. It's like the words burrow their way up through the dirt in his mind.

The lyrics are suddenly there, totally complete. He just needs to remember them, just needs to get them down on paper as soon as he gets home.

Daniel glances up, holds his breath.

There's that dog again.

Closer now.

And voices?

Daniel catches sight of the substation, not too far off. He slows down. There're people behind the tall weeds. Two of them. He hears one of them say:

'Calm down, man! Make the dog shut up! Listen to me now!'

Daniel comes to a halt. He looks right, then left. He takes a few steps into the woods and gets behind a tree. He squints.

There're two of them. Two men. Both around forty or something. One of them, who's really lanky, must be all of two metres, is waving and swinging his arms around, he looks like a tree in a storm. The other one isn't that tall and he's kind of difficult to see. He's the one with the dog on a lead.

'Okay,' he hears the guy with the dog say.

'Good,' says the tall guy in a raspy voice. 'You need to calm down, Påli, if this is going to work out. That's one of the fundamental principles right there. Keep cool! What's important here is to think, you get me?'

What's going on here?

'Okay, you're a Motörhead man, so that probably makes you a Metallica man, am I right?'

'Yeah, or I used to...'

'Darkness imprisoning me, all that I see, absolute horror, I cannot live, I cannot die, trapped in myself – is that how you feel, hombre?'

'Well...'

'Where do I take this pain of mine – I run but it stays right by my side?'

'Well I...'

'Maybe you're a Judas Priest man too, eh Kåli?'

'Ehh...'

'Breaking the law, breaking the law...'

'Can't really—'

'Too bad Rob Halford turned out to be a queer, but there are a lot of things in life you have to turn a blind eye to, or whaddayasay, Gnåli?'

What's going on here?

Daniel hears footsteps, he turns around – it's Sandra. Reacting as quickly as he can, he hurries on to the path, nods in the direction of the men behind him and pulls her into the darkness of the woods, whispering: 'Don't make a sound.'

He points. Sandra twists herself loose. She looks angry, her eyes are red, but there's no time for him to think about that, he points again in the direction of the two men and whispers as quietly as he can: 'Just listen!'

She looks over at the men behind the substation. The taller one lays his hands on the shorter man's shoulders.

'Okay,' they hear him say. 'You think I'm a magician. A wizard. You're right, and you're wrong. You've got problems. It's understandable. What we'll do is...'

Sandra gives a start, takes a step forward, craning her neck.

'Th—'

'Shhh!'

She mouths something.

There's that light again. That expression in her face. Sweet Jesus. There's not one girl, not in the whole world, who's as beautiful. What's she trying to say?

I know him.

Feeling how bloody gorgeous she is, feeling it all through him, Daniel mouths a reply.

Do you know him?

She opens that beautiful mouth, still without uttering a sound:

Yes.

He moves his lips soundlessly once more:

Who is he?

'...I'll go back to my people, Tråli. You go back to yours. I'll see what I can come up with. And I'll see you tomorrow. All right?'

Sandra stands on tiptoes, crying, she takes hold of Daniel's face, kisses him and then whispers: 'He's the father of Tiril, the one I work with, and Malene, a girl in my class, he's their dad.'

'She's in your class?'

Sandra nods. 'Mhm.'

'Okay,' says the shorter guy. The one who's the father of these girls. 'Where will we meet? When?'

'It'll have to be here. No surveillance cameras in the woods, y'know. Same time. Then we'll see if we have a solution to your problem. And remember: the internet is the root of all evil. So don't you go turning on that computer now, dude! Set aside a little time with a few good records instead. Number of the Beast! Overkill! Sabbath Bloody Sabbath! Or what do I know, maybe you listen to Coldplay when nobody's around? Ha ha, fucking bedwetters. Okay, brother. See you tomorrow!'

Then he spits, spins around and leaves.

He staggers out on to the forest path not too far from Daniel and Sandra, tall as a tree, looking neither right nor left, just walking like some sort of Frankenstein in fast motion.

Over by the substation the shorter guy emerges from the bushes. He looks around as though he doesn't want to be seen. Then he crouches down in front of his dog. He puts his nose against its snout and stays like that for quite a while. Eventually he straightens up, heaves a sigh with his whole body and begins walking. With heavy steps at first, which become gradually lighter. Then he bends down and unhooks the lead from the dog's collar. He picks a stick up off the ground. The dog freezes, its ears standing straight up. The man holds the stick in the air in front of the keyed-up dog, holds it until the animal is about ready to burst. Then he hurls it in the direction of the football pitch by the school and calls out:

'Go Zitha! Go on! Good girl!'

The man disappears from view. Daniel turns to Sandra. They look at one another, pupils flitting from side to side in an attempt to capture each other's gaze.

'What was that?' he whispers.

'I don't know.'

'Have you ever spoken to him?'

'No ... I think his name's Pål or something, but no, I've never really met him,' she says.

They hold hands, fingers entwining.

'But you know the daughters?'

'Well, yeah, a little.'

'It seems like they're in trouble.'

'Yeah'.

They squeeze one another's hands, tight.

'What are we going to do about it?'

'I don't know.' Sandra sobs. 'I'm not able to think about it right now. What about us? Are we in trouble? Daniel?'

Daniel looks at her for a long time. Then he says:

'We're not in trouble, baby, no fucking way.'

She sobs involuntarily and feels her knees give way.

'But you need to be getting home,' he says.

'Yeah, Mum and Dad are going to kill me, I'm way too late.'

'Listen, sexy. We'll talk about this tomorrow. All right? I'll see you tomorrow, okay?'

Sandra nods.

'I'll come by the shop,' he continues, 'you text me when Tiril has gone and then I'll come. Then we'll think about what we can do. Okay? Don't tell anyone about what you've seen, no one, okay?'

She nods again.

'Every day,' she says, 'every day for the rest of our lives, just you and me.' She strokes him across the cheek. 'And it felt amazing,' she adds.

'That was only the beginning,' Daniel says proudly, 'shame we were disturbed.'

'We have the rest of our lives,' she whispers, giving him yet another kiss, a long one, and Daniel thinks about how he wants a kiss like that every day, then his life would be in order, then everything would be okay.

She tears herself away from him, reluctantly, and runs off.

Look at that girl.

Look at that ass.

That's the meaning of life running off right there.

When she's out of view he begins searching for the moped

helmet. His arms are tired, as though he's been chopping wood all day. Life can be so fucking good. Play the drums. Work out. Party with Dejan and the others. But if your woman wants you to stay home with her then you better know what to say. *Sure thing, baby.* Because when you've found a girl who puts up with a lot and gives back so much, you need to hold on to her, hold on tight.

But what is the father of those two girls up to?

There's my helmet. On the gravel in front of the substation.

Girls. They're taking over the whole world.

To the right of the sea-green cell door hangs the torn-out page of a notepad. There's nothing written on it. It's just hangs there, sellotaped to the wall, at head height next to the light switch.

There's a cork notice board on the wall between the door and the bed. No pictures pinned to it, no family photos, just two postcards and three pornographic clippings. Mina from Flekkefjord, a cheerful brunette with a navel piercing, small tits and an African ass. And two other girls, without names, kissing one another.

There are tinned foods, bottles, ketchup, a couple of sandwich spreads as well as some toiletries lying on the end of the desk. Along with two packs of chocolate chip cookies. *CSI: Miami* is playing out on a 24-inch flatscreen on the centre of the desk. A few binders stand along the bookshelf, in addition to a couple of crime novels. Harlan Coben. Wilbur Smith. A book about meditation: *Meditation, Path to the Deepest Self.*

He stands in the centre of the room. Feels the weight distribution on the soles of his feet. Three points. Under his big toe, under his little toe and on the edge of his heel. Takes a deep breath, closes his eyes and exhales slowly while he feels the balance strengthen his body. Neck straight. Muscles tensed from his armpits to his fingertips. Knees active, thighs strong. Silent.

There's enough jabberers, in here as well as out there, and if they're not talking your head off then they're telling you what you want to hear and one is just as bloody annoying to listen to as the other.

Tong opens his narrow eyes. Tightens his fists. He propels himself towards the torn-out page taking only a couple of purposeful strides. He opens his palms, kicks out with his right foot and makes contact with it before landing with precision on the floor again. Bullseye.

He straightens up, bows as though a master stood in front of him and walks the few steps to the little bathroom, where he – unlike many other inmates – has his own shower. Tong is in newly renovated A3 and he's a guard's helper, two advantages in so old a prison, with so many dingy cells, run-down blocks, poor ventilation and often times four men to a room.

He bends down and takes hold of the blue-and-white towel with the words 'Correctional Services' written across it. Squeezes it before lifting it to his forehead and wiping the small band of sweat below his hairline from the half-hour of training he's been doing since he was locked in for the night.

A day and a half, then he'll be out. Then a new life begins. A new style. A new Tong. Quit the drugs. Quit working with Jani and Rudi. He's moving up a notch. Get the situation with Cecilie sorted out. In or out. All or nothing.

Third conviction. Åne prison is all right but he's tired of it. The first time, in the mid-nineties, was okay. A good bunch on C2 back then, the older screws still say it. 'Jesus, Tong,' Hangelanden says, 'what you lot had going on in C2 back then, best block we've ever had.' Were good, those times. Almost everyone was someone you knew. Rune, Espen, Diddien and ... anyway. All in the past. Only immigrants here now. Back then it was ninety per cent white and ten per cent black. Now it's the other way around. Now it's ninety per cent immigrants. The blacks sitting in for rape, the paedos and then the Lithuanians, the Polacks and the Romanians. Idiots who can't pull off a real job, the ones who stand in your room at night rummaging through your handbag. The ones who smash your windscreen and take your stereo. The ones who are happy to get into a fight, who bump off one another all the time and who send the daily wage they get at Åne home to Poland and think life's hunky-dory in here. Fifty-six kroner. Fantastic immigration policy. What are they doing here? Tong is adopted but no way does he see himself as a foreigner. He's Norwegian, he just has the wrong complexion. Simple as that. Send the fuckers home. Close the floodgates. Full stop.

Doing time in Åne isn't like it was. Things were slacker, there were more fights in the exercise yard and the screws weren't as extreme about doing everything by the book as they are now.

Tong has stayed clean this time. He's kept away from the others, been strict. Not that he's become a Christian or anything, but simply because he couldn't face it any more. And he's tried to get that into that kid Bønna's skull. But he doesn't get it. He thinks prison is fucking great, you can relax here and it's a lot less stress than outside. 'Bønna,' Tong says, 'listen to an old dog, that's what I used to think too. But when you land in here for the third time, then you start to see you've screwed up. You realise it's a pile of shit, the whole thing. You're fed up with it.'

Tong turns the tap on, lets the water run for a few seconds, bends down, opens his mouth and drinks. He's got an okay bathroom at least. Was a relief coming here after the first few months in the old block. Rooms without ventilation, rooms without a bog.

Being in the nonce wing is different from doing time for assault or dope. First time he was sent down was for complicity in trafficking of grade A drugs. Four years, got probation after three. That was all right. The second time, aggravated assault, eighteen months, probation after a year. No problem for Tong to get out on probation once he's inside. No difficulty adapting to the system. But this time it's different. Being stuck on the nonce wing is very fucking different. Even though he's not a paedo, even though every inmate in the prison knows who Tong is – he's not even on the paedo wing – it's different. The looks the other prisoners send him, they're different. It's as though they enjoy it, the fact that he's not serving time for drugs or violence. As though they want to make him out to be a bit of a paedo all the same.

And if he runs into that girl, that little fucking whorebag, if he so much as catches sight of her again, then she'll be sorry. No fucking way she looked like she was fourteen. No fucking way she behaved like she was either.

Everything had gone well. They were partying after the warehouse job in Orre. They'd made off with over sixty laptops and a load of other equipment. Then they headed over to that horny bastard Hansi's place, and there's always a young crowd there, girls and boys, and line after line on the glass table. She sat on his lap, wanted cocaine and speed and everything she could get, rubbed her crotch against him like he was a car and her pussy was the car wax. He took her into the bedroom and banged her in every hole a woman has. What's wrong with that?

That's what he said to the lawyer: 'Listen, Hanne, no fucking way did she look fourteen, I was off my head, but I didn't do anything wrong. She wanted me and I wanted her and what's wrong with that?'

Hanne did her best. She was his prosecutor last time and like he told her: 'I've had you as a prosecutor, Hanne, you were one vicious bitch, now I want you on my side.' Ah well. Not her fault. It was that slut's fault.

What he's going to do about Cecilie, he really doesn't know.

But he's done working with those idiots. Rudi and Jani. All done.

Tong gets to his feet. He takes a chocolate chip cookie from the open packet and chews it slowly. His hair is jet black, his facial features are sharply carved as though someone had cut them with a knife. He swallows the biscuit, making sure there's no crumbs left in his mouth. He straightens up, tenses his body, opens his eyes wide, doesn't blink. Assumes the stance. Finds balance. Propels himself at the wall.

WEDNESDAY 26 OCTOBER

> *The only card I need*
> *Is the Ace of Spades*
> Motörhead

32. MORNING AT THE HOME OF THE CRIMINALS (Jan Inge)

Up with the lark. Up with the light.

Yet another mystical day in the wealthiest city in the world.

Look at everything glowing.

Feel that heat.

I, a morning person.

Jan Inge can often feel an almost violent sense of joy when the early morning sun rises behind the hedge. When it's just about to break through the morning mist, streaming towards him like a ball of celestial madness. Then he feels a shiver on the back of his neck and a pressure behind his eyes, and he hears an airy voice call. It's the sun. It's that brilliant white fog lamp calling, it's voice an almost orbicular timbre, spinning like a merry-go-round of sound, and then he has no choice, he has to walk barefoot across the morning dew, across the cold lawn, whispering to the light:

Yes? Master? Yes? I'm here. What would you have of me?

It's like being married to the earth.

But when you've hit 120 it's not so easy to wish the morning welcome any more. There's a lot to lug around. The fat has resulted in a depression of sorts, as well as having given rise to a not inconsiderable laziness at being this big. The wheelchair is handy but things have gone too far. He needs to get down to a 100. Maybe 90.

But he doesn't have to put the wheelchair away of course. It's not the wheelchair's fault he's fat. David Toska wasn't exaxtly sylphlike either when he was operating in Stavanger. To draw a comparison. And not a bad comparison at that. Toska, our Charles Peace, our Dave Courtney, our Clyde Barrow, our Stanley Mark Rifkin. After all, what do these masterminds have in common? They thought big, they aimed big, and like Toska, they were caught.

He needs to start taking some exercise. Tong's a demon for the training. Cecilie says he doesn't do anything in Åna but train. Rudi is naturally thin. Like Cecilie, she's naturally scrawny. They never need to exercise. While he, the leader, is predisposed to getting fat, really fat. The problem is that Jan Inge has no desire to start working out, besides, what kind of training would he suddenly start at age forty-three, when he hasn't actively exercised since he dropped out of PE in third year.

Yoga?

He saw a programme about yoga on TV the other day.

Something about the idea of the individual self and the universal soul becoming one.

He saw people sitting on mats with their eyes closed listening to tranquil music from faraway places. A yoga master stated that even though you're merely sedentary it has the same effect on the body as a half-hour jog.

Yoga Yani.

Not a bad idea, he thinks, feeling he might have arrived at something. And that's what he likes most of all. Think, think, think, result, result, result.

Complaining, that's easy.

Who gives us positive individuals attention?

It's important to look at things in a positive light, like Dad said so long ago, when Cecilie was crying her eyes out at the airport. 'Come on, kids,' he said. 'Houston's not a million miles away. A hundred years ago it took weeks to get to America. Think about all the people who left, think about all the emigrants!'

Indeed.

Yoga Yani has thought about the emigrants many times.

For the simple reason of his father having uttered that sentence out at Sola Airport, Jan Inge is pretty knowledgeable when it comes to the emigrants. And it's true what his father said, the world has changed.

But for the better?

Jan Inge isn't sure.

Wouldn't it be better if it still took weeks to travel to the other side of the globe? Then folks might think things over before they headed off to foreign climes, where the food they eat and the language they speak is completely different, and left lots of heartbroken people in their wake.

1982. It was the year *Time* magazine named the computer Man of the Year. The war was cold but Jan Inge's thirteen-year-old heart was warm: in February the house in Hillevåg had got a video player. With a mother in the graveyard and a father in the oil business a horror escapist was born. Jan Inge spoke in hushed tones to the guys in the video shop, got hold of uncensored versions from the golden age of the last ten years and watched videos until his head grew large, dark and replete. He became acquainted with the thinking of Dario Argento, Wes Craven, Tobee Hooper, George Romero and John Carpenter, he watched *Amityville Horror, When a Stranger Calls, The Brood, Suspiria, The Shining, Night of the Living Dead, The Texas Chainsaw Massacre, Friday the 13th* and *Last House on the Left.*

While Cecilie was at school he sat on the sofa at home, pulled the blanket over his knees, brought the bag of crisps closer, his watery blueberry eyes shining in the light of the TV screen, and they loved one another, horror and Jan Inge, and he often had the feeling that he wasn't watching the movies as much as the movies were watching him. And loving him. He watched zombies come at him, watched deviant murderers raise their axes, degenerate rednecks slaughter everything they came across, watched frightened girls light up the screen and scream down the house, multicoloured lights and the jaws of the abyss open up.

Two years prior to Jan Inge and the video player finding one another they'd lowered Mum into the earth. And thank goodness for that. She was an animal. Brought kids into the world and ended up a dunghill stinking of liquor. She would have fit right into a horror movie. *Mom from Hell. Hellmom.* Life brightened up when she disappeared, and it was at its brightest when the video recorder and Jan Inge were alone in the house. He has a lot of good memories from that time. Cough a little in the morning, struggle with the asthma, get Dad to ring school and tell them Jan Inge has to stay home. But then came autumn 1982 and one day Dad came into his room, stood in front of his *Jaws* wallpaper and announced that new times were here, and these new times were lubricated with oil. The company was sending him to Houston.

'But I'll be back every fortnight,' he said, giving Jan Inge's hair a tousle, 'everything's going to work out just fine, so it is.'

And then came the day at Sola airport.

Cecilie was ten.

Yeah. Ten.

Jan Inge can remember her asking him to put her hair in pigtails that morning. He told her he didn't know how. But she showed him and out in the hall Dad ran back and forth with suitcases and bags, ties in his hands, his passport in his breast pocket and his toothbrush in his mouth. A few hours later they were standing in the departures hall, Cecilie with her untidy pigtails, both of them with their hair wet from the morning rain and their father trying his best to explain to them that this is all going to work out just fine, so it is. He opened up the doors to that big, warm smile of his, threw his arms out wide to show them how easy things can be in the world, and he said: 'Jan Inge is a big boy. He can make your school lunches for you, Cecilie. And then Dad will be home in a few weeks.' Their father clicked his tongue against the roof of his mouth and winked at them. 'The two of you will manage this,' he said. And that was when Cecilie began to quiver and shake all over and then started screaming and shouting so loudly that Dad got embarrassed, and Jan Inge couldn't help himself either, so he began to howl as well, like a little kid.

That was when Dad added the thing about Houston not being a million miles away and to maintain a positive outlook and think of all the emigrants in the olden days.

A few weeks later he rang up and said it would take a little longer before he was able to get back home, and he reiterated that Jan Inge had to be a big boy now and think positive, that no big boy ever suffered from having to look after a house and a sister. On the contrary, he said, if he'd found himself on his own when he was thirteen, what a dream that would have been.

Up with the lark. Up with the light.

Another scintillating day in the wealthiest city in the world.

Jan Inge wheels blithely over the worn lino. The sun is showing up the dirt on the kitchen windows, where some kids have scrawled 'cock' on the pane with their fingers. Jan Inge sits in his pyjamas, smiling; that's kids for you. He turns the wheelchair and veers towards the fridge, opens the door, his mind falling into new exciting thoughts while he reaches for the sliced meats, cheese, jam and juice.

What a night.

After watching *Three on a Meathook* and taking what he likes to think of as 'internal notes', he trundled out on to the veranda. The evening chill surged to meet him and he let his thoughts move slowly as he allowed his eyes drift from the light of one star to the next in the deep sky. The problems he sometimes feels are almost tangible seem to have blown away. The whole 120 matter, the fear of Rudi and Cecilie contriving to move, the issue of them needing an extra car, or two, the job Rudi was checking out in Gosen Woods, Tong getting out on Friday...

He fell asleep. A solitary individual in the world. Resting in front of the cold, starry sky. A criminal life. The David Toska of petty crime. But a life all the same. His chin hanging down. His head slumped to the side on one shoulder. Some saliva at the corner of his mouth. Laid bare in front of nature. Deep meditation. Cosmic intelligence. An airplane passing high up in the dark, night sky. Red lights blinking. A neighbour putting the rubbish out on the road below.

These kinds of things. Just like a poem, all of them.

I, a child. Yoga Yani and the universe.

Jan Inge was awoken by voices floating in the air in front of him:

'Is he asleep?'

'Oh, has he wheeled himself out here?'

'Oh Jesus, I'm dying for a smoke.'

'So why don't you start again?'

'Why don't you just quit?'

'Did he manage to get out here all by himself?'

'I could see you liked that Pål dude.'

'What do you mean, I liked him?'

'Christ, I really want a smoke right now.'

'Are you sure he's asleep?'

'I'm only saying, you liked that Pål dude.'

'Just look at him, would you?'

'Are you going to that face ... treatment ... thing tomorrow?'

'Mhm.'

'Nice.'

'Mhm.'

'You'll be one sexy bitch after it.'

'Heh heh.'

'Would you screw that Påli dude?'

'Shut up.'

'Some brother you've got.'

'Yeah.'

'Look at that.'

'Wha?'

'He's got a bald spot here, Jan Inge.'

'Runs in the family. All the men get one.'

'Yeah, yeah, there's enough age discrimination in society without us needing to pick on that too.'

It was in this atmosphere, with Jan Inge slowly began to orient himself, while he remained with his eyes closed dwelling upon the humanity and compassion he was surrounded by; in this atmosphere that yesterday ended.

Whilst he experienced a kind of totality of love.

Cecilie and Rudi wheeled him across the living-room floor. They said *shhhh, you don't need to get up, shhhh, we'll talk about that Pål thing tomorrow, shhhh, all you need to do now is just hit the hay, master,* and as they jostled and bumped him into the bedroom, Rudi made mention of a skirting board that would have to go. They helped him, in the frozen and deeply moved state in which he found himself, into his bed, where he could carry on sleeping, and with his eyes closed, as if he were an old man in a con-genial nursing home, Jan Inge heard Rudi's last words of the night:

'Good night, maestro.'

And Cecilie's last words that night: 'Sometimes I think it's a shit life being your sister, Jani, but right at this moment you're fucking intense.'

So naturally enough Jan Inge is experiencing a considerable amount of emotion this morning. All people who feel loved do, he thinks as he takes out the cheese and places it on the old earthenware plate from *Stavangerflint*, which makes him think malicious thoughts of his mother in the graveyard and painful thoughts of his father in Houston.

Soon he'll wheel into the hall and wake them. Call out in the direction of their room: 'Good morning! Wednesday! Breakfast meeting!'

It's a good ritual.

Wednesday = Morning meeting.

If there's one thing Jan Inge has blind faith in, it's rituals.

For example: Cecilie always washes the bath. Rudi takes care of all things electrical. He himself always prepares breakfast. When it comes to breakfast, the thing to keep in mind is that it's all about setting a certain standard for the day, and it's about quality time, which is something of a basic necessity if this company is to succeed. Meals have a surprisingly large role to play. People need to get up and eat breakfast and they need to have dinner. They listen to Motörhead when they sit down to dinner, way up loud, so everyone can feel a sense of peace and calm within, but when they eat breakfast it's quiet. It's a time for evaluation, strategies and pep talks, and if it's a Wednesday then there's a morning meeting. That means an opportunity for anyone to bring up whatever they might have on their mind, and an opportunity for Jan Inge to be a visionary, if he so wishes.

Which he often does.

Lately Jan Inge has spared no effort at mealtimes. He's bought more expensive cheese, meats and spreads, taken great pains when setting the table, purchased better coffee than usual and has even procured candles. All in order for them to see that being part of this household, of this company, is no bad thing. So any talk of moving, they'll put that right out of their minds.

Jan Inge brings the wheelchair to a standstill.

'That is one very nice spread I've prepared,' he whispers, his crisp voice filling the early morning light of the room.

Three glasses. Three side plates. Knives for everyone. Coffee for him and Cecilie. Chocolate milk for Rudi. A candle glowing in the centre of the table. In a lot of ways you could say it's nicely set off by the sun outside. A platter with cuts of meat. A platter with cheese. Jam for Rudi. Liver pâté for Cecilie. And the beetroot slices she likes to have on top of her pâté. An egg for him.

He raises his heavy behind off the wheelchair and takes a folded sheet of paper from his pocket. He reads:

1. Film of the week: *The Abominable Dr Phibes* (R. Fuest 1971).
2. Pitch in and fix up the garden. This weekend? If so who's getting hold of a trailer for all the shit?
3. Are we going to W.A.S.P. in Oslo on 24th October? If so who's sorting out tickets, transport and somewhere to stay? NB: We're not sleeping over at Tom B's in Holmlia! Remember what happened last time!
4. Update on yesterday's meeting w/ Pål. What's happening? Progress?
5. Friday. Tong. What are we doing? Party? Dinner? Just let him relax? Suggestions?
6. Misc. Anyone have anything they want to share?

Jan Inge folds the note, and feeling primed and strong within, wheels himself out into the hall. And just as he's about to call out 'good morning, Wednesday, breakfast meeting', he hears creaking from the bed in Rudi and Cecilie's room. He swallows and trundles a little closer, hears a kind of banging on the floor, then Rudi's deep voice: 'Jesus! Chessi, turn round, let me see that ass. Yess! Lift it up, chica, come on! YESS! Live porn from Hillevåg! Hands up, your pussy or your life, yess, right there, yeah, my little whore, oh yeah, here comes Mr Cock, oh you're so big, hips like shelves, oh, heeeelp, mamma, ooh it's so big, ooh it's ready to burst, ooh mamma, you don't need to come after all, I can come myself! It's a *partay* on my ass! Into the darkness, for the twenty-seventh year in a row! And-peo-ple-go-and-get-div-or-ced! Sitting on the internet pulling their plum and going to nightclubs for strange cock. Ahh. I'm yours till the mountains fall into the sea. Okay, okay ... now ... now ... okay ... we're on our way, my soldiers and me ... Can you hear the artillery thunder across the battlefield? WE'RE A MILLION STRONG AND WE DON'T NEED NO WORLD WIDE WEB TO SPREAD US! HERE IT COMES, THE WORLD WIDE FUCK! SweetjesusIfuckingloveitwhenIgettoslapthatfuckingass!'

Jan Inge remains quiet and motionless for a few minutes.

Sits there weighing things up against one another.

'But my horror movies,' he whispers to himself, 'I'll never lose them. And Johnny Cash, he'll never stop singing. And Cecilie's pigtails, they're burned on to my memory. And the sun,' whispers Jan Inge, becoming aware of a rapid blinking in both his eyes as he hears Cecilie begin to whimper from inside, as he hears Rudi's voice get even louder, 'the sun, that will never leave me. And on my grave,' he whispers, feeling his eyes well up, 'on my grave it'll say: This is the last resting place of the Master, here lies the Son of the Sun, 120 kilos of cosmic love, Yoga Yani, Jan Inge King, the Thinker from Hillevåg.'

33. **SOCKS ON TOP OF THE STOVE** (Pål)

No: a new day. The switches in his brain come on, crackling and flickering, like fluorescent tubes lighting up one after the other down a long corridor. His thoughts revive him. They're painful, they're fraught. They arrive along with feelings of self-contempt and nausea. His ears pick up a sound from the street, a neighbour's car driving past, maybe it's the guy in number fourteen who works as a builder. A noise from the bathroom increases in strength, one of the girls turning on the shower. Morning is here, the ground emitting a citrus smell as the temperature rises. But Pål feels no joy. He's unable to participate. When was the last time he woke up happy, feeling rested and rejuvenated? He can't remember. It feels like he's waking up inside an egg, it's felt like that for an eternity and it's as though he's never going to get out. He doesn't want to be here, doesn't want to be this man and wishes he never woke up again. Don't flick on these switches in my head. Don't come to me with this darkness. No: not a new day.

'Dad?'

If he only had one more chance.

'Daaad!'

Pål props himself up on his elbows, throws back the duvet, swings his body round and sits on the edge of the bed. His holds his head in his hands, then drops them on his knees, lets his blood settle.

Footsteps. Then stomping on the stairs. Tiril.

The door's going to be opened in a moment. He gulps, tousles his hair and plasters a smile on his face. His eyes. There's still sand in them.

If he only had one chance to erase everything he's done.

There. The door's opening.

'Hi, Tiril,' he says, smiling. 'Good morning, love. Come here and give me a hug.'

He stretches his arms out towards her, noticing straight away how weak they feel. She remains standing in the doorway. She's wearing so much make-up, so black around the eyes. Her clothes, the red-and-black skirt, the cut-up tights, the braces, all the button badges, skulls, band names and slogans, the lank hair.

Zitha comes scurrying in. Pål takes a hold of her under the snout, looks in her eyes and she licks his face before lying down obediently, expectantly at his feet.

'There's no bread,' Tiril says, folding her arms and planting her feet apart. 'And there's no milk or fruit. And you're never up out of bed.'

He shrugs awkwardly, reaches for his trousers on the chair and takes his wallet from the pocket.

'Here, look—'

She sighs. 'That's just great, Dad.'

'What do you mean—?'

'Whatever. Give me the money. That'll fix everything. Why not just leave the fridge empty?'

She stands with her hand out in front of him, refusing to meet his gaze.

'But Tiril, honey, I just forgot ... it'll be fine, listen, I'll get to the shops after—'

She remains unmoved, her hand out. She reminds him so much of his wife sometimes. Barging into the room, no hug, no good morning, nothing, just instructions and demands. Pål hands her the hundred kroner note, wants her to know that he has money, that he's taking care of what needs taking care of.

'Will that cover lunch too?'

She crosses her arms again.

'Imagine we ate a normal breakfast now and again,' she says.

'But ... but we do?' He rubs his eyes, pulls on his trousers. Holds out another hundred. 'Don't we? I mean, at the weekends—'

New footsteps on the stairs. Sounding easier, lighter. Malene. Zitha raises her head, wags her tail. Malene walks in the door, glances at both of them and then at the hundred kroner note he's waving.

She goes over and stands beside her sister. Both of them look at him as he pulls on his T-shirt, puts on his socks.

'What?' Pål tries to laugh but can't manage. 'What is it?'

Malene's chest rises and falls. She doesn't make a big deal of it as she takes the money from his hand. She tilts her head slightly to one side. The fact that the two of them are sisters. Hard to comprehend sometimes. He remembers taking them to the playground when they were small. Tiril triggered into life as soon as she caught sight of the place, the colourful apparatus, the sandbox, sprinting towards them with almost frightening excitement, jumping on to the swings, never getting enough, *faster, Dad, faster*. Malene would walk in calmly. Go over to a swing. Sit down upon it. Examine it. Begin to sway, carefully, *that's high enough, Dad, that's enough*.

Tiril's eyes are red, she turns on her heels and leaves the room. While she's tramping down the stairs she shouts: 'Zitha's been fed! I won't be home for dinner! Be back late! Got rehearsals!'

'But—' Pål tries to raise his voice a notch. But he lacks the strength.

Malene remains standing in front of him. He knows he treats her as though she was an adult and not his daughter, but he can't help himself. 'What was that?' he asks. 'What is it now? Have I done something wrong? I forgot to go shopping, but there's a lot happening in work at the moment, Malene, you've no idea – do you think I deserve that kind of treatment? Hm? Do you? I've done my best for the two of you, you know I have, and it hasn't been easy either—'

What am I doing now?

'...as I'm sure you know, it hasn't always been so easy ... Being practically a single parent, for the both of you, that's not easy either, Malene, trying to keep things together, I do my best, you know that, right? You know that, don't you? Honey? That I'd never do either of you any harm? That I'm doing the best I can? And she comes in and then storms back out accusing me of all sorts...'

What am I thinking of?

'...you understand, don't you, Malene?'

He forces himself to cry. Jesus, I've sunk so low, he thinks, while he squeezes out a few crocodile tears. What kind of father am I, what am I doing. Why can't I get out of bed, check the day's school times, wake my girls up and make them both a packed lunch, what am I doing?

The tears come, he almost believes they're real.

Malene puts her arms around him, hugs him, in that grown-up way of hers.

'Dad,' she says. Runs her hand up and down his back. 'Shhh. I understand.'

He lets her hold him tight. It feels good.

Then he sniffles, breaks free of her embrace.

'Oh dear,' he says, 'your Dad is such an fool, eh?'

Pål bends over to Zitha.

'Dad's such a fool, eh, Zitha? Yeeah, good girl, yeeah.'

Malene nods and smiles. 'Go downstairs now,' she says, 'get yourself some coffee, put on your Adidas and get off to work. How are your eyes?'

They make their way to the kitchen. The coffee is made, he pours a cup and drinks it quickly. Takes a look in the fridge. Must fill it up today. Get to work. Things are going to be okay. Pål turns around, his head doesn't feel as heavy, his troubles are absent, he watches Malene put on her coat and shoulder her schoolbag.

'Tiril,' she says.

'Hm?'

'It's just that concert tomorrow. The thing is Mum isn't going to be there, she ... I think the reason she's so worked up is just that she really wants you to be there.'

Pål throws his arms wide in exasperation. 'Jesus, I mean I've told her I'm coming. Does she think I've forgotten? I might seem like a bit of a scatterbrain sometimes but that's because there's so much happening at work. Of course I'm going to go along and watch her sing. I'm going to be sitting in the first row clapping every chance I get. Isn't that what I've always done?'

He takes a big, warm slurp of coffee and shakes his head.

'I'm not too sure Tiril feels you've told her that,' Malene says, 'the way you did just now, I mean.'

Pål takes a Ryvita from the corner cupboard and starts eating it. Not that he likes Ryvita, but he needs something in his stomach.

'No, I guess I haven't. I'll make sure I do.'

'You are going to work, right?'

'Yeah, the usual time, yeah of course I'm going – work? Why are you asking that?'

Take it easy now, he thinks, easy, Pål.

'You got in late last night.'

Easy now. He pictures Rudi and Cecilie, feels shame well up inside for what happened in 1986. Jesus, that girl was younger than Malene is now.

'Late?' He clears his throat. 'Was I?'

She's talking to me like I'm the kid here.

'Yeah.'

'Right, yeah, maybe I was. Took a longer walk than usual, I guess.'

Easy now.

'By the way,' says Malene, fixing her hair in the mirror, readying herself to go, 'I was down in the basement this morning emptying the washing machine—'

'Oh good, yes, must have slipped my mind—'

'Anyway, there was a light on in the study and a pair of your socks were lying on top of the stove, they were really hot, Dad, I mean roasting hot.'

'Oh, gosh—'

'Were you up all night? The computer was on.'

'Well...' he hesitates, turns his head, looks out at the garden. 'I was just ... well, I couldn't sleep. Just sat surfing...'

'You shouldn't dry your socks on the stove, Dad. You don't want to start a fire.'

He remains standing with his back to her.

'No, of course,' he says, looking out over the garden. Only now catching sight of the good weather, only now getting the chance to ponder how nice it is outside again today.

'You took the socks away, then,' he asks, his voice mild.

'Yep,' he hears from behind him, 'I threw them in the wash.'

Pål nods. He can make out something in her voice but he decides not to turn round, decides to push it away.

He points towards the garden.

'I know I'm going on about it,' he says, 'but every time I see that tree I keep thinking the two of you should really hang up a new milk carton for the birds.'

34. **CAN YOU KEEP A SECRET?** (Sandra)

Sandra's body is sore. She's tired, the schoolbag on her shoulders feels heavy. When she woke up she had bags under her eyes. But she clenches her teeth, brings her fingers to the silver crucifix in the hollow of her neck and walks on. Up King Haralds Gate, on to Madlamarkveien, past the church, across Jernalderveien and on towards the school. She'd rather bunk off. But she's never done that, and she'd never dare, because that's not how she is.

Dear Jesus, she whispers, my stomach is so cold, I'm so frightened. Her mother and father told her off when she got home last night, she just about managed to fix her hair and check her clothes in the hall mirror before they were standing there in front of her. Her mother, eyes jittery, her father with his arms crossed. *Have we not been clear about this, Sandra? Did we not agree on this? You're tired, you can't concentrate, you're getting in late, was that what we agreed on? Hm? You know how much we love you, dear, we're telling you this for your own good.*

If she wanted to keep this job, which, strictly speaking, she was too young to have, then she had to prove herself deserving of the trust they placed in her. That meant responsibility. If she came home late at all, if there was the slightest sign of it affecting her schoolwork or how much sleep she got, then it had to come to a stop. She could go up to bed, they could all have a think about it, but she had to be aware that under their roof nobody was allowed to behave that way.

She straightens up as she makes her way along Sophus Bugges Gate towards the school. She still has the chance. She hardly dares to think about it. Just run away. Send Daniel a text – *I'm not at school. Come and meet me. Now!* – and run away. Rush off to the woods. Rush off to the ends of the earth, totter on the edge in

SEE YOU TOMORROW   167

the arms of the one she loves. She still has the chance. Just run between the villas, behind the terraced houses, past the old school, until she reaches the block of flats he lives in and call out to him, *Daniel, I'm here, come on.*

But she doesn't dare. Sandra feels as though she has a lump of ice in her stomach. Is this how love's supposed to be? Are you meant to feel cold and fearful? – *Do you love me? Did I do it right? Will it be as nice tonight? Tomorrow? Am I doing what you like?*

Dear Jesus, she whispers, I don't have the strength for this, I'm shit scared, I'm so fucking shit scared, sorry, sorry, I don't mean to talk like that.

Sandra fixes her fringe, takes a deep breath, her eyes flashing, she smiles into the empty air. It went well, after all, she whispers. He said it was good. He said he wanted to see me again. I'm not the one with problems, it's those sisters, Malene and Tiril, they're the ones with problems. What did he say again ... *that was only the beginning* ... his voice, that bright mouth of his ... what else did he say?

We have the rest of our lives.

Dear Lord, she whispers as she reaches the lean-to at the front of the low, grey school building, is love really this hard?

It's nearing half past eight and pupils swarm about her, all on their way to the first class of the day. Those first-years, God, so annoying, the fact she was actually like that herself, it's hard to fathom. Jostling around, like they're still in primary school, their arms and legs all over the place, no wonder you can never find a spot to eat your lunch in the yard, first-years have no control over any part of their bodies, or of their stuff, all hanging halfway out of their bags, and they're so tiny, they look like goblins and the only cute one is Ulrik Pogo, he's sweet enough to eat, just makes you want to hug him like a teddy bear. Still, poor sister, Kia, hard to talk to someone who's paralysed. What are you supposed to say? How's things today?

'Hi, Sandra.'

Malene's voice. She turns around, quickly. She feels her throat tighten, forces a smile. 'Hi ... hello...'

She's never really hung out with Malene. But the fact she's

standing in front of her the morning after she saw her father in the woods makes her feel she ought to say something. She feels sorry for her but what's she going to say? It's not like she wants to snitch on anyone.

Daniel, why aren't you here. What will I do?

'How's it going?' asks Malene, an expression coming over her face which she trys to hide.

'Oh, y'know,' says Sandra. 'Okay. Lots to do.'

'I know what you mean,' Malene says.

The girls remain standing under the edge of the lean-to while the other pupils stream past on their way in. The most natural thing would be for one of them to start making their way towards the doors and mingling with the rest. But they stay put. Malene is looking at her as if she knows something.

'Did you manage the maths?' asks Malene. It's like she's trying to wrestle with her own facial expression, making her look like E.T.

'Yeah,' Sandra says, 'but I thought it was hard.'

Is she able to see it, the fact that I know something about her?

'Yeah, it sucked.'

'How's the foot, by the way? You going to get back to the gymnastics soon, or...?'

'Dunno. It's taking its time to heal.'

Malene stands there. She makes no sign of wanting to go. Everything about her says she's going to stay put. What is it she wants?

Daniel, what will I do?

'Your sister, Tiril – she's singing tomorrow, right? At that International ... Inter...'

'Cultural Workshop,' nods Malene. 'International Cultural Workshop. Some kind of student exchange thing. She's a good singer—'

'Seriously good—'

'But she needs to sort her head out. Drop all that emo stuff.'

'Well, y'know, she's only in second year.'

'Mhm. YOLO.'

Sandra smiles. Malene has nice features. Those high cheekbones give her a beautiful face, she looks kind and she's very different from her sister. Sandra feels her knees growing weak, her forehead becoming warm, oh no, is she going to start sweating? Is she going to start crying? She realises how long it's been since she's been face to face with a girl she feels can understand her, and she has a sudden sense of having a friend. It's stupid, they've only stood together talking a couple of minutes, only bumped into one another on the way into school, but there's something about Malene's voice that makes Sandra feel safe, so she opens her mouth and hears herself say:

'Can you keep a secret?'

The school bell sounds, ringing out over the yard.

'Can you?'

Malene nods.

Dear Jesus, Sandra thinks, grabbing hold of her arm, I hope I'm doing the right thing. She lowers her voice, takes a step closer:

'I'm seeing Daniel William Moi. I've met him almost every night the last few weeks.'

Malene looks at her.

'I tell lies the whole time,' Sandra whispers. 'To everyone.'

Malene nods her head slowly.

'I met him again yesterday,' Sandra says softly. 'I had sex with him. In Gosen Woods.'

35. A TIME-HONOURED CLASSIC IN THE BUSINESS (Rudi)

The little lady on top of the lanky man.

He's worked it out: if you've been together with your woman for twenty-seven years, and you've screwed her on average twice a week, then how many times have you screwed her? And: if it's lasted a quarter of an hour each time – on average – how much of your life have you spent at it?

Hm?

2,808 times.

42,120 minutes.

Or 702 hours

Or 29.25 days

You get to know the terrain.

The arithmetic is only approximate, of course. Calculations for the first few years are bound to be a bit ropey, given that, strictly speaking, Chessi gradually went from being an underage whore under Jan Inge's control to his girlfriend, and also that she was quite young. Girls don't like screwing so much when they're thirteen, so you have to subtract a little to make up for the first couple of years.

Still, not one day too many.

The little lady on top of the lanky man. That bony body of hers on top of that skinny body of his. All those freckles, across her back and arms. Her shelf-like hips, that Rudi calls 'God'. Those little tits. He likes them. Little girly tits. Rudi has a wild look in his eyes, makes fearsome movements with his mouth: his tongue sweeping across his front teeth, biting down on his lip and sucking in air, clicking his tongue against the roof of his mouth. His compulsion to talk all the time, talk and talk and talk – and there's no situation he feels more like talking in than when he's having sex with Chessi: 'Jeeeeesus! This pussy is never going out of style. Chessi, come on, sit yourself down on Rudi, spin that wheel, come on! Twothousandeighthundredandeight! Eh?! What do you say to that, you sexy slut! Eh? I'm already looking forward to nine! Oh Jeeeeesus, you just don't know how much I love you. Give it to me. Is that ass getting bigger the older you get? Yeah! Come on, MILF!'

Ah.

Feels good to get it out.

Rudi rolls off Cecilie and over on to his back. He stretches right out and releases a satisfied groan. He entwines his fingers in hers. Rudi is soft and spent, and he doesn't say anything right away, doesn't feel like it, just holds Cecilie's hand. After a while his breathing becomes more regular, and then he feels like talking a little.

'That was bloody good,' he says, in a low voice.

'You say that every time,' Cecilie says soberly.

'Well, that's because it's bloody good every time.'

She doesn't reply. It took him a while to get his head around that. While he might have an absolute motherfucker of a need to talk while he's riding her, and just as much of a need afterwards to hear her say how great it was, it's still a need *he feels*. Not her. For years it was a touchy subject, the fact that she never said anything, not a single word. Not for ages afterwards, and then she wanted to talk about other things entirely. They'd be there, getting it on, and it was so good to ride her, sometimes he'd worked himself up all day, but would she say anything when they finally got under the duvet? Like maybe wrap her lips around his dick and mumble something while his knob pumped against the inside of her cheek, like how rock hard he was or how damn good it felt and that she'd been dreamingaboutrudiscocksinceshewokeup or that she was sofuckinghornyshecouldntthinkstraight or that he was the sexiestmanontwolegs, sexier than Steven Tyler and Lemmy put together? Just imagine, how amazing it'd be, listening to her slobbering and muttering down there, his prick getting in the way of the words, *ab at ock mm am it up my sy,* whatdidyousayyousay?

Please say it again? *Ab at ock mm am up my sy.* Can't hear you, *Pfläumchen,* can you say it one more time? GRAB THAT COCK AND RAM IT UP MY PUSSY.

But no. Not one word. Hurtful really.

It took him ages to figure out how to live with it. There was a time he wondered whether he should rough Cecilie up or take her to see a psychologist, because it all felt so unfair. Him being so attentive, giving her cash, lavishing her with love, saying so many nice things to her and getting so little in return. A cut-price feeling. A cap-in-hand feeling. But he weathered the storm, didn't send her to a psychologist or beat the shit out of her; *hear that, Gran? I never laid a finger on her.* Rudi learnt to live with it. Acknowledged that she was a person with her own qualities, her own surly, introverted way of being, while he was a person with qualities of his own, his own talkative and extroverted way of being. Now everything's just fine, obviously, twenty-seven years speaks for itself, but it still hurts a little.

And still, even now Rudi can't help but feel it niggle a little. So he says:

'Yeah, yeah, I know you love me, even if you're as quiet as a baseball bat.'

Cecilie sits up, leans over to the bedside table and grabs hold of the cigarette pack and the hair elastic she took out while he screwed her, because he likes to see her hair cascade across the pillow.

He studies her. Damn bony and damn sexy. Rudi puts on his most boyish smile, hoping she'll look his way. But she doesn't. With her eyes closed and the cigarette in her mouth, she raises her eyebrows and sets her hair in a ponytail. She puts on her knickers, her bra, her top and her socks before standing up. Cecilie opens her eyes, gazes at the wall and fixes her jaw into place with a sort of fish-mouth movement. She's been doing that since she was thirteen. It's like catching sight of an old friend for him. Nice to have things like that. Safe things. But she's not looking at me, he thinks.

'Good morning! Wednesday! Morning meeting!'

Rudi rolls his eyes and sees Cecilie do the same. She calls out to her brother, whom they both know is right behind the door:

'All right, all right! Take it easy, Jani. We're coming.'

'Okay, okay!' they hear from outside in the hall. 'Just thought I'd let you know. Morning meeting.'

'Okay, okay,' Cecilie says, 'you always just think that, little darling!'

Rudi doesn't think that *little darling* stuff is really necessary, even though the fact that he's so *on* first thing in the morning does annoy both of them. Standing outside their door shouting about those endless breakfasts of his. Still, she doesn't need to say it, it just seems downright patronising, and he doesn't like her picking on him. *Little darling?* Why does she have to say that? She is his sister and everything. Particularly when Jani isn't the slightest bit little. If there's anyone in this house who strives and deserves respect, it's Jani.

Cecilie turns to him as she's pulling up her jeans. Ash balancing on the tip of her cigarette. 'What's with that two thousand stuff?'

'Eh?'

'With all that, y'know ...' she shrugs, the ash falls on to the duvet, 'two thousand stuff you were on about?'

Rudi laughs and gets to his feet, pulls on his T-shirt, socks and jeans. Then he gives Cecilie a kiss on the cheek, slaps her on the ass and says: 'The number of times I've banged you, honey, that's what that is. Two thousand eight hundred and eight.'

'Jesus,' she says, extinguishing the cigarette in the glass of water beside the bed. She opens the door. 'Have I had that huge dick of yours up me that many times?'

'Yes indeed, baby. Two thousand more to go.'

Cecilie isn't smiling. She's stopped with one foot on either side of the doorsill.

'But... Rudi says, again trying to make his voice as soft as possible. 'There's ... nothing ... wrong, is there?'

'More than two thousand times ...' Cecilie looks pensive. 'It's just that it's so long, that dick.'

He runs his had up and down her back.

'I know,' he says, guiltily. 'It started in sixth class. I woke up every morning and though, shit, that's going grow to some size. And it did.'

'It goes so far up me.'

'Yeah, it does all right,' he says, tilting his head to the side. 'But I really like it, y'know, feeling you right up against me.'

Cecilie sighs, 'But imagine you damage something up there, what then?'

He screws up his eyes. 'Damage something? What do you mean, damage something?'

'No, I...'

There's a scratching at the door. Jan Inge's fat finger:

'Don't mean to go on about it but ... breakfast meeting!'

'No, it's fine,' Cecilie says, actually giving Rudi a little smile, an almost apologetic smile, and it makes him feel good. 'It's fine,' she says. 'It's lovely and big, that dick of yours. Come on. Big brother is getting impatient.'

The sun shines through the kitchen window, shining upon a well-laid breakfast table, glinting on knife blades and making the jam glisten. Rudi runs a large hand through his hair, yawning, almost fatigued by the sight of all the food. Neither Rudi nor Cecilie eat a lot in the morning, but lately Jan Inge has been preparing breakfasts as though he were running a twelve-star hotel. There's more and more every day, food no one's ever fucking heard of, cured mutton and French herb sausages, dill-marinated shoulder butt, weird cheeses and whatnot, and today he's gone that little bit further.

Cecilie sits down at her usual place by the window. She pours herself a large cup of coffee and brings it to her face, allowing the heat to steam her skin.

Jan Inge comes wheeling in from the living room.

'Sleep well? Everyone?'

Rudi nods. Cecilie clasps her hands tighter around the coffee cup and shuts her eyes.

'Great,' says Jan Inge, 'I did too. After the two of you pushed me back inside last night. Thank you for that, by the way.'

'Don't mention it,' says Rudi. 'But what's with you and the wheelchair? Isn't that the one I nabbed for Chessi when she broke her foot?'

Jan Inge nods. 'That's right. It's just been sitting here since.'

'Yeah, it was just parked inside the door of the Intensive Care Unit. They were practically fucking giving it away. What's the story, then? With you and the wheels?'

Jan Inge gets a look in his eyes. 'Weell,' he says, sucking in one cheek a little, 'to be honest, I just find it a real effort hauling this 120 kilos around...'

'But you're not fat!'

'Rudi. Stop it. I'm fat.'

'He's fat,' Cecilie confirms.

'It's all in the eye of the beholder.' Rudi shrugs. 'I think you look good with a bit of weight on you. But okay, I rest my case. Safe to say you're a bit fat.'

'Exactly. And now the wheelchair is being put to proper use. It simply solves quite a few problems for me. And you know how much I like solving problems.'

'Oh yeah, we know that.'

'That's what you like more than anything.'

'Then there's nothing else to say about it,' Jan Inge concludes. 'A problem and a solution. That's the reason we've all got as far as we have. It's because we're problem solvers, and we don't mess things up for ourselves and that's why we're able to look at a nicely laid breakfast table and not a desk in a cell in Åna with some dry foods and instant coffee. That's the reason we've managed to work so many years in this town, under the radar so to speak, and been able to make a living from it. Not on a grand scale maybe, but on a safe scale. We know our stuff when it comes to break-ins. When it comes to cars. To alarms, keycards and locks. We can handle cash machines. Carry out extortion. And we're able to move goods. Well, Buonanotte's able to move goods and we know Buonanotte. We have contacts that the junkies don't even know exist. We know our stuff and do you know what that means? Knowledge. Expertise. A problem and a solution.'

'Genius,' says Rudi, 'that's what I've got to say to that.'

'The cheese is getting moist, let's eat,' says Jan Inge, his voice even more high-pitched than usual. 'I rustled up some meagre fare for the morning meeting.'

Meagre fare? Rudi frowns. It's not just at work that you need to keep your eyes and ears open. But within the safety of your own four walls. Is there something going on here? Has someone got cancer? Is it somebody's birthday?

He looks over at Cecilie.

Is there something going on with her too?

That thing she said about his dick? Was there something in her voice? She isn't usually so considerate, she usually just moans about it being way too big and making her ovaries hurt like hell.

He turns his gaze back to Jan Inge.

All this food.

Whatthefuckisgoingonhere?

Cecilie closes her eyes and drinks her coffee. Her brother spreads some pâté over a slice of bread for her, then places some beetroot on top. Just as he's done since she was little. Rudi's well aware of that. He's well aware of how much Jan Inge has done for her. He wants to look after her. And now he's put a little extra effort into making a good breakfast. That's probably all it is. And Chessi is a little emotional. Is it next week she's getting her period? Or was it the screwing? Rudi leans back in his chair. Smiles to himself. It was the screwing, it was particularly good, that's it, that's what it is.

'Right,' Jan Inge says, after a few minutes of coffee, chocolate milk and silence round the breakfast table. 'I think we'll get started with the morning meeting while we're all fresh in the noggin.' Jan Inge produces the folded note from his pocket. 'This week's list. We'll take it from the top.'

He leans on the windowsill and puts on his reading glasses, the ones Rudi pinched in an opticians on Kirkegata and gave him as a Christmas present, after he'd been complaining about his sight for so long.

'Something enjoyable to begin with,' Jan Inge says, producing a DVD that he's actually *sitting* on, Rudi notices. 'Our Saturday movie for the week. A classic starring Price and Joseph Cotton, *The Abominable Dr Phibes*. I'll give a short introduction after pizza on Saturday, as usual—'

'As usual—' Cecilie sighs.

'...exactly,' Jan Inge says, ignoring his sister, 'and then we can cosy up for a night of gore.'

'Great, good man.' Rudi clicks his fingers and points at his friend. 'Always a new movie. Can count on you.'

'Item number two,' Jan Inge says, adjusting the spectacles on the bridge of his nose. 'Item number two concerns all the clutter and mess. Our weak point. The garden. It can't continue. We're attracting attention. We're wallowing in crap. We need to start taking care of this house. It's our headquarters. As well as,' he says gravely, looking at Cecilie, 'our childhood home. This is where Dad wanted us to live. So. A clean-up. That's the question.'

'I think it's a good question,' says Rudi.

'Sure is,' says Cecilie.

'Okay, then we'll say this weekend. Sunday? Sunday it is. Who's doing what?'

'I can tidy a little,' says Cecilie.

'Good, positive attitude. Anyone else? We need a trailer. Who'll sort that out?'

Rudi shrugs. 'We are going to have a lot to do now, what with that Pål guy—'

'That's item four—'

'Okay, right—'

'But if you've both got your hands full with item four, then I'll take care of the trailer. We've people within our network with a trailer. No problem.'

'Tødden must have a trailer,' Cecilie says.

'We're not talking to Tødden,' Jan Inge replies sharply, 'not after what happened in Sauda. Sick hippie. But. Anyway. Great! Clean-up. Sunday. I'll arrange the trailer. I'll have a chat with Hansi. Everybody happy.'

'Hansi? Like all of a sudden it's better to go to Hansi than to Tødden?' Cecilie says, rolling her eyes.

'Maybe not,' Jan Inge concedes. 'But Hansi owes us, so we'll go to him.'

'Will Tong be going along?' Cecilie asks, casually.

'That actually pertains to item five—'

'Jesus! Jani! Fuck your items!'

'Listen, if we didn't itemise—'

'Itemise my ass.'

'Itemise my ass!' laughs Rudi. 'Sodomise my ass. I'll sodomise your ass, baby—'

'Moving on,' interrupts Jani. 'Item three. Are we going to see W.A.S.P.?'

Jubilation round the table, even Cecilie's face breaks into a smile. 'W.A.S.P.?! Are they playing?'

'Yes indeed, in Oslo on the twenty-fourth of October,' her brother says, in a satisfied tone.

Rudi shoots his hand in the air and bangs his fist on the wall behind: 'We're totally going to W.A.S.P.! I fuck like a beast!'

'God, I love W.A.S.P.,' sighs Cecilie. A yellow glow spreads across her forehead and she sings: 'Hold on to my heart, to my heart.'

'Yeah,' Rudi says. 'He's one, big, lawless lyricist is Blackie. L.O.V.E., all I need is my love machine tonight ... I can't fuck, I can't feel, I'm one bizarre motherfucker, what the fuck's inside of me, those lines especially, so fucking intense. The thing about what the fuck's inside of me.'

'I'm guessing that's settled then,' Jan Inge says. 'A trip to Oslo for the three of us. W.A.S.P. That's going to be amazing. But we're not staying at Tom B's in Holmlia, just so we're clear on that.'

'That goes without saying,' says Rudi. 'I mean, we're not Nazis.'

'And that—' Jan Inge says, nodding to Rudi, 'that brings us to item four. The update on yesterday. What happened, where do we stand, what's going on.'

Rudi takes a gulp of chocolate milk. He realises it's his turn to talk. He clears his throat and straightens up in the chair. 'Yes, well,' he says. 'There're a couple of things—'

'Nice guy,' Cecilie suddenly cuts in. 'Pål.'

'Nice?' Rudi turns to look at her.

'Yeah, well he was, wasn't he? So?'

'Nice schmice,' Rudi pouts. 'Do you want to fuck him as well? Anyway, we're not here to talk about how ni—'

'He needs money,' interrupts Cecilie.

Rudi clears his throat again, 'Right, they—'

'A million,' Cecilie says.

Rudi gapes at her. 'Jesus, you're very talkative all of a sudden!'

'Am I not allowed to speak now either!'

What has gotten into her? They've had a good night's sleep. They've had a good screw. She's got that skincare shit to look forward to. Yet here she is, all thorny and difficult. Besides which, she's sitting there talking about riding that fucking Pål guy.

Rudi swallows and looks at Jan Inge.

'Long story short, brother, what we're looking at here is a man with a problem. He's run up a large amount of gambling debts, we're talking a million, like Cecilie just mentioned. The problem is further complicated by women, two daughters, and he's come to us for a solution. Is there any way we can help him get hold of a million kroner. That's the situation.'

Jan Inge begins to nod. His head rocking back and forth.

This is good. Always a good sign when Jani moves his head back and forth.

Jan Inge takes hold of the egg slicer, places his egg in it and brings the thin wires down through it. He leans forward and picks up the mayonnaise. Hellmann's. Unscrews the lid. Puts his knife inside, then spreads the mayonnaise across a slice of bread. Lifts up the egg and distributes the slices on the bread. Takes a tomato. Cuts it up with the knife. Places the slices over the egg.

This is good. Always a good sign when Jan Inge goes quiet and concentrates.

He brings the bread to his mouth. Takes a bite. Chews. Continues nodding and rocking his head. Then he looks at them, takes another bite and says:

'This is just right.'

Rudi raises his eyebrows, sends an expectant glance towards Cecilie, who makes an odd grimace.

'This is just right,' Jan Inge repeats, nods, chews and goes for his third mouthful of egg, mayonnaise and tomato. 'You know what?' he says, getting up from the wheelchair and moving towards the window, the slice of bread in his hand, 'you know what, I had a feeling about something like this when I woke up today. The sun was shining down on me and I thought: there's something good on the way.'

'What's going on in that brilliant mind of yours?' Rudi asks, cautiously.

'Firstly,' Jan Inge says, taking a large bite of his bread, continuing to speak with his mouth full, 'firstly we can make use of a time-honoured classic in our business.'

'We can?'

Rudi turns once again towards Cecilie, whose face has taken on an odd yellowish tinge.

Jan looks at them, and with pride in his voice, says: 'We're talking classic insurance fraud. Does this guy have a house? Good. Does he have money? Good. No problem. We borrow Hansi's Transporter at the same time as we get a loan of the trailer on Sunday, we drive up at night, reverse into the garage – does he have a garage? Good. We back into the garage, smash up his house, wreck his car, take everything we can find, break one of his arms, a leg, the usual. Rudi gives him a black eye and maybe a gash under the ear, we tie him to a chair – and *voilà*, this guy can cash in all his insurance, household contents, personal injury. That should go a good way towards the million, and then we can drive the stuff out to Buonanotte's barn, take ourselves a coffee with a little something in it and have a chat.'

Jan Inge swallows the last piece of bread. Rudi shakes his head, impressed. It's just nuts, he thinks, this man has always got a solution.

'What about Tong?' Cecilie asks, her hand over her mouth, looking out of sorts. 'He ... will he be going along?'

'Yes,' Jan Inge says, with a note of satisfaction, 'and that ties in with item five on the agenda. Tong gets out on Friday. It's perfect. Because what would Tong like better than walking out the gates at Åna and getting straight to work?'

Rudi downs the rest of the chocolate milk in one and gets to his feet. He walks over to where Jan Inge is standing. Puts his arm around him.

'If you were from Oslo you'd be famous all over the country. And everyone would call you The Brain of Crime. Jo Nesbø would base a character in his books on you. A time-honoured classic! That is seriously sweet!'

Cecilie suddenly gets up and holding her hand over her mouth, she dashes in the direction of the bathroom while mumbling: 'Sorry, sorry, I have to...'

Rudi and Jan Inge look at one another.

'Hey, are you sick?'

They both shrug.

'And now,' Rudi says, straightening up, 'now Rudi is going to remove the rest of the skirting boards in this house, in your honour, so you can go just where you want in the wheelchair.'

Then he trots from the kitchen, stooping like an eager horse, into the hall and down to the basement to fetch the crowbar, while he feels his chest bubbling with delight and then that song kicks in again: Du-du-du-du-du-du-du-du-du.

'Thank you!' he hears from behind him.

'*Kein problem*!' he shouts back. 'Shit, it is a mess down here, we need that clean-up now! Hey, Chessi? Are you *puking*? Bit too much coffee and too long a pole, eh? Felt those ovaries getting poked right up to your throat! Heh heh! Nice guy ... Pål, Pål ... I'll give you nice all right. You just stick close to Rudi, that's what you do, and I'll make sure it's *nice*. Christ, we really need to tidy up this house. Nah, listen, I liked that Pål guy, two daughters and a woman problem, a time-honoured classic comes sailing in. L.O.V.E., all I need is my love machine! Skirting boards, come to daddy. Are you *puking*? Heh heh! Just ring Doctor D. Ick! Did I say I'm meeting him again tonight? Did I tell you that? Jani? Did I tell you? Jani? Wasn't that crowbar down here someplace? Crow ... no problem! Found it! The metal cock crows! It was under the balaclavas!

36. **HIT HARD** (Daniel William)

Daniel hears the front door open and close, Inger's steps growing fainter as she descends the stairwell.

He's been through two foster homes. He goes ballistic when people pester and nag, and he knows what he is. He knows he's a bastard to have in the house when he first gets riled

He hooks his bag off his shoulders. Sets down his moped helmet. Takes off his shoes. Throws off his jacket. He hears the sound of the shower from the bathroom and not for the first time is about to call out – 'Veronika! Don't use up all the towels!' – but he stops himself; she can't hear him.

He just can't stand people getting on his back. The last foster father was a right pain, breathing down his neck all day long, forever hassling him about homework and timekeeping, and always going on about him not being allowed to behave this way or that. Shut your fucking hole, or do you want a taste of the poker?

Hm?

Would you like to feel the bleeding iron, foster father?

I know how much money you make on me. I know what you're at when no one sees you, when your wife's asleep, when you think all the lights in this city built on oil are out, when I'm lethal and painful; I'm the poison that's poured in your ear.

He was a real asshole. Was carrying on with a woman living three streets away. Daniel William heard him clear his throat, saw him put down his paper, and caught him saying he was heading out to take a look at a sofa he'd found on the net. He watched him go out the door, out into the stinking darkness, and walk three streets down to where the slapper spread her legs and he put it up her.

I saw you, you horndog. I saw you.

He had said it and all. During the last meeting. Child Welfare, him and the foster family sitting in that pathetic living room where they were supposed to sort everything out or some shit. He had got to his feet, the god of true darkness, and said: 'I know where you've been putting your dick, you randy bastard.'

Then Daniel William Moi left. Because if there's one thing he knows how to do, it's leave. If they nag at him, get on his case, then he knows exactly what he'll do: Give them a taste of the poker. Put the sword to the forehead. Leave.

And no chance in hell of him ever going back.

Daniel enters his room, closes the window that's been open all night. He sits down behind the drum kit. Takes hold of the sticks.

He's tackled living with Inger and Veronika so far. Not that they ought to feel too secure, he knows there's no point being naïve: Inger's nice, she's kind and friendly, but she makes money on him. Same as the rest. No fucking matter how nice she is. Veronika knows that too. That her mother earns good money having him in the house. But it's gone well so far. Not much nagging. Not much fussing. He's actually gone as far as staying home with them some evenings. Even at the weekends. At least up until he met the Christian girl anyway. That's the thing about Inger and Veronika, they need him. Daniel can notice it, how they need a man in the house, because they're not that strong. That's what Inger says, *it's good having a real man around.* She laughs when she says it, those dimples showing, and she signs it at the same time, making Veronika break out in that laugh of hers, but neither of them are picking on him, neither of them bugging him: they mean it.

Daniel starts hitting the drums. As hard as he can. 'Battery.' That was really mad in the woods yesterday. Stupid about that with Sandra, but he straightened things out. And the guy with the dog. What the fuck was that. *I'll go back to my people. You go back to your people. I'll see what I can come up with. And I'll see you tomorrow.* Dad of that girl in Sandra's class. Your people, the tall guy said. Your people. Who was he talking about? My people, he said. And who are they exactly?

Daniel's room is soundproofed. It was the only condition he set out when Inger turned up as a possible foster mother. He was so pissed off that he wasn't bothered who was put in front of him; he'd gone through two foster families, he was ready to tear through a third, but she looked all right, that deaf daughter of hers looked all right, kind of pretty in an off-the-wall way. 'But there is one thing,' he had said, sitting there with arms folded in the social worker's office, 'I want a drum kit in my room.'

'There's not much of a chance of that,' they said, 'we live in a block of flats, it wouldn't be allowed.'

'Well then, that's that,' he said, 'I can't'. So Child Services coughed up the money to get the room soundproofed. Fucking idiots. They're understaffed, there's stories in the paper every second day about how stretched they are, yet they still have the money to soundproof a room.

Cannot kill the family, battery is found in me, battery.

On the one hand it's like he knows Sandra and she knows him. On the other hand it's as though she has no idea who he is. None. But she was good at screwing. Felt just like it ought to, like diving into eternity. Manage to hold out in time. Was just some sort of shock to the system was all. No problem. Just wait, soon be banging away at you for hours on end.

He'll have been marked absent by now. Daniel can't face going to school today. The upshot will be them ringing Inger, then ringing Child Services and after that there'll be a parent-teacher meeting. They'll sit down in the guidance counsellor's office. The student-teacher liaison, the maths teacher, and no doubt that Sivertsen guy, going on about how if Daniel doesn't buck up then he won't pass his maths exam, and then he'll fail his finals, and then ... he's been listening to it since he was in first class. Your attendance rate, Daniel, that's what they'll start on about.

Yeah, he'll say. What about it?

He'll soon be eighteen. They won't be able to touch him then.

The handle on the bedroom door turns slowly and the door opens. Daniel hits the drums as hard as he can, the Metallica lyrics whirling round his head, and then he looks up.

Veronika comes into the room. She has two towels around her. A big baby-blue one, fastened above her big tits and reaching down to below her hips and a smaller, pink one, done up on her head like a turban.

She's often in his room, there's nothing peculiar about it. At the start it was a bit weird. For the first few weeks he didn't know how to behave round the girl with the hollow-sounding voice and the strange hand gestures, but then he realised she was just like everyone else, only deaf, and the reason she was a little shaky was that idiots had treated her like an idiot. All she actually needed was someone who saw her for who she was. Is that so hard to grasp? After a while he began to enjoy the silent attention she gave him, so he allowed her to come in. He let her sit on the floor in her Buddha posture and listen – *yeah, listen* – to him as he played the drums, as well as allow her to sit in his room and do homework.

'Big bruv,' she called him a few weeks back.

Daniel had nodded. He could be her big brother.

'You know what?' he said, speaking slowly so she could read his lips.

'No?'

'I'm going to buy you a car. And a house. You won't need to worry about anything. I'm going to be rich, Veronika, I'm going to be filthy fucking rich. Your big bruv will look after you.'

Her whole torso, her tits – which are pretty huge – had wobbled under her sweater, her eyes narrowed to lines and her weird laughter had filled the room.

She's good-looking, Veronika. Tidy. Big eyes. Awesome body. Long legs. But she's got something intense about her, as though she were water on the boil.

He puts down the drumsticks, looks over at her.

'Are you going to go to school?' he asks slowly. Daniel knows he should really use his hands, use sign language, but he couldn't be bothered.

'Are you?' Veronika smiles. Two small dimples play in her cheeks. She shrugs.

He smiles back. Shrugs.

He likes that about her. Her sense of humour. She's quick.

'So, what's up then?' Daniel says, and clears his throat. He has to look away. He's seen her half-naked plenty of times. But right now it feels a little weird. Her just standing there. Like that. Now. In the morning. Water beading on her shoulders. Her breasts look enormous beneath the towel and he's having trouble averting his eyes.

'So, what's up then?' he hears her say.

Shit.

Now she's sitting on the floor. In her Buddha position.

Fuck.

He can see everything.

'No, nothing much,' he says, attempting to smile.

'No, nothing.' She smiles.

Daniel swallows.

He tries to take his eyes away but he can't manage. They're drawn towards her sitting there cross-legged, towards the towel pulled tight across her open thighs, towards her crotch. What is she doing? She must know he can see it?

'Play,' she says, making the sign for drums.

He shrugs. Is she just going to sit there like that? Is she doing it on purpose?

'Okay,' he says, making to begin. 'Wait, hang on.' He motions to her. 'Come here. You try. Come on.'

She laughs. 'No, no.'

'Yeah, come on, come on.'

Veronika laughs again. She shows no indication of knowing what he can see. She merely laughs, waves her hand in refusal and again says: 'No, no.'

He stands up, takes a step to the side and points at the stool. 'Come on, sit down. I'll show you.'

She rolls her eyes but gets to her feet and makes her way over to him. She sits down.

He sees the nape of her neck below the coiled towel. The red hairs beneath. Her shoulders. Her skin. Her cleavage. Her hips, her ass, heavy on the stool. Veronika turns her head, reads his lips. Mouthing slightly what he says with her own.

Daniel speaks slowly: 'Pick up the drumsticks. That's right. Grip them like this, as though you were holding a fishing rod. That's right. Good. Okay, I'm going to show you four-four time, straight beat. Completely straight beat.'

'Bit?'

'Take your right hand, yeah, like that, bring it over to the left, yeah, there, and now you hit the high-hat four times...'

He stands right against her back. Holds her arms, her hands. Helps her with each beat.

'Like that, yeah.'

She laughs. Tries to keep on hitting.

Daniel feels his pulse begin to rise.

'And steady. One two three four, one two three four ... then you take your left hand, here I'll help you, the drumstick in your left hand, and on the third beat you bring it down on the snare, like this...'

He takes her other arm. Stands pressed against her. Holds both her arms, both her hands.

'Okay, good, like that, nice and steady, one two *three* four, one two *three* four...'

Daniel's breathing is heavy. It's the caveman panting inside, can't stop this, it's the stone man panting within.

Veronika lets go of the sticks. She removes the towel from her head. Her long copper-red hair falls down, looking darker now it's wet, lying like thick knives down along her back. She turns, her eyes gleaming for a second before she closes them, gets to her feet, stands on her tiptoes and gives him her mouth.

No, he thinks, kissing her. Sandra, he thinks, feeling Veronika's tongue, fresh and strong. He gives her his tongue, feels the electricity in his mouth. She brings her hands to her chest, fuck, she's undoing the towel, it falls to the ground, her breasts brush against his sweater. Veronika's hands go behind his back. She takes hold of his T-shirt, lifts it up and presses her breasts against his skin. Fuck, Sandra, fuck, Veronika – Daniel pushes her away.

He clenches his fists and visualises himself beating her bloody.

Daniel runs into the hall. He grabs his moped helmet, slips hurriedly into his shoes, leaves his bag lying where it is. He snatches his jacket, hears Veronika's muffled crying behind him, opens the door and leaves.

Quit that snivelling, he thinks as he rushes down the stairs, his footfalls slamming against the walls of the stairwell. Stop that blubbering, stop it, do you want a taste of the bleeding iron, bitch?

37. **GO NEAR THE DEVIL** (Malene)

The school bell sounds like a fire alarm. The pupils begin making their way inside, while Sandra stands there, her face almost unrecognisable. There's sweat on her brow, her big frightened eyes stare at Malene, pleading for help, as though she were suddenly her lifeline in a rough sea. Sandra's hand is trembling, the bell is ringing furiously in their ears, and she won't let go of her sleeve, but what is Malene going to say?

She can't bear to lie, she's unbelievably bad at it, and acting surprised is the hardest thing she knows. *Daniel Moi? No way. Have you had sex with him? Wow? In Gosen Woods?*

Sandra would see through her right away.

Malene has never slept with anyone. She likes boys, it's not that, and she's aware she's nice-looking, she knows they like her, it's not that either. She's just not ready. She hasn't met the right guy yet. The One. Tiril always says she's going to screw the first guy that comes along, makes no odds, really. But Malene can't think that way. She knows people call her names. Ice queen. Gymnastics queen. But she pretends not to hear. She doesn't take it to heart. At least not much. A little, maybe.

What's she going to say to Sandra? It's no surprise, what she's hearing, Tiril already told her, but all the same it's bonkers that the biggest swot, the most Christian girl in school, lawyer daughter Sandra Vikadal, is together with Metal Daniel. Moped Daniel. Crazy Daniel. Foster home Daniel. And what's just as mental is that Sandra is standing in front of her – why her? – telling her that she's had sex with him.

Outside. In the woods.

That is mental.

Daniel is hot, no question about it, but he's hot in that

dangerous way. All the girls know who he is, *those eyes*, but would anyone dare to do what Sandra's done? Go near him? It's so mad it makes Malene's heart pound, a heavy hammering inside: *I met him again yesterday. I had sex with him. In Gosen Woods.* And not only is Sandra saying it, she's picked Malene to say it to. She's told *her* everything – why? They've been in the same class for years but they've never really spoken. Not before today. It gives Malene a pain in her chest. She's entwined in Sandra's world now and she doesn't want to leave it.

Daniel Moi has done some crazy stuff, they say. Killed someone, they say.

'Jesus,' says Malene, thinking she needs to look natural, 'is it true? With Daniel Moi? Wow!'

Sandra's eyes are watery. 'You mustn't say it to anyone, you have to promise—'

'No, Jesus—'

'I've been seeing him for two weeks.'

'But,' Malene takes a quick look around at the dwindling number of pupils around them, 'we need to go in—'

Sandra retains her grip on Malene's sleeve. 'Do you think I'm gone in the head?'

'No,' says Malene, 'but ... I mean, he's seventeen, he's – well, it's not so much his age as – y'know ... people say things about him, stuff...'

'Yes. But I love him.'

Love him

Malene feels the thumping of a pulse in her ear. 'We need to go in,' she says, avoiding her eyes, 'but ... you know what people say?'

Sandra relaxes her grip on her jacket, her eyes narrow.

'I mean,' Malene goes on, 'as long as you know what you're doing. Then it's probably all right. If you ... love him.'

Sandra wipes her forehead. 'I do,' she says. 'So, what is it they say about him?'

'Weell ... you know ... you do know, right?'

Sandra nods.

'Don't say any more. I love him.'

Malene has seen this prim, proper girl every day since first class. She's always had a naïve look about her, but also balance and poise. Now everything's off-kilter. Malene shudders. She becomes suddenly aware of wanting to feel like that too and it scares her. Because she's never thought about it before, about wanting to go out there, out there on that sea where everyone can drown.

'Look,' – Malene pushes yearning to one side – 'we need to be getting in, but are you sure that he's not just using you, I mean ... what about him, does he love you?'

Sandra suddenly gives a start, a look of panic filling her eyes, she looks like she's about to keel over.

Malene turns to look. There's a moped coming down the street towards the school. A tall boy with a black helmet, black jeans and a leather jacket riding it.

Sandra gasps for breath, and drags her fingers like a claw from her forehead to her chin. 'Sorry, Malene, I ... talk to you later, okay? I won't forget this. You won't say anything, will you? I've got to—'

Sandra rushes off towards the boy, who's pulling up by the bicycle racks. Malene stands looking at her. She recognises that knock-kneed run from PE class, the one people snigger at, one hand under her tits, the other swinging through the air.

Daniel pulls off his helmet and runs a hand through his hair. Sandra throws her arms around him.

Can't stand here. I'll get a demerit.

She loves him.

Malene opens the doors and dashes down the corridor, a sudden burning feeling having come over her, a sudden uncertainty; *I want that too.* She stops for a moment – religious studies? Art and crafts? Pull yourself together, Malene, it's Norwegian ... she's out of breath as she enters the classroom. Malene nods to the teacher, is conscious of being spared a demerit by a whisker and hurries to her desk.

'Thank you, Malene,' Mai says. 'Nice of you to join us.'

Mai Jensen Bore is fairly young, and she's a canny, kind teacher. She was off for almost six months last year, for what some claim was an operation on her uterus, while others maintain she had ME, or CFS, which Mira said was the proper name, because that was what her mother had; she lay on the sofa for nearly two years and didn't have the energy to do anything. But you'd never know it to look at Mai. She teaches Norwegian and social science and she's one of the most popular teachers, the girls look up to her and the boys make gestures to one another when she walks by in the corridor.

Mai switches on the digital blackboard, clicks on Wikipedia and says something about continuing on today with some texts by contemporary writers. 'You'll all recall we read a short story by Frode Grytten—'

'Pussy Thief!' shouts one of the boys.

'That's right, Jokki, Pussy Thief,' says Mai without blushing, 'and you'll also remember we talked about Tove Nilsen. Well, today we're going to take a look at something by Johan Harstad, the Stavanger writer who'll also be paying us a visit in two weeks' time, so that's something to look forward to...'

Malene smiles at Mai, tries to follow what she's saying, *Johan Harstad, writer, point of view.* But she can't manage to concentrate. Her head is full to bursting. Sandra and Daniel Moi, Dad and his eyes, the mess in his room, his crying, Tiril, whom she slapped last night...

Malene looks around. There's a growing disquiet in the classroom, a buzz and murmur spreading throughout. People turn to one another and whisper. Mira has stood up and gone to the window. More and more people get to their feet to follow her. Mai has stopped talking about Johan Harstad and even she's walked over to take a look. Malene cranes her neck.

'Jesus,' one of the boys exclaims. 'Check it out!'

'Wicked,' says another. 'Yeah, baby!'

'Whoop whoop!' a third calls out.

Malene stands up to look out. Sandra is standing by the moped making out with Daniel Moi.

'All right, everybody,' Miss Jensen Bore says, 'let's try to settle down, okay?'

Malene holds her breath. The white sun shines on Daniel's moped. His hands are around Sandra's waist. His head is bowed down towards her and he looks like he's going to eat her alive.

Take him, Malene urges.

38. I'D DO FUCKING ANYTHING FOR YOU
(Cecilie)

The house is situated at the end of a cul-de-sac, close to the rail-track, and anybody would have difficulty guessing what colour it is any more. It hasn't seen a lick of paint since Thor B. Haraldsen leaned the ladder against the wall in the early seventies and ran a brush across the planks. It could do with new windows, six of them have condensation between the double glazing, the ground around needs to be drained, it's got so damp in the laundry room that the boxes of old clothes down there will soon decompose.

Mum drank herself to death in this house, lying there at the end like a dung heap with a death rattle, hardly a tooth left in her head. Dad moved to Houston a few years later, telling his kids to be positive in life and since then things have hobbled along in their own lopsided way. Jan Inge's reputation spread over half the city, people called him Videoboy. Some dodgy characters began hanging around the house and he started to rent her out when they came to visit. He let them eat crisps and watch video nasties which they paid for by putting cartons of stolen Marlboros on the table, and in this way it developed into a little community in a run-down part of Stavanger, a little company where people have come and gone and which today is comprised of her, Jan Inge, Rudi and Tong.

It wasn't that horrible, she thinks.

Having all those boys on top of her.

But it wasn't good either.

It was just something she was forced to do.

The house lies a few hundred metres from the old *Riksvei* 44, the main road into Stavanger city centre, which goes from Sandnes, through Forus, Gausel and Hinna. The stretch of it passing near to where Cecilie lives is called Hillevågsveien. For a long time it was a dismal area of the city. While the oil ran down through the region and lubricated Stavanger, added lustre, it was as though Hillevåg was forgotten. Nobody pumped money into Hillevåg. The whole suburb, along with its small factories, car showrooms and wholesalers, was left to lie and rust. And these grey streets have been Cecilie's streets. This is where she's bought her cigarettes and cinnamon buns, the treats she brings with her down to the quay behind the grain silos, while she looks out at the oilrigs lying in the sea at Jåttåvågen.

But it's strange being a Hillevåg girl now. Property prices have shot up, there's a new road, a new shopping mall, an odd place called Hillevåg Business Park, a newly opened fitness centre, a skincare clinic and God knows what else. 'It's Stavanger that's come to Hillevåg,' Jan Inge says. 'I'm fucking sceptical' says Rudi. 'View over the fjord,' was how it was advertised the time Thor B. Haraldsen bought the house in 1971. What would the wording be if Cecilie's childhood home was put up for sale today? 'Attractive detached residence with huge potential, close to Hillevåg Shopping Centre, allowing partial views of the fjord and within a short distance of the city centre.'

Cecilie finds it sort of scary but also sort of nice. A central reservation with pretty trees. Clean streets. People look happier, she thinks. But it's still safest going down to the sea. That doesn't change. The waves come in, one after the other, and the mountains on the horizon don't move an inch, because they belong to what is eternal, while she belongs to what will fade.

Cecilie has never had a job, never had any friends, and at times she's felt like she can't tell the days apart. She likes power ballads, because they make her eyes mist over and she likes fags and cinnamon buns because they help her muscles relax and she is carrying a child in her stomach. But she doesn't know whose it is. Rudi could be the father, because she's slept with him thousands of times, and Tong could be the father, even though she's only slept with him four times, in the visiting room at Åna.

She's tried feeling guilty but the bad conscience won't come about. When Tong asked if she could wank him off or give him a blowjob, she'd only thought about it for a second or two. The thimbleweed lay in wreaths beneath the trees out at Åna. 'Like a favour of sorts?' she'd asked. 'Call it whatever you want,' said Tong. 'Rudi mustn't get to hear about it,' she said. 'Jesus,' said Tong. And then Cecilie had felt a kind of burning in her chest and a tingling in her mouth, and she said: 'Okay, I'll suck you off so.' She went down on her knees, shoved the round table to the side, opened Tongs flies as he sat on the sofa with eyes wide-open, pulled his pants down around his ankles and gave his dick a quick glance before taking it in her mouth.

She didn't mind. He needed it, she could tell. After all, Cecilie knows something about these things, a professional insight of sorts, or whatever she ought to call it. She knows men's bodies are bursting from within. It was nice, in an odd sort of way, sucking off someone she knew so well, someone who'd always looked straight at her but had never made a single pass at her. She thought about it while she tensed the muscles at the tip of her tongue and licked the underside of his knob, that she'd probably known Tong for close to twenty years and that he'd always behaved like some kind of soldier, pretty much like Steven Tyler sings about in 'Amazing', an 'angel of mercy to see me through all my sins'. Not that she'd thought about it before, but as she'd knelt there blowing him, allowing her tongue to relax and widen, giving him wet, doglike licks, it struck Cecilie that Tong had always looked after her. He'd always watched out for her, in an entirely different way from either Rudi or Jani.

Could it be that Tong had always liked her and she hadn't noticed? Was that possible?

Cecilie stroked him gently with her fingers while she tongued him, tightening her grip now and then, listening to him gulp and breathe, noticing herself becoming aroused, becoming warm at the thought of one of the guards passing by out in the corridor, pulling the curtain in the window on the door aside and seeing her like this, on the floor, with an inmates's prick in her mouth.

After that Wednesday in March she began visiting him regularly. Seeing as she was the only one in the house in Hillevåg without a criminal record it was left to her to head out to Åna, get the latest from Tong, check how he was, make sure he was staying clean and fill him in on how things were with the rest of them at home. 'Get him to look on the bright side of things,' as Jan Inge said. 'Give him faith,' as Rudi said. And after that Wednesday it seemed strange not to wank him or suck him off. After all, they didn't have that much to talk about. Tong has never been a chatterbox, on the contrary, he 's always been the silent type.

Cecilie would get behind the wheel of the Volvo, drive past Sandnes, past Bryne and out to windswept Jæren. She would turn off the main road after crossing the River Hå, drive through Nærbo, over the flat expanse of Opstadsletta towards Åna, watching the old prison building rise up on the barren height, thinking how from a distance it resembled a German concentration camp she'd seen on TV. She had a strange sensation as she drove up the grand tree-lined avenue flanked by dry stone stone walls, before she drew to a halt, pressed the button and said: 'Cecilie Haraldsen, here to visit Tong.'

She liked driving to Jæren in sunshine, in wind or rain, listening to Aerosmith on the stereo, smiling to the guards at the entrance, who began to recognise her after a while, and she liked the feeling of being a known face. It felt like they knew why she was there and that she was swathed in a kind of respect. Jealousy even. She liked nodding to the guards, feeling their eyes upon her as she walked down the hall to the visiting rooms. She liked to open the door and see Tong sitting there, see that body of his, strong from all the work-outs, with his jet black hair shining. She liked closing the door behind her, going down on her knees, sucking him and pulling him off. She got to know his breathing and his body, she saw the veins on his sprawled forearms thicken. Over time she saw a light and colour in his eyes she'd never seen before, and one day, just as he was about to come in her mouth, he said: 'Jesus. I'd do fuckin' anything for you.'

Rudi talked and talked and talked without stopping, never more so than when they were having sex; she was so fed up of all that blather. Tong hardly ever spoke. But when he first opened his mouth, the words that came out, they were perfect.

He just seems so bloody smart, she thought.

So why is he with us?

Maybe it's because of me?

Cecilie hid the thought away in her heart and she looked forward to going to Åna once a week, but she never allowed Tong to touch her. She never let him undress her. That's where she drew the line. If she took her clothes off, allowed him to see her and put his hands on her – that would be wrong. It'd be unfair to Rudi. Because no matter how browned off she was with Rudi, he is the one she loves, that's the way she's always seen it. Up until last summer. Then she'd sat astride Tong. She'd just done it. It wasn't like she had her hands on the wheel listening to Aerosmith while the countryside of Jæren flew past and the thought of having sex with him had popped into her head, she had just come into the visitors' room that particular day and done it.

I couldn't help it, she told herself. I wanted him. It was the first time in my life I ever actually fucking wanted a cock.

Since then they've had sex four times on the brown leather sofa. And Cecilie has to admit that now there's a lot going on in this life that, until recently, was just drifting imperceptibly along. The father of the child could be Rudi, or it could be Tong. She has a grown-up problem on her hands. Because Rudi trusts Tong one thousand per cent. And Rudi loves her. And Tong says he'll do anything for her. And Tong is strong, he can smash anything with his bare hands, he's stronger than Rudi, but the fact of the matter is that Rudi is crazier than anyone she knows and that makes him the strongest of all. If Tong wants to do anything for her, then he ought to be aware there's also another who will, and his name's Rudi, he's out there and he's got ADHD.

On top of all that there's Jan Inge, and he's not strong but he's the one who runs everything, without him none of them are anything, and Jan Inge loves them all. If he knew about this he wouldn't go get the shotgun and blast somebody with it, he'd burn down the whole house. Set fire to everything and let everybody die, including himself.

And all these people, they work together. And none of them know she's pregnant. So what's she going to do? Sit and wait, see what kind of kid comes out, if it has Korea eyes or ADHD eyes?

'What do I feel?' she whispers in a low voice while she listens to Rudi making a racket down in the basement, while she puts on her shoes and opens the front door on the bright, clear September day.

'In love?' she says in a low voice as she comes out on to the street. She takes out a bag of Fisherman's Friend, needs something to get rid of the taste of vomit. Surely she won't be throwing up every morning from now on? It was probably the sight and smell of Jani stuffing his face with those eggs. He's way too fat now. He needs to go on a bloody diet, that brother of mine.

Am I in love?

In love with Tong?

At the same time as I love Rudi?

Cecilie glances down at her stomach, gives it a rub and whispers: 'Don't you worry about it. Mummy will sort it out. Somehow or other. But right now we need fags, a cinnamon bun and skincare.'

Cecilie walks up to *Mix* on Hillevågsveien every day and buys twenty Marlboro Lights. She's tried to bring it under twenty a day but seeing as how she likes smoking so much she's just not able. She's set a limit at twenty, which she maintains by smoking precisely one pack each day. She's pleased with having made the switch from ordinary Marlboro to Marlboro Light, that's a step in the right direction.

After she's bought the fags, she usually goes into Romsøes' Bakery next to the Mattress Master and buys a cinnamon bun. Then she crosses the street, passes Kvaleberg School, cuts over the playground by the old German bunker, wanders over the waste ground, out on to Flintegata, down to the bend in the road by the corn silos and along the street towards the sea where she sits down and looks out over the fjord, towards the heights of Li and Storhaug and at the water in Hillevågsvannet. She smokes two cigarettes, one before and one after eating.

And thinks.

Just thinks.

For years this has been what Cecilie's liked best about her life. Getting out for a walk, buying cigarettes and cinnamon buns, sitting down by the fjord and thinking. To avoid being at home, to escape listening to Rudi's prattle. And she still likes it. But now a lot has changed.

She began to notice them pretty much around the same time she started sleeping with Tong. Women in high heels and fancy clothes. They had handbags with gold fastenings. They started appearing in Hillevågsveien. They came in and out of a building across the road from *Mix*. They looked stylish and pretty. They looked like they came from leafy Eiganes or somewhere.

Mariero Beauty, it said in the window, even though strictly speaking it wasn't in Mariero but Hillevåg. Spa, it said. Universal Contour Wrap, it said. Classic Skincare, it said. And the women in the high heels and the gold clasps on their handbags, they went in and out of there. Looking radiant, she thought.

One night, after they'd watched *Evil Dead*, she looked at Rudi with her softest expression and said in her most mellow voice, 'Rudi boy, baby, I was wondering if I could maybe go down to that skincare place?' Rudi's eyes widened: 'What?' At first he was in a huff and then he grew angry. What the fuck did she want to doll herself up for? Cecilie thought about how right his family were, about how it wasn't strange they didn't want anything to do with him. That greedy brother of his with the psycho wife out in Sandnes. She should have just done it. Should have just gone down to the basement, fetched the axe and planted it in his back while he was asleep. But Cecilie isn't stupid, so later that night, after she had sucked him off and taken it so far down her throat that she nearly puked, she made it clear to Rudi that it was him she wanted to look good for, then Rudi nodded his approval over and over. After a while he began to smile. Then he began singing the opening lines of 'Dream On': 'Every time that I look in the mirror, all these lines on my face getting clearer.' Eventually he said: 'I get what you're saying. You're knocking on forty. You feel clapped out. Okay, baby, you'll get five hundred kroner, once a month. All sweet. On the house.'

Now she's walking along. Pregnant. On her way to the skincare clinic. To beautify herself. For who? Meandyou, Chessi, says Rudi. I'll do anything for you, says Tong, and he'll be out on Friday, and tonight she's going to visit him in Åna for the last time.

Cecilie halts. She brings her hand to her stomach. She'll need the car tonight. Rudi's heading out on a job, meeting that sweet Pål guy, the one with the nice dog. That'll piss him off no end, he hates public transport. But she needs to have the car. It's too much stress trying to get to Åna without a car.

She whips out her mobile, writes a quick text: 'Visiting Tong tonight. Need the car. XX. At the skincare place now.'

Cecilie puts the phone back in her jacket pocket, sets it to mute. She arrives at Hillevågsveien. She walks over the pedestrian crossing, into *Mix,* smiles to Geggi and says, 'Twenty Marlboro Light, please,' and he says, 'The day you quit smoking is the day this place goes out of business,' and she says, 'No danger of that, Geggi, I need my fags.'

Cecilie walks down the street to Romsøes, buys a cinnamon bun from the woman who works there, the one who talks about all kinds of things in a way that makes them sound amazing. Then she walks out into the light, heading for Mariero Beauty, with a feeling that there's going to be a lot of change in a very short space of time.

So much to think about.

A nursery in the basement.

A dog, maybe.

But what if the baby has Korea eyes?

Then there won't be any nursery.

And there won't be any dog.

Then the whole house will go up in flames.

'It's going to be okay,' she whispers to her stomach as she opens the door to Mariero Beauty. 'I'm your mummy and I'm going to look after you forever.'

39. I'VE GONE AND DONE SOMETHING REALLY STUPID (Sandra)

All she wants to do is throw herself into his arms, *take me away from here, I can't stand it any more*, and that's almost what she does when she sees Daniel driving into the schoolyard. She feels a sensation in her body, like a lead weight plunging down through it, but she tells herself she's a good girl, that she needs to practise restraint, but she can't manage: I've no control over myself.

Sandra makes Malene promise not to say a word, sweet Malene who feels like a friend all of a sudden, poor Malene who doesn't know what's going on with her dad, and she runs towards Daniel.

He dismounts and pulls his helmet off. Daniel looks flustered. His limbs seem uneasy, he rubs his fingertips against each another and he has a worried look in his eyes.

You know what people say about him.

Sandra wants to say something nice to lighten the atmosphere, to make them both smile, but she's tongue-tied. Is it time for her to hear the truth – what they whisper about him? *Something to do with his parents. Something mental. So mental it's fucked up his head. Daniel Moi has killed someone.*

She's never seen him like this before, as though he's present but he's not. Everything about him seems strange. She has the sudden feeling that everything she's doing is dangerous, that her decision to ignore what he's gone through is dangerous, and that there's truth to the rumours about him.

Sandra doesn't like being suspicious, but she can't ignore the thoughts gorging on her mind. She can't think of anything to say. Daniel stares right into her eyes. What is it he wants?

She closes her eyes.

Are you going to strike me, Daniel?

She opens them: he hasn't hit her. She can see the muscles in his jaw bunching tightly as he grinds his teeth.

What is it?

Everyone can see me, she thinks. The school building is just behind me, the classroom is right behind me. *Get a grip*. She can't stand here, not with Daniel William Moi. But if she isn't brave enough to do that, then it means she also lacks the courage to stand up and fight for love, and then she won't be his girl: Be electric in what I love.

All of a sudden, he takes hold of her head with both hands. His grip is firm. She's scared but then she feels his mouth on hers. He kisses her. But his mouth isn't soft, it's rigid. His kiss isn't gentle, it's rough, she can feel he isn't breathing down in his stomach but up in his head.

I'm making out with Daniel Moi, thinks Sandra. I'm snogging Daniel Moi outside the classroom window. Everyone can see me. I'm doing it. I want to do it.

He lets go of her. Sandra steps back.

'What is it? Has something happened?'

'No,' he says, without looking at her, 'I just had to see you.'

Sandra feels a jolt of happiness. Say it once more, she thinks.

'Listen ... look, I've got to get a move on, classes have already started—'

'Heh heh. Maybe it's about time the good little Christian girl got a demerit.'

He laughs. Is it nice? Is a pleasant laugh? Was he being nasty now? Ironic? She brushes her suspicions aside, laughs herself.

'Heh heh, yeah, maybe it is. But listen – did you see the girl who just went in?'

He nods. 'The one you were talking to?'

'That was Malene,' Sandra says, then blinks. 'I mean, that was one of the daughters of the guy in the woods last night. I didn't know what to say to her, I just ran into her—'

Daniel smirks. He points behind her. 'Is that your class?'

She doesn't turn around. 'Are they looking at us?'

'You can say that all right. Heh heh.'

That laugh. She's never heard it before.

'Forget about it,' Daniel says. 'You just need to keep your mouth shut, act like nothing's happened. Don't mention it to her. We need to find out more, know what I mean? See you tonight, okay?'

She nods. She'll do as he says, that's what she wants to do. She wants to trust the person she loves.

'Sure. But ... I've told her.'

'Told her what?'

'About...' She draws a breath. 'About you and me. That we're ... that we...'

'Heh heh. So what? Makes no difference to me.'

Makes no difference to me? Why is he talking as though it didn't mean a thing? Sandra doesn't like that laughter, doesn't like those words, but she thinks about how she has to be careful, how she has to respect him for who he is, because that's what love is: to strive to do your best for the other person.

He laughs and kisses her again.

She pulls away. She doesn't mean to but she does.

'But,' Sandra stammers, 'but ... why did you come here? Why now?'

'What are you asking me that for? I told you, I had to see you.'

She gives him a quick kiss, to rid his voice of the hurtful tone.'

'No reason,' she whispers, trying to bring her lips to his, but he avoids her kiss. 'No reason,' she whispers again, 'I didn't mean anything by it, I just didn't quite understand...'

'What? What the fuck was it you didn't understand? Me coming here? Me having to see you? What's so hard to understand about that?'

This can't happen

'Nothing,' she says, seeking out his lips once again, that bright mouth, wanting to kiss away all the bad, 'I understood, I won't bug you. You probably have lots on your mind. You've probably been through loads of stuff that you don't want other people to bug you about, I realise that ... People say so many weird things after all, but I've never asked you about anything ... I just don't always understand what's going on with you, but I won't ask any more questions, I won't—'

He tears himself away. His features are cold. He puts on his helmet. Climbs on to the moped.

'So shut up, then,' he says, starting the Suzuki.

Daniel rides out on to the street.

A window opens behind her and a voice calls out: 'Way to go, Sandra!', followed by another voice, just afterwards: 'Joachim! That's uncalled for. Now, close the window, leave her be.'

Dear Lord, Sandra thinks, I've gone and done something really stupid. She feels the oxygen leave her body, as though she were a balloon someone had stuck a hole in. Dear Lord, she whispers, have I ruined the most beautiful thing there is? If I have, I want to die. If that's what I've done then I don't want to live on this earth. I'm sorry for my horrible thoughts, I'm sorry for being suspicious of the one I love, but love doesn't tolerate anything at all.

40. **BEVERLY HINNA** (Jan Inge)

'Right, I'm heading out for a little while,' he calls out in the direction of the kitchen.

Jan Inge stands in front of the hall mirror checking his hair. It's always been thin and now there's a bald patch to boot. The Haraldsen curse, Dad always called it. My granddad, his dad, the whole bunch, scraggly bird-nests atop the lot of them.

But we make up for it in other ways, Jan Inge!

That's what Dad always said.

Is that right, what ways were you thinking of, Dad?

He runs a pair of plump fingers through his fringe, trying to work the small tuft into some kind of style, to give it some pizzazz.

'Hitting the gym, hombre?' Rudi's voice is cheery. 'Probably take a mosey on out myself later, after I've removed the skirting boards. Little bit of air under the flippers of the old seal.'

Rudi appears in the kitchen doorway, his hair sticking out in all directions, his eyes lively. He leans his long body against the doorframe, an almost-eaten slice of bread in one hand, the crowbar in the other. 'Chessi's at the skincare place. That's the way things are going – soon she'll want me to pay for facelifts and botox. But, you know. You're not a man if can't meet a woman's needs.' Rudy gives Jan Inge a gentle tap on the shoulder with his fist. 'You and your workouts. Every week. The gym bag is taken out, come rain or shine. Respect, brother. Lift those weights! Work those pedals!'

Jan Inge hooks the bag over his shoulder, the one they found at Metro Bowling in Åsen in 2007. They'd been tipped off that there was plenty of cash in the place. A paltry 3,700 kroner. Max. Might as well face it. There's less and less real money around. Bloody cashless society. The human factor matters less and less, no matter where you look. The bag had been left behind by a customer. They took it with them. It had been full of kids' clothes.

Jan Inge nods. 'We'll drive over to Hansi afterwards, then.'

Rudi nods in response. 'Have you talked to Buonanotte, by the way?'

Kein Problem, mein Sohn,' Jan inges says, opening the front door. 'All good in the hood.'

He hears Rudi's laughter behind him. *'Gute Reise, Bruder!* The gym awaits, see you in a couple of hours!'

Jan Inge walks out to meet the day. Heads uphill towards the main road, toward Hillevågsveien.

As soon as he rounds the corner and is out of sight of the house, his breathing quickens. Jan Inge walks as fast as he dares without running the risk of sweating – he doesn't want to arrive with patches under his arms, with sticky hair, as well as being out of breath. He reaches the bus stop in time, waits a few minutes under the shelter. Beside him, an old man in a cap stands staring vacantly into the Stavanger air, on the bench behind them a girl sits with her knees together and her fingers on an iPhone.

Jan Inge sees his face reflected in the door of the bus as it swings open. It looks how it looks, he has the time to think, before ascending the steep steps and paying a bus driver with a hearty Stavanger grin and a large moustache. Never been anything he could do about his face. He's always had those tiny, little dark eyes. Always had those short, chubby fingers. Always felt there was no getting away from himself.

As the bus sails out on to Hillevågsveien, he settles into one of the seats down the back. Low centre of gravity. Chin resting on his chest. Shoulders hunched over. He takes a quick glance out the window. No one sees him.

A little over a quarter of an hour later, Jan Inge alights from the bus on Randabergveien. At the stop near the filling station, close to that woman Åse's antique shop, right next to Toril's Clothes. Nice, that Åse one. Always a smile and a story to tell. He's been in there a few times. Bought a couple of things. Jan Inge heads into the petrol station. Bending down to the red plastic bucket by the newspaper stand, he picks out a bouquet of flowers.

'That'll be sixty-nine, please,' says the young man behind the counter, a Turk or an Indian or something like that. Jan Inge has never seen him before. There's usually a woman with a blotchy face behind the till.

'Sixty-nine it is,' Jan Inge says, placing a hundred down on the counter.

Five minutes later he's making his way up the hill behind Tastaveden School. Jan Inge feels hot, but not from sweat or physical discomfort, the warmth is due to other things. Because when all is said and done, this is the high point of his week. Even the street names make him feel happy, as though he were from here, as though he were in the wonderful vale of his happy childhood; Sjoveien, Granlibakken, Soltunveien, Fredtunveien, Høgeveien. So snug, so cosy.

And cosy is underrated.

Within certain circles, at least.

Within metal circles, criminal circles and horror circles, for example.

Maybe not within choir circles, tupperware circles or tweed-cap and waxed-jacket circles.

But in our group. We do underrate it.

Jan Inge has views on the matter. He's a firm advocate of the fact that cosiness is important, and he's reminded of that every week as he walks the streets in this area, which he ranks as his favourite in Stavanger. Tasta. Now this is Stavanger, Jan Inge thinks, feeling the warmth in his body, his thoughts flowing fast and philosophical and a firm pounding in his stride. All these ordinary houses. All these ordinary cars.

Jan Inge stops a few metres from the house. In order to swallow.

Will he come closer to his goal today?

Less than a minute later, his podgy index finger releases the doorbell and he hears it chime loudly in the hallway. He smiles to himself as he looks at the wavy glass in the panels running alongside the door. He smiles too at the rosemaling on the nameplate hanging under a painted garland: B. HINNA. He smiles again as he looks at the beautiful, flowery mat beneath his feet, and again when he sees the ceramic pot next to the mat with the colourful plants inside. And a shiver passes through him when he hears the familiar footsteps from inside, making such a wonderful *shuffling* sound, as though they belonged to a domestic angel, and don't they, after all?

Jan Inge straightens up. He clears his throat. Sucks in his cheeks and runs his tongue over his teeth and gums. Adopts what he thinks of as a handsome, positive and slightly teasing smile – the kind Dad wears so well – and the door opens.

'Jan Inge! So nice of you to come,' she says in broken Norwegian. 'Always nice. Look at you, fresh-faced, rosy-cheeked and darn fine. Come in. Oh now, did you bring me flowers? Oh, the gentleman caller, you didn't need to do that, bringing flowers along to old Beverly—'

'You're not old,' he says, as she steers him into the hall, which is bursting with the fragrance of perfume and flowers.

She clicks her tongue and bats her eyelids at him, takes his coat and slips it over a coat hanger. 'Fifty-four next year, and this girl don't lie about her age, you know that.'

'I know,' he says, looking at her admiringly.

It's unbelievable.

Every time Jan Inge sees Beverly Hinna, he's struck by an indescribable feeling of awe. He thinks he's standing at the gates of Heaven, the way he imagines it must be. He can hardly breathe. *It's like he becomes a different Jan Inge* as he walks down the hall on the middle-aged woman's heavily decorated carpet past her baroque-filled walls.

Her big hair, lending her a glorious Elizabeth Taylor style. Her full lips, always looking like they're anticipating something to eat, or have just eaten. The heavy golden earrings hanging down alongside her neck. Her eyes, with their listless intensity, accentuated by that purple eye shadow. And her outfit? Never easy to predict what Beverly will be wearing when they meet on Wednesdays. He can sit on the bus with his eyes shut and salivate at the mere thought of what kind of exciting ensemble she'll have on. The woman is a surprise package. On certain days she might open the door in a pair of tight jeans and an elegant blouse, usually with gold sequins and big shoulder pads that are almost lifting her off the ground, other times she'll stand there in a gorgeous dress and red high-heels, while sometimes there's the off-chance she'll turn up in what she's wearing today. A pink dressing gown with embroidered motifs: pelicans.

'Well,' says Beverly, laughing, and speaking in equal parts Norwegian and English, 'you'll just have to excuse me, but I have not gotten round to fixin' myself this mornin', you'll have to take me as I am.'

He lets out his reedy laugh but can't think of anything to say. Beverly reaches out her right hand, the one with big rings on all the fingers and leads him into the richly furnished living room. The deep red sofa with the large flowery pattern and a full skirt, the genteel rugs on the floor – what kind could they be? Persian, Oriental ... who knows what a woman will come up with. The beautiful table lamp with the fringe, all the wonderful pictures on the walls; a cosy painting of a typical garden on the south coast, a picture of a girl plucking flowers in a meadow, the framed poster with the image of Jesus and the inscription 'Lo and Behold! Our Saviour Cometh! Presbyterian Church of Poplarville'. On the corner table, lots of interior design magazines, a novel with a photo of a broken vase on the cover, and little bowls here and there with sweets, Belgian chocolates, small caramels, marzipan and he can only guess what else. Everything is so, it's...

It's so...

LOVELY.

LOVELY AND SEXY.

AND FEMININE.

AND COSY.

It makes him want to screw.

To say it straight out.

Not out loud.

But within.

He says it within.

That the combination of all these things – a buxom, plump woman nearly fifty-five years old, with heavy make-up and long painted nails, on both her fingers and her toes, with a lovely twang to her accent, in these ample surroundings, filled with patterned

sofas, snacks, interior magazines, pictures of gardens and Jesus and
flowers; that the combination of all these things give him an enormous urge to screw. Jan Inge isn't the type to go around all week
thinking about sex, as he has the impression a lot of guys do. He's
been aware of that since he was small, that it's like that for a lot of
boys. Just look at Rudi. He says as much himself: 'Hell, yeah, I pretty
much feel like just one big cock. And I like it.' But for Jan Inge? All
this sex in society today. He thinks there's something undignified
about it. That we, in many ways, live in a society of screwing. He's
sceptical. He wonders if it can be a good thing. In the long run.
What about the people who fall outside this society? What about
his own milieu, where there's no shortage of creativity but there is
a distinct lack of cosiness. Isn't there way too much sex in that, too?

Jan Inge feels left out.

He can go a long time without thinking about sex, days can
pass where all he thinks about is horror and interpersonal relations. But. When he gets in close proximity to Beverly Hinna he
can't control himself. And the more she offers, the plumper she is,
the more of her form being pressed out, the more lace tablecloths
lying out, the more ornaments decorating the fireplace, the more
Jesus posters covering the walls, the more interior magazines she
has lying around, and the more listless her eyes are, the more he
wants to get inside.

Her.

If she opens the door someday wearing a Norwegian national
costume, he'll break down in tears.

'Make yourself comfortable now,' says Beverly, who had come
to Norway arm-in-arm with Alfred Hinna, an oilman from Tasta.
He had found her behind the counter of a Shell station in Poplarville when he was working for that very same oil company back
in the early eighties.

Beverly sashays to the kitchen, her hair dancing in the air. 'You
ready to boogie, boy?' Jan Inge sees that powerful behind of hers
under the terrycloth gown and feels almost fatigued with admiration. He hears the tap run and a few seconds later she returns with
the flowers he's purchased standing up in a pretty crystal vase.
'Wasn't it you who gave me this vase, Jan Inge? Last year?'

He nods, happy she remembers. 'That's right,' he says, as politely as he can, 'that's right. I bought it from Åse on Randabergveien – it's from Hadeland, early nineteenth-century.'

'Beautiful,' Beverly says, leaning in captivating fashion over the table, allowing one breast to come into full view in the plunging neckline of her morning gown. 'Howdy, girl,' she says, laughing as she tucks it back into place. 'So,' – she fixes those sultry eyes on Jan Inge – 'how are things with you this week? Business okay?'

'Oh, business is booming, the money's rolling in, lots of new ventures I can tell you—'

'Lovely, and pleasure?' Beverly moves closer to Jan Inge. She takes his hand in hers, continues making small talk while slowly entwining her fingers in his – 'Hm? Jan Inge? How is my boy?' – and pretty soon she's massaging his middle finger as though it were a pastry she was kneading. 'Hm? Tell Beverly how my Ramblin' Man is.' She's right up against him now and he can't manage to reply, he can't manage to think. What is it she's asking? Jan Inge isn't able to hear her voice, he can only see that beautiful skin, feel that increasing warmth, her hand, her fingers kneading his finger, the breasts he glimpsed a moment ago, the breasts he's seen every week for over a year now, which prove just as exciting every Wednesday, as though he'd never seen them before, and he can't control himself.

'Beverly,' he says, his voice cracking, 'I worship you. You're the whole of America, you're fifty states and then some.'

'Oh,' she waves off the comment in mock embarrassment, before gently buffing her perm with the heel of her hand, 'now you're exaggerating. It's just my ass you like, Old Hinna liked it too. Yeah, wouldn't like to bet against it being what tipped the scales when he saw me bend down behind the counter back there in Poplarville.'

Jan Inge doesn't like her talking about Old Hinna, but he manages to push him from his thoughts and he continues: 'Don't talk like that, Beverly, don't put it like that, you mustn't trample on my love – it's huge, it's overwhelming. I'm asking you, marry me. Make me the happiest man in the world.'

'Now, now, now, you know we've talked about this—'

'I mean it, Beverly, I have a well-run business, I can increase the staff, I could be a good husband to you, I can provide considerable sums of money, I—'

She pouts and slaps her tongue against the roof of her mouth, as though there were poultry in the room. She tilts her head slightly forward and Jan Inge sees her eyelashes quiver. Beverly undoes her dressing gown. It feels like womanhood itself issuing forth and filling up the whole room as he watches her breasts spill out from behind the terrycloth; he gasps and forgets what it was he was going to say.

'Shh,' she says, 'you need to be released from whatever it is which is stirrin' up such a thunderstorm in you. Come now and let Beverly from Louisiana take you for a little stroll into the master bedroom.'

Jan has begun to cry, like he does every Wednesady. He sniffles and nods to Beverly, and she takes a gentle hold of his left hand, guides it to one of her naked breasts. He puts his other hand in his pocket, pulls out fifteen-hundred kroner which he places on the coffee table, while his left hand still rests on her breast. Beverly closes her eyes, brings her hand down to his crotch, and Jan Inge takes a big gulp as she takes her hand away, as he watches her walk across the floor towards the bedroom.

41. **AND THIS IS SUPPOSED TO BE A RECORD SHOP?!** (Rudi)

Rudi parks the Volvo outside Food Story in Hospitalsgata. Free parking for a quarter of an hour.

He removed five skirting boards. It'll be nice for Jani to be able to wheel freely through the house. You have to respect him for exercising as much as he does, hauling himself off, week after week. Although it's sad never to see any results. Just as flabby and overweight.

Rudi crosses Klubbgata towards Dropsen the confectioners, passes Ostehuset Café, which he thinks is for wankers. He was in there once, asked them for a simple raisin bun but could he get it? No problem ordering an ecological cock with a wreath of gash marinated asparagus on a bed of spinach with sprinkled herbs, but a classic raisin bun, that was beyond them.

He peels off into Laugmannsgata up the hill in the direction of Sølvberget. It's a little unpleasant being in such close vicinity to the Nokas building, scene of the biggest heist in Norwegian history. Nobody in the company talks about that. Kind of a touchy subject, especially when they felt they were close to being picked by Toska and his gang. When such a high-profile team comes to town, takes on such a big job and manages to bag over fifty mill, then not being picked can be a sore point. Even though they're opposed to hold-ups. And to violence. Still, you have to draw the line somewhere as far as principles are concerned. They could at least have kept watch or contributed in some kind of consultancy role. They are sitting on a lot of know-how and a good deal of knowledge about the region after all. What did Toska want with Swedes and people from Sandnes? Maybe a few of them would still be at large if they'd been along? Who knows, maybe that policeman never would have been killed if they'd been in on it. All in all, it's hard to be passed over. Everybody needs to be noticed.

Rudy passes a beggar in a knitted sweater, an apron and head-scarf sitting outside 7-Eleven. Her face looks blackened from soot, her hair is jet black, she's holding a paper cup between her hands and she looks at him with two sad eyes as she holds it out and shakes it. Rudi feels her looking at him but he restrains himself; remember what Jan Inge says: *No matter how much you babble away within these four walls, we can live with it, but when you're out in public you need to button your lip.* But his mouth won't obey and Rudi halts abruptly in front of the beggar.

'You there,' he says resignedly. 'Come on. Eh?'

She looks at Rudi, puzzled, and says something in a language he doesn't recognise.

'Seriously,' says Rudi, arms out in an expression of exaspera-tion. 'Where are you from? Lithuania? Romania? Andorra? Eh? Listen, I'm in a hurry, but this disappoints me. You sitting here. In a foreign country. In tatters and rags and looking the way you do. In broad daylight. You're sitting there, messing up our city and waving a paper cup from 7-Eleven around collecting halfpennies. Jesus. How low can you sink? Look at yourself, honey. Once you were a sweet little girl with pigtails. Once you sat in your Chechen granny's lap while she sang you nursery rhymes. What is it that makes you think you can get up in the morning, go out and receive – RECEIVE – money from people, while the rest of us have to work to earn a wage? Self-respect, have you heard of that? Would I go off to your country, find a nice spot to sit with a paper cup and beg for money? Jesus! And don't go telling me that you've an uncle from Azerbaijan who beats the shit out of you and your thirteen kids if you don't sit here degrading yourself. You have a choice, Miss Poland! You can stand up, right this moment, and walk from this with your head held high. You can walk into ... Christ ... you see that shop there? Ting? Yeah, Ting it's called. You can go in there and you can say: *Hi, I'm a washed-up woman from Estonia. My husband was blinded in the civil war, I have cervical cancer and my kids have tapeworms but I want to do something with my life. Give me a job, I'll do anything at all.* But no, you just want to sit here polluting the cityscape. Fuck me. You make me feel so depressed.'

'Excuse me?'

Rudi shakes his head and clicks his tongue with a disapproving *tsk*. He rummages in his pockets. Produces a five kroner coin and drops it in her cup. The woman casts her eyes downward and bows her head.

'And the next time I'm walking through my city, I don't want to see you. By then you'll have returned to the loser land you're from and participated in it's reconstruction, or else you'll have got your act together, found a job and gone on a course to learn Norwegian. Yeah, who knows Aunty Bulgaria, before you know it you could be standing for a political party in elections in our country and speaking up on behalf of the immigrants' cause, and then I'll hear you say: *Don't abuse people's hospitality! Pull yourselves together! Put away the paper cup!*'

She bows again and Rudi hurries off towards Arneageren Square. He stops when he reachs the open area in front of *Kulturhuset*.

Fuck, really *in your face*, this city.

Too much bloody ruckus, pain in the hole with people pestering, trying to get you to do one thing or another, people putting on plays, writing books, arguing in the papers and kicking up a fuss about one thing or another, not to mention them earning so much money. In that respect it's not so strange Toska and his gang decided to head here.

The quiet, peaceful times are gone, thinks Rudi. Back when you could sit in Granny's garden, look around at nature and think deep thoughts.

Rudi realises he's lost in thought and he hurries on towards Platekompaniet record shop. He comes to a halt as he walks in the door. It's a long time since he's been here, hasn't bought a lot of albums in the last few years and the ones he has he's picked up at Statoil. He looks around in surprise. He walks along the shelves. Games, DVDs, Blu-ray. Fuck's sake, where the hell are the CDs? Jesus, isn't this supposed to be a record shop? He goes further down the aisles, films, films, games, games, reaches the counter and at the very end on the right-hand side he spots a few shelves of CDs.

A shop assistant walks past, a smallish guy with a crew cut.

'Oi,' says Rudi. 'Not too many bloody albums in here. What's going on?'

The assistant smiles. 'No, well, we don't sell many CDs any more—'

'You don't sell many?' Rudi says, raising his voice slightly. 'Well, that's not so strange, seeing as you don't have any.'

The guy in the blue Platekompaniet T-shirt shrugs: 'So what is it you're looking for?'

'Ah, you know,' Rudi says, lowering his voice and taking a glance around to see if there's anybody he knows around. 'Metallica, Motörhead, Slayer...'

'We do have a selection of metal, lot of Maiden on special offer, for instance—'

'Don't you think I've got Maiden? The entire collection!' says Rudi, with a dismissive wave. 'No, you see, it's a present, for a niece of mine, and y'know, kids today, they only like pop—'

'Well, actually a lot of them are into metal too, they—'

'Maybe they are,' Rudi says, in an irritated tone, 'but my niece isn't. She wants...'

Rudi clears his throat.

'Yeah?'

'Well,' he says. 'Coldplay'.

'Coldplay, yeah,' says the guy, 'great band. Which album were you thinking of?'

Rudi squirms. He bends towards the guy.

'Y'know ... that one ... eh...' He clears his throat again. Then, in a low voice, he hums: 'Du-du-du-du-du-du-du-du-du...'

The record shop guy smiles and Rudi feels an urge to plant a fist in his face.

'Viva La Vida,' the guy says. 'The Beatles couldn't have done better. We've got it over here.'

'Hm,' Rudi says, nodding while the guy goes to get the CD. 'Yeah, that's the one.' Then, raising his voice says: 'But listen, record dude, you really need to do something about this shop!'

The guy walks back around the counter with the CD in his hand. 'Is it a present?'

'Yeah,' Rudi hastens to reply, 'you don't think I bloody well want that shit for myself, do you? You don't actually think Rudi—' He stops himself, no names. 'You don't actually think a metal man like me is going to sit in the Volvo—' Again he checks himself, no details. 'You don't actually think a regular guy who works in an office...' – that's nice, yeah, an office – '...has a good job in an office listens to that kind of poppy shit on his PC while he's shuffling papers around?'

The record shop guy laughs. Again. Rudi clenches his fists. What the fuck is he chuckling about?

'No,' Rudi says, restraining himself, producing his wallet and extracting a two hundred kroner note, 'I'll tell you this – back when I was a kid, this was a cool town to live in. When I moved in with my granny after my folks split up, there must have been at least five record shops in Stavanger, and they were *record* shops, *capisce?*'

The guy laughs. Again. 'Yeah,' he says, 'I worked in a few of them so I know what you're talking about.' And then he gets a kind of serious look on his face. He leans across, begins tapping the gift-wrapped CD lightly on the counter. 'No,' he says, 'things are really going downhill. I had to remove a whole rack of CDs just a couple of weeks back. It's just the way things are. People don't buy music any more. Now they download everything, you know. They steal.'

'Jesus,' Rudi says, feeling a degree of sympathy for the guy with the crew cut. 'Hard times.'

The guy nods. 'They are indeed.'

'Just constant grief,' says Rudi, looking around. There're hardly any other people in the shop. 'But what can you do? We've all got work to do, don't we? We all try and land the good jobs, and sometimes the big fish come to town, but you don't always—' Rudi stops himself. 'No, it's not as though an office job in local government is that great either, if you know what I mean.'

The guy behind the counter nods. 'I remember the old days. Fåsen Records. Fona. Platon Discs. Free Record Shop. Toots Music.'

'The good old days,' Rudi says with a sigh.

'Yeah,' says the guy. 'Thousands of records.'

Rudi places the two hundred kroner note on the counter. 'I feel for you, hombre. You're upagainstsomerealshithere and I think you know what I'm referring to. The internet. The black death of the modern age. If you ever need any help, all you have to do is pick up the phone and—'

Rudi stops himself again.

'Respect to you and your loved ones,' he says. 'And fuck Coldplay, metal up your ass!'

'I like Coldplay,' says the guy behind the counter.

'Heh heh,' Rudi chortles, 'that is your massive problem! No, but seriously, my niece is going to be made up when she gets this pop shit from Uncle Rudi.'

The guy behind the counter laughs. 'Yeah, if she has a CD player, that is.'

Rudi leans towards him. 'Listen, mate, I'm going to level with you. Rudi – this is Rudi here in front of you. Come here, let me shake your hand. Rudi's going to level with you. I don't have a niece. That's just some shit I made up. I'm an honest-to-God metal man. A pen-pusher. Have to work hard to earn a crust. Shuffle papers for the council. At the moment we've got our hands full with that new crossroads in Tjensvoll. Tonnes of people complaining about how it takes twice as long for the lights to change since the new intersection was finished. And who is it has to deal with these complaints? Who is it has to answer the calls when people ring up to give out yards about us regular local council employees? And who do you think suffers? It's the little people. The old and the sick. It's the old people who ring us up, desperation in their voices because their hearing aid isn't working, because they can't find their bedpan or because they don't have a grandchild to go and look after them. That's my working day. I'm a straight-up metal man. Got a best friend who weighs 120 kilos. Got a woman I'm never planning to let go. You know. It's like Judas Priest say, you remember, "Fever"? "Fever. You set my soul on fire. You fill my nights with desire." And people say there's no soul in metal? People sit around listening to Coldplay? Christ, I'm telling you, here we are, living in the wealthiest city in the world, the city David Toska and his handpicked crew chose to .... and ... well, you can just get so bloody depressed thinking about it. Where's the humanity? Yeah. No. You could go on about it all day, eh? Pleasure meeting other people who are sound. There're not many of us left, brother! I thought you were a tosser, but you're not – you're the last man standing. And now I'll give you a little quiz here – what two metal tracks am I thinking of?'

'What?'

'Last man standing. Two metal songs called 'Last Man Standing'.

'What?'

'Hammerfall. Bon Jovi. You've a lot to learn. And I've a lot to do.'

Rudi takes out his mobile. He feels buoyed. He may have shot off at the mouth a bit, but first and foremost he's aware of having done a good deed, offered a little inspiration to a working man in his daily toil, in a business on the way down.

Text message. From Cecilie.

'No, for fuck's sake!'

The guy behind the counter clears his throat. Rudi looks up.

'Christ, if it's not one fucking thing then it's another.' He draws a deep breath then exhales slowly. 'Okay,' he says. 'Sometimes you've just got to suck it up, like the man said. No, you take away a man's car, you take away his freedom. So it's a good thing to have a friend with a van. Okey-doke! Rudi signing out.'

At which point he sets off, more agitated than when he arrived, out the doors of Platekompaniet, in the direction of Hospitalsgata. By Havana department store he catches sight of the beggar who had been sitting outside 7-Eleven and, reaching her in a few quick steps, bends down into her terrified face, tears the paper cup out of her hand, plucks out the five kroner he gave her a few minutes earlier and scatters the rest of the small change she's received on to the cobblestones. 'Seriously,' hisses Rudi, 'didn't you understand a word I said? I just ran into a real working man and here you are!' Rudi spits on the ground. 'I despise you,' he whispers, 'you and everything you represent.'

Rudi leaves the beggar and strides past Ostehuset Café. When he reaches the car he sees a parking ticket for five hundred kroner under the window wiper. He rips it into pieces and gets in. He feeds the CD into the player, taps forward to 'Viva La Vida', leans back and closes his eyes.

I used to rule the world?

Rudi stops the CD. Presses the back button. He listens one more time.

I used to rule the world.

And then?

Seas would rise when I…

What is it he's singing? Rudi rewinds.

Seas would rise when I … gave the word.

Now in the morning I sleep alone.

Rudi opens his eyes wide. He tightens his grip on the wheel. Cecilie. All this skincare. The thing she said about his cock. The puking. Something's up. Something's fucking wrong.

'God,' he whispers, a thickening feeling in his throat, 'is my girl sick? Is there something wrong with her?'

42. I'VE GOT YOU NOW (Veronika)

The first time she saw him, Veronika thought he looked like a wolf.

They'd talked about it a lot. It was important to Mum that she was happy enough to take it on too. It's not something I want to push on you. No, of course not, said Veronika. It might be a nice experience, don't you think? Yeah, sure, said Veronika. Like having a big brother? Yeah, said Veronika. He knows that you're deaf. Okay. He says it doesn't bother him. Right. It's nice to be able to help someone out, isn't it? Of course, Mum. But, thought Veronika, there's no doubt you could use the money. You work for the health services, Mum. We live in a block of flats. She googled it. Idealism is nice and all but you don't say no to 13,000 a month.

Child Welfare's response was positive. It wasn't a big draw-back, then, that Inger was a single mother? No, on the contrary, it might be advantageous, they believed. Foster children have often had such bad experiences with parental relations that it can actually be a good thing for them to have fewer adults to deal with. With regard to the boy in question, they were sure it wouldn't be anything other than good for him. It was no easy matter finding a suitable home for a sixteen-year-old, and it was only made more difficult by the fact that the boy could admittedly be a hard nut. He was intelligent. He was talented. But he had been through some things. He had what they referred to as baggage. They made no secret of the fact that this would be the third – assuming they said yes, of course – the third foster home Daniel William Moi had had in under two years.

Mum listened to the Child Welfare Officer. She attended meetings, she took walks with her best friend and talked about what was on her mind. After a while she was able to meet the boy concerned. Mum came home, sat down in the kitchen with Veronika and painted a picture of a boy who was strong, had lots of wonderful qualities, a boy who could at times be unpredictable but who was vulnerable, sensitive and intelligent. A boy who'd been through a lot and was in need of a place to stay until he turned eighteen. A stable environment. Preferably with someone who has experience of looking after others. Mum didn't say what she or Child Welfare meant by that, but Veronika picks up on those kinds of formulations. She knew they were comparing her to Daniel. As though the facts that she was deaf and he was a foster home kid had something to do with one another.

'He's a fine boy,' said Mum, on the day last of autumn when they were on their way to meet him. And then she shot her that teasing smile of hers, the one which always draws people in, before she said: 'And he's very handsome, *very.*'

Veronika shook the case worker's hand and looked at the guy in the chair across from her. He was really tall, probably one ninety. He was wearing black clothes and sitting with his arms folded. This isn't going to work, she thought. He didn't even acknowledge me. He's not saying a word to anyone. Veronika saw Mum and the case worker smile at one another. She read their lips and understood how in agreement they were, but the one who really mattered, Daniel William Moi, just sat there looking like a wolf.

He'd obviously made his mind up beforehand not to say a word and not to look at anyone. But Veronika didn't think he ought to get off so easy. 'That's a funny name you've got,' she fired in when there was a short pause in the conversation between Mum and the man.

She knew how taken aback people could be when they heard her voice for the first time, so hollow and strange. But in that meeting it was as though that stupid voice gave her an advantage. 'William,' she continued, snickering. 'Did you add it on yourself? To sound like a prince?'

Mum shot her an angry look.

'It's a cunty name,' Daniel said, finally piping up.

'I'm practically deaf,' said Veronika, 'I can hardly hear a thing. But I'm good at lip-reading, so if you want me to understand what you're saying you need to look at me, and if you're bothered to, you could learn sign language.'

Veronika felt her lips tingle as she spoke. He was terribly, terribly beautiful. His eyes narrowed, took on a yellowish tinge; he opened his mouth and enunciating each letter slowly said:

'I-t-s-a-c-u-n-t-y-n-a-m-e.'

Mum shifted uneasily in her chair. The case worker smiled, in an accustomed manner, and said: 'Veronika is no shrinking violet, I see. That probably suits you, Daniel.'

'I need a smoke,' said Daniel, his eyes still on Veronika; she felt he was going to devour her. 'Are we done here, or what? C-a-n-I-m-o-v-e-i-n?'

Veronika kept her gaze fixed on him and said slowly: 'W-h-a-t-i-s-w-r-o-n-g-w-i-t-h-y-o-u-r-v-o-i-c-e-d-o-y-o-u-h-a-v-e-s-o-m-e-s-o-r-t-o-f-s-p-e-e-c-h-i-m-p-e-d-i-m-e-n-t?'

A few days later Daniel William Moi was standing at their door. He arrived with four large bags, a drum kit and a moped. Inger had signed the contracts, she'd also been informed by the social worker that she needed to exercise caution where his past was concerned – he didn't like people bringing it up. Advice she also impressed upon Veronika. Inger welcomed him, tried to make him feel at home as best she could and Daniel appeared to like her manner; in any case the situations that Child Services had warned them about never actually arose. Veronika's and Daniel's interactions continued being confrontational in style, their exchanges cheeky and in your face. She ventured closer and closer every day and before long she took his chin between her finger and thumb, turned his head to face her and said: 'I need to see your mouth when you're speaking to me.'

She noticed him looking at her. At her copper-red hair. At her dimples. At her long legs and at her tits.

After a few days, Veronika said to herself: I'm in love. I want him.

Soon she'll have waited a year. She's sat on the floor of his room with her legs crossed when he plays the drums. They've lain on the sofa together watching TV, their bodies just barely touching. I'll look after you, he says, my little sister. There's been more and more of that kind of talk and Veronika doesn't like it. A car? Do you want a car? Daniel will sort it out.

Little sister.

That's not what she wants to be.

It's the wolf she wants. She wants him to place his paws on her stomach. She wants him to sink his teeth into her neck. She wants him to lick her with that red tongue of his.

It was last week when she realised something was up. Daniel had begun to stand in front of the mirror fixing his hair, was coming and going at funny times, and went straight to his room when he did come home, avoiding eye contact with Mum when she asked where he was off to. She should have realised sooner, but she didn't cop on until he asked her if she knew a girl called Sandra.

'Sandra? Who's that?'

'Nah. Nobody.'

'*Nobody?*'

'Just a girl a few streets over. Lives someplace near the church.'

'And what about her?'

'Nothing, just wondering if you knew her is all.'

In the space of those few seconds her fantasy world came crashing down and Veronika felt her skin begin to burn. She was so jealous she could have gone for him, torn strips off him, pushed him through the living room, out on to the balcony, tipped him over the railings and watched him fall to the ground and smash his skull on the tarmac twelve floors down.

What do you take me for? Do you think you can get as much as I've given you without it costing you? Do you think you can head off to some cuntbucket of a Christian girl – *I know who she is* – without your fur catching fire, when I've been waiting a year for you?

Veronika pretended she'd something in her eye and ran off to the bathroom. She locked the door, turned on the tap, switched on the hairdryer and sank her nails as deep into her cheeks as she could.

She cried it all out.

Then she sat down to think.

What is it I've done wrong?

Veronika has made good use of her self-control the last week. If there's one thing being handicapped has instilled in her, it's patience. An existence as a deaf person has provided her with ample opportunities to be exposed to inertia; sluggishness from public services, from school. She's had to wait. For all the good-will, which is overwhelming on paper, but which always comes slowly.

She has self-control. But she's made an error. What boy is really attracted to a girl he's mates with?

She's made herself too trivial. She's lain beside him on the sofa, eaten breakfast with him without thinking about how she looks, she's done all the things adults do when they've been together ten years and are tired of one another. She hasn't been attentive. She hasn't sold tickets.

Veronika took great care with herself when she went to the bathroom this morning. She told her mum she didn't have classes before second period and wanted to wash her hair. Then waited for her to get ready for work and go out the door. She took a long shower. She scrubbed thoroughly. She shaved her legs. Her crotch. She breathed in calmly and then breathed out just as calmly. She got out of the shower, went over to the mirror. She looked at herself. The strength in her eyes. Her hair. Her ass. Her legs. Her tits.

You won't be able to resist this, she thought, and smiled as she wrapped one towel around her hair and another around her body. She tucked it in above her breasts. She left the room and walked down the hall, in the direction of Daniel's room. She felt a faint pounding in her stomach: He's sitting at the drum kit.

She had turned the door handle and gone in. She had lifted her coccyx. She had hiked the towel up her thighs. She had felt his breath on the back of her neck. She had felt his body against hers. She had pulled off his T-shirt, pressed her tits against his skin: *I've got you now.*

Now Veronika is lying in the bath. She's crying through closed eyes. Her right hand resting on the side of the tub, between her fingers a razor blade.

She's not pretty. She's not beautiful. She's not sexy. She's not smart. She's deaf and she's dumb and she's ugly and no wolf wants to put his paws on her.

43. A RAGING TORRENT IN THE HEAD
(Daniel William)

Daniel puts his visor down, closing out the white light. He turns the ignition.

If that's how things are going to be, then all you can do is ride. If one girl is going to attack you and the other can't keep her mouth shut, then he can't deal with it. Every man has the right to turn around and leave. Who the hell is going to look after you if you don't look after yourself? Girls are dangerous. You couldn't trust them and they can get you to do anything at all. Heroin? Acts of terror? Heroin and terrorism are nothing compared to girls. Girls control the entire world and they're all too fucking well aware of it. They're always the ones in the driving seat.

Your job: look after yourself.

Your job: go.

Your job: get out of here.

You've only got one shitty life. It might well be that it's supposed to smell of sulphur, might well be that every day is supposed to be like sailing on a lake of burning silver. But it's yours.

Daniel zips his jacket right up under his chin, puts his foot on the gas and leans slightly forward. He sees Sandra in his wing mirror. Her arms are hanging limply by her sides, she's crying and he can see that she's unable to move. He can almost feel her despair and that's the way he wants it. He wants her to be in pain.

Is there a hole opening up in the ground beneath you?

Talk, talk, talk, talk, talk, talk, talk.

Am I torturing you, bitch?

Daniel rides.

He can explain it. And he can't explain it. How things turn inside out within him.

He wants to be that way and he doesn't want to be that way. He wants to be the hardest metal and doesn't want to be the hardest metal. Once he feels things begin to twist inside, he can no longer do anything about it. Then he needs to leave, he needs to ride. It's as though a fuse has been lit in his head and as it starts to sparkle and crackle, there's no other option but to shut out all the light: go, ride, get away.

I have my limits and you crossed the line.

Daniel feels the air press against him. He rides down to Hafrsfjord, past Liapynten and whizzing along the seashore at Møllebukta, sees the sculpture of the three swords, dark against the clear horizon, and thinks how they look like they're going to take off and rocket into the sky. He rides past Madlaleiren barracks, sees the soldiers lining up, sees people walking and cycling and cars cruising on the tarmac. He shuts his thoughts out. The mobile phone in his inside pocket vibrates but he doesn't take it. He rides further on, out to the junction at Madlakrossen, takes a left, passes the golf course, on up towards the church at Revheim, out towards Sunde. Daniel leans into the onrushing air, letting nothing inside. Before Hafrsfjord Bridge he swings off towards Kvernevik, takes the turn off to the sea, in the direction of the finger of land at Smiodden and thinks about how out there in the blue of the ocean peace is to be found. When he reaches the ribbon of road that is Kvernevikveien his phone begins to vibrate again and he hunches over the handlebars a little more. Where's he going? Nowhere. Just far away. He heads over to Randaberg and rides through the small village centre. He's aware of people, both old and young but he doesn't see them. He simply rides, all the way out to Tungenes, passing farms, fields, cows and sheep.

Daniel doesn't stop before he's rounded the headland and is on his way back towards the city. He turns off at Stokka and brings the moped to a halt beside Stokkavannet Lake. He removes his helmet. Walks along the lakeshore. After a few minutes he sits down on a bench. He throws a few stones out into the water before taking out his phone.

Two messages. The first is from Sandra.

Dear Daniel, what have I done wrong?

The other is from Veronika.

You're a wolf, Daniel. I'll never forgive you.

He takes a breath. Writes back to Sandra.

You talk too much.

A few seconds pass before she replies:

Yes, I know. Sorry! I'll do anything you say!

He closes his eyes. Takes a deep breath from far down in his stomach. It feels right. That she should apologise outright.

He sends her another text:

OK. Fine.

A few moments later:

Will I see you tonight? Usual time?

He answers:

OK.

Then a few seconds after that:

Thank you, I love you. Yours forever.

He goes back to the text from Veronika. He looks at it as though it were a photo. *You're a wolf, Daniel. I'll never forgive you.*

He places the phone on a rock, squints out over the calm water. He takes out a cigarette and lights it. I'm in love with you, Sandra, he thinks. I'm not in love with you, Veronika, he thinks. But I like you better than Sandra.

He grabs the mobile, types in:

Sorry Veronika. I didn't mean to hurt u

Then he takes out a well-used notebook and pencil stub he has in his pocket. He writes. A few lines.

Me the wolf, you the rabbit
Go deep, go deep
Me the sword, you the casket
Go deep, go deep
Dearly beloved, truly disgusted
Go deep, go deep
Do not think I can be trusted
Go deep, go deep.

Into the slicing dark

That's where it ends. He likes the rhythm of it. He likes the dirty humour. It's from something he read on some blog a while back: a girl was asked what she liked least about sex and she said, 'When the guy applies pressure to the back of my head as I'm blowing him so it's not me who decides when I'll go deep.' But he can't think of any more lyrics to add. And he doesn't know if 'slicing dark' actually works. Is it good enough English? He can easily picture it, how the darkness could be a knife. It might be dead good. It might be shite. Sometimes the stuff he writes is like that, wavering between genius and crap and it's impossible to say where it actually falls.

Daniel closes the notebook and puts it back in his pocket along with the pencil. Zips up his jacket. He's starting to get into this writing thing. When he manages to put it down on paper he feels the pressure in his head ease. At first they come cascading, the words, the sentences, and a lot of the time he doesn't have any idea where they're coming from or where they're going to, but it makes for a raging torrent in his head, and then, when the words flow on to the paper, bringing other words with them – it's a kick. He feels a tingling in his fingertips, just like when you push yourself to the limit lifting weights.

Daniel makes his way back to the bike. He puts the helmet on, sits down and starts to ride.

A wolf? He thinks, watching the needle of the speedometer rise.

A few minutes later he dismounts outside the block of flats.

In the lift he feels the upward motion tug at his stomach.

Not long after that he walks in the front door.

He stops, looks around the hall. Everything is the same as it was this morning. The lights are on. Her clothes are there. Her schoolbag is there. He kicks off his shoes, hangs up his jacket and tosses his helmet on to the hall bureau. He walks into the living room.

'Veronika,' he calls out, as though she could hear him.

Daniel feels his pulse rate rise. He sticks his head into the kitchen, the sight of the fridge door ajar gives rise to a feeling of faint unease. He shuts it. He makes his way back through the living room and out into the hall. He walks towards her room.

'Veronika?' he calls out again, as though she really could hear him, and opens the door. There's nobody in there. Just a half-made bed, her books, her posters, the computer and her clothes.

He returns to the hall.

He glances at the bathroom door.

He takes a few steps then halts outside. He puts his ear to the door, listens.

Daniel takes hold of the handle, presses down. The door is locked.

44. **BUNNY'S LITTLE BROTHER** (Tiril)

Bunny's bloody little brother. He is such an unbelievable douche-bag. What does he want? Every single day it's one thing or the other. Tiril just wants to lamp the guy. After all, he is only a dwarf – he looks like a little duplo man. Are his parents retarded? Were they on heroin when they conceived him? If it's not something about her clothes then it's her make-up, and if it's not that then he's poking or prodding her. Jesus, he's annoying. He can't pass by her without bumping into her or making some moronic comment – the other day he *spat* in her hair during music. She was trying to follow what the teacher was saying about the difference between major and minor, really interesting as a matter of fact, and then she felt something wet in her hair and heard Bunny's little brother's toady laughter behind her. Christ, how much of a mongo can you possibly be?

Here he comes now, with the wigger walk, the crappy hoodie and the unlaced trainers, and those eyes of his, blinking nonstop, is there something wrong with them? Soon be able set your watch by the pint-sized reject. Lunch break. Pling, and he appears: 'Hey, Hanna Bad Karma, been talking to your sister, have you? She's suddenly all best mates with Daniel Moi's slapper!'

Tiril's just about to open her mouth, just about to tear into him.

'Don't even bother, like,' says Thea.

Tiril extends her middle finger, narrows her eyes as much as she can and says: 'What is your problem?'

'AIDS!' shouts Bunny's little brother. 'Do you want it? Come on, I'll smear it all over your tits!'

Thea takes a hold of Tiril. 'Lets go. Just ignore him.'

Jesusfuckingchrist. Tiril just stands there, even though Thea's expression is imploring her to move. What is with him? There's definitely something wrong with him. God, she's glad she's not in the same class. Tiril feels her heart pound, feels it thump with wicked clarity when he talks about Malene. That's how it's always been. She and Malene might argue like mad, fall out all the time, like yesterday when Malene clobbered her, but if someone says a bad word about her sister then Tiril flies off the handle. She'll clench her fists, go for them and beat the shit of them.

'Come on,' says Thea once more. 'Just drop it.'

'Just let him stand there shooting his mouth off?'

'No, but ... don't bother your ass, like.'

Tiril makes her way towards Bunny's little brother. She walks as quickly as she can. The silver chain, which loops from her hip down the outside of her thigh, jingles in time with her strides. Little bastard. He can say what he likes about her singing, can call her an emo until he pukes, but no way is she going to listen to this. There have been rumours flying all around the school since this morning, loads of people saying one thing and the other about what happened. Some are saying Daniel rode into the school-yard, got off his moped and hit Sandra, while others are saying he snogged her, some people are saying he grabbed her between the legs, others that he bawled her out, but Malene was there. And Malene told her, loud and clear: 'We're the only ones who know anything, Tiril. Understand? Suddenly we – you and me – are the only ones Sandra has. Do you understand? She loves him. He loves her. No snitching, okay? Sandra isn't like we thought she was.

That sank in. Sandra can't help who she is. Sandra can't do anything about where she comes from: Sandra's one of us now.

'Hey, Shaun!'

She continues walking towards him. People are looking now. They begin to flock around.

'Oh oh! Emo alarm!' says Bunny's little brother loudly. He's standing together with Fredrik and Hassan in front of the tree by the gymhall.

'Hey, Shaun,' she repeats. 'Hey! Shaun the Sheep! I'm talking to you!'

Tiril stops right in front of him. Bunny's little brother stands there sneering but she notices he can't meet her eyes. She maintains a steady gaze.

'Something on your mind, Amy Lee?'

'Yeah,' she says, 'there is.'

'Hey! The emo actually has a mind! Word!'

Bunny's little brother raises the palm of his hand to Hassan and they high-five.

'See these?' Tiril lifts her hands and holds them in front of his face. 'Can you read?'

'Funny.' Shaun's gaze sweeps across her fingers. 'Love hate, wow, scary.'

She lowers her voice, brings her face right up to his: 'You're a loser, Shaun Payne, and you know it. You're going to end up smoking crack in a couple of years. You think you're hot shit because your family comes from the US but you're not. We don't buy that crap. You're from a shithole where people think the death penalty is the solution to their own problems and invading other countries is the solution to other people's problems; you're a lowlife and an idiot; you're the only person I know who's managed to get busted swiping stuff in Spar twice in two weeks. Jesus, look at yourself, you're the same height as a wheelie bin and you still get clocked trying to steal chocolate. You can't open your mouth without coming out with something stupid. What's wrong with you? Can't you do anything other than slag people off?'

Bunny's little brother's face is red, he shifts his weight from one foot to the other, tries to grin but can't quite manage. Tiril whispers: 'Shaun? You've bad breath. You hear me? Loser. Have you got a crush on me?'

He swallows; she sees his Adam's apple rise and fall.

'Well, have you?'

'Jesus,' he says, but there's a tremor in his voice.

'These are my hands,' Tiril says, clenching her fists. 'The next time you say a fucking word about my sister, or Sandra, or me, I'll plant them in your face. And when I get my period – and that won't be too long – I'm going to smear blood all over your ugly mug. And tomorrow I'm going to stand in the gym hall and sing, and I won't forget one single line. And you are never, you hear me, never going to get so much as the tiniest little piece of me.'

She turns on her heels. Starts to walk. A crowd of people have gathered round. Nobody says a word. She sees Malene standing amongst them, and behind her, Sandra. She gives them a quick nod.

From behind her comes the sound of laughter. It grows louder the further away she gets. She slows down. She closes her eyes.

'Emo bitch!'

Bunny's little brother.

'Emo slut! Do you think you can talk to people like that and get away with it?'

Oh, you stupid little shit.

You couldn't let it go, could you?

Tiril turns. Thea makes an attempt to restrain her but Tiril runs at him, her fist raised, and when she punches him as hard as she can in the face, she connects cleanly.

45. **MARIERO BEAUTY** (Cecilie)

She is so beautiful.

She's behind a desk, dressed in a white lab coat; she could be in her late thirties, maybe early forties. She's slim, but in a strong way, her skin golden and Egyptian, her mascara moss green, her nails are painted, her lipstick is deep red and she's wearing her hair up.

Cecilie feels like a hedgehog, she wants to turn around and go back out the door, run down to the fjord and never come back.

The lighting in the room is low. There's a chandelier with yellow twirly light bulbs hanging from the ceiling and a pale pink candle on the woman's desk radiating warmth over her smooth, wrinkle-free hands. The scent of essential oils, plants, lavender and herbs pervade and a piano and panpipe version of 'Für Elise' is sneaking out of speakers someplace.

Cecilie's stomach feels cold and her palms are sweaty; she needs to pee but the woman behind the desk looks up, smiles and says, 'Hello, welcome, you must be Cecilie?'

A peeping sound like that of a bicycle brake escapes her mouth as she emits a 'yes', in an attempt to keep her lips from opening too wide and revealing her yellow teeth.

The woman gets to her feet and walks round from behind the desk, her whole being still smiling. The corners of Cecilie's mouth twitch when she sees her green eyes. Fine green rays spread out across the iris, and in her left eye, below the pupil, she has three or four red flecks resembling tiny pearls.

'Lovely to see you, Cecilie – is this your first time with us?'

'Yes...'

The woman motions with her hand towards a coat stand and Cecilie begins removing her jacket even though all she wants to do is leave.

'Your hair really is a fantastic colour, I envy you that!' She glances at a sheet of paper lying on the desk. 'Cecilie Haraldsen. Classic skincare treatment, wasn't it?'

'Ehh ... yeah,' Cecilie brings her hand to her hair, awkwardly, 'I thought I'd...'

'Für Elise' is replaced by the strains of 'Imagine', also being played on piano and panpipes. The beautiful woman seems to be strewing something across the floor as she gestures towards a hemp basket with pink, sea-blue and white slippers in it.

'Feel free to take off your shoes and slip into a pair of these,' she says, letting out a gentle laugh that almost seems to materialise, like a colourful ball rolling over the floor and up the walls. 'Just heaven.'

'Okay...'

Cecilie bends down, self-consciously, and takes off her shoes. Two old, worn-out black socks. She curls her toes and tightens her lips.

'Good, Cecilie, this is what we'll do. You come along – silly me, I forgot to introduce myself, I'm Hege...'

Cecilie gives her clammy palm a quick brush of her thigh and takes the woman's hand. Warm and soft, like everything else in here.

'I just have to say,' she says, smiling again, 'that hair colour. Smashing! Now, we have eight cubicles in all and if you'll just follow me down here then we'll see what we can do.'

'Okay...' Cecilie blushes and raises, without meaning to, her hand to her hair.

'Are you married, Cecilie? Kids?'

Cecilie looks away, shakes her head.

The woman smiles, almost conspiratorially, and says: 'Still not too late to have a few little ones, but all the same, we have to admit we are of a certain age, and we need to look after our skin—'

'We do, yeah...'

'But a boyfriend – you do have a man, Cecilie?'

'I do, yeah...'

'And of course he wants to see you looking nice, hm? It's just the right time for you to take care of yourself. You deserve it.'

Cecilie follows on the heels of the beautiful woman into what she'd called a cubicle – a small room containing a bed at an angle with a pillow covered in a towel at the head. There's a small stool with wheels beside it and a shelf along one wall. Beneath the shelf stands a small table with an assortment of skincare products, bottles and jars on it. And once again a pale pink candle, the same music as out in the reception, the same soft smells, and a strange looking contraption on wheels.

The sight of the bed makes Cecilie nervous – is she supposed to undress?

'Now, Cecilie, here we are. Everything okay? Good. You lie down and make yourself comfortable. You can take off your sweater – leave your bra on – and then just relax. There you go.'

Cecilie pulls the sweater off over her head, turning it inside out, her pulse climbing, shivering as she folds it before lying down on the bed.

No other girl has seen me like this since PE at school, she thinks.

'Now we'll just put this little hairnet on,' the beautiful woman says. 'Oh, you seem to be a little tense today, try to relax. That's it. You're a tad pale at the moment, don't you think?'

'Weell, maybe a bit, yeah...'

The woman smiles and leaves the room but returns after a few moments. She's carrying a bowl of water. She puts it down on the little table and dips a cloth into the water, wringing it afterwards. She places the cloth on Cecilie's face and begins wiping her skin gently while talking about a purifying cream she's going to apply, one with several functions – it peels and cleanses as well as acting as a tonic.

'You know, Cecilie,' she says, removing the cloth and moistening her own hands with the purifying cream. 'We need something pure, simple and effective. We only use ecological products here. Adverts will always try to convince you to buy the cheaper ones but they're just stuff and nonsense. When we get a little older we...'

Cecilie shuts her eyes.

The beautiful woman begins to touch her. Soft fingers smear

on a light cream and massage Cecilie's skin in gentle, circular motions.

Cecilie's breathing becomes shallow.

Nobody has ever touched her like this.

The beautiful woman talks and talks while she cleanses her skin but Cecilie can't follow what she's saying. All she can focus on is how unpleasant it feels to have someone touch her in this way.

When she's finished with the cleansing, the woman wheels the big contraption closer. It's a steam machine, and she positions it above Cecilie's head, pretty much like a large hairdryer.

'Now, Cecilie. You just lie there, okay? Do you feel a little more loosened up now?'

'I ... wha?'

'Your muscles, have they loosened up a bit?'

'Ehh ... yeah...'

The woman runs her hand across Cecilie's shoulder and smiles.

'Stressful time at the moment, perhaps? At work?'

'Suppose...'

Her fingers leave her skin.

Don't touch me.

'What do you work at, Cecilie?' the woman asks and turns on the machine, the steam rushing into Cecilie's face.

Touch me.

'Work?' Cecilie clears his throat, blushes, sweats. 'Well, I ... work in a video store.'

A video store? Why did she say that?

'Ah, well, there you go,' says the beautiful woman, 'you're on your feet all day. That can be tough, standing so much. Tough on your back, tough on your shoulders. It's only proper you're taking a little time out for yourself. Good. Have you done any yoga?'

'Yoga?'

'Try to get into a yoga frame of mind. Is it hot? Try to imagine you're becoming soft and heavy all over, that you're accepting all the peace and relaxation you can get. Don't worry if you find it a little bit difficult to breathe, that's quite normal, it's the steam – just turn your head ever so slightly away. Okay, Cecilie?'

'Okay'.

I need to pee, Cecilie thinks.

I want a smoke, Cecilie thinks.

A gush of heat hits her face.

Touch me.

In a little while, after the beautiful woman has left the room with the bowl of water and returned with it again, the steam machine is turned off and wheeled away from her face. The woman cleanses Cecilie's skin once more and once again she touches her and again she tenses up, from her feet all the way up to her neck.

She hears the woman's voice: 'Okay, Cecilie, peeling.'

'Huh?'

'Peeling,' says the beautiful woman, opening a small jar and scooping a thicker cream on to her fingertips. 'You may as well throw out all those expensive creams if you don't peel the skin.'

Are you going to put your hands on me again?

Cecilie looks at her. Doesn't she realise who I am?

'There's no doubt,' the woman continues, her hands moving slowly towards Cecilie's face, 'we all face stress and strain in our daily lives and that affects our skin, giving rise to impurities and blemishes. Do you use sun factor fifty? I do. Skin cancer is a real danger in the Nordic countries, you know. The skin needs to breathe – cosmetics block our pores and cause a build-up of grime, which is why you need to use mineral make-up.'

Her hands hang in the air in front of Cecilie.

Is she not going to touch me again?

'Mineral ma—'

'The skin is better able to absorb it and it contains fewer particles than cream. Doesn't it feel lovely? Can you sense the dialogue between you and your body?'

'Huh?'

The woman smiles. She just smiles.

You're so beautiful, Cecilie thinks, not quite understanding why everything turned out this way, why this woman should have the life she has while Cecile is stuck with her own life.

The woman spreads the coarse cream over Cecilie's face, it feels like grains of sand and causes a slight burning sensation.

'Does it feel okay? Some people find it a little bit rough, a tad prickly.'

No, Cecilie thinks, I only feel your fingers.

'Okay, great, now for a little tonic...'

She's touching me.

'And some serum...'

Even softer motions, a light tapping on the skin.

'Anyway, Cecilie,' the woman says after a few moments of silence, 'now we're ready for a face mask, a moisturising mask with hydralin acid – which our bodies produce less of the older we get – and collagen, to build the skin back up. Okay?'

I can't breathe, Cecilie thinks, nodding with her eyes closed. With calm movements and supple hands, the woman applies a cream with a faint odour to her face and places cotton wool pads on her eyes .

'Now you just lie there and relax for fifteen minutes while the mask takes effect. I'm stepping out for a little while. What about this fantastic weather we're suddenly getting? You know, I just have to say again, that hair colour of yours? Smashing. I'll be back soon. Think about something nice, Cecilie, think about the nicest thing you have.'

The beautiful woman leaves. Cecilie can feel the movement of her fingers across her skin, like an echo.

The nicest thing I've got?

Dad. The SodaStream.

The nicest thing I've got?

Rudi. Tong.

The nicest thing I've got?

Fags and cinnamon buns.

The nicest thing I'm going to have: my kid.

The music coming through the speakers changes. 'Bridge Over Troubled Water' has been playing since 'Imagine' ended, now the lapping of waves and the chirping of birds can be heard and the lighting above Cecilie's head is dimmed.

She falls asleep.

Cecilie dreams, she dreams in strong colours – she dreams of Tong.

She's woken up by the sound on the CD of the waves and the birds jumping. Cecilie's body feels hot; she pictures Tong, hears his breath in her head and she feels sweat form under her hairline. The CD has caught on a loop in the middle of a wave breaking on a beach; she hears a machine out in the hallway – a coffee machine? – and then voices. Two woman talking. Slightly disoriented from having slept for a few minutes in the middle of the day, she gathers herself, and then catches bits of what the voices are saying. It's the skincare woman and another girl: 'Yeah, everything's so expensive now...', '...we're going to re-landscape the whole garden next year...', '...oh, poor thing...', '...a complete wreck, I think she's a drug addict...'

Cecilie pricks up her ears.

'...you think?', '...oh, yeah, poor thing...'

The CD stops, the jumping subsides, and the skincare woman re-enters the room. Her smile is just as warm as it has been the entire session.

'Wonderful, Cecilie, now just wait. We'll cleanse ever so slightly again, apply a little tonic and serum, a few drops of oil and some eye cream – and believe me, you're going to look great.'

The skincare woman wrings the cloth over the bowl and brings it to Cecilie's face.

Cecilie keeps her eyes shut. Her lips taut and pressed hard together.

'There. Try to relax. Hm? How do you feel?'

Cecilie opens her eyes.

'Cecilie?'

She can't manage to say anything.

'Is everything all right ... are you crying?'

Cecilie turns her head away. She looks at the wall. She brings her hand to her eyes, runs a finger beneath the bottom lid of her right and left eyes and realises she's crying from both. And then she says: 'You're not the only one with a child. I'm going to have a child, too. And I'm not a junkie. But my boyfriend will steal your car while you're asleep. He'll beat up your husband when he doesn't pay up what he owes. I'm not pretty, I'm never going to be, and you're only lying when you say how nice my hair is. I listened to you talking, I can hear that you never tell the truth. You might well walk around thinking you're gorgeous and you and your friends might well think you know everything about everyone, but you're all just fucking high-heeled heifers, and I, I need a smoke and I need a cinnamon bun.'

Cecilie gets up, puts her feet on the floor. The beautiful woman stands in front of her, fright in her eyes.

'Shall we…' she says, clearing her throat, 'shall we schedule another appointment?'

'Your CD is scratched,' Cecilie says and walks out of the room.

46. **RAINING BLOOD** (Daniel William)

Locked. Daniel feels his breath being forced up his throat. Veron-ika. Don't be messing about now, okay? He presses down on the handle again, shouts, and bangs on the door, even though he knows it's pointless.

He jiggles the door handle. The only way to get her attention is if she sees it going up and down.

Nothing happens.

Daniel puts his ear to the door. He holds his breath and listens. Nothing. He would have heard if the shower was on, if the tap was running, if somebody was moving around or someone flushed the toilet. Nothing.

The lock clicks.

He gives a start, takes a step back and stands looking at the door. Nothing happens. It doesn't open. Fuck, he thinks. Am I supposed to go in? Is this a signal that I'm welcome in after all? Eh? And what does she mean by it? Am I supposed to go in all puppy-eyed, with my tail between my legs? Am I supposed to get down on my knees in front of her and apologise?

I can't be bothered with this, he thinks. I can't be assed playing along. Daniel curses himself for having landed in this situation, curses himself for not having said yes to an institution instead of a new foster home. This was bound to happen when he was left living with women.

He opens the door.

Oh Jesus.

He's unable to move.

'Veronika! What have you *done?*'

The girl is sitting on the toilet lid. She's wearing a T-shirt, the metal one, the white *Kvelertak* one he gave her for her fifteenth birthday. Her hair is dishevelled and her legs are bare.

Veronika turns her face towards him. It looks like a grid, a fine-lined mesh. There are vertical lines from her forehead down to her chin and jaws and horizontal lines going straight across her face. She's also cut her arms, streaks running down each forearm. Most of the blood has congealed and assumed the same colour as her hair. The long parallel incisions are nasty-looking and rust-coloured.

'Veronika...'

He tries to hold the tears back but can't manage, and begins to cry. He sniffles, dries his eyes and takes a step forward. She just sits there looking at him. She shrugs, gives him a lopsided grin. There are bloodstains in the bath. A razor blade lying beside the drain.

Why do I always have to see things like this, he thinks, feeling anger rise. Why can't I be left alone? Why can't I leave without things catching up with me again?

Daniel reaches out, puts his arms around Veronika and pulls her close. She's stiff at first but her body begins to warm up the longer she remains in his embrace. She places her arms on his back.

What will I do, thinks Daniel. What the hell will I do. He tenses the muscles in his jaw, squeezes his eyes shut, wanting more than anything to leave, get to the Suzuki and ride, but he can't do that now.

After a while he relaxes his embrace and pulls his head back a little to look at her. The lines on her face are straight, she's carried it out with precision, cut herself up carefully and thoroughly, from top to bottom and side to side, with her eyes open, in front of the mirror.

Daniel opens his mouth.

'How deep are they?'

No reply.

'How deep?'

He brings his hand to her face, traces the incisions with two fingertips. The cuts are superficial, not extending far below the surface. 'You have to promise me never to do that again,' he says.

She turns her head when he speaks. That's what she does when she doesn't want to listen to people. He takes hold of her chin, feeling the cuts against his fingers again, turns her to face him and says: 'Veronika. Look at me. You have to promise never to do that again.'

She closes her mouth, tightens her lips.

'Well? Say something.'

She shakes her head.

'What is it I've done to you?'

She's crying. Fuck, that's almost worse.

'Don't cry,' he says. 'I didn't know about this. How could I have known?'

Veronika raises her right hand, sniffles, the tears cease. She extends her index finger and pokes him on the chest with it. 'Your heart,' she says, 'it's raining blood in there.'

She does this sometimes, says zombielike things – they just fall out of that sky she has inside her head.

'Jesus, you're one unusual girl, Veronika,' he says.

She taps her fingers on his chest. 'Say it once more.' Veronika moves a little closer to him. 'Say it once more.'

You're not the one I want.

'Say it again. Say that I'm one unusual girl.'

He smooths away a wisp of hair from her cheek, it was stuck in the moisture from her tears.

'You have to promise me never to do that again. I won't stand for it. Once more, and I leave.'

'Don't speak so fast.'

'I'll leave,' he repeats. 'And I'll be gone for good. And when I go for good, I never look back. Do you understand?'

She nods.

'Say it. Say it once more.'

'You're one unusual girl, Veronika,' he says, conscious of meaning it.

She nods.

'Doesn't it hurt?' He strokes her gently across the face.

'No,' she says, 'it doesn't hurt now.'

'Christ.' Daniel exhales heavily.

'I like this T-shirt,' she says, pulling at it a little, making the cotton taut against her tits.

'Mhm,' he says, nodding. 'It's the bollocks.'

'The bollocks?'

He nods. 'The dog's bollocks. A deaf girl going round wearing it.'

'Yeah,' she says, and moistens her lips. 'The dog's bollocks.'

Daniel runs his hands through his hair. 'But what are you going to say to Inger? Are you just going to ... what are you planning to say?'

Veronika shrugs. She sits down on the edge of the bathtub. 'I don't know. She'll just have to deal with it. I'm not dead. I'm just deaf.'

She giggles, the atonal laughter resounding more than usual. He laughs too, he can't help it. Stuff she comes out with, sometimes she really hits the mark.

'God, you're weird.' Daniel shakes his head, looks at her sternly. 'You do know that I have ... that there's another girl that I'm ... going out with. Yeah? You do know that?

She nods.

'Yeah?' he shrugs. 'And so? Don't you respect that?'

'We're competitors.' Veronika looks him straight in the eye. 'Does she have a *Kvelertak* T-shirt?' Veronika shakes her head. 'No, she's slavers after Jesus. She wears a cross round her neck. I know you think you love her. I know you think that she's the one you want. But I know that it's raining blood in your heart, Daniel. I know who you are. Does she know who you are?'

He swallows.

'Hm? Does she?'

47. **PAIN** (Sandra)

Caught up in something.

That's what it feels like.

Strange sitting here now. The teacher talking, the pupils sitting with their books open in front of them. But none of them are listening. They're all thinking about her. The teacher too. She can feel it. Nobody in the room is thinking about anything else.

From one second to the next, Sandra has gone from being the most well-behaved, conscientious girl in 10D to becoming the object of everyone's open-mouthed attention. She'd cracked a few hours ago, lost herself, snogged Daniel and cried when he rode off, while everyone stood at the windows watching. Then the rumour began racing through the school like a fierce wind, the teachers tried to hush it up but it was just as though she'd unleashed a force of nature. When she went into the yard during the break it was like she was a magnet. Malene had walked alongside her as if they were blood sisters; comments had been shouted in their direction, as though both of them had done something crazy and within a few hours it had got completely out of control.

The rumour was that he'd hit her, it was also going around that she'd hit him, that she was pregnant, that she was on something...

She was just caught up in it.

Then at lunchtime, right out of the blue, Tiril had hit that little guy in second year, Shaun, and she had done it for her. Everything has been turned on its head. *Tiril?* If there's one person Sandra feels has never liked her, if there's one person she's almost been afraid of, it's Malene's sister, her co-worker at Spar.

She just let him have it, Shaun the smurf.

So, what, now it's like, her and the sisters? Her and Malene and Tiril? And where's Daniel? His replies were so curt. *Okay. Okay, fine.* Where is he? She realises she's done something he's not able to take, but why is he so angry? He said he'd be there tonight although she's not sure she quite believes it.

Sandra sits with her maths book open in front of her, hardly daring to breathe.

Not to mention Mum and Dad. If they don't already know everything by the time she gets home, then it won't take long before they hear about it and that won't be good. They'll tell her off, issue more warnings and deliver another lecture, but the worst of it is they won't allow her to see him. *That bright mouth. Daniel William Moi.* And if they do that, she'll just die. She can't go home. Sandra knows that. She can't go home today.

There's a sound of laughter in the classroom.

'Mira? Something you wanted to say?'

The teacher.

'No, Miss. Nothing,' Mira says.

Sandra can hear her sniggering. She can hear it spreading. Other girls laughing. Other boys. Joachim, he's laughing too.

She glances up furtively, trying to make eye contact with Malene.

Malene nods to her.

Her chest rises and falls. Sandra gets quickly to her feet. She packs her things together as fast as she's able. The entire class is looking at her. Mira's cheeky face. Joachim's smirk.

'I don't feel too well—'

A ripple of laughter.

'I think I need to—'

'Ooh, I need it! Daniel, I need it!' Joachim.

'That's all right, Sandra,' she hears the teacher say.

She walks towards the door. She stops at Malene's desk on the way, her friend smiles at her and takes hold of her hand a moment. Sandra's seen that smile before. She's seen it on a grown man's face. Malene's father. She feels like a fraud, she isn't sure if it's right, what Daniel said, about not telling her anything about her father, but she has to trust the one she loves.

'See you,' Malene whispers. 'Where are you going?'

'Dunno.'

'Text me, okay?'

Sandra nods.

'Say hello to Tiril,' she whispers.

Malene smiles. 'Hey,' she says. 'Don't worry. Okay?'

'No,' Sandra whispers, hearing her voice beginning to crack.

She runs. One hand under her breasts, the other waving in the air, slightly knock-kneed, through the corridors, out the front entrance, into the mild September day.

48. **A FRIEND WITH A VAN** (Jan Inge)

It looks like a wading bird and a duck out for a walk.

The sun is low in the sky, its light casting long shadows along the streets as Jan Inge and Rudi make their way uphill from the house by the rail tracks. It's not that far to Hansi's place; he lives on the far side of Hillevågsveien.

Jan Inge is conscious that he's developed a somewhat rolling gait of late. He tries to avoid doing it, but he just sort of swings, from side to side, no matter how he tries to adjust it.

There's been something agitated and unfocused about Rudi ever since he got back from town. He hurried into the house, went straight to his room, rummaged around a bit, then came out and stood in the middle of the living room looking at his mobile. When Jan Inge asked if anything was wrong, he'd replied: 'No, what the hell would be?'

But there is something wrong.

After they've passed Sun City tanning salon and started up the hill towards Hansi's, Jan Inge asks again: 'Rudi, what is it, you're not even talking?'

'Man, people don't need to talk all the time, do they?'

No, but when people who do talk all the time suddenly stop, that's when you get nervous. So Jan Inge tries once more: 'We're here for one another, you know that, right?'

Rudi halts. His long form swaying to and fro in front of a wheelie bin. His eyes are restive.

'I don't know, Jani. I just got it into my head.'

'What?' Jan Inge wheezes, taking out his inhaler and sucking in air.

'Chessi,' Rudi says.

Jan Inge raises his eyebrows. 'Chessi? What about Chessi?'

'What the hell do I know.' Rudi leans his hands on the bin behind him for support. 'Probably just some bullshit. The puking. That skincare shit. And ... well, some private stuff.'

'Private stuff?' Jan Inge cocks his head to the side. 'Is it your brother?'

'You don't bloody well have to mention him! No,' Rudi says. 'Very private stuff. Shit, I need a fag.'

'What kind of very private stuff?'

'No,' says Rudi shrugging, 'we are amigos, my friend, but there're things even brothers don't discuss. Woman things, Jani. Anyway. She's heading over to see Tong and she needs the Volvo. So we really have to get hold of Hansi's Transporter.'

Rudi is seldom like this. Calm, almost. Normal, almost. Talking in short sentences. Chiselling them out of himself as though he were of stone. Even though Jan Inge does often want Rudi to calm that electric head of his and stop talking holes in peoples' heads, it is disturbing when he's not acting like himself.

'Well,' Jan Inge says, 'I'm sure it'll sort itself out. But we probably shouldn't drive the Transporter around Gosen two nights on the trot...'

Rudi's eyes flash.

'Oh yeah, great, what are we going to do? Take the fucking *bus?* Is that what you want to do, busfuck?'

He's cross, clearly angry. He's never usually like that either.

'Rudi, listen to me. You've got something in your system. I know you. Get it out or get shot of it. We've a sweet job on tomorrow, a classic in our line of business. So we can't drive around in the work van in the same area two nights in a row. You know that. It's not going to kill us to take the bus.'

'They can stick their public transport up their hole as far as I'm concerned, Rudi says. 'I hate buses, I've always hated buses.'

Jan Inge tries to make eye contact with him. '*Hei, mein Freund,*' he says, trying to lighten the atmosphere with a little German, '*ein Pfennig für deine Gedanken.*'

'I'm not thinking about anything,' Rudi sighs, 'It's ... *Scheisse.* It's just feelings. Feelings feelings feelings! You just can't always bloody well describe feelings.'

Well said, Jan Inge thinks, and they continue on their way up the incline. The mystical sun warms their faces. I'll leave it alone, he thinks; right now it's all about solid leadership.

'It's like I'm always telling you,' he says, in as mild a tone as he can muster. 'You're an emotional person, Rudi, you do your best, day in, day out, and then a whole army of feelings invades your body, and that's just how life is. Come on, let's wake up Hansi.'

Hansi is a thin guy, whose slightly mangy appearance tends to put people in mind of a dog. He's been in and out of prison since he was nineteen, and on opening the door to his two old friends, he scarcely raises his eyebrows, before motioning with a wan hand for them to come in while he shuffles back into the house.

'Hi, man, feeling a bit rough today?'

Jan Inge and Rudi exchange a look and follow him. They enter the living room, where Hansi plonks himself down in an old sofa centred behind a coffee table covered with liquor bottles.

'I'm drinking a bit at the moment,' he mutters. 'Working a lot. Been over and back to Sweden loads, to Gothenburg. Not right in the head, those Albanians. How are things in Toyland? What's going on in the lives of Sly and Gobbo? Any break-ins lately?'

Hansi grins, brings a liquor bottle to his lips and takes a large swig. Jan Inge bunches the muscles in his jaw tightly. You look like my mother, he thinks.

'What do you g—'

'We need a loan of the van,' interrupts Jan Inge. 'And the trailer.'

Hansi looks at them askance. 'And so the two of you turn up here and think everything is going to be sitting waiting for you?'

Rudi keeps his mouth shut. Jan Inge doesn't move a muscle.

'Okay, okay,' Hansi says, 'fine. And what if I say I need them myself? If I tell you that you can't have a loan of them?'

'Then we'll say—'

'Then we'll know where we stand with you,' says Jan Inge curtly. 'You owe us, Hansi.'

He gives Rudi a brief nod.

Hansi looks from one of them to the other. 'And how long am I to go on owing you?'

'Listen.' Jan Inge's eyes narrow. 'We've been fair to you. We could have smashed your kneecaps. After what you did. We could have let people know the kinds of things you like to get up to. We haven't done either.'

Hansi gets to his feet, takes another quaff of the bottle and picks up a pair of trousers hanging over the back of a chair. He rummages through the pockets, pulls out a key ring.

'You're a loser, Jani, and you know it. You've been at it for thirty fucking years or something, and you haven't ... yeah, fuck it, whatever. Here.'

He chucks the keys to Jan Inge. Rudi inhales quickly, takes a few steps, grabs hold of Hansi's head, glares in his eyes and headbutts him.

'You never fucking talk that way to Jani, you hear me!'

'Shit, I'm bleeding!'

'Fucking right you're bleeding, motherbleedfucker! You want to bleed some more? Eh? You want to bleed out your ears? You want to bleed out your ass?'

Jan Inge smiles. He loves this. He fucking loves this.

Rudi. Rudi. Rudi.

'You want to bleed inside your head?'

'No! No! Rudi! Jesus!'

It's just like Jan Inge is at a football stadium and thousands upon thousands of people are standing with their arms in the air and their mouths open, shouting: Ru-di! Ru-di! Ru-di!

Rudi's body tenses, almost to the extent that Jan Inge can see the adrenalin surge through his arms and legs as he kicks Hansi repeatedly in the back, as he crouches down, lifts Hansi up by the hair and plants his fist in his face.

'Now,' Rudi says, straightening up. He grasps his knuckles, then shakes off the pain and spits on Hansi: 'You keep your mouth shut, cockbreath. Loser? Who the hell's the loser here?'

Hansi lies on the floor writhing in pain.

'Rudi can't hear you,' Rudi grabs hold of the bottle Hansi was drinking from. He stands over him. 'Open your gob, daisy-picker.'

'W-wha?'

Peeping at him in terror, blood all over his face, Hansi opens his mouth.

'Wider!'

'Wwwider?'

'Wider!'

Hansi opens wide and Rudi empties the remaining contents of the bottle down his throat. 'Hey, cockaholic! You drinking a bit at the moment? Drink some more! Hey, buttaholic, I didn't hear you? Who's the loser?'

Hansi coughs and spits, blood and booze. 'Me,' comes the meek voice from the floor.

'Toofuckingright,' Rudi snorts. 'And the next time you say anything out of order about the Master, I'll skin your dick, and the next time you put your cock into one of the schoolboys round here, I'll be fifteen metres away, and fifteen seconds after you're finished I'll jam fifteen cactuses up your ass.'

Jan Inge clenches his fist tighter around the key ring.

This here, this is what makes life worth living.

'Hansi,' he says, 'you're a really good ... what is it they say in Sweden ... a *jättegod* ... friend. You'll get the Transporter and the trailer back over the weekend. No problem. Really appreciate it.'

They walk back out the front door, to the front of the house.

'About fucking time, that there,' Rudi says, glowing.

'Felt right, no doubt about it,' Jan Inge says, lumbering towards Hansi's grey Transporter.

'Tong would have enjoyed that,' says Rudi, opening the driver's door.

'Cecilie would have enjoyed that,' replies Jan Inge.

'That's my woman,' Rudi says, getting inside. 'What are we having for dinner?'

'Fishcakes,' says Jan Inge, landing in the seat, the van listing with his weight.

Rudi sticks the key in and starts the engine. 'Fishcakes,' he says, reversing out the drive, 'remind me of Granny. The good, old days.'

'I know,' says Jan Inge. 'And listen, what you were brooding over earlier, the private stuff and all that, you need to just shelve that.'

'Hell yeah,' Rudi says, as the sun, low in the sky, hits the windscreen and dazzles him momentarily, making the whole world gleaming and white, 'it's just I'm so fucking sensitive sometimes.'

The van glides down the street.

'Ah.' Rudi lets out a deep breath. 'Jumping Jiminy, that felt good. Jesus, it's been a long time since I've used my fists. Right, I'm going to make a call here!'

Rudi takes out his mobile, turns to Jan Inge and gives him a nod and a wink. He chortles to himself as he leans over to the glove compartment, roots around in it a little, fetches out a pen and paper, tosses it into Jan Inge's large lap and says, in a low, rasping tone: 'Now, pay attention, busfuck.'

49. **ADD TO CART** (Pål)

That the days should be so filled with lies. He doesn't understand how he has managed to sink so deeply into it. One lie. Okay. It's no big deal. It feels uncomfortable, like sticking your hand into a compost heap on a warm day, but the discomfort soon passes. Two lies. Fair enough. You shake them off. And then a third lie to cover up the preceding ones. Not quite so pleasant, what that entails. The stories need to correspond, need to fit together. Your face, it needs to fit too; it needs to match who you are. But who are you? What world are you living in? A fourth lie to correlate all the stories. It starts getting heavier, starts to whiten. It starts snowing inside you.

What happens is that you begin to get good at it. You loosen up, your gestures become uninhibited and plausible, and your face, which was nervous the first few times, takes on a similarly assured look. In a surprisingly short space of time none of the original distress is visible. Your face melts together with the lies. You start to see the world the way the lies explain it, and it doesn't take long before you defend them, tend to them, and cuddle them, ugly children that they are.

He doesn't think about anything else. He gets up, makes breakfast, and drives off in the car, doing 30 in the morning traffic, and the lies fill his whole head, his whole being. It has become a world of its own. Once they were necessary stories, sentences uttered to wriggle free from a situation. Then they became the narrative of a life. Then they became something to live. Something true. *I just stayed up last night surfing the net. I'm just going to take Zitha out for a walk.* Is that how it fits together? That the lies are now the truth? That without them he does not exist, because they are what he resorts to every day in order to keep it together?

A little earlier he went into his boss, smiled, and said: 'I need to take off for a couple of hours, one of my daughters is sick.'

It felt good to say it, as if there was a girl lying at home with a temperature, who needed her daddy. He saw the lie materialise in front of him. He saw it take effect, spring to life and become real.

'Poor thing, by all means, you take off home, Pål.'

He turns off the motorway, drives uphill at Ullandhaugbakken. To tear down an entire life. It's so easy.

Three things have ruined everything. The wife. The money. And the lies.

Day one for the whole thing, was when Christine came home and said *I need to talk to you, Pål*. She spoke calmly, almost in a whisper, and told him that it wasn't working. *Wasn't working*. There's no passion. *No passion?* I've met somebody. Hell opened up around them, kids dissolving in tears. Jesus, he'd never forget Malene's face and the feeling of having smashed a child to pieces. But Christine managed to see it through. She had the strength to go ahead with it. She left, for Bergen and another bloody man. As though she wasn't a mother at all. She managed to *leave her kids*. That took some doing. Everyone he has talked to agrees. Everyone – especially women – agree that it's an action bordering on inhuman. Jesus! They exclaim. She just left? And you're stuck here? Yeah. It was that situation, and everything it ushered in. A single dad, just like that. Who had prepared him for it?

But he coped. Touch wood.

Then came the next phase: money.

Never being able to buy the kids anything extra. Always having to search the papers for special offers on mince, on sausages, frozen pizza and fuck knows what else. That horrible feeling when he and the children were round at Mum's for Sunday dinner, and all he could think was: free meal. That horrible feeling of gladness when the girls were invited round to school friends' homes during the week: they'll get something to eat there.

Before he started winning, and losing, there were no lies to be found in his life. Perhaps there was shame, perhaps an insidious desperation, a sense of relief when the kids got plenty of gifts at Christmas and on birthdays, but there were no lies. Or were there.

The lies came with the money – or did they come when he started losing it?

Is he thinking clearly now? Has he always had them in him? The lies?

No, I haven't, he says to himself as the tower blocks come into view.

I'm not thinking very clearly now.

He drives down Folkeviseveien. Past the bin at the bus shelter where he usually gets rid of everything he can't face opening. Letters from debt collection agencies. Bills. His hands are sweating, sticking to the leather of the steering wheel. Someday they'll be at the door. The police, the betting companies and the debt collectors. They'll soon be there.

He brings the car to a halt, puts on the handbrake, releases the seat belt, grits his teeth, rubs his eye with the back of his hand, and then hurries into the house. Down to the basement. Over to the computer. His pulse is pounding like a fist. He needs to get a move on, get a move on before things catch up with him, he just needs to do it, one last time.

Username: Maiden.

His fingers stiffen, they are cold. He performs a quick wrist stretch and finger flex, blows on them, places them back on the keyboard: do it, one last try, there's still time to get out of this, there's still time to avoid meeting Rudi.

Password: Zitha

Blackjack.

'Dad?'

Pål gives a start, moves the mouse to click on the little x in the top right corner of the screen, but the arrow veers here and there, and his fingers tremble.

Footsteps coming down the stairs.

Shit, shit, shit. This bloody machine, it's so slow.

'Dad?'

He hears her in the hall, just outside the door.

There. He manages to close the webpage. And there. He manages to open the one he always keeps minimised, just in case.

'Dad? You home? I saw the car...'

Malene walks into the room.

'Yeah, I...' Pål sighs wearily, offers her a quick glance and taps his feet against the floor. 'Well...' He begins to laugh. 'No, it's kind of stupid, Malene, I...' His laughter gets louder, gets dangerously close to seeming unnatural. 'Well, I've been thinking a lot about what you said about Tiril, about me not giving her enough attention ... so I was sitting here trying to see if I could find an Evanescence T-shirt for her.'

He laughs. Loudly. She looks askance at him.

He types quickly: www.evanescence.com. Trying to make it look as practised as possible. Enter site. Merch.

'There, eh? Nice T-shirts, eh?'

He points at the screen. Malene leans forward, squinting over his shoulder.

'They look good, don't they? What about that one?'

'I think that band is stupid,' she says. 'But she'll love you for it.'

She looks at him obliquely. He gets to his feet, pulls her close, hugging her so she won't see his face, which right now is not able to keep the lies in place.

'So, school?' he says. 'Everything going okay?'

'Yeah, fine,' says Malene. She frees herself from his embrace, avoids his eyes. 'Nothing special happened. Had an all right day. Just doing my homework now. Tiril won't be home for dinner, but you haven't forgotten that. She's rehearsing for tomorrow.'

Malene jogs up the stairs. 'You do the shopping, yeah?'

'Yes!' He calls out, admiring the tone and high pitch of his own voice. 'No problem!'

Pål sits back down in front of the computer.

There is no collection agency, no online gaming, no tears, nothing.

Women's. Dark Angel Babydoll T. Front and Back Print. $20.00. Add to cart.

50. **LUDVIG NILSEN AND ALBERT JENSEN**
   (Rudi)

'Yes, hello, this is Ludvig Nilsen speaking. Now, I wanted to get from Hillevåg to Gosen tonight, heh heh.'

'By bus?'

'Yes, by bus. Public transport. Knights of the environment. Nature's best friend.'

'Okay, then you must take a number 7.'

'Must I?'

'Yes, and you must hop on that either at Tjensvollkrysset – a number 3 will take you there from Hillevåg – or...'

'Didn't you just say a number 7?'

'Yes, but in order to get the 7, the easiest thing for you to do would be to hop on at Tjensvollkrysset, and to get there you'll need to take the 3 from Hillevåg, or take it into the city centre and then catch a number 1. From Hillevåg. To Stavanger Station.'

'Stavanger Station?'

'Yeah, Stavanger Station.'

'The train station, you mean.'

'No, or rather, yes, by the train station, yes. You could say that.'

'Listen, Jani! We either need to take the number 3 to Tjensvollkrysset, or the number 1 into town, write that down! And then ... hold on a sec ... then take the number 7 from town, at the train station?'

'Yes, from Stavanger Station.'

'Jani! From town. Down by the train station. The number 7 to Gosen! Whoops, shit! What? No, no. We're just out for a drive, hands-free! Heh heh. Okay. Next question, Miss Bus. If we want to be at ... what the hell's the name of ... Madlavoll school and—'

'Then you must get off at Gosen Kindergarten. At the turnaround there.'

'The turnaround, right! Okay, if we need to be there at ten o'clock then what time do we take the bus from town? And what time should we catch the bus at Tjensvollkrysset? Assuming we choose that alternative.'

'Ten o'clock...'

'Yeah, ten o'clock. Now we're talking.'

'Yes, then that would be ... no, I seem to have read that wrong...'

'It happens.'

'The best thing for you to do would be take the number 2 from Hillevåg to—'

'So it's the number 2 now?'

'The 2, yes, the 2 from Hillevåg to—'

'Hey, Jani, cross out the 3 and 10 there. It's the number 2 to—'

'Yes, so it's the number 2 from Hillevåg, departing 21:01—'

'And when you say Hillevåg, just so we're clear, you mean—'

'The stop on the main road, just after Baneveien, travelling into the city—'

'*Kein Problem*, you're talking to a local here – so that's the number 2 from Hillevåg at 21:01 – hey, you writing this down, Jani? Yeah I know it's bumpy, that's why they call them speed bumps. The number 2 from Hillevåg at 21:01 – right, and then?'

'And that'll drop you off in the city, by—'

'Hey! Girl! We're not talking by the cathedral here, are we? The Nokas building?'

'No, you must go to the other side of Breiavannet Lake, you'll arrive at stop fourteen, which is close to what you refer to as the train station—'

'I see! We're back there again!'

'Then you walk a few metres to stop ... nineteen, and you wait there until 21:15—'

'Jani, write this down, get off at stop fourteen, walk to stop nineteen, wait until 21:15 – okay, we wait a while?'

'Yeah, and then you take the 7—'

'Heh heh! There she comes! The 7! I'd say the 7 has been going to Gosen for more years than anyone can remember, the bus never goes out of fashion – heh heh, I could tell you, girl, a thing or two about what doesn't go out of style! Fishcakes, to give you a little clue! The good, old number 7, a stalwart – and then Ludvig Nilsen and his friend Albert Jensen will be at Gosen Kindergarten at what time exactly?'

'21:25. In ten minutes.'

'Do you get that, Jani? Ha. Ten minutes. Eh? Not bad. Public transport.'

'Oops, oh no, I'm afraid I've given you—'

'No need to apologise, *Fräulein*! Don't stand with your cap in your hand! Don't bow and scrape like you were a Romanian beggar! It's fine – we're all only human. Now let's take it smoooooothly one more time – was it the 3? The 6? The 1? Do you want it up where your number two comes from? Heh heh!'

'Eh, it doesn't go right up to the kindergarten. You must get off in Madlamarkveien, and from there you make your way to the kindergarten. It will take you ten minutes by foot.'

'By foot? Do you know what Granny called that? The Apostles' horses. That's from the Bible. Deuteronmomy. Or Acts of the Apostles! Oh yes, The Good Book. There wasn't too much bussing back then, so to speak, *Fräulein*! It was all camels and sandals! But now that I've got you on the line, do I detect a slight accent? And the thing you keep saying about what Nilsen and Jensen *must* do?'

'Heh heh.'

'Heh heh, your Norwegian is flawless, I'm guessing you've lived here for quite a while ... Might we be talking Germany, *Mädchen*?'

'Hannover.'

'Hannover, to be exact. And who else is from Hannover?'

'What do you mean? I'm from Hannover...'

'Yess, baby, you and Scorpions.'

'Ha ha!'

'Heh heh, you got a little laugh out of that, Gerda!'

'My name isn't Gerda...'

'No, that's just something we say. Oh! Gerda! *Ja*! *Bitte*!'

'Ulrike, my name's Ulrike.'

'Okay, okay, no names, honey, no names.'

'Well, have a *gute* trip to Gosen Woods then.'

'The same to you, Ulrike! And now you could say that Nilsen and Jensen are back home; now the light of this bright September day is shining down on us all; now the whole of society is heading home for dinner, and I've had a chance to employ my fists, you've had an opportunity to employ your expertise and Jensen here, he's had occasion to put that big brain of his to a little use. And if that doesn't make for a good day, then we may as well bang it all intoouterspace – trip, Gerda? Did you say trip? This whole life's a trip! *Ich habe eine grosse in die Hose*! Rock you like a hurricane!'

51. **MALENE UNDRESSES** (Malene)

Malene walks into the bathroom. She locks the door and takes a step towards the mirror. She fixes her gaze on its surface and focuses on the reflection of her own eyes. 'Am I pretty?' she whispers to the face she sees, and the face mouths back. 'Am I beautiful?' She narrows her eyes, squints. She sucks in her cheeks, sees her cheekbones become even more prominent and she pouts tentatively. 'Am I sexy?' Malene takes her hand to the back of her head, takes hold of her hair and lifts it. A boy said that to her once: *You should always wear your hair like that, looks well cute.* Oliver in 10B. Cockwad. Gamer. He goes to LAN parties and stays up all night. He won some endurance contest recently, played for hours on end in a big hall, fell asleep and was woken up by the laptop burning the side of his face like a hotplate. Retard. But even idiots have eyes in their heads and maybe he's right?

Malene can see what he's talking about. She does have nice hair, always has had, shiny and strong. It takes on a whole other look when she tousles it, takes it up and avoids letting it just hang straight down. And a nice body, she knows she has that. A gymnast's body. But unlike a lot of the other girls she's always found it hard to relate to that sort of thing ... nice body, yeah, so? It's like the cheekbones; should she go round trying to show them off all the time? Or draw attention to them? What if you don't feel comfortable with that, sticking your tits out, being so much about your body all the time. What do you do then?

Quit biting her nails, she'll have to do that in any case.

Aunt Ingrid has no problem with it; she walks around in extremely tight tops and pants, she has the deepest cleavage in Rogaland, and she's loud and brash. The girl is such a hussy, Gran always says, and then she'll explain what it means: hussy, that's what we used to call girls like that. They're so full of themselves and into themselves, all flirty and shameless – and my daughter, she's like that. Ah, give it a rest, Aunt Ingrid says, I've been listening to that since 1980. I'm a woman and I choose how I look and how I dress, Mummy.

Is it Gran who's right or is it Aunt Ingrid who's right?

Sandra: *I love him.*

Tiril: *The next time you say a fucking word about my sister, about Sandra...*

She planted her fist right in Bunny's little brother's face. She's always been like that. She's always gone that little bit further than the rest, always been a bit extreme. What is it Mum says: *Tiril can be a little over the top sometimes.* Then again she could just as well be describing herself, couldn't she?

There have been times Malene has been jealous of Tiril. She's witnessed her explode and experienced admiration and astonishment in equal measure, but she's never once wished that she was like that. She wouldn't be able to handle it, having such a tumult going on inside. No control. The feeling that anything can happen. But now?

She lets go of her hair. Lifts the toilet lid. Unzips the flies of her jeans, pulls down her knickers, sits down and pees.

There's something creeping around inside her.

Something making her body tingle.

She's warm.

What is it?

It's been a day of surprises; Sandra left her flabbergasted, Tiril has gone further than usual, and as for herself ... she's even been taken aback by her own actions. It's as though – she tears off a sheet of toilet roll, dries herself – as though ... she stands up and presses the handle. As though there's another Malene trying to force her way out. As if something has come loose. Or something is running wild. A little animal ... is it a little animal? It's as though every thought she's ever had about being careful, about not wanting any change, no longer counts. As if they're no longer true.

She's so hot. Something is tingling inside.

She goes back to the sink, lathers the soap and turns on the tap.

She lets the water run over her hands while looking in the mirror again. Am I pretty? Am I sexy?

'Malene? You there? Listen, I'm off to the shops, okay?'

Dad's standing in the hall. She can picture him. Eyebrows raised a fraction. Head cocked ever so slightly to the side. His kind eyes.

'Yeah, okay,' she replies while looking at how flushed her cheeks are.

'All right! Great! See you!'

The front door slams.

What is going on with Dad? Something's up. Is he surfing porn on the net? Is he chatting with women? Maybe that's why he's so distant. Jesus, as long as it's not a woman from the Philippines or something.

Malene wipes her forehead. What is she so warm – is she getting sick? The tingling, what is that?

Her mobile rings. The display lights up. Sandra. She answers it: 'Hello, Malene speaking.'

She hears sniffling on the other end of the line.

'Hello,' she says again, as if she doesn't know who it is, 'Malene here.'

'Hi, it's me,' Sandra's voice is meek.

'Hi, where are you? How are you feeling?'

Sandra sniffs once more. 'I...'

There's a sudden loud noise on the line, then a pause.

'Hold on, such a racket here ... they're digging up the road ... just going to ... that's better. You there?'

Malene lets the cold tap run for a while, then places her free hand under it before bringing it to the back of her neck.

'Yeah.'

'I'm in town,' says Sandra.

'Okay?' Malene feels the water cool her down, she shuts her eyes.

'I'm, eh...'

'But where have you been? Since you left?'

'Nowhere. All over. I went into town. I—'

Sandra begins to cry.

'Hey, hey, don't cry, what is it?' Malene opens her eyes, looks at the mirror, her cheeks are red.

'I don't know ... I ... Sandra sniffles, 'I just can't take this, I don't know what I'm going to do, he ... he—'

'Who?'

'Daniel...'

Malene takes her hands to her face. She's burning up, her cheeks, her forehead, her lips. 'What about Daniel,' she asks. 'Has he done something to you?'

'No, he just ...' Sandra sniffs again. 'He's not here. He's not even answering his phone. We're supposed to see each other tonight, but ... can you come and meet me?'

'Where?'

'In town. I was thinking of buying a headscarf...'

'Okay. I'll come. I might be a little while though...'

'That's fine. I'll be sitting outside *Kulturhuset*. Or I might go to McDonald's. Just text me.'

'Okay, Sandra. I'll be there. Just give me a little time, okay?'

She hangs up. The gymnastics queen, ice queen, silver queen. Malene opens the cabinet above the sink. She takes out the lipstick. Removes the top from the holder. Pouts. Feels a tingling inside.

Malene undresses, runs a bath, steps into the tub and touches herself.

52. BUNNY'S BIG BROTHER (Tiril)

Tiril is standing in Thea's kitchen, her chin thrust forward and resting on her hands, elbows leaning on the worktop. The light outside assails the window, almost in desperation, as though it'll fragment into something unknown at any moment. Tiril tries staring at it, but has to give in. She squints, blinking such that her eyelashes quiver in front of her vision, like a jittery fog.

'Thea, you coming or what?'

They're always able to hang out at Thea's after school, never anyone else home until late. Her parents work so much; her dad is part of the management of Schlumberger and her mum works in marketing or advertising – they've no problem with Thea having people over. They're cool, Thea's folks. The family might be moving to Brussels, actually, something to do with her dad's job. Thea takes private piano lessons. Her parents like Tiril, even though her dad is always slagging her off, saying there are other colours in the world besides black. No, she says, black isn't a colour – black is the absence of light. Heh heh. That makes him laugh, he likes those kinds of answers.

'Thea! Jesus, are you planning to get a move on?'

They have a lot to do. They're going to go through the plan for tomorrow, discuss all the things they need, what's left to do, and they're going to fine tune the choreography before tonight's dry run.

The radio plays on the windowsill, Thea's in the bathroom. Tiril traces her nail along the slit in her skirt and glances down at her hands. Can just about make out the faint lettering. She scrubbed off the tattoo – it just felt wrong somehow – after she gave Bunny's little brother a wallop. Almost as if the act itself had made the letters fall off her fingers.

She'd never hit anyone before. It hurt like hell when her hand made contact with his face, but at the same time it felt great. Right after she landed the punch a taste spread through her mouth, a pleasant taste, like vanilla. Tiril hopes Sandra and Malene realise that she did it for them. Because Malene struck her. Because Sandra needed help. She did it for Dad too, in a way. Shaun? Shaun's a maggot; it wasn't about him, that whole family are maggots. If they kick up a stink at school she can say it was about Shaun, that she acted in self-defence, that he's been pestering and picking at her for about a year, that she had to defend herself.

But it's not true. She did it for Malene. For Sandra. And for Dad.

Not that Tiril is superstitious. But.

It's a feeling she has.

Of things being connected.

For instance, if something is up with Dad – and Malene could be right – then her standing up for him might help. Even though the action she carries out may not be directly related to him, that's what she feels: that when she walloped Bunny's little brother, it made Dad's heart stronger.

Malene can sit in his lap. That's how it's always been. Tiril can't. It doesn't feel right. The few times she's tried to copy Malene and crawl on to his lap it felt like she was sitting on sharp stones. She can't do it. But she can do this.

Besides, nobody's said anything. She hasn't been told to go to the principal's office. People stared at her. They whispered and pointed. They were afraid, they didn't know what to say, they didn't know what to do. But everyone understood that she had a right to do it.

Tiril runs her nail quickly along the slit in her skirt, as though she were striking a match. She feels like having a smoke now, but there's no chance. Thea's parents are complete Nazis when it comes to smoking. If they knew Thea smoked now and again they'd hit the roof, and if they found a cigarette butt outside the house, even some flicked ash, they'd be furious. Once, she was out smoking on Thea's veranda and Thea was almost in tears; she said they'd smell it when they got home. Smell it? They won't be home for another three hours. It'll seep into the house, said Thea.

'Hello! Thea! Are you coming or what?'

She turns off the radio as Rihanna's new single comes on, can't bear that slut or her music.

'Thea! Come on! Let me have a look at you!'

What was that?

Tiril straightens up and looks out.

She catches sight of some movement in the garden.

She cranes her neck and squints against the strong light above the lawn. The sun shining in beams through the branches of the apple tree. No, nothing. A cat, probably. She gets to her feet, walks over and opens the fridge. It's filled with food. Always is in Thea's house. Apple juice and orange juice. Always both. Milk and yoghurt. Cold cuts, several types of cheese and lots of vegetables. A bowl of fruit on the table. As well as one in the living room. Fresh grapes. They've plenty of money, Thea's family. They've two cars. One for each parent. They've a cabin, up in Ålsheia. Big place. Bigger than their house. Always smells nice in their home – they have a cleaning lady who comes once a week, a Polish girl. They've paintings on the walls, the whole hall is filled with framed family photos. Sort of prim, in a way, but nice as well. Thea has an iPad with retina display and she's ordered an iPhone 5. It's difficult not to be jealous of her.

Tiril takes out the apple juice, reaches for a glass in the cupboard above and pours herself some.

There it is again.

She stands stock-still. Squints.

A disturbance in her field of vision once more, as though something or other passed by out in the garden.

Tiril takes a sip of juice while her eyes narrow. She scans the lawn, between the trees and lets her gaze sweep along the hedge.

No, there's nothing.

'Thea!' She turns towards the hall. 'What is taking you so long, you coming or what?'

Tiril gives a start when she hears a thud, a loud one, as if something fell against the house. As though someone hurled a hammer at the wall. She feels a chill take hold and spread across the back of her neck, right below the hairline, like a cold hand was just placed there. Her chest tightens.

'Thea!'

She takes a few steps backwards across the floor of the kitchen, reaching the table and remaining there, one hand on the back of a chair, her eyes flitting from window frame to window frame. A door opens behind her, she turns quickly. Thea comes gliding across the floor all in white.

'What was that?' she asks, knitting her brows. 'Did you hear it?'

Tiril swallows, doesn't manage to comment on the outfit, just nods.

'What was it?'

Tiril shrugs, Thea draws up beside her.

'Tiril, what is it? Say something – do I not look good?'

'Yeah, yeah, you look good,' she mumbles.

Thea follows her gaze as Tiril turns to look in the direction of the window. They remain standing beside one another. Thea is dressed up in the clothes she's going to have on when they perform. It looks just like Tiril had imagined, because white isn't a colour either: white top, white dress, white tights, new white shoes, bright red lipstick, her hair up and black nail polish on her fingernails.

'What was that banging? What is it you're trying to see?'

Tiril takes a step closer to the window. 'Nah,' she says, 'nothing. Just some sounds was all. Probably some building work or blasting going on someplace. I took a glass of juice, by the way.' She looks her friend over. 'Really good, Thea. The shoes are lovely. Your mum's?'

Thea nods.

'It's exactly how I pictured it,' Tiril says, nodding. 'It's going to be brilliant. A black piano. You in all white. Your lips all red. Heh heh, you'll be able to put that pout of yours to good use.'

'Lay off.'

Thea waves a hand in protest.

'The black fingernails.' Tiril nods in satisfaction. 'The hair. It looks amaz—'

It comes out of nowhere. Slamming into the kitchen window like a bullet. In a microsecond everything turns red, the white pane of glass covered in a viscous, red pulp. The girls jump, spin around. Thea lets out a shriek and they both stagger backwards into the kitchen. Then the banging begins again, the thick, red muck runs slowly down the windowpane, the thumping builds, it intensifies, it's as though there are a load of people pounding on the house, striking it with hammers on all sides.

Tiril takes hold of the sleeve of Thea's dress and pulls her into the living room. The banging continues, they breathe in short gasps. Tiril places her hand over her mouth, she tugs Thea in against the wall, out of sight of the windows.

They both breathe heavily, and in time.

'You know who it is, right?' Tiril whispers.

Thea is shit-scared, her lipstick is smudged above her top lip, she's shit-scared. 'No,' she says, shaking her head. 'Who?'

'Don't you know?'

'No!'

Tiril nods, as if confirming it to herself: 'Bunny's big brother.'

Thea's eyes open wide. If she looked scared shitless a second ago she looks absolutely terrified now. 'Bunny's big br— Fuck! Are you ... are you ... s-s-sure?'

The banging stops abruptly.

Tiril nods her head slowly.

'Yeah, certain.'

'How can you be certain?'

'Because I am.'

'What do they want,' Thea whispers. 'Bunny's big brother and them?'

Tiril crouches down, takes hold of her sleeve again and leads her back into the kitchen. The loud pounding noises haven't resumed. Most of the red muck has run off the windowpane, with only a few leftovers still sliding downwards in slimy streaks.

'What do they want?'

'Come on,' says Tiril. She turns quickly and makes her way into the hall with Thea scurrying after.

'What if they're still—'

'Come on!'

Tiril slips on her shoes and opens the door. Thea stands behind her hesitantly, but when her friend walks out to the front of the house she follows reluctantly. Tiril can feel the tick of her pulse in her throat, the blood pumping in her fingers and she sucks on her tongue. She rounds the corner of the house to the garden. Takes a few steps on to the lawn.

Thea follows after, stepping gingerly, her white outfit shimmering as she walks across the grass. She looks like an elf.

Tiril's gaze sweeps the garden; it seems deserted. The lawn bears the imprint of feet. She looks at the window, soiled and smudged from the red pulp.

Thea's scream fills the garden.

Tiril turns to look. Her friend is pointing towards the big apple tree. Tiril follows her finger. Somebody has driven a huge nail through a cat's head and into the tree trunk behind. Dark blood still drips from the skinned, feline body.

'Bunny's big brother,' Tiril whispers, looking at the dead animal. She feels a shudder at the back of her neck. She takes her cigarettes and lighter from her shirt pocket almost by reflex.

'You can't smoke here,' Thea sniffles. 'Mum and Dad will go spare.'

Tiril lights the cigarette.

'What will we do now?' says Thea and swallows, her make-up running over her cheeks. 'What if they come back?'

'If they come back,' Tiril says, taking a deep drag of the cigarette and exhaling, 'if they come back, they come back. We'll handle that. That family are seriously fucked up, Thea. Because I gave his little brother a wallop, he's sent his big brother after us; now all we're missing is Bunny.'

Thea closes her eyes.

'Relax,' Tiril says. She looks around. 'Have you got a garden hose? And a hammer? That's what we need, a hose and a hammer – and a black bin bag.'

'Yeah, I think so,' Thea says, reaching out her hand. 'Here, gimme a drag.'

53. **THE TRANQUILITY OF MOTÖRHEAD**
(Cecilie)

Cecilie sat behind the silos, looking out over the fjord, for an hour and a half. No wind, scarcely a boat and hardly any people. Only a jogger who ran by in skintight gear. Only an old woman in a green coat out walking her dog. Only the calm water glittering in the white sunshine. Cecilie felt empty, she couldn't manage to collect her thoughts; she couldn't even manage to make out what she was thinking when she was thinking it. She tried to recall some old memories; maybe Mum had taken her here ages ago, while she was still in good health. Maybe she and Dad had come here once, while she was still a tot? Cecilie couldn't remember anything and she felt a chill on the back of her neck when she thought of never having been here before, even though she's sat here so often that she considers herself almost part of the landscape. She ate the cinnamon bun slowly, smoked, ate more of the bun and smoked some more. Then she gave a start, got quickly to her feet, suddenly frightened that some harm may come to the child from her bottom being so cold.

And now she's here. Now she's home, indoors, her bum is warm, the living room is warm, the house is quiet and her head is filled with thoughts. Her hands rest on her stomach. What kind of kid is inside her? Who's growing, who's going to be born into the world? Is it a healthy kid? Is it a mongo kid? Is it a horrible kid, as horrible as her? Is it a little shit of a kid? Is it a professor kid? Is it a Korea kid? Is it a Rudi kid?

Soon be dinnertime.

This house is poisoned.

She's lain on this same sofa, year in year out, thinking exactly the same thoughts. Watched horror films. Watched Rudi or Jani walking in and out, carrying boxes of cigarettes, carrying TVs, carrying all kinds of shit. Lain here thinking the same thoughts: get away. And now she's lying here again, and not just by herself; she's two people and the problems are piling up around her. So much has happened in such a short space of time and Cecilie doesn't quite know who she is or what she's going to do. That's the thing about love, she thinks. It's so bloody difficult. She loves Rudi, just the idea of not being with him makes her so sad, but still the thought of him makes her want to throw up. And Tong? Is *that* love? She pictures him clearly, standing there, sees his rigid stare, hears the chugging of his breath, sees the sinews straining on his forearms: *I'd do anything for you.*

Would you, Tong?

Anything for Cecilie?

Would you kill Rudi for me, Tong?

She puts her hands in front of her and pushes at the air, as if to shove her problems away. She feels like having ice cream. She felt the same way yesterday, and the day before that as well, and she has to smile because now she realises what it is.

'Baby,' she whispers, gets to her feet, scoots into the kitchen, opens the freezer and says, 'of course you can have ice cream.'

She takes out a three-litre of Neapolitan. Then quickly grabs a spoon from the cutlery drawer. She opens the tub, using all her strength to sink the spoon into the firm ice cream, sees it bend back, the ice cream yielding. She sits down and starts to eat. Can't manage to stop, can't manage to stop.

Cecilie closes her eyes.

Ah sweet Jesus, that's so good.

'Fuck's sake, what are you at now?! Ice cream? Right before dinner?!'

Weird – she didn't hear them coming in. She didn't hear the car, the stomping, the slamming of doors. Rudi stands in front of her shaking his head. She doesn't dignify him with a glance, just brings another spoonful to her mouth.

'Oh yeah,' Rudi says, smiling, 'you're my woman, Chessi, from here to eternity and the whole way back, and I'm damned if I'm going to come between you and your ice cream. Let me look at you.'

He reaches both his hands towards her face but she recoils, can't stomach the thought of him touching her, just can't stomach it.

'Heh heh,' says Rudi. 'Jani! Come on in and take a look at this girl who's all sexied up from the skincare shithole. She's radiant! Hey, Jani, there's a sunbeam sitting in our kitch—'

Jan Inge walks in and Rudi lowers his voice.

'Yeah, a sunbeam, in our kitchen.'

They look at her.

'We'll have to have you do this once a month,' says Rudi, then bends over and gives her a peck on the cheek, and once again she recoils.

'She doesn't want her make-up ruined, all fancy now,' Rudi laughs. 'Just how it ought to be. That's why we have women in the world, so they can look good. Yesss – and we've had a killer day, I can tell you that. Rudi has been able to knock some sense into Hansi's head, we've got a van and a trailer, so you don't need to worry about the car, baby. You can drive out to Åne and have a real good time.'

Cecilie is momentarily thrown. 'A good time?'

'Aerosmith, the open road, good humour ... you know. The lot!'

She puts the tub of ice cream down. No one, absolutely no one, can be so simple and good and as full of energy as Rudi. When he stands in front of her, his face lit up like a little boy's and he showers her with loving droplets from his heart, then it's completely impossible to imagine a single day without that bloody idiot.

She smiles at him.

She hadn't planned to.

But she does.

'Moron,' she says.

'Yup! That's me,' Rudi says, laughing. Then he walks into the hall. 'The moron is heading down into the basement to get a few things ready for tomorrow – how many baseball bats? Three, I guess. Tong is coming along after all, nothing he likes more than smashing things with a bat. Fuck me, this moron can't wait to see that little Korean again!'

Sometimes she thinks that he's jabbered away so much in this house that sooner or later the walls and the floors will learn how to speak, and the day they do, they're going to sound like Rudi. Cecilie gets up. He can't wait to see Tong again, that's what he says. What a fucking mess. What'll I do? Maybe I'll just tell him, right now? *Hey Rudi, I'm screwing Tong! He might be the father of the baby you don't know about!*

She stretches out.

Then we'd see a murder.

It's not criminals who are behind all the killings in society.

It's love.

Jan Inge has already started making the food. He's put on the apron they bought in Houston the last time they visited Dad, seven years ago, the purple-and-white one with 'Fuck Y'all I'm from Texas' written across it.

'I'm going to have a kip for a half-hour,' she says, and leaves the room. 'Call me when dinner's ready.'

'Don't I always?'

She sighs and walks down the hall.

'Yes, you do,' she says in a low voice. 'What is it, by the way?'

'Fishcakes!' comes the reply from the kitchen.

Cecilie opens the door, falls on to the bed. Fishcakes, she thinks, I couldn't face a morsel of fishcake.

She knows things will be different in the future, but how exactly, she doesn't have a clue. She wants ice cream and she wants to sleep. Her body is so heavy. She never had many muscles, but now it feels like she has none at all.

She sinks into the mattress.

She takes out her mobile, pulls up her list of contacts, and presses on a number. It takes a little while before a click sounds and a voice says:

'Hi, you've reached Thor Haraldsen and Southern Oil. I'm not here at the moment. Please leave a message and I'll be sure to call you back.'

She takes a breath. 'Hi Dad,' she says. 'Just Cecilie here ... well, not calling about anything in particular. I just remembered ... I was out stretching my legs today and ... didn't you and I used to take walks down behind the silos? I was just wondering if you, like, remembered that? All right. Hope everything's good. Talk to you again. Bye bye. Feel free to give me a ring. Talk soon. Bye bye.'

She sinks down into the mattress, sinks and sinks.

A half-hour later Cecilie is sitting at the dining table in the living room with Rudi and Jan Inge, the table that's been there since she was a child. This is the nice time of the day, but not for her. She might have thought so before but not now. Motörhead fills the room, *Iron Fist* at full blast, and nobody speaks; they just relax, as well as they can, all of them. That's how it is every day. Rudi and Jan Inge love this part of the day, peace and calm and heavy metal. Not everyone understands just how peaceful Motörhead can feel, Rudi maintains. Jan Inge says that even though he's a country man in his heart of hearts, that it's actually this time of the day that all his thoughts take shape.

This used to be really nice, I used to enjoy it too, thinks Cecilie. But I'm not able to feel that way any more.

Maybe I shouldn't go on living, she thinks, feeling just as tired as before she slept. Maybe not, little baby. Maybe that would be for the best. That neither you, nor I, lived. That we were the ones to die. We, who don't know who your father is. You, who have an ugly slut of a mother. Me, with a slut's baby in my tummy. Maybe that would be best? My little baby? So people wouldn't have to be bothered with us? So they wouldn't have to beat each other to death? Wouldn't have to hate each other?

Hm?

Baby?

Just a little?

Just die a little?

You and me?

Baby?

54. **YOU NEED TO BREATHE EASY** (Sandra)

She walks by the clothes racks with her hand out, her fingers running along the material of garment after garment.

The light in Hennes & Mauritz is cold and glaring; she's been there a half-hour without really looking at one single article of clothing. Other customers have come in, the clock has ticked, past five o'clock, getting on for six, work and school are finished, outside the sun is sinking on the horizon, the afternoon is slipping into evening.

She's had to stop several times and draw breath, close her eyes and swallow so as not to burst out crying. If this is love, she doesn't understand what it wants with her. She thought love would make her feel good. But what it's doing is dishing out pain, rending and tearing at her and thrusting her into something unknown and dangerous.

We were supposed to be good to one another, Daniel.

Sandra holds an ocean-blue headscarf between her fingers. She can't remember having picked it out to look at. Blue, her mother always says, blue suits you, Sandra, nice colour on you, brings out your eyes.

She pays. 69.50. She goes out of the shop and down the escalators, out into the fading light on Domkirkeplassen, the square in front of the cathedral. A normal day in Stavanger. Market traders selling fruit and vegetables, a thin man with a hot-dog stand at the entrance to the SR-Bank chatting with passers-by, a beggar wearing a shawl, a 7-Eleven cup in her hands, sitting cross-legged in Laugmannsgaten, and over by 'Ting', a junkie in light-coloured jeans and a tracksuit top selling *Asfalt*.

Sandra notices daily life around her, but doesn't take it in. She feels small, she feels afraid. She keeps her eyes lowered, tightens her grip on her H&M bag, enters Arneageren Square, without looking at anyone and steering clear of the teenagers sitting outside *Kulturhuset*; she opens the door to McDonald's.

Sandra hopes Malene comes soon, because right now she needs a friend. She's taken out her mobile a thousand times and begun writing a text to Daniel, a thousand times she's pulled his number up on the screen to ring it.

Dear, precious, Daniel. Nothing matters, nothing apart from you and me.

Daniel, you're everything to me. I love you.

She hasn't sent either message. She doesn't like what she has written. Is this how it is? Does love bring out all the pain inside people? Is *that* love's secret, the one the Bible doesn't dare talk about? Maybe this is what every grown-up knows, but avoids saying to their children. Maybe that's why all grown-ups have something of an ash-grey look in their eyes. Because they know that love is the same as pain.

Sandra orders a cheeseburger and a coke. She sits down with her back against the wall, sets the tray on the table in front of her. She takes a sip of her drink, but can't taste anything. She lifts up the cheeseburger, brings it to her mouth, takes a bite, not good. Pain in her stomach.

Suddenly something jolts in her mind.

She sits up straight.

Has it been like this the whole time, has she just been blind to it? Facial expressions and words spoken begin detonating in her head, bursting like soap bubbles; an ugly sneer playing on his mouth, his eyes turning steely all of a sudden, his hands going limp, the reticence that sometimes comes over him. Is he toying with me? She feels something spread across her chest, feels her mind begin to clear. The risk of weeping begins to subside. Is this the truth? That he caught sight of her that night in the shop, and what he saw was a stick of candy, something he wanted to taste, as long as it had some flavour? In her mind Sandra goes though the times she's tried talking to him about something other than exactly what he wants to talk about. What does he do then? He just shuts off, closes down completely.

Sandra clears her throat, almost loudly.

The sick stuff he's done. Beaten people up. Killed his parents. Whatever it may be. The way he just rides around on his moped. She knows he bunks school a few days a week.

He's dangerous is what he is.

It's strange how her heart settles when she has these thoughts. Gradually she begins to notice the people around her, the single father in the Smiths T-shirt sitting with his son over at the steps; he's finished his food and he's waiting for his son to do the same, they're probably going to the cinema. Outside the window, four teenagers, sixth-formers, talking, laughing and waving their hands about, one boy constantly bumping up against a very pretty girl.

Malene opens the door. Her new friend walks with her back straight, with colour in her cheeks and red lipstick on. She's very pretty, with a body a lot of girls at school envy; it says as much on her Facebook page – *oh, such a nice bod, Malene.*

'Hi Sandra, I came as quick as I could...' Malene sits down, bringing fresh air with her. 'How are things with you?'

'Okay.' Sandra nods and takes a sip of coke to conceal her thoughts.

Malene looks surprised. 'But you didn't sound so—'

'I bought a headscarf.'

Malene leans back into the seat. 'Cool ... let's have a gander. Hennes?'

'Mhm,' Sandra nods, 'it's all right.' She takes the headscarf out of the bag. Hands it to her friend. Malene examines it.

'It's nice ... blue suits you.'

'I think I'll break up with him.'

Malene's eyes open wide.

'With Daniel, yeah, I—'

'What?'

Don't start crying now. Sandra takes another sip of coke, a bite of the cheeseburger.

'Jesus, Sandra, what's happened—'

Sandra looks at her friend. 'I can't handle it,' she says, taking back the headscarf and beginning to tie it around her head, under her hairline. 'I don't know who he is. He ... I just can't handle it—'

'But, I mean, you love him, he loves you, you—'

Sandra nods. *Don't say it*, she thinks, *don't say it.*

'Don't you? Do you not love him any more?'

Sandra ties the headscarf at the nape of her neck.

'But if you love him, if he is the love of your life—'

'Yeah, but what if all that love of your life, the one stuff, is just a...'

She can't manage to finish the sentence. The tears are coming. Shit. Sandra tries to hold them back but they won't be bossed. She shuts her eyes, places her fingers over them, inhales and exhales.

When she opens them again, she catches sight of him. And her. Daniel and Veronika are standing a few metres from the window, between McDonald's and the fountain in the square. No doubt about it. It's them. Sandra has a rushing sensation in her head, as though a thousand tiny spears are flying from one side of her brain to the other: his head tilted to one side, his hand going to her hair, his fingers moving a lock from her cheek.

Daniel and Veronika.

'Sandra, what is it—'

That's it. That's what it's all about.

Malene turns and looks out the window.

'Oh my God, isn't that—'

'Yes, it is.'

'But—'

Daniel puts his arms around Veronika. He pulls her close and runs his hand up and down her back. She leans into him, resting her head on his chest.

Malene looks at Sandra in confusion.

'But I don't understand, is he, have they—'

She turns back towards the window.

Daniel lets go of Veronika. They stand looking at one another. The deaf girl's face is covered in lines going up and down and across, as though it were divided into pieces. Daniel brings his hand to her face, tracing the lines with his fingers, opens his mouth and says something. Veronika nods and smiles and then they leave. Walking past the fountain, out of sight, into the gathering darkness.

'You need to breathe easy,' Malene whispers.

'I can hardly breathe at all,' Sandra whispers back.

55. **GIRLS' MEETING** (Tiril)

Thea unrolled the hose from the basement, Tiril sprayed the entrails off the window, feeling cool standing there with her feet apart and a cig hanging from the side of her mouth as the jet of water hit the pane. Thea fetched her father's hammer, but looked away as Tiril pulled the nail from the tree and out through the cat's head. She had to stand on a lawn chair and use all the strength she had, the bark of the tree made a whining sound as the nail came free, the head and pelt of the cat landing with a smack at the foot of the tree. Tiril was satisfied. They had withstood the attack from Bunny's big brother. Thea fetched two big black bin liners. As if to demonstrate it was no problem for her, Tiril put out her cigarette in the carcass of the dead cat before lifting it up from the ground – uuchh, Tiril, disgusting – and throwing it into the bag. She tied the bag tightly, double-wrapped it in the other bin liner and then said: 'I'll take care of this.'

'So, like, what are you going to do with it?'

Tiril held the bag up in Thea's face and shook it about.

'Uhhyuu! Quit it!'

Tiril threw the bag to Thea. She reacted as though a live rat had landed on her lap and flung it quickly back.

'Tiril! Quit it!'

'I said I'd take care of it, didn't I?' Tiril laughed and began to make her way out of the garden.

'Where are you going?'

Tiril halted. 'Are there any of the neighbours you don't like?'

'What?'

Tiril put one hand on her hip and swung the rubbish bag round in the other.

'Do you think this is all a joke? Do you think my mum and dad aren't going to twig that something's gone on here? Do you think the neighbours aren't going to discover what's happened if they find a cat in their rubbish?'

Tiril walked back to her friend. She placed her hand on her shoulder. 'No,' she said. 'I don't think so.'

A little over an hour later, Thea's parents arrived home. The girls were practising, Thea by the piano, edgy and ill-at-ease, Tiril seated beside her, singing, better than ever. She felt something had loosened in her chest when she sang the lines she loved: this pain is just too real. When the parents first entered the living room they stood still and listened. After a while they sat down on the sofa by the window and when the girls finished they clapped and said it was one of the most beautiful things they'd ever heard, and as the four of them made their way to the kitchen, Tiril mouthed 'I told you so' to Thea, before she turned to Thea's parents and said: 'It's so great we get to practise here, we've been at it for hours now.'

'Yeah, I can definitely hear it,' said Thea's father. 'You've got at least two fans that can't wait to hear the two of you tomorrow in the gym hall. Isn't that right, dear?'

'Absolutely,' said Thea's mother. 'By the way, it's really wet in the garden. What happened?'

Tiril saw a nervous twitch at the side of Thea's mouth and hurried to say: 'A few brats came along and threw eggs at the window. We brought the hose out and washed off the mess.'

Thea's father clicked his fingers. 'Heh heh,' he chortled, his eyebrows dancing up and down a little as he turned to his wife. 'Eh? There you go. Girls nowadays,' he confirmed with visible satisfaction, 'they don't take rubbish from anyone. Are you both hungry?'

'Yeah – we wouldn't say no,' Tiril replied and noticed how everything just fits into place when you feel self-confident.

They walked into the kitchen, where, a few hours earlier, the girls had witnessed the cat's entrails hitting the windowpane. Thea's father opened the fridge door. He does resemble Dad, Tiril thought, around the same age, same sort of build, but whereas Dad does everything with a kind of reluctance, Thea's father does it all with such ease. In a matter of seconds he'd taken out broccoli, carrots, a fillet of chicken, and in no time he had heated up the wok, cut up the vegetables, kissed his wife on the neck and made a risqué joke as she tied the apron round his waist.

Tiril didn't find it gross, the way they flirted with each other. Although it wasn't so long since Tiril couldn't stand that kind of thing, not long at all since the sight of two happy grown-ups made her livid, particularly if they were the parents of someone she knew. But Thea's parents, she can handle that – perhaps because Thea's father always makes her laugh.

That was awesome.

Pulling the nail out of the tree, out of the cat's head.

Thea hadn't noticed, but Tiril had: Bunny's big brother, that sick fucker, had hammered the nail through the cat's eye. Right through his left eye. The sound when she had extracted the nail, like putting your foot into a waterlogged welly.

The feeling she had had, it was good.

When she held the cat's furry skull, when the limp body hung from the dead head, like a figure from a puppet show. She hadn't felt sorry for the cat. She'd just looked into its dead eyes and all she was able to see was the sick, but nevertheless fantastic, act. His hands. Bunny's big brother's hands. One of them holding the head against the tree. The other gripping the hammer. The nail in his mouth. The wail of the cat as the blows rained down.

Because he wanted to make it clear that nobody touched his brother.

No matter, Tiril thinks, no matter what way you look at it, he's one sick fucker, but a strong fucker, and in one way he did what was right. Just like she did what was right. So the only question is: who's stronger? Who can sing more beautifully?

It was getting on for six o'clock and the girls left the table; it was still a while before they were due at rehearsals. They went to Thea's room where, for probably close to the thousandth time, they sat down to watch Evanescense videos on YouTube. They talked about what an insane day it had been, they felt content and happy with themselves, they laughed about how they'd handled Bunny's big brother, how they'd handled Thea's mum and dad, and now, now they're looking deep into one another's eyes, speaking in hushed tones, as they talk about how exceptionally well they performed the song in practice today.

'If we can sound as good tommorrow...' Thea whispers.

'We'll sound as good,' whispers Tiril.

'I'm just, like, really nervous. Aren't you?'

'Why should I be?'

Tiril clicks on the mouse and leaves the live version of 'Haunted' from Rock Am Ring behind. She's not so into that one, nor does she care much for Amy's shorts, hair or eye make-up in it. She likes her better when she's Gothic and exalted, like in the video for 'Call Me When You're Sober' for instance.

'We'll sound better, Thea,' she says. 'We'll sound even better.'

Text message. She leans towards the desk, looks at the mobile. From Malene.

R u @ T's? Can we come over. Pls. Sandra and me.

'Who is it?'

Tiril shows the message to Thea.

Thea taps her chin with her middle finger, like she always does when she's unsure. 'What's happened?'

Tiril gets to her feet, like she always does when her heart begins to tick. 'Dunno.' She texts back: *Just come. We're here.*

A few minutes later the doorbell rings and Thea, with Tiril right behind, hurries down the stairs to answer it, calling out to her parents that it's for her. As they'd suspected, they open the door to the sight of two girls in crisis mode. Malene leads a clearly shattered Sandra over the threshold and they steer her up to the bedroom: 'Just Sandra and Malene!' Thea calls out in the direction of the living room.

'Great!'

That's the thing with Thea's father, thinks Tiril, as she hears his voice ring out. Everything's great as far he's concerned, and if it's not great then he insists on it being great.

Once they're in Thea's room, Sandra collapses on to the red beanbag on the floor. The other three stand in front of her.

Tiril looks at Malene: 'What's going on?'

'We're not quite sure, but it's Daniel, in any case.'

Tiril can see Thea swallow, like most girls do when his name is mentioned. But Tiril doesn't have any need to swallow. 'What is it he's done, then?' she asks.

'We were in town,' Malene does the talking, Sandra slumps unhappily in the beanbag, her make-up running down her face, 'because it was all a bit too much for Sandra today, so I met her there, at McDonald's—'

'McDonald's,' Tiril rolls her eyes and crosses her arms, 'have you started going there as well now—'

'Can you just drop the environmental shit today?'

'Okay—'

'Anyway, we're sitting there and Sandra's trying to get a grip on things and suchlike and that's when we see them—'

'Who?'

'Them...'

'Who?'

'Daniel and—'

'Daniel?'

'Daniel and Veronika.'

'Veronika?' Thea takes a step forward. 'The foster sister?'

Malene nods. 'But that's not all, because when she turns round—'

'Turns round?'

'Yeah, we were sitting inside and they were outside—'

'With their arms around one another,' comes a sobbing voice from the beanbag.

'They had their arms round one another?!'

'Yeah, they did, but anyway—'

'Like – I mean, they were wrapped around each other—'

'Yeah, but anyway, when she turned around her face was all ... all...'

'She'd cut herself up,' says the voice from the beanbag. 'Out of love.'

They all turn to Sandra.

'How...' Malene crouches down beside her. 'How do you know that?'

Sandra makes a fist, thumps it against her chest and with a sobbing voice says: 'I understand everything now.'

The girls sit down in a ring around the beanbag. They tend to Sandra. They run their hands over her hair, fix her fringe, straighten her necklace so the crucifix rests in the hollow of her throat, stroke her gently on her forearms. They speak to her softly. They let her relate. They listen. They let her tell them how fantastic these past weeks have been, about his bright, electric mouth, about how he's given her his heart and she's given hers in return, about how she felt that life has been filled with a colossal love – I haven't needed sleep, I haven't needed to eat, all I've needed was him! They nod and they listen as she fills them in on the last twenty-four hours, how everything has twisted, how everything has become harsh and ugly and how fear has been hammering at her door.

Tiril gets to her feet. She paces the floor in thought. She feels she's the one who needs to assume responsibility. They need to be at rehearsals very soon. Sandra needs to pull herself together. Tiril halts in front of the beanbag and makes eye contact with Sandra.

'You need to go see him. You need to tell him what you think and what you've seen. You need to take the fight to him. And to her. Veronika.'

Sandra sniffles, wipes her nose with the back of her hand.

Malene nods.

Thea nods too.

'You're going to send him a text,' Tiril says.

Sandra shuts her eyes, shakes her head quickly from side to side. 'No, I won't...'

Tiril raises her voice a notch: 'You're going to send him a text, do you hear me?'

'But, I...'

'Gimme your phone.' Tiril puts her hand out.

'No, Tiril, I...'

'I said, gimme your phone.'

Sandra reluctantly hands her the mobile.

Tiril begins to type:

Daniel, you are a coward. It's time you showed me who you are. Who it is you want. I'll wait for you...

'Where do the two of you usually meet?'

'Mm, by the electricity substation—'

...by the substation. This is your last chance. Sandra.

Tiril presses send. She tosses the mobile back into Sandra's lap and walks towards the window. She stands there with her back to them. She can feel their eyes on her.

'By the way,' she says, without turning around, 'Bunny's big brother was here. Y'know, Kenny. He nailed a cat to the tree. Put the nail right through the cat's eye. He was trying to put us in our place. He failed. Look. It's beginning to get dark.

56. **SNIFFED LIGHTER FUEL AND LISTENED TO LATE-NIGHT RADIO** (Jan Inge)

Dark clothes, of course. No need to attract attention. Casual attire, obviously. Just a couple of blokes taking the bus. Just two guys doing their bit for the environment.

Rudi and Jan Inge have changed, they've followed the timetable Ulrike from Hannover gave them, taken the bus into town and hopped on a number 7 by Breiavannet at 21:15. But Rudi's not in good humour. The cheerful mood he'd been in after beating up Hansi evaporated after dinnertime. They'd listened to Motörhead and then settled down to watch *Driller Killer* while they digested their food, but Rudi couldn't get into it. He twisted and turned in his seat and talked about what a deprivation of liberty it was being packed on to a bloody bus. And Rudi in bad humour is a pain. But what is a leader going to do about it? When the employees are in a bad mood?

Jan Inge sometimes feels this is his lot in life. Cecilie is in rotten humour so often that he's firefighting day in, day out. And she hasn't been the only one. He's had many grumpy people in the organisation over the years. At times he's felt like he's been running a kennel for sick dogs. It's a common flaw amongst so many of the criminal element, such a large number of them are angry and obstinate. They lack stability in their lives. Positive surroundings.

And what can you do about that? What, for example, would my kindred spirit David Toska do about it? What sort of steps would a big shot like Toska take in order to reinvigorate and re-energise tired troops? Would a seminar be a good idea, the kind of thing where you rent a place and book some speakers, possibly out at Sola Strand Hotel or in the basement of Atlantic Hotel, have some food on the table, get in a motivational speaker, maybe a Pia Tjelta or a Kristian Valen, or a guy with a guitar? Tjødaen, he played in that band before, what were they called ... Hundvåg Racers? And Dabben, that boy can talk, more than one person's remarked on that, and if only he wasn't so ill-suited for ordinary working life he could have been a stand-up comedian or a politician. Might be an idea. Rent out part of Sola Strand Hotel. Get Dabben in to tell a few jokes and pep up the team. Have Tjødaen play a few songs. A Cash number for Jani, something by Aerosmith for Cecilie and a Metallica ballad for Rudi.

These are good thoughts. Positive thoughts.

Shouldn't the criminal element, in general, work a little harder at raising awareness at the need for a good atmosphere in the workplace?

In any case, Rudi has always been useful with regard to that. Sure he can be a hassle, going on and on, but he's rarely in bad humour.

But now the atmosphere here is really going downhill. Of course he's got a point about being robbed of his freedom, that public transport is out to suppress the individual, everybody knows that. All the same. There's something else.

All this couldn't possibly just be about the bus.

'I'll grant them one thing, the people who work with this,' Rudi says, as they're tipped sideways in their seats at the roundabout by the theatre, 'they know their fucking systems. Look, Jani,' he continues, 'now we're coming out on to Madlaveien, and I'm nauseous, being on a bus always makes me nauseous – but let's not talk about me, let's talk about the guy driving. You can be sure that that fucker sitting up there holding the steering wheel between his knees, he is drilled in this. System, system, system. Do you think bus drivers get heavy balls, my friend? The amount of time they spend sitting? I do. In a lot of ways, you could say he's a German, couldn't you? A brother of Ulrike. *Ordnung. Ordnung. Ordnung.* Now this busfuck knows that we're going to stop outside the bicycle shop at such and such a time. Andsoonandsoforth. And he's one thousand per cent set on it. Jesus, I feel sick! Anyway, I'll give them that, the people involved in this; they've made a plan and they've gone for it.'

'Well—' Jan Inge reckons he can agree with those sentiments, that it's something positive, that in many ways it's similar to what he himself is busy doing in their own firm, making plans and going for them. But Rudi has no time to listen.

'But,' Rudi says angrily, 'what does it do to a person, being squeezed into these seats, breathing this stuffy air and having their insides bounced around like they were in a bloody tumble dryer, and constantly stopping then driving then stopping then driving again. Eh? Jesus, I'm nauseous. Brother of cunt! I ask you that, Jani, on top of it being a fundamental infringement of our rights when two working men like you me have been robbed of the symbol of our freedom. The Volvo. Eh? You can bet that creates tension. I'm pretty certain that if you take a look at the statistics for people with muscular aches and ailments and compare the ones who have their own car with those who take public transport, then you'll see that amongst those who travel by bus there'll be a lot more instances of people suffering from fibromyalgia, wear and tear, migraines and even long-term sick leave.'

Jan was thinking of saying that Rudi may possibly be right, but that on the other hand it is conceivable that these bumpy trips, with all the stops along the way, may have a relaxing effect on some people, but he's gets slightly confused, so he asks: 'Yeah ... but ... are you talking about bus drivers now?'

'Aren't you listening to me, brother of fuck?'

'Yeah, I—'

'It's the passengers I'm thinking off, in this tunnel of nausea we're inside. And I've been thinking about it a hell of a lot today,' Rudi says, as they near the stop on Holbergsgaten. 'A hell of a lot, Jani. And what I'm getting at is that we need to sort out the vehicular situation.'

'The vehicular sit—'

'Don't go interrupting me, Jani, not yet, brother of impatience! What we need is a new vehicle, which both you and I can have the use of. We can hand over the Volvo to Chessi and then we get our own van. No matter how good it felt laying into Hansi, giving him a working-over for old times' sake, we can't do that whenever we need a van.'

'But we—'

'I don't want to hear it, Jani, I don't want to hear any protests. Those are my final words on the matter. I feel really nauseous now. But I'm hanging in there. Can you see that? I'm hanging in.'

Jesus, this is a bit much, Jan Inge thinks. He places his clammy hands in his lap and looks out the window.

'I can't talk any more now, brother,' Rudi says, 'because I feel so sick at this stage that I actually just really need a little time to myself. I need to look straight ahead. In both senses of the word. Straight ahead at the road. Straight ahead at the future.'

The bus passes Mosvannet lake, then the junction at Tjenvollkrysset, continues up Madlakrossen, driving past the ice rink in Siddishallen, past the gymnastics hall, out to Madlakrossen before turning into Molkeholen and heading towards Madla and Gosen.

Nausea? This can't just be about being on a bus and feeling sick. Jan Inge feels he's displaying poor leadership qualities at the moment. What would David Toska have done?

The bus pulls in at a stop not far from Madlamark School. Two teenagers hop off, a woman in her thirties gets on.

'Rudi?' Jan Inge turns to his friend. 'How you feeling?'

'I'm concentrating. I'm looking straight ahead.'

'Okay, good.' Jan Inge speaks in as calm a tone as he's able. 'I promise you. Next week, there will be a new car standing outside the house. And a van. We'll have to find somewhere else to park the van though – it'll draw too much attention if we make such striking changes simultaneously, and nobody's going to go near the moving van. But I promise you that, Rudi. And listen, Rudi. No one, no one, is going to leave you.'

Rudi's long, narrow head sways gently as they drive up towards Gosen Woods and their final stop. He doesn't open his mouth to speak.

When the bus pulls in they step off, out into the chilly evening.

Rudi breathes in the fresh air and says, 'I conquered myself there, brother, conquered myself, my own body and my own fear. Look at me. Am I throwing up? Am I alive?'

Jan Inge smiles: 'A mighty display, Rudi,' he says. 'Mighty.'

'Yep,' Rudi clicks his tongue on the roof of his mouth and checks the time. 'I looked straight ahead. Jan Inge? You can say a lot about bus people in general and that bus in particular. But take a look,' he says, tapping the face of his wristwatch, 'ten minutes this bus trip was supposed to take, according to Ulrike, and that's exactly how long it took. But they felt like long minutes, didn't they? For you and for me? Long, my friend. I went through a lot. You went through a lot. You don't get any deeper than that. *Mano a mano*. Sink or swim. The feeling of making it to the last bus stop, so to speak. And that thing you said, about nobody leaving Rudi – I can tell you, right from the fuckin' heart, that helped solve a problem that's had me tied up in knots all day.'

Rudi takes hold of Jan Inge's head, bends over kisses him on the forehead.

'You should have been a shrink,' he says. 'Nausea? Who knows where that so-called nausea comes from. The internet? Come on, lets head up to Gosen Kindergarten, meet a man with a problem and offer a solution.'

LEADERSHIP ABILITIES.

How many marriages could be saved if families had only one person in charge, man or woman, with leadership ability, instead of a woman who's a lush and a lardass and a man who's a rough-neck and a coward, neither of whom, let's be honest, should ever have been allowed to bring kids into the world.

'Shit, maestro,' Rudi says, 'I really need a piss. Is it all right if I just nip into the woods here and whip out the schlong out for a sec, or would that attract a bit too much attention, do you think?'

'Yeah, just wait to piss until we're a little out of plain view.'

'I hear you, boss,' Rudi says. 'Fantastic night. Imagine. Uncle Autumn is here, but he looks like Aunt Summer. And before we know it we'll be up to our knees in Grandfather Snow, and then it all begins all over again.'

Jan Inge looks at him in admiration. 'Lyrical, brother. If you weren't working for me, you'd probably be a poet.'

'A poet?' Rudi says, slowing his pace, nodding to himself. 'Yeah. Yeah. Maybe so. I am sensitive, you know. Getting more and more sensitive the older I get.' He stops, grabs Jan Inge by the lapels and looks at him gravely. 'Where's the eleven-year-old who smashed the windows of Hafrsfjord School in 1981 and made off with his first stereo, a Philips with double cassette decks? Where's the twelve-year-old who took 1,450 kroner from Mathiessen's banana wholesalers on Løkkeveien in 1982? Where's the Rudi who beat the shit out of a thirty-year-old at Tjensvoll Shopping Centre in 1983?'

'You know,' says Jan Inge, 'back then you were a diamond in the rough. Now you're mature and rich with experience.'

The friends continue walking. The night envelops them, the woods seem warm.

'Yeah, I feel more mature and all,' Rudi sighs. 'They were great times. Out at the weekends. Gathering in the light beneath the lampposts. Hanging around and messing about, waiting to see what would come our way. Took my first car when I was twelve, have I told you that?'

'Yeah.'

Rudi's cheeks take on a hearty glow. 'Out in Bryne. At Rieber-Thorsen Auto Dealership. An Opel. Could just about see over the windscreen wiper. Frax and me parked it out near the airport. Sniffed lighter fuel and listened to late-night radio. Fell asleep in the back seat. Great times. Free and easy.'

'To your grandmother's great disappointment. And your brother—'

Rudi exhales heavily. 'Jani. Please. It's still painful for me to think about that there.'

'Right, I didn't mean to...'

Rudi nods and waves his hand as if to brush it away. 'Not like I'm proud of everything either. Fucked if I know what went on in our heads half the time ... Did I ever tell you about that one night we knocked over twenty-nine gravestones in Tjensvoll cemetery? Ungodly. If somebody tipped over Granny's headstone. I'd fucking brain them.'

'That's just how boys are,' Jan Inge says. 'You shouldn't take it so seriously.'

'You're right. I've become so soft. Tip over a gravestone. So what. Put it back up again, Mr Grave Minder! Get over it. Let boys be boys. You're right. Where will it end? Do you think I'll be floating beneath the ceiling someday, crying twentyfourseven?'

Jan Inge laughs. 'Who knows?' He stops and looks at Rudi. 'Okay. Quiz. Blood! Blood!'

'Ha ha. Easy. Not only blood! Fulci, 1981. *House by the Cemetery.*'

'Correct. And what does Fulci teach us? That one day it'll all be too late. Before you even know it. And what lesson should we take from that? That we...'

'...must always nurture love,' they say in unison.

'Justaboutright, brother of wisdom!'

'Heh heh.'

And in this buoyant mood, filled with memories and musings, they trudge on uphill towards the substation, where they are to meet Pål in just under half an hour.

57. WENDY, DARLING, LIGHT OF MY LIFE
(Cecilie)

The Volvo drives slowly through the small centre of Nærbø village. Street light after street light, not many people. Two cars, an old Kadett and a rusty Carina, are parked beside each other outside Statoil, their windows rolled down.Two boys sit behind the wheel of both, chatting to one another. A girl sits in the passenger seat of the Opel, twiddling her boyfriend's long hair between her fingers while blowing a chewing-gum bubble. A tattoo on her forearm: *Salve I love you you nutcase.* There's a man in a boiler suit from the farmers' co-op in front of one of the houses; he's smoking and teasing a dog with a stick. Two motorcyclists tear past her car, the harsh engine sounds piercing the darkness. What do people do in such a small place? Work at a plant nursery? At a newsagents? Maybe it's a good place to bring up a child?

The headlights stream ahead, dissecting the night as Cecilie drives out on to the flat expanse of Opstadsletta. It's deserted here. A deep darkness extending towards endless open country.

They did a job out here once. It was while they were working together with The Shabby Ones. That was a mistake. Some loan-shark shit that took place in a barn, something to do with a kid and drugs. Rudi nearly killed the guy, kicked him in the head and beat him with big logs of wood.

Cecilie can't be bothered listening to music right now. She just wants quiet. She told them she's going to Åna to arrange things with Tong, fill him in on the job tomorrow. But what is it she actually wants to do?

She closes her eyes. Drives blindly for a few seconds.

Say it like it is?

Tong, I have something to tell you.

And what's he going to say then?

She opens her eyes again.

Jesus. I'd do anything for you.

Did he mean it?

Or is he like all the other boys, who only love you before they come? Because that's what they want, frigging boys, their eruptions. That's when they're weak, that's when they're strong, that's when they'll wait on you hand and foot, the world over, when they're tensed, when you have them inside you, when you have them in your mouth, when you have them in your hands. Then they'll do anything for you, then everything they own is yours. She once screwed a biker with a tic from Hommersåk – the guy that carried out all the motorcycle robberies in the early nineties, held up places all over Rogaland, made off with millions. What was his name, Bjørn Roger Kydland? While she was riding him, he said: *I'll give you two hundred thousand if you promise to fuck me every week for the rest of my life.* And the Fokkt Brothers? Cecilie remembers them well, Poster and Sorry, Pål Stephen Vogt and Stein Eskil Vogt. Poster and Sorry were from Eiganes and they always came together – like, they always *came* together. There was no end to their prattle before they did either, *Cecilie, fuck you're gorgeous.* But afterwards? Neither of them would wait on her hand and foot. She'd just lie there, fourteen years old, jizz in her hair from one and jizz in her face from the other. They were sick in the head. They first worked as bouncers at *New York.* Then they were fitness instructors at S.A.T.S Training. After that they started a hairdressers in Kvadrat Shopping Centre. Then they disappeared. But hey, they still exist. Just google them. Put in Brothers of Porn and you'll find a webpage. Sorry and Porno have done well in the brother porn business. *Brothers in Arms, O Brother Where Art Thou, He Ain't Heavy He's My Brother, Big Brother, The Grimm Brothers, Brother Oh Brother.* Did the mother not kill herself when she heard what her boys were actually up to in Hungary; thought they were running an IT company, and later she saw a scene from *Brother Beyond* with Poster dressed in a tennis outfit, ramming a racket up Sorry's ass? Yeah, that's right, she did.

Both Cecilie and the Fokkt Brothers' mum have learnt by experience. You can't rely on boys.

Apart from Rudi. Cecilie can depend on him.

He's an awful idiot, she thinks. But he'll never leave me.

He'd die before he'd leave me.

Cecilie sees the silhouette of Åna rise up in the darkness. She slows down and indicates, sees the long, impressive driveway come into view. If you didn't know what this place was and you happened to drive up in a dim light you could easily believe it was the avenue to a castle

Wendy, darling, light of my life, I'm not going to hurt you...

The telephone rings.

...you didn't let me finish my sentence, I said, I'm not gonna hurt you...

She needs to change that blasted ringtone.

...I'm just gonna bash your brains, I'm gonna bash 'em right the fuck in...

It's not funny any more, no matter how much she loves both Jack Nicholson and *The Shining*. Cecilie leans over to the passenger side, turning on to the approach road while fumbling for the phone with her right hand.

Wendy, darling, light of my life ... I'm not going to hurt you, you didn't let me finish my sentence, I said...

She gets hold of the phone, looks at the display.

Dad calling.

Cecilie puts her foot on the brake, stops the car halfway up the driveway to Åna.

...I'm not gonna hurt you...

She kills the engine. It grows darker in the car. Only the glow from the mobile remains, casting a blue light on her hands and making them appear dead.

Dad calling.

Cecilie turns off the phone. She opens the door and gets out of the car. Stands there looking at the prison rising up out of the darkness. She takes out her lighter and a cigarette. She tenses the muscles at the back of her mouth, like she did when she was small, right behind her tongue, in order to empty her head of air. Then she lights the cigarette, sucks in the smoke and feels her body relax. She rubs her hands over her stomach to warm up the child.

'That was Granddad,' she whispers. 'He'd probably be happy to find out that you exist.'

Another drag of the cigarette.

'But we don't have time to talk to Granddad right now. We're going in to say hello to the guy who might be your father. And then we'll have to see what we do. Would you like to live out here, hm? In a little place like this? With Tong and me? Maybe Mummy could get a job at a newsagents. Mummy is good with people. Or would you like to live in the city, with Rudi and me and Uncle Jani? Or would it be for the best if we died, baby?'

The telephone beeps. Answerphone.

A weak and solitary breeze hits her, the first hint of wind in days.

Cecilie rings up her voice messages. She hears her father's crisp voice:

'Hey, girl! It's Pop! Houston calling, and nope, we ain't got no problem! Great you called, honey, great to hear everything's going well. Okay, gotta run, busy, you know, say hello to Jan Inge, always thinking of you guys, great to hear everything's good. Sure we took walks down by the silos, of course we did, allthetime. I'll stick a bit of money in the account one day soon. Hugs and kisses! Tits and asses! Nah, justajoke, honey.'

She begins to cry.

58. **ALTERED STATE** (Pål)

When he was young, he liked the darkness. Autumn, the evenings, the nights. Now he's not so fond of it any more, but he needs it. Pål feels scrawny. He feels lean in both mind and body. He's lost a lot of weight in the last few months. You look good, people have told him, it suits you, have you been hitting the gym? No, I've hit the wall. He's bought in food for the kids. Where are they? Out. Was Malene heading into town for something? Was Tiril calling round to a friend? Was it something to do with that performance tomorrow? He isn't sure. The words they say to him. They come out of their mouths, he nods, he smiles, but then they're gone.

Pål puts the lead on Zitha.

'Yeaah, come on, you're going out with Daddy.'

Yet another few steps further into the darkness.

He walks out on to Folkeviseveien. No unopened envelopes to toss in the rubbish bin at the bus shelter today. A victory. A day without debt collection. What is Zitha so jumpy about? Why is she whimpering like that?

'Zitha!' he says, louder, and in an angrier tone than normal. 'Simmer down, bad dog.'

Pål halts as he turns on to the path behind the tower blocks. Zitha is still agitated and he feels a terrible pang of conscience as the reason for it dawns on him. The dog hasn't been fucking fed.

'Yeaah,' he whispers. 'Daddy's a dolt.' Pål crouches down, pulls Zitha close. 'Poor you with a daddy like me, eh? Cries crocodile tears in front of his daughter and looks to his dog for forgiveness. Yeaaah, yeaah. Come on.'

He picks up the pace, puts on a spurt with Zitha for about a hundred metres or so. He gets her worked up, as if something's going to happen, something of relevance to her as well. But it won't. What will happen will only be of concern to him. It's getting on for five to ten. Pål hasn't heard from Rudi today. That means he's going to go ahead with this. Further into the forest. Listen to how they're planning to help him. Christ only knows what they intend to suggest. What can people like that offer? Pål has no idea. He has no clue about the workings of the criminal world, no more than what he can imagine from films and TV series. Do they have a set menu with a list of options? *Okay, Pål, here's a suggestion: you smuggle a quantity of heroin to Germany. No? Then we've got something else: you join us on a bank job. No? Then you'll have to sink your fingers further in the shit. There are people who are willing to pay others to use violence. We can arrange something along those lines.*

'Zitha! Can you quit your bloody whimpering?' Pål grabs her firmly by the scruff of the neck and presses her snout hard against the ground, and he sees the fear come into her eyes – she's not used to this. 'You'll get food. Later.'

Pål releases her and shakes his head. He's made it as far as Mad-lavoll School. He's noticed himself becoming more and more sentimental as the years pass. Maybe that's just the way of things? At least in a life like mine, he thinks, where the future isn't exactly burning bright. He walks over to one of the classroom windows. 'Yeaah, Zitha,' he says, 'that's where Dad sat, all those years ago.'

He takes a furtive look around. He has to cross the football pitch. He needs to get to the turnaround by the substation. It lies in front of him, illuminated by streetlamps.

Pål hurries across the gravel pitch, passing one set of goal posts and striding briskly into the light. He can't see Rudi anywhere.

'Here, Zitha, come on, girl,' he whispers, leaving the light, rounding the substation and entering the shoulder-level thicket. 'Yeaah, come on now.'

No Rudi. Pål stands there for a few moments. Zitha is still uneasy, but she's quiet now, his trepidation having rubbed off on her. It's still possible for him to call the whole thing off. Turn around and leave. But he doesn't. On the contrary, Pål has the same sensation in his head, the same tingling in his fingers as when he opens the laptop at night, the feeling of wanting this.

Voices. Footsteps.

He remains quite still. Zitha begins moving ever so slightly, but Pål is assertive and she obeys.

' ...you're still thinking about that, yeah?'

' ...well, now and again, but yeah, mostly as a sort of ... retirement idea, almost...'

'Retirement idea! Nice. Hey, I see you've retired, so what are you filling your wrinkly days with? Well, I'm busy writing my horror book, is what I'm doing, analyses of Argento and Fulci for the most part ... Blood! Blood! Listen, when I totter into the ranks of the coffin dodgers, I'm going to have enough saved up for me and Chessi to spend six months of the year in Spain—'

'Okay, let's keep it down now, Rudi...'

'Surethingboss, we'll keep it down...'

' ...and not so much blabbering, okay?'

'Who, me?'

They've stopped in front of the substation. The unfamiliar voice is very high-pitched – it sounds like that of a child in a grown man's chest. Pål brings his hand up and fixes his shirt collar, as though he were going to a meeting where he has to look smart. The sounds of whispering carry to him now. He can't make out what they're saying. Movement.

There they are. Pål has to make an effort not to stare at the corpulent form lurching through the brush, manoeuvring with an effort between leaves and branches.

'Påli! He-hey! Just like I was saying, only a few moments ago, yessir, Påli will be here, I said, you can count on it—'

It's him. It's Videoboy. Big and fat. With the same empty eyes as over twenty years ago. Small and black. He gives Rudi a quick look of admonishment, who in turn nods and draws his lips tight.

Videoboy offers him a brief smile as he puts out his hand. He's incredibly like his bygone self. Time hasn't affected him.

'Jan Inge Haraldsen,' he says, in a quiet tone, making his voice almost more high-pitched, 'nice to meet you.'

Videoboy himself. Pål tries not to show how thrown he is, attempts to conceal any form of recognition. He puts his hand out.

'Pål,' he says, and clears his throat, 'Fagerland.'

'There you go, ' says Rudi, 'now you've met the man himself, the—'

Jan Inge gives Rudi yet another look of reproach. Pål needs to gather his wits. It's Videoboy standing in front of him. Even though he's met him before, that damn week in 1986, it's just like encountering a celebrity from childhood. One of those you always heard about but never met, almost like it was, well, Kevin Keegan or Phil Collins. Pål has always been nervous around celebs, they make his hands sweat. *Videoboy.* He's really fat. His skin is wan, like ash. His hair is thin. And that freaky high-pitched voice.

I can't let them recognise me, thinks Pål. They mustn't remember what I did.

'I'm not entirely comfortable about you bringing your dog along,' Jan Inge says, glancing down at Zitha, who's sitting by Pål's feet.

'No, I'm sorry about that,' Pål says, fidgeting nervously with the lead, 'but it's the only way I can get out of the house without arousing too much suspicion. I've got two daughters, you see, so...'

'I understand. I'm not heartless. I have a family myself. I trust the dog will stay easy?'

'You know what, I was just thinking exaaaactly the same thing—'

Rudi speaks loudly and gesticulates. Videoboy glances at him for a third time. 'Anyway—'

Videoboy slips his hand into his trouser pocket, producing an inhaler which he proceeds to shake. He presses down on it, breathes in.

I'd forgotten that, thinks Pål. The inhaler.

'Anyway,' repeats Jan Inge, 'I understand you're having financial difficulties.'

Rudi folds his arms, nods in a manly fashion.

'Yes.' Pål swallows, but notices this situation isn't as horrible as he thought it was going to be. Jan Inge seems genuine. 'Yes,' he says again, 'I've tried everything but I just can't find a solution.'

'Right,' Jan Inge says, nodding. Causing his jowls to wobble. 'That's where we come in.' He places a hand on Pål's shoulder.

'That's how you need to view us, as a solution. You need to get your life back on track. You require a service. We – in all probability – can provide that.'

'Eh?' Rudi nods contentedly, his arms still folded. 'Schnåli? You hear that? What did I tell you?'

'I'll get right down to business—'

'Right down to business—' Rudi uncrosses his arms and snaps his fingers.

'Rudi, would you let me speak here?'

'*Kein Problem.*'

Jan Inge inhales. He lets his gaze wander. Peers into the woods, as though he heard something. Then he fixes his eyes on Pål again: 'We had a meeting today. About you and your situation and what we envisage could help. And we came up with something which I believe will solve your problems. But first, a question: are you well insured, Pål?'

'Insured, mmm ... yeah, I suppose I am? My ex-wife, she...' Pål shoots Jan Inge a hesitant glance. 'Insurance ... right ... well, if you're thinking—'

'Yes, that is what I'm thinking,' says Jan Inge.

'Heh heh. Blood! Blood! Not only blood!'

'Oh, shut up.'

Jan Inge fixes Rudi with a harsh stare. He checks himself and nods affirmatively.

'Right,' Jan Inge continues, 'you're well insured. Both household and contents as well as personal injury?'

'Yeah...'

'Excellent. That makes everything much simpler. This is the scenario we envisage: when night falls tomorrow and *the suitable hours of calm* arrive, roughly between half past seven and eleven, then we'll drive over to your place. Where do you live?'

'Well, in Ernst Askildsens Gate, up by the low-rises, not too far from here...'

'Do you have a garage?'

'Yeah, sure, I've got one...'

'A spacious garage, would you say?'

'Weeell, yeah, I suppose it is...'

'Perfect.' Jan Inge slaps his bloated palms together and Pål notices how they hardly make a sound. 'It's a good time to work,' he continues, enthused. 'It's dark. People are busy with their own thing. No one pays any attention to the presence of an extra car or not. Some people are watching the news. Others are at club or association meetings. Shadows and shapes and incidents. There're many who believe that the poetic hours occur later, in the middle of the night. I say it's these hours that are lyrical.'

'Heh heh. You listening?'

'Daily life is taking place,' Jan Inge goes on, without allowing Rudi to perturb him, 'it's dark but not too quiet. That's when we'll come driving down the street. A plain, grey Transporter. A Trojan horse. And the only thing you need to do is to make sure your kids are out of the house.'

Pål nods with interest. There's something about the way Jan Inge presents it that makes it feel right. His confidence is reassuring, he's genuine and proper, reflective and experienced. It's the same impression he gave in 1986, but he seems more reliable now.

'We park the Transporter at your place, we'll number between three and four people, depending how many the firm have at work that evening. We will of course have some equipment along with us, you'll usher us in and then we'll get to work on your house. Our goal will be to make the damage look as realistic as possible. Basically, you understand: to make such a good job of it that the entire insurance amount is paid out to you. We'll take your possessions.'

'Possessions...?'

'Possessions.'

'Possessions!'

Jan Inge puts his head to the side and narrows his eyes. This is a joint effort, Pål. We can't risk this much without getting something in return. You understand that.'

'Eh ... sure ...' Pål clears his throat. 'That's probably – well – how it has to be. So. You'll take everything, I presume, TVs, computers...'

'If it's your laptop you're thinking of, I'd imagine you should be happy to be rid of it. The internet isn't for you, Swalli.'

Jan Inge takes a step closer to Pål: 'There's also the added detail of us being obliged to leave you in a somewhat altered state.'

'What do you mean?' Pål says, knitting his brow. 'Altered?'

'Heh heh. Altered.'

Jan Inge's laughter is as shrill as that of a little girl.

'Professional jargon, Pål. Altered.'

Pål looks from one of them to the other. Rudi must have a condition of some kind, but still he's a cordial type, the kind of guy everyone wants to have in their gang of friends. Jan Inge is impossible to place, obviously talented and very intelligent, but all the same ... stupid?

'Hey, Uli?'

Rudi places a fingertip firmly on Pål's chest. Jabs him four times in the solar plexus.

'I can feel that this is going to go fucking great,' he says. 'We definitely have a connection here. Am I going too far when I say that this could be the beginning of a long friendship between you and our company? What do the stars have to say about it? What do you think Gran – rest in peace, old patchwork quilt – would say, sitting up there in Heaven, knitting socks for the lot of us? Respect to you and respect to your kids and respect to your dog, and death to your woman problems. What's his name again? Zitha? He's been sitting there now, obediently, for fucking minute after minute after minute after minute, and I've noticed it. While the two of you were talking I was on the dog's side. And what does a dog get out of a human's conversations? Wellmyfriend, there's more between people and dogs than we suspect. That dog has participated. You have a true friend there, Huli.'

Videoboy nods to Rudi and places a fat arm around Pål's shoulder. He leads him a few metres alongside the substation wall. Walks with him a little. Gives him a few pats on the back. Nods. Both of them with eyes downcast.

He stops abruptly and looks Pål in the eyes. Then the high-pitched voice wafts into the darkness of the woods: 'Have I seen you before?'

'No,' Pål replies hastily, 'I don't think so.'

'No? Hm. Are you scared, Pål? You don't need to be. You

should know that you're surrounded by friends. You should know that you're working with someone who wishes the best for you, someone who is going to give you the chance to get your life back in order and get you back on your feet. Fear? Let me tell you. I know all about fear. It's what you could call my area of expertise. You're at the point where it's still not too late. You're not alone in this. We're going to lift this weight as a team, Pål. A collaborative effort.'

There's a shine in his blueberry eyes. His voice carries out into the woods, with an unworldly tone.

'Are you with us, Pål? Will we do this? Go through with, what I like to call, a time-honoured classic?'

59. **DO YOU WANT TO KNOW WHO I AM? HM? DO YOU?** (Daniel William)

This here – this is a hassle. That last foster father was a run-of-the-mill asshole, but he was right about what he said: if it's hassle you want, just get yourself a woman. Daniel has two of them now and they're both psychos. One has cut herself up and the other is hysterical. *Daniel, you are a coward. It's time you showed who you are. Who it is you want. I'll wait by the substation.* Daniel feels the lift suck him down through the block of flats, and looks at the display on his mobile for around the twentieth time. What the hell's happened to Sandra? The fact that Inger flipped out when she saw Veronika's mesh-face, screamed and wailed and wanted to ring the hospital and Child Welfare, and send Daniel off to some outreach camp for kids and God knows what else – that he gets. But he managed to calm her down. He has a knack for that sort of thing. Look deep into the eyes, keep a good hold on the shoulders, wait for the breathing to slow: *Inger, Inger, we'll sort it out.*

But this here?

You are a coward

Daniel exits the entrance to the flats and walks out into the darkness.

He's not an idiot either. He's got good hearing. He can pick up when other people are talking through your mouth. When you open your gob and they're not your own words spewing out from between your lips. When you can see in people's eyes that there's a psychologist in the background dictating the words.

Get rich. Get a woman with her head screwed on once and for all.

That's all Daniel wants. Two small things. How difficult does it have to be? Every time he nears his goal it's like some fucker comes along and wallops him in the face with a club, sending him back to his own stone age. Inger seemed all right. Sandra seemed all right. Veronika seemed all right. But no. They were all too good to be true. That's the hidden truth. Nobody is as they make out. They sell themselves as beautiful fucking buttercups, but when you unwrap them they snap at you.

Give them cancer, cancer, cancer.

He walks with purpose, his arms paddling through the air, as though to sweep aside anything that gets in his way.

He can handle Inger. A grown woman screaming because her daughter has transformed her face into a hundred small bloody squares, who says she regrets ever having taken him into the house. *There there, Inger. It's going to be all right.* He can also handle Veronika. When he left them, mother and daughter were sitting on the sofa with their arms round one another. They feel they've been through something together. But Sandra. He can't handle her or his own feelings for her. They brim over, he's unable to hold them down. Whenever other girls pass him he doesn't react. They can be as hot as may be, they can have jugs that are heaven-sent, legs and asses that are primo, but it makes no odds. When she comes running along from side to side with those knees of hers, then he just has *no control over himself.*

But now.

Now he's in control of himself.

Daniel, you're a coward. It's time you showed who you are.

All right. It's a deal, bitch. You asked for it.

He runs. The last metres through the schoolyard, over the football pitch. It's already dark all around. There isn't the slightest breeze, no friction other than what he himself creates against the world.

'Daniel!'

He stops dead.

'Daniel!'

A dark figure appears over by the school, becoming clear under the lights by the football pitch. Be angry now, he says to himself. Be hard.

She runs quickly towards him. Fast, small feet across the gravel.

The pulse in his necks throbs, he clenches his teeth. Sandra speeds up, she looks a wreck, her hair is dishevelled and her eyes tired.

'Daniel!'

She stops just in front of him. They look at one another. He bends over slightly, she raises herself on her tiptoes. They throw their arms around each other, kiss.

'Fuck,' he says, feeling her soft lips, how they take shape to fit his, her warm, wet tongue, how it seeks his, 'fuck, fuck, fuck.'

'Fuck,' she says, sniffling.

'Fuck,' he says, closing his eyes, 'fuck, fuck, fuck.'

'Fuck,' she says, sobbing.

'It's you and me, baby,' he says, placing his hands on her behind.

'Touch me,' she says, 'never stop, Daniel William Moi.'

'Fuck,' whispers Daniel, 'I didn't mean it. You know that.'

'I know,' she whispers, 'I know.'

'I just get so fuckin'...'

'I know,' she whispers again, 'you don't need to say anything.'

They break off from the fantastic kissing he can't live without and stand looking at one another under the lights of the football pitch.

'Daniel?'

She reaches her hand out, strokes him gently across the cheek.

'Yeah?'

'Have you seen Malene and Tiril's dad?'

'No...'

They look in the direction of the substation.

'What do you think is going on?'

He shrugs. 'I don't know – did you say anything to them?'

'No,' she says, 'but I think it's kind of horrible ... I feel I know something I shouldn't, and I feel I ought to say it, but—' Once more she brings her hand to his face again, strokes his skin with her fingers, and once more he loves it. 'But Daniel,' she says, warily. 'Am I the one you love?'

Is she going to start this again?

He can't believe his ears. They've been snogging each other for two minutes, they've forgiven one another – and she starts this again? He feels like beating her senseless. Can she not fucking leave well enough alone?

'Veronika,' she says, nervously, 'you need to tell me what's going on. I saw the two of you, in town. I saw her. You have to tell me what's going on.'

He breaks eye contact. Okay. That's how it is.

'Sandra.' He shifts his weight to his other foot. 'Don't worry about this. Will we go into the woods and look for the father of those girls? Just, don't be concerned about this—'

She just stands there. 'I need to know, Daniel. I have to know if it's me you want.'

He sighs and looks up towards the sky. 'Please. I need you to trust me now.'

She nods. 'Yeah, and I need you to be honest with me. You had your arms around her. You live with her. I have to know—'

'She fancies me.'

Sandra takes a step backwards. The corners of her mouth begin to quiver. She stammers: 'Does she want ... but ... so, do you want to be with her?'

'I—' he stops himself, this has to come out right. 'I'm not able to protect myself when I'm with you.'

Furrows appear on Sandra's forehead, her hands begin to clench.

'When I'm not with you I sometimes think I should break it off, that we shouldn't be together.' Daniel is conscious these words aren't coming out right, he can hear how dangerous it is saying them out loud, yet he's unable to stop: 'But when I see you, then I just want to have you.'

Sandra weeps inaudibly. Her body is limp. He doesn't like looking so he turns his head and continues: 'I didn't know she wanted to be with me. Not like that. Not in that way. But she did. I can get on fine without her, but at the same time it's like she ... fuck, you know? It's as if she's good for me somehow, while you're not good for me, even though you're the one I need. Do you understand?'

Sandra has closed her eyes. She looks like she's going to keel over, as though her knees are going to give way any second.

'Do you understand?'

She doesn't say anything. She just stands there with her eyes shut, crying. Fucking hell, she looks so beautiful. Okay, he thinks. Not so strange she has to mull it over a bit. She's just got a considerable dose of honesty right in the face. But if she managed to listen to what he was saying, then she's understood who he needs. That was what she wanted to know, wasn't it? *Who it is you want.* He's said it as clearly as he could, without lying. He likes Veronika, he's not planning on letting her down. If Sandra's thinking of a life with him, then she'll have to learn to deal with Veronika. Just like Veronika will have to face the fact that it's Sandra he needs.

'Sandra?' he says in a soft voice. 'Are you all right with this?'

'Did she cut herself for you?'

She opens her eyes, they're overflowing with tears.

He nods.

Sandra swallows. 'Just one more thing, Daniel, then I'll let everything be.' She brings her hand to her throat, fiddles with her necklace. 'I need to know who you are.'

'Hm?'

'I need to know who you are. What you've seen. What you've done.'

Ponderous beasts surround the football pitch, crippled mongrels. They've emerged from out of the woods. Groups of small boys stand just behind them, all dressed in beige wadmal, all barefoot, all with horses' heads, all with bleeding eyes. One of the boys holds a lance in his right hand. He raises it and at the same moment the horse heads begin to scream, a piercing, depraved shrieking, and the sky overflows with a rapacious light, and there, in the heavens, the sun is on fire, burning with raging flames. The boy with the lance summons the muscles in his body, tenses his arm, brings it back and sends the lance up into the sky.

'A wolf,' whispers Daniel and sees the beasts withdraw, moving backwards into the woods, followed by the boys in horses' heads.

'Hm?' Sandra juts her chin out. 'I didn't hear what you said.'

The sound of footsteps coming across the gravel behind them. Daniel and Sandra turn around. Malene. It's Malene.

60. **INTERNATIONAL EMOTION** (Tiril)

She should sit at the front of the stage playing piano. Sing. Just her, a piano and the audience. Like Amy Lee. But she can't play the piano. It's just as well Thea is taking care of the music so she can concentrate totally on vocals. There's a video like that on YouTube, where Amy is sitting on a stool singing while the guitarist in the band is responsible for the music. But Amy is kind of fat there and doesn't look too good, and the backdrop isn't great either.

'Candles?'

Tiril has pictured it. That they can cut out the spotlight and the coloured lights. It would be a lot more intense if they bought a load of candles – pillar candles, purple and white – and turned off the lights in the hall.

'Yeah, good, eh?'

Tiril and Thea walk through the double doors into the gym hall. Lots of people are there, things are already underway and Svein Arne is busy helping with rehearsals. He's the one responsible for organising things, Svein Arne Bendiksen. He's in charge of the school revue and he's a musician – good at everything. People say he held the county record in playing fast on the guitar when he was younger and he's able to play the saxophone, the piano and the oboe, and one time a guitarist from a really huge band, Tyler Straits or something, heard Svein Arne play, and he said that Svein Arne was a mega talent.

'I'm certain it would look good,' Tiril continues, as they hurry into the hall. She unbuttons her jacket and waves to Svein Arne.

'Tiril! Thea! Great!' Svein Arne comes towards them smiling. 'Good stuff, we can have you on soon.'

'Listen, we were thinking,' Tiril says, 'about the lighting...'

'You'll have to talk to the lighting crew about it...'

'Yeah, I know, but you're the director,' Tiril laughs, 'or the manager. Anyway, what about if it's all totally dark, right, when we're introduced. Then we, like, come on stage, Thea in white, me in black, and I go and light up ten or twenty big candles while Thea plays the intro...'

Svein Arne nods, clearly impressed. His long curls bobbing about his enthusiastic face. 'But if it's going to be that dark, then maybe you should consider wearing something other than all black...'

'Nah, I'll have some candles right beside me...'

He laughs. 'Right, just make sure you don't catch fire then. Great. That sounds atmospheric. You're on in about twenty minutes. We're going through the programme in the same order as tomorrow. I'm just going to finish up with the dancers from Eksilstuna. You have to see them, they're really good.'

He jogs back to the stage: 'Right, okay, we'll go again. Ingrid, Susanna, wasn't it, yeah, Susanna, Kadi ... Kadija, yes, Malin, Badra! Mina! Ulrik! Okay, let's take it from ... let me see ... what is it Taylor Swift sings there ... *we are never, ever, ever*, yeah two times on *ever*, no wait, actually it's three times here...'

'Taylor Swift,' Tiril snorts. 'Candles. Thea, you play the intro. I'll go and light them. It'll look cool, yeah?'

Tiril takes off her jacket. Then she gets a look in her eyes. Money. Twenty pillar candles. That'll cost a bit. She can't afford it. She's not getting paid before next week.

'Thea?'

'Mhm?'

'I was wondering ... can you get the money for candles?'

'Sure,' Thea says, with a facial expression as if it were an odd question.

'Cool. We'll buy them tomorrow. He's really good, Svein Arne, isn't he?'

'Mhm, yeah, he can play so many instruments.'

They survey the gym hall. Strange when it's filled with people from other countries. They're all being put up in pupils' homes. There's one in Tiril's year who has a Finnish girl from Jyväsklä staying with her, another in Malene's year who has a girl from Antsirabe in Madagascar living with her – she's really cool, she's going to give a speech, apparently, and recite a poem. And Ulrik, he's going to play the guitar; cute, little Ulrik, so popular he makes all the girls melt.

'They're all from twin towns of Stavanger,' says Thea. 'Do you know anyone?'

'Well...' she wrinkles up her nose, 'spoke a little with a girl from Denmark...'

'They're from, let me see,' Thea counts on her fingers, 'Fjarda-byggd, that's in Iceland somewhere, Esteli in Nicaragua, Houston, in Texas of course, and from Esbjerg in Denmark, Nablus, that's in Palestine...'

'Yeah, yeah, Brainy, I know, you're so good at...'

Thea continues: 'And from Aberdeen in Scotland, from Eksil-tuna in Sweden, and Jyväskylä and Antsirabe...'

Somebody pokes Tiril on the shoulder. She turns around.

Bunny's little brother.

What the hell is he doing here?

'Can I have a word?'

There's something different about him. For one thing, he's on his own. He never usually is. He's always with those annoying friends of his. For another, he doesn't have that cheeky grin on his face. And thirdly, he's just standing calmly. He has a pair of headphones around his neck. She can't remember ever having seen him stand quietly.

'I don't have the time.'

'It's all right – we're not on for another twenty—'

Thea. Great. You had to open your mouth.

'Just a couple of minutes,' says Shaun. 'Five. Tops. Promise.'

'Listen,' says Tiril, folding her arms, 'you've ratted to Kenny, you've spat in my hair, you've—'

Shaun shakes his head. 'I didn't rat to Kenny. I wasn't the one who told him.'

'Yeah. Right.'

'Can you not just come outside with me for a sec? Just for a bit. Five minutes. Two minutes.'

'Where Kenny is standing waiting with your idiot mates to beat the shit out of me. Do you think I'm stupid, Shaun?'

He remains standing, quite still. Tiril tries to remain firm, but can't maintain it. Some old memories well up inside her, from primary school, when she and Shaun used to have pretend fights in the snow, when he tripped her up, when she threw snowballs at him, when she sat on his chest and gave him typewriter torture.

'One minute.'

She gets to her feet.

'Okay. One minute. Max.'

Shaun nods and begins walking towards the door. His body isn't swaying from side to side as much as usual. He's small, almost a foot shorter than her. He walks with his hands in his pockets and his head down. She follows him. Out through the foyer, out the front doors. Shaun walks a little away from the gym hall, over behind a tree.

She comes to a halt when she reaches him. 'Well, what is it?'

'I—'

'He's bang out of order, Kenny, you are aware of that? Do you know what he did?'

Shaun nods. 'I can't do anything about it, some others told him, and Kenny ... Kenny's not quite right in the head, it's not my fault.'

'What do you want, so?'

'I—'

Tiril takes a deep breath. Her chest rises.

'Have you got a fag?'

Shaun nods. He takes a ten-pack from the pocket of his baggy hoodie. They sneak around to the side of the gym hall. He produces a lighter, lights one for her and then one for himself.

'We're probably the only ones in second year who smoke.'

He nods. 'I was the only one who smoked in sixth class too. Going to try to quit soon.'

'Me too. Not good for the singing voice.'

Tiril is pushed for time, but she looks him over. Small, scared and strange, that's what he is. Her eyes fall on his headphones. 'What are you listening to?'

Shaun gives an embarrassed shrug. 'Ah, nothing.'

'Give me a look at your phone, then.'

'Eh,' he says, shifting his feet.

'Give me a look.'

Shaun takes his phone out of his pocket, makes a face, not eager to let her see. But Tiril grabs it, begins to scroll. Just hip-hop, just shit music. Eminem, Rihanna and a load of bands she's never heard of – David Banner, Khia, Akinyele... what the fuck? Her finger stops moving. She glances up at Shaun.

'Eh...' He blushes.

'Put it in my mouth?'

'Eh, yeah, that...'

'What the fuck is this ... smell your dick? We fuck virgins?'

She removes the headphones from around his neck, puts them on and presses play. A sleazy drumbeat. A siren. A creepy man's voice whispering: *Cum girl, tryna get your* ... what's he singing? Tiril raises one eyebrow at Shaun while she taps the next song on the playlist. A faint drumbeat, another creepy voice, a woman this time: *All you ladies pop your* ... what is she singing?

Tiril takes off the headphones. Her cheeks are flushed, she tries not to swallow but can't manage. The little, embarrassed halfwit stands there in front of her and she doesn't have time for this.

'*Awesome Pornrap for Shaun,*' she says.

'Eh, yeah...'

She shakes her head.

'You are a sick slacker,' she says, handing him the phone.

He takes it and shrugs again, as if that's the only thing in the world he's able to do. 'Yeah, I suppose I am, all right,' he says in a low tone.

'That music,' she says. 'It's, like – Jesus, Shaun.'

Again he shrugs. 'I know. That's the kind of stuff I like.'

Shaun gazes at her, looks at her for longer than any boy has ever done.

'What was it you wanted to talk to me about?'

'Huh?' His eyes flit about.

'What was it you wanted to talk to me about?' Tiril asks again, aware of an antsy warmth in her body and suddenly realising what all this is about. Without quite being able to explain it to her herself, without being able to take it in her hand and look at it shimmer, she decides to say yes when he asks if she'll be his girl-friend. No, she decides to be the one in control, so she blows out the smoke and says: 'Shaun. Do you want to go with me, or what?'

His eyes grow large.

'What? Do you want to get down on one knee or something? Are you not able to speak now?'

She gives him a thump on the shoulder, but Shaun stands there, as though rooted to the spot, his eyes growing larger and larger.

'Come on,' Tiril says, 'now you've got what you want. You need to cut back on the porno rap. There's proper music out there. Have you heard Evanescence? And don't make such a big deal out of this here. Kiss me. Make it quick. I haven't got all night.'

Shaun blinks a few times, raises himself ever so slightly up on his toes, and gives her a kiss, a slightly awkward one, but nice all the same.

61. BRILLIANT, SPOFFI! THIS IS GOING TO WORK LIKE A DREAM! (Rudi)

Granted, at first sight, yeah. At first sight Jan Inge may not cut such an impressive figure as he does when you see him in action. But then we're talking discrimination, Rudi thinks, and isn't that a mortal sin? What we're looking at then is a type of racism, a type of Nazism, *obesity Nazism*, and what was it we learned in primary school about not judging people by their appearance, their race or creed? It's bullying, pure and simple. And Rudi's seen it so many times when he's been in the presence of the great Jan Inge, and he doesn't mean 'great' as in fat, but 'great' as in brilliant, and what would Gran have to say about that? Shame on you! People who meet Jan Inge and look away, people who talk shit behind his back, call him a hobbit, or people who quite simply talk shit to his face. Do they not think he's hurt by that?

Great men have feelings too.

The worst Rudi's experienced was the time they had a job on with the Tornes Gang from around Haugesund. A shower of bastards. Doped out of their minds all day long, swapping women all the time, swindling each other, no conscience and no love, either for the profession or for the people engaged in it. It had seemed so promising, a nice decent break-in up in Haugesund. They'd come by information, they needed people, they'd heard about Jani's gang – naturally enough, word gets around. But Jesus, Mary and Holy Saint fucking Joseph. It started from the minute they met them. 'Whataboutye,' said the Tornes guy, the one with ears as big as an elephant, 'fat ass there is Jan Inge, is he?' 'Whataboutye,' his brother chipped in, Tornes guy number two, the one with such a tiny nose you'd think he'd snorted it away, 'all right hi, Porky, you going to drive the Skoda, are you?' 'Whataboutye,' Tornes guy number three takes over, the youngest brother, the one with the mental big wart on his forehead, 'all right hi, Fatso, are you the one called Videoboy?' Oh fuck, Gran, wash my mouth out with Domestos. I'm happy you didn't have to see that. That's how they went on, for two whole days, and if it hadn't been for Jan Inge himself refusing to let Tong and Rudi do over the whole Tornes Gang and cut them into pieces, then that's what would have happened to them, and they would have been messed up and smelt even worse.

It's only fair and proper, thinks Rudi, that I stand in Jani's shadow.

Der Führer, without making invidious comparisons.

Look how he puts his arm around Pål. Strolling along in the lee of the substation. Seems like a sound bloke, Pål. Heart in the right place. Feels like one of us in a lot of ways, thinks Rudi, as he hears Jan Inge say: 'Are you with us, Pål? Will we do this? Go through with, what I like to call, a time-honoured classic?'

When they meet people they're going to cooperate with in some way or another, Rudi often feels that he can't really talk to them, like they're living in a world far removed from his. But Pål. Top bloke, plain and simple. Really good feeling, knowing they're not just doing this for the money, but also to help their fellow man.

Fellow Man.

That was a book, so it was. Granny was always on about it. She had books on the brain, Gran. Sitting there with her books. Hamsun and Agatha Christie and whatever their names were. Nothing wrong with that, total respect for book people, Rudi thinks, even though I've chosen the real life and everything it has to offer, instead of the book life with all it has to give.

Pål doesn't reply. But Jan Inge allows him time.

It's all about being calm, pensive and dignified.

'Let me tell you a story,' he hears Jani say, from over in the thicket. 'A little story. My father – I won't mention his name or where he lives – my father had some problems once. Lets put it like that. Some problems that his kids, my sister and me that is, weren't completely aware of. If you and I were to walk the miles together, I could tell you all about it. About what a child sees, about what

a frightened little child understands and what a grown-up understands, and what a person who sees an axe coming down on their
throat understands. You like horror, Pål? No? I could – and maybe
I will? – show you some films one day. *Suspiria?* No? You haven't
seen *Nightmare in a Damaged Brain? The Thing?* No? *Carnival
of Souls?* You haven't seen it? *Night of the Living Dead? The Hills
Have Eyes?* Hm. You sure I haven't met you before? Anyway. My
father. He had an insurmountable number of problems. And this
is in spite of being a happy-go-lucky guy. If there's one thing that
characterises him, it's his unbelievable good humour. It's almost
mystifying. But problems. Big problems. But you know, we were
just kids, and I mean, what did we know about adult life. I mean,
what were we? A trifle, blades of grass in the field. So, we're talking
the very early eighties here – keywords are Blondie, Wham!, *Blade
Runner, E.T., Raiders of the Lost Ark,* John Holmes, Desiree Cou-
steau – and let me make it quite clear that we're anti-porn. We're
feminists, twenty-four hours a day. At your service, women! The
eighties – reminds me of Speedos and tight shorts, Rossignol skis
and Björn Borg, things your kids will never know anything about.
Smells they won't associate with anything. I mean, who remembers
Kim Carnes? Me, Pål. Me. Or, hold on ... 'Bette Davis Eyes' ... no,
now I'm getting mix— Rudi! Eighty? Eighty-one? Eighty-two?'

'No idea, that's your area of expertise.'

Jan Inge nods: 'I think I might be wrong, forget that about
Kim Carnes.' He plods on for another few steps with Pål, who
still remains silent. Rudi has begun patting Zitha, the dog breathing calmly to his touch.

Jan Inge breathes in and out heavily. 'I'm showing faith in you
now, Pål. Because I like you. But also because I want to show you
that in our firm, we're different. We're not some cocaine-snorting
gang of idiots from around Haugesund. We work with, and for,
people. We don't bow to the Hell Angels or the Bandidos. We
don't jump for joy because David Toska and his gang come to
town. We work away quietly. We're almost like part of the very
bedrock of the city. Anyway. My dad. So he had a large number of
insurmountable – is that what it's called? Insurmountable? Rudi?
Insurmountable or insuperable?'

Rudi pouts while pondering the question. 'Errrr,' he says, 'I think you could use either of them.'

'Right. They were the problems he had. Insurmountable and insuperable. I can just say it right out: the biggest problem was my mother. A she-devil, Pål. The mother of all fears. A heart of glass. We can talk about it another time, when the two of us are sharing a pipe by the ocean – I'm speaking metaphorically now – then, we can talk about it. But now we're discussing my Dad. And I'm getting to the point. Around this time, he was made an offer. An offer, Pål. Just like you.'

Now Rudi feels a tugging in his chest. This is precisely what he loves about Jan Inge. Standing here, on an ordinary Wednesday, watching him in action. His thoughts flying hither and thither, his words too, and who knows what he's after but then it comes, the point.

'Yes,' he hears the master say. 'My father got an offer. This was the oil age now, Pål, not the internet age—'

'Mayhem! Get thee behind me!' Rudi makes the sign of the cross with two fingers and holds them towards the sky.

Jan Inge laughs his reedy laughter. 'It's the era of oil, and my father is in that business and he gets an offer. While he's up to his neck in problems. Will he accept a job over there?'

'Over there, land of the brave, hom—'

'Will he? A lucrative position, Pål, good money, a new life. He gets an offer, a time-honoured classic, if you think of life as simply time and this as a classic.'

'Hah. You listening, Poffi?'

'You follow me, Pål?'

Pål nods.

'Simple as that. Dad went to Houston. Difficult for us as kids to understand back then. Easy to understand now. And you? Now you're being made an offer. What do you say, Pål?'

Rudi can't manage to keep still any longer. This is just too much. He lets go of the dog, who responds by following him. He stands in front of Pål, looks him in the eyes, grips his jaws in both hands and says: 'Brilliant, Spoffi! This is going to work like a dream! Hallefuckingluja! Can I kiss you?'

Pål looks bewildered. Rudi gives him a friendly shove. Jan Inge takes out his inhaler, shakes it and sucks on it.

'So. Now we can listen to what you have to say, Pål.'

'I'm in. But...' he pauses uncertainly.

'What are you thinking about, brother?'

'Well...' He runs a hand through his hair. 'No, it's just – what were you thinking of doing to me?'

Rudi smiles. 'Listen,' he says, 'it'll be fine. We're experienced. Don't worry about it.'

'Right ... but ... will it ... hurt?'

'Look, Joffi, there's being hurt and there's being hurt ... you can take a little bit of pain.'

'But ... will I wind up in hospital? Will I be able to walk afterwards?'

'Shit,' Rudi says. 'You're a nice guy, Toffi. Don't think about that. Think about the money! Ah. See this here, this is one of the best days of my life. When I die, I'll remember four things: Chessi's face, Jani's face, Lemmy's face and that beautiful face of yours, Schmoffi.

Zitha barks.

'Yeah, yours too, fuckmutt,' Rudi says and in his head Coldplay begin blaring at full volume: Du-du-du-du-du-du-du-du-du.

'It's so bloody good,' he says 'to feel that you're alive. I can't wait to tell Chessi.'

'What?' Jan Inge shoots him a dubious look. 'No details, not before you've cleared it with me.'

'No, no,' laughs Rudi. 'Jesus, I mean, I can't wait to tell her that it's time we started thinking seriously about things – kids, y'know, maybe getting a place of our own, taking the relationship a step further!'

A darkness brims in Jan Inge. It flows from his little blueberry eyes and washes down over him.

62. **HONEY** (Malene)

Malene walks out the front door and out into the street, heading in the direction of Folkeviseveien.

She went home when Thea and Tiril left for the rehearsal, the same time as Sandra disappeared into the darkness to meet Daniel. The wild sensations the day had thrown up vanished quite abruptly, the tingling of her skin, the heat of her body, which had made her feel strong and new. She couldn't manage to take control of the situation. All of a sudden, Sandra didn't need her any more; suddenly it was Tiril who had taken over everything, as though she were the big sister. Malene no longer felt at ease wearing the bright red lipstick.

'Will I go with you?' she'd asked. Sandra had shook her head. 'No, no, course, you have to do this yourself.' Malene had hastened to add, 'Don't let him ride roughshod over you, Sandra, okay?'

Dad wasn't at home when she got in. The house looked like it was abandoned right in the middle of something. The living room door was wide open. One slipper at an angle to the other in the centre of the kitchen. A single saucer with a slice of bread on the kitchen table. A half-empty glass of juice. Zitha's rubber bone on Dad's pouf.

Malene cleaned up, but the sight of her hands annoyed her. She thought they looked like the hands of a forty-year-old as she loaded the dishwasher, as she hung up damp towels in the bathroom and as she placed Dad's shoes beside one another.

Soon it was nine o'clock. She looked over her homework. She flicked through the channels on the TV. Clicked around on Facebook.

Now she's outside. It's daft. It's idiotic. Out spying on Sandra and Daniel. But she can't help herself. Sandra is having a torrid time and Veronika has it rough ... is she jealous, is that it?

She walks quicker.

'You're such an idiot, Malene,' she whispers.

She hurries along past the tower blocks in Jernalderveien and comes out on the plateau above the primary school, from where she's afforded a view. There they are. Daniel and Sandra. In the middle of the football pitch, underneath the lights. She slackens her pace, lets her feet move slower across the tarmac. She knows she should turn around, but she's can't manage to.

Malene straightens up. Walks as naturally as she can out on to the gravel pitch. What will she say when they spot her? She doesn't know Daniel. He hardly knows who she is. He's a dangerous boy – who can tell what he's capable of.

She draws closer. He's so handsome. Everything about him is beautiful and strong. It's hard to act naturally when people are so good-looking. How are you supposed to act, when the presence of another person is so overwhelming? She would never have dared go out with a boy like that. He gives a lot but he takes more. What he touches would always be left dazzled but also diminished. It's not possible to come away from Daniel William Moi intact.

Malene scuffs her feet on the gravel so they'll notice her. She's only a few metres from them. What's she going to say when they ask her why she's here?

Sandra turns. So does Daniel. What eyes he has, what a mouth. If he opens it up the whole world will disappear down his throat

'Malene?'

She raises her hand in a clumsy greeting and refrains from looking at Daniel.

'Hello, fancy meeting you two,' Malene says, trying to make her voice sound as unaffected as she can.

'Hi...' Sandra looks nervous. 'This is Daniel...'

He gives her a quick look, a look that says she should get out of here as quick as she can.

'Well,' she hastens to say, 'I'm heading to the school to listen to Tiril. Not too many people paying her much attention at the moment, so I figured I'd better be there for my little sister.' Malene knows she's speaking too fast, and she knows she's a bad liar. 'Yeah,' she giggles nervously. 'Y'know, Evanescence, heh heh, have to support little sis.'

You need to go, Malene.

It's in their faces, it's in their body language.

She sees two men come into view down by the substation. They're coming out of the woods, they resemble characters in a computer game. One of them is ungainly and as tall as a tree, the other quite small and fat. They're momentarily lit up by a street-lamp outside the kindergarten, before they disappear from under it, heading in the direction of the main road.

'I see,' Daniel says, 'you're one of the sisters. The gymnast? Heard about your tumble. Bummer. Ankle was it?'

One of the sisters? Has Sandra been talking about her?

'Yeah...' Malene nods.

She looks at Sandra with uncertainty, whom for her part, avoids Malene's eyes.

'Okay, but anyway, Malene,' Sandra says, with an affected smile, 'we're just going to have a chat...'

Another figure appears beneath the light outside the kinder-garten. And a dog. They look like they're part of the same com-puter game. First the towering figure, then the little, fat round guy, and now a normal man with his head down, and finally a dog sniffing along. Malene juts her chin out and squints.

It's Dad.

She feels something shoot through her stomach, a needle-thin pain.

She points at the substation, 'I'm...' she says to Daniel and Sandra, 'I'm just ... that's my dad.' The others turn to look. 'He's out walking Zitha, our dog, that is...'

Dad bends over. Picks something up. It's a stick. He holds it up high in front of Zitha, who's wagging her tail expectantly. Then he stops dead, his head turns in their direction, his hand suspended in the air.

He looks like he doesn't want to be seen, Malene thinks. It's completely obvious. Dad doesn't want to be seen.

He relaxes his body, his face breaking into that nice smile of his, shouts 'Come on, Zitha!' and throws the stick toward the goalposts.

Zitha sets off in pursuit. Dad strolls towards them.

This is embarrassing.

'Hi!'

Dad's big, warm smile.

'Malene, didn't expect to see you.'

Dad's big, false smile.

He puts his hand out as he reaches them. He whistles for Zitha. Daniel shakes his hand and introduces himself. 'I'm going out with Sandra.'

Dad smiles. 'I know Sandra all right. Nice evening, eh?'

Zitha comes running over with the stick in her mouth, drops it at Dad's feet and he commends her.

'Out walking the dog?' Daniel asks, bending over and running two hands along Zitha's snout.

'Oh yes,' Dad says, 'every day. What are you lot up to?'

Daniel's grins and he says: 'Darkness imprisoning me, all that I see, absolute horror, I cannot live, I cannot die, trapped in myself.'

Dad gives a start, as though someone had hit him in the face.

'Heh heh,' laughs Daniel, 'Metallica. Your T-shirt.'

Dad laughs and looks down at his chest, the old T-shirt barely visible under his jacket.

'Best band in the world,' says Daniel.

Dad smiles. 'Well, I better be getting home,' he says. 'Enter Sandman, y'know. Heh heh. Are you heading home, Malene?'

She nods, knows she's been given away, but it makes no difference.

She smiles at Sandra, gives her a hug.

'See you around,' says Daniel.

The windows of the tower blocks are lit up in the darkness. All those people crammed together. It looks cheery and sad at the same time. Malene is aware of her father's heavy form beside her. He walks along, making small talk about something, but she's not following what he's saying. She's just aware of him plodding along, aware of something being terribly wrong. She stops as they get to the last tower block. She stares at him for such a long time that he's forced to make eye contact with her.

Malene puts her head to the side.

'Honey,' he says, 'everything's going to be fine.'

63. Y-E-A-H-W-E-A-R-E-J-U-S-T-F-I-X-I-N-G-O-U-R-S-E-L-V-E-S-A-C-O-U-P-L-E-O-F-S-A-N-D-W-I-C-H-E-S-H-E-R-E-T-H-A-T-S-F-I-N-E (Veronika)

She can feel his breath in the room. Soon he'll steal around the corner, soon he'll come and lick her face. Veronika straightens up on the sofa beside her mother. They've been lying beside each other for almost two hours. Neither of them have stirred, nor said much. Sweetheart, you must never do that again. No. Do you promise me? Yeah. You'll tell me, won't you, if anybody does something bad to you? Yes. You'll let me know, won't you, if Daniel seems dangerous?

Her mother has stroked her hair, taken her hand and entwined her fingers in her own. They've breathed in and out together. Watched an episode of *CSI: Miami*. And now the wolf is here. Veronika doesn't know how this day was born or how it is going to die. She doesn't know if it's been a horrible day or a fantastic day. She's proud and she's embarrassed, she feels whittled, she feels sharp. But he's here now.

Veronika runs a hand through her hair: here is Daniel. He's been to see his slut of a girlfriend. Has he licked her face? She fixes him with her eyes.

Daniel smiles. Not so much self-assurance.

'Do we have anything to eat?'

Her mother shakes her head, shrugs, takes a deep breath.

'No, there's not much, I'm afraid. Some bread, maybe. You'll have to take a look.'

He nods, doesn't meet her eyes and walks to the kitchen.

Are you scared, Daniel? You held me close, you caressed me and you put your arms around me. But you don't want me. You're letting me down, Daniel William Moi. Don't you know who you want?

Veronika gets to her feet. She signs the word for 'eat' and makes her way towards the kitchen. On her way she tucks her T-shirt into the waistband of her trousers so the material is taut over her breasts.

There he is. Standing with the knife in one hand. His other hand on top of the bread. He's slicing it. She opens the fridge, takes out the ham slices, as well as the butter, and places them on the worktop. Then she stands beside him. He smells of outdoors, he smells fresh, doesn't smell of his slut girlfriend. The blade of the knife flashes in his sinewy hand and slices through the bread. Daniel cuts slowly. Veronika moves a tiny bit to the side, her body just barely making contact with his. Daniel doesn't move.

Hm? Can you feel this?

He doesn't move. A vein appears in his neck. He clenches his jaw, his teeth grind. Veronika reaches for the ham, allows her forearm to brush against his.

Daniel doesn't move. She can hear his breath, she thinks she can see claws growing out of his paws. She can see his mouth opening, fat glistening on his lips, his tongue slipping out between his teeth. His head turns in the direction of the living room, she reads his lips: 'Y-e-a-h-w-e-a-r-e-j-u-s-t-f-i-x-i-n-g-o-u-r-s-e-l-v-e-s-a-c-o-u-p-l-e-o-f-s-a-n-d-w-i-c-h-e-s-h-e-r-e-t-h-a-t-s-f-i-n-e.'

She catches his eye, mouths: 'I-a-m-n-o-t-y-o-u-r-l-i-t-t-l-e-s-i-s-t-e-r.'

His ears stand on end, his snout narrows. He mouths: 'W-h-a-t-a-r-e-y-o-u-t-h-e-n?'

She takes his hand and presses it against her crotch. She mouths: 'I-a-m-w-h-a-t-y-o-u-n-e-e-d.'

His lips move towards her, kiss her.

That's what I thought.

I see your yellow eyes.

Nothing is settled yet.

Veronika feels his hand, slipping around her pubic bone, and feels the fingers of his other hand gently stroking the cuts on her face. She gives him her tongue.

64. ME AND TOMMY POGO, MADLAVOLL SCHOOL 1983 (Rudi)

'Jesus fucking Christ.'
  'Huh?'
  'Shitshitshit!'
  'What?'
  'Holy mother of God.'
  'Huh?'
  'Tampon!'
  'Huh?'
  'Tampon!'
  'Where?'
  'There!'
  'Where? I can't—'
  'There!'
  'Huh, where?'
  'There, for fu—'
  'I'm telling you, I can't see—'
  'By the shop!'
  'Oh.'
  'Yeah.'
  'Oh holy fuck.'
  'That's right.'
Rudi and Jan Inge have stopped at the edge of the woods, Rudi feels his adrenalin pump as he points down towards the shop on the corner, at the man standing there.
  'Oh no,' says Jan Inge in despair.
  'Oh no, oh no, oh no, oh no.'
  'Has he seen us?'
  'Youcanfuckinbetyourasshehas,' says Rudi. 'I can feel his eagle eyes on us.'

Jan Inge wipes his forehead with a clammy hand.

'Tampon.'

'Tampon.'

'Pogo.'

'Tommy.'

Rudi spits and grates his canine teeth against one another. 'That's torn it, like my Dad, that badger used to say. And you know how seldom I mention him, or any of the other voles in my family. What the hell is Tampon doing here? Doesn't he live on Mosterøy?'

'He must be working so, you gobshite.'

'Don't call me things like that, Jani. It's hurtful.' A line forms between Rudi's eyes. He doesn't dare take his eyes from the man standing on the corner. 'Working?'

'How would I know,' Jan Inge hisses, 'what a guy from Mosterøy is doing in Madla. It's a free country.'

'Sure, all too free. Jesus!'

'Keep it down, he's looking at us,' Jan Inge says. He's speaking with the voice of a thinker now. The voice of a leader. Rudi finds that reassuring. 'Look at him,' Jani continues, 'look at him standing there trying to psych us out.'

'Pogo. Jesus fucking Christ.'

'Please,' says Jan Inge. 'Not God and not His Son. You know I don't like it when you're profane.'

'Sorry, it's that foul mouth of mine. I'll never get shut of it. You know as well as I do that if there's one person who respects the Lord, it's me.' He shakes his head slightly. 'Look at him. Standing there staring at us. That bloody beard and all. He was really young when he first got facial hair, did you know that?'

'No?'

'Oh yeah. Must have been in sixth class.'

'That is young.'

'Was a hard bastard, Pogo. None of us saw it coming.'

'Jan Inge gives Rudi a quick glance, 'The force?'

'Rudi nods. 'One day he's laying into Ullandhaug-Remi with a nail-bat – you know Remi's back was never the same? One day he's laying into Remi with a nail-bat behind the greasy spoon, because he happened to glance in the direction of Elisabeth from Spring-arstien, and the next thing he's applying for—'

Jan Inge nudges Rudi in the side. 'He's on the move.'

Rudi blinks rapidly. 'Andwhatarewegoingtosaywearedoing-here? We're screwed now, amigo.'

'Not so fast,' says Jani, irritably. 'Smile.'

'Hm?'

'In the name of Saint Catherine of Siena – smile! And let me do the talking.'

'Youcanbloodywellbetyourlifeonit. And I hope you have a good explanation as to why we're here. Leadership – now.'

Rudi puts on his broadest smile, but he gets the feeling it's no more convincing now than when people ask him to smile for a photograph. 'Shit,' he whispers as he watches Tommy Pogo approach. 'He's kept away for months – you'd almost think he'd been on paternity leave or quit the force, and then he shows up here.'

'Shut it. Smile. And let me do the talking!'

'Yo! Tampon!'

He's only a few metres away from them. Tampon keeps himself in great shape. He's so in form and fit-looking it's almost threaten-ing, thinks Rudi. A healthy mind in a healthy body, as Granny used to say when she saw Rock Hudson on TV. Look at that. The beard covers up his harelip. The bright, blue eyes. The tanned, healthy skin. The shiny hair. Guy's got muscles coming out of eve-rywhere. Impressive looking, there's no getting away from it.

'Tommy Tang! Well, well, what's the long arm of the law doing on the old stamping ground?'

Tommy gives them a cheeky grin, a grin Rudi can remember, a grin which made all the women in Tjensvoll, Madla and Gosen melt and dream of going on a date with Pogo.

'Heh heh, indeed, was just about to ask the two of you the same thing.'

'Heh heh,' Rudi laughs in reply, 'after you, sir.'

'Heh heh. No, by all means, Rudi.'

'Heh heh.'

'Heh heh.'

'Tam-pon. It's a long time since we met around these parts. They were the days, eh?'

'You're right there,' laughs Tommy Pogo. 'Yeah, so I've just moved back. Living on Sommerstien.'

'Hah.' Rudi slaps his palms together. 'There you go. Back to the land of childhood. You hear that, Jani, Tampon has moved home.'

'I heard,' says Jan Inge, in a strained tone.

'And what are you two doing here?' Tampon lets his gaze drift from Jan Inge to Rudi and back again.

Jan Inge's face breaks into a broad, self-confident smile. 'Will we tell him, Rudi?'

Rudi looks at his friend uncomprehendingly, his thoughts running around confusedly in his head, but he understands by the look Jani gives him that all he needs to do is follow his lead. 'Yeah, let's just spit it out.'

Jan Inge laughs. 'We must be getting a bit sentimental in our old age, just like you. We were sitting at home – we've had lots to do recently, a load of work with our removal company – and it was almost as if all this moving we were doing for other people made us aware of how little we move ourselves, if you know what I mean—'

'Yeah,' says Rudi enthusiastically, 'that we're just over there in Hillevåg and never get the finger out—'

'And then Rudi said: "Jani, I wonder how things are out in Madla these days. In Tjensvoll. In Gosen. In Haugtussa." You know how it is, he's from around here.'

'I know that, heh heh.'

'So here we are. Breathing in the diamond air of the eighties.'

'Diamond air?'

'Yeah. A comparison.'

Tommy Pogo's smile lets them know he doesn't believe a word.

'So you're living here. Your kids are going to school in Gosen then?'

'Yeah, Ulrik's in third year. Kia's in first year. They've got a good set-up for her there.'

'Oh, yeah, forgot about that acc—'

'Yeah.'

'Something to do with ski—'

'Slalom. In Ålsheia. She's paralysed from the neck down.'

'That's tough.' Rudi shifts his weight from one foot to the other. 'So. Heard about how things are with Remi, by the way?' Rudi grins, but he can feel Jani's eyes burning into him.

Tommy Pogo takes out his mobile and looks at it. 'No,' he says, putting the phone back in his pocket, 'but listen, Rudi, now that I have you here.'

Pogo takes a step closer. He cocks his head a tiny bit to the side. Rudi moves backwards.

'That key,' says Tommy.

'Key?' Rudi says, his eyes flitting about.

'The key to the centre.'

'The key to the centre?'

Tommy Pogo smirks. 'Rudi, come on, I've been wondering about it for almost thirty years. Where did it get to?'

'Oh! The key to the shopping centre!' Rudi relaxes and slaps the palm of his hand off his forehead. He laughs, and thirty years seem to disappear, and for a few seconds he feels like it's old times, and he almost has to stop himself from giving Tommy Pogo a hug. 'Heh heh,' he chortles. 'The key to the shopping centre. Christ. I'll tell you where it's got to.'

Rudi produces a bunch of keys, begins flipping through them and finally holds up an old Union one.

Pogo sticks his chin out. 'Jesus,' he says. 'Is that it?'

Rudi's eyebrows dance up and down.

'You've held on to it,' says Pogo, nodding. 'Well! I'd better be off home,' he adds, reaching out and shaking both their hands. 'I'll drop by one day.'

'Yeah, by all means,' Jani says, 'by all means.'

Rudi smiles: 'Sure thing. We'll be home all right.'

'Tomorrow,' says Tommy Pogo, 'why not tomorrow?'

'Hey, why not,' says Rudi, feeling Jan Inge's eyes boring into him.

'Good,' Tommy Pogo says, 'it's agreed. See you tomorrow. Steak, chanterelle mushrooms and Brussels sprouts?'

'Wha?'

'My favourite meal.' Tommy turns to go, but stops as though he's just thought of something, spins back around and asks: 'By the way – Tong, isn't he getting out soon?'

'Yeeah...' Rudi notices his voice doesn't sound right.

'That's right,' Jani says swiftly, 'he's out tomorrow. Big day for us.'

'Right, yeah,' Tommy Pogo says, smiling. 'Had a feeling he was out around now. Great. Then I'll have a chance to catch up with him too. Apparently he's had an okay time in Åna, or so I hear. All right. Talk tomorrow.'

Pogo walks off in the direction of Sommerstien.

Rudi shakes his head. Harelip Pogo. Strange to think of. Once he was in the Tjensvoll Gang, now he heads up Project Repeat Offender for Rogaland Police District. It's screwed up how life goes. Once Tampon was his best mate, now Pogo is one of Rudi's biggest problems.

Tomorrow,' he sighs. 'What are we going to do now? Call the whole thing off?'

Jan Inge shuts his eyes for a couple of seconds, before slowly opening them again. 'We go through with things as planned. Tampon's not going to suspect us after meeting us here and then calling in tomorrow.'

Rudi nods. Go through with it. Masterly.

Jan Inge looks at Rudi. 'What was the story with that key?'

Rudi smiles. 'Tommy and me,' he says. 'We got our hands on the key to the backdoor of Tjensvoll Shopping Centre. Nicked it from a coat in the break room. At first we used it to get in and knock off fizzy drinks and beer. But after a while we rented it out to people. We put a limit of two crates of beer each. Me and Tommy sat up in Vannassen and ran the whole thing. The police didn't know what was going on. The alarm would go off, they'd drive down, but there was never anybody there. People just unlocked the door, got in and got out. The cops thought there was something wrong with the security system. Heh heh. It all went to hell when Janka couldn't control himself. He filled a whole shopping trolley with beer. They copped on then.'

'Nice all the same though,' says Jan Inge, nodding. 'That kind of style is right up my street.'

'Yeah,' says Rudi. 'One of our better moments. Was Tommy who came up with it, of course. I probably would've just broken a window, gone in and picked up the beer.'

'Yeah, that you would.'

'Hah. The dark side lost a good man there.'

'True. A kind of Anakin Skywalker in reverse, that Tommy.'

Rudi looks down at the bunch of keys, rubs the old Union one between his finger and thumb. 'I've never been able to bring myself to throw it away,' he says. 'It felt pretty intense seeing him. Back here, like. Same old Tampon in a way. Somewhere or other inside that buff cop's body is the mate I once had. Steak with chanterelle mushrooms and Brussels sprouts. Wasn't a lot of that when Tommy was a boy. Did I ever tell you about the time we broke into Madlavoll School?'

Jani shakes his head. 'No, don't think so.'

'Middle of the night. 1983. Tommy was always so bloody angry. You can't see it any more. But he was, a fucking ball of rage. Hah. 1983. Middle of the night. Madlavoll School. Me and Tommy Pogo. We just ran through the empty corridors roaring and shouting. That was so fucking great.

65. **PRAYER** (Sandra)

Dear Lord, I don't know who you are any more. I don't know who I am any more. He's hurting me, he's tearing me apart, but I try to tell myself that if I am to be ruined, then I'll be ruined by something beautiful. I'm not able to think about anything else. I hate the here and now, I want to go back to when I was small and you were standing in front of me. I no longer have the feeling you're there. When I was little, I always knew you would come to me. All I had to do was wait, all I had to do was close my eyes. Now I don't know where you are. But now is the time I need you. Why don't you say something? Do you want me to suffer here on my own; is there some purpose behind it? You let me feel love but now you're taking it away from me. I don't understand the purpose of that. Please, I'm closing my eyes now, I'm lying here in bed. Breathe on me. Mum and Dad are upstairs in the living room. They're pacing the floor, I can hear them. They're talking together, you know that, talking about me. Mum is crying; can you hear that, she's crying. She's not used to this, she's protected me her whole life – Sandra has never done anything to make Mum cry. But she doesn't recognise me now. It's not our Sandra, she says. You've skipped work, she says. Who is it you're meeting, Sandra? Why don't you talk to us? Why are you pulling away? We're your parents, Sandra, all we want is to help you. The scary thing is Mum's right – I'm no longer their Sandra. I'm Daniel's Sandra. So breathe on me, Lord. Breathe first on me, then go up to the living room, get Mum to sit down and breathe on her eyelids and say: She is not your Sandra. She is Daniel's Sandra. Is he leaving me? Is he not who he said he was? He's not going to Veronika, he's not going to her. Say it. He is not going to her. I'm the only one who knows who he is. Breathe on us. Breathe on Malene and Tiril's father. Breathe on the sisters.

Breathe on Mum. Breathe on Dad. Breathe on me. Now I'm calm. I'll try to sleep, I know you'll come and lie down beside me a little later tonight, like you always used to do. I know you'll come. I know that it will be a new tomorrow and I know that everything will be fine.

66. **0162** (Tong)

He sits on the floor with his legs crossed. He's switched off the TV and the light in the ceiling. The dark of night lies beyond the bars of the cell. He has his shoulder blades lowered, his arms hang limply by his sides and the palms of his hands face upwards. His head is perfectly straight. There's a calmness around his eyes, around his mouth, in his arms, his stomach and his feet. Heavy hands, heavy fingers, eyes shut.

The prison liaison officer had escorted him back from the visiting room just before half-past eight. Piddien is from Loddefjord, skinny as a rake, talkative bugger, a guy Tong has always thought could just as well be in a cell himself. Piddien had given Tong a cheeky grin, as he had done each time he'd walked him back the last few weeks. He knows well that Tong is getting some action every Wednesday.

'Well, Tong,' he had said, giving him a slap on the back, 'last time you'll need to get dressed in Åna-issue clothes to get your end away. You're out tomorrow, that'll be good, eh?'

Tong hadn't reciprocated the smile, or the slap, or anything else.

'That'll be good, all right,' Piddien went on. 'You wouldn't exactly talk the hind leg off a donkey, but you've had an all right stay. Prisoner number zero one six two. You won't be needing that any more.'

Tong had stood motionless in the doorway with his back to him.

'You'll be looking for something in carpentry, then?'

Tong nodded. 'I'll give it a go.'

'Yes,' Piddien had said, 'that would suit you down to the ground, that would. Strong lad like you, likes physical work. Worn out at the end of the day, tired muscles. Heh heh, yes indeed. So, will your little lady be coming to collect you then?'

He feels the weight in his palms, the weight on his coccyx.

'She's not my lady.'

'Heh heh, no, no, of course, ha ha.'

They should have meditation classes in prison. Tong has said as much to the people in administration. Everyone who lands in here has their body in a tangle. Their shoulders are so tensed up they're practically scraping the ceiling. Being locked up isn't the worst thing – it's the waiting. The months between waiting to be sentenced and the time you first come in. That's what screws you up, that's what wrecks your head. When you first arrive, you're hardly a person – you're a knot. It's not medication you need – it's meditation. It's not Subutex you need – it's contemplation.

Tong meditates every day. A short session at midday and for an hour after lock-up. Then press-ups and a workout. He used to have a mop handle in the cell, to which he tied towels, then attached big industrial soap dispenser refills to the towels, making for an effective barbell. But they took that from him. They don't like people getting too big.

Cecilie, Tong thinks, relaxing his jaw and feeling a softness in his throat, in his face. It was as though she was going to devour him. He entered the visiting room; she was there, as usual, but it looked like she'd been crying. He didn't say anything. Nor did she. Her bony hand just trembled a little. Looked at the wall as if it were something other than a blank, white surface. But she stood up abruptly. Jumped like a little animal, right over to him, took off his trousers, then took off her own and sat on top of him and screwed him like it was the last time, or the very first. It all happened just like that, the whole thing. And then, while he was inside her, she started going on about her dad in Houston, and she talked about Rudi, something about her being so fed up with him she wanted to puke, and then she went on about not knowing what to do or something.

It seemed like she meant what she said. Tong listened to her, but as time went on and she went up and down on him he had difficulty following, her pussy was eating him and he just said what he always does when he's about to come – that he'll do fucking anything for the woman he's riding. Then she opened her eyes wide, stared at him and said: 'Do you mean that, Tong?'

He shut his eyes, clenched his teeth so hard it made his jaws ache.

When he was finished, she kissed him and said: 'That was lovely, Tong. Listen. We've something on tomorrow. An insurance job. Do a guy over, cause a bit of damage, make it look like a clean break-in. Are you in?'

She's fucked up, but gorgeous all the same: 'Yeah, yeah, sounds good.'

Tong takes a deep breath through his nose, then exhales through his mouth. Last night in Åna. He's leaving in the morning. As of tomorrow he can do what he wants. Just have to get that pathetic job out of the way. Rudi and Jani. It is so the last time he's going to work with them.

His body rises. He no longer feels the floor beneath. He glides above a jungle landscape, green treetops drift by below him, a soft, warm wind brushes across his skin. He ascends, descends, and ascends again. He floats in the air over a waterfall, sailing over the plunging water, and there, close by, an eagle is wheeling, Tong opens his mouth, goes for the bird, sinks his teeth into its neck, hears it screech, feels the taste of metal in his mouth, and there, in the wild sky, stands a burning sun.

THURSDAY 27 SEPTEMBER

There are friends who point the way to ruin,
others are closer than a brother
Proverbs 18:24

67. **SHELLEY WAS RIGHT** (Sandra)

She wakes up in the dark. Neither tired nor teary-eyed. Her body feels ready, as does her mind. She reaches towards the night stand and takes hold of her iPhone. The light from the display illuminates the room. 05:57. She sits up.

I'll do it, she thinks, and plants her feet firmly on the floor. Taking care to avoid the floorboards that creak, she goes to the wardrobe by the window and takes out a clean pair of knickers. She grabs the clothes she wore yesterday off the chair, slips quickly into them, tights, jeans, bra, and top and creeps out on to the landing. She opens the door to the toilet, pees, throws some water on her face and, unconcerned about how she looks, goes downstairs, leaving all the lights off, letting Mum and Dad sleep.

She picks up a shiny red apple from the glass bowl on the kitchen bench.

She pours herself a yoghurt drink and downs it in the light from the fridge.

I'll just do it, she whispers as she opens the front door. It's cold, but night is about to give way to morning. It'll soon be light but it's still too dark to make out the fjord. Some small birds perch in the trees, only just having begun singing the day in. Otherwise the streets are quiet. No lights on in the neighbouring houses. No one to be seen.

She hastens down Kong Haralds Gate, passing Madlamark-veien and continuing to the bottom of the hill. She crosses Mad-lavollveien, hurrying between the low-rises, the time getting on for half past six. The tower blocks rise up in front of her, dead and desolate, as if nobody lived there any more, as if those poor, stupid people who once did because they couldn't afford anything better were, fortunately, all now dead.

The night has done her good and now she intends to cause another girl harm. She slept for no more than four hours, but is as rested as though she slept twice that. You can be as deaf as you like, you handicapped ginger bitch, she thinks as she walks by Coop Prix supermarket. You think you're sweet and innocent just because you can't hear. You think you can cut yourself up and then everyone will feel sorry for you.

That's not how it works.

You've taken my man from me.

You're going to pay for that.

Sandra leaves the shop behind and walks calmly towards the tower blocks. Her body is of steel; she's never felt so cold. You must never, her mother has said, make any room for envy and jealousy. Well, Mum, here I am, I've let it take root.

A man passes by, wearing a bicycle helmet and tight training gear. She makes her way up the last hill, towards the last block in Jernalderveien, the one facing the Iron Age Farm. She approaches the buzzers. She slides her fingers down over all the buttons, without pressing them, like she did as a little girl, together with Shelley in 4A. Shelley was from Norwich, had lived a few years in Stavanger while her father worked for Mobil, had a big mole on her top lip and had never managed to learn Norwegian. One time they had rung all the doorbells, ran their hands down over the buttons and felt the hairs on the back of their necks stand up at the thought of the buzzers going off in all the flats in the block, and while Shelley thought it was *wicked*, it had given Sandra a pain in her stomach. She had let her mother down and let Jesus down by doing such a mean thing, by playing ring and run. But now she knows that Mum is a nervous wreck and that Shelley was right and Jesus isn't a coward, Jesus is the master of vengeance: He spins the cylinder of the revolver and turns the other cheek to hate.

Her finger stops.

There's a dull thud from inside like someone unloading a pallet off a truck. The lift reaching the ground floor. A figure behind the glass. It's coming towards her. Shit. She makes to move, but doesn't have time to run and ends up crouching down to tie her shoelace. Who is it? Sandra is on one knee, the door opens and a woman in a red jacket and tight jeans comes out, a woman in her late thirties.

It's Veronika's mother. Daniel's stepmother. She mustn't recognise her. Sandra keeps her eyes fixed on her shoes, her breathing rapid. The woman glances at her, but is in a world of her own and doesn't take in what's in front of her.

The door slams shut behind the woman, who walks quickly away along Jernalderveien.

Sandra straightens up. It's getting bright. Day is dawning. She brings her finger back to the panel of doorbells. She moves it, purposefully, across to the occupants of the twelfth floor.

'Inger and Veronika Ulland. Daniel William Moi.'

This is what hate is. It's good to know it's alive and kicking.

68. MUMMY'S JUST TALKING RUBBISH (Cecilie)

Just like little fish. Small, glittery fish darting through the water, stopping, beating their tails a little, then turning around, bodies twitching before swimming to another part of the ocean she carries within.

That's what they say. She's read it in magazines. Fish. Or bubbles. As though little bubbles are bursting inside her. After sixteen weeks, they say. Then you can feel life. When is that? Sixteen weeks? How far along is she? She doesn't know, maybe five weeks, maybe six. She has to go to the doctor soon, needs to get that cleared up.

Cecilie lies quite still with her eyes closed, like her own mother must once have lain, with a little girl inside her. She can sense the day approaching, a thin strip of light slipping into the room. It's going to be warm again today. What time is it? Seven? Waking up early these days. Must be the baby, I suppose.

In a few months there's going to be an infant lying beside her. In its own cradle perhaps, alongside the bed. Maybe it will look like her, might come into the world with crooked lips and ash-grey skin. Maybe it'll have a rattle in its hand and a mobile hanging over its little baby head. Maybe it'll lie there whimpering. The way she herself must have lain, beside her own mother.

Cecilie opens her eyes. She raises herself on to her elbows, feels the nausea spread. She looks over at Rudi. His long form, stretched out beside her, half covered by the duvet, his huge cock like an eel dozing on his pale stomach. Lots of scars and blemishes to be seen on that body. Marks, all over the skin, covered in moles, nicks, pocks and craters from old spots. Handsome, he most certainly is not.

The baby might not survive, may well die inside. Wouldn't

surprise me, she thinks, if it croaked in my sea of ash – not as if anything could grow there. And if it is Rudi's kid then there's no telling what kind of creature it will be. Might be just as well it dies before the world gets to see it. Maybe it'll be an alien pops out of her in seven or eight months' time. Maybe an alien head is going to be sticking out from between her legs. Euuuugh! Sister! What an ugly fucking kid! Jesus, what a pigugly smurf!

Nobody wants to look at kids like you.

Nobody wants to be with kids like you.

Cecilie sighs and rubs two sleepy, clammy hands from her hairline down to her chin.

'Sorry,' she whispers. 'Mummy's just talking rubbish. Mummy's always a little like this in the morning. Mummy doesn't mean anything by it. We're going to get up now, you and me, get some coffee. Your granddad, the one who lives in America, he needs his coffee first thing in the morning too. Says he goes nuts otherwise. Once he gets his coffee he's a funfair for the rest of the day. Did you know he runs his own company, your granddad? That's right, baby, he does. Southern Oil. He's the president, yessir, Thor, president of Southern Oil. Yeah, yeah, but don't spare him a thought, he's a spineless shit. Now, we're going to have our coffee, baby, take a quick shower and then get out of this house of horrors, because we have to go pick up the man who may be your father.'

Rudi turns, half-asleep.

'Mmmmm, Chessi...' he mumbles, 'who are you talking to ... lying there yakking away ... Southern Oil ... Granddad?'

Breathe in. And breathe out.

Cecilie leans over to Rudi. She places her hand on his forehead. Then brings it slowly down over his eyes, his already quivering eyelids, straining to open at the approaching day. She kisses him, even though he stinks.

'Rudi,' she says, in a low voice.

'Oh yeah,' he murmurs, 'just talk away to it, then I'll impale you, just say the word and I'll be ready...'

'That wasn't what I meant,' she says softly, 'you just sleep. I'm getting up to go get Tong. Sleep some more, Rudi needs it. You're so tall, you know, you need a lot of sleep.'

'It's my cock takes up all the blood...'

'Yeah, I know,' Cecilie whispers, 'go to sleep now. It's early, even Jani isn't up yet. Go back to sleep now.'

Rudi focuses his gaze on her, his eyes are gleaming. 'Like being in a nursing home, this is,' he says, in a raspy, morning voice. 'Care. A care home. That's what you should've been, Chessi, a nurse. You're one awesome lady, you know that?'

Rudi raises his head. Keeps his eyes fixed on her.

It's hard to hate a man who loves you much.

But not impossible, she thinks, sending him a kiss with pouted lips before picking up her jeans and bra and making towards the bathroom.

'Just watch out,' she hears from behind. 'After that job tonight there's going to be cock in your house. He's going to be hunting through your halls tonight! Jesus! There's a mad dog here! Holy shit, he's got the biggest cock in the world! Heh heh. You're one awesome lady. We should get a place of our own soon, eh, Chessi? Tonight, Lady Gaga! Tonight!'

'Go to sleep now,' she says. 'If you want some pussy after work then you need your sleep.'

'Ooops! Surethingboss.'

Cecilie shuffles along the carpet in the hall. It's hard and dirty. It needs to be changed. She yawns, the nausea is heavy and constant. She doesn't need to throw up, but it feels as if everything would be better if she did. So, when she's moving around, is the baby staying still, is that how it is? Or has it already begun to move around itself? It soon will. If it's not already dead. Dead baby. Soon start moving. Tiny fish. Soon stretch out its tiny fingers and tiny toes, its little head will turn around, its little eyes will try to figure out what's going on. But the baby's asleep right now. It's following Mummy's movements. Just as though it's holding its breath. What is Mummy up to? Where are we off to?

Was it like that for Mum as well? Back when she was a little mite inside her own mother? Did she wonder if the baby was already dead?

Cecilie opens the bathroom door. She gives a start when she catches sight of Jan Inge. He's sitting fully clothed on the toilet seat, his feet dangling a little above the floor. He has dark, blue rings beneath his eyes, one finger stuck into his mouth. He's chewing on a nail and doesn't look up at her. He blinks, his eyes going from side to side. He's been crying. He looks about twelve years old. He looks like he did when he was twelve. Back when he was in here biting his nails, crying and shouting to her outside in her nightdress: 'Cecilie! Don't come in! I need to think! I need to think!'

69. **MORNING IN THE HOME OF A FATHER OF TWO TEENAGERS** (Pål)

'Tiril? Malene? Breakfast!'

He has his foot placed in a jaunty fashion on the bottom step, his chin tilted towards the first floor. Zitha stands beside him, her tail wagging, the end of her snout also raised, as though imitating him. Pål lifts his eyebrows, elevates his cheeks, arranges his features into a pleasant expression, as if this were a summer day and he were a father from a film on children's TV. In his hands he holds a milk carton and a plate of sliced cucumber, tomatoes and pepper.

'Come on, girls! Breakfast!'

That's the way. He keeps his back muscles tensed as he returns to the kitchen. Setting down the milk and the plate on the already set table, he takes the matches from the mantelpiece and strikes one off the box. He lights the candles and glances at the coffee maker gurgling by the window. Sides of meat, cheese, pâté, sliced fruit and veg, lettuce even, as well as milk, juice and coffee.

This looks good. This'll do the trick.

'Zitha! Good girl. Lie down now.'

This day exists. And it doesn't.

He hears Tiril's footsteps, firm and lively, coming down the stairs, ostensibly saying everything about his youngest daughter, *the trampoline kid*, as Christine once called her. She could be like that now and again, original in her choice of words, as if she ought to have been a writer as opposed to a businesswoman. Behind Tiril he hears Malene's footfall, steady and mature. The difference in their footsteps is like hearing his wife and himself. Back before the break-up, back when she jumped out of bed in the mornings, after a good night's sleep, already at work long before she had actually stepped out the front door and got into the car. He takes a little longer to wake up – usually about twenty minutes before Pål is ready for the day. Christine was awake before she awoke. As soon as she opened her eyes her energy level was running at maximum. He smiles to himself at the memory, which was annoying back when it was reality and not reminiscence. The recollection of Christine drinking coffee while she dressed, putting on make-up, preparing the kids' lunches, reading the paper and hey presto – suddenly she was in front of him, radiant and ready, car keys in hand, giving him a routine peck on the cheek before telling him he had to 'have a nice day' and then disappearing out the door.

A mutual tempo of sorts was something they never shared. Pål would make an effort now and again to get up to her speed. He convinced himself that somewhere within him lay a kind of variant of her that he could be. He planned the day in accordance with her pace, attempted to imitate her. If she took it upon herself to start vacuuming on a Saturday morning, he would let breakfast wait while he got stuck into the dishes from the day before. But it just drove Christine round the bend. Jesus, Pål, please, this here is just weird – do you have to shadow me?

Tiril's body is electric, she has headphones on and she's sharply defined in black-and-red attire.

'Hi, honey,' he says, in as friendly a tone as he can, stopping her with his arms outstretched, but she ignores his invitation to hug. He drops his arms without making a fuss about it. Tiril forces a smile, he can hear the music from her iPod, stripped of bass; she has no time for Dad now, she needs to concentrate.

'Christ,' she says, pointing at the breakfast table, 'somebody die?'

He laughs, even though he doesn't find it funny. 'Just wanted to make you a nice breakfast, with you having such a big day and all,' he says, feeling a swelling in his chest as though what he was saying was pure and true. 'Sit down there and I'll get you some coffee. Can you take off those headphones, just while we're eating?'

Tiril raises her darkly pencilled eyebrows, but leaves the head-phones on. She takes her mobile from her pocket, flips the cover up and begins texting.

'I need an iPhone 5, Dad,' she says, without looking up, 'but I don't suppose we can afford that?'

The door of the hall toilet can be heard opening and moments later Malene appears. She looks tired and unwell. Pål grows anxious and forgets Tiril's complaint, but he thinks how he mustn't allow the feeling to take root, probably just a morning thing, soon blow over – talking about your troubles only makes them materialise.

'Hi, Dad.'

Malene bends down to greet Zitha, giving her a rub before coming over to Pål. She looks towards the kitchen table.

'Wow, what an amazing-looking breakfast.'

He strokes her hair. 'Sleep well?'

'Not really,' Malene says. 'Do we have any bread?'

'Yeah, of cour—' Pål stops himself. 'Hold on, of course we've got bread...'

He scurries over to the breadbin, feeling the girls' eyes on his back as he lifts the lid up. A little bag with a stale heel. He places his palms on the worktop. Turns to the girls. Malene has dark rings under her eyes, it won't soon blow over. Tiril's thumb works away at the screen of her phone, the treble from her iPod hissing about her head like a swarm of wasps.

'Ryvita?' Pål asks, hearing how poorly his voice is carrying.

Malene shrugs. Tiril scrolls on her mobile and moves her lips, but no sound escapes her.

Pål breathes in, fastens a smile on his mouth, brings his palms together with a clap and says: 'Ah, it's going to be a lovely day. Thursday. I've taken the day off work, thought I might get us something really nice for dinner, tidy the house and live it up, the three of us, and then, yes, then it's – eh, Tiril?'

He walks over to her. So much make-up, where's the girl under there?

'Eh?'

He stands in front of her.

'Eh? Your big day, isn't it, eh?'

She removes the headphones, puts down the mobile: 'You coming to watch?'

He keeps his smile fixed and brings his hands to her face, one on each cheek: 'Of course I am, honey. I wouldn't miss it for the world.'

Tiril's phone vibrates, reverberating on the tabletop. She frees herself from his hands but he can see the joy in her eyes, the effect his assurance has had. She picks up the phone, taps the screen. Her features contort and she rises from the seat, her head shaking. Then it vibrates again and she reads once more.

'Jesus,' she says, not looking at them, 'asshole.' Tiril breathes through her nostrils and looks up from the display. 'This here, this is seriously screwed up. Sorry, I gotta go. Kenny has kicked the shit out of Shaun and Sandra is flipping out. Malene, you need to come along, let's go. See you tonight, Dad.'

70. **THAT'S THE WHOLE POINT** (Veronika)

Night arrived with creeping darkness. It covered Madla, covered Stavanger, the west of the country, Norway, Europe, the world and the universe in the same ever-increasing circles she's pictured since she was a little girl, back when she could hear. She was six years old when she lost her hearing and her memories of sounds are as clear as glass, but she doesn't like them; her mother's voice, the sound of a toilet flushing, a car starting. It's nicer to think of the noises she's never heard.

Mum seemed knackered when she said goodnight. She stood in front of Veronika with her head to one side and placed two fingers on her cuts, tracing her fingertips along them, just as Daniel had done in the kitchen minutes previously.

'Don't stay up too late, okay?'

'I won't.'

It was as though his very hand had sowed desire in her groin. The firm grasp he had taken of her was hard and insistent, painful almost, but the craving in his palm, the hungry pressure he put against her pubis, made her body ignite, and when he took his hand away all she could think was *do it again*. She felt a flailing warmth spread throughout her, also in the form of increasing circles, beginning in her crotch, describing a ring round her loins, a ring round her stomach and thighs, around her breasts and calves, a ring around her entire body.

The bathroom door opened. The sound of her mother's feet going in the direction of the bedroom and out of sight.

'Night, Mum.'

'Good night, Inger.'

Daniel was sitting at one end of the sofa, feet up on the table, neck resting on the back of the cushion, one arm over the end of the sofa, the other resting on his stomach. Veronika sat up for a moment, pretended to fix her clothes, then sat down again, closer.

He got to his feet without looking at her, his lips moved, but she wasn't sure if he said something or merely sighed, snapped for air, like a guppy. He went over to the window, closed it and remained standing looking out at the darkness with searching eyes.

He did say something, but she couldn't make it out. 'What?'

He turned his mouth away again. *Too much shit here now?* Was that what he said?

Veronika got up and went over to him. 'What are you saying?'

He avoided her gaze. 'Dunno. School. Can't face school tomorrow. Need to think.'

She drew as close to him as she dared. There was a long pause. Veronika's breath had less and less space to draw in air from.

'And what is it you need to think about?' she asked.

He turned to her. His face glistened, his teeth shone like polished ivory, his eyes had yellow spears in them and his tongue was long and cruel.

'You fuck me up,' he said.

'You fuck me up,' she said.

Daniel put his hand back where it belonged, he pressed harder and she felt how that was the way it was supposed to be. Her hand went to his jeans, rubbed him across the flies and she saw his mouth open, saw his chest heave and his jaw clench.

'You really fuck me up,' he said, gritting his teeth as his torso rose and fell.

'I know,' she said, as she took her fingers away, saw him take sharp intakes of breath, took hold of his belt, undid the buckle and saw him gulp and blink, 'and that's the whole point.'

'Shit, we have to be quiet,' he said, placing a hand on each of her breasts.

'We have to be very quiet,' she said, feeling a throbbing dick in her hands for the first time.

Veronika wakes up. Her cheeks are warm and it is Thursday morning. She opens her eyes and closes them right after, as though what she's going to see is an enemy of that which has occurred.

She has no choice but to go far today, too far perhaps.

71. MOON AND SUN, WIND AND CLOUDS, SISTER AND BROTHER, DEATH ENSHROUDS (Jan Inge)

'Oh ... Jan Inge ... I didn't know you were in here.'

Jan Inge swallows. He looks up at Cecilie. She has those threadbare jeans of hers in her hands, as well as an old bra. She's only wearing the large Europe T-shirt. It looks like a tent.

She crouches down.

'Hey? You okay?'

Jan Inge nods ever so slightly. He meets her eyes for the briefest moment, then looks away again. It's not a good idea to look deeply into Cecilie's eyes, too much to see in them.

'Oh God, Jani, bruv, are you crying?'

It's not so easy after all. Always having breakfast ready. Never falling apart. Forever being in good humour. Being in control at all times. He saw it. In that programme on TV, the one about leadership. A Microsoft executive. *Show emotion*, he said. *Demonstrate that you're a person and not a machine.* It makes for a good leader. And why? asked the Microsoft guy. I'll tell you why, because you work alongside people. They need to see that you're like them.

Jan Inge reaches out and tears off a few sheets of toilet paper. He blows his nose. Swallows.

'What's wrong? Why are you sitting here crying?'

Jan Inge raises his bulk from the toilet seat. He takes a few steps towards the bathroom mirror. He sniffs, clears his throat, spits in the sink and rinses his mouth. In the reflection of the mirror he can see Cecilie pulling down her knickers, flipping up the lid of the toilet, sitting down and peeing. She actually looks quite nice when she's sitting like that. Those eyes, set far apart, open up her face kind of like a book; she looks like she did when she was small, when they roamed about the house wondering what to do, when Mum had died and Dad had gone to Houston.

Those compassionate eyes. More gut-wrenching looking into them than meeting those tetchy eyes she glares at you with most of the time.

Jan Inge finds a spot in the air and fixes his gaze upon it. He straightens up: 'Cecilie. I'm sitting here in the toilet. It's an important day. I'm here enjoying a few moments of peace early in the morning. I'm meditating. I'm like the Chinese. Do you see the bowl of rice between my hands? Do you see the wind playing in the hazel trees?'

Cecilie gets up from the toilet, flushes it and tries to make eye contact, but he avoids it.

'Jani,' she says, sitting down on the edge of the bath, 'you know I'm not always able to follow what you're saying when you talk like that. What do you mean?'

'I just mean that I'm thinking.'

'Yeah?'

He looks her in the eye. He's able to now. 'About my life,' he says. 'About our lives. About Tong getting out today. About Dad in Houston. About Mum in Hell, barbecuing rats with the Devil. I'm picturing the grease dripping from the side of her mouth. Is she riding the Devil, Cecilie? It wouldn't surprise me. I'm thinking about the job we have on tonight. I'm sitting here in the toilet – the last bastion of privacy. And yes. Perhaps I shed a tear. Yes. Perhaps life overwhelms us all at times.'

He turns to the sink, puts both taps on, waiting for the water to become lukewarm before placing his hands under the jet. Warms them up.

'Yeah, of course it does,' says Cecilie.

'Do you not think I harbour dreams?'

'Sure, of course I think you do.'

Jan Inge turns off the water and takes hold of the towel hanging beside the sink. 'Do you think it's fun for me to have become so fat and got a bald patch to boot? Do you not think I'll do anything to keep this gang together?'

'But Jan Inge—'

He sits down on the edge of the bath, beside her.

'I'll tell you something, Cecilie,' he says. 'When Dad went away … one night after I'd put you to bed, I went down to the basement. Dad had left behind some tools in case we had to fix something in the house. We did become independent, you and I, by the fact of him leaving. I'll give him that. I found the toolbox and took out the hammer, Cecilie. I took it in my hand and carried it with me up the stairs, carried it through the hall here, held it while I opened the door to your room, clasped it as I made my way over to your bed. And once there, I raised my hand over my head and saw the shadow of the hammer on the wall behind you.'

Jan Inge pauses.

He is aware of the heightened atmosphere in the bathroom.

Cecilie sits camly beside him. She listens as though what he's saying is on celluloid. An intense film about a brother who's going to take his sister's life. Because their mother has kicked the bucket and their father has moved to Houston.

But it isn't a film.

It's this shitty life.

But that's just how it always is.

It's never a shitty film.

It's always life.

Cecilie nods, as if remembering what he's telling her.

'I don't know,' Jan Inge says, turning to look at her. 'I can't explain what I was thinking. Maybe I thought things would be easier if you were dead. Maybe I was afraid of having to look after you for the rest of my life.'

'But that's what you hav—'

'Yes, I have.'

'You've really looked after me, Jani.'

'Yes, I have.'

'Good thing you didn't crack my skull open with the hammer anyway.'

'Yes, it was.'

'But listen, I need to take a shower and be on my way to pick up Tong.'

Cecilie puts her skinny arms around his big body. It feels good.

She radiates warmth even though she's ever so small. Jan Inge remembers the song he made up that time he was standing over her bed with the hammer in his hand. *Moon and sun, wind and clouds, sister and brother, death enshrouds.* He stood there with the hammer raised and sang. He can still hear the choirboy pitch of his own voice. How nice it sounded. While he looked at the shadow of the hammer thinking that now Cecilie had to die. *Moon and sun, wind and clouds, sister and brother, death enshrouds.*

Cecilie loosens her hold around him, her body gives a jerk and she lets go of him. She swallows and gulps, then makes an abrupt dive for the toilet where she leans over the bowl and throws up.

Jan Inge blinks. Repeatedly. 'Yeah,' he hears her wheeze, her head down the toilet bowl, 'yeah, yeah, yeah, I hear you, Jani, I know what you're thinking.'

Blimey.

Jan Inge picks up his inhaler from the washstand. Breathes in.

Hah.

Sometimes life is fascinating.

It's right in front of you, day in, day out, but no danger of you catching sight of it.

Jan Inge nods to himself. This is fantastic news. He can feel a swelling inside. He's aware of tears in his eyes. A child. My God. Now there's going to be some life in the house. Now things are going to happen. Revenge. That's what he feels, a sense of revenge, like an axe cleaving a skull, because now the Haraldsen name will be carried on, yes, it's almost as if it's his own child coming into the world. There'll be life in the house, the genes will be shuffled and who knows what the child will be like. Will it inherit Cecilie's capricious nature? Jan Inge's characteristic astuteness? Its father's levity?

'Uncle Jani?' he asks. 'Me? Uncle Jani?'

Cecilie, her back to him, nods. She reaches into the shower and turns on the water.

'Wow. Chessi, I—'

Cecilie turns her head and fixes her brother with a fiery look. 'Yeah,' she says, while holding her hand under the jet of water. 'But you're not to tell a bloody soul.'

'No no, I—'

'Because I don't know who the fucking father is.'

'Wha?'

'Don't be so dramatic.'

'But—'

'Listen,' Cecilie lowers her voice, which doesn't serve to reduce the intensity. 'I don't know if it's Tong or Rudi—'

'Ton—'

'You're not to say a single word. Not one word, you hear me.'

'No, but to ... to ... I mean he's in—'

Jan Inge stops himself.

'Åna,' he says in a quiet tone.

'Not another word now,' Cecilie hisses. 'Not to me or to anyone else.'

Jan Inge nods. She's right, he thinks. Sometimes you've really just got to shut up. Keep your lips sealed and gulp down.

'You go out and think about what you've heard,' continues Cecilie. 'Go out and let me shower and be alone with my own thoughts and my own life and you get your own ass in gear. You don't need to go round feeling sorry for yourself, Jani, because you're not the one with problems – I'm the one with problems. And put on some coffee will you – aw! Bloody shower! Either too cold or roasting! Why can't things in this house just work like they do in normal peoples' houses!'

'Right, I'll—'

Cecilie pulls off the Europe T-shirt. Takes off her knickers. Gets into the bathtub. Pulls the shower curtain across. Jan Inge sees her silhouette, hears the running water, the sound of her voice: 'And don't start crying, all right? No crying, okay? We've done enough crying, you and me, yeah?'

72. THEY'RE SO PERFECT, THOSE TITS OF YOURS (Daniel William)

Veronika is standing in front of him as he comes into the hall. She's leaning against the wall as if waiting for someone to take a photo of her. Jesus, she looks good. Her hair tousled, sticking up in all directions, her mouth haughty and red. He makes to go past her towards the kitchen, force her to cede this edge she has over him, but she takes a step forward, blocking his path.

She grins.

'Manage to sleep?'

He shakes his head with a fatuous smile. He doesn't like to appear so exposed, feels like a bit of a wuss, but there's nothing he can do about it.

'Me neither,' Veronika says, leaving her lips slightly parted when she's finishes the sentence.

He returns her smile, but again his is puerile and foolish, while the smile blossoming in the lattice of fresh cuts on her face speaks of self-assurance, and rather than divesting her of authority – it bestows it.

Ah.

This business of being in love with two girls at the same time is a right pain. One of them is going to lose and one of them is going to win. It's the flesh that decides. The fuckplan, what happened to that? If the whole point of living was to fuck and get rich, find a woman willing to put out once a day, then how's the plan looking now?

Which of them will win?

Daniel tries to swallow his smile like it was a morsel in his mouth. He needs to ward off his weakness with something so he lets his gaze wander over her body, the body he possessed a few hours previously. The feet he held in his hands, the long legs he ran his fingers over, the thighs he parted, the loins he kissed, the tits he tongued and cupped in his hands, the ears he panted into, the red hair he clutched and the mouth he couldn't take his eyes from as they had sex.

Veronika closes her mouth as he looks her over. She puts her head to the side, her eyes are pert and alive, anything flushed or childish about her disappears.

Daniel takes hold of her hand, she backs against the wall.

'Listen,' he says.

'Yeah?'

Fuck, she's gorgeous.

'I've been doing a bit of thinking,' Daniel says, aware of how right it feels when he utters the words, even though it's a lie. *Thinking*? He hasn't thought at all, he's been fucking. To put it bluntly. Veronika was a whole lot different from Sandra. Sandra made him small and uncomplicated. Veronika made him big and uncomplicated.

'Me too,' she says.

'Okay,' Daniel says, surprised, 'you first, so.'

'No, you,' Veronika says.

'All right ... well, you know. Sandra.'

Veronika nods.

Good. She could have gone for him.

'Yeah,' Daniel continues, 'she's going to lose it when she hears about this. So, we're going to have to, well, deal with that. Some way or another.'

Veronika nods.

'And then there's your mother. How do you think she's going to react? And then there's that business with the father of those two girls, Tiril and Malene...'

Veronika stops him. 'Don't speak so fast,' she says. 'What did you say?'

'I don't know. I'm just stressed out. Tiril. And Malene.'

'What about them?'

Daniel walks towards the kitchen and she follows after. He turns on the tap, places his mouth under it and drinks. His mind is reeling. There's too much going on. Why should he care about that Pål guy? The people in the woods, the loser in the Metallica T-shirt, the sisters – how come he's not able to sweep it aside?

'What is it, Daniel? I don't understand?'

That hollow, deaf voice of hers; is he going to have to put up with that for the rest of his life? Christ, his throat is dry. He puts his mouth back under the water still running from the tap and drinks; it's like he's dehydrated, and now his vision is beginning to flash, no, not this, not now, he sees blood, sees hands being raised in front of a face, hears screams and his body is so dry, his body is so dry it feels as if it'll crack like parched earth and tiny brown animals will emerge: 'Shut up!'

He turns to Veronika. He moves swiftly towards her, one hand clenched into a fist while he uses the other to take hold of her hair, pulling her head closer to his, roughly: 'Can you just shut the fuck up?'

Veronika smiles.

'Are you going to hit me, Daniel?'

He pulls her head back forcefully, making her yield to his will. Or does he? Is it he who's won now or is it her?

'Daniel? Are you going to hit me now?'

He can't make out what's what, but Veronika continues smiling at him and he hears her say: 'Daniel, I'm going to look after you. Listen to me. Breathe in, breathe out. Let go of me. That's right, yeah. Sit down, listen to me. Daniel, Daniel. Tell me what happened to you.'

Fuck.

Is he going to start crying in front of a girl?

He puts his head against her chest, feels her breasts against his cheek.

It's part of the fuckplan, Daniel thinks. It's bigger than you think, that plan. More dangerous than you believe. It's carrying a whole world of shit along with it and in the end you'll stand there watching the blood flow.

Daniel sniffles. 'Jesus,' he whispers, 'they're so perfect, those tits of yours. I'm not really into big tits, but fuck, I like yours.'

Veronika nods.

'I'm in love with two girls,' he sighs.

'I know,' Veronika says. 'But it won't last long.'

He looks up at her, gulping back mucus, his teeth clacking together. His mouth foaming. He says: 'Come on, we'll hop on the Suzuki and just leave, okay? We'll go as far from here as we can and never look back.'

73. **TOUGH JESUS** (Sandra)

Maybe you were right, maybe DW is a coward. Outside his block of
flats now, have no clue what's going to happen. If I die, I die for love.
   Xx S.

Yet another brisk September day. The sun has come up, white
and reigning supreme in a sky where not a cloud is to be seen.
People have begun going about their morning business, a few
early risers have already exited the tower block, mostly adults on
their way to work. It's still too early for any schoolkids to put in an
appearance. Fortunately. Sandra doesn't want anyone to recognise
her standing here.

She puts the phone back into her pocket.

If he comes out with that skank of his it makes no difference.
If he has that slashed-up slut with him, then the blood will gush
from those faulty ears of hers and if he comes out alone, then he
better have an answer for her. She doesn't want to hear any more
bullshit, what she wants is a simple *yes* or *no*, and the question
she's going to ask is: *Am I the one, the only one you want, for all*
time?

She's going to be tough. Both she and Jesus are going to be
tough.

Sandra brings her finger to the panel with the doorbells. She
buzzes. A few seconds pass before a click sounds on the intercom
and his voice, metallic and uncertain, can be heard: 'Yes?'

Sandra doesn't reply. She takes two steps backwards. Stands
there looking at the name below the buzzer.

'Yes, hello?'

She's not going to answer. You're going to have to come down,
Daniel, and show who you are.

The line goes dead. She approaches the panel again. Lifts her hand. Rings once more. Longer this time, keeping her finger pressed hard against the button.

The response comes quickly: 'Yes, hello?'

Not nice, that voice. It has been so warm and deep at times, spoken right to her and she's trusted it. But this voice, she's not about to reply to that.

'Hello? Anyone there?'

Once again, Sandra takes two demonstrative steps back from the panel of buzzers.

'Listen, enough of the dinging already, yeah?'

The intercom goes silent again. A woman passes behind Sandra, walking a drever on a lead; it makes for her legs but the woman gives the leash a yank and they continue on. Sandra steps up to the buttons for a third time, breath rising in her throat, sweat beading on her hairline. She presses the buzzer.

A couple of seconds. Intercom crackle. A girl's voice. The skank: 'Give it a fucking rest, all right?'

The fact that she even dares open her mouth. It sounds so retarded. She talks like a mongoloid. Sandra puts her lips to the intercom, bunches her tongue against her uvula and imitates Veronika: 'Give it a fucking rest, all right?'

It goes quiet on the other end. That gave them something to think about. Sandra smiles, puts her mouth to the speaker again, makes her tongue thicker, her voice quaver, trying harder to mimic the deaf tone: 'Huuunnh? Are you able to speak? But you're not able to hear what I'm saying. Huuunnh? Maybe you've got someone there to translate for you, have you?'

The line goes dead again. That should do the trick, thinks Sandra. Now they'll come down. She hurries round the corner of the tower block, puts her back against the cold brick and her feet on the grass, banking on them not catching sight of her. Now she'll be able to see how they behave. Before she snares them, she wants to see what happens.

A minute crawls by; she counts the seconds like she's counted the seconds while waiting for Daniel in the last few weeks, waiting in smitten bliss. That naïve girl seems far away now, as though they had never been the same person. Then she hears the door open. The sound of footsteps emerging. One person. Two people. The footsteps stop.

'No one here.' His voice

'Little shits.' His voice

'Fucking cheek of them.' His voice

'If I get hold of them I'll beat their faces to a pulp.' His voice.

Sandra feels a swelling in her throat and she tries to swallow. Daniel is sticking up for the deaf girl. His voice is clear, deep and warm. The words sound just as real as they were when he spoke to her, in the woods and at the shop. Sandra gulps once more, the tears come; she gasps and presses her tongue against her crooked front tooth. She hears footfall. The sound of a jacket being unzipped. Is he opening her jacket, putting his hands inside, comforting her? Sandra goes as close as possible to the corner of the block: is it her opening his jacket? Putting her arms around him? Are they kissing?

'Is there anyone who's got it in for you?' His voice.

'Veronika. Answer me. Has this happened before?' His voice.

'No.' Her voice.

'We won't give a shit. Okay?' His voice.

'Yeah.' Her voice.

'Let's just leave, all right?' His voice.

'All right.' Her voice.

Leave?

'You and me.' His voice.

'Yes, Daniel.' Her voice.

Leave?

'Daniel is going to look after you, you know that, right?' His voice.

'Yeah.' Her voice.

Sandra's knees are giving way; she just about manages to remain standing and has to support herself against the wall. Leave. You and me. She hears the trust implicit in Veronika's reply; she hears how steady his voice sounds. Sandra feels pulverised; there is no tough Jesus here, just this caustic pain.

'Right, come on.'

Footsteps. They're moving. Quickly.

Sandra takes a few small steps towards the corner, puts her head around and sees them. Daniel William and Veronika, jogging along in front of the tower blocks, hand-in-hand, him slightly in front of her.

Why am I not strong? Why don't I shout out to them? Why don't I lift my hands to the sky and scream? Why am I just standing here?

Sandra sniffs, then draws as much air as possible into her lungs and begins to run. She keeps close to the wall of the buildings so as not to be seen, running as fast as she can, her knees touching and hips swinging. What's important now is not to think, just act, just be a seething jealous heart. When she gets to the end of the third block she sees them. Daniel has his helmet on and he's mounting the moped, Veronika standing beside him. After he's straddled it she climbs on behind. They haven't spotted her. They're too preoccupied with one another. Veronika puts her arms around his waist. She leans into him. Her chest presses against his back.

He starts the engine, reverses with his feet a couple of metres, then rides out of the car park, her red hair lifting up on the air like a pennant.

Just where Daniel and Veronika come out on to Folkeviseveien, there's a bend in the road by a bus shelter before it continues on towards the big roundabout on Ullandhaugveien. Sandra has no choice. She can't let the one she loves ride off with the one she hates. So she runs. She runs right across the green area backing on to the bus shelter and emerges on Folkeviseveien at the same time as the moped rounds the bend. Sandra runs on to the road, halts suddenly, and the rider of the moped can't manage to stop. He is unable to manoeuvre round the girl who has dashed right out into the road and he runs her over.

It doesn't hurt, Sandra thinks at the moment of impact, not me anyway. She takes a heavy blow to the head as her body is thrown to the ground. She tries to keep her eyes open because she wants to see what's going on, but it's difficult when it feels like something is cracking inside your head. What she thinks she sees is this: A boy, he's called Daniel William Moi and she loves him, a boy running towards her with a moped helmet in his hand, a terrified-looking

boy, a boy who shouts: 'Fuck! Sandra! What the fuck?' Behind
him a girl standing beside a moped, a red-haired girl with a cut-up
face, waving her hand about, shouting: 'Leave her there! She did
it on purpose! Leave her there!' The boy she loves brings his hand
down over his face, shakes his head and runs to the moped. Starts
it up. Rides away. With his girl on the back.

You were tough now, Jesus, she thinks, and loses consciousness.

74. KEIN PROBLEM, MEIN SOHN (Rudi)

We may well be criminals, Jan Inge always says. We may well live outside the law. But that doesn't mean we live without laws. We are prinicipled criminals, says Jan Inge, we have some ground rules. Which we live by. We won't have any divergence between theory and practice, got it? They'll be as one, you hear me?

Jefe Haraldsen.

One prize idiot after the other has come and gone. If the gap between theory and practice has been too wide then Jan Inge has asked them to sling their hook. Hansi, Tødden, Donald, Kjabbe, Sorry and Poster. Every one of them was kicked out over something that violated the fundamental priniciples. With the exception of Tong. He's the only one who's been let be even though there's been a pretty big gap betwe—

Rudi shakes the urine off his cock. No, he thinks, there hasn't been a big gap between theory and practice with Tong. He puts his cock back into his briefs, reflects on how cute and snug it looks all limp and curled up, and he washes his hands. The fact of the matter is that Jani has accepted Tong. Sort of like how it is with Lemmy. He can knock back as much Jack Daniels and do as much speed as he likes, but that doesn't mean that other people can do it. Even Lemmy himself has been clear about that.

Rudi leans towards the mirror, opens his mouth wide, bares his teeth and picks out some food wedged between them.

Whilst the others have abided by Jani's management priniciples, Tong has been allowed to step outside. Porn, dope and what have you. It's a bit annoying and Rudi does feel slightly jealous. But what can you do. Solo-playing virtuosos have to be allowed to live outside the law.

And one of the management principles, Rudi thinks as he dries his hands and opens the door to the hall, is going into play today. We're not junkies, but when we're on a job we rack up a few lines. It's a great fucking principle. Not so much as a gram in normal, everyday life. Just at work. An ever so little line of speed. Rudi loves amphetamine. Who doesn't? Show me the man who can stand up and say, in all honesty, that speed isn't a gift to mankind.

'If everyone was as principled as us,' Jan Inge says, 'there'd be precious few problems in the world.'

Rudi enters the kitchen and is surprised not to be met by the sight of a table laid for breakfast. The wheelchair sits there, forsaken. Breadcrumbs on the worktop. An opened tin of pâté. A carton of apple juice with the cap off. The menstrual odour of a coffee machine that's been on for hours. The time? Soon be half eight. Looks like people have been up a while. Chessi is probably just about arriving at Åna. Rudi rubs the back of his neck, opens the fridge and takes out the milk. He feels his faith being restored. Christ, she was great this morning, Chessi. No way she wants to screw that Pål guy.

Rudi makes himself a big glass of chocolate milk.

Where has Jan Inge got to?

He downs it in three gulps while looking out the window.

Another cracking day. Global warming, you're more than welcome. Tong. Speed. A time-honoured classic. Ride Chessi.

'Hey, *caballero*?' He plods into the living room. '*Jefe*? *Mein Führer, wo bist du*? *Dein Schweinhund ruft dick an*!'

He looks in the direction of the hi-fi. There's a bag on top of it, half-hidden under the shelf above. Rudi takes a few quick steps, gets hold of the bag, takes out the CD, opens the cover, presses eject, waits for the drawer to slide out then places the CD in. He does it all quickly so he won't have an opportunity to stop himself. About time. He scans the back of the CD cover. Number seven. He skips forward. Turns the volume up. Waits two seconds.

Jesus. That is so good. Du-du-du du-du-du du-du-du, du-du-du...

'Hey!'

Du-du-du du-du-du du-du-du, du-du-du du-du-du du...

'Hey!'

The sound of Jani's high-pitched voice cuts through the music. Rudi blushes and grins. 'What the hell? What are you doing jumping round singing along to ... what is that? The Bee Gees?'

The state of Jani. Dark, heavy rings under his eyes. Eyes flitting this way and that.

'No, I – okay, brother. Mea culpa. You're going to hate me for this, but – sorry. I must be getting old! I've hit the mid-life MOR crisis. I'll soon be sitting here with a monocle and a bowl of lentil soup listening to Radio 4. It's Coldplay. And yes, Rudi loves it. Kill me. Do away with me. That's just how it is.'

Jan Inge shrugs. 'Whatever,' he says.

Huh? Rudi screws up his eyes.

'We need—' Jan Inge clears his throat and looks out the window, 'we need to make a start on the day. Look at that garden. We'll have to clear it out soon. But anyway. We've got a busy Thursday ahead. We have to drop round to Stegas—'

'Hell yeah! Stegas!'

'Yeah,' continues Jan Inge, still somewhat awkwardly, 'and we have to welcome Tong back—'

'Fuck yeah! Tong.'

'Can you calm down a little? Welcome Tong back – and then we have a moving job.'

'Have we?'

'A grand piano. Over in Våland. Furras Gate.'

Ah, for Christ's sake.

'A grand piano. I fucking hate humping pianos around. Seriously, Jani, how much longer do we have to—'

'Rudi! I'm not getting into this right now. We need to make clean cash, you need to get that through your head! How many times do we have to talk about this? We run a moving company, that's what it says on your tax returns, on my tax returns – it's the reason no one can nab us, don't you get that? You know, sometimes I wonder if you're retarded. We're respectable people, we have jobs, and as you're well aware, there's nothing better than having a moving job on the same day as we have ... well ... other jobs!'

Rudi takes a step back. What's up with the guy? Jan Inge has sweat rings under his arms, all worked up and giving out like a headmaster or something.

'Hey, brother,' Rudi says cautiously. 'Take it easy, yeah? What's gotten into you? You need to use the wheelchair. Every day. You just tire yourself out spending so much time on your feet.'

Jan Inge takes a deep breath. He nods. 'Yeah. You're probably right,' he mumbles. 'Sorry. It's nothing. Didn't get enough sleep is all. You know yourself. Too little sleep will stress anyone out. You remember Tone-Tone? The one who hanged herself, remember her?'

'Mhm.'

'Yeah, hanged herself in the kitchen, and people said it was because Donald was having it off with Kjabben's girlfriend and she walked in just as he was rimming her, but that wasn't it. It was because she slept too little. She lost it. Put the noose round her neck one morning when she couldn't take it any more.'

Rudi nods. 'Tone-Tone, yeah. You remember her sister? What was she called again? Li ... no, Lu ... no—'

'Lene-Lene.'

'The very one. Whatever happened to her?'

'Something in IT, I think.'

'Like most of them. End up working with computers. You liked her, eh? Lene-Lene. Fuck, Jani. Maybe that's what the matter. You should find yourself a woman. You know what Gran said, a man without a woman is half a person.'

Jan Inge nods. 'Yeah, maybe. But I've got enough on my plate. Will we get a move on here?'

Rudi straightens up. *'Aber klar, mein Führer!'* He performs a Nazi salute and laughs.

'Tong will be here,' Jan Inge continues, 'that'll be good. We'll score some speed. We'll move a piano. We'll work a nightshift. *Kein Problem, mein Sohn.* But enough of the Bee Gees. This is a house of horror. A house of metal and country music. That Coldplay stuff isn't even funny. It just makes for a bad atmosphere.'

'No, no,' Rudi says sullenly, turning off the CD. 'Did you see Chessi this morning?'

Jan Inge turns around and starts walking towards the kitchen.

'Mhm. Why?'

Rudi squints. 'Dunno,' he says. 'She was in such a great mood.'

'Yeah, she's in good humour all right.'

Jan Inge disappears into the kitchen.

Rudi ejects the CD, puts it back in its case. No, he thinks. Becoming more and more obvious that this house is beginning to get a bit cramped for all three of us. More and more obvious that Chessi and me need to find a place of our own.

'Did she not have a massive pair of jugs?' Rudi calls out in the direction of the kitchen.

'Who?'

'Lene-Lene!'

'No, that was Tone-Tone.'

'You sure?'

'Yeah. I notice that kind of thing.'

'Yeah, you like that.'

'Huh?'

'Big jugs!'

'Wouldn't say I dislike them.'

'Frank and forthright.'

'Wha?'

'Frank and forthright, I said!'

'That?'

'Wha?'

'Wank what?'

'Frank and forthright, I said! That you like big jugs! I think they can be a bit much. Speaking of which, do you think Cecilie's tits have grown bigger lately?'

'What?'

'Your sister! Her tits! Gotten bigger!'

'No, no!'

'Fuck. Probably just in my own sick head.'

Jan Inge walks back in. 'Enough about tits now,' he says, looking serious. 'We've also got this thing with Tommy to take care of.'

'Shit,' Rudi exclaims, slapping his palm to his forehead. 'Shitshitshit.'

'You'd forgotten about that, I take it.'

'Shitshitshit.'

'We're just going to have to deal with it. Simply go about our day as though he could show up here at any given moment. And the sooner he does the better.'

'Okay, what about Cecilie – have you told her he's coming?'

'No, I have not, the fewer people that know about it the better,' Jan Inge says, heading back towards the kitchen.

Rudi takes a breath and lets it out; he feels the urge to spit and spin right round. Difficult to deal with when the atmosphere in a room changes. When the boat rocks. That's the reason he's never believed in all that stuff about revolution – it makes people so insecure.

'You should at least listen to the lyrics,' Rudi says in a lower tone, to himself really. 'Seeing as how you plan to become a writer and all that,' he adds, as he stows the Coldplay CD on the shelf behind some old magazines. 'It's about a king who's no longer a king.'

75. I SPIT-ROAST MY OWN SQUIRRELS HERE
   (Tiril)

'Seriously, Mally, this is insane, Kenny has beaten up Shaun!'

Malene hurries after Tiril as they rush along Ernst Askildsens Gate, up towards the green area overlooking the neighbourhood of Tjensvolltorget.

She can't take much more of this. Malene wants to return to the world where she goes to school, does her homework, eats her dinner and then heads to gymnastics practice and hears Sigrid's voice resound through the hall: 'Malene, now! The double!' Train until it's late, sail through the air and enjoy the sensation of it. Focus her mind and body, shut everything else out and feel herself growing stronger. She doesn't want to be in the midst of this muddle of unpredictable interpersonal relations that's been stirred up over the last couple of days, with Dad acting so strangely and Tiril going off her head. Malene herself feels as though she's being opened and closed every other minute, to the point where she hardly recognises herself.

'And Sandra – holy shit – here, check out this text.'

Tiril comes to an abrupt halt and hands her the mobile: *Maybe you were right, maybe DW is a coward. Outside his block of flats now, have no clue what's going to happen. If I die, I die for love. Xx S.*

'What'll we do?' Tiril continues. 'Eh?'

Malene lifts her hands in a gesture of resignation: 'I've no idea...'

'And what about Dad, breakfast banquet for no good reason? He really needs to get a girlfriend. Or a new car. Something.'

Tiril stops when she sees a football lying on the tarmac. She looks at it as though it's a person who's done her wrong, knitting her brow before giving it a boot with her right foot.

'Where's Shaun?' asks Malene, watching the ball go in the direction of the tennis courts. 'What did he write?'

'That was all,' says Tiril, while they watch the ball disappear out of sight. 'He didn't write any more. *Kenny beat the shit out of me.*'

'Where is he?'

The sisters walk up the hill towards the green belt of land around the pumping station, known locally as Vanassen. There's a park of sorts up there. It's laid out as if the local authority had intended it to afford outstanding views over the area: lying high up, on a grand scale, with the water of Hafrsfjord in the west and the peaks of Ryfylkeheiene to the east. But it's almost as though the people in the council lost interest midway, they couldn't stay the course and what remains seems half-hearted and hopeless. A miserable gravel path, a dry-stone wall, four garish benches with two matching tables and the land around always overgrown, any surfaces invariably graffitied. It's windswept up there, even when there's not the slightest hint of a breeze anywhere else.

The girls slow down when they catch sight of him. Tiril keeps a cool head, a moan escapes Malene's lips. Crouched in the corner, behind the tables and the benches, is Shaun. He's wearing the grey top with the hood up. The laces on his trainers are untied, the tongues hanging loose and languid on the insteps. His ripped, baggy jeans are stained with muck and blood. In his hand he holds a grimy rag and a tube of glue. He lifts his head as if in slow motion. Big, black rings under his red eyes, a colourful shiner, a cut on his cheek.

'Ok-aay,' he says, grinning, 'Shaun reporting for duty. Heh heh.'

Tiril plants her feet on the flagstones in front of him and crosses her arms. Malene looks away. It's not far to the gymnastics hall. It's right down the hill. Maybe her foot is okay now? Maybe that's the best thing for it? Just take off, run?

'Come on, Tiril,' Malene says sternly, 'we don't need this. Enough's enough. Come on. Let's go.'

Tiril brushes her aside. She squats down in front of her boyfriend.

'Jesus, Shaun. What did he do to you?'

'Tiril.' Malene feels her irritation mount. 'Let's go.'

But Tiril pays her no attention, merely leans closer to Shaun, who sits sniffing: 'Hey, get rid of that.' She takes the glue and the rag from him and tosses them over the stone wall. 'What's up?'

I could just run, Malene thinks. I don't need to be a part of this pathetic scene.

'Heh heh.' The boy simpers again. 'I'm like just … heh heh. Shaun reporting for duty, baby.'

'Come on.' Tiril takes hold of him, but his body is too limp and she can't lift him alone. She turns to Malene: 'Well, you going to stand there all pissed off and thinking of yourself or are you going to give me a hand here?'

Malene shakes her head heavily. A stinging pain in her ankle. She can't run. She takes a step forward, even though she doesn't want to, and helps Tiril get Shaun on to his feet.

He sways once he's standing up. Malene can see that he's really been given a working over – the cut looks nasty, the bruising even more so, like a lava landscape on his face. What is it with that family?

Shaun leans his back against the table. For the first time he opens his eyes properly, for the first time something akin to clarity appears in them. He looks at Tiril.

'Have you got a cig?'

Tiril nods and puts her hand in her pocket, produces a packet and her lighter and offers him one. Lights it for him. Lights one for herself.

'Kenny,' says Shaun, smoke seeping out from between his lips. 'Kenny doesn't stand for snitching, you know.' Shaun raises his unsteady hands, holding them up in front of his face like a boxer. 'And he was like: *Hey, Shauny! Fuck did you say to that bint of yours! Eh?*'

Shaun launches an inept punch at the air, connecting with nothing except his own memory.

'Hey, Shauny.' Tiril takes him by the hands and holds them tight.

'Yeah?' He looks at her, eyes clearer now.

'You're not your brother. All right? You're just you. Okay?'

Shaun nods slowly.

'Can you manage to pull yourself together?'

He shrugs. 'Dunno. Never been too good at that.'

Tiril tugs at the cuff of her sweater, draws it over her hand and spits on it, then she wipes his face. Removes each mark and blotch while he looks at her.

Jesus, Malene thinks. These two are so far removed from me. She tilts her foot to the side and puts a little weight on her ankle. The stinging pain is still there, like a needle beneath the skin.

'We've got to go,' Tiril says. 'If the text Sandra sent is anything to go by, there's something very screwed up going on but I don't know what. She's down by the tower blocks. We need to get all this sorted out and then I can't deal with any more distractions after that, because I'm going to sing tonight and I need to focus, okay?'

Shaun sniffles.

'Jesus, Shaun,' she says, 'you're such a loser, you know that?'

He nods. 'But I have cut back on the porno rap.'

'That's good, smurf boy,' she says and takes a long deep drag of her cigarette. 'You've got me, after all.'

Loneliness is the land I live in, thinks Malene. Where I spit-roast my own squirrels. Where I put my feet in the tall grass. Where Dad lies on his back in the warm sand. But I'm the only one who sees it, all of it. Double backflip tucked.

76. **SAME OLD SAME OLD** (Cecilie)

The waves wash over the ancient beaches with a steady rhythm, the sun, a ball of light high up in a sky that itself seems proud: look at me. Look what I can do, how vast I can be.

Cecilie pulls into the lay-by, not far from the turn-off towards Nærbø. She puts the car in neutral, listens to a few bars of 'Jump' by Van Halen before killing the engine. She rolls down the window, feels the briny wind from off the North Sea against her cheek, stretches her hand to the rear-view mirror and tilts it to look at her face.

You could have met a farmer's son, got married and lived out here. Farmers have whole barns full of money. You could have gone into a byre to milk the cows and been taken from behind right there near the pens by your wealthy farmer, him smelling of manure with soil under his fingernails. Or you could have met a guy in the oil business and lived in a big house in Stokka. Roughnecks, they have money. Just ask Mr Thor. Then you would have avoided your man for two weeks at a time, screwed him every day when he was back onshore, and probably spent your time wondering if he was cheating on you with a woman in the kiosk out there on the rig.

Cecilie looks in the mirror and applies her lipstick.

But you didn't, she thinks. No farmer, no roughneck.

You got Rudi. And he got you.

Yellow teeth and crooked lips. Not much to cheer about. Looking at it objectively, her hips are probably the only cracking thing about her. Or her ass maybe, that does it for the guys that like them large. That's the card she can play. Some girls have the legs. Some have the lips. Some have the tits. Well. I've got the ass. And there's no point in listening to what Rudi has to say;

according to him she's a deck of cards where every one is an ace, but she knows that's just bollocks. She just has to make the best of a bad lot, and lipstick can help draw attention away from what doesn't shine.

Cecilie cups her hands, brings them to the back of her head and tries to inject a little volume in her hair. She tousles it. Applies some blusher, puts on some eye shadow.

A little bit sexy.

That's what she's aiming for today. Slightly sexy. Because she knows. Sexy isn't about being pretty. Every girl can be sexy. Dirty. Hungry. She realised that long ago, over twenty years ago. She might not have understood it in so many words but she understood it with her eyes. Because the boys came back. She was far from the prettiest girl in the neighbourhood, but they wanted to sleep with her. They needed to have her. Why? Because she was lying there on her back, obviously, but also because she was something the really pretty girls weren't. Sexy. And if there's one thing Tong likes, it's to see her looking sexy. A pair of high heels. A bit of cleavage, even though she might not have that much to put on show. Just the thought of it. That she's done it. That she wants to look like that. He likes that.

Cecilie lights up a cigarette and starts the engine.

What is it she wants?

Does she want Tong?

She doesn't know. She just wants to be sexy. She just wants to hear Van Halen. Those synthesisers. Those drums. David Lee Roth. Chessi just wants to drive a car and be the kind of woman people turn to look at.

'Isn't that right, baby,' she whispers as she comes out on to the flat expanse of Opstadsletta. 'Isn't that right? You don't give a shit, do you, who your father is?' Cecilie presses her foot down on the pedal and feels the old Volvo accelerate. 'We'll take the strongest of them, won't we? Deary me, you don't like Mummy smoking, do you, hm? Sorry, promise I'll cut down, baby. But Van Halen, you like them, hm?'

A few minutes later, Cecilie slows down and takes the turn up the avenue to Åna. She's a couple of minutes late and is well aware Tong doesn't like that. It pisses him off when people aren't punctual. She remembers him nearly choking Donald to death that time he showed up twenty minutes late. A jewellers. Out in Sola. One of their best heists ever. Drove the van right through the window, smash-and-grab. Serious money. If Donald had arrived five minutes later they would have been busted. Tong took such a hold round his neck he puked in the car. She was the one who had to clean it up of course. Jittery fucker, Donald. Couldn't control his habit, impossible to trust.

Someone said he'd died.

That they found him in the back of a bus to Randaberg.

Kind of strange to think about. Donald was only thirteen when she had him. Pretty sweet actually. He had one of those cleft chins. One of the first she had. Really shy. Tripping up as he took his trousers off. Yeah, yeah, sighs Cecilie. I've probably screwed just about everyone who's died from heroin in this city. I was the one who had them first. And heroin had them last.

If Rudi didn't kill Donald, that is. He never could handle the fact that he had to work with someone who'd banged her so many times. He might well have done. Not inconceivable that Rudi sent Donald to meet his maker and said it was a heroin overdose on the back of the bus to Randaberg.

Cecilie stops by the intercom, identifies herself, drives up and parks. She gets out of the car and makes her way towards the main building. She feels a light breeze on her face. Always like that out here. No matter how little wind there is, it's blowing out in Åna.

There he is. Outside the main entrance.

He doesn't look like a person.

He looks like an iron man. A sculpture. Cecilie suddenly feels slightly afraid. The figure standing over there doesn't appear human at all. Everything seems a little scary – what has she got herself into? Cecilie draws closer. Tong isn't wearing prison-issue clothes and it's unpleasant to see him like this, in his old jeans, with his shiny leather jacket, the blue veins bulging out of his neck.

His features are impassive. Is this the guy she's been wondering if she's in love with; is this the guy she's put on lipstick for?

'Deary me,' she whispers, her lips barely moving, 'looks like Mummy's a little nervy.'

She halts in front of Tong. He doesn't move.

'Hi, Tong.'

They begin to make their way towards the car. Cecilie has no clue what to say. Is this playing house? She feels she should relate some news, tell him something, say anything, but she has no idea what. She needs a cinnamon bun; she needs a fag. Cecilie gives Tong a brief glance, but looks away again quickly. His eyes are like scorched stone. How's it possible to be so intense and so withdrawn. Is there a person in there?

She opens the driver's side. Lets out an exaggerated breath. Peeks up at the sky as if to say: Look, lovely out. She opens the passenger's side. Tong throws his bag in the back seat, gets in.

'Maybe you want to drive?'

Her voice is thin and feeble.

Tong shakes his head.

'Right, just thought you might like to, seeing as it's been a while since you've driven a car. Anyway.'

She should stop talking. Tong has never liked small talk and he seems to like it even less now.

Cecilie starts the car. Drives down the avenue.

'Nice day, though.'

Why did she say that?

'But,' she tries to laugh it off, 'doesn't really matter. If it's nice or not. The weather, I mean. Makes no difference, I suppose. Now. I'll just get them to raise the barrier here. Hello, yeah. Cecilie Haraldsen, going out.'

He just sits there. To look at him you'd never know it was his first day of freedom in years.

'So, good to be out?' she says, after they've driven a while.

No reaction. Black, charred eyes.

'Yeah,' she hastens to add. 'Of course it's good.'

'Can you just shut up?'

She gives a start, swallows and nods.

Tong takes a hold of Cecilie's hand. Tightens his grip around it, the blood vessels above his knuckles appearing in front of her eyes, her hand feeling like it's about to be crushed. He brings her hand to his crotch, slides down further in the seat, spreads his legs and rubs it against the bulge in his trousers.

Okay, she thinks. Of course. Same old same old.

77. **YOUR OWN FIRE** (Veronika)

She leans into him. Her arms around his waist. Presses her cheek against his back. She doesn't want to be anywhere else but here, leaving everything behind, just the two of them. She couldn't help it, but the sight of Sandra doing a somersault in front of the moped, the sight of the girl hitting the tarmac, filled her with a burning happiness. That's justice: *It all came too easy to you – you don't deserve him. You would never have understood him, you've met your match, bitch, and it's me.*

The moped heads towards Madlakrossen, taking off to the left at the roundabout, out towards the golf course, following the road as it begins to climb towards Revheims Church. The land around them begins to open into fields, two horses run alongside a stone wall, a tractor disappearing in the distance.

Sandra could be seriously injured; if the worst comes to the worst she might lose her life. But Veronika feels only that pull, helping her see things clearly, giving her that feeling of elation; she's not afraid. She clings even closer to his back, wrapping her arms more tightly around his body. His heart is pounding under her hands. She loves his fear, loves his despair. She knows he needs her, because she has longer eyelashes than him, she's softer and slyer than him.

The landscape stretches out further as they ride uphill towards Sunde, the vast Stavanger sky parading above their heads. Daniel slows down, turns his face half towards her and she sees how wildly agitated his eyes look behind the visor, but it doesn't frighten her, because she knows it's her he needs to turn to now.

Daniel veers off to the left, down a steep incline into a small estate of seventies-looking houses facing the sea. He steers the moped towards a colossal grey, grafittied concrete building. An old bomb shelter. He brakes, brings the moped to a halt and they dismount. His breathing is fast; he looks about nervously as he searches through his pockets. After a little while he finds the key ring. He sets it between his teeth as he quickly pushes the moped over to the large entrance door. He mumbles something or other, but she can't see what it is.

'What did you say?'

He doesn't reply. Removes the key from his mouth, opens the door and, pulling it wide, wheels the moped into a windowless concrete corridor.

Of course. The rehearsal room. Is he mumbling again? She hurries after him, he leans the moped against the wall and she closes the door behind her while he chooses another key from the bunch and walks in total darkness towards the next door. He fumbles with the lock, tries to locate the keyhole.

Veronika walks over the hard floor, feeling her way to Daniel, places her hands over his and notices he's trembling. She clasps them until they steady. She says: 'It wasn't your fault. She ran into the middle of the road. She wanted it to happen.'

It's dark. She has no idea if he's talking to her, but it feels as though he's saying something. She reaches out towards his face, touches his full lips, feels his warm breath against the palm of her hand. The door into the practice room opens and a faint light flows in their direction. Her eyes adjust quickly to the surroundings. She sees quite a large room, threadbare carpets on the floor, egg cartons and posters for gigs on the walls – obscure or forgotten local bands that have played at *Grevlingen*, at Metropolis, on Music Day or at *Folken*: The Substitutes, *Lillemor*, Rag Doll, Arlie Mucks, *Røde knær, Luftskipet Noreg, Hekkan, 60-Sone Satan*. Guitar amps, a drum kit, bass amps, a microphone stand and mics, a mixing desk, a Wurlitzer, an old analogue Yamaha synthesiser, loudspeakers. Along one wall there's a sofa covered in a coarse-looking brown-and-green material, a tarnished, scratched teak coffee table littered with ashtrays, cola bottles, chocolate wrappers, guitar strings, plectrums, magazines, *FHM, Us Men* and comics.

Veronika takes up position in his field of vision. She meets his eyes, holds his gaze and repeats: 'It wasn't your fault.'

His chest rises, not sinking again before he plonks down on the end of the sofa. He takes hold of a couple of drumsticks lying on the armrest, twiddles with them before looking at her and saying: 'What would you know?'

Veronika sits down in a worn-out leather armchair. She takes his hands, stopping the sticks that want to strike at the empty air. His hands are cold from the ride, she rubs them between her own the way her mother has always done with hers. He twists free of her grip, gets to his feet, walks resolutely over to the drum kit and sits on the stool behind it.

Daniel looks at her. 'So, what are we going to do? Hm? What do you suggest?'

'Daniel, I—'

He interrupts angrily: 'You've got my head completely fucked up, you know that? Run a girl over – run Sandra fucking over – and just leave her there? How do you think that's going to sound to her parents? Or the police? What the fuck is with you?'

'Daniel, listen—'

'No! No, I'm not going to listen to you any more!'

He gets up, turns to the wall and slams the base of his fists against it.

Veronika, remaining as composed as she can, walks over to him. She puts her arms around him, presses her breasts against him. With all the assertiveness she can muster, she turns him around, forcing him to meet her gaze.

'What if she dies,' he says.

'She won't.'

'You can't know that. They'll figure it out. People will talk. They'll find us.'

'I was there, Daniel,' she says. 'I saw the whole thing. She flung herself into the road. I'll speak up for you.'

Daniel looks at her. His eyes are as shiny as wet glass. His mouth narrows and his top lip begins to quiver. He sucks his cheeks in, his mouth is dry.

'I like your red hair,' he says.

Veronika kisses him.

'I don't stand a chance,' Daniel says.

78. **DAD ALWAYS SAYS IT WHEN HE SMACKS US AROUND** (Tiril)

They walk towards the tower blocks. A small guy wearing baggy trousers and his hood up. A girl with a determined gait and a look in her eyes to match, another with a troubled step, looking just as troubled around the eyes. Tiril can feel the strength within, can picture the evening ahead: She's going to stand there, the song is going to come from her heart, Thea will play and the roof is going to lift free of the beams and be blown sky-high.

'So, she was just going to stand by the tower blocks, was she?'

'Yeah,' Tiril answers, irritated by the tone of scepticism in Malene's voice. 'That's right, she was just going to stand by the tower blocks.'

Shaun jogs along between the girls, small as a pixie, thinks Tiril, daft and from a psycho family but he's so cool, and he's mine.

They pass the bus stop on Norvald Fraȷ́ords Gate. It's morning all around, people are off to work, or heading to school and buses and cars move along the road. We'll just behave normally, Tiril thinks, then nobody will see anything other than three kids on their way to school.

Then they catch sight of her. A girl. She's huddled by some large rocks not far from the road. She has her head in her hands and her clothes are in disarray.

Malene squints. 'Is that Sandra?'

Tiril runs, the others close on her heels.

'Sandra, what is it?' Tiril halts in front of her. Her cheek and forehead are bruised, her trousers have a large tear and her jacket is ripped.

'Oh my God,' Malene brings her hands to her face.

'Wow,' says Shaun.

Tiril bends down to Sandra and takes her by the arm, makes to help her to her feet but Sandra cries out in pain.

'What the fuck happened?'

'It was Daniel,' she says chokingly. 'And Veronika. They ran me over.'

'They ran you over?!'

Sandra nods and brings her hand across her chest to hold her other arm, which looks completely stiff. 'I went to the tower blocks, then they came out and I followed them and then ... I jumped out on to the road, and they knocked me down.'

'You jumped out on to the road?'

Sandra nods once more.

'Have you been run over?' Shaun raises his eyebrows.

'Fuckssake, Shaun, didn't you hear what she said?'

'Yeah, but Jesus—'

Tiril gathers her thoughts, she needs to react quickly. 'Can you move?'

'I don't know—'

'Stand up.'

'I don't know if I—'

'Sandra. Get up.'

Sandra raises herself slowly using her hands. She looks in real pain. Tiril brushes grass and earth off her clothes, takes her face in her hands, turning it left then right, examining it. Then she looks at Malene, who's speechless, and Shaun, who can't seem to decide where to look.

'Does this look like she fell off her bike on the way to school?'

'Wha?' Malene shakes her head. 'She just told us, she got run—'

'I'm asking if it could look like a bicycle accident.'

'Yeah, but—'

'Then it is a bicycle accident.'

'Eh?' Sandra hobbles a bit and Malene helps to hold her up.

Tiril is aglow. She senses that anything can be what you want it to be if you know how to bring the world to its knees.

'Tiril,' says Malene, 'you need to get a grip. This is insane. Sandra has been run over by Daniel and Veronika, and they just – I don't know – rode off?'

Sandra nods.

'They just rode off,' continues Malene, 'and you want us to – what? What is it you want? – for us to go to school and make out that she had an accident on her bike? She might have broken something, she may have concussion, we need to call—'

Tiril stares at her sister. Fixes her with her eyes until she stops talking. A girl from 9C, Rebekka, goes by, stopping for a few moments and looking at them strangely. Tiril raises her hand, gives her a friendly smile and the girl continues on her way to school.

'Shut up,' she says calmly. 'Shauny. Have you been sniffing glue?'

'Weell, y'know, I just...'

'Have you been sniffing glue?'

'Yeaah, like, I did...'

'Shauny.' Tiril places a hand on each of his shoulders. 'Have you been sniffing glue?'

'Eh ... no?'

'No, you have not. Shauny. Did Kenny beat you up?'

'Yeah, he did...'

'Shauny. Did Kenny beat the shit out you?'

'Eh ... no?'

'No.' Tiril nods. 'He did not. And you, Sandra. Have you been waiting for your boyfriend outside his block of flats? Have you hurled yourself into the road for him? Have you been knocked down?'

The girls look at one another. Shaun grins, making his brown teeth gleam like dirty diamonds.

'No,' Sandra whispers. 'I haven't.'

'Heh heh.' Shaun gazes at Tiril, admiration in his moist eyes. 'It's called leverage in America. Dad always says it when he smacks us around. Leverage, he says.'

'Your dad is a dick and he should be in Åna,' Tiril says, 'but now we'll gain the upper hand. Over all of them. Over Kenny. Over Bunny. Veronika. And Daniel, the liar. And we'll psych them the hell out. They're going to be sitting there thinking they've won. And then they'll start sweating. And then they'll get nervous and start looking over their shoulders. And that's when we take our revenge. Understand?'

They nod. Even Malene nods.

'We don't need any doctors, we don't need any teachers, we don't need the police or parents interfering here. A bicycle accident. The two of you collided on the way to school.'

'The two of us?'

'Yeah. You and Shaun.'

'Awesome.'

'We found you. Malene and I. We'll get a plaster for that cut.'

'But what if I have concussion?' Sandra says in a meek voice. She performs a few tentative movements with her jaw then massages her temples carefully with her fingers. 'What if I've broken something?'

Tiril shakes her head. 'You haven't. Come on, let's go put in an appearance at school.'

The four teenagers move off and head down along the low-rises. Two young women with buggies stand smoking outside Coop Prix supermarket. They pass by them, then by Jan Petersens Gate, and on by Anton Brøggers Gate. The sun is warm on their faces, Tiril can see that Sandra is limping, that Shaun is beginning to come down.

She slips her arm around his waist.

'Hey, you got any chewing gum?'

He delves his hands into the pockets of his hoodie and nods.

'I learnt that from Mum,' Tiril says.

Malene looks at her. 'What do you mean?'

'Domination,' says Tiril. 'That bitch didn't give a shit when people were in pain. And that just made it more painful.'

'You're not like that,' says Malene.

'Oh yes, I am,' replies Tiril.

The sun is high above the fjord, above the roof of the school, over the church spire and they turn off, in the direction of the schoolyard.

79. **BUNNY** (Jan Inge)

That hurt. A king who's no longer a king.

Loneliness. A lot of horror movies centre around loneliness.

Is that to be my life?

Jan Inge glances across at Rudi, sitting beside him in the Hiace.

Tommy Pogo hasn't shown up yet. Jan Inge had expected to see him relatively early. The police love to turn up in the morning. Disrupt the atmosphere. But he still hasn't come. Maybe that's his whole plan, to delay his visit in order to keep them sweating as long as possible?

Loneliness. Rudi and Chessi moving out. Getting themselves a garden. Making a life for themselves.

Jan Inge in a little flat. In a block of flats. Sitting in the wheel-chair. Day in. Day out. Listening to the postman come. The echo out in the hall. An old woman in the neighbouring flat.

It's slipping through my fingers, thinks Jan Inge, and I'm not able to do anything about it. Nothing other than be myself.

He lifts his head slightly and takes in his surroundings, as if to assure himself that he's on his guard. Strømsbrua Bridge. A normal Thursday in September. Cars moving to and fro between the different parts of the city. A view of the neighbourhoods of Paradis to the east and Våland to the west. The sun strong in the sky. A black man pushes a punctured bicycle along the pavement. His dark skin in sharp contrast to the pale blue sky. That's prob-ably what poets call poetry. In the distance: a siren. In the dis-tance: the mountains. In the distance: Asia, Africa, Australia. In the distance: a god, watching over us all. In the distance: our dead, monstrous mother. In the distance: our living, cackling mysteri-ous father. In the distance: one's own demise?

TO BE MYSELF.

That's the solution.

BUT WHO AM I?

'Rudi,' says Jan Inge, as amiably as he's able, 'listen, I was a bit sour this morn—'

'Fuck! Sour as an old snatch!'

'Yeah. Well, you know. This thing with Tommy. And. Well. I shou—'

Rudi gives him a soft thump on the shoulder with his fist. 'Jesus, Jani.' He shakes his head. 'You think Rudi harbours ill will all day?' He raises his eyebrows and gesticulates: 'Christ, you're talking to the man who's going out with Chessi here! I know everything about bad humour. It drags you down into the shit, but it blows over. All you need to do is look the other way. You need a bed to piss in? Be my guest! Pogo? Let him come. But yeah, you were in a lousy mood, I'll give you that. Speed! Just the thought of pepper makes me feel like we've already done a line. Do you know if Stegas is home by the way?'

Jan Inge laughs. 'Stegas is always home.'

'Heh heh. Mr Kush! Isn't his name actually Steffen? Fredriksen?'

Jan Inge shrugs. 'No one knows what his name is.'

'If there's one person you can count on in this oil village,' says Rudi, taking a deep breath, as though drawing ganja into his lungs, 'it's Stegas. This is where it's at, Jani. Scoring speed. You and me.'

Jan Inge feels his pulse rate begin to even out. The lines on his forehead fade away. That's all you need to do. Face unpleasantness with heartiness. Make those around you realise what they've got. Appreciate that it's precious and irreplaceable.

THE IRREPLACEABLE

A Study of Horror Films

By Jan Inge Haraldsen

He should keep the surname. Now that he thinks about it. There's something conceited about changing your name. You are who you are.

'And just think, brother,' he hears from the seat beside him, 'just think that Stegas still lives in the same place. Eh? *Der Meister* of Weeds. Been selling his spices there for twenty years now. Right next door to the school. You've got to respect that.'

'Don't want you becoming a junkie now,' Jan Inge says, feeling obliged to offer a gentle reprimand. 'Remember, our fundamental principles. We're against drugs. It's the main reason we make out as well as we do. Tommy Pogo is also aware of that. And he knows that's why they're never going to nail us, because we don't let drugs get the better of us.'

'*Aber klar*!' says Rudi. 'If I see another dude selling *Asfalt* I'll break his kneecaps and grind them into sand. I only meant to point out how cunning Stegas is. What a shrewd businessman he is.'

They park a few blocks away from the dealer's house. Jan Inge slips the car keys into the roomy pocket of his jogging bottoms and feels them tickle his thigh. They slow their pace as they reach Nedstrandsgata. Keep a lookout for parked cars that don't look like they belong there. Surveillance vehicles. Hold a careful watch for people who don't look like they should be walking there. Plain-clothes policemen. They cross the street, smile as they see the children in the schoolyard next to the house, as though they were old pals, walk up to the front door and ring the bell. After a few moments the door opens a crack and Stegas' flaky scalp and head, or half of it rather, appears.

'Jesus,' he says. 'The Dalton Brothers.'

Stegas looks just like he always has. Bumming around in a white string vest, an old pair of 501s and some worn-out felt slippers, which he got from his mother when he left home and is never going to get rid of. His prominent Adam's apple is just as pointy as it was in puberty and his characteristic concave temples are just as evident. Nobody is quite sure how old Stegas is, seeing as he looks the same as he always has, is involved in the same thing as he's always been, speaks the same way he's always spoken and lives in the same place he's always lived; people have lost count. Stegas is a natural phenomenon of sorts.

He invites Rudi and Jan Inge in with a waggish smile. They are old acquaintances and even though Stegas could not be classified as a friend, it pleases Jan Inge to see him receive them as though they were family. It's those kinds of things Jan Inge needs to be alive to. They need to take care of the few people they do collaborate with. And their relationship with Stegas is a shining example.

He supplies them with what little they require of speed, tells them things they need to know and they protect Stegas whenever there's call for it. They've roughed up a few people for him, individuals who were slow to settle their debts and so on. No money has ever changed hands between them. Merely information and services.

Jan Inge and Rudi are guided into Stegas' living room, which like the man himself, looks the same as always. The big, deep leather sofas. The TV in the corner. The IKEA shelves holding cookbooks and a sizeable collection of DVDs. A lot of musicals, in fact. A complete collection of *The Eurovision Song Contest*. Cosy. It always has been. Something Rudi isn't slow to comment upon.

'I'm always inspired, Stegas, when we visit you – you keep your place so clean, bright and homely.

Stegas nods. 'Just can't stand being surrounded by crap. Probably something I inherited from my mother.'

'Oh yeah, Jesus!' Rudi almost jumps up off the sofa. 'Sorry for your loss, fuck, we heard about that. Cancer?'

Stegas brings his hand across his face, nodding slowly. 'Embedded itself in her liver,' he sighs. 'Began eating her up. Three years it took.'

'Sorry, man,' Jan Inge says, while at the same time being aware of how unimaginable it is to be in Stegas' shoes, to actually miss his mother. Difficult, even for a person with as much empathy as Jan Inge.

'We're all headed that way,' Stegas says, his eyes moist. 'But she lives in my heart.'

'Intense,' says Rudi.

'Anyway,' Jan Inge says, hearing the gush of a cistern somewhere in the house. 'How's the foot?'

'Ah,' Stegas says, giving it a slap of his hand. 'Same old. Not really able to use it. Getting disability benefits for it. Never griped. Could've had whiplash, you know.'

'Intense,' says Rudi.

'Benefits,' repeats Stegas, 'they keep me afloat. Fuckin' good thing we live in Norway and not Romania. Things wouldn't be looking too bright for Stegas.'

'Words of truth.'

A chubby guy in jogging bottoms and a hoodie comes padding into the living room. He's wearing a headset, the thin microphone arm bobbing up and down in front of his mouth, making him look like some kind of pilot. He nods to Jan Inge and Rudi, walks past, sits down in front of the TV and resumes *Battlefield 3*.

'Bunny,' says Stegas. 'He's crashing here at the moment. Doing a few odd jobs for me. That right, Bunny?'

'Sure,' says the chubby guy.

'That right, you're doing a few odd jobs for me?'

'Sure, that's right,' says the pilot guy. 'Freeze, fucker! Freeze!'

'Good bloke, Bunny,' Stegas says. 'Aren't you, Bunny?'

'Sure,' comes the voice from the TV corner. 'Boom! Hell awaits, my friends.'

'So,' says Stegas, reaching for a teacup he has on the coffee table, 'you want a few lines? Got a job on?'

Rudi slaps his knees and gets a warm look in his eyes. 'A time-honoured classic,' he says. 'We're going to give a guy who's in need of cash a beating. Insurance.'

'Mmm,' Stegas drinks from the cup, nodding appreciatively, 'very fucking nice to do something by the book now and then. Too little of that in the times we live in.'

'Fuck, if that's not the truth then I don't know what is,' exclaims Rudi. 'Way too much computer crime for my taste nowadays, often feel like I can't put myself to use. So safe to say we need a few lines. Jani, Tong, Chessi and me.'

'Two hours,' says Stegas. 'Drop: Stokkavann, the large lake. By the boulder.'

'You've changed it around? Thought you always used the old cannon emplacement up on Hinnaberget.'

Stegas nods. 'Alternating arrangement.'

'Jesus,' Rudi says, 'you've such a good system.'

'A system is the key to success,' Jan Inge says.

'Good spot all right, eh, Bunny?' says Stegas.

'Die, Mofo!' says the podgy guy with the headset. 'Here comes Bunny! Die! What?'

Rudi and Jan Inge get to their feet. Stegas follows them into the hall. Jan Inge gives their old friend a hug. 'And you make sure to get in touch,' he says. 'You know we'll be there for you, pronto.'

'Appreciate it,' Stegas says. 'Say hello to Tong, that Paki bastard. Tell him welcome home.'

'Pronto,' Rudi repeats. 'Anyone needs doing over, we're there. Any supplies you need, TV, washing machine, whatever, give us a call – let your fingers do the walking. Stokkavannet. The boulder. Only a good thing for us to be seen out and about today taking a walk round Stokkavannet – that is supersupersupersmooth, Stegas, that is ... You know what? Coming here today, it makes me feel two things, and both of those emotions are pretty tightly linked. One is of entering a church. Of walking into a church, finding your place amongst the row of benches and sensing the light of Jesus warming up your bones. And the other, brotherof-dope, the other, it's – and this is very personal – it's the feeling of coming home to Gran. Walking through her door. Noticing that good old smell. Coffee and Swiss roll. Going up the steps. Seeing her sitting in her chair listening to, fuck, Franz Liszt or something.'

Stegas nods slowly during Rudi's emotional outburst. Jan Inge watches the dealer. He can see something's going on behind those eyes.

'Strong words, fucking intense,' says Stegas. 'You know, Rudi, my mother used to listen to Franz Liszt too. Sweet Jesus. The old masters. He was the Elton John of his day, that guy. The two of you need to get the hell out of here before old Stegas starts blubbering. I'll stick in an extra four grams and I won't hear any more about it. Franz Listz. I'll never forget that. I'm going to bring Bunny along this afternoon and pay Mum's grave a visit. That's what I'm going to do.'

Jan Inge and Rudi walk out into the harsh light.

This is what we have, Jan Inge thinks as they amble along towards the car. This is what we have built up. Good relations. And everything is just going to be torn down?

RIPPED INTO PIECES, TRAMPLED AND STOMPED ON.

Rudi looks at him. 'Shit, man, are you crying?'

'It's just the light,' Jan Inge says, and clears his throat before turning to Rudi: 'Think about it. Tea. Musicals. *The Eurovision Song Contest*. Frank List.'

'Eh?'

They stop in front of the car and Jan Inge takes the keys out. 'You don't see it?'

'No, wha?'

'I always knew there was something about him,' says Jan Inge and sighs. 'Slightly prissy. And it's been there, right under our noses, all these years. A homo. A little fairy. A proctologist. A rear-gunner. Elton John. Bunny. Frank List. Hm, Rudi? How many surprises is this life going to have in store?'

RIPPED INTO TINY PIECES.

Rudi shakes his head slowly. 'Jesus,' he says, 'that's tough to take, Ironside. You remember Gaupa's mother? She was never the same after she found out her son was gay. Trine, Gaupa's sister, said their mother sat chewing tree bark throughout her entire menopause. That's how I feel now. Betrayed by one of my best friends. Society is on the road to hell; we'll soon be surrounded by ass bandits and Muslims playing computer games, and you and me, brother, we'll be out in the cold, searching for a place to breathe freely.

Jan Inge opens the car door. He gets in.

TRAMPLED AND STOMPED ON.

She has a talent for that there. A delicate touch, rhythmic, not too rough, not too hard but firm and sensitive. Dynamic.

Tong comes as the Volvo passes the IKEA in Forus.

When you're inside it's not a good idea to think too much about women. But after Tong started having it off with Cecilie in the visiting room it grew impossible to shut out that part of his life. If you have no access to women, you manage to pacify the need after a time. In the beginning it's hell, you can't imagine how you're going to manage a week without a woman. But after a while it calms down. Something happens to your body. At least that's how Tong's experienced it. The opposite to how it is when women are plentiful – then your body wants more. And everybody knows how much space women can occupy. At worst they can fill you right up. They can make it impossible to think straight. And the thing is you just get hornier and hornier the more women you get. She doesn't need to be pretty, doesn't have to be smart, doesn't have to be kind. Say what you like about Cecilie, but screw, that she can.

Tong lights up a cigarette. He rolls down the window and looks across at Cecilie, who's steering with her left hand. He takes a dirty T-shirt from his bag and holds it out to her.

'Thanks,' she says and wipes her right hand.

He turns and looks out the window. The mountains in the distance. She did it on purpose. Got all dolled up before she picked him up. She knew well he'd turn into a hyena once he saw her. She knew well he'd be wound up when he walked out of the prison gates. People think sitting inside is stress, but it's not. It's monotonous, but it's a simple life. You soon get used to it. Being outside, on the other hand, that's stress. The first days of freedom are hard ones. Where are you going to stay, who are you going to talk to – paranoid is what you are, you think everyone's going around talking about you.

'Laurel and Hardy,' says Tong. 'They home?'

Cecilie tosses the T-shirt on the floor. She indicates a turnoff on the motorway after the Ullandhaug tunnel. Down towards Hillevåg. 'They're at Stegas' place, I think, scoring speed.'

Tong nods. He'll give speed a wide berth.

'Cool that you're going to come,' Cecilie says, smiling. 'Along on the job, I mean. The old gang, together again, and all that.'

He continues looking out the window. The mere thought of seeing Jan Inge and Rudi again makes his insides churn. He's been weak. He had promised himself a new life when he got out. He was to ditch this gang of idiots from Hillevåg. He was going to work with better people. HA maybe. Now he's sitting here. In this fucking car. With this slut. On his way to those losers.

'Do you remember anything from your childhood, as a matter of interest?'

Cecilie gives him a quick glance. They're driving through Åsen down towards Kilden Shopping Centre.

'I mean,' she goes on, 'weren't you four when you came to Norway? No, you'd be doing well if you remembered that.'

The Volvo trundles down to the junction by the shopping centre and Rema 1000 supermarket. Cecilie stops and puts on the indicator.

'I just mean, it must be like, strange to think about. That you had a life there. In Korea, like. Parents and, yeah, maybe brothers and sisters and that. But no. You probably don't remember anything. I mean, I only remember tiny bits myself and after all, I had a mother, a father too, until I was...'

The indicator ticks loudly. The sun hits the windscreen.

'You haven't started giving any thought to finding yourself a woman, then?' asks Cecilie and smiles archly. 'A woman, a house, even,' she laughs, 'a kid, maybe?'

Tong reaches out his left hand and seizes Cecilie's throat with his fingers. He squeezes as hard as he can. He sees her head bow under the pressure of his hold, sees her grip tighten on the steering wheel.

'Shut your cunthole,' he says. 'Sit up. You've got a green light. Drive.'

'I bruise easily, Tong,' Cecilie says meekly, as she changes gear and puts her foot on the accelerator.

81. IT FEELS AS THOUGH HIS FEET ARE LEAVING THE GROUND (Pål)

One of the hardest things, people often say, is to be the father of
teenage girls. Bjørn Ingvar Totland goes on about it constantly.
How he's going to get his rifle out the day his girl turns thirteen,
how he's going to be prepared for the ring of the doorbell and a
boy outside asking after his daughter. That's sure to scare the little
prick out of his wits. What do you say, Pål? We know all too well
what we were like when we were sixteen, eh? Get the rifle out, Pål,
eh?

Pål likes practically every person he meets, something Christine always found annoying, but he doesn't like Bjørn Ingvar
Totland. He doesn't like his car salesman's grin, doesn't like the
way he winks, and he doesn't like the way he slaps people on the
back. Pål really wants to tell him to quit comparing them. They're
not at all alike. Because it's never been that way for Pål. Neither
when he was sixteen nor now. The fire within Pål has always
smouldered rather than raged, burned slow and long. Now that
Tiril has a boyfriend all of a sudden, he feels no sense of alarm,
on the contrary, he feels relieved, as if the fact a boy has come on
the scene will serve to protect her. Is that cowardice? Maybe it is.
Now the job passes on to someone else, the job of looking after my
daughter.

Shaun, his name is. Tiril's boyfriend.

American? Irish? Only just happened apparently.

He's expecting visitors in a few hours. The Hillevåg Gang are
going to come through the door. They're going to beat him. Tie
him up? Where exactly? He looks around. Maybe they'll tie him
to one of the kitchen chairs. Will they blindfold him? How far are
they going to take it?

What was it he said? That he was going to tidy the house. Get something nice for dinner. That this was such a big day for Tiril that he wanted to make it a little bit special. And then the girls dashed out the door, something about some friend and her boyfriend.

Pål sits languidly in the armchair, the one beneath the living-room window. He has Zitha's dozing snout under the sole of his foot. He brought her out for a quick walk after the girls left; since then he hasn't done anything at all. The cheese on the table is soft and warm and the cold cuts of ham are glistening. His jaw is sore. He's been grinding his teeth for several hours without being aware of it.

He leans over towards the little table beside the armchair and Zitha trots off across the carpet. The remote controls for the TV, the one they'll probably steal tonight, lie on the table, along with his mobile phone. He scrolls down to a name, rings.

'Yes, Christine speaking?'

'Hi, it's Pål.'

'Yes, I can see that – listen, I'm in the middle of something here. Was it important?'

This is just a completely normal phone call.

'No, just that I forgot to let you know that Tiril is performing at school tonight. Kind of a big deal for her, this here, she isn't expecting you to come or anything and she hasn't asked me to call you, it's—'

'Pål?'

'Yeah?'

'This is a bit strange.'

'Is it?'

It's just like we're still married.

'Yes, Pål. It is.'

We speak to one another the same way we did as when we were married.

'Well, that might be so.'

'Well, it is. What are you trying to say? That you've just remembered that Tiril is going to perform and that I should be there? And then you call me at – what time is it, half eleven in the morning – and expect me to rush out to Flesland Airport, jump on a plane and make it to her school in, what is it, six hours it begins?

The tone of her voice. Just like it's always been.

'Yeah. No. I don't know. I'm just...'

Then the line goes quiet. It takes him by surprise, to the extent of making him nervous, as though something unpleasant is going to happen. It only remains quiet for a short time, Pål feels his heart pounding in his chest, and then he hears her say: 'Is anything wrong, Pål?'

'No, good gracious, wrong? With the kids? No, no, God.'

'No, Pål. With you,' she says. 'With you, Pål.'

He lived with her so long, knew her so well. She lived with him so long and knew him so vexingly well. Pål's eyes fall on the spruce tree in the garden.

'You remember that spruce tree?'

'Huh?'

'I'm standing looking at the old spruce tree in the garden. The one the girls hung milk cartons from, you know, with food for the birds.'

'Pål, sorry, have you been drinking?'

He smiles. Holds the phone out, as though it were a torch, before he brings it back to his face and says: 'No, listen, sorry about this, stupid of me to call. A whim, really.'

She laughs, exactly the same old laughter. 'Are you becoming impulsive, Pål?'

He laughs in response. 'Yeah, that'd be a turn up for the books, wouldn't it?'

'So, have you everything you need? The girls I mean, everything they need?'

'Yes,' he answers, quick as a flash, and thinks: what if I just say it? Tell her everything. How little money I've got. What I've done. Household and contents. Personal injury. What's going to happen.

'Good,' Christine says. 'So when is it Tiril's on stage again?'

'Oh, I'm not sure, I think it's seven it starts, isn't it?' he replies, realising he doesn't actually know when it begins. He walks over to the board in the kitchen, sees the note pinned there, reads: 7 p.m. 'Yeah, seven.'

Oh Jesus, he thinks, as he hears her breathe into the receiver.

'Well,' he hears her say.

Oh no.

'Why not?'

No no.

'I mean, I would actually manage to make it.'

'Wow,' he says, closing his eyes. He should have anticipated it. That she would consider doing it. Actually come.

'Okay, listen, Pål, I'll check it out, all right? I have a meeting now, but I'll get Ragnfrid to look at the flight times, and then I'll let you know, okay? Keep it to yourself, in case I don't make it. What's she's singing, by the way? Will you have time to pick me up at Sola airport?'

'Eh?'

'Will you have time to pi— no, forget it. The kids will notice. I'll get a taxi. What's she going to sing?'

'Evanescence,' Pål says, in a meek voice.

'Oh Christ, that's awful. Does she still like that?'

'She loves it. "My Immortal".'

'For fuck's sake. What about Malene, is she okay?'

'Malene, yeah she—'

'Okay, I'll be in touch.'

Click.

Zitha's snout brushes the back of his hand. Pål stands with the telephone in his hand staring vacantly ahead without looking at anything at all. Is she going to come? Here? Today? It feels as though his feet are leaving the ground and there's nothing he can do about it.

82. **FINE YOUNG PEOPLE** (Malene)

Frida Riska's meticulously applied red-varnished toenails gleam like a row of pearls protruding from under the vamp of her shoe. Her navy skirt sits tightly on her hips and narrow waistline, around which hangs a thin, coquettish belt, which lends her an air of youthful ease. The same air she has exuded in the class-rooms and corridors of Gosen School since she began there thirty years ago, and had the reputation of being the prettiest teacher at the entire school, maybe even in the whole area, if not in all of Stavanger.

Dad laughs every time Malene mentions Frida Riska, he can't help it: is she still there? Everyone was head over heels in love with her, we weren't able to follow what she was saying in class she was so pretty, but she was edgy too, heh heh, is she still there? You know, one day she came in, those high cheekbones of hers almost glowing from the moment she stepped into the classroom, and she was wearing these really sexy tights and she stood in front of the blackboard and said, without any preamble: 'You know what, I woke up this morning and I thought, Jesus, I'm going to have to face those hopeless pupils again, and I just about managed to drag myself to school – well, now you know, so you can get down to proving me wrong.' Is she still like that?

Yes, Malene thinks, as they enter the schoolyard and see Frida Riska hurrying across it with two ring binders pressed to her chest; she's still like that. The prettiest and most unconventional, but also the best teacher they have, she's always on the fringes of what is acceptable; like she has no respect at all for the Norwegian school system. Malene said to Dad once: I think she really wants to run everything herself and doesn't care a jot about what she's been tasked to teach us. Yeah, he said, laughing, you can be sure she does. She might look very middle class, Frida, but in reality she's an anarchist.'

'An anarchist, what's that?'

Dad laughed. 'Ask Tiril,' he said. 'Or better yet, just look at Tiril and Frida, then you'll know.'

Frida stops up as she catches sight of the quartet walking past the bike racks. Typically, she remains unruffled, merely tilts her head slightly to the side and drums her fingers on the ring binders she's clutching to her chest, before approaching them with that characteristic sway of her hips on her high heels. Malene casts a quick glance at Sandra, who is attempting to stand unaided, but being supported by Tiril. Shaun looks somewhat better than previously, but his pupils are still swimming like tiny fish in his glassy eyes.

Frida's hips come to a halt. She stands in front of them, her back straight. Her eyes move in measured fashion from one of them to the other, her gaze resting just long enough on each of them to let them know they've been seen, singled out and exposed.

'Yes?' she says.

None of them manage to respond. Malene expects Tiril to pipe up, but for once – perhaps because of Frida – she doesn't seize the chance.

The middle finger of Frida's left hand taps a steady rhythm on the ring binders. 'Yes,' she repeats, 'what do I have before me?' She raises her right arm gracefully and checks the slim silver watch on her wrist. 'A quarter to twelve. It's a long time since I've worked as a babysitter, but it goes without saying that when four such distinguished students – distinguished and talented each in their own way – when four such students arrive in school so late in the day, it is not atypical for it to warrant surprise, or what do you think yourselves? Particularly when two of you look like you've been involved in a fracas. Shaun? Sandra? And perhaps even more so when one of these two – you, Sandra – is the last person I could imagine being in a fight. You, Shaun, on the other hand, I can easily envisage being embroiled in all manner of conflicts. What do you have to say for yourselves?'

Tiril comes to life and takes a step forward. 'Sandra took a tumble on her bike. She crashed into Shaun on the way to school. Me and Malene saw it—'

'Malene and I,' Frida interrupts, 'go on...'

'Malene and I – yeah, it happened by the tower blocks, not far from where we live, and we saw them, on the way to school, they crashed. Really badly.'

Frida Riska checks her watch again. 'A quarter to twelve. Almost ten to twelve. And so you've used several hours then, to reflect upon this bicycle accident?'

Sandra shifts her weight on to her other foot and wheezes audibly. Malene sees they've now aroused other people's interest, the faces of more and more pupils are appearing in the windows of the classrooms. Sandra looks pale. Frida – Dad once termed her a hawk – takes a step towards Sandra.

'Are you feeling all right, Sandra?'

Sandra smiles. Her eyes look blurry.

'She bore the brunt of it,' says Tiril, placing an arm around her friend. 'That's why it took such a long time. We sat down. Took it easy. Went back home to get water and that.'

Sandra smiles again and nods. 'Yeah, fine,' she says, 'my head's a bit sore, that's all, feel a little tired. I'm okay though.'

Frida looks at them. Once again letting her gaze wander from one to the next, fixing each of them momentarily with her eyes, and once again they feel both examined and exposed.

'Listen to me,' she says. 'I don't believe what you're telling me, not for one second. You all know that. Judging by the body language on display, coming to expression through your beautiful, young physiques, and judging by what I'm seeing in your eyes, those beautiful, young pairs of eyes, there was no bicycle accident. But that's just how it is. The lot of you are up to something. It may well be something completely innocuous, which a grown-up ought to disregard. It may not. Perhaps it's something none of you realise the gravity of, perhaps something you should entrust to somebody who's lived longer than you. But here's what do I know. You are the ones responsible for making that decision. I'm going to take my leave of you in a moment and then you'll either end up making a good decision or a bad one. One of you, most likely you,

Tiril, will take control of the situation, and the rest of you, Shaun and Malene, will follow the course Tiril marks out for you. And well, what can I say? I wish you luck, you fine young people.'

83. **THE BOTNEVASS GANG** (Jan Inge)

Autumn 1996. Brother and sister were sitting at home in the living room, well wrapped up in old blankets and well stocked with crisps and cola. The light of the TV tinted the room, screams filled the air, and Jan Inge and Cecilie watched horror film after horror film while they listened to the stormy weather pummel the house in Hillevåg. Rudi was working a few hours east in Kvinesdal, he had been subcontracted out to the Botnevass Gang. Exactly what he was doing wasn't clear, but the money was good and Rudi's skill set was required. After he had been up there a couple of weeks the telephone back in Hillevåg rang late one night. Cecilie was having a bath while Jan Inge was sitting in the living room listening to his father's old country records. He picked up the receiver. It was Rudi. His voice screeched like a circular saw. 'No way I'm staying here a minute fucking longer, Jani.' He said. 'That whole Botnevass family are completely out of their tree. They're hanging out in a bus parked in a field, they have the interior all decked out like a movie set and they're filming one sick porn film after another, and their mother, she won't have anything to do with them any more, while the rumour is that Grandpa Botnevass, that Solomon guy, the priest, is going to come down from the mountains and tear strips off the lot of them.'

'Take it easy, calm down,' Jan Inge said, and after a while he managed to talk Rudi around and to persuade him to stick it out for a couple more weeks. They needed the money.

He rang again a fortnight later, and this time not from Kvines-dal, but from a public telephone in Ben's Kafé, after narrowly avoiding a head-on collision with another car in Gyadalen Valley and now there was no going back. Torleif Botnevass had shot his brother, Gordon Botnevass, over – according to their sister, Mary

Botnevass – a quarrel about how to rob the Chinese in Flekkefjord. Or – if their cousin Anton Botnevass was to be believed – due to an argument over which Maiden album was the best, or as Hilde from the shop said: because of a spat over my snatch. 'Christ,' said Rudi, over the telephone from Ben's, 'this has gone way too far, Jani. I was standing just four metres from the little brother Torleif when he pumped bullets into the side of his big brother Gordon's head. I don't fucking like murder, Jani.'

'Not good, that sounds awful, come on home.'

One hour later he walked in the door of the house in Hillevåg. 'Christ,' Rudi sighed, when he saw them, 'it's good to be around normal people again,' and then he lifted Cecilie up in the air, held her close and told her there wasn't a sexier woman on the planet.

A half-hour later, as they were sitting in the kitchen eating a supper of cured salmon and scrambled egg, Rudi pointed out the window at a van standing parked beneath the street light. 'What's that?' he asked. 'Someone visiting?'

'That,' said Jan Inge, smiling to Rudi and Cecilie, 'is our new company transport.'

'Company transport? Ours? That sweet ride?'

'That's right,' replied Jan Inge and pointed down the hall. 'You see that door there?'

Rudi let his weary eyes wander in the direction Jan Inge indicated. There was a sign on the door of the spare room. He squinted. 'Office,' it read.

'That is our office, Rudi.'

'Eh? Have the two of you lost your minds while I was dicing with death?'

Cecilie smiled and put her arm around her brother. 'You know,' she said in a soft voice, the way she could sometimes speak, as though filled with deep affection, 'you can't expect to be gone for three weeks and come home without this man here devising something of genius.'

Jan Inge got to his feet – he was fifteen kilos lighter back then – and said: 'Rudi, that was the last time you're going to be hired out to some unknown nutcases. We're putting things in order here at home. There's a telephone in there. A separate line with it's own number. You'll find it in the phone book under *Mariero Moving*. Inside that office you'll also find paperclips, folders, a pencil sharpener attached to the end of the desk, a ruler and a fax machine, everything an office worker could dream of. And our company car is parked out there on the street. A car which never – you hear me, never – will be used for anything other than this.'

'And what is *this*?'

'It's our moving company, brother. The moving company I run, with Cecilie responsible for cleaning and you as primary driver.'

Cecilie laughed, she really was in fine fettle around that time, and said: 'Now you see what happens when you're away for a couple of weeks, Rudi! Congratufuckinglations, you've got a new job.'

Rudi was a little piqued at first. He sure as hell wasn't up for some ordinary job. He was fucked if he was going to go round breaking his back lifting big boxes full of books just because old women were on the move to sheltered housing in Lassa, no bloody way was he about to start paying tax, and he was sure as fuck not going to drive around wearing a stupid hat with Mariero Moving on it for the whole city to see – and so on. But he was quick to reconsider, he began to change his mind pretty much at the same time as he was speaking: He didn't want to have this job in removals as a way to conceal his actual identity as a crook – even though it was undeniably a clever idea. Yes, only Jan Inge could come up with something so smart, give him his dues; open an office, set up another phone line, sort out a company car, company clobber, a logo, convert the garage, fuck, now that was what Rudi called genius. He had only been away a couple of weeks in Krazy Kvinesdal, where at this very moment Grandpa Solomon was probably pointing a shotgun at his progeny, who were no doubt lying around in the bus drinking hooch after yet another day of porn, picking them off one after the other while spewing Bible quotes from his mouth like spit, while old lady Rose Marie Botnevass was in all likelihood standing outside counting the gunshots and gobbing on the ground for every fallen son and daughter and niece and nephew – only a couple of weeks, and then to come home to...

Rudi threw his arms around Jan Inge: 'Fuck, brother. I thank the Lord and Gran that you exist. When's the first moving job? By the hour or fixed price?'

Jan Inge is proud of how he handled things in those tough few weeks back in 1996. If he hadn't hit upon the idea of establishing a company and presenting them as law-abiding citizens they'd all be wearing Åna-issue clothing and answering to a number by now. The scheme had occurred to him while he and Cecilie were sitting in the living room gorging on horror film after horror film and the rain hammered on the roof and transformed the garden into a pool. *Watch out, Jan Inge. Do something before it's too late.* So don't come here saying horror harms the mind; horror is a wellspring of creativity, *horror yields unity,* horror makes you see what's important here in this world and helps you choose the right path. And he's going to write about that in his book; how pain brings about good.

Ever since those rainy days in autumn 1996 there's been a steady stream of calls on The Other Telephone. Marketing? All you need is a number in the phone book, a listing under Removal Services and it takes care of itself.

'Yes, Mariero Moving?'

'Yes, hello, me and my wife need help moving from Hundvåg. Do you provide a cleaning service as well?'

'Specialist cleaning? *Kein Problem*! We have a highly trained cleaning consultant, she can take care of everything while you sun yourselves on the veranda.'

Last Thursday: The Other Telephone rang again. Jan Inge walked to the office with a wobbling gait, sat down in the old leather chair and picked up the receiver: 'Mariero Moving, Haraldsen speaking, how can I help?'

A grand piano. On Furras Gate. In Våland. Stavanger. Not exactly their favourite kind of job. Good thing Tong is going to be here; Jan Inge's abilty to lift and hump things around has become somewhat limited since the weight piled on.

Jan Inge and Rudi trudge to the garage and open the large door. They still haven't seen any sign of Tommy Pogo, and Jan Inge can feel it beginning to prey on his mind. Knowing he's going to come is worse than him turning up unannounced.

Rudi sighs as his eyes fall on the white van. 'Shit,' he says, 'my heart aches every time I see the Hiace. We have *ein tolles auto* right here and we only ever use it for moving.'

'Rudi,' says Jan Inge, 'no one is touching the moving van. This is half the reason we can live like we do. You remember autumn 1996?'

'Course I remember autumn 1996,' says Rudi, a dark look coming over his eyes: 'Did you hear what happened to the Botnevass Gang, by the way?'

'No,' says Jan Inge and switches on the ceiling light in the garage, producing a nice sheen on the roof of the vehicle. 'Presumed they were still doing their thing.'

'In hospital, all nine of them. Brothers, sisters, cousins and I don't what else. Torleif, Mary, Anton, Jo-Lene, Salve, Odd Harald, Ånen, Steven, and ehm ... what's her name ... the one in those films ... ehm ... yeah, Nancy Rose. Crushed both legs, she did. So that's the movie career finished.'

'Hah.' Jan Inge opens the van door and peeks inside. 'Nancy Rose. She could be doing with my wheelchair.'

The van is spick and span, ready to go to work in.

'Went how you thought it would, then?'

'Not quite,' says Rudi, peering over Jani's shoulder. 'They hit a rock face beside the road on the way home from Sweden Rock. They skidded after Ånen, swerved trying to avoid hitting a fox waltzing along the road. So they say, anyway. The bus broke through the crash barrier not far from Liknes, slammed straight into a rock face. Hilde from the shop says that stuff about the fox is bollocks, she says Grandpa Botnevass fiddled with the brakes because he thought they were bringing shame on the family name. But apparently old Father Solomon told her that if she opens her mouth one more time, he's going to come down from the mountain and make sure she never sees the light of day again. They say Grandma Rose Marie couldn't care less, never liked her kids anyway, apart from the one she lost when he was a baby, Kjell Ivar. They say she regrets ever marrying that mad priest, was so beautiful she could have had her pick of anything in trousers up there, whether they were called Botnevass, Øyvass, Kissvass, Vedvass,

Sandvass, Skjerlevass, Storevass, Vestvass, Krokevass, Svodvass, Grunnevass or Movass. And she had to choose the biggest head-case of them all. Solomon Botnevass.

'Not good,' Jan Inge says, turning around, 'not much luck in that family.'

'Well, you know, brother, better to be good than lucky.'

'Words of truth.'

'It's how it is; some families are haunted by demons and evil spirits. Wouldn't surprise me if they were back on their feet in a year's time. Wait and see, back on track with bus porn for the handicapped. They still haven't hit the Chinese in Flekkefjord. Torleif is sure the owner is sitting on a few hundred thousand in cash. Probably only a question of time.'

'Everything, Rudi, can be transformed into a question of time,' says Jan Inge. 'It's the essence of every good horror movie.'

'Philosophy again,' says Rudi, nodding. 'It's so you, while the rest of us are discussing nuts and bolts and baseballs and batons, you're hovering above in the clouds.'

'You don't find it odd that Tommy hasn't shown up yet?'

They look at one another.

Rudi nods.

'Yeah,' he whispers. 'Now that you mention it.'

Jan Inge nods. 'Kind of stressing me out, I have to say.' He points towards the back garden. 'Speaking of stress,' he says. 'There's still that there.'

An overgrown garden that hasn't served as a garden for decades, old mattresses, two rusty wheelbarrows, hubcaps and tyres, rotten planks, a broken lawnmower, Cecilie's old Raleigh bicycle, Mum's washing machine, the couch from the basement, which was once red, now the colour of sun-bleached vomit, snapped spades and rakes, a broken TV, a video recorder, the three panel radiators Dad bought right before he left, a total of eight pallets, an enormous amount of smaller pieces of scrap, half a pair of shears, screws and washers, a door handle and in the south corner a rusted rotary clothes line, the one Jan Inge always thought looked like an umbrella when he was small, the one he always thought he was going to lift up in his little hand, hold up in the rain.

'Looks like a bloody tip. How long has that fridge been there?'

'1987.'

'Big clear-out so.'

'Sunday.'

Rudi spits on the ground and accepts the inevitable.

Jan Inge hears the familiar sound of the Volvo behind him, the splutter of its engine coming down the street. He straightens up and looks at Rudi. A smile spreads across both their faces and they consign Tommy Pogo to the back of their minds for the time being. They walk out into the white sunshine.

The Volvo comes to a halt by the bins and the car doors open. Cecilie gets out from the driver's side. Jan Inge is struck by an uneasy feeling as he watches her walk with an unsteady step and a wavering look in her eyes. Tong gets out from the other side. He looks like a walking chunk of iron, and Jan Inge realises that he's in no way happy that Tong is home, that he is in no way happy that Tong may well be the father of the child Cecilie is carrying.

'Hey! Fuck yeah! Holy shit!'

Rudi vaults the porch wall, opens his arms and pulls the Korean close while slapping him repeatedly on the back: 'There you are, you sick bastard! Shit, we have missed you! So bloody good to see you! Hell, *wilkommen zu Hause*! Toooooooooooooooooooooog-ong-ong-ong-ong-ong-ong-ong-ong-ong!'

84. THEY CAME FROM THE FOREST (Sandra)

Her eyelids keep slipping down. Her chest rises and falls, and Sandra wants so badly to sleep. Put her arms on the desk, form them into the shape of a heart, lay her head on them and slip into the heavy sea. Sea? Yes, Lord, you are mine. Her cheeks are warm, like she's been watching TV for a long time, and her fingers are heavy, like her arms have been hanging by her sides for a long time, and her head is woozy; is it Thursday? She forces her eyes open, smiles listlessly at Malene who's just turned around in her seat further up the classroom. Are you there? Her jaw muscles, it's as if they're missing. Is it Thursday today? Or is it Wednesday? Is it maths, is it English? Yeah, English with Frida Riska. Hi, Frida. *To* talk *too* much. Everyone understand? The difference? Or is that proving too much of a challenge for you all? Sandra feels queasy now, there's discomfort in her stomach and chest and she's so unbelievably tired. Must be Wednesday. Fingers are so heavy, eyes are so slanted, cheeks are so warm: once. *Today's paper.* Has something happened? She can't remember any more. Wait. Wasn't she in an accident? Yeah. With Daniel? No. Once. No, he loves me and I love him: youandme. Was she? My bright boy, I will serve you the rest of my days, because that's how love is: yes. Once they came. A peal of thunder across the sky, you could feel the rumble beneath your feet. They came from the forest. They were sons of Lucifer, because they were naked, and in their arms they bore the severed limbs and small hearts they had gathered from the sons and daughters of man. A little distance behind them, the daughters of Lucifer came, also naked, also promising fire and torment. Yes. Blood ran down their thighs, from between their legs. These fingers are so heavy. Thursday? Meandyou, Daniel. My bright boy, your bright mouth. Sandra thinks she needs to throw up, throw up and fall asleep at the same time, as if that was something that went together, she ponders sluggishly, throw up and fall asleep. Once they came from the forest. Daniel. My Daniel. For what could be right here in this world if love was not right? What would speak the language of truth if love did not? Warm up our church, light this candle. I have to sleep now. I really have to sleep.

'Sandra?'

'Hello, Sandra?'

'Sandra!'

'Oh my God!'

'Frida! She's not breathing!'

'Get help!'

'Sandra?'

'Malene! You need to tell me the truth now! Malene! What happened earlier? Malene!'

85. WHENEVER WE VISIT GRANNY ON FURRAS GATE SHE ALWAYS GIVES US ELDERFLOWER CORDIAL AND IT'S THE BEST IN THE WORLD (Rudi)

The white van pulls out on to Hillevågsveien. It has a red logo on the side with the motto, *Mariero Moving – Your problem is kein Problem*. Four people are sitting inside, all dressed in the company's light blue overalls, the motto of the firm written diagonally across the backs of each.

Rudi, Tong and Jan Inge sit in the spacious front seat, in that order, and Cecilie sits behind smoking.

Rudi turns the large steering wheel, but he doesn't feel at ease. The oxygen inside the vehicle is too thin. It's not like before. Tommy Pogo stresses him out. He still hasn't shown up. And the atmosphere in the van, that's also stressing him out. Is something funny going on? It's about time Tong started loosening up a little. Understandable if he has got some issues, maybe it was rough being inside this time, even for a rock-hard fucker like Mr Korea, but isn't he going to say one single thing?

Get released from prison, come home to your best mates – *your Norwegian family* – and don't utter a bloody word. Here we are throwing our arms around him, hugging him, putting beer on the table, breaking out chocolate chip cookies and doing one thing after the fecking other, but the guy is behaving as though we don't exist. It's not natural.

'Ah well, Tongi!'

Rudi makes an expansive gesture as they go around the roundabout by Strømsbrua Bridge.

'I'd say you must be overwhelmed to see the old stamping ground again, eh? The city of Stavanger, best place on earth! Yessir!

Everything's the same as it was, apart from even more internet, and the financial crisis giving the globe a good seeing to from behind, not that it affected us, people have more than enough money for all the break-ins we could ever imagine—'

Rudi speaks extra loudly and in the back seat Cecilie giggles, albeit slightly nervously. Jan Inge smiles too, but Tong just stares straight ahead. A sheen coming off his jet-black hair. No movement from him at all, as though he isn't even breathing.

'Well,' Rudi tries again, 'anyway, it's good to have you back again, because heh heh, I don't think we'd manage this piano without you!'

No reaction at all from the great warrior. Is he a zombie? Is it just Rudi who thinks this is weird? Cecilie? Jani? Hello-o? This can't be put down to morning tiredness; this isn't Cecilie when she wakes up snapping like a hammerhead shark. Is he just going to sit there like a fighting fish?

Rudi gives Tong a nudge as they crawl up Tors Gate in Våland. 'Hey, Tongo man. Time you came out of the freezer now. Come on, bushman. Hey, yellow peril! It's us! Your people! Did somebody die? Did you get a letter from Korea, someone calling you son, all of a sudden? Come on. Out with it, *caballero*!'

Silence. The Hiace turns on to Furras Gate.

It's pointless. Rudi nods to himself. Fine. No one can say he hasn't tried to be the life and soul of the party, as Gran used to refer to him. Or the clown, as she also used to call him.

'Here we are,' Jan Inge says, pointing to a white wooden house on the left hand side. 'Thirty-nine.'

Rudi slows down and pulls in slowly to the kerb. They open the doors and a bent, old woman appears by the gate.

'Everyone behave themselves, now,' Jan Inge says, 'and we leave with our flawless reputation intact. As usual.'

He takes a step towards the elderly woman. She's wearing a blue dress, has wavy, white hair, glowing cheeks and strong blue eyes.

'Ludvigsen?'

She's a small woman, must be over seventy years old, and even though she doesn't look like she was ever as tall as a tree, she must have shrunk a little as well.

'Yes, that's me,' she says smiling. 'Splendid you could come, yes, let's see now, the piano is in there. I don't know how you intend to do it, but anyway it's to go to my daughter's. I don't have the space for it any more, or rather I do, but I don't feel I can really have it here any longer, so I thought—'

'You know what,' Rudi says, dazzled by the beautiful old woman who in every way reminds him of Gran, 'you know,' he repeats, bending down to her, 'this will be no problem.'

'That's our motto, all right,' says Jan Inge, taking charge, '*your problem is kein Problem.*'

'Such lovely young people,' says the elderly woman and shows them to the living room. She offers Tong a rather wary glance, but Cecilie notices and gives her an extra large smile.

'Oh, there's not a pick on you,' the old woman says, 'you need to eat, girl.'

Cecilie laughs. 'I eat plenty, so I do, just have a fast metabolism.'

'Ah,' the old woman says, 'I've always wanted a fast metabolism, but it wasn't my lot in life.' Then she lowers her voice and leans towards Cecilie: 'Constipation. Takes three days.'

Rudi makes a brief attempt to follow the indistinct conversation before heading for the living room, Jan Inge and Tong following behind him. The grand piano, which he quickly estimates to be close to seven feet in length, is standing in the centre of the room. There are high ceilings in the old house, but lots of tricky little corners.

'Ludvigsen?' he hears Jan Inge say. 'You don't have any other exits on this floor, do you? A veranda or something?'

'Oh, yes,' replies the little woman. 'There's one back here...'

'Detachable feet,' Rudi mumbles, bending down to the piano. 'Heavy as hell. Still. We'll manage it.' He turns to the old woman and speaking slightly louder in a friendly tone asks: 'Is it old?'

Tong stands stiff and straight by the door.

'Oh heavens, yes,' the woman says, 'it's so old now. I inherited it from my grandfather – it's a Steinway, as you can see...'

'A Steinway,' nods Jan Inge. 'No, they're not exactly giving them away.'

The woman laughs, her face lighting up.

'Apparently I could get half a million for it if I sold it.'

Over by the door, Tong shifts his weight from one foot to the other. Cecilie gulps. Jan Inge clears his throat. Rudi doesn't know where to look.

'But I'd never sell it, not for all the money in the world, no, what would I do with that kind of money? I can hardly spend what I have as it is.'

Tong shifts his weight again. Cecilie sweeps her tongue over her front teeth and Jan Inge fumbles for his inhaler, which he locates in the trouser pocket of his overalls. Rudi's gaze flits around the room.

'Asthma,' says Jan Inge.

'No, I'm going to give it to my daughter,' says the woman, then lowers her voice a notch, 'I've discovered I can pass it on to her as an advance on inheritance, and that's probably just as well,' before lowering her voice even more, drawing closer to them, almost gathering them in a ring, 'it's my grandchildren, you see,' she says.

'What about them?' Rudi asks, when the woman doesn't appear to intend finishing her sentence and lapses into thoughtful silence. She moves even closer.

'They're drug addicts,' she says. 'Apparently they steal from everyone. That's what happens with drug addicts,' she adds. 'They lose the run of themselves, stop being the people they once were, and so it could well come to pass, my daughter tells me, that they end up trying to rob their own grandmother.'

Rudi can see Tong's arms twitching. His veins are visible, as are his muscles.

'Imagine,' the old woman says. 'Their own grandmother. Jørgen and Svein Anders. I just don't understand it.'

Rudi can hear Tong breathing now.

'Well,' Rudi says loudly, 'we need to go out to the van to fetch some equipment, the Haraldsen siblings here will remove the legs and go through the practical details with you, and hey presto, this expensive Steinway piano will be on its way to your daughter's house and out of the clutches of those monsters you have as grandchildren!'

Rudi seizes Tong by the arm and hisses: 'Come on!'

He halts on the steps outside and throws Tong up against the wall: 'What the fuck is wrong with you? Were you planning on flattening the old biddy and taking her piano? Hm? What the fuck is your problem! Here we are, after picking you up – or Cecilie did – and laying on chocolate chip cookies and beer and good humour, and what do you bring? Have you ever heard of manners, for Chrisssake?'

Cecilie and Jan Inge emerge from the house behind them, both looking anxious, shutting the front door quickly behind them.

'What's going on,' Jan Inge whispers. 'What the hell are you two up to?'

Rudi feels the pulse in his throat throb and releases Tong.

'I've had enough of this bloody Korean simpleton. He was all ready to bash in grandma's brains there. And has he said anything all day? Hm? This has gone too far!'

Jan Inge studies Tong, who's standing completely still. Cecilie looks at him too.

'You need to say something, Tong,' says Jan Inge. 'Rudi has overstepped the mark, I know, but he does have ... well, a point.'

Tong makes some movements with his lower jaw, opens his mouth and spits in the direction of an elderberry bush beside the driveway.

'What's the deal?'

'Ehh ... I don't quite follow you now,' Jan Inge says.

'Tonight. What's the deal.'

'With Pål, you mean. Simple enough job. Smash up the house, give the guy a few bruises. Take what we find.'

'Alibi?'

'God, what is with everyone today?' Jan Inge shakes his head. 'Of course. I have an address in Sandal. We drive the van there. We're at work from 6 p.m. to 10 p.m. We're moving the contents of one terraced house to another. Witnesses all arranged. Watertight.'

'And the deal?'

'I told you, Tong. Smash up the house. Alter the guy. Take what we find. What are you getting at?'

Tong closes his eyes. 'That's the deal?'

Rudi is livid. 'Yeah, that's the deal, but first Tampon is going to pay us a visit!'

Jan Inge looks at him resignedly. Cecilie's eyes grow larger. Rudi throws his arms up. He just couldn't contain himself.

'Yeah,' he says. 'We ran into him yesterday. He said he was going to drop by.'

Tong shakes his head slowly.

'This is unbelievable. You've got Tampon on your back? And you're still going ahead with it? And the insurance money? That is so incredibly lame. You haven't demanded a cut of the money. You waltz straight into a house with a piano worth half a million inside while Tommy Pogo is hiding behind the bushes watching us. This is my last day with you lot. I can't stand you, Rudi, or you, Jan Inge. You're just ... you're nothing to me. Understand? I'll go along tonight, but only if you agree to us taking half of the insurance sum. After I've taken my cut we'll never see each other again.'

Tong turns to Cecilie.

'And you?'

He shakes his head.

'Jesus,' he says. 'You are the fucking ugliest woman I've ever seen.'

Rudi's fists begin to clench, his teeth begin to tap, but as he's about to head-butt Tong the front door opens. The old lady's head appears.

'Ah,' she says, 'I was almost beginning to think you'd left. It was so quiet. Look, I've defrosted a little apple pie.'

She holds out a tray with some slices on it.

'Yes,' she says, 'and elderflower cordial. You must try some. All that hard work you do. My grandchildren used to like it so much, Granny's elderflower cordial.'

86. **HE DEALS WITH IT** (Daniel William)

Veronika strokes him across the wrist. His veins are swollen, as though lying ashamed beneath his skin. Daniel withdraws from her caress. He puts a cigarette between his lips and lights it up. He leans towards the teak coffee table and takes hold of his helmet. He fiddles with the strap. She reaches for his hands, grips them tightly and kisses him. She tastes of seaweed, of icing sugar and iron and he can't stand it.

Daniel tears himself free and gets to his feet.

'What is it?' asks Veronika.

He can't bring himself to answer. His shoulders rise as he takes a deep breath. He doesn't want to talk any more. He just wants to strike out. He opens the door to the concrete corridor and the light from the rehearsal room floods out to where the moped is standing. The Suzuki gleams. Daniel walks over to it, runs his fingers along it.

Why must it be this way?

Why must everything go down?

Why must everything go under?

'Daniel?'

He's a matter of seconds from whirling around and going for her, seconds from sinking his teeth into her throat and biting down until she loses her deaf life. But he doesn't. He remains standing looking at the Suzuki.

He can tell by her footsteps that she's coming closer. She really shouldn't, he thinks.

Veronika pokes him on the shoulder.

He doesn't look around, but she continues jabbing him.

Eventually he turns. She looks shattered, and he says: 'Don't poke me.'

He takes a step towards the Suzuki, takes it by the handlebars, kicks the stand up and points to the entrance. 'Will you get the door?'

'Daniel, you have to remember to think straight. I understand that you're angry, I understand that you're afrai—'

He merely continues to point and Veronika doesn't say any more. She does as he signals. Walks to the door, opens it and lets the September light in.

'You're not easy to understand,' she says. He can see she's trying to make eye contact, but no fucking way is he going to let her.

'I haven't asked anybody to understand me.'

She reaches her hand out, but he ignores it. 'Only a little while ago you said we should stuff everything. We should just leave. Together. But now – what is it you want to do now?'

He doesn't reply.

'Daniel, things change so quickly with you.'

'Right,' he says, feeling power in his own self-contradiction.

He sees her let out a heavy breath. He can see she actually wants to crack. But he can also see she's restraining herself. She nods. Smiles.

'Where are we going?' she asks. Her smile is feigned, but he likes the fact that she makes an effort.

'Are you one of those people who need to know everything?'

He sees her eyes mist over.

That brought her right back down.

Are you going to cry, deaf girl?

'Didn'tyouunderstandwhatIsaid?Didyounotmanagetoreadmy lips, thought you were a world champion at it? A-r-e-y-o-u-o-n-e-o-f-t-h-o-s-e-p-e-o-p-l-e-w-h-o-n-e-e-d-t-o-k-n-o-w-e-v-e-r-y-t-h-i-n-g?'

She continues to look at him. But she doesn't begin to cry. She folds her arms.

'Answer me,' he says. 'If you're the kind of person who goes on and on asking questions and needs to know everything and can't trust a guy, then you can just forget about me, got it?'

'Daniel, I—'

'I asked you a simple fucking question. Can you not answer?'

Veronika brings her hand to his face, letting it rest there until his breathing regulates.

'Yes, I can,' she says. 'I'm not the type who needs to know everything. Take me with you, wolfman.'

'What the hell is with the wolf stuff?'

'That's what I like to call you,' she says and lets out a laugh, intended to lighten the atmosphere, like her mother always does when she and Veronika argue. 'Where are we going?'

'A place.'

'Okay. But you know that right now we ought to stay put? That there's probably lots of people looking for you and me at the moment—'

He doesn't listen. He wheels the Suzuki out into the light, wishing it were deadly. He wished the light would bring a violent end to Daniel William Moi, wished the rays of the sun were like scalpels, making an incision in his skin, folding it aside and opening into a snapping, chomping, howling mouth, and he wished it caused unparalleled pain.

Daniel tosses her the keys and climbs on to the moped. She locks the door, then gets on behind, putting her arms around him.

'Daniel?'

He turns his head.

'Are you going to see her? I'm up for anything, but I won't go along with that.'

He puts the key in the ignition.

Veronika narrows her eyes. 'Do you love her?'

Daniel feels his fists tighten on the handlebars. 'There's someone I need to talk to before it's too late,' he says.

It's just a normal day all around us, thinks Daniel, trying to relax his grip on the handlebars. He tries thinking about how he doesn't need to hit her. He sucks on his tongue, as though it were a damp cloth or a snowball.

'Veronika,' he says. 'I'm never going to tell you or anybody else what happened to me. If I do, it'll happen again.'

They ride up the hill from the bomb shelter and he swallows back saliva while he lets his gaze sweep over the housing estate they're leaving behind, the little houses that grow smaller and smaller the further away they get. There are people inside them. Some of them are off school sick. Some of them are asleep, because they've worked a nightshift or couldn't sleep the night before. And maybe somewhere, in one of those terraced houses, there are people in bed together, in the middle of the day, in the bright light, and maybe somewhere there's a person daring to raise a gun against all that light that's just too strong.

Daniel deals with it. He doesn't hit her.

87. SCRAT (Tiril)

The ambulance travels at speed as it drives up to the front of the school, and Tiril feels a bolt of guilt slide back in her head as the sound of sirens fills the air. It's as though a closed fist is pounding at her from within. The very thing she denied and dreaded has come to pass.

Sandra.

When someone like her is brought down, things are bad.

And it's her fault.

Tiril isn't the only one peering out the window at the ambulance that's come to a sudden stop outside the entrance and thrown open it's back doors, at the medics readying a trolley stretcher, at the headmaster and deputy head running out, at Frida Riska gesticulating and taking control; the entire class has got to its feet. Mai has put down the book she was holding, a murmur spreads through the classroom, eyes wander, and hands and feet shift and shuffle: 'What is it?' 'What's happened?' 'Jesus!' 'No way?!' 'What are they doing?'.

Tiril knocks over a chair on her way out of the classroom. Mai casts a wavering glance in her direction, but refrains from saying anything. Tiril runs out into the corridor, hating the linoleum under her feet, hating the stupid charts along the walls, hating the framed photographs of past pupils, hating the teachers, hating everything that's happened and is going to happen, hating The International Cunty Wankskop and hating herself as she emerges into the strong sunlight at the same moment that Frida Riska shouts: 'Tiril Fagerland! Can you please move!'

The flash in Frida's eyes: 'And someone will be speaking to you afterwards. You and Shaun and Malene.'

Tiril moves to the side and is almost mowed down by the

ambulance crew wheeling a stretcher. One of them, a young woman with a ponytail and a hawk nose, holds an oxygen mask over Sandra's face; a white face, thinks Tiril, a white face with dead eyelids. The woman says something as the stretcher is rolled into the back of the vehicle, but she can't make it out, and just as quickly as they arrived, they're off again: the double doors slam shut.

Frida Riska stands in front of the headmaster, nodding, 'Yes, of course, I'll call the parents, right away,' and she takes out a mobile phone.

Malene comes over to Tiril and puts her arm around her, but doesn't say anything. Shaun shows up – or has he been there all along? She looks dejectedly at the glue-sniffer she's fallen for, who all of a sudden doesn't seem so attractive, standing there, nodding, unable to meet her eyes, looking like that squirrel in *Ice Age*, Scrat, with his hands in the pockets of his hoodie and nothing at all to say.

'Frida?'

Frida Riska presses the buttons on her phone. 'I can't get hold of them...' She turns, visibly irritated, to Tiril: 'Yes?'

'Yes?'

'What happens now, I mean, like—'

'We don't know, Tiril.'

'But... she'll live?'

'We don't know that yet,' says Frida, and then fixing her eyes upon her: 'All you should be thinking about is that it's time you started telling the truth, and stopped playing with somebody's life.'

Then she hurries off.

Tiril feels her face smarting from Frida's words. Malene runs her hands up and down her back and says: 'Guess we're the ones who need to breathe easy now, aren't we?'

'Yeah...'

'What are we going to do?'

'I...'

'Tiril, you have to say something, what will we do? I mean, we said it was Shaun and Sandra, that's what Frida's told them, but ... Tiril? What are we going to do?'

Then Tiril begins to cry.

All she manages to think is that it must be years since she has, since she's cried. Then she moves off. Twisting away, determinedly, but without anger, from Malene's consolatory hand, and walks across the schoolyard.

Shaun runs after her. 'Hey, baby, do you need, like, help? I mean, we can't be sure that ... you know, it could turn out all right, all this.'

He's sweet again now, sweet and small and stupid as a smurf, and cool in a way, but what does that matter when you've killed a person, what does that matter when you've chosen lies in order to satisfy your own rage, what the fuck does it matter when you're the one who's pressed The Big Red Button, the button that opens a trapdoor in the floor under another person, when you're the one who's done it, all because you're so wrapped up in yourself, so busy thinking about being first, being biggest, being best, what does it matter then that Scrat stands in front of you asking if you want his nut?

Tiril shakes her head, rebuffs him with a wave of her hand and walks towards the gym hall. Scrat stands looking after her.

She walks towards the large building and the others let her go. She rounds the corner, sniffles and spits, takes a cigarette from her packet and wonders what in the hell she's going to do. Just say balls to everything? Screw the singing. Don't be bothered about Dad, about Malene, about the songbirds, about Mum in Bergen, about love, to hell with everything; and she means *everything*. This old school, this Stavanger suburb, the telecom tower on top of Ullandhaug, the hill at Limahaugen, these streets, everything.

If you take another person's life, you have to offer your own.

She hears the sound of footsteps while standing there. She sees a little guy scurrying towards her. He has an awful running style, not even bothering to take his hands out of his pockets. He has a fresh shiner, a daft-looking body and his head wobbles as though not properly attached to his neck. He draws closer and he's only thirteen years old, but pants and puffs like he has lung disease and he clearly won't give up.

Shaun comes to a halt in front of her. He's sweating and needs to swallow, put his palms on the wall and gather himself before he manages to say anything: 'Just wanted ... fuck ... okay, give me a sec here ... just wanted ... awh ... shit ... people don't always die because their consciousness faints ... or ... yeah ... I just wanted to say that you have to sing tonight and ... well ... you'll figure out what we should say, y'know ... you'll figure out what's right, because that's your style ... and everyone says you should all go ahead and sing ... that no matter what happens, we'll sing, because it's ... shit ... like solidarity and international and the environment and that ... nobody's going to give up, we're not going to let fear ... get the upper hand, or something like that .... Anyway, the head-master says the international, like, workshop is going ahead and everyone's talking about unity, and fellowship and solidarity ... and you're going to sing ... because it doesn't help not to sing ... or ... I can't exactly sing myself ... but that's probably just me ... anyway ... yeah ... I just wanted to ... hear if you needed help with anything ... I'm like really into you ... Tiril?

88. RUDI HOLDS A SPEECH ON THE EAST SIDE OF STOKKAVANN LAKE (Cecilie)

Men? Cecilie walks a few paces behind them. They're not real men, not that lot. A fat guy who's always eating crisps, watching horror movies and thinks he's a business executive. A beanpole with ADHD who walks around with a constant hard-on and lies in bed crying at night. A twisted Korean brute without any feelings at all. They're just little boys. They haven't grown up at all, they're just like they were twenty-five years ago, the only difference is that any charm they had then is long gone.

That's how boys are.

They never grow up. They grow down.

I'd do anything for you.

Cecilie has her eyes fixed on Tong's back as they walk along Store Stokkavann. The white sun shimmers on the surface of the water, one or two people out walking pass in the opposite direction. She wants to explode. The fact she had sex with him the whole summer. The guy is just plain evil.

She lets her gaze drift from the back of Tong's taut neck, via her brother's bloated neck over to Rudi's unsteady bird neck. A feeling of guilt spreads in her stomach; the way she's treated him over the years. He's been there right in front of her with that glittering intensity of his, waiting upon her every single second, and what has she done?

Cecilie dries away a tear from under one eye as they enter the wooded area along the east bank of the lake, about a kilometre and a half along the trail, and the boys slow down and exchange glances.

'Yeah,' says Rudi, his voice a little despondent, 'feel a little ashamed now, fetching that stuff. I mean, with that woman and her piano and everything. Those grandkids of hers. Jørgen and whatever the hell his name was.'

Jan Inge pokes at the gravel with the tip of his shoe. 'Svein Anders.'

Tong looks out at the lake.

'We need to pick it up anyway,' says Jan Inge. 'Did you hear, Tong, what we found out?'

Tong looks at Jan Inge with disinterest.

'Yep,' Jan Inge says. 'Stegas is a homo. Eh? You wouldn't have guessed that. Sits at home baking muffins, lighting candles and climbing on top of Bunny.'

'Each to their own,' Rudi mutters, 'but it's not natural.'

'Amen,' Jan Inge nods, 'amen to that.'

Tong spits on the ground. 'And you're still working with him all the same?'

'Listen,' Rudi says, 'I'll tell you something. Stegas ... I agree. It's against the word of the Lord. It's against nature. It's disfuckingust-ing.' He pauses and turns to look at Tong. 'But when you get older, when life begins to ... when life begins to ... how can I explain this ... okay: when I was five, life was simple. It was like this: Get up! Go out! Play with something! Get fed! Sleep! When I was fifteen, it was like this: Get up! Go out! See if I could get laid! Get fed! Sleep! Y'know, simple, yeah? Nothing to get philosophical about. But then. Okay. Tong. And you need to listen fucking closely here. And there was me thinking you'd had time to do some thinking in the joint. I have to say, I thought you'd become richer, not poorer in there, but fair enough, our time as colleagues will soon be over, so hey, I can say what I think: You understand, after a while, that *simple,* that is the one thing which life is not. It's ... shit, I don't know what you'd call it...'

'Ambiguous?' Jan Inge says. 'Is that what you're thinking of?'

'Ambiguous ...' Rudi sways his head from side to side, 'yeeeah ... but...'

'Multifaceted?' Jan Inge inquires. 'Could that be the word?'

'Better,' says Rudi, continuing to move his head from side to side as he sucks on his lip, 'but...'

'What you might be thinking of,' says Jan Inge, sweating in the sunshine, 'is the sense of majesty. Of gravity. A feeling of interminable complexity.'

Rudi stops swaying his head, bends down, picks up a stone from the gravel path and throws it out into the lake.

'You've put your finger on it,' Rudi says solemnly, before turning again to Tong. 'It's probably true that you don't fit in with us. We're on a different level from you. We're alive to the feeling of gravity, to the feeling of majesty. What is it Deep Purple sing? "I'm a blind man and my world is pale." Well, I can see very well, as Elton John sings on "Madman Across the Water", and yeah, I'm not quoting Elton because I like him, I'm quoting him out of reluctant respect for his fellow bumchum Stegas, and I'm not quoting him because my brother, that jackal, didn't listen to anything but Elton when I was small, before he became a Cars fan, but that's another thing entirely. But anyway, my brother – who I have a *serious* problem even talking about, in fact even the *mention* of my brother makes me bristle, so when I bring him, that rat, up, you know that I've something important to say, something that surpasses my hatred for him, *burninhellyoubastard*. He used to sit there going on about Elton this and Elton that ... shit! Now I've forgotten what I was on about. Why am I even talking about that git, get thee behind me, carpenter! I hope you drown in your own puke! I find it so fucking hard ... my own brother ... and to think we slept in the same room when we were small ... in the bunk beds ... not to mention my own fam ... my own fam—'

Rudi gasps for breath.

'Listen,' Cecilie says, 'you know you don't need to talk about them, not if you don't want to, you know how worked up you get.'

'That my own fam—'

'I know.'

'That my own famil—'

Cecilie rubs the back of his hand. 'I know, Rudi.'

'Rikki and Ben ... and Kate...'

'I know.'

'Rewind!' sniffles Rudi, and slaps his hands together. 'Where was I? Yeah, Tong: Elton. John. An openly homosexual man. And friend of the British royal family. Yes.' He clears his throat. 'And that's what he sings, my Korean friend, or rather my *former* Korean friend: "I can see, very well." And that's what Deep Purple sing: "I'm a blind man and my world is pale." And to take it slightly further, what is it The Cars sing: "Oh, heartbeat city, here we come." Hm? Tong. Have you been there? In heartbeat city? And what is it Marillion – yeah, I know you hate Marillion, and I'd be only too happy to sit down and discuss the strengths and weaknesses of that band – what is it Marillion sing? "You've got venom in your stomach, you've got poison in your head." Well, I'll tell you one thing, brother of evil: I was blind, but now I can see, and my address is in heartbeat city, and my stomach isn't full of venom, my head isn't filled with poison, I'm rich. How is your stomach, yellow adder? How is your head, my furious friend? That's the way it is, Tong, you have to accept that your best friend sucks cock, no matter how fucked up it seems.'

It's quiet after Rudi's flood of words lets up. Four pensioners pass by, one of them smiles, raises his hand to his forehead and gives them a three-fingered scout salute and says: 'Lovely day, isn't it?'

Cecilie feels warmth spread across her skin. Her eyes are moist.

'In prison,' says Tong calmly, 'I read a good bit of psychology. And psychiatry. There's a diagnosis for people like you, Rudi. It's called manic. A lot of unstable people suffer from it.'

Cecilie continues looking at Rudi. The warm feeling on her skin increases, like a friendly fever. Please, whispers Cecilie to herself, please baby, don't be Tong's kid. And please, baby, please never let Rudi find out what I did. He's my man, she whispers to herself, and now finally, I'm in love with him.

It just took a little time.

Then she approaches Rudi, places her hand in his, and says: 'Hey, Rudi boy. Manic?' She turns to Tong. 'So what? Manic, my ass. I love manic.'

Rudi stares at her, his eyes look like they're going to fall out of his head.

Cecilie continues to look at Tong.

'Hey, Tong,' she says, her voice clear and distinct. 'Can you see how ugly I am?' Then she goes up on her toes, reaches towards

Rudi, takes hold of his head, finds his mouth, gives him her tongue and whispers: 'I'd do fucking anything for you.'

His kiss is stiff. His eyes flit about. 'Shhh!'

'Wha?'

'Pogo!'

She turns and looks in the direction he's staring. About fifty or sixty metres from them, Tommy Pogo is approaching along the path. He's wearing white trainers, blue jeans and a black belt with a shiny, silver buckle. A freshly washed, black T-shirt sits tight across his torso. Kia is rolling alongside in a motorised wheelchair. She has wavy, blonde hair and curling eyelashes to match, and she's almost alarmingly pretty; imagine having a daughter like that.

'No way,' Rudi whispers, kissing Cecilie back as naturally as he's able, 'there's no way this is a coincidence.'

Tommy and his daughter draw closer. Kia turns her head to her father and says something. He nods three times in succession. They've recognised them.

'Tampon is sticking *so* close to us,' Rudi whispers. 'So bloody close. Come on, baby, let's show him a bit of tongue here.'

And so Rudi snogs his woman, with such passion and intensity that his whole body is shaking as he hears Tommy Pogo's resonant voice: 'Well hello, didn't expect to see you lot up here. I didn't get a chance to pop by. Kia was off school due to some rehearsals, so I took the day off too, and *voilà*, here we are, and what do you know, you lot are here too. Tong, you're back again. Did you have an okay time in Åna? Hi, Jan Inge, seems like either we never meet or we can't stop bumping into each other, eh? You know, I've often thought about it, how you and Cecilie were left there in Hillevåg in the eighties; that'd never happen today, Child Welfare would have intervened, we would have stepped in, but maybe you're happy we never did?'

Jan Inge smiles, but doesn't reply, and Rudi merely continues making out with his girlfriend.

Pogo laughs. 'Will there be wedding bells in the near future, Rudi? See, Kia, love can work out too, can last a long time. Good thing Rudi isn't inside, the way the two of them carry on, eh?'

His daughter laughs, a mellifluous sound, she's obviously inherited her father's vocalisation. Tommy Pogo is a very handsome man. His beard is trimmed, his harelip barely visible beneath, not that it mars his appearance – it's more of a liberating feature under the straight nose and piercing eyes.

Cecilie smiles mischievously and Rudi frees himself from her lips. Buoyed by self-confidence, he stares fixedly at Tommy: 'Not that I believe for one second that you're here by chance, Tommy. But I'll tell you this, man, here we are, four friends, four bloody good friends, it's Thursday and we've just had a heavy moving job, a grand piano in Våland, and we have one more job this evening, entire contents of a terraced house in Sandal, and now we're taking a walk, and that, sir, we intend to continue with, and love, which I heard you talking about while I was giving Dolly here a little taste of things, yes, love, that's the flag blowing in our breeze.'

Tommy Pogo nods.

'It's a free country, Rudi. Good to hear. Well, what do you say, Kia, will we be getting on?'

And so they part, Tommy and his daughter in one direction around the lake, the four crooks in the other. They stop and fall silent just five minutes from the car park, they look around, and on Jan Inge's signal, Rudi runs up into the woods towards a large stone where he sticks his hand into a crevice and locates a bag of speed. Cecilie observes him from a distance, she feels like her face is burning up and she thinks about how strange this life can be, where one day the sight of a certain person makes you want to puke, and the next he's your god, and she turns abruptly and looks straight into Tong's face with utter disdain.

Pål reads the text once more as the sound of the doorbell fills the room: *On my way. Heh heh! I'll get a taxi.* Zitha's ears stiffen and her tail begins to beat against the floor. Pål checks that his answer is sent, *OK, great,* and looks out the window, which could really use a wash; when was the last time they did that? They had it on a list once, Malene was to wash the windows, Tiril was to do the shopping, and he was to, yeah, what was he supposed to do? They disappeared, those lists. They couldn't manage to run such a tight ship.

So she is coming after all. Here. Today. *Great.*

How's that going to go?

He squints: a moped?

Pål's mouth runs dry, he hears Rudi's agitated voice in his head, Jan Inge's reedy voice, Cecilie's warm voice, and he begins breaking out in a sweat. Is that them? They're not supposed to be here before tonight. Now? On a moped?

It starts to sink in. He's agreed to this scheme with people who cut their teeth in the Tjensvoll Gang, people who've been hardened criminals for over twenty years, and he's put his *trust in them.* Christine should have been here now – she will be soon of course, *great* – she would have shaken her head as hard as humanely possible, she would have lowered those sexy eyelids of hers, sighed heavily and said: Pål. What is wrong with you. How naïve can you possibly be? Will you never learn?

He walks slowly into the hall, holding Zitha tightly by the neck, firmly enough for her to understand how quiet she needs to be.

In for it now. He takes a furtive peek through the glass beside the door.

He pulls his head back quickly. A young girl with her face all cut up. Flaming red hair. Pål slumps against the wall and closes his eyes. He grabs hold of Zitha's snout as she begins to whine. 'Shhh!' What is it Rudi has sent my way now? His psycho niece? A heroin addict he's planned to include in this insane scheme?

The doorbell rings again. Zitha beats the floor with her tail, uneasy in her body.

Pål orders Zitha to sit. He places two fingertips on the bridge of his nose, then sweeps them under each eye while opening his mouth and feeling the skin tightening over his gums. Okay. He rehearses a few opening lines in his head, grabs hold of the dog and opens the door.

Before Pål can speak he recognises the guy from under the floodlights at the football pitch the night before. The beautiful, young man with the disquieting eyes, the one that laughed at his Metallica T-shirt. What's he doing here with a girl who looks like a patient from a psych ward?

'Hi,' Pål says, holding Zitha back as she makes to go closer to the visitors, and keeping the door only half open to indicate that this needs to be quick: 'Tiril and Malene aren't home yet.'

'Good,' says Daniel.

'Eh...?'

'I didn't come to see them,' says the boy.

A unpleasant feeling begins to takes hold of Pål. Young people, strange how they can knock adults off their stride. Are they working for Videoboy?

'Okay?'

The girl looks terrible. Someone has slashed her face. She's freaking Pål out the way she's just standing staring at his lips, studying his face intently.

Daniel takes a step closer.

'I don't know what you're up to,' he says.

Pål feels like he has a lead apple in his throat.

'What I'm up to?' Pål straightens up. 'Listen, I don't think I need to stand here and—'

'I don't know what you've got yourself mixed up in,' Daniel continues, as though he didn't hear what Pål said. The girl keeps on staring at his lips. 'But I—'

'Listen,' Pål cuts in, 'I really think you need to g—'

'I saw you in the woods.'

'Eh?'

The girl bends down to Zitha, pats her.

Daniel shrugs. 'You might be getting yourself into something stupid.'

'What is this? I think you better—'

The girl continues rubbing Zitha's snout.

'I get that you can't stand here and admit that something fucked up is going on, but I did see you, and I thought about it afterwards, without really knowing if I should say it to anybody – I haven't, by the way – but I decided to ride up here. And tell you straight out. That I don't know what it is you're involved in. But it might be stupid for you to see it through. And I know what I'm talking about.'

She opens her mouth to speak now, the girl with the cut-up face. Her voice is strange and her eyes shine like burnt copper. She says: 'It's true. He knows what he's talking about.'

Zitha barks and Pål feels saliva accumulate in his mouth again. He shakes his head. 'It might well be you know what you're talking about,' Pål gives Daniel a gentle, lofty pat on the shoulder, 'but I don't know what you're talking about. And I have to make some food for Tiril and Malene now, because they'll soon be home and it's a busy day. Tiril is going to be singing at the school in—' he checks his watch, 'yeah, in just over a couple of hours. All right?'

Daniel smiles. 'That's fine,' he says. 'You have to lie. You need to protect yourself. I know. That's the way it works.' He extends his hand to Pål, who shakes it, remaining nonplussed, as Daniel puts his helmet back on, climbs on to the moped together with his girlfriend and disappears down the street.

Pål sinks down on to the doorstep.

Zitha places her snout in his lap and emits a faint whimper. He runs his hand over her warm coat. 'Dad was seen, Zitha,' he whispers.

God, I should never have got mixed up in this.

Pål takes out his mobile and composes a text: 'I'll let you know when the girls have left. Just have to make them something to eat and then you can come. It'll be a real blast!'

Five, ten minutes pass, Pål sits with September light all around and he's barely aware if he's alive or dead, then he hears them. He has a sinking sensation in his chest and wishes it were a simpler day, say around six years ago, when the girls were small and he was the safe, secure dad. A plain, maybe slightly boring dad they could count on, one who could look his own girls in the eyes.

He jumps up, affects an air of energy as he sees them approach. Tiril has a pained expression on her face, Malene is calm and collected and alongside them walks a guy who looks like a warped ball, with moist eyes and a hoodie. Zitha runs towards the girls.

'Hi! I haven't had a chance to sort out food today, things just got on top of me, but we'll throw a frozen pizza on, will we? So, getting excited? Eh?'

'Dad, this is Shaun,' says Tiril, patting the dog.

Pål looks at the little guy, who gives him a crooked smile, revealing a row of rust-coloured teeth. He isn't exactly what Pål was expecting; is Tiril actually going out with that there?

'Okay? Hi, I'm Pål,' he says, putting his hand out and feeling a feeble grip, like shaking hands with a mollusc.

He accompanies them inside, he can tell by their body language that something is up, he sees them exchange uncertain glances, but he neglects to ask what's happened. He understands that they have something behind them that's hard to put aside and just as hard to talk about, as though he realises it's not for grown-ups' ears. That's how he's raised them, always allowed the girls plenty of space, never went into their rooms and asked what they were up to, but has made himself available to them whenever they feel the need to talk. Sometimes it's gone too far, and Pål has been left standing at a distance when their world has begun to catch fire.

That may be how it is now, but he can't face going into the flames today. All he wants is for them to eat some food and be on their way, because they need to get out of here; what's going to happen is just too degrading.

It doesn't seem as if Daniel or the girl with the face have spoken to them.

Zitha has taken her place on the mat, safe and secure; for a dog the house is as it usually is. Dad is here, the girls are here. Pål lets the kids go to Tiril's room. He puts a pizza on and stands facing the oven for a quarter of an hour watching the cheese slowly begin to bubble, and he finally takes it out and carries it into Tiril's room where the three teenagers sit in a sort of youthful darkness that somehow seems to glow.

The voices fall silent as he enters, all expression on their faces wiped clean and their eyes dim.

'Pizza, girls.'

'Great, we'll just eat and head off.'

'It's going to be exciting, this here,' he says.

'Very,' says Malene.

He can see she's lying. Or rather, keeping something to herself.

'Dad?' Tiril turns to him, looking lost.

'Yes, honey?'

'Do you know what happens to people who suffer concussion?'

It's a strange question.

'What do you mean?'

'Well, just if they're concussed and everything seems fine, but then they get problems. Do you know what can happen?' Tiril's eyes are moist. 'Like, could she, you know, die?'

Pål looks at Shaun. Is Tiril really with this guy? He doesn't seem able to speak, his teeth are rotting in his head and he has a black eye, what sort of boy is he?

'No,' he says, 'I don't know about that kind of thing. Who's *she*? Has someone got concussion?'

Malene nods. 'A girl at school. She collapsed.'

'I see,' he says. 'Well, I hope she's all right anyway. Get some food in you, okay?'

He leaves the room. He can't face being with them right now.

A quarter of an hour later, all three of them thank him for the food and get ready to leave. There're no feelings in the air other than those of pretence, thinks Pål. Everybody in this room is holding something back.

'See you soon, then,' he says, smiling. 'Really looking forward to it, Tiril.'

'See you later,' she says.

'Gonna be a real blast! Love you both!'

Malene turns as though he has said something strange. Pål lifts his hand up and waves vigorously with his entire arm, as if trying to catch their attention in a school parade: 'Love you!' he shouts again.

The door opens, warm air floods towards him and they disappear.

A little while later, the mobile in his pocket vibrates. Pål takes it out, reads: 'Can I come?'

He sends a reply: 'Yes. All clear now.'

Pål crouches down in front of Zitha and scratches her under the chin. He's not quite sure how he's going to get through the next hour. He has no idea how this whole thing is going to end. But he can't picture anything other than it turning out badly.

Zitha rolls on to her back, asking to be rubbed on her stomach.

90. WE SEND HELENE CHRISTMAS GREETINGS EVERY YEAR IN CONTEMPT OF THAT MANGY MONGEREL OF A FATHER SHE HAD (Jan Inge)

'So, Jan Inge Haraldsen, this must be a big day for you?'

'Heh heh, well I suppose you'd have to say it is.'

'Indeed, what went through your mind when you heard you'd won the prize in the category of non-fiction?'

'Well, I felt like a little God, to draw a comparison.'

'*It's Too Late, a study in Horror Films* has sold thousands of copies and been translated into a host of different languages. What would you say was your main motivation in writing it?'

'Motivation? Well ... an exceptional number of research hours have been put into this...'

'Yes, the material is overwhelming. Is there, in fact, any horror film you haven't seen?'

'I doubt it. But what you're asking me about motivation ... you have to picture an ordinary boy. Slightly overweight perhaps, mildly asthmatic, without a mother and practically fatherless. He's captivated at a young age by the horrible world of horror.'

'I see. And this boy, it's you?'

'That's right. But then, after a few years sitting in front of the screen, I began to gain some valuable insights, and I hit upon what today forms my main thesis...'

'You refer to it as a thesis?'

'Indeed, a thesis. Let me paint you a picture, since you've come all the way from *Frankfurter Allgemeine* to interview me. Many years ago. An ordinary day in my ordinary life. A dark living room. An armchair. Me. And a glowing TV screen. I was re-watching one of my favourite films. It was Dario Argento's masterpiece,

Suspiria. Horror, which I love so much, filled the room, and it filled me. And then all of a sudden I began to weep.'

'To weep? You're telling me you began to cry?'

'I'm telling you I began to cry.'

'Why?'

'Safe to say I wondered about that myself. Tears were streaming down my face and I was incapable of stopping them.'

'My word.'

'Yes. I was on my own that day. My sister, whom I live with, was out at work with my best friend, Rune Digervold, whom I also live with. The tears just flooded down my face. Eventually I had to stand up and pace around the room. And that was when I began to ask myself what it was that these tears contained. Do you understand?'

'Yes ... or rather, no. Did you find an answer?'

'Yes. It was the feeling that it can all suddenly be too late. That was what the tears were telling me. That was what I had understood after so many years in the world of horror, that it's not a horrible world, but a world of goodness, a world that struggles to lead us into kindness before it's too late, and that this is what every real horror film is about.'

'A remarkable thesis, Jan Inge Haraldsen, which you explore at length in your book, through in-depth analyses of a number of films, *Evil Dead, Suspiria* which you've already mentioned, *A Nightmare on Elm Street...*'

'They're all there. As well as less well-known movies like *Rosemary's Killer*, also titled *The Prowler*. Joseph Zito, 1981. The Golden Age of The Nasty. An important time for the slasher film in particular and the horror genre in general. What about the scene in the shower, when the girl is stabbed in the stomach with the pitchfork, just below her breasts – have you read my thoughts on that? I don't go on about how well made it is and the type of things horror fans often do. I focus on what it's about, in a philosophical sense. I take a large part of the horror fan base to task, the ones who sit grinning at body counts, the ones who view horror as a form of ironic humour and the people who believe it's all about the amount of gore, which in my view, it isn't.'

'Exciting.'

'Exciting. That's the word.'

'But moving on, this is after all not just an interview with you about your book but also a profile: Who is Jan Inge Haraldsen?'

'Oh, he's just an ordinary, slightly overweight boy. A butterball. The Coca-Cola Kid from Hillevåg. Heh heh.'

'What else have you done, where are you from, indeed, who are you, Mr Haraldsen?'

'Oh, a bit of everything, this and that, heh heh.'

'Come now, give us some impression of who you are.'

'Let me see, an impression...'

'Yes, an impression...'

'Well, I can tell you this: I've run my own company since I was quite young. I've had a good number of employees along the way. My sister, as well as my best friend Rudi have always worked with me.'

'And what does it do, this company?'

'What does it do?'

'Yes, what sector is it involved in?'

'Eh, sector ... we're in removals.'

'So the rumours which have reached us at *Frankfurter Allgemeine*, that you are all actually petty criminals and that Mariero Moving is just a front for your activities, these aren't true? That for years now, ever since you were a small boy and lost your mother, and then your father abandoned you and your sister in a most inhumane manner, leaving for America to pursue his own selfish interests and start up a business, Southern Oil – that ever since you were young you've been involved in criminal activity, been behind many break-ins, many scams, quite brutal instances of debt collection, yes, that for a time early in your career you even pimped your sister, whom you rented out within the confines of your own home; is that also incorrect? Jan Inge? Mr Haraldsen?'

Jan Inge looks up from his plate, where potatoes, broccoli, carrots and meatballs swim in gravy, and a dollop of lingonberry jam wreathes the rim. The sun is low, casting a wavering light into the room, shining skittishly upon the old Coca-Cola poster hanging beside the fridge, in which a sailor with white teeth holds up a bottle, and shimmering tentatively on the salt and pepper pots standing on the table, one in the shape of a reindeer, the other a seal; both from Dad's childhood home.

Motörhead blasts from the living room, 'Stone Dead Forever.'

Nobody has opened their mouth for a long time.

SOMETIMES THINGS ARE SO DELICATE.

You would think the future would be looking brighter now.

Rudi giving his big performance when they were on their way around Stokkavannet.

Cecilie responding so quickly and with such passion, such affection, of a type she rarely reveals.

But then.

They get into the Volvo, everyone refreshed, except for Tong. Everything seems flushed, the sky, the tarmac, the car and its occupants, but as they drive past the allotments near Byhaugen, it's almost as if it becomes too much to take. Suddenly there's a clearing of throats and coughing in the back seat, the shifting of feet, people looking in all directions but at each other and mumbled half-sentences abound. The oxygen disappears from inside the car. Cecilie stares out the window. Rudi's eyes remain fixed on his lap. There has to be some terminology within psychology for it. Suddenly Cecilie and Rudi are so unbelievably awkward. They had been snogging in full public view, then they were like two lovesick teenagers in the back of the van and now they are utterly out of sync. Both of them look like frightened birds, maybe that's what its known as in psychology? Frightened bird syndrome?

And Tong?

Tong is sitting silent as a stone by the window, longing for a chocolate chip cookie.

EVERYTHING HAS BEEN TURNED ON ITS HEAD, thinks Jan Inge, massaging his front teeth with his fingertips. One moment everything is *allt i lagi*, as Buonanotte says, the next it's all fallen apart. Not to mention Tommy Pogo, who's also obviously got them in his sights. Taking a walk around Stokkavannet, coincidence?

Jan Inge can't handle this. Now is the time he should show them who's wearing the pants, but he sinks back down into his own thoughts, while the world he's created heads for ... what's it called again...?

Jan Inge pictures himself getting up from his chair, offering his hand to the interviewer who has come all the way from Frankfurt and thanking him for the visit. He imagines the photographer taking two photos of him, one in front of the van, with him dressed in Mariero Moving working attire, and one in the video room, with him standing in front of his vast collection of films.

'Atlantis,' he whispers.

Cecilie looks up. 'Wha?'

Jan Inge clears his throat. 'Oh, I was just thinking about something. How's the food?' He checks the time. 'After five,' he says, 'nearly ten past. We'd better start packing the stuff together. I don't think we need to concern ourselves with Pogo. He's been on us. He was smart. Caught us on the hop. But he's not going to strike twice in one day. We'll be at Pål's place in a couple of hours. We'll leave the moving van in Sandal before making our way there. And I just want to say one thing: there's a weird vibe in the air today. I can't say I like it. But I would ask that all of you, to the extent you're able, not lose your composure, and please try and remain focused.'

Cecilie has put down her knife and fork. Rudi chomps his food pensively. Even Tong has his eyes on Jan Inge.

'What do you say each of us try to bring to mind some happy memories to cheer us up?'

Yes.

They're listening now.

'Personally, I'm going to call this memory to mind,' continues Jan Inge: one day in the eighties, Cecilie and I received word that our uncle, our father's brother, had passed away. John Fredrick Haraldsen. He was a mangy mongerel, who had brought pain to the entire family by interfering with his daughter, Helene, our cousin. She's never recovered and lives in a flat paid for by Social Services somewhere up in Trøndelag – and, as you're all aware, we send her a Christmas card every year, something she no doubt appreciates. You'll remember we sent her a lovely gold ring the year before last, Rudi, which we took with us from the job out in Sola.

Well. On this particular day in the eighties we were informed that he was dead, her father that is. John Fredrik had been killed in a bicycle accident. That's a good memory for me. Cecilie and I looked at one another with relief, and she made waffles while I – I was a few kilos lighter back then – I ran out into the garden to cut the grass. Which reminds me, we need to have a big clear-out on Sunday.'

Cecilie has tears in her eyes.

Brilliant.

You tell a good story.

And the audience weep.

They're moved.

That's the whole point of a good story right there.

The journalist has one final question as Jan Inge is showing him out: 'Tell me, Haraldsen, is it all horror with you?'

'What do you mean?'

'Is it all horror films, do you not like anything else?'

'What, do you think I'm just a fat guy with a one-track mind who sits in a wheelchair watching horror all day?'

'I don't know, you tell me.'

'*E.T.* I love *E.T.* And everything it stands for. And I'll tell you something else: I love everyone who wants to phone home.

91. **KINDA LOOKS LIKE A WAY OUT** (Shaun)

Shaun tilts his head back and looks up at the sky.

Those sisters are close. But they're so frigging different.

He walks a little behind them. Shaun is good at that. Knowing when to hang back.

Kenny just laid into him. Unleashed blow after blow after blow as though Shaun were a punching bag. Mum was asleep on a cocktail of pills and Dad had already gone out, because it's so long since he cared. Kenny just came into his room, his hair sticking up as if he'd been struck by lightning. He came barging in, and it was obvious he'd only just woken up, because that's when he's at his worst, always been that way with him, a big fucking bunch of energy building up in his body when he sleeps and then he's like a sharpened pencil or something in the morning, and that's how he was when he burst into the bedroom. Shaun lay sleeping and woke up with a shock, just managed to make out it was six-thirty on his mobile, before he felt Kenny's hands pulling him out of bed and dumping him on the floor like he was a sack of potatoes, grabbing him by the neck, forcing his head down, and rubbing his face against the rug before turning him over and pounding and pounding and really beating the shit out of him, all the time repeating: 'You need to learn to shut up, Shauny! You don't fuckin' get it, Shauny! You need to learn to shut up, Shauny! You don't fuckin' get it, Shauny! You need to learn to shut up, Shauny! You don't fuckin' get it, Shauny!'

Bunny should have been here now.

That was what he thought while he lay there listening to a continuous whistle in his head.

Everybody says Bunny is a nutcase.

But he's not really.

That's just hearsay.

Bunny is just Bunny. Kenny is the nutcase.

Look at them.

Sisters.

So nice to look at.

The way Malene runs her hand up and down her sister's back, speaking so calmly to her after their falling out, after everything has been turned upside down.

'Yeah, Tiril. Yeah. But listen to me. We'll take it easy now. One step at a time.'

Shaun has no rock of a sister, not like Tiril has. He only has preoccupied Bunny and psycho Kenny.

'Listen to me,' says Malene, when they've walked about halfway to the school, 'listen to me, Tiril,' and Tiril's features go all small like a cat and she listens, really listens, when her sister says: 'There's nothing we can do for Sandra. We made a choice and what's happened has happened. And we'll sort it out, I'm sure. But now it's time for the performance. And Dad is going to come. And you're going to sing. You got it? *My Immortal.*'

Tiril sniffles. 'I don't want to any more.'

Malene stares fixedly at her. She says: 'My immortal sister. You will. Will. For me. For Dad.'

'And for Shaun!' he shouts from behind them, because he thinks it fits in well. Heh heh. 'For Shauny!'

Tiril turns. Not in her pottiest dreams would she have believed that she would be together with him. She turned, looking super cute – fuck, Bunny, you should have seen that – when she said: 'For Shauny.'

Bunny is gay.

No one else knows.

Just Shaun.

And he doesn't give a shit.

If he wants to stick his cock up guys' asses it's no business of Shaun's. Bunny's not the one in the family there's something wrong with; Kenny's the psycho. Kenny and Mom, she doesn't even have eyes for fuck's sake. Shaun has never seen any, just eyelids falling down over pupils that swim; it's all the pills she stuffs down her throat – *fo sho, honey*, is all she says, *fo sho, precious*. Soon that's all she'll be able to say. That's what she'll say when she's dying, thinks Shaun, when he's standing over her, and she's breathing with a rattling sound, on her way out and he asks if she's all right, then she'll say *fo sho, precious* and then she'll throw up or something and die, and it won't be too different from how it is now, *fo sho, honey*. But there's nothing in those words. She just longs for her dope and for the United States of Shit, as Dad calls it. Bet you he regrets picking up Cindy Wilder from North Dakota and trying to make a Norwegian out of her, yessir. Like he says, beware of the titties, they're pointing right at you, but they're loaded.

Heh heh.

For Shauny.

Gonna be fine, this here, Shaun feels, as they near the school. That one Sandra is going to come around and everything will be okay. Heh heh. It's the first time he's actually been happy about heading to school. It's the first time Shaun has felt as though this tarmac is a friend and not an enemy. The first time he notices houses and fields and doesn't just see a shithole all around him. He was all right, Tiril's father. Nice guy, no hassle, no fuss, pizza man.

He looks at the girls. Seems like Tiril has got it together now. Straightened up a bit. Her sister has got her back on track. Yeah. This is going to be fine too – there's that Thea one running out of the gym hall, heh heh, people are a little wired now, whoa, Thea is totally stressed out, calm down, girl, no biggie.

'Tiril, seriously, I was starting to get worried.'

Tiril smiles. Yeah. She's all set.

'Chill out,' Tiril says, 'relax, just got a little delayed. Heard anything about Sandra?'

Thea shakes her head. 'No,' she says, 'but Frida and the headmaster are saying we're all still going on, that we're doing it for her.'

Tiril nods.

Heh heh. Tiril's taking care of business.

'Svein Arne is shitting it,' Thea says, motioning for Thea to follow her to the gym hall, 'he's been asking for you, plus we sent you heaps of texts and—'

Heh heh. Look at Tiril. Heh heh. Hands on her hips. Feet apart.

'Thea. Please. Enough. Jesus.'

Heh heh. Now she's found her voice.

'What do you think? That I can't handle a rough day? Got any gum?'

Heh heh. Way to go.

'Shaun, Malene,' she says, gathering them around. That's sort of how it is with these sisters, Shaun notices; while Malene is the one who steps up and holds the fort when a typhoon is blowing, Tiril gets the plaudits. Her eyes are all steel and flowers now, thinks Shaun. She is so ready to go and it's no wonder she rocks my world.

'Shaun, Malene,' she repeats. 'Go in and find a seat, Thea and me have about eight minutes to get changed backstage before we go on. For Sandra. Okay?'

Heh heh. Tiril. Niiiiiice, girl.

Kinda looks like a way out, like Dad said once when it was completely quiet in the living room, which it isn't so very often. Bunny was out, probably round at that guy Stegas' place, and Kenny wasn't home either – he was beating up some Chechens in Sandnes. Mum was strung out on something in her room, him and Dad were watching that movie, can't remember what it was called, but it was about a guy who takes his kid and goes to another country after he kills his wife with sleeping pills and buries her in the garden. Kinda looks like a way out, said Dad, giving Shaun a thump on the arm.

'Okay,' Shaun says, giving Tiril a hug, 'sing like a fucking star. We're on your side.'

Malene smiles. A really confident smile. And says: 'Go on, get going. We'll keep a seat for Dad.'

Shaun tilts his head back and looks up at the sky.

It's just something he needs to do now and again.

92. ONCE IT WAS YOU AND ME (Pål)

At some point, although he can't remember when exactly, Pål realised that life wasn't one ever brighter journey, the way he often pictured it when he was young, but was composed instead of phases. Different phases that arrived with age, circumstances and settings. He realised at the same time, at some point after Christine left, that neither is life some marvellous path onward towards ever increasing maturity, as he had also imagined when he was young and observed those around him with curiosity; his parents, uncles, aunts, grownups on TV, teachers and football coaches. He can't remember when it sank in, that everything happens in phases, and maturity is not a reality but a cultural ideal, yet as he sees Christine again, as she alights from the taxi in front of the house he once shared with her, when he witnesses that outrageous alertness of hers that seems to fill the whole driveway, he is emphatically reminded of it. Once she meant everything to him. Once he was so in love with her that he trembled when he woke up in the morning. That was that phase. Then they lived together for a few years, not beneath the roof of the first flush of love, but under the roof of routine; school lunch boxes, washing machine, MOT. That was that phase. Then she left him and Pål experienced hate for the first time. That was that phase. And now? What is it he feels as she approaches him? A black, waist-length jacket, a tight, dark skirt, a white blouse, those high cheekbones and healthy-looking hair. It's not forgiveness, and certainly not a rekindling of love, although his feelings of hate are long extinguished; so what is it then? Some sort of ... sufferance? He's unable to put his feelings into words as she sallies towards him, like she's always done towards the whole world, but there's a surprising measure of kindness in his feelings, even on such an unprecedented and downright dangerous day as today.

'Pål!'

She's so stunning, Christine. She really is quite beautiful, maybe even more beautiful than before. She's one of those women who look better with age, even when it arrives with an extra few inches around the waist, even when it arrives with wrinkles – everything looks gorgeous on her.

'Pål, Pål, Pål,' she says, throwing her arms around him, firm, warm and friendly, and he's surprised at experiencing the same sensation, the one he underwent on a daily basis so many years ago, of feeling that no matter how unreasonable this woman is, she still possesses an incredible ability to make him feel safe, in the sense that being in proximity to her makes it seem as though nothing troubling can occur. It is of course erroneous, but the feeling is real.

She pulls back and looks him up and down. Presses her lips together and nods twice with one eyebrow raised in an expression that combines both sincerity and jest: 'You're skin and bone, man! Are you eating at all? I'll have to have a chat with those girls of ours – what are their names again?'

Her sense of humour, always bordering on indelicate. The words couldn't come from someone else's mouth without sounding cheeky; from hers they sound fine.

He laughs, just like he used to; for her.

'It's all good,' he says, lying, 'conscious dieting. You know. Middle-age spread. Have to stay trim. Cut back on frozen pizza. Watch the carbs. Working out a good bit lately, actually.'

'Hm,' she says, in disbelief. 'You haven't become a spinning instructor too, have you? So, how much time do we have? Enough for a coffee in my old house before we have to go?'

He smiles again, aware once more of how she manages to make imminent events disappear from his mind, but shakes his head. 'No,' he says, lying again, 'we're a little pushed for time.'

'Oh,' says Christine, and pouts before extending her tongue, 'you know how tetchy I get without coffee. You've been warned, ex-hubby.'

'Yeah, I'm bricking it,' he says, laughing as he revels in how nice it is to be with someone he can be effortlessly flippant with; it's how he and Christine were at their best, it was precisely this tone that drove the days onward. He smiles warmly and for a moment forgets all his anxiety. He says: 'But you'll have to go without, unless you want to skip seeing your daughter perform, and just have a cup of coffee in Stavanger before you fly back out again.'

He's aware of how, in the space of a few seconds, he's begun to speak differently; speak like her. At her speed, with her tongue. As though he were imitating her.

Was that how it was?

'Hm,' Christine says, 'I think I'll choose coffee.'

'Come on,' he says, locking the front door. He's been standing outside the house with the key ready for almost a quarter of an hour, because he doesn't want her going inside. She'd only walk around passing remarks on this and that in the brusque, effortless manner she has.

His plan is a bad one. But it's the only one he's got.

They walk down Ernst Askildsens Gate and Pål feels a composure in his stride. Perhaps one of the neighbours can see them from a kitchen window, and thinks it strange to see them together again. Maybe it was already strange back when she lived here. An odd couple – him so timid and ordinary, her so outré and out-there. The fact that the two of them got together was surprising to themselves; it must have been surprising for others.

'What is it she's going to si—' says Christine, halting in mid-sentence: 'Oh Jesus. Evanescence. It's so turgid.'

He shrugs. 'What did you like when you were thirteen?'

She ponders the question for a moment as they peel off to the right, cross the street, and continue along by the low-rises. 'Thirteen? We'd be talking Wham!, for the most part.'

Christine stops for a moment. She takes in the surroundings. Her eyes are calm, as is her body, that fabulous concentration of hers has stirred, that ability she has to dedicate herself to one purpose, which has got her where she is.

'Yeah,' she says, mainly to herself. 'Yeah.'

'What?'

'I can hardly fathom it, Pål, that I used to live here.'

He looks away, towards the trees.

'What the hell was I thinking?' she sighs.

Pål feigns interest in the trunks of the trees, letting his eyes linger on them.

'I don't particularly remember that much of it. Of my time living here, I mean. It all feels very distant to me.'

That's one thing you were always adept at, he thinks as he allows his gaze to sweep down a tree trunk and fall upon the ground, you were always adept, Christine, at trampling on things other people liked. He refrains from responding, takes a few steps to indicate they're pushed for time, and she snaps out of her musing just as quickly as she'd fallen into it, and soon she's the one in front of him as they make their way down towards the school.

Then he suddenly stops in his tracks, just as he's planned. He tries not to overdo it, does his best to be just as good a liar as he has been for months, and the slight put-down, the earlier remark she made, has provided him with that little extra he needs. Then he lifts his hands up and takes a sharp intake of breath: 'Aw shit.'

He says it as though talking to himself.

It looks real.

'What?'

He looks at her, shakes his head a little.

It looks genuine as well.

'Sorry, I'm such a numbskull—'

'What?'

'The candles. I—'

She rolls her eyes.

It's working.

'Pål, Pål, Pål.'

'Yeah, I know.'

'Candles in September?'

'Mhm,' he nods and points. 'I won't be long. You go on ahead, that'll be even cooler, you coming on your own. Five minutes, tops, that's all it'll take me.'

Then he runs.

'Candles in September,' Pål mumbles while he looks at the tarmac blur under his feet and has a horrible feeling of having deserved all of this, the hate Tiril is going to dish out when she realises what he's done, the disappointment Malene is going to dish out when she realises what he's done, the disgust Christine is going to dish out when she realises what he's done, and the violence Rudi is going to dish out to him very soon.

Pål makes it to his own street. As he nears the house, he hears Zitha barking and he remembers how that was the first thing that entered his head the day Christine told him she'd had enough: I'm going to get a dog. You've refused me that all these years and that's what I'm going to get and it'll be such joy. Four weeks later a little puppy was running around on the carpet, gnawing at chair legs, chewing on slippers, paring its teeth down until they were sharp as scissors, snipping holes in the carpets, peeing on the parquet flooring, wagging its tail every day the girls came home from school, jumping up in their laps, licking their faces and looking up at Pål with almost unbearable trust as it lay in its basket whimpering for fifteen seconds before falling asleep. And it turned out to be true, what that idiot Bjørn Ingvar Totland said during the Christmas party at work a couple of years ago, when he knocked back a beer, looked over at Pål and said that a dog is man's best friend and a woman man's worst enemy.

'Yeaah yeaah, Zitha, Daddy's coming, yeeah.' Pål looks at his mobile.

18:45.

93. **NANCY ROSE BOTNEVASS** (Rudi)

Rudi has a secret. He has it tucked away in a place of such impenetrable darkness that it's almost hidden from him. He's dug a hole in his soul and consigned it to the depths. Then he covered it with earth, with stones and cemented it over. He's promised himself never to go down there again. But the mind cannot be compelled to be silent. The foulness seeps from cracks and fissures no matter how much Rudi tells it to remain below. The foul matter comes before him, presents itself. Oh no. What is it the Gospel of Luke says about repentance? 'If your brother sins, rebuke him, and if he repents, forgive him.' Wise words, Luke, but to whom can Rudi speak of the unspeakable? How can forgiveness come about when what we're speaking of is the unspeakable? Who can Rudi apologise to? And if he was to be granted forgiveness, how can he undo the thing he has done?

It isn't possible.

That's the truth, Luke.

What you have done can never be undone.

Some nights are like that: Rudi cries. He lies beside Cecilie, weeping as silently as he can while listening to her breathing in the darkness. He clenches his powerful fists and whispers: 'I'm sorry, my love. You must never find out, that your Rudi did the unmentionable. That your Rudi went with another woman into the deepest woods. That your Rudi went down on her, and she went down on your Rudi, that once, for a few weeks, almost fifteen years ago I was not myself. I did everything a man is capable of doing with a woman, and that woman was not you, but the daughter of the Devil, Kvinesdal's very own poisonous flower, Nancy Rose Botnevass.'

Then Rudi sniffles. As quietly as he can. 'What is it the Lord says,' he whispers. 'Keep thee from strange women'. He strokes Cecilie across her tattooed back, running his fingertips along the eagle's wings of the Aerosmith logo, feeling the tiny goosebumps on her skin and listening to her heavy breathing. 'And you must never,' he whispers even lower, 'you must never get to hear of this, Cecilie. Or to put it another way, you must never catch sight of my cock – your cock – on a TV screen. Thank God nobody in this house can stand porn.'

He gradually slips into her rhythm and falls asleep. And every morning he awakes. The sun rises in the sky and he's aware of his own breathing, aware of Cecilie being grumpy and close by; he's happy he gets to live yet another brilliant day on earth, and in high spirits he breaks bread with pleasure and plunges into the day.

He wept last night, but now he's ready. The beanpole stands in the basement. He's dressed in black. He's confused. He hardly dares think his own thoughts. Outside the sun is sinking, the evening is on its way. Jan Inge and Cecilie are back after parking the moving van in Sandal. Rudi has two fully packed bags in his hands. Baseball bats, hand weights, knuckle dusters, balaclavas and tools. A roll of blue plastic shoe covers, a roll of tape. Scissors. Everything they need to go to work. But he just does not understand what is going on. The way Cecilie has suddenly been behaving. Snogging him as though he were Steven Tyler. It scares the pants off him. And the way her eyes were sparkling and one thing and the fucking other, and acting all sexy like she never has before. And then complete silence. Total shut off. And Tong? He should have stayed behind lock and key. And Tommy Pogo? Turning up all over the place?

Fucking Thursday.

Right, time to get to it. A man needs beating up.

'Are you lot almost ready?' he calls out in the direction of the stairs while he scans the room. At some stage this screwed-up family probably harboured ideas about what this room would be used for, a pool table for the kids, carom, board hockey, maybe a cosy den, a little bar, who knows, some kittens in a basket. Now it smells strongly of mould and it's minging everywhere. Rudi relaxes his facial muscles and shakes his head before setting his foot on the bottom step and ascending the staircase.

Tong is in the hallway, dressed in black, his body taut. Everything has gone to hell since he came home. You'd think it was Tong's fault that troublesome air abounded. Rudi can't be bothered saying anything to the little Korean. He just nods and avoids looking at Tong, who bends down and begins to tie his shoelaces without responding.

Jan Inge waddles out, dressed in black and looking fat – he needs to consider cutting back on guzzling now, bit much flab bursting out. Jani doesn't say anything either.

Eventually Cecilie joins them, dressed in black and looking anxious. She slips her little feet into her shoes.

Rudi knits his brows when he sees Jan Inge open the closet door beneath the stairs and take out the pump-action shotgun. Cecilie stops tying her shoelaces. Tong raises one black eyebrow ever so slightly.

'What's the story?' Rudi asks, as he watches Jan Inge put a box of shotgun shells into the bag.

Jan Inge gives a faint shrug.

'Is there a meeting on in the Arms and Armour Society? What's with the shooter? Are we not anti-violence?

'Yes, we are.'

'So? We're not planning on putting someone in a coffin, or have we started with that now?'

Jan Inge shakes his head slightly. 'Rudi, Rudi. Take it easy. We're just raising the level of security a notch. You know. Pogo. Tampon.'

'You're going to shoot a cop?!'

'Rudi. Look at me. I'm not going to shoot anyone. It's just for ... security.'

Cecilie finishes tying her laces, Tong listens with his mouth shut and Rudi yields to the leader.

'So we're ready?'

Jan Inge's eyes sweep each of them in turn.

'Yeah,' says Cecilie.

'Can't wait,' says Tong in a sarcastic tone.

'Headgear, hairbands and hairnets, footwear and shoe covers, handgear, gloves, tape?'

Cecilie nods.

'Knuckle dusters, baseball bat, table leg, hand weights, speed?'

Rudi gives the bags in his hands an affirmative shake.

'Good,' says Jan Inge, 'then we just need to get on with it.'

This is depressing. The lousy atmosphere is so thick it fills the room like exhaust fumes. No more snogging now. Not even Rudi, who prides himself on his ability to raise a smile, could turn this room around. Strike a warm blow for love.

Because everything, Rudi feels, is a matter of love.

Nancy Rose Botnevass didn't have hips like shelves, or nubbly skin, or eyes set far apart that made her look like a burrowing animal, or crooked lips and tiny little mollusc eyes. She smelt of randy soil and salt ore, had lips like a bitch, drove a tractor and went elk-hunting like a man. She was a poisonous flower with a gap between her two front teeth, a she-devil with enormous thigh muscles, so greedy she ate your house clean and it was impossible to keep your hands from her skin, because it was nature at work. Everyone who'd been near her knew that she was born with an electric fervour and if she wanted something, she got it. In the valley, people said that nobody had ever seen a smile cross Nancy's face, they said she never slept at night, but went up on the heath, sniffed at the moss, talked to grouse and killed adders with just a look, and there were rumours that it wasn't Solomon the priest who was her father, but a lynx from up on Krokevasshei, and that Rose Marie wasn't her mother but an eagle from Mjauntjønn.

You smell like a bull, Rudi, she had whispered.

'Okay,' Jan Inge says, opening the door on the last light of the September day and on the van outside, 'let's drive up to Pål Fagerland's and give him a good working over.'

The loudest screams you hear can be your own.

94. THAT'S NOT GOING TO BRING YOU AROUND (Tiril)

Tiril enters the backstage area with her jaw muscles tensed and her eyes narrowed. The room is packed with people, the air buzzing with different languages and diverse English pronunciation. The make-up group fit masks on the Finnish girls who are going to perform a dramatic piece, the wardrobe group have put out the clothes people will wear, numbered the hangers and hung up an information sheet at the entrance. People tiptoe nervously around, Svein Arne wanders this way and that, curly hair dancing and forehead sweaty, some people are biting their nails, and everyone has a serious look in their eyes because they all know there's a girl in hospital and they all agree with Frida and the headmaster: we'll perform for freedom, democracy, solidarity and for Sandra.

Tiril doesn't want any help. Not with make-up. Not with clothes. She doesn't want smiles from people and she doesn't want to smile back. She has no idea who a third of them are and she doesn't have time to get to know them. This is make-believe, but my day is authentic. I am Amy Lee. I've grown up by the Arkansas River and this is much too real. I'm going to fill the hall with pain, let it bleed out of my mouth and eyes so those poetry-reciting, guitar-playing, dancing kids know they've been totally *parked*.

'It's not really on, arriving so late, Tiril,' Svein Arne says. 'You do know that?'

She looks at him, feeling her gaze send a spear between his eyes, penetrating the flesh.

'Yeah,' she says, 'I know everything.'

Thea hurries past: 'Have you seen my shoes?'

Tiril gets changed. Because now she's going to be someone other than herself. The black tights. They have a nice sheen to them when they're stretched tight across her skin. The black shoes with the high heels. The black skirt. The black top. The black shawl. The bold, red lipstick. The purple eye shadow. Her fringe, which she takes right above her eyebrows. The shawl she'll let drape down over her face.

Tiril studies herself in the mirror while people scurry all around her. The foreign kids Thea is so friendly with. Ulrik Pogo. Svein Arne, who's more nervous than anyone; does he not realise how hideous those curls look, doesn't he have a wife and don't they have a pair of scissors in their house?

Sometimes it's such a pain being a part of something.

Just twenty-fours ago this was all she wanted.

Now it's the exact opposite.

They're the fourth act on. First out is a girl from Nicaragua, who's going to deliver a speech on peace. Then Ulrik, who'll play 'Stairway to Heaven'. People will no doubt sit with their heads cocked to the side, thinking he's so cute that it'll seem like the whole hall is dipped in honey. Everyone remembers what Frida Riska said the day he began at school, and some said she was actually talking about herself: *You are so pretty, Ulrik Pogo, that a lot of people are going to have trouble being in the same room as you, so your challenge, young man, will be not to allow the dazzling looks you've been blessed with to govern your entire life.*

After Ulrik, the two Finnish girls from Jyväskyla are performing a drama about fair trade.

Then they're up. Tiril would have liked to be last, she said as much to Svein Arne, but it wasn't up to her to decide. You two will be number four, Svein Arne had said. Yeah, who's going to help us take the lights right down, then? The volunteer helpers will take care of it.

Tiril applies the eye shadow.

Mum, that witch, has said a lot of stupid things, but there's one thing she said that Tiril will never forget: if you want something done, Tiril, then do it yourself.

Light the pillar candles. Look at the frightened faces in the audience. Walk up to the microphone.

I'm so tired of being here.

I'll bring you round, Sandra. Watch out, Daniel, I'm not finished with you.

Tiril takes a step back from the mirror. She narrows her eyes, feeling she can shoot sparks from them. Then the corners of her mouth begin to quiver. At first she doesn't understand what it is, and she brings her hand to her mouth as though something strange is emanating from her body, and presses two flat fingertips to the side of her mouth, but then in the mirror she sees that her eyes are shiny and she feels it in her throat, how something's growing and she realises she's crying.

She closes her eyes and orders herself to count to twenty.

Opens her eyes again.

There we go. Her mouth is taut. Her eyes are normal.

The headmaster and Frida Riska enter the backstage area. Frida claps her hands twice to quieten people down. She nods to Svein Arne.

'Only two minutes to go, folks.' Svein Arne talks in a low voice and gathers the teenagers around him. He calls each and every one of them by their name and says, in his impressively poor English, how proud he is of this production, how hard they've worked, and how positive it is that so many talented, hard-working people from Stavanger's twin towns have come to make this very special cultural evening about solidarity, democracy and freedom: 'Okay, all ready?'

The kids whistle and clap, Tiril remains rigid, and then Svein Arne's face takes on an idiotic expression that makes him look like a mother admiring her little girls as they stand in front of her, dressed up for a Christmas dinner. He straightens the red-and-white shirt he's put on for the occasion, turns to the teenagers one last time, lifting his eyebrows twice in rapid succession, before slipping out between the gap in the stage curtain.

Cheering and clapping greets his entrance. 'Yeah! Gosen! Hello everybody! Wow!'

'You ready?' Thea shifts nervously from foot to foot beside her.

'Of course I'm ready,' says Tiril, while they hear Svein Arne give a speech to the audience about the value of unity and the exchange of experience across national boundaries.

Tiril looks at her. 'Stage fright?'

'No, just...' Thea shifts her weight on her small feet again. 'Hasn't been the most ordinary of days.'

'So?' Tiril entwines her fingers, twists her hand around at arm's length and cracks her knuckles.

'Okay,' Svein Arne says from the other side of the curtain, 'I'm going to hand you over to the headmaster who wants to say a few short words.'

Frida nods to the headmaster and he walks out on to the stage. 'I don't want to keep you,' he says, 'but I have some information to share. Earlier today there was an accident at the school. One of our pupils, Sandra Vikadal, lost consciousness and was taken to hospital in an ambulance.'

There's silence in the hall, as well as backstage.

'We've decided to go ahead with this evening of culture...' says the headmaster, pausing slightly. Frida Riska nods. '...Because we don't wish to allow despair to defeat us.'

The audience claps. Tiril can hear from the sound of it that they clap the way people do when they feel they have won. But what is it they have won?

'We haven't heard anything new from the hospital,' says the headmaster. 'I spoke to them not too long ago. Her condition is critical, but stable.'

Silence spreads through the hall again.

'We can do this,' says the headmaster, placing emphasis on each word. 'Now, would you please welcome back, our very devoted teacher, the man who's put this wonderful evening together, Svein Arne Bendiksen!'

Tiril's throat is itchy. We can do this. We? The clapping grows louder and the stage curtain is drawn aside, the headmaster and Svein Arne swap places and Frida Riska hastens to her seat. Svein Arne introduces 'a brave girl from Nicaragua', and the show is underway.

Tiril takes a small step forward. She puts her head slightly to the right and glances out into the dimly lit hall. There's not one chair free. There are people standing along the walls. She directs her gaze along the rows of faces trying to catch sight of Malene, Dad and Shaun, but she can't spot them. She sees other parents,

Ulrik's mum and dad, Tommy Pogo and his wife, along with Kia in the wheelchair, Thea's folks, her dad with that irresistible smile of his, and there, in the first row sit the teachers, Frida Riska, Mai and the others.

Tiril sees Sandra's face. It enters her mind with such clarity, such intensity, that she almost feels the girl is in the room. She shakes her head, shoves the image aside and concentrates. She holds the matchbox tightly.

The curtain is pulled aside again; Tiril hears the foreign tones of the girl from Nicaragua fill the room and thinks how it sounds like talking soil. Svein Arne catches her eye and lifts his eyebrows enthusiastically, twice, as if to say *eh, exciting, eh.*

A taut sensation takes hold of her body, a false sensation, her head feels dizzy and she wishes she could think clearly. We? What is it we can do? Poor Sandra, kind Malene, psycho Veronika, dangerous Daniel, distracted Dad, bloody Mum, cool Shaun, screwed-up Kenny and weird Bunny.

'Shit, I can feel it in my stomach,' Thea says, rubbing her hands together.

There's applause from the gym hall, Tiril's throat itches and Svein Arne pats Ulrik on the shoulder. He's standing with the guitar in his hand, an Idol hairdo and admirable self-assurance in his eyes: 'You're up next, Ulrik, good luck!'

Svein Arne disappears out to the enthusiastic parents: 'Wasn't that fantastic? *Salve a ti, Nicaragua!*' Fresh applause. 'And now, one of our own, Ulrik Pogo from 10A with his version of Led Zeppelin's timeless classic "Stairway to Heaven"!'

Ulrik, glistening slightly above his top lip, where he's begun to perspire at the last minute, unveils a gleaming set of teeth and walks towards the stage curtain. It's drawn aside and once again Tiril catches a glimpse of the audience; Ulrik's parents, the parents of the people in her class, Frida Riska, looking close to tears.

Tiril lets her gaze wander and then stop abruptly.

It can't be.

While the black curtain is still drawn, while Ulrik is given a stool and the lighting is being adjusted, she has time to confirm it: Mum.

It's Mum sitting there. Between Shaun and Malene. It's not Dad.

The curtain comes together, Ulrik picks the first notes of 'Stairway to Heaven' and Tiril clenches her fists.

Fucking Led Zeppelin.

She grinds her teeth. You leave us behind without giving a shit, you stay away year after year, and now you show up? And think everything's okay?

'What is it?' Thea whispers. 'Is something wrong?'

'No,' Tiril replies brusquely. 'What would be wrong? Are you ready?'

Thea nods. 'Nervous. But, like, yeah. I'm ready.'

'Good,' Tiril says. She turns to Thea. 'And when you catch sight of my mother out there in the hall, don't flip out. I have no idea what she's doing here. But forget it. She can do whatever she wants as far as I care. We're going to be amazing, okay?'

'Your mother?'

'Forget it, all right? Are you ready?'

'Stairway to Heaven' finishes, to rapturous applause, whistling and whoops, *wow, the length of that boy's nails, he can sing, takes after his mother there, poor thing, must be tough for Kia having a brother like that, I mean, he's almost unnervingly good-looking that boy, but you know what, I think there's nearly something scary about him.* No matter what Ulrik Pogo does he bowls people over.

'Eh?' Svein Arne calls out above the tremendous response of the crowd in the hall. 'If that didn't blow you away, then I don't know what will, Gosen! Okay, now we're moving on to something different, to the world of theatre, to a little piece about taking care of our planet, where we'll witness the talents of two fantastic Finnish girls!'

Fresh applause.

'I'll be back in two minutes,' she says, turns on her heels and leaves. Thea gawks at her as though Tiril has told her she's off to murder someone, but that can't be helped right now. She's nauseous, her throat itches and something's just not right. She walks quickly towards the door. Her throat feels blocked and her head is swirling and she needs a smoke. The sharp evening air snatches at her skin as she emerges outside.

She goes around the back of the gym hall and lights up a cigarette with unsteady hands.

I need to calm down.

That's what Mum always said.

Don't lose your head.

That's rich, coming from her.

People have always said that Tiril is like her mother.

She inhales the smoke, feels it tear at her throat.

No frigging way I'm like Mum.

Sing now? And where's Dad? Solidarity? Freedom? Democracy? Song? That's not going to bring you round, Sandra.

Tiril takes one last drag and flicks the cigarette away. She walks around the building and up to the front entrance, where she can see into the hall. She leans towards the glass and makes out her mother's profile. The slanted, yellow streak of a moped headlamp lights up her back.

95. **ELECTRA** (Tong)

Jan Inge sits behind the wheel, dressed in black from head to toe. Hansi's Transporter, a grey 1998 model, will soon have 300,000 on the dial; it splutters a bit in low gear, and one of the back windows leaks, but it's not a bad van for an old banger. Tong is in the passenger seat, also all in black, and Rudi and Cecilie sit in the back.

Tong is so pissed off that he can barely keep a lid on it, but he's told himself that this is something he just needs to get through. Make a bit of cash, because he sorely needs to, and then turn his back and walk the fuck away from this gang. There are better people to work with out there. And if that doesn't pan out, he can go solo, like Melvin Gausel. Melvin was head of the Kvernevik Gang, did a great job, but suddenly one day chubby chops and his shrill laughter were gone, some people said he'd been snapped up by the crowd around Toska in Oslo, some said he'd been sighted in Gothenburg, others maintained he'd been killed by Mini from Haugesund in a drunken quarrel, but then some genius began to put two and two together after a series of outstanding robberies were carried out in the region, several in the space of a month, all impeccably executed and unsolved: Melvin had gone it alone. Impressive. Lives up in Randaberg now, has an Asian wife, and works for himself. Tong could do that. Do it even better than Fat Melvin. Is there anyone in the district who knows more about security and breaking into places than Tong?

No.

Cecilie deserves a kick in her slut stomach. If it wouldn't cause such trouble, he'd have beat her until she was lying on the tarmac and then stamped on her until she was dead. Sitting back there holding hands with Rudi. And he doesn't have a clue, the idiot, but that's not surprising; trust her? Trust women?

Tong leans his elbow on the door and looks out the side window as Jan Inge changes gear to ascend Ullandhaugbakken.

Those letters. Not easy to get your head around. Shouldn't Sverre and Ragnhild have let him know about it? He left home – his Norwegian parents' home – a long time ago. Tong was in and out of Child Welfare institutions from the age of thirteen, and those poor parents in Bømlo couldn't keep up. Wasn't their fault. Sverre and Ragnhild did what they could, but sometimes what you can do isn't good enough.

They told him his Korean parents were dead, but they failed to tell Tong he had a sister out there somewhere. They could have mentioned it. They could have told him she lived less than fifty miles away in Egersund. They could have told him that she had two kids and played in the Stavanger Symphony Orchestra. Must be talented. Sharp-witted. Precise. Tong is too. Must be in their genes. A violinist in a symphony orchestra. Intense, able to concentrate, with an ability to focus. What was it she wrote? 'We have opened the new concert hall now, it's absolutely beautiful, we're going to perform *Electra*. Are you familiar with that opera?'

Tong went to the prison library and asked if they had anything called *Electra*. Greek tragedy, said the librarian, Iselin Vasshus, and gave Tong a strange look. He really wouldn't mind fucking her, he thought, and nodded. Whatever, he said. Sophocles, Iselin said, gathering her nut-brown hair into a bun in her hand. All right, said Tong, so do you have it? No, said Iselin, and gave a lopsided smile, mostly crime here. Well, can you get it, Tong asked, and pictured himself taking hold of Iselin by the hair, pushing her face down on to the desk and taking her from behind. Yes, I can order it, she said. What's it about? Tong asked. It's about revenge, Iselin answered – nearly all the Greek tragedies are about that.

'Revenge?'

'Mhm.'

'Revenge for what?'

'Electra and her brother, I can't remember his name, take revenge on their mother, Clytemnestra.'

'Why?'

'Because she killed Agamemnon. The father.'

'So how do they take revenge?'

'The brother – Orestes, that was his name – murders her, I think.'

Tong clenched his teeth and nodded.

'With a knife?'

'I don't know.'

'But why did the mother kill her husband?'

'He sacrificed their daughter.'

'Sacrificed?'

'Yes, before the war. Iphigenia. On the orders of the gods.'

'Hm.'

'That's how it is in the Greek tragedies.'

'Hm. Sound good – the Greek tragedies.'

'Yes, they are. They're our heritage in many ways. But – why are you so interested in this?'

'What do you mean by our heritage?' Tong asked, leaving her question unanswered.

'Well, our cultural heritage. Many people are of the opinion that everything we do and think is to be found there, in ancient Greek culture.'

'Hm. So, it's the daughter, this Electra one, and her brother Orestes who bump off the mother, this Clytemnestra.'

'Yes, at least that's how I remember it from lit crit.'

'Lit crit?'

'Literary theory and criticism,' smiled Iselin, and once again Tong pictured holding her hair tight and pressing her cheek down against the tabletop as he took her from behind. 'I studied it at one stage.'

'Do you think you know more about life than me because you went to college, is that it?' Tong cocked his head to the side and looked fixedly at her.

Iselin swallowed, gave another lopsided smile and said: 'No, I don't think that, Tong.'

'I want to borrow that book. Order a copy. I know someone who plays it. In the symphony orchestra.'

The Transporter makes it to the top of Ullandhaugbakken and the view over Hafrsfjord stretches out before them. It's beautiful.

Tong has had plenty of time in Åna to reflect upon what's beautiful. He's received three letters from his sister, Jin Eikeland, as she's called. Three letters. That too is beautiful. He hasn't managed to reply. But Jin has continued to write. As though she knows that he reads them. As though she's used to talking to people who don't respond.

'Hey,' says a voice from the back seat.

That big gob of Rudi's. Tong would like to pour cement down it. Years ago, Rudi was funny, stupid and entertaining. Then he began to get slightly annoying, then he became really irritating, and soon it grew into hate and during his time in prison it's become unbearable, even the mere thought of his face, of the way he takes up all the space in a room, the thought of that continuing to be a part of Tong's life; it makes him want to puke.

'Hey!' says the voice again from the back seat.

'Yes, Rudi, what's on your mind?' Jan Inge replies as he takes a right turn and drives alongside Haugtussa, with the tower blocks on the left, only a minute or two from Ernst Askildsens Gate.

'What is on my mind,' says Rudi, and Tong can hear how it's kind of bubbling up in the guy's throat, 'is that we need to put down the hatchets here. We can view life as a billy can, yeah? Sometimes it can be a bit much. And I've been sitting here thinking. We are such friggin' old friends, we have gone through so much feckin' shit together, and then today has been a bit screwed up, and yes, I'm willing to take a share of the blame, I mean, what kind of buffalo am I who can't accept love when my woman offers it to me on a silver platter? Yeah, I'm—'

'But Rudi I—'

'No, don't interrupt me, Chessi – like I said, I'm a reptile, but I'm talking now, I'm lifting the words over my tongue, and I see all you guys, I see our shared past in my head, and I'm asking you, as we make our way towards our friend Pål Fagerland, a man we have to do over for his own sake: can we air out this foul atmosphere before we get out of the Transporter?' Rudi takes a short pause and looks around at them. 'Can we wash our mouths out with Fairy Liquid and remember what advice Solomon gave us, what The Good Book says? *A gentle answer turns away wrath, but a harsh word stirs up anger.* Hm? Can we try and recall some good times and enjoy a pleasant hour on the job? Eh?'

Tong can see Jan Inge nodding his head. He puts the van into second and turns into Ernst Askildsens Gate. Jan Inge smiles. Everyone sits smiling and it's revolting, it's utterly revolting.

'Rudi,' Jan Inge says, 'you've got a real gift when it comes to people, you know that?'

Rudi shrugs proudly, 'Weeell, I don't know about that...'

Cecilie gives him a rub on the cheek.

'Okay,' Jan Inge says, bending his head down a little and looking out the windscreen. 'There's the house. We just need to reverse in ... Everyone ready? Beanies on, gloves on. The tape, you have the tape, Rudi? We don't want to leave any traces behind.'

Rudi nods, finds the roll of tape in the bag and takes it out. He picks at the roll with a fingernail to work the end free and then tapes over the gap between his gloves and sleeves, before passing it to Cecilie.

'Electra,' Tong says.

'Hm?'

'I read a book in prison.'

'Hey! Tongo! Man of books now, too!'

'A Greek tragedy,' he says coldly.

'Wow! A Greek tragedy! Mr I-Read-A-Lot from Korea!' Rudi thumps him on the back and lets out a loud laugh.

Tong wants to pulverise Rudi's face. But he controls himself. 'There's a woman,' he continues while putting on his gloves, 'in this book, who kills her mother. She's called Electra. And there's a line in it where it says: The result excuses any evil.'

Jan Inge shrugs. 'Well. I have heard better quotations than that, to be honest with you, so if that's the level of Greek tragedies these days I can't say I'm overly impressed. Your suffering will be legendary, even in hell, to put it like that.'

'Heh heh! Brother of quotes! There you go, Mr Reader, you'll never reach Jani's level.'

Tong has never killed anyone. No one in the gang has ever killed a person. That has been one of their most important principles. *Life will not be lost due to our work.*

Jan Inge has reversed the Transporter into the drive, backed right up to the garage door, which is opening from the inside. 'Okay,' he says, and backs into the garage, at the same time as Tong catches sight of the outline of a small man in the rear-view mirror. It looks like he's trying to hide in there.

'Let's get to it,' Jan Inge says. 'Everyone all set? Everyone sharp? Hairnets on, everyone?'

You must come visit Egersund sometime, Jin wrote, when you get out of Åna. It would be so nice to see you. Sometimes I feel like I know you, even though we have never met one another. Ofttimes I feel like I would understand more about myself if only I had the opportunity to meet you, my brother. I won't judge you by the life you have lived, that you should know. Come to Egersund, we have a big guest room with a comfy bed.

Why not?

Why not leave all this behind and go knock on a door in Egersund? The garage door comes back down and shuts, and Rudi rubs his hands together before taking out the small bag of speed he has in his pocket. His eyes are sparkling as he uses his driving licence to set up a few lines on the dashboard. Tong has a ticking sensation in his temples. He ought to keep away from this stuff. But he accepts the speed as it's offered round, placing a finger over one nostril, sniffing it up the other and feeling it hit.

Rudi is electric. He takes hold of the blue roll of shoe bags Cecilie hands him, pulling a pair over his shoes while he laughs. He opens the side door of the Transporter, that long, bloody body of his tottering out into the garage like Pinocchio on speed, and he calls out: 'Pål Schmål! Well? Been keeping away from the internet?'

Tong has never killed anyone.

But there's a first time for everything.

96. **DANIEL'S WISH** (Daniel William)

Daniel slows down the Suzuki a little way off from the gym hall. Veronika, riding pillion, shifts uneasily behind him.

'What do you think you're doing?' she asks. 'We shouldn't be here, can't we just go back to the practice room and—'

'Shut up.'

Daniel dismounts. He sets down the kickstand and parks. There's a girl standing over by the gym hall.

'Daniel, you can't just ride around thinking I'll go with you without having a clue where we're—'

'I'm squaring things up,' he interjects.

Veronika squints in annoyance. 'And I'm supposed to like, understand that? That we come here? Were we not going to leave—'

'We will leave,' he says, cutting her off again. 'But I have to square things up first.' Daniel throws his hands up in frustration: 'I've asked you before and I'm asking you again, are you type who needs to know everything?'

'No, I—'

'Well shut up, then.'

'But you said you wouldn't go to her—'

'I'm not going to her! I'm squaring things! Shut up!'

The girl by the gym hall turns to look at them. It's that Tiril one. Pål's daughter. She's dressed in an emo get-up, black from head to toe, her eyes are teary and she doesn't look too good.

He starts to walk towards the gym hall and Veronika follows.

'What the hell are you doing here?' she asks when they reach her, fixing two purple eyes on Daniel. 'Are you sick in the head? And you,' she points at Veronika, 'you should be locked up.'

'Give it a rest,' Daniel says, noticing how easy it is to talk to this girl, 'how's Sandra doing?'

'What the hell do you care?' Tiril answers, taking out a stick of gum before beginning to make her way round the other side of the building. 'Start reading the obituaries if you're that interested.'

Daniel feels a hand close around his heart and squeeze it.

'Relax,' Veronika says, 'I know her. She's a drama queen.'

Daniel draws a breath. 'I need to know if she's alive or not,' he says.

'Please,' says Veronika. 'We can't be here. Don't you understand anything? If they see you it's all over.'

Daniel walks towards the heavy doors, opens one and hears the applause grow inside the gym hall. Veronika goes after him. It's packed, not one seat free. Daniel keeps his eyes down and sidles along the wall bars together with Veronika, hoping not to be noticed.

Within a few seconds they've gained the attention of the entire hall. Face after face turns to look in their direction, as though he and Veronika were magnets. One set of eyes after the other stare at them. Whispering, muttering.

A wildly enthusiastic guy with socialist curls and round glasses comes on stage. He says that that was just amazing, *fantastic girls,* and then he spreads his arms wide: 'And now we're going to enter the world of emotion! Into the darkness! Please give a big welcome to Tiril and Thea, who are going to perform Evanescence's "My Immortal".'

The attention of the audience has been divided. A lot of eyes are focused on the stage and a lot of eyes are looking directly at Daniel and Veronika. The teachers are talking together in hushed tones.

'W-e-n-e-e-d-t-o-g-o,' Veronika mouths. 'N-o-w.'

He doesn't reply.

A girl has taken up position beside Daniel. He turns his head slowly, bringing it around as though on a rail, while keeping his eyes on the stage, where Tiril and Thea emerge from between a gap in the curtain. One black and one white angel. The lights in the hall dim, turning everything red, then green.

Daniel's eyes settle on the girl beside him. It's Malene.

'Yeah?' he whispers, as if he doesn't know what she wants.

'What are you doing here?' she whispers harshly. 'How have

you got the nerve to come here? Have you turned yourself in to the police?'

'Malene,' he whispers, his forehead lowered, 'please.'

'Haven't you two caused enough problems?'

'Malene,' he whispers, rarely having seen such an angry face. 'Have you heard anything about Sandra? Tell me what you know, and I'll do what I need to.'

'She's in a coma,' Malene says. 'That's all we know.'

He nods. Then he says: 'Please. Go home.'

Malene is taken aback, a line bisects her eyebrows.

'Go home,' he whispers, beginning to move towards the exit. 'Okay? Go home. There's something seriously fucked-up going on with your dad.'

The room is bathed in a dim, dark red light. Thea sits by the piano. She's white as aching snow that makes your eyes smart. She places her fingers on the keys and plays the first notes. Tiril stands in front of her holding a lit match. The flame trembles in front of her, casting a reflection on her skin, making troubled waves on her face. The girl stands with her gaze fixed and face impassive, looking like some black, twisted progeny of Satan, thinks Daniel, and the hate she radiates is not foreign to him; on the contrary, it feels soothing, stimulating and welcome. If the girl on the stage was to open her mouth and say *Daniel, come with me, and we'll make the pain worse*, he would obey.

Tiril lifts her chin, lets her gaze sweep over the room as the flame burns closer and closer to her fingers, before bringing the match to a pillar candle and the wick begins to glow, and Daniel hopes she manages to burn the whole world down.

'Sorry,' he whispers.

The music increases in volume. Daniel opens the door, with Veronika right behind him. They run towards the Suzuki.

97. **SHALL WE MAKE A START?** (Jan Inge)

'So Pål, you in form?'

'Heh heh, formformform?'

'How's the form, Pål?'

'Heh heh, form schmorm?'

Pål stands with his arms hanging loosely at his sides in the dimly lit garage. His eyes are as they should be, puppylike. He stands at the back wall radiating docility. Offering a reassuring impression immediately.

Jan Inge walks across the concrete floor. 'What do you say? In form?'

Pål is dressed casually. He doesn't appear to have worked himself into a tizzy deciding what to wear. Jeans. A simple, stripy shirt. He's newly shaved. That's good. His complexion looks clean and fresh. Which means he slept last night. That's a good sign. No one needs Pål roving around like a nervous wreck. No one needs Pål with bags under his eyes and his head all a frazzle when they're going to work him over.

Jan Inge nods and smiles. 'Hm, Pål? Good form?'

'Heh heh, form the norm?' Rudi draws up alongside Jan Inge and slaps Pål on the arm. 'Good to see you, Mr Poker Joker! Sprouted more grey hairs lately? What does the word of the Lord have to say about that, Pål Kål? *Grey hair is a crown of glory; it is gained in a righteous life.* And what else does God say: *A truly wise person uses few words; a person with understanding is even-tempered.* Well, that's sure not me the Good Book is talking about!'

'Rudi. Easy now.'

Rudi mimes a gun with his finger and thumb and shoots himself: 'Relaxed Rupert. Heh heh.'

'Well,' Pål says, 'I'm ... yeah, suppose I'm in form. Just want to get this over with. Y'know.'

Cecilie approaches Pål. She smiles warmly and places a gloved hand on one of his arms hanging limply by his side.

Jan Inge feels his chest swell with pride as he watches her do it in such a gentle, maternal fashion. Generate stability. Offer him assurance. He's also aware of how little Rudi likes her doing it, so he takes a quick hold of his friend as he makes to move towards his girlfriend.

'Rudi. This is work,' he whispers.

Rudi exhales through his nose and nods.

'Are you scared?' Cecilie asks, presenting her most feminine side.

Pål shrugs. 'Scared ... I, well...'

'I can understand that,' she says. 'Where's the dog? That cute dog, what was it call—'

'I,' Pål gives a lopsided smile, 'I left her in the basement, figured maybe—'

'That's good.' Cecilie pats him on the arm. 'This is going to work out just fine. Okay? You're among friends. Rudi, Jan Inge, my brother, and Tong.' She points to the silent Korean who's closely inspecting the garage and its contents. 'It's the four of us who are working today. And in order for this to go well, you need to view us as your friends. Okay?'

Pål clears his throat.

'Okay, Pål?'

He nods.

'Good. Then there're just a few things we need to go through with you, okay, Pål?'

Pål raises his eyebrows.

'Okay, Pål?'

This truly is Cecilie at her absolute best. It's just a shame that this social, feminine and tremendously perceptive side only comes to the fore when we're at work. Imagine if it was more evident on the home front, if she was like this when the house needed cleaning or when she got up for breakfast. But, it's important to look ahead. Jan Inge harbours hope that she'll be filled from top to toe

like this after she gives birth. He has faith that this child, who may
be Rudi's, or Tong's, but for God's sake must remain unspoken of
for the next while, that this child will fill her with maternal joy.

Pål sniffles and clears his throat again. 'Yeah,' he says.

'Great,' Cecilie says, reminiscent in no small measure of a nurse
who has done something unpleasant to a patient, but who still has
the ability to coax a smile, 'great.' She turns to Jan Inge, giving
him a barely perceptible nod. 'Jan Inge? Will you present Pål with
a quick run-through of what's going to take place?'

Jan Inge takes a step forward. Out of the corner of his eye he
notices Rudi has wandered over to a workbench at the end of the
garage where he is standing messing about with something. A bird
table?

'Rudi!'

'Heh heh. Oops! *Ich komme, mein General*!' Rudi puts the bird
table aside. 'Yess, the Rudi reporting for duty. What's going on?'

Jan Inge ignores him, he knows this is how Rudi reacts to
speed, straight into his bloodstream at the start, but stabilises
pretty quickly.

'Yes,' Jan Inge says, hiking up his black work pants, taking hold
of the belt and trying to almost hook the trousers over his ample
hips, 'shall we go inside?'

'Sorry,' Pål says, showing the way, 'it's through here.'

'A door from the garage right into the house,' Jan Inge remarks,
clicking his fingers. 'I like that. Pål. I like it a lot.'

They enter a hall. A series of family photos in IKEA frames
hang along the walls. Two girls aged about ten with a large cod
in their laps, a girl with a ponytail wearing a purple leotard with
silver stars on it, holding a trophy in her hands, a girl sitting in a
little car in what must be Legoland. The four of them are dressed
in black and focused, they carry their black bags, all having taped
the gaps between footwear and trousers, between sleeves and
gloves, all wearing blue shoe bags, all with hairnets and hats. Pål
leads them into a spacious kitchen. An ordinary kitchen table.
Five chairs. A plastic tablecloth. A coffee maker, toaster and radio.
Curtains drawn, very good. Pål pulls out the chairs and the four
of them sit down at the table.

'Great, Pål,' Jan Inge says, with a satisfied smile and a real warmth in his cheeks, 'we're off to a good start.' He glances at the clock on the wall. 'Okay. We need to be relatively efficient here. As I'm sure you understand.'

Pål presses his lips together and rests his elbows on the table. A padding, shuffling sound comes from the stairs to the basement and a moment later a dog's head appears in the doorway.

'Pål!' Jan Inge lifts his hands up in exasperation. 'Did we not talk about—'

Pål hurries over to Zitha and grabs her by the scruff. 'I must not have – sorry, I'll make sure to—'

'You'd better,' Jan Inge says sternly, watching Pål pull Zitha down the stairs while admonishing her. He returns a moment later.

'There. Now she's well secured to—'

'We won't talk about it any more, Pål,' Jan Inge says calmly. 'Now. Before we start, would you put some coffee on, just so it looks like we've barged in while you were going about your daily routine? You could also put out a loaf of bread on the worktop, you might want to take it from the wrapper and cut a slice, and place some salami beside it and leave the fridge door ajar, then it won't look too far off.'

Pål jumps up as though having received strict orders, nodding with reassuring appreciation, does exactly as he's asked and does it quickly: takes out the filters, measures out the amount of coffee, fills the water, turns on the coffee machine, takes the bread from the bread bin beneath the window and opens the door of the fridge.

'Very good, Pål,' Cecilie says.

'Cheese, is that all right?'

'Can't go wrong with cheese, Pål. I like your willingness to cooperate,' Jan Inge says. 'If everyone was like you, things would be a lot more tidy in our line of business. In any case,' he continues, feeling an almost Mediterranean warmth spread through his stomach, 'our purpose is to leave you in a sufficiently altered—'

'Altered!' Rudi bangs his fist on the table. 'I love that fucking word so much I want to screw it!'

'Rudi! That's enough!' Jan Inge clicks his fingers loudly at Rudi. 'I beg your pardon, Pål. The purpose, as I was saying, is to leave you altered to the extent that there's no doubt as to what has taken place. It's in your interest and our interest. You need the money. We don't need the attention. And the dog stays in the basement.' Jan Inge sees Pål nod energetically. 'That's great. You maintain the first impression you make. Have you always done that?'

'Eh?'

'Have you always maintained the first impression you make?'

'No, I don't quite – what do you mea—'

'Something I often think about. That a person presents themselves in some way or another. Appears to be a certain way. And then a winter passes and spring rolls by, and suddenly the birch trees are in bloom and you see that this person isn't what they sold themselves as. While in other cases – yours? – you get what you pay for.'

'Well, I, yeah—'

Jan Inge holds up the palm of his right hand to signal that they don't have time to get any further into this, in itself, compelling topic.

'The alteration. We have to cause you sufficient damage so that nobody can suspect it's self-inflicted.'

Pål clears his throat once again, deeper this time. 'Right. Sure. Okay.' His gaze wanders over the surface of the table. 'Are you going to have some coffee too? Or will I just leave it on?'

Jan Inge casts a quick glance in Cecilie's direction, to let her know that she may perhaps need to step in again and behave in a soothing, maternal fashion as the subject is displaying nervous tendencies, but now she doesn't appear to be paying attention.

'You can let it sit there,' he says. 'We're not exactly eager to leave any DNA traces. Crime scene investigators these days, they're a skilled bunch. We do have to cause you some damage. But we're no more fond of violence than you are. On the contrary, we're anti-violence, almost pacifists in fact; you don't need to be worried about permanent injuries. Come and sit down now, Pål. Don't stand there getting all worked up. No good will come of it. Are you worried?'

Pål lets slip a despairing smile and shuffles back with his head hanging limply, which makes him resemble his dog, before he sits down at the kitchen table with the others.

'It's quite understandable,' Jan Inge says, becoming aware of a mild irritation creeping into his gut over Cecilie no longer being at the ready with that nurselike warmth. 'But listen.' He places a soft hand on Pål's wrist and gives a gentle squeeze. 'You. Dogman. Father to two beautiful girls. The man who will soon be free.'

'Hear, hear! Cry freedom!'

'We know how to punch and kick a body,' Jan Inge continues, 'we know what can be broken and what can't without it having serious consequences.'

'Youbetya, Pål Wall!'

'Rudi, could you exercise a modicum of calm?' Jan Inge speaks slowly to Rudi, letting his eyebrows dance up and down to make him understand that he's marring the current tactics. 'You will,' he goes on, 'you will feel pain, but it shall pass. My advice to you is to think about how good things are going to be for you and your daughters.'

Jan Inge raises his corpulent form from the seat. He's definitely going to start working out after this job is over with. He begins to swagger across the floor, doing his best to resemble a barrister or something along those lines. Pål follows him with anxious eyes.

Jan Inge stops. 'What's going to happen,' he says, 'is the following. Cecilie is going to explore the house. She'll take a close look at your possessions, point out what we're going to take with us and what we're going to wreck. Isn't that right, Cecilie?'

Cecilie turns to Pål, her face tracing a pretty arc, making her resemble Beverly Hinna, and serves him a smile of class. Good, she's singing from the same hymn sheet again.

'The last part,' Jan Inge continues, 'is mostly for the sake of realism. It's important for it to look like the crooks who broke into your house and beat you up were looking for stuff to steal. People like that usually leave a trail of senseless destruction in their wake.'

A hmph sound escapes Rudi, 'Hopeless sorts.'

'They're on drugs and they take pleasure in wrecking things,' Jan Inge says. 'They have a need for destruction, Pål. Have you heard of that?'

'No, can't say—'

'It's the same as when a gang of youths kick the wing mirrors off parked cars. They're generally acting out after a painful upbringing. They've experienced maltreatment and abuse. We're talking about failure of care a lot of the time. These people have something inside that has to come out. A need for destruction. The crooks that were at your place tonight suffer from something like that. Do you understand, Pål?'

'Yeah,' he says. 'It sounds ... well, realistic.'

'Good, Pål. You catch on quick.'

'I think so too,' Cecilie says.

'While Cecilie carries out an evaluation of your household contents,' Jan Inge says, smiling, 'the three of us will get started on you. We'll leave a few signs of forced entry, we need to fake a modus operandi so it looks like we've broken in. We'll smash the window beside the front door to make it look like that was how we gained access, we'll mess up the hall a little – what do you think, Tong, smash the mirror? Evidence of a struggle?'

Tong nods. 'Enough with a crack in it. Turn a chair over.'

'If Tong says it's enough with a crack and an overturned chair, then it's enough with a crack and an overturned chair.' Jan Inge nods. 'So. We'll rearrange the hallway a little, make it look like a scuffle has taken place, same goes for the kitchen here, where I think we'll let the main action play out. Or actually.' He stops to think for a moment. 'Let me have a look at your living room.'

Pål shows Jan Inge and Pål into the living room and they take a look around. A corner sofa, an armchair, a table, large windows facing the garden.

Tong shakes his head. Jan Inge does the same. He points to a framed photograph standing on a sideboard. The same two girls from the pictures in the hall. They're about ten or twelve years old in the photo. 'Your daughters?'

Pål nods gravely.

'Lovely girls. Think of them. The living room is a no go,' Jan Inge says as they walk back to the kitchen. 'This is where we'll let it all go down. We'll tie you to one of the chairs. You'll be in some pain overnight, and sore for a few days after, but without serious injury. And we'll break a few things around us—'

'The Tjeeeeensvoll Gang! The Tjeeeensvoll Gang!' Rudi exclaims, grabbing Cecilie on the behind. 'Sorry, capo,' he says, as he receives a stern look from Jan Inge, and removes his hand from her behind, 'I'm just so happy today. Job satisfaction! *Arbeit macht frei*!'

'So,' Pål says meekly. 'This ... I don't know what you'd call it ... this...'

'The actual violence, is that what you're thinking of?' Jan Inge folds his arms, noticing at the same time that he actually has a pair of tits now.

Pål nods.

'I don't know what to tell you,' Jan Inge says. 'Would you like to know what we're going to do beforehand?'

Pål rubs his palms against one another and shifts his weight. 'Weeell, em ... can I get a cup of coffee?'

Jan Inge nods and Pål pours himself a coffee, immediately warming up his nervous hands around it.

'You don't want to know,' Cecilie says, again producing that motherly warmth that impels Jan Inge to believe, truly believe, in the future.

'Pål,' she says, with the air of an old-time continuity announcer, 'it's not worth it. You'll only work yourself up and that'll make the pain worse.'

'Right,' Pål says, 'I see...'

Cecilie strokes him across the cheek and Jan Inge sees Rudi's eyelids quiver.

'That is,' Tong says, 'if you don't find it reassuring to know what's in store. People are different. Some people work in the symphony orchestra, some study lit crit and some specialise in break-ins.'

'True,' Jan Inge says, taken aback by Tong's comparison. He turns to Pål again: 'It's something you'll need to decide for yourself. We'll blindfold you after we've tied you up anyway.'

'Shit,' Pål says, putting his hand to his hair, 'not easy to decide.'

'That I can well understand,' Rudi says, seeming more together now.

'You need to make a decision,' Jan Inge says, glancing at the clock, 'we have to get started.'

He leans down to one of the bags by his feet.

'What have you got inside that?' Pål asks nervously.

'That's sort of what you either want to know or don't want to know,' Jan Inge says impatiently. 'What's it going to be?' He looks at Cecilie. 'Will you start taking a gander round?'

She straightens up and nods. Stroking Pål across the cheek one last time she says, 'Trust me. Think of your daughters, what were their names again?'

'Malene and Tiril.'

Cecilie's forehead relaxes and her face takes on a faraway expression, that of an expectant mother. 'Malene and Tiril,' she says, a growing colour in her cheeks, 'such gorgeous names. I'm sure they're lovely daughters.'

'Yeah,' Pål says, and Jan Inge can see that he's having a hard time swallowing.

'Think about them,' Cecilie says, 'and just go with it. Think of it as giving birth.'

Jan Inge clears his throat unintentionally.

'A birth?'

Cecilie nods.

'Okay,' Pål says. 'I'll go with ... that. I don't want to know anything.'

Tong takes a step forward. He demands attention from everyone in the room, just by the look in his eyes, and he gets it. 'One last thing,' he says, 'there's been a bit of a misunderstanding about the insurance money.'

'Yes, that,' Jan Inge says, producing his inhaler from his pocket and sucking in air.

Pål frowns. 'What do you mean?'

'We've discussed it within the company—'

'We're taking a cut,' Tong breaks in. He places both hands on the table in front of Pål. 'Half.'

Pål's eyes widen. He looks from one of them to the other. 'But – but – the deal was – the whole point of it is ... I need ... but, I need a million! It's not enough with – we made a deal—'

Jan Inge shrugs. Tong keeps his eyes fixed on Pål.

'We made a de—'

Again, Jan Inge shrugs.

'But we have—'

Pål stops talking. His chest rises and he exhales slowly, his pallid hands poised for a moment in front of his stomach before falling on to his lap like leaves.

Jan Inge nods. 'Good, Pål,' he says, 'no point making a song and dance about it.'

Rudi bends down to the bag containing baseball bats, hand weights, pliers, knuckle dusters and table legs. Jan Inge takes a bandana from his pocket and hands it to Rudi. Tong holds Pål tight and Rudi ties it around his head. Cecilie turns and walks towards the basement.

'Hey, we agreed that ... I can't ... this isn't on—'

'Pål,' Jan Inge says assertively, 'that's enough! Sit down so we can make a start here.'

Rudi tightens the bandana over his eyes. 'Can you see anything?'

'You can't see anything, Pål, can you?'

'All dark, Pål Wall?'

'Looks good, Jan Inge! Loads of good stuff to take with us!'

'Tong, can you hand me that eh ... yeah, that...'

'Has the tape come loose? Look, just hold it here and...'

'Rudi, see this, can you not...'

'No, but I was actually thinking of using...'

'Oh right, you wanted...'

'Yeah, maestro, I mean, whythehellnot?'

'Won't that be a little ... all right, yeah, why not?'

'There's a nice big TV down here, Jan Inge! And a computer!'

'Darkness imprisoning me! You there, Pål Nål?'

'Think of your daughters!'

'Aww, here's where that cute dog is. Yeaah, good doggie.'

'Shall we make a start?'

98. **SHE CARRIES HER OWN WEIGHT** (Malene)

Tiril glides towards the microphone. She moves as though her feet aren't touching the ground, a glimmer in her eyes.

There's something unreal about such a quick-tempered person suddenly becoming so balanced and self-possessed, as if she wasn't of this world, but of another; and which would that be?

Malene has palpitations and the sound of Daniel's whispering voice still in her head, *there's something seriously fucked up going on with your dad.* Her thoughts race this way and that like scatter-brained pups, not realising what's going on, other than that something terrible is happening, *right now.* Ordinarily this gym hall is packed with kids running, climbing ropes or lifting weights, now it seems drowned in pain as it glows in that deep red light; what, Dad, what?

Daniel and Veronika have slipped out, the moped has ridden off, Frida has got to her feet and is tapping something into her phone; is she calling the police, has she realised we were lying?

Malene remains standing by the wall bars. Mum is sitting on a black, plastic chair looking at the stage and Malene's devil sister is standing in front of the microphone.

Is her head going to start smouldering? Will her skin crackle like a porcelain glaze and smoke begin to seep from the fissures in her head? What is Tiril planning? The people in the gym hall are silent, not seeming like they dare to breathe, not seeming like they dare to swallow, chins forward, cheeks sunken, their hands resting on their laps and between their fingers they have a frail hold on their own hearts.

The first bars of 'My Immortal' resound through the room, Thea's fingers playing them over and over again. The girl at the microphone just stares at the audience. She doesn't blink.

Dad? What is it?

Tiril raises her hand to her mouth.

What is she going to do?

Tear out her own teeth?

Tiril puts the top of her thumb and finger in her mouth. Takes out some chewing gum and without taking her eyes from the audience, she sticks it to the microphone stand.

'Sometimes it hurts so much you can hardly breathe.'

Tiril's voice is deep and flat.

What did she say? Unease spreads through the hall.

'I'll say it again: Sometimes it hurts so much you can hardly breathe.'

Tiril keeps her voice clear and cold, as though it were ice.

The audience grow increasingly restless, people begin to shift in their seats, look at those seated next to them. The curtain behind Tiril moves, Svein Arne's wimpy head comes into view.

Tiril just continues staring at the audience.

Is she not going to sing?

Hold on. It's not the audience she's looking at. It's Mum. Tiril is staring at her mother and the empty chair beside her.

'Do you hear me?'

Oh, Jesus.

Tiril.

'Do you hear me?'

Malene peers along the row of chairs. Mum looks small and afraid, almost unrecognisable. Her cheeks are shiny, as though someone's polished them. She's crying, and it strikes Malene that she's never seen her do that before.

'There's a girl lying in hospital,' the icy voice says. 'We know her. Everyone knows her.'

Now people breathe again. Their hearts are back in their chests, they've swallowed, the oxygen has returned to their heads and they breathe again. They move their feet cautiously and nod.

'Sandra, I've been an idiot. You don't deserve this song, Mum, and you don't deserve it, Dad.'

Malene gives a start. She feels panic well up in her throat, takes out her mobile, finds Dad's number and calls.

It's ringing.

Come on, pick it up.

'You were run over, Sandra. By the one who said he loved you.'

Frida Riska's head and neck give a jerk and she sits up in her chair.

'Daniel William Moi,' Tirils says. 'You know who he is. Veronika Ulland sat behind. You know who she is.'

Frida looks at the headmaster, he nods and she gets to her feet, almost stumbling as she makes her way along the row of chairs, mobile phone in hand.

'They ran off,' Tiril says. 'That was gutless.'

Frida punches in a number, runs her hand through her hair and brings the phone to her ear.

'We lied,' Tiril says. 'Sorry, Sandra. We'll breathe on you now.'

Still ringing. Pick it up, Dad.

Voicemail: *Hi, you've reached Pål, I can't take your call right now but leave a message after the beep.*

I have to run, Malene thinks, as her body becomes aware of something her mind can't comprehend, as she hears Tiril's thin, birdlike, but beautiful voice begin to sing the song Malene hasn't understood before now: 'I'm so tired of being here.'

Malene throws open the doors, Mum sits in the hall watching one daughter sing and the other one run, and Malene gets out in front of the gym hall, places her feet on the tarmac, feels how strong her tendons are, feels how her body obeys her, not the slightest stinging, nothing. She carries her own weight across the tarmacked schoolyard, through the small streets, along the lane separating the terraced houses in Anton Brøggers Gate, across the playground and the green area beyond, ringing again, running with the phone to her ear, but her father doesn't pick up and she slips on the grass as she nears the road by the low-rises, skids and falls, but gets back on her feet, and has the feeling of doing the right thing, but of getting there way too late.

99. **STRAIGHT TO VIDEO** (Jan Inge)

'Ow! Fuck! Owwwwwh!'

'Pål?'

'Owwwaaaah, owwahhhh, ouchouchouch!'

'Hey, Pål?'

'Arrrrghiiii, arrrrghiiii, ouchouchouchouch!'

'Pål, we've talked about this, you can't make this much noise.'

'Woof, woof!'

'Pål, didn't you say that mutt wasn't going cause any problems?'

'Brrrr! Brrrr!'

'Hey, Rudi! Can you turn off that mobile?'

Jan Inge extends both arms straight out, striking as much of a superior officer-type pose as he possibly can, to signal that he has now reached his limit. Pål writhes in pain, his mouth closed, blood running from his ear and over his neck, from the cut left by Tong's knife across his cheek.

Jan Inge listens. The dog has quit barking. The mobile has stopped ringing. He lowers his arms and nods to Tong, who has folded the knife and put it back in his pocket. Tong takes a step closer to Pål. He raises his hand and plants the knuckle duster in his face. It is a clean blow, but once again Pål screams like it is the end of the world.

'Pål! Keep it down! Will you please try and remember what we talked about? Go ahead and scream, but do it on the inside!'

The whimpering from the dog can once again be heard from the basement. Pål swallows his own sounds, his head hangs by tensed muscles in his neck, and all that escapes him are grunts.

'Good, Tong,' Jan Inge says, pleased, and he turns his head nearly 180 degrees and shouts in the direction of the stairs: 'You find anything down there? You got the dog under control?'

'No problem, it was just the screaming he didn't like! Some nice stuff here, Buonanotte will be happy!'

Jan Inge nods and tightens his grip around the baseball bat he has in his hands.

'Brrr! Brrrr!'

He is about to bring it down on Pål's fingers when once again the telephone vibrates loudly on the table. 'Rudi? Can you help out a little here? Could you at least turn off that damned mobile phone so I can get on with my job?'

'Holy Mary, Mother of God, Jani, help out? I'm not even—'

Jan Inge stands with the bat raised above his head while he turns to look at Rudi who's on his way to the kitchen, sulking over Jan Inge lavishing all his attention on Tong. 'Hold on a sec,' he says. 'Who's calling?'

Rudi lifts his hands in despair. 'Was I supposed to turn it off or not to turn it off? I've switched it off now! You told me to switch it off!'

Jan Inge raises his eyebrows. 'Fuck it,' he says, and sets his jaw. He slams the bat down on Pål's fingers; Pål twists his face in pain and howls even louder. The dog barks in the basement.

'Pål. I'm going to get angry soon.'

Pål splutters noisily and the dog begins whimpering again.

'Cecilie! Shut that dog up!'

Jan Inge places the end of the bat on the floor and leans on it, like a golfer. He listens. It is quiet again. The dog is calm. 'All right,' he says. 'You need to learn to answer people when they're talking to you, Pål. Things just get messy if you don't. All right. Focus. Next step.'

'Focus!' Rudi says in encouragement, but Jan Inge is just not able to deal with his friend now, so he turns instead to Tong and offers him an inquiring look. Tong folds his arms and cocks his head.

'Hmm,' says Tong. 'The fingers?'

He bends down and takes a pair of pliers from the bag.

'I don't know if we need to,' Jan Inge says, 'surely they're already broken?'

Tong shrugs and puts the pliers down. 'The nose?'

'Hello? Lionel Ritchie? Am I not here?'

Once again Jan Inge ignores Rudi. He checks to see if Pål's fingers are broken – four of them are – and then stands next to Tong. They both study Pål. He is not screaming, but he snorts as though in labour.

'Well, yeah,' Jan Inge says. 'The nose. We probably ought to do that.'

Rudi peeps over their heads while he waves a broken-off chair leg casually around. 'Why wouldn't we?'

'*Why wouldn't we,*' mimics Jan Inge. 'What kind of answer is that? Is that your assessment, Rudi? Round and round we go and where we stop nobody knows?'

Cecilie comes walking up the basement stairs. She sighs when she sees Pål's battered face, the wound from the corner of his mouth and the blood dripping on to his jeans.

'Oh dear, Pål,' she says in a gentle voice, 'you should be glad you can't see it. Can you keep it down a bit? Hm? For the sake of the dog?'

'I think so,' Pål replies breathlessly. 'It's just that it's pretty tough going, this here.'

'I understand that.' Cecilie looks at Rudi, who has sat down on one of the kitchen chairs – after having first turned it demonstratively to face the window. He's crossed his legs and folded his arms, one bagged foot bobbing up and down from the knee.

She leaves him be and turns to Jan Inge. 'The nose?'

'That's what we're standing here discussing.'

She lines up next to Tong and Jan Inge and studies Pål.

'We need to do the nose,' she says, in a firm voice. 'The people that were here tonight – they would've done that, I think.'

'They would,' says Jan Inge, allowing himself time to reflect briefly on femininity and motherhood, how much he has missed them down through the years and how nice it will be to have them in the house.

'We need to,' says Tong.

'Of course we need to,' Rudi says, getting up from the chair.

'But we hav—' something between a sign and groan escapes Jan Inge.

'True, but we can—'

'We don't really need to tal—'

'Pål stamps on the floor. Jan Inge turns to him. 'Yes, Pål? Did you want to say something?'

'What are ... what ... are ... you talking ... about?'

Jan Inge shrugs. 'Well,' he explains, 'it's just that we have had a mishap with a nose before.'

'Mishap? Whatkindamishap?'

'It's not really something we ought to be discussing with you, Pål. That just wouldn't be right. Now we're going to break it, it will hurt, but Tong knows what he's doing. Put it this way, the mishap wasn't his fault—'

'Yeah, rub it in!' Rudi shouts.

'Rudi, don't be so touchy. Remember what we talked about. Little good comes from taking affront. You only have to look at your brother.'

'Rubitinbaby! You had to bring up that toe rag in Sandnes as well? One mistake and it haunts you for the rest of your life! I'm here too y'know, I do exist! What is it you're always saying? That we're a team? You'll never walk alone? Well then, Mr Bullshit Writer, Mr Horror, what do you think it's like not to be noticed? Just because that little Korean is back again? Have you forgotten your chocolate chip cookies, Manchurian Candidate? I WON'T STAND FOR THIS! ONE MISTAKE AND YOU'RE HAUN—'

Jan Inge fixes his gaze on a point picked in the air at random. He inhales and exhales, feeling like an adult in a nursery.

'Rudi.'

'Yes.'

'We've talked about this.'

'I don't remember that.'

'We have.'

'Don't remember.'

'Rudi. We have. Talked about it. About you being touchy.'

'Yeah, and? So are you.'

'Yes, I can be now and then. But they're two different conversations. We're talking about you now.'

'Okay, okay, but all the same. You can be touchy too. If we don't like a film that you like for instance.'

'Fine. I'm willing to accept the criticism. But. The thing is Tong is home. It's his first day back at work. So it's hardly unreasonable for him to get a bigger slice of the pie.'

'The pie?'

'A metaphor.'

Rudi nods. 'Right, okay.' He fills his mouth with air and it looks as though he's playing the trumpet when he blows out.

'As I was saying,' Jan Inge says, regarding the situation as retrieved. He turns to Pål: 'As I was saying, Tong knows what he's doing. As opposed to certain other people,' he adds, realising at the last moment it's a bit much, but sometimes you have to tell the truth. 'You'll experience severe pain now,' he concludes, 'but then it'll all be over. Can you live with that?'

Rudi is staring at the window again. But to no effect. Cecilie has noticed him sulking, and runs her hand up and down his back.

Pål nods.

Jan Inge raises a forefinger to his nose and taps it lightly. Tong lines up, a few feet from Pål. His concentration is a joy to watch, his Asian body perfectly balanced, before he takes a single pre-paratory step and plants his foot full in Pål's face.

'That was act one, in a way,' says Jan Inge and watches the blood cascade from Pål's nose. 'Act two,' he continues, 'is somewhat shorter. Put your head back, Pål, it'll help stem the flow of blood a bit. Act two. All that's left to do, is break a couple of your ribs, and then we'll go and get your stuff – how many things have you got on the list, Cecilie?'

'Twenty-two in total'

'Twenty-two. Great. And then we'll be out of here in no time. Okay, Pål?'

Tong straightens up, assumes the stance in the centre of the room again.

'Okay, Tong,' Jan Inge says, laughing, 'that's enough now.'

Tong remains poised. His muscles flexed.

'Tong?'

He takes one quick step and again lands his foot in Pål's face.

This time making his whole head fly backwards, as if he has been shot, and Pål screams.

'Tong! What the fu—'

He straightens up a third time, the others not managing to react before he again kicks out and strikes Pål full in the face. It is a slab of blood and mucus. The sound of Zitha barking comes from the basement.

'Owwwwwwwwahhhhhhhhh!'

'Je-sus,' says Jan Inge and throws his hands up, 'what are you doing?'

There's a racket from the basement. Something falls over, something breaks, and the next moment the sound of paws coming up the steps. The door is pushed open and Zitha comes storming into the kitchen. The dog stops for a second, her head going from side to side, a feral look in her eyes, but when she catches sight of her master sitting beaten up and bound to a kitchen chair, she darts across the parquet. But before she gets there, Tong shoots out an arm, takes a vice-like grip on her by the scruff of the neck and holds her tight. The dog writhes beneath his hand, paws flailing and mouth snarling, and then, before anyone can blink, a blade flashes and a split second after, the knife is planted, the handle vibrating, in Zitha's throat. She lets out a howl before she lies ruptured on the kitchen floor with her tongue hanging out and her front paws stretched out towards Pål.

'Tong!' Cecilie shouts. 'What have you – Jesus Christ!'

Tong grins and turns to her. The knife is sticking out of Zitha's neck.

'Jan Inge! He's killed the dog!'

Pål's head rolls from left to right, his mouth twisted. 'Zitha?! Zitha?! What's happened? Zitha!'

Jan Inge gapes at Tong.

Tong points at Rudi and smirks.

'Zitha! Hello? What's happened?'

Tong pulls the knife from the dead dog and dries the blade on the arm of his jacket. He leans over to Pål. 'Pål,' he says, 'let me tell you something. I've screwed Rudi's woman. In prison. Once a week.'

The room is silent.

Jan Inge cannot form a single thought. Rudi's eyes slowly enlarge. Cecilie's head sinks towards the floor and she takes her hands to her cheeks. Pearls of sweat form on Jan Inge's forehead, and then run from his armpits, his mouth is dry. He fumbles in his pocket for his inhaler, puts it to his mouth, sucks and feels the sweat trickle, and he does not resemble a company executive in the slightest.

I've seen this in movies, Jan Inge thinks. People letting you down when it counts.

'Zitha,' Pål sobs. 'You've killed Zitha.'

Rudi begins to quiver. The towering man starts to shake, his eyes look like they are ready to burst out of his head.

'You know what, Pål?' Tong says calmly, 'it was like coming in old lettuce.' The room is even more silent now.

Tears run down Cecilie's cheek.

Rudi is just quivering.

Pål swallows, several times in a row, while whispering: 'Zitha. Zitha.'

'And you know what else, Pål?' Tong whispers. 'I'm never going to work with this crowd again. Something new has come into my life, a symphony orchestra, and I'm going far away from here.'

This, thinks Jan Inge, sweating from every pore, while he has that gruesome feeling of being unable to open his mouth, of being unable to do anything at all, as though it were Mum lying in front of him like a damned compost heap and he was just standing there, looking at her, sweating, frightened, eight years old and unable to do anything at all; this is going straight to video.

100. **SIBLING LOVE** (Cecilie)

The nausea seethes like boiling milk. Suddenly she's afraid of vomiting up the child, it's as though she can feel the little baby kick, punch and cry in there.

'Fucking yellow peril!' Rudi shouts, eyes blazing.

Tong stands sneering, some blood still dripping from the edge of the knife in his hand. 'Come on then, birdshit skin, I'm right here.'

Cecilie hears Pål crying quietly, he's stretched his feet out to locate Zitha's form, which is still warm, the bandana around his head is damp with tears and he whispers: 'Zitha, Zitha, oh Jesus, what has Daddy done.' She understands that she only has a few seconds to halt a crisis no one will be able to handle. But what will she do; is there anything that can restrain a man who finds out his mate has slept with his girlfriend?

'I'm going to reach down your throat and rip your tongue out!'

'Yikes.' Tong tosses the knife back and forth between his hands. 'I'm shitting myself.'

Rudi is snorting like a horse and shaking like a drill, and in a matter of moments he's going to explode. Fly at Tong's face and tear it to pieces with his teeth, rip his heart out and rend it into small pieces, and nobody's going to be able to prevent it, not her, not Jan Inge, not Jesus, not God, not Steven Tyler and not even Lemmy, but she needs to come up with something, so what will she do?

It's like Jan Inge has dropped out of himself, or the opposite; he has sunk into himself. That happens sometimes, he loses everything he's built up, and when Jan Inge diminishes there's nobody smaller, as a result Bro isn't going to be of any help; what will she do?

Rudi stands like a cat ready to pounce, facing Tong, still calmly tossing the knife back and forth between his hands. 'I've never fucking liked you, China man.'

'Same here,' Tong smirks, 'same here, I've detested you from day one.'

Hey Dad, what is it you always say?

When storm clouds gather, what is you say to do again?

Just tell the truth, honeybunch, then everything will be just fine.

Vein after vein is becoming visible through Rudi's skin, his teeth are chattering.

The truth, Dad?

Cecilie clears her throat and shuts her eyes for a second. Then she reopens them, and looking at the man sitting sobbing on the chair says: 'I'm pregnant.'

Her voice carries clearly and her words fill the room.

No one looks at her at first. Rudi just quivers, Tong just sneers. It's as though the sentence is spoken in a language nobody understands, slowly catching and drawing them in. Jan Inge's near-void blueberry eyes, Tong's iron stare, Rudi's coffee-brown ADHD eyes, even Pål turns his face towards her.

Rudi sways, looking ready to collapse like a house of cards. 'You're what?'

Tong snorts.

Cecilie dries a tear from under one eye. 'I'm pregnant. With—'

'But—' Rudi raises the back of his hand to his mouth, wiping it hard across his lips as if he had shit on them.

'Yeah,' she repeats, watching Rudi as his brain labours, his face reflecting each step until it dawns on him.

'But—'

'Yes, Rudi. Yes. By one of you.'

Laughter. Lean, derisive laughter.

Cecilie sinks down on to one of the dining chairs near Pål, perhaps in the place where one of the sisters usually sits. Who knows, she thinks, picturing a home life she wishes were her own, before looking at what she has in front of her: three boys – one crazy and wild, one scornful and hard-hearted, one at a complete loss; a badly beaten man with a broken nose, dangling blood and mucus dropping on to his thighs, broken fingers and a cut-up face, and a dead dog.

She places her hand on her stomach, not because the baby bids her to, but because she's frightened.

Rudi grinds his teeth. There's just as much chance of him letting loose on her and the child as there is of him going for Tong. She hadn't considered it before, but now it's obvious.

'Rudi, you mustn't, you hear me,' she gets to her feet, reaching for his hands, trying to make eye contact, 'are you listening to me, you mustn't. I can see what you're thinking ... you know I'm Chessi ... listen ... Rudi ... please—'

There it is again, Tong's laughter.

Rudi shuts his eyes, like he does at times when he looks truly beautiful, then turns his head to the left, stretching it around until the muscles make a cracking sound. He opens his eyes again, places his palm on the left side of his chest while keeping his gaze fixed on Cecilie. He thumps his hand resolutely over his own heart and says: 'Sometimes, Chessi, I wonder if you know who I am.'

'Huh?' Her mouth trembles. 'What do you mean, sweetheart?'

Rudi's eyes spin. He's really high and really scary.

'If you know who I am, Chessi. I wonder about it sometimes. If even after having lived with me for all these years you know who I am.'

'I kn—'

He bends down, his face right up in hers, his warm breath on her skin and she doesn't know whether she's going to live or die.

'I'm a man of love,' he whispers.

She feels the touch of his finger, stroking her across the cheek.

'Meandyou, baby, from here to heaven,' he whispers.

She nods.

'I don't give a shit who you've screwed,' he says, and turns to Tong. 'You know what Gran used to say: *I can trust you, Rune.*'

Then he bounds at Tong. He shoots through the air like a vengeful dog, sending Pål and the chair tumbling to the ground, the back of his head seeming almost to rattle, but nobody has time to attend to him as he lies moaning.

Tong protects himself as he's knocked to the floor, bringing a knee up into Rudi's stomach, who in turn tenses his abdominal muscles, the way he learned in the eighties fighting the Ulland-haug Gang, thwarting the worst of the intent. Tong gets hold of his face with his fingers, tightening and squeezing as hard as he can, searching for Rudi's eyes with his thumb and middle finger, but Rudi has the upper hand, has the advantage of his bodyweight on Tong and he's in possession of the strongest weapon a person can have, raging love. He quickly raises his right arm, angles it and plants an elbow in Tong's mouth, filling the room with a crunch-ing sound, while he employs his legs to try and gain control over the wriggling body beneath.

'What the fuck have you been playing at!' Rudi pounds his elbow repeatedly into Tong's mouth. 'What the fuck have you been playing at!'

'I haven't been playing at anything,' Tong screams, his mouth bleeding as he spits out a tooth. 'She's a slag! She's the one who came on to me.

'Like I'd fucking believe you,' Rudi yells. 'She loves me, you twisted fuck!'

Jan Inge stands looking immobile, flummoxed and tiny next to where the fight is taking place. He has given up. His eyes have always been small, it's one of the few things Cecilie can remember her mother saying, *That boy's eyes are so small they scare the life out of me*; now they resemble minute little pebbles.

Tong exerts himself and manages to tip Rudi off him. Rudi is sent rolling across the floor, crashing into the kitchen table, both feet smashing into Pål's head, which is still resting on the ground. The table is knocked on its side and Tong is nimbly back on his feet and within seconds is astride Rudi, pinning him to the floor, the knife in his hand.

'Jan Inge!' Cecilie screams.

Her brother turns his head slowly towards her. He's broken out in a rash, the same purple blotches he had so often on his cheeks when he was young, which vanished when Rudi started coming to the house. He has those red streaks in the whites of his eyes, which she hasn't seen in years either. He looks like a little boy who's going to walk out a door alone, into darkness, never to return.

'Jani! You have to do something!'

Tong straddles Rudi, immobilising him with his thigh muscles. He pauses to bring the knife to his own mouth and pick at his incisors with the blade, just like he always did in the eighties when they sat in the living room watching video after video, when boys were in and out of the house, boys with cartons of cigarettes and VCRs, boys that Jan Inge paid with her.

'Aren't you going to fucking do something!'

Jan Inge strokes Cecilie across the cheek.

What a useless pile of shit to have for a brother.

Is he thinking it would be best if he could rent her out again, like before? How could she have been so stupid, why has she never just left?

Then Jan Inge goes down on his knees, reaches his hands to the bag by his feet, unzips it and takes out the pump-action shotgun. He nods to Cecilie, lifts up the shotgun and holds it at stomach height.

'Tong,' Jan Inge says, 'you've gone too far. This is precisely what all good horror deals with. And you haven't understood anything I've taught you.'

Jan Inge puts the muzzle of the gun to Tong's temple.

'Get up.'

Tong smirks and gets to his feet. 'What are you planning to do? Shoot me? Like you fucking have it in you.'

'Move,' Jan Inge says, poking Tong. 'Move.'

Rudi gets up stiffly, Cecilie wobbles on her skinny knees and watches her brother push Tong into the hall, prodding him in the back with the shotgun, towards the door that leads to the garage.

'This is ridiculous,' Tong says, 'what the hell are you going do?'

Pål lies writhing on the kitchen floor. Cecilie gives him an apologetic look before she and Rudi follow Jan Inge.

At the end of the hall, Jan Inge puts his elbow on the door handle, presses down and pushes the door open, still holding his hands on the shotgun. Then he orders Tong to step through on to the cement floor inside.

'Rudi?'

'Yeah?'

Jan Inge motions with the shotgun in the direction of the van. 'Will you open the back doors?'

Rudi scurries past his best friend and opens the doors. Jan Inge places the muzzle to the back of Tong's neck and compels him to walk towards the open doors. When they reach them, Tong resists slightly, but Jan Inge presses the barrel harder against the nape of his neck. Tong gives in after a couple of seconds, squats down and climbs into the van.

'Jan Inge,' he says, sneering, 'you're such a fucking idiot.'

'Sit down,' Jan Inge says.

'Jesus,' says Tong, shaking his head. Then he sits down.

Jan Inge shoots Tong in the face.

Rudi looks at his best friend with a mixture of admiration and horror.

Tong lies stretched out on the floor of the van, his face torn asunder. The roof and sides splattered in blood, skin and flesh.

Jan Inge lowers the shotgun, the rash on his face beginning to wane.

In the kitchen, Pål's thighs shudder when he hears the powerful, resounding bang from the garage. He swings his head from side to side, making the mucus and stringy blood swing under his chin. 'Wha? Hello? What's happened?'

Cecilie takes a step forward. She looks at her brother.

'I couldn't very well spray-paint the kitchen with his DNA,' Jan Inge says calmly.

What a fantastic brother.

See, little one, see what a fantastic uncle you've got?

Then Cecilie hears a click in her ear as a switch from the past is flicked on. She pictures the man who's lost his dog, the man who's lying in there on the kitchen floor and she remembers him, Pål Fagerland, from an afternoon in 1985, an afternoon smelling strongly of vanilla. She can picture the room as it was back then, the poster of the ochre cat hanging to the right of the window, the pink hairbrush on the desk, the hair elastics beside it, the red desk lamp and the globe, a crack going from north to south, the Aerosmith poster, the Foreigner poster, the Lois jeans sticker on the door, she can hear the muffled sounds from the living room, a horror movie on the TV, and she can see Pål's young body, so thin and hairless, and she can see his gentle, frightened face, and she can hear her own voice saying: 'Come on, I don't bite.'

101. **PURE METAL** (Daniel William)

'Seventh,' she whispers.

Daniel raises his head, but his eyes remain downcast. He should never have got messed up in this. He should have done what Dejan suggested a couple of months ago: *Hey, Dano! What do you say – me and you, we rob a bank, get the fuck outta here, go and live like kings in Dubai, eh, man?*

But the girls came into the picture and Dubai went out the window.

Minutes from now, maybe a few hours, and he'll be sitting in the police station.

Daniel brings his finger to the button and presses it.

She knows her way around here. Veronika has been in and out of hospital since she was a little girl. She's been back and forth together with Inger, check-up after check-up at the audiology clinic. Seventh floor, said the woman at reception, and nodded to Veronika the way you nod to somebody you're used to seeing, but she struggled to maintain a natural expression when she saw the mesh of cuts on her face.

'Sandra Vikadal? Seventh floor.'

The lift is slow and heavy. Veronika seeks out his hand, finds his fingers.

'My finger friend.'

What is she on about? Daniel shoots her a puzzled look.

She laughs. 'Just popped into my head.'

'You come out with some weird stuff.'

'What did you say?' She looks at him with that expression she always gets in her eyes when she doesn't catch what's been said. Vigilant, the tiniest bit offended.

'Nothing,' Daniel says, 'nothing.'

The lift ascends, passing floor after floor. A sterile smell pervades, even in here, the odour of hospital and of unease. People go quiet when they use lifts, doubly so in hospitals.

The doors slide open.

'Hey?' She squeezes his hand.

'Mhm?'

'It's okay, you know. I'm with you, all right?'

Daniel nods. He can't bring himself to speak.

'We'll go in, you get to see her, and after that you're mine. Yeah? We'll just ride. You and me. Far from here. We still have time.'

He nods, but he doesn't believe what she's saying. They exit the lift and set their feet on the linoleum of the seventh floor. It's almost as though the ground is swaying beneath them. There are double doors to either side of them and Veronika points to the ones to the right. Daniel doesn't say anything, just nods and lets her lead the way.

She wants to hold him by the hand, reaches for his, but he avoids her attempt. He speeds up, noses a few inches ahead of her as they walk down the corridor. A doctor and a nurse are walking towards them. Daniel looks down. They pass empty chairs, doors and rooms, people inside with pain in their bodies. Veronika draws level with him, tries to take hold of his hand once more. Daniel brings his fingers to his eye, pretends to have something in it.

Then they halt. A man and a woman are standing outside a room about fifty feet in front of them. Daniel takes an audible intake of breath and makes as if to turn back.

'Who's that?'

He gives her a quick glance and she understands who it is.

The man is tall and slim, wears a suit and shirt and has polished shoes. The woman is petite, slender, dressed in a blue jacket, with a neckerchief and her hair neatly styled.

'Relax,' Veronika says, 'do they know who you are?'

Daniel tugs her with him, back towards the lift, but she resists.

'Wait, stand still. Don't look at them. Look at me. Have you met them?'

'No, I haven't met them,' he says, angrily.

'Take it easy, Daniel,' she says. 'They're talking to a doctor. Look. He's quite calm. The father has his arm round the mother. She's crying.'

Daniel brings his hands to his head. Massages his forehead with his fingertips.

Then they see them. Two uniformed police. A man and a woman. They come out of the same room. The woman tilts her head to the side, says something into the radio mounted almost at her shoulder. The other speaks to the doctor and Sandra's parents.

Daniel and Veronika turn and walk quickly away. They don't stop until they make it around the corner by the lift.

'What are we going to do?' Daniel's eyes flash fiercely.

Veronika takes a step to the side, looks down the corridor.

'They're talking,' she says.

Daniel swallows.

'Wait,' she says, 'wait, they're leaving.'

'What?'

'They're going the other way.'

'The other way?'

Daniel sticks his head round the corner to take a look. She's right. The doctor and the police are accompanying Sandra's parents further down the corridor. The doctor opens a door and shows them in.

'Come on,' Veronika says, giving him a tug, 'now.' She begins to walk towards the room Sandra is in.

Daniel hesitates, but she's stronger. Veronika won't hear him. She doesn't want to hear him. That's how this girl is. She says weird things and has no trouble crossing boundaries others wouldn't dare contemplate. She lacks something other people have. She possesses something they do not.

Daniel is on the verge of letting her go into Sandra's room on her own, on the brink of turning around and leaving. But he's unable to resist her. She's too much. That copper-red hair. That pursuable body. She's like pure metal.

They reach the mint-green door and Veronika reaches for the handle, pressing it down gently.

Daniel wavers as she enters, but follows her in.

It's a single room. A narrow entrance with a bathroom to the side, a window ahead with the curtains opened. The late September light shines into the room. A poster of a flower arrangement hangs on the wall to the right. To the left, a bed with curtains drawn around it. A low hum from the air conditioner. A chair facing the bed.

'I can't do this.' Daniel closes his eyes.

'You can,' Veronika whispers, reaching her hand towards the curtain.

102. SING SONGS OF PRAISE (Sandra)

The sound of the curtain rings sliding along the pole. A soft swish. The material is drawn aside. It's her. The burnt hair, the slashed face. It's him. The bright mouth, the deep-set eyes.

They approach the bed.

Sandra is lying under a duvet with the hospital emblem on it. Her head is turned to the right and she can't move it. Her hair is lying neatly across the pillow the way her mother arranged it. Her lips are dry and cracked, even though her father has applied lip balm to them. She has bruises on her face, a cut under her cheekbone, because the people standing in front of her knocked her down. There's a glass of water on the table beside the bed, as well as a vase with three red roses; one for hope, her mother said, one for faith, she said, and one for the future.

Sandra can't feel a thing. Not anywhere. Her senses, with the exception of sight and hearing, are gone. She doesn't know if they can see that she sees them. She doesn't know if her eyes are moving.

'Jesus.'

Daniel brings his hands together, fingertip to fingertip. He sinks down into the chair.

'She's in a coma,' Veronika says, leaning down so her face is closer to Sandra. Studying her.

'What have we done?'

'Don't you want to talk to her?' Veronika brings her eyes up close to Sandra's, scrutinises them, as though she suspects Sandra of pretending to lie so still.

'Aren't you going to say something?' Veronika doesn't take her eyes off Sandra. 'Get on with it, so.'

'What will I say?' Daniel's voice is meek.

'I don't know. Say what you need to say.'

Veronika gives a short nod to herself, as though confirming her belief in what she sees: Sandra is in a coma. She can't move. This is not an act.

Daniel clears his throat, 'Sorry, Sandra,' he says in a stilted voice, 'you should never have met me.'

The bright boy isn't able to look at her. He isn't able to talk naturally. He closes his eyes when he speaks, hardly opens his mouth. He backs away from the bed.

The corners of Veronika's mouth begin to turn up into a smile as she sees Daniel move away. He walks over to the wall by the door and hides his face in his hands.

The girl who's ruined Sandra's life comes closer to the bed again.

What is she doing?

Sandra sees her lift her hands, bring them towards her neck. Her fingers curl, as though she were feline, her nails are long and painted; what is she doing?

The cuts on Veronika's face glisten, a triumphant smile appears and her eyes are aglow. Her fingers touch Sandra's throat. The crucifix. She takes it between her fingers, inspects it. Sandra can feel the disgusting breath on her face, and she wants to spit on her, wants to open her mouth and bite off her head, but she can't do anything. Veronika loosens the clasp of the necklace, takes the crucifix and leans forward so her mouth is up to Sandra's ear. Veronika lifts away a lock of hair, disturbing her summer blonde fringe, and whispers: 'Hi, Sandra. Are you in pain?'

Sandra pictures kneeing her in the cunt.

'It's Veronika,' she says, her lips millimetres from Sandra's ear. 'You're nothing now. Nothing. Your tits are too small, those Met jeans suck, your thighs are too fat and your mouth makes you look like a weasel.'

Sandra pictures tearing her apart with her bare hands.

'You can't move,' Veronika whispers. 'You're nothing now.'

Sandra imagines carrying her dismembered limbs. She walks across a dry stony landscape and after a while she reaches a fire-scorched rock-face. She crouches down and lets the body parts roll from her arms, as if they were logs of firewood. Then she lights it, sees Veronika's skin start to melt, watches the flesh begin to drip, smells the rising fetor of marred meat and makes out the bones beginning to appear.

Veronika straightens up. She breathes calmly. A summer of sorts has taken hold of her. A barrage of sunbeams shine through her very being.

Veronika turns to Daniel.

But he is not there. He is no longer by the door. He is out in the corridor. There is a doctor standing beside him. Not the same one as a little while ago. A different doctor. Now Veronika is nervous. Sandra tries to see what's happening, but it's beyond her field of vision. She can only hear voices and see Veronika's form moving towards the door, nearer to the doctor and Daniel.

'And who are you?'

'I'm just a friend of hers.'

His voice.

'A friend?'

'Yes. I know her.'

That bright mouth of his.

'Okay—' the doctor looks slightly puzzled.

'How is she?'

My Daniel.

'Well, it's too early to say,' the doctor looks even more uncertain now, looks from Daniel to Veronika and says: 'And who is she?'

Sandra sees Veronika draw closer to Daniel and the doctor.

'No, she's nobody,' Daniel says.

'Just a moment,' the doctor says, 'wait here for a second, I need to check something.'

Daniel turns his head to look at Sandra. So deep, those eyes of his, she feels she could fall into them.

He puts two fingers to his bright mouth, and leaves.

Love, Sandra thinks, as she notices her vision begin to fail, love bears all things, believes all things and hopes all things. And love, she thinks, and sees that she no longer sees, love endures all things. Sing songs of praise for my bright boy.

103. **SOIL WITH LEAVES ON** (Veronika)

Veronika places the necklace around her neck. Fastens it. Lets it rest in the hollow of her throat.

She watches Daniel go down the corridor, walk away with a heavy footfall. She sees the lift doors open and him disappear inside. She moves to the window on the seventh floor and waits. A minute goes by, maybe two, and then she catches sight of him below. He emerges from the main entrance. He walks towards the Suzuki.

She knows how to do this.

Don't look, don't listen.

It's been like this a thousand times before and it can be like this again.

My wolf man, you called me one unusual girl, but you didn't exist and here's the rule I made when I was small, when I lay under the duvet and thought about how I was always alone, how there would never be anyone for me:

Trees with bark on
bark with soil on
soil with leaves on
leaves with water on
water with boats in
boats with people in
people with clothes on
clothes with me in
me with bark on
me with soil on
me with leaves on
me with water on

water with people in
people with soil in
soil with leaves in
leaves with trees in.

104. **SILLY DADDY** (Pål)

'There you are, girls. Could you give me a hand here? Yeah, I know. Some people were here, I just came home to put out the candle – silly Daddy, leaving it burning, eh – so I sent Mummy on ahead. Wasn't that a nice surprise, Tiril, Mummy turning up, you weren't expecting that, eh? You might have seen a van driving off, yeah, that was them, they just broke in, I think they must have been a motorbike gang or something, they were masked, they tied me up, beat me and took a load of our stuff, but never mind, fortunately we're insured, and I'm here, Daddy's here, it's fine, it's fine, I've only a broken nose, as well as some fingers and ribs, along with a few cuts and bruises, it's fine, unbelievable what a body can take, don't cry, Malene, hi Tiril, it's fine, Daddy's sorted everything out now, things will be good now, we're a nice little family so we are, we'll be all right, we'll get a new dog, it'll all be okay.'

He hears the front door open.

The sound of Malene's steps. Then Tiril's. And Christine's stomping.

Like she lived here.

'Dad?'

Pål sits with his back to the oven. Aching pain all through his body. He's lost feeling in parts of his back and he's not certain, but it's like something in his mouth is smashed. His hands are still tied behind his back, but he lifts a finger, an unbroken one, as though they could see him.

'In here!'

Sounds in the hall. Crunching, crackling.

'Jesus, Dad! What happened here!'

'Oh, it—'

'Shit! There's glass everywhere!'

'Hi, Tiril, how did it go? I'm in here!'

The footsteps near the kitchen.

'Dad?'

They've entered the room. The footsteps have stopped. Breathing. A gasp. Someone says, 'Jesus.'

It'll be good to see light again, good to get the blindfold off.

The worst is over now.

'Hi, are you there?'

Pål hears Malene begin to sob, the same sound as the night she lay with her face buried in a pillow after injuring her ankle. He hears Tiril scream, *Zitha, Zitha, Zitha,* and he hears what he thinks are her knees hitting the floor with a thud as she sinks down in front of the dead dog. He hears Christine's silence, which only occurs when something has gone completely awry.

Well, she might move back home now? Who knows, never say never.

He clears his throat. 'There you are, girls,' he says, feeling a stinging pain in his mouth as he speaks. 'Could you give me a hand here? Yeah, I know, there were some people here, I was just coming home to put out the candle, silly Daddy, eh?'

105. LURA TURISTHEIM? DOLLY'S PIZZA? HINNA BISTRO? (Rudi)

Cecilie is lying with her head in his lap and it feels pretty damn good. Rudi becomes aware of a growing erection developing against her cheek and that feels pretty damn good too. They left in a hurry, managing to hump some of Pål's possessions from the house, a couple of computers, a TV and some other odds and ends, not exactly the haul of a lifetime, but like Jan Inge said: 'It'll do given the day that's in it.' Tong is lying in the back of the van under an old dog blanket they grabbed on the way out, faceless and bloody, and Jan Inge is sitting behind the wheel of the Transporter, as they drive uphill in the darkness towards Ullandhaug.

A strange mix of emotions.

Rudi can't feel it inside. He doesn't feel as though he's been cheated on. He has no emotional reaction to his woman having been unfaithful to him for months. Nothing. Almost the opposite, and that's what's so weird, he feels only happiness. As if he had won it all, and maybe he has!

What did Gran say that time?

'Rune, dear,' she said, 'you'll soon be a man.' He was sixteen or seventeen, sitting in Gran's, drinking decaf, outside it was raining cats and dogs, she'd served him Swiss roll and she had that crafty expression round her eyes that made her look like an owl, and she said: 'And you know what it means to be a man?'

'No, I mean, yes, well...'

'It means you have to be big-hearted, Rune,' she said. 'Kind and big-hearted. That's what the girls like, you know.'

Chessi's eyes are shining. She is so bloody gorgeous.

The Transporter slows down as it reaches the top of Limahaugen, Jani puts on the indicator, pulls up to the kerb and turns around to them, and Rudi can't help but feel everything is just perfect as their conversation unfolds: 'So. What'll it be? Lura Turistheim?

'Brother? You mean?'

'Well, just figured, before we get home and take care of this—'

'Reindeer stew with Waldorf salad and lingonberry jam. That was good. You can't go wrong with meatballs and mushy peas. Salt cod with bacon and onion, you liked that, brother.'

'I think they close at six.'

'Ah shit.'

'Dolly's Pizza?'

'We're always ordering from Dolly's.'

'Thai Summer number two, baby, Thai Summer number two, you know how much you love that. Lime and coriander.'

'Yeah, I suppose.'

'No no. Hinna Bistro, then.'

'They only do pizza too.'

'Yeah yeah. But we do like pizza. Number fifteen – Gringo?'

'Is that the one with chicken, chilli and salsa?'

'Mhm.'

'I can't help but feel we've made idiots of ourselves.'

'Yeah yeah. Depends how you look at it.'

'Word.'

'Just think of George Michael.'

'Whaddayamean?'

'If you want to compare. People who've made idiots of themselves.'

'Poor guy.'

'I have no sympathy for him.'

'Yeah, yeah. It's cosy at Hinna Bistro. Long time since we were there. Must have been before the summer.'

'Aww. I'm looking forward to the summer.'

'Eh, yeah. But summer has just been.'

'Well. Y'know, I'm a summer kid, baby.'

'Yeah, but it's a long way off.'

'So, Hinna Bistro?'

'Hinna Bistro.'

'Be just the ticket. Some pizza, a nice kip, and then – Christ, I just realised we'll have a baby by the time summer comes.'

'Wow, yeah. Imagine that. Running around the garden.'

'He'll like that.'

'How do you know it's a he?'

'Heh heh. Daddy just knows.'

'You don't even know if you are the daddy, you nitwit.'

'I can feel it.'

'That it's a he or that you're the father?'

'Both, Chessi, both.'

'Oh, good.'

'So that's the reason your tits are bigger.'

'Mhm.'

'Hinna Bistro, so.'

'Weather's been nice for days now.'

'Yeah.'

'I like this time of year. Brisk and bright. Kind of like summer but autumn.'

'How do you think Pål is now?'

'Well, not great, I suppose.'

'Poor dog.'

'I have a feeling this isn't going to be any problem.'

'Me too. No chance of Pogo suspecting us.'

'Probably not. And I think we can rely on Pål.'

'Good thing you shot Tong in the van though.'

'Yeah. Otherwise we'd already be in Åna.'

'You know, he was at our place once.'

'Eh?'

'Oh?'

'At our place?'

'Eh?'

'In Hillevåg?'

'Mhm. In the eighties.'

'Gosh.'

'Gosh.'

'There was something familiar about him though.'

'There was.'

'So. You mean—'

'Yeah.'

'When you say he was at our place.'

'Yeah.'

'Does that mean that, that you—'

'We're not going to talk about it.'

'No. Ah. That's what it is to be a man.'

'Eh?'

'Big-hearted and kind.'

'Oh.'

'I'm considering cutting out the speed.'

'Oh?'

'Something about kids and drugs that doesn't really go together.'

'Mhm.'

'Something about our line of business and drugs that doesn't really go together either.'

'Mhm.'

'Yeah. Reindeer stew with Waldorf salad and lingonberry jam. Now they go together.'

'I wish Lura was open.'

'Yeah yeah, but it's not. Hinna Bistro is cosy.'

'Strange seeing Tong like that. Without a face, I mean.'

'Yeah, but makes things better in a lot of ways.'

'I can't get George Michael out of my head now.'

'That's so you, soon as you get something on your mind, it just sticks.'

'Our first murder.'

'Not good.'

'Not good.'

'Not good.'

'Do you think there was something wrong with Tong?'

'Eh?'

'Well, I mean, he has always been a vicious bastard, but like, I don't know, just wondering if there was something up with him now.'

'Nah, that there had been coming a long time. Sick in the head, sick all over.'

'You're going a bit far now. To be fair, we did have a lot of good times together.'

'Yeah, but did we though.'

'I thought the worst thing was the dog.'

'Not good.'

'Killing a dog. I don't know. I just feel like it's not on.'

'You're not wrong there.'

'It was so cute. Doing that to it, horrible.'

'We'll get him a new dog.'

'That makes two murders then.'

'Three with the hedgehog.'

'Now you're being unfair, mamacita. That was an accident.'

'Yeah.'

'Yeah.'

'Okay, we're agreed. Hinna Bistro it is.'

The telecom tower on top of Ullandhaug, Rudi thinks, has always been one of the most beautiful things in the world. But most people probably feel that way, it occurs to him as he feels his erection twitch against Cecilie's cheek, as though she were a door he was knocking on. Most people must have something bolted on tight inside of them, something so dear to them that it never disappears, something that just grows and grows for every strange day that passes.

SUNDAY 30 SEPTEMBER

106. CHANGE

After a good pizza at Hinna Bistro, with beef, bacon, onions, chilli, nachos and extra cheese, and a long, warm night filled with plentiful sleep and fertile dreams, they took it easy on Friday. They slept almost until noon, had a nice breakfast of chocolate milk, pâté, beetroot and eggs, and for the sake of propriety, Cecilie put Tong's chocolate chip cookies at the back of one of the kitchen cupboards, while at the same time she threw out his black Puma trainers, which were lying in the hall. After they had drunk some coffee and Cecilie had consumed a large portion of Neapolitan ice cream, they rolled Tong up into an old carpet in the basement and spent the rest of the day on the sofa with their feet up, with crisps and soft drinks on the table, watching a couple of good films, a repeat viewing of *The People Under the Stairs* and *A Tale of Two Sisters*. They lounged and loafed about the house, Rudi entertaining and adding to the ambience by quoting lines from the Korean film, not without his thoughts drifting to the homeland of the recently departed, while he contorted his Mick Jagger mouth into horrific grimaces: *That woman is strange! And so is this house!*

They listened to Motörhead and Aerosmith, and later on that night Jan Inge put on a record from his dad's old vinyl collection, *Best of George Jones*. They ordered a takeaway from Peder's, deep-fried pork with curry sauce for Jan Inge, Chinese pepper chicken for Cecilie and Peder's Burning Peppercorn Biff Pizza for Rudi, who, when Cecilie pointed out that they had had pizza yesterday, replied that just because he gets pussy the one day it doesn't mean he's tired of it the next. They changed into jogging pants and sweatshirts, ate, enjoyed the warm feeling of relaxation and refrained from talking too much, a fire engine drove past the house, and they went to bed, worn out, around midnight.

Saturday ambled along at the same leisurely pace, punctuated only by Jan Inge taking a spin in the car to deliver the haul to the island of Fogn and the barn of one Halldór Buonanotte Ljótsson from Isafjördur. The people out west just call him Buonanotte, because those Icelandic names are, as Rudi says, apaininthefuck-inghole to pronounce. He did not come by the name through saying 'good night' every time he shot somebody, he was given it because for years he said 'Buonanotte' when he met people, due to Halldór thinking it meant good day. But no matter, when it comes to shifting loot, Halldór knows his stuff, can read people and make sales: Buonanotte on Fogn? He could sell tinned sweat. If you want your stuff dispersed far and wide on this side of the country, Halldór is the man to talk to, Buonanotte's barn is where it happens. He sits in there like a Scrooge McDuck of the underworld, presiding over a sea of stolen goods, some space at the entrance for the tractor, but otherwise there's little room for anything else; a vast horde of PCs, Macs, iPods, iPads, valuable car parts and everything a man could want, even a painting by Munch. Halldór came to Norway at the beginning of the millen-nium because he was weary of sheep, writers, fish and alcoholics, 'and there's nothing else in Iceland,' as he put it, before adding, 'yeah, and bloody Isbjörg, who I caught riding the neighbour one day, Ólafur from Sudureyri'. That Halldör has managed to stay under the radar since arriving in Norway is no inconsiderable feat; he's never been inside, and remains unknown to the people in Lagårdsveien 6, they have no idea that the Icelandic 'sheep farmer' with an Alsatian named Geysir has a barn off the coast of Ryfylke filled with everything that has disappeared in the region since the turn of the century, and Fogn, well, what can you say?

An island with 300 inhabitants in the municipality of Finnøy, a tiny place with an athletics club, a youth club, a farmers' club and a prayer club, not to mention an ever enthusiastic scouts troop – a transparent little society, in other words. Truth be told everyone out there knows what else Halldôr is up to, in addition to his greenhouses full of tomatoes and his hen house by the church, but sure, the islanders are proud of the few who have put up sticks out there, who have chosen to tough it out, who, like them, can pick up a pair of binoculars from their windowsill and glower over at the lights of Stavanger in the night-time, where the city slickers dwell thinking they are something. When the people of Fogn find such an enterprising man in their midst, a capable Icelander with his sleeves rolled up all year round, who never pisses in his toilet, but insists on relieving himself in the open air, who will turn up in his tractor ready to lend a hand to anyone on the island, who trains the boys' football team, with a grin like a beaming equator around his head, a big, burly man who comes with Geysir by his side and good humour to boot, always has something sharp in his pocket and a good bit of salted sausage in his hand; when the people of Fogn are gifted such a fine man on the island, then they figure that what he gets up to and what he doesn't get up to in his barn may be of concern to others, but it is no business of theirs. Because nobody has anything against Halldór, and it is obvious he must give these fellows who arrive on the ferry and drive up to him late at night strict instructions, because they may not be the best behaved individuals, but when they are on their way to Halldór they know how to conduct themselves, so what, then, is the problem?

Jan Inge had a pleasant trip. While he drove across Rennesøy, he pictured Cecilie's pregnant stomach and Tong's blasted face, and thought about change and what it actually is. He saw the landscape open up, drove on towards Fogn, where the terrain shifted to undulating hills, and when the Volvo neared its destination he could make out Halldór's outline against the side of the barn; a dark giant. Jan Inge smiled at the familiar sight, got out, greeted the big Icelander, felt the wind on his bald patch, which seemed to be expanding by the day, and together they heaved the stuff inside.

Halldór looked it all over, nodded, mumbled and counted on his perpetually dirty fingers, before Jan Inge and the Icelander sat down for a chat in the barn, just inside the large doors, where he has a seating area consisting of an old green sofa, a pair of good leather armchairs from the seventies, and a table. Halldór served coffee with a splash of spirits while he chewed on a Viking sausage from Svindland's of Flekkefjord, patted Geysir, and stroked his beard while listening with interest to Jan Inge's account of his eventful Thursday. '*Það er nefnilega það,*' he said, again and again, a sentence he utters so often that the whole of Fogn now uses it; when one of the boy scouts does something noteworthy, the scout leader can be heard to say *það er nefnilega það*, and when one of the pupils at the school distinguishes himself, the teacher will not be long in uttering *það er nefnilega það*, and the same goes for the prayer group, when one of the members informs the rest that the 400 kroner they sent to Somalia before Christmas has been used to build a church, then Hilde Østhus folds her arms across her sunken breasts and says: *það er nefnilega það*.

'Yeah,' Jan Inge says. 'It was actually a time-honoured classic. Impossible to go wrong. But. Well. The human factor.'

'*Það er nefnilega það*,' Halldór nodded, and poured some more coffee and spirits.

'But we'll be okay. We have an alibi. We avoided leaving any trace behind. Pål has everything to lose if he gives us up. Our problems are inside of us. Murder. Living with murder.'

'That can be hard.'

'A scratch in the mental paintwork,' Jan Inge said, 'to make a comparison.'

'Well well,' Halldór said, 'if anybody can manage, you lot can, Jan Inge.'

'Good to hear you believe in us, Buonanotte.'

'*Það er nefnilega það*,' Halldór uttered once again as he dropped a piece of sausage for Geysir. 'So Tong is *daudur. Jahérna*. In the graveyardium.'

'Yes... there was that, of course.'

'You have to bury him,' Halldór said, raising one bushy eyebrow and sipping from his cup. 'Even if he was a *djöfulsins djöfull*.'

'*Djöfulsins?*'

'An evil man.'

'I understand.'

'Yes, you do,' Halldór said, rising to his feet. He pointed at Jan Inge. 'Bald spot. I think you're getting a bald spot.'

'I think so too. But, Buonanotte?'

'*Já, hvað ertu að spá, feiti hlúnkur?*'

'Change. That's what I'm thinking about. What do you think of change?'

'*Jæja*,' Halldór said, rubbing Geysir under the ear. '*Breytingar*. I think it's God's gift to *okkur dauðlegra*.'

Halldór paid a few thousand kroner notes for the haul, asked Jan Inge to say hello to the others and tell them they were always welcome to the barn whether for business or a party, because he appreciated having such good colleagues and nobody should deny themselves a knees-up now and then, and before Jan Inge had rattled off over the hills and sailed round the corners from Eidsbrotet in the direction of the ferry, Halldór threw a stick which Geysir loped after and mumbled *helvítis djöfull* and *það er nefnilega það*, before telling him that he would spend his evening reminiscing about the only Korean he had ever known, a silent one with jet-black hair: 'Because you know, Jan Inge, in Isafjördur we don't have many immigrants from far-off places, but we have a music school and an amateur theatre group and for two months we don't see the sun and it's not uncommon for planes not to take off or land for days at a time, so change, well, us Icelanders are so used to it that we don't know what it is.'

When Jan Inge made it home that afternoon, he was greeted with the spectacle of Rudi and Cecilie lying on the sofa snogging, practically eating each other's faces, in the old way, a sight he had not seen in years; when Jan Inge made it home, his mind was really bubbling, it was as though the winds of change themselves were attempting to outrun one another up there, and it was clear to him that important matters had to be taken care of the next day. He cleared his throat in the doorway, thankful for the good atmosphere that had marked the last all-too-warm days of September, and when Cecilie had untangled herself from Rudi, sat up and buttoned her jeans, when Rudi had finished grinning, clicked his fingers a number of times and said, 'You were seconds from viewing an adult movie there, brother,' Jan Inge sat down in the wheelchair and said: 'We're going to have to make some changes here.'

Sunday dawned with a long-awaited downpour over Stavanger and an equally long-anticipated westerly wind.

The familiar sky was back, the sky people from Rogaland

County are so used to it that they don't stop as they walk along the Vågen inlet – like the tourists always do – and gape at the changing clouds, at the curious formations taking shape, scudding along before dissolving into constantly new figures. *We have cats and dogs and trolls and goblins above our heads*, Gran used to say to Rudi when he was a little boy, *do you see them, sweetheart?* But on this morning the people of Rogaland stopped, one and all, not least Jan Inge who got up before the others, went out on to the veranda and witnessed the ground beneath the scrap heap of a garden receive the wondrous drops of rain. He stopped. Now that the habit was broken, he realised that all through these white, cloudless days at the tail end of September, he'd missed the vault of the sky, and perhaps never realised how dependent upon it he'd been. His heart missed a few beats and he realised that it was because he had longed for the vast, variable and regularly stunning sky over Stavanger.

Jan Inge stood with his coffee cup to his lips and let the rain pour down on his head. He watched the water cleanse the veranda and listened to it splash and splatter against all the clutter in the garden while he marvelled at how a man like himself, so concerned with order, could have allowed such disorder to fester on the property. He breathed in the smell of wet autumn, looked up towards the sky and determined the wind direction; clearer skies lay off to the east and the gusts were carrying them this way. In a few hours, he thought, the rain will pass. He closed his eyes and pictured the days ahead in strong colours as he drank a mouthful of coffee and performed a few tentative knee bends as a foretaste of the workouts he would put himself through in the near future.

Different times, he thought.

Change, he thought.

Buonanotte is right. God's gift to mankind.

Jan Inge went back into the living room. He put on a record by Hank Williams, the performer he and Beverly are so fond of, he pictures them listening to Hank one heavenly day when she gives him her hand. He will sit with his arm around the generously fragranced and just as generously formed woman and they will look at the opalescent flame of a candle flicker on the table before them, her blouse not quite adequate to keep her breasts concealed, and Hank Williams will sing like he sang for Jan Inge this morning: *I can't help it if I'm still in love with you.*

He drank himself to death, Hank, wasn't even thirty when he died.

Big changes.

While Rudi and Cecilie still lay sleeping, or swapped body fluids, who knows, Jan Inge went down into the basement and got out the three navy boiler suits they had knocked off from a warehouse while on a job in Nordfylket in 2007, garments which had seen plenty of use at break-ins since. He brushed the dirt off them and laid them out on the kitchen table, then he fetched the work shoes from the closet in the hall, which he lined up on the floor between two table legs, first Cecilie's small ones, thereafter his medium-sized and lastly Rudi's enormous pair. He went and got the work gloves from the storage room in the basement, they smelt somewhat musty, the storage room had been subject to some mould problems that they needed to sort out soon, but in spite of that they could still be used. Finally he got a roll of black bin bags – never any shortage of those in the house – placing them beside the boiler suits just as Hank Williams sang *I heard that lonesome whistle blow* and Jan Inge felt a lump in his throat and pushed that wondrous image of Beverly to the back of his mind so as not to allow the pain and longing to gain the upper hand on a day with so much to do.

What will it take, he thought, unable to dismiss the image, what will it take for her to be mine?

More wealth than I can offer?

A toned physique?

Once again he pushed away the picture of Beverly in his mind's eye, now clothed in a fluttering, almost transparent dressing gown, and attempted to concentrate on what was going to take place. He went to the bookshelf and took down the Bible, the only real book there, with the exception of *The Encyclopedia of Heavy Metal* and *Sound of the Beast: The Complete Headbanging History of Heavy Metal*, a book about Lemmy, *White Line Fever*, and around thirty titles on horror movies; *The Art of the Nasty,*

How to Survive a Horror Movie, The Golden Age of Crap and so on. Jan Inge appreciated the reassuring weight of The Good Book in his fleshy hands and settled into the wheelchair to leaf through the thin Bible paper. He read a few pages about Moses, the man of God, whom near the end of his life was told by the Lord to go to the top of Mount Abarim and look out over Canaan at the land the Lord had given to the Israelites, and he found himself strangely moved by the poetry that shone from the pages when the Lord told Moses, in no uncertain terms, that he would die while he looked out over the land and would not enter it since he had been faithless to the Lord. Jan Inge thumbed further and read a few pages about Saul, whom the Lord commanded to go out and punish the poor Amalekites for what they did to Israel, and it sent shivers down his spine as he read how the Lord instructed Saul not to show any mercy but kill men and women, children and infants, oxen and sheep, camels and donkeys. After that he read about Nathan visiting King David. Nathan recounted a terrible tale of a rich man who had slaughtered a poor man's only lamb instead of taking something from his own abundant livestock, and King David burned with anger at this and said to Nathan that this man must die. But then the situation took an abrupt turn because Nathan pointed his finger at King David and said, 'You are the man!' and accused him of having scorned the word of the Lord and having killed Uriah the Hittite and taken his wife, and so the Lord, according to Nathan, decreed that misfortune would rain down on King David, that his wives – so he had lots of them, Jan Inge thought and again the image of Beverly came gliding into his head, this time attired in a smart waist-length jacket and high heels with golden pearls – that these wives would be taken from him and given to another man and this man would lie with them in broad daylight, because David had acted secretly, and to top it all, the son he had with Bathsheba, the wife he had taken from Uriah, would not be allowed to live. And so it was. The Lord allowed illness to strike down the newborn boy and he died, but David lay with his wife again not long after and they had another son and he was called Solomon. However, a prophet turned up who wanted to call him Jedidiah in honour of the Lord, whatever that means, Jan Inge thought, and became aware of that feeling he sometimes gets when he's reading up on things, that he is lacking in a little knowledge here and there.

They were disturbing, compelling stories. Jan Inge was struck by the magnificence of The Good Book, how rewarding it always was to peruse it, equally as gratifying as watching a horror film, and for the same reason, because they both spoke about truth, about goodness, about how after one blow it's all too late; and didn't both of them speak of change? As disturbing and captivating as the stories might be, and as much about truth and change as they may be, neither the one about Moses, nor the one about Saul nor the one about Nathan, David and Bathsheba could be used this Sunday. On the whole, the task – finding an appropriate eulogy for Tong – presented problems. It seemed almost like The Good Book didn't have anything to say about one such as Tong, had no words to sum up his life and act as encouragement in the wake of what had happened on Thursday. Jan Inge turned page after page while Hank Williams sang about loneliness, while the clock ticked on past nine, around to ten and then half past ten, but no stories and no quotations with the right wording or content seemed to stand out. He sat enthralled in the wheelchair for a long time by the words of Job, *who can bring what is pure from the impure*, but to use a quote like that, which would obviously be directed towards Cecilie's child and the question of whether it was Tong's, would be pure madness. Job's words about there being hope for the tree, because it can grow again after being cut down, while all hope is lost for the dead man because he will not, also seemed too harsh for such an occasion.

Weary of reading the gauzy pages, Jan Inge put the book in his lap and tried instead to listen to the sound of his own heartbeat.

He had often felt the pace begin to slow after a while.

Thump-thump, thump-thump.

It was not something he took lightly.

To close one's eyes, lean back, listen to one's own heart and interpret one's own inner voice: he had frequently found this to be the path to solving many problems.

The first problem it cleared up, quite literally, was the weather

outside. After a few minutes in the wheelchair with The Good
Book in his lap, it stopped raining. Jan Inge noticed the changes
in the sound around him, the rustle of the rain suddenly gone.

Thump-thump, thump-thump.

Again he shut his eyes so he could listen to his own heart and
decipher his inner voice.

Thump-thump, thump-thump.

He tried to keep his eyelids at rest, which he often found difficult, as they had a tendency to quiver faintly on his eyeballs, and
he listened as intently as he could.

Cold, cold heart, Hank Williams sang.

Jan Inge opened his eyes. He got up out of the wheelchair. He
paced up and down the living room a number of times shaking
his head. Hank sang about a woman with a cold heart, and it was
a long way from a love song about a cold woman to the story of
Tong, but still. Jan Inge's heart began to pound as the felt the
truth foray forward: the story of Tong wasn't a story of warmth.
The story of Tong wasn't the story of a good person. It was – and at
this point Jan Inge was contrite for having such terrible thoughts
– the story of a cold heart.

And it has to be said, he hurried to add, that there can be many
reasons for a person to have a cold heart.

But there they were. There were the words his own heart had
tried to communicate to him. Thump-thump, thump-thump.

The various parts of the breakfast Jan Inge had prepared several
hours earlier had either begun to dry up, melt or go stale, so he
went into the kitchen to make another at the same time as he
decided that since it seemed like Cecilie and Rudi were going to
sleep the whole day through, he would have to wake them. He
cut some fresh slices of bread, he put on fresh coffee and brewed
a little tea, threw out the tomatoes and cucumber slices he had
put out some hours before, cut up a few new ones as well as some
fresh cheese so everything appeared more pleasing. He read a few
pages of the Saturday edition of *Stavanger Aftenblad*, which had
lain unopened all of yesterday, running his eyes over a piece about
a serious assault and robbery in Madla, taking note of the fact that
the police were without any leads, and as he perused an article

concerning a girl (15) who had died in the early hours of Saturday morning as a result of injuries sustained from being hit by a moped, he reflected on how sad it was when people died so young.

Then he went into the hallway and walked to their door. He put his ear against it. There was the sound of whispering within. He held his breath and tried to listen, but it was impossible to hear what they were saying, so he gave up, took a few steps backwards and mustering as much energy in his voice as he could, called out: 'Breakfast!'

Dressed in boiler suits and accompanied by the peal of a church bell in the distance, with minds set firmly on the future, Rudi and Jan Inge carried the carpet with Tong inside up from the basement after breakfast, which Rudi had praised as being fit for a king. Cecilie walked in front, making sure they did not trip on the ends of the rolled-up carpet which brushed each step, and they managed to manoeuvre Tong's body up the narrow, steep staircase that had not been built with that kind of thing in mind back in 1972 when Thor B. Haraldsen and Veslemøy Sivertsen hung up a sign beside the front door which read 'Welcome to Veslemøy, Thor, Jan Inge and Cecilie'.

There'll be many more breakfasts like that, Jan Inge pointed out, in his most optimistic tone of voice, while at the same time being conscious of sweating like a pig from actual manual labour, many more breakfasts, yes indeed, when there're four of us living in the house. He hoped for a response to confirm that there actually would be four of them *living in the house*, but it was not forthcoming and he thought about how there is a time for everything, and now was the time for work, not confrontation. *Show, don't tell*, as they say in the world of the scriptwriter, a term they'd had a good laugh about once when it turned out that Rudi had misunderstood and presumed it meant to put on a real show as opposed to talking. In spite of his error, Rudi still maintained that the two could often be one and the same, because as he said, what could make for a better show than a good talk?

They stowed Tong and his carpet beneath the curtains by the door to the veranda and went to fetch all they could scrape together of picks, hoes and digging equipment, because it was a deep hole that needed to be dug. None of them had any expertise in the area, but Jan Inge knew this much; if you were going to bury a person in your garden – a comrade with a cold heart – you needed to put him a long way down. That much was obvious. That body, it would have to be laid far below. In a garden a child would soon be running around playing. A garden that would soon be fixed up and made neat and tidy, a garden that would be used in the future. The mere thought of Tong lying just beneath the soil while they played croquet for example, or barbecued pork chops made him feel unwell.

But there was little to bring croquet or pork chops to mind for the time being. The old mattresses Mum, poor cow, had dozed on before she died, lay there, bearing little resemblance to mattresses any more, as well as the two wheelbarrows, riddled with rust, from when Mum and Dad worked in the garden, from when Dad had plans for the house. Some hubcaps and tyres lay over in the east corner, along with the remnants of some car parts they had stolen from a parking lot in Forus around the turn of the millennium, so worn and in such bad condition that not even Buonanotte could offer anything for them, while in the west corner a load of planks lay rotting from the time Rudi got it into his head to extend the veranda; nothing ever came of it, but who knows what might happen now. The broken lawnmower was just as rusted as the wheelbarrows, and Cecilie's old Raleigh bicycle equally so, all of them strewn like dead tin soldiers against the west side of the hedge, not far from Mum's washing machine, which she never used, old witch, and the sofa from the den. It's seen its fair share of video films, that sofa, Jan Inge said, from the time it was new and red and bought at a flea market in Kannik School. And then there was all that assorted junk, broken tools and equipment, the smashed TV Jan Inge used to have in his room together with the VCR, which also lay there as a reminder of the old, difficult days, as did the three panel heaters Dad bought before he left, but why there were eight mouldy pallets at the end of the garden was something Jan Inge could no longer recall, nor what the broken shears had to do with anything, nor the door handle, but the rusty rotary clothes line, that awoke strong memories, and was in many ways the most acute image of his childhood, because when he was small it always put him in mind of an umbrella, and he always thought about lifting it up in his little hand against the rain.

But soon they would have a big clear-out and everything would go. There was a skip in front of the house, and there was no point offering prayers up to old memories now.

Change.

They cleared the odds and ends off the centre of the lawn, where Jan Inge had decided that Tong would be laid to rest. Rudi remarked on that particular detail of the plan; why he should lie under the middle of the lawn and not in a corner, he didn't get that, but he nodded as Jan Inge held forth about not sidelining old friends, the way we do here in this country. Look at Italy, said Jan Inge, they honour their old, while we, we're embarrassed by them and their drooling, bingo and walking frames.

It was hard work digging such a deep hole. They counted themselves lucky that Thor B. Haraldsen had planted a hedge back in the day, a hedge nobody had trimmed for years, so at least no one had a clear view of all the hacking and digging they carried out that afternoon, because it took considerably longer than they had imagined. How hard can soil be, exclaimed Jan Inge in amazement, while being conscious that manual labour was something he did all too seldom, because the pounds were running off him at record speed.

After a few hours of hacking and digging, punctuated by some short breaks to drink and smoke, which saw Rudi actually crack and begin to smoke again, who knows why, perhaps because Cecilie smiled at him with such love; after a few hours' work, Jan Inge stood at the side of the two-metre-deep hole and signalled that they could stop. He placed his feet apart and put his hands on his hips, which almost felt slimmer already to him. He looked down into the darkness of the hole beneath. Rudi came to join him from one side and Cecilie from the other. All three of them stood looking down into the soil.

'Yes,' Jan Inge said.

Rudi nodded. Cecilie nodded.

'I think now we can say that Tong has got his temple.'

'Temple, brother?'

'Tomb, might be a better way of putting it.'

'I'm getting a bit of an Egyptian vibe here,' Rudi smiled.

'Heh heh, indeed. I had such a crush on her, what was her name, the little one—'

'Susanna Hoffs,' Rudi nodded.

'Yeah, Susanna Hoffs,' Jan Inge said. 'She was cute as a button, so she was. "Eternal Flame". Was she small? Or were the other girls just really tall?'

Cecilie tapped the spade against the ground and inquired as to whether they were planning to discuss the Bangles all day or what, and that was certainly true, Jan Inge affirmed, they didn't have a single minute to waste jabbering, before he looked towards the veranda door, a meaningful expression on his face that both Cecilie and Rudi understood: It was time to fetch Tong and lay him in the unhallowed ground.

'Tempo, tempo,' Jan Inge whispered as he and Rudi lifted the carpet with Tong, because speed was 'of the essence', as he put it, just hotfoot it across the veranda and heave him in the hole. With or without the carpet, Rudi wondered, and Jan Inge and Cecilie weighed up the pros and cons, but seeing as none of them could picture themselves using the carpet after Tong had lain dead in it for almost three days, they decided to bury it with him. Jan Inge was of the opinion there was a certain dignity about that, which Rudi agreed with, because if there was one thing in the world he held in high regard it was a sense of dignity.

Tong's face, which they had not looked at since it was blown apart on Thursday night, had congealed into a decomposed mask. All three were struck by a feeling of detachment upon viewing it, because, as Rudi pointed out, it simply did not look real. It did not even resemble a face. If someone had shown this to him, Rudi said, and he didn't know what it was, he would have guessed it was some sort of half-thawed minced meat. Or a heart, Cecilie said. Ironic, Jan Inge added.

Tong's body resembled a puppet without a puppeteer as it

rolled out of the carpet and into the hole. There were no muscles, nothing in the arms or legs to take the fall, and it was both frightening and fascinating to see it collapse upon itself, joint by joint, as it slid down to meet the ground below.

'Rudi, spade,' Jan Inge whispered, and Rudi picked it up hurriedly and began shovelling earth, while Jan Inge moved a couple of steps away, took up position on the adjacent side of the grave and cleared his throat.

'Earth to earth, ashes to ashes, dirt to dirt,' he said.

'I think it's dust to dust,' Cecilie remarked.

'We don't have the time to be so particular,' Jan Inge said, and while Rudi threw spadeful after spadeful of soil on top of Tong's body, Jan Inge pondered how this must be how priests feel when they go to work. Day in, day out, carrying out their sombre duty.

When Rudi was finished patting down the earth, Jan Inge requested their attention. Cecilie nodded and took Rudi by the hand and together they looked like a navy-clad bride and groom.

'I've spent the morning and afternoon in contemplation,' Jan Inge said, in a solemn tone.

'That's not in the least bit surprising,' Rudi said, blithely.

Jan Inge raised his hand, palm open, to indicate he had something important to add, and Rudi nodded without saying anything more.

'I've been pondering,' Jan Inge said, putting his hands into the pockets of the navy boiler suit, 'what took place on Thursday. We have to face to it. Our plan was good. The Trojan horse worked. You, Cecilie, and you, Rudi, delivered. But our dead friend, he ran amok and exploded.'

'Ran amok and exploded. You hear that, Chessi?'

She nodded.

'I have to admit it took me by surprise,' Jan Inge continued. 'I'm no stranger to shocks or twists, I often feel I can see the glint of the blade before the knife leaves the hilt, but this time the surprise was genuine. I hadn't foreseen any of this.'

'We didn't see it coming either, bruv,' Cecilie said, consolingly.

'No,' nodded Jan Inge. 'Tong was one tough nut, we knew that. We also knew that given certain circumstances, he was capable of doing the unexpected. But this? After being such a model prisoner in Åna? After all that meditation?'

Rudi's Adam's apple bobbed up and down visibly, but Cecilie assuaged any emotion by lifting his hand to her mouth and giving it a kiss.

'No,' Jan Inge repeated, 'the conclusion I've reached, dear friends – dear Tong, if you can hear me – is that—'

Jan Inge broke off and cleared his throat. Cecilie and Rudi remained holding hands, Rudi with eyes narrowed and ears pricked.

'That,' Jan Inge attempted to continue, obviously moved by what he was thinking, 'well, I'll just say it straight out: Tong walked the earth with a cold heart.'

A gust of wind swept through the garden and clouds gathered above their heads.

'It's not a nice way to put it,' Jan Inge said, slowly and deliberately. 'I mean, is how I feel now the way the mother of a rapist feels, as she has to come to terms with the fact that her son, the boy whose nappies she once changed and has loved for so long, had a cold heart?'

Neither Cecilie nor Rudi had anything to say in the light of such a grave comparison.

'I mean,' Jan Inge said, bending down to the ground and picking up a rusty spanner, which he began to turn in his hand, 'I mean, of all the people we know. Hansi, for instance. A prize idiot.'

'Such an asshole,' Rudi snorted.

'But a cold heart?' Jan Inge said, continuing to rotate the spanner. 'No. Hansi has a stupid heart. And Melvin, for example, who went solo. A cold heart? No. An extreme heart, perhaps, but not a cold one. Buonanotte?'

'No.'

'No!'

'Right. Buonanotte. An amusing heart. And Stegas?'

'Ha ha.'

'A wet heart,' Jan Inge said in a fluty voice, laughing, and tossed the spanner away. 'And Pål,' he added, clipping the wings of the laughter he had spread, 'what about Pål?'

'I liked that Pål guy,' Rudi said, promptly. 'A good heart, I would've said.'

Jan Inge nodded in agreement. 'And Cecilie, if I may ask – what would you say about Mum and Dad, if you're able to talk about them without upsetting the child in your stomach?'

Cecilie let go of Rudi's hand and lit up a cigarette. 'Well,' she said, 'you couldn't say Dad had a cold heart, maybe more of a ... I don't know ... a stuff-and-nonsense heart, I think? And Mum ... it wasn't hard, just weak. A fish heart.'

Cecilie turned to Rudi. 'What about your people?'

'Who do you mean,' Rudi knitted his brows, 'you mean ... are you talkin' about ... do you mean my fami ... is it my fam—'

'You don't need to say anything,' Cecilie smiled, blowing out smoke before stretching up on her toes to kiss him.

'Anyway,' Jan Inge said, seizing the chance to speak as the sky above them grew more and more unsettled, 'anyway, the way I see it, Tong had a cold heart. And it's awful for me to have to say these things, because I don't want to be seen as a racist or anything, and it's unpleasant that having now broken one of my fundamental principles and shot someone, having taken my place in the murky ranks of the men of violence, it turned out to be an immigrant. It's horrible for me to have to say these things, because standing here, I have difficulty thinking of anything positive to say about the man lying beneath us.'

It grew quiet in the garden.

'And it pains me to say,' Jan Inge said after a while.

Once again there was silence.

'He had too little love in him,' Jan Inge whispered, after another pause. 'And that is the knowledge we can glean from this.' He added, pensively, 'That it's all about love.'

Rudi nodded and looked at Cecilie. 'That's what I always say,' he whispered. 'He got that from me.'

'What was that, Rudi?'

'Nothing,' Rudi said. 'Well put, brother,'

It grew quiet around the grave as the first raindrops spattered on washing machines, VCRs and spades. They stood there and let it come down upon them, both the rain and the scary feeling of having buried a person they had, or thought they had, known so well; a person who ate chocolate chip cookies and hardly ever spoke, and when it came down to it – they now understood – had never allowed anyone to get close to him or allowed himself to express too much. A person they had not known at all. About whom they could not think of anything good to say. And in this atmosphere, images began to float through Cecilie's mind. She pictured the flashing intensity in Tong's eyes as she sat astride him, the animalistic hunger and snapping of his mouth when she offered him hers to kiss, pictured Tong, smiling, pulling into their driveway years before, with the window rolled down and a cigarette dangling from his lips, proud of coming home with thirty-five thousand after a simple break-in in Eiganes. There was a Tong they were on the point of forgetting, Cecilie felt, and because of this she turned to Rudi, whose shoulder-length hair was damp and lined face wet, and to Jan Inge, and said: 'But even though he didn't have enough love inside him, either for us or for anyone else, that doesn't mean we're going to be just as bad.'

'That's beautifully put, baby,' Rudi said.

Jan Inge stood beside them, conscious of a tear perched precariously in his eye.

They remained there, all three of them, as the rain grew heavier, in front of Tong's grave, each wrapped in their own thoughts. Three people dressed in boiler suits by some freshly dug ground, surrounded by old junk. On impulse, Rudi began to stomp on the soil, bringing his large soles down on the grave as he walked, after a fashion. Having gone back and forth like this for a while, he turned and looked into Jan Inge's tiny blueberry eyes.

'If Tommy Pogo shows up again,' Rudi said, 'I wouldn't like the thought of him coming out here into the garden.'

'Calm down,' Jan Inge said.

'Easy for you to say,' Rudi said, 'you're the laidback type.'

'Should Pogo,' Jan Inge said, 'turn up, we'll tell him we know who he is and what he's trying to do, we'll tell him we have nothing to hide, and if he, or any other investigators from Lagårdsveien 6, ask where we were on Thursday, we have an alibi, and we'll make sure to let them know that we think it's a pretty lousy thing for Lagårdsveien to be harassing ordinary removal people and putting the frighteners on us or whatever it is he thinks he's up to, and then we'll point out the garden and the clear-up we've carried out—'

Rudi shook his head, flabbergasted.

'Jesus, you are one hell of a managing director.'

'And then,' Jan Inge continued, 'then we'll make sure to tell him that from now on there's going to be some changes out here in Hillevåg. Changes, Rudi, you hear me?'

Rudi clapped Jan Inge on the back. 'Well said,' he whispered.

Jan Inge filled his lungs with air and then exhaled.

'I just don't want any more grief,' whispered Jan Inge.

'There won't be any more grief,' Rudi replied, in a soft tone.

The rain grew heavier, turning the ground wet and muddy.

Jan Inge turned to Cecilie. He had broken out in a nervous rash, his eyes were red, the corners of his mouth were quivering and she saw him as she had seen him so many times before so very long ago.

'Are the two of you moving out?' he asked, trembling.

Cecilie looked at him askance. 'Moving out?'

'Moving?' Rudi said, looking puzzled. 'Wherethefuckdidyougetthatideafrom, brother of tears?'

Jan Inge sniffled. 'I dunno,' he said in a low voice. 'Have you thought of any names for the baby yet?'

Cecilie and Rudi looked at one another, the way parents do when they ask each another, wordlessly, if they are going to reveal their secrets to the world, and Cecilie nodded to Rudi.

'Steven,' Rudi said, 'if it's a boy.'

'Jambolena,' Cecilie said, 'if it's a girl.'

'Jambolena?' Jan Inge whispered and cleared his throat. 'Isn't that ... a tree?'

There was a sound in the distance.

'It's going to be fine,' Cecilie whispered. 'Changes, right? There's a lot that's going to happen soon and we're going to be happy together. It begins now, Jani, you hear me?'

'Yeah,' Jan Inge said, 'yeah, you're right. A nursery. Mariero

Moving. Clear-up. We're going to take everything up a notch. Everything is going to be good.'

The sound grew louder, came within earshot, and their eyes turned in the direction of the source. It was coming from the front of the house. It was the revving of an engine, a motorcycle, or moped perhaps on the street outside. They looked at one another.

'Hm,' Jan Inge said.

The sound ceased. Most likely the ignition being turned off.

'Okay,' Rudi said.

Cecilie cocked her head to the side. 'Is that outside our place?'

Jan Inge exchanged looks with the others. They put down the spades and other tools, walked up on to the veranda, signalling silently to one another with seasoned expertise while removing their muddy footwear and slipping out of their boiler suits, before going into the living room. Cecilie gave the boys a quick once-over, fixing Rudi's hair a little and wiping some dirt off Jan Inge's face, and then they made their way into the kitchen. Jan Inge gave Cecilie and Rudi one last look before drawing the curtain carefully aside and peeking out.

There was a moped in front of the house. An old Suzuki, red with a black leather seat, the kind people drove when Jan Inge was small.

His attention shifted to the front door.

There was a boy standing there.

'What is it?' Cecilie whispered.

'I don't know,' Jan Inge whispered back.

'Who's out there?' Rudi said in a low voice.

'I don't know,' Jan Inge replied in a hushed tone.

'What does he want with us?' whispered Cecilie.

Jan Inge shook his head resignedly. 'More changes, maybe,' he whispered.

'Looks that way, headmaster,' Rudi sighed, as the doorbell rang. The three of them walked slowly in line out into the hall. Jan Inge opened the door.

A beautiful boy with deep-set eyes, wearing a leather jacket, stood before them. He looked gaunt and tired. He did not look like he had slept in several days. He held a black crash helmet in his hands.

'Hi,' the boy said, with a quick nod.

'Hi,' Jan Inge said. 'What do you want?'

The boy looked at them, 'I know who you lot are,' he said.

Jan Inge cleared his throat. 'Okay?'

Oh Jesus, he thought, are we going to have to open up the grave again?

The boy tossed the moped helmet from one hand to the other.

'You have something I want,' he said, 'and I have something that none of you want.'

Rudi took a step towards the boy.

'Is it the internet you're on about?' he said sternly.

Jan Inge put a hand on Rudi's shoulder, but he paid no heed. 'Listen,' he said, 'you can't go round knocking on strangers' doors talking like that, you get me? One more word and I'll get my baseball bat and clobber you with it. Youhearmebirdseed?'

The boy remained unflustered. 'You have something I want,' he repeated.

'What exactly do you mean?' Jan Inge asked.

'I want in,' Daniel said, 'in to where you lot are.'

'Jesus,' Jan Inge said. 'What are you talking about?'

'I know what you've done,' the boy whispered and stared right into Jan Inge's eyes.

'Excuse me?'

'Pål Fagerland,' the boy said.

Oh no, Jan Inge thought, clenching his teeth as hard as he could, do I have to get the shotgun, do I have to murder again?

'I don't need any more changes right now,' Cecilie whispered while she looked over the unusually beautiful boy with his deep-set, hungry eyes, his bright mouth, sharply defined jaw and long-fingered hands. Then she brought her hand to her stomach to safeguard her child against this terrible, ineluctable world it would one day be part of.

Acknowledgements

See You Tomorrow asked for hard work, patience and a lot of research, and I have been fortunate to have the generosity and devotion of intelligent and empathic people during these six years of writing.

Thanks to my editor Kari Joynt and everyone at Forlaget Oktober in Oslo. Thanks to Aschehoug Agency for their work with my books abroad. Thanks to Karen Sullivan and Gary Pulsifer at Arcadia, Amélie Burchell and everyone at Faber Factory and Faber Factory Plus, my translator Séan Kinsella, and all my foreign publishers and translators for making this happen around the world. I am grateful for the generous support of Norla and the Norwegian Embassy, who have made so much of this possible.

My love goes out to my lifelong friend and internet-dude, Kristian Fjermestad, and thanks to my designer Asbjørn Jensen, the directors Stian Kristiansen og Arild Andresen, and Motlys and Yngve Sæther for making films of my books.

For invaluable information, I thank investigator Eldfrid Vestbø at Stavanger Police Station, lawyer Anne Kroken, inmates and workers at Åna Prison, pupils and teachers at Gosen School, and everyone else who so generously shared and listened.

A big round of applause to my colleagues: Karl Ove Knausgård for years of inspiring friendship and reading, Jo Nesbø for advice and interesting talks, Frode Grytten for so much support and joy, and Tønes and Janove Ottesen for all those great songs.

It often feels as if my energy comes from listening to music. I'd like to take the opportunity to thank a handful of artists who have meant so much over the years: Nick Cave, Jarvis Cocker, David Bowie, Ray Davies, The Flaming Lips, David Sylvian, Morrissey, Pet Shop Boys, Tom Waits, Kate Bush, Duran Duran, Phil

Collins, Bob Hund, Depeche Mode, XTC.

Without family, there would be no great books. Thanks to my lovely mother, Mirjam Elisabeth Renberg, to my beautiful children, Petra and Allan, to all the cowboys and Indians in my family, and to my shimmering girlfriend, Hilde.

First and foremost, thanks to my great readers. You are the reason.

(And thanks to the Tjensvoll Gang. You sure did frighten us back then. You wrote this.)

This book has been selected to receive financial assistance from English PEN's Writers in Translation programme supported by Bloomberg and Arts Council England. English PEN exists to promote literature and its understanding, uphold writers' freedoms around the world, campaign against the persecution and imprisonment of writers for stating their views, and promote the friendly co-operation of writers and free exchange of ideas.

Each year, a dedicated committee of professionals selects books that are translated into English from a wide variety of foreign languages. We award grants to UK publishers to help translate, promote, market and champion these titles. Our aim is to celebrate books of outstanding literary quality, which have a clear link to the PEN charter and promote free speech and intercultural understanding.

In 2011, Writers in Translation's outstanding work and contribution to diversity in the UK literary scene was recognised by Arts Council England. English PEN was awarded a threefold increase in funding to develop its support for world writing in translation.

www.englishpen.org